LEGENDS OF IMYRIA

ASHES OF AETHER

HOLLY ROSE

RED
SPARK
PRESS

LEGENDS OF IMYRIA

ASHES OF AETHER

HOLLY ROSE

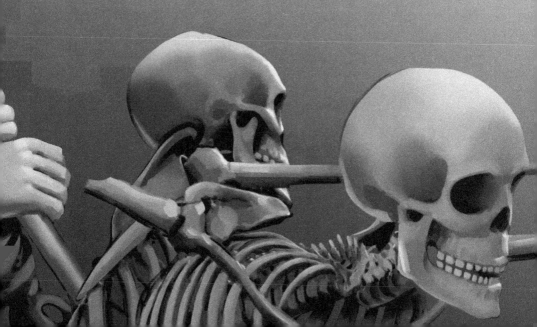

BELENTRA

Nimira

Ruins of Ithyr

Aesari · Mithrys

Olona Island

LUMARIA   FENYR
             WOODS
Shalandril

Althira

Verethia   Tarethel   Eldasil

                          Caelis   ALANOR

                                      Talmira

The Shimmering
Isles

WORLD OF
IMYRIA

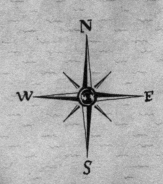

TALIÐOR

KRALAXXAS

N
W E
S

Uldren Isle

Odela

VALKA

DROMGAR

Zol Arrod

Arnvik

Jorga

Boldred

Avrak

Ðalry

Gerazad

JEKTAR

Lowrick

The Ghost
Woods

NOLÐERAN

TIRITH

Ðul Kazar

Lenris Port

SELYNIS

Nezu

Esterra

Tuylon

Meran Island

Copyright © 2021 by Holly Rose

Published by Red Spark Press

The right of Holly Rose to be identified as the author of this work has been asserted in accordance with the Copyright, Designs and Patents Act 1988.

Cover artwork by Jay Villabos
Illustration by Kolarp Em

ISBN (hardcover): 978-1-914503-02-3
ISBN (paperback): 978-1-914503-01-6
eISBN: 978-1-914503-00-9

To my sister, for helping me to believe.

CHAPTER 1

FIRE FALLS TOWARD ME. Blazing flames spread into ferocious wings. There's no time to escape.

I reach through the air and gather all the aether I can. Violet sparks crackle in my fingertips, and the magic amplifies as it joins with that which flows through my blood. Together, the power is great enough to fuel my spell.

I thrust out both hands, my palms facing the oncoming fiery blast. Despite the aether dancing across my fingers, I feel the sweltering heat. It's close enough to blister my hands and singe the edges of my cerulean adept robes.

But I will not be defeated. Not on my birthday.

"*Aquir'muriz!*" I shout. My voice rings through the empty arena and echoes off the highest stone seats.

The aether heeds my command. Violet sparks turn to swirling sapphires, and the spell blossoms into a shield of blue light. Flames lick at the edges and gnaw holes across the emerging magic.

My breathing slows to a halt. I fear it's too late.

But then my shield becomes corporeal. The sapphire light materializes into a whirlpool so violent it hides the raging inferno beyond.

Flames sizzle as they meet the tumultuous water. Steam billows through the arena, and water sprays out as my shield weakens.

I grit my teeth and fuel the wall with more power, willing for it not to disintegrate and leave me entirely exposed, but the defensive spell soon falls apart. Water splashes onto the smooth marble slabs beneath my feet, and the freshly made puddles glisten in the late noon sun.

The fiery wings are also gone. Not even embers remain.

Kaely tosses her mousy brown braid over her shoulder. An ugly sneer contorts the countless freckles splattered across her cheeks. Her eyes, violet like mine, smolder with relentless hatred.

We were friends once. That seems a lifetime ago, despite it being only last year. I don't know what I did to deserve her hatred. Surely breathing isn't a crime?

Her glare is so venomous, with magenta flames blazing in her eyes, that I think she may kill me—though we are only dueling in the arena as part of today's Combat Class.

My attention drifts from Kaely to our spectators. Archmage Lorette Gidston sits on the lowest row of stone seats, our peers gathered around her. Lorette's talon-like hands rest on her lap, and her expression is a mask of cool indifference while she watches us, as if we aren't trying to kill each other. She appears to be in her mid-thirties, but I know for a fact she is much older than that. Her platinum hair is scraped into a bun so neat not even a single strand strays from its place. While this is my second year as an adept—a mage in training—I've never once seen Archmage Gidston wear her hair down. I imagine she would look quite pretty with her hair falling loose across her face, softening her severe features.

Remembering that now is not the time to be scrutinizing the Archmage's appearance, I return my attention to Kaely. But I'm a moment too late.

"*Telum!*" Kaely commands.

A blast of raw aether hurls from her fingers and surges toward me far quicker than the fiery wings did.

I could counter her spell with another aether shield, but I doubt mine will be powerful enough to fend off the attack. Kaely is much stronger than me. The only reason my previous spell nullified hers is because I wielded the element of water against fire. Aether is not one of the four elements, so I can't adopt a similar strategy.

Since shielding isn't an option either, I focus on the spot a few paces from me, far away enough that I'll be beyond the blast's range. I close my eyes, doing my best to ignore the magic racing straight for me, and picture my chosen position. I draw aether into my palms and let it run freely through me.

"*Laxus!*"

At my shout, the teleportation spell claims me, and my body glimmers away into aether dust.

I fade too slowly.

As I slip through the folds of time and space, Kaely's blast slams into me. Pain rips through my shoulder, white-hot and blinding. Though it hurts, I'm lucky the blast caught me mid-teleport, or else the sheer force of it would have torn me apart.

I stagger from the teleportation spell, emerging exactly where I envisioned, and clutch my shoulder. No blood wells out, at least not externally, but the pressure of the blast will have probably ruptured my vessels, and my entire shoulder will be starting to blacken with a hideous bruise.

Kaely prowls toward me, and her footsteps shatter the tense silence enveloping the arena. The other adepts no longer murmur among themselves, their attention entirely focused on our deadly duel.

She raises her arm, and aether gleams in her hand like a lethal torch. My stomach broils with acid as I guess at which spell-words she may next utter. I can barely straighten, let alone defend myself.

Is this how it will end? Am I to die on my birthday?

I don't know why Archmage Gidston hasn't intervened yet. I've never seen a duel taken this far. Maybe among magi, but not among adepts.

"*Gelu'gladis.*" Kaely's voice is both a sneer and a whisper. A promise of death.

Ice. She has chosen to end me with ice.

I can only watch as she stretches sapphire light into a sword. My heart pounds furiously against my rib cage as the frozen blade solidifies.

I squeeze my eyes shut and brace myself for the caress of death. But it does not come. Neither does the bite of the frozen sword.

"*Ignir'muriz.*"

My eyes snap back open. Archmage Gidston stands between us. A fiery shield encases her, and it blazes so brightly the amber light glints across the arena's marble.

Kaely's frozen sword dissolves as it touches the flaming shield. Disappointment descends over her expression as a dense shadow. Disappointment that she could not defeat me once and for all.

"That is enough!" Archmage Gidston booms, her shout tremendous enough to make the clouds tremble. Even Kaely flinches. "Your victory has already been earned, Adept Calton. If you continue, you will end up killing her."

Shame brands my cheeks, as scorching as the inferno Kaely hurled at me.

Kaely raises her brows in apparent surprise. "Reyna should be able to withstand my attacks. She is the Grandmage's daughter."

Her words might sound unassuming—respectful even—to everyone else, but I can hear the mockery in her voice. I clench my left fist. My other hand still clasps my shoulder. Through the cerulean fabric of my adept robes, I feel my skin throbbing where the blast struck. She was so close to killing me.

"Indeed," Archmage Gidston says, turning to me. "She is."

Her words are cold and pensive, and I can't tell what she's considering. Perhaps how unlike my father I am. When he was an adept at the Arcanium, he was known as a prodigy, while I am a useless and lazy adept.

"*Conparios.*" Magic bursts from the Archmage's hands and radiates out. When the light fades, a small vial remains on her palm. It's barely larger than her little finger, and frothy green liquid churns within like fluorescent slime.

As unappetizing as it appears, the sight of the healing elixir relieves me enough to straighten my posture. But I continue clutching my shoulder to suppress as much of the pain as I can.

"Catch, Ashbourne," the Archmage says as she tosses the vial to me. In the next breath, she mutters *ventrez* and a wind spell swirls from her fingers, blowing the small container across the arena and into my hands.

I tear off the cork, tip back my head, and deposit the entire contents into my mouth. The potion tastes like rotten eggs and has a lumpy texture that reminds me of liquified slugs, but I swallow it all in a single gulp and try to cough none up. Hopefully the potion will work quickly enough to banish my pain and minimize any bruising.

Archmage Gidston doesn't watch and instead turns to address the other adepts. "Now that the last pair have finished dueling, your lesson is over for today. You are all dismissed." She offers us no words of praise, but she never does. I'm yet to see the Archmage of Knowledge impressed with any of our performances.

The adepts scramble from their seats, and one by one they murmur *laxus* and disappear into clouds of violet light. Aether scatters across the arena and glitters in the wind.

Archmage Gidston follows them, likely teleporting back to somewhere inside the Arcanium. In addition to overseeing its daily running, she also calls it her home. She lives somewhere in the upper levels, but I don't know where exactly. That part of the Arcanium is banned to mere adepts. Actually, most of it is, aside from the teaching rooms and the library. While my father is the Grandmage of Nolderan, and arguably the most powerful sorcerer in the world, even I am forbidden from entering areas restricted to official magi.

When all the other adepts have teleported out of the arena, only three of us remain: me, Kaely, and Eliya.

Eliya bounds over to me with such speed she almost sends me flying back onto the stone floor, and her unruly crimson hair dances around her heart-shaped face. Fortunately, she brings herself to an abrupt halt before reaching me.

"Reyna!" she exclaims, clutching my shoulders and shaking me. "Are you all right? Are you hurt?"

I don't mention that her fingers are pressing deeply into my left shoulder, the one which was injured by Kaely's aether blast. The healing elixir hasn't yet kicked in. Maybe in ten more minutes it will, but I expect my wound to be tender for a few days.

"I'm fine," I mumble. If Kaely weren't here, I would be more honest. I try to stand tall and proud, but I'm somewhat hunched because of the injury.

Kaely lifts her chin, doing her best to look down at me. Only figuratively, though, since she is much shorter than me. Sometimes I wonder whether she hates me because I'm almost twice her height.

Our eyes lock together. I think she will say something, but she instead draws aether into her fingers and mutters *laxus*, fading away without another word.

Then only Eliya and I are left standing here, surrounded by the arena's towering walls and thousands of empty stone seats. Against its sheer size, I feel as insignificant as an ant. Perhaps I am. Today I was horribly defeated by Kaely and failed to put up a decent fight against her.

I let out a heavy sigh.

"It wasn't *that* bad," Eliya says.

"It was terrible."

"Well, it's not just you. None of us have ever gotten close to beating her."

I gaze over to where Kaely stood moments ago. Aether dust still swirls there. "She's so strong," I say wistfully.

If only I were as strong as Kaely. Then my father would not be ashamed that the only heir to the Ashbourne family was a sorry excuse for an adept. Maybe I would be a better sorceress if I tried harder and spent more time studying, but what's the point? Kaely will always be far stronger than me. I never understood why she took to hating me when we started at the Arcanium. I should be the one who hates her, since she represents all that I am not.

"Her father is the Archmage of Defense." I suppose Eliya is trying to reassure me with a reminder of that fact, but it has the opposite effect.

"My father is the Grandmage of Nolderan." The words taste like ash on my tongue. "And yet look at me."

"Don't think like that," Eliya says, grabbing my hand and squeezing it. "You'll make a great mage when you graduate from the Arcanium."

"But not as great as Kaely."

Eliya presses her lips into a grim line, clearly knowing that nothing she can say will convince me otherwise.

"Please try to smile, Rey-rey," she says after a pause. "It's your eighteenth birthday today. You shouldn't be sad on any birthday, let alone your eighteenth."

I try to smile, but it must look as forced as it feels since Eliya sighs. My fake smile falters, and I replace it with an expression which matches my sour mood.

I know I would be a better adept if I tried, but even if I pour my heart and soul into studying, it still won't be enough to defeat Kaely or to make my father proud. I've long decided that it's better by far to hide behind the mask of idleness than to have my lack of talent laid bare for the world to see. I can never meet my father's expectations, be the prodigy that he was, so I would much rather be a mediocre mage out of choice than because of fate.

At least I can say the reason she defeated me so horribly today is because I don't work hard enough.

"You can't let Kaely spoil your eighteenth birthday." Eliya swings my hand back and forth as she pleads me. "Think how gleeful she would be if she knew you were this upset."

"I'm not upset. I'm just angry she dared to take the duel so far."

It's a lie, and we both know it, but Eliya doesn't point it out. Her expression continues to silently implore me not to let Kaely ruin my birthday. Eliya is right. I shouldn't let Kaely make me miserable. Not today.

"Anyway," I say, "what are you doing tonight? No one's made any plans with me yet."

"Not even Arluin?"

Her question strikes a raw nerve. "No," I grind out, "not even him." When I saw him last night, he mentioned nothing about my birthday. Not a single thing.

"What about your parents?"

I huff a strand of long, dark hair from my face. "My father has important meetings until late tonight. So, I was thinking the two of us could do something instead? Something that involves getting really, really drunk."

Eliya shuffles uncomfortably, not looking me in the eye, and focuses on the marble floor. Her guilt is plain to see. "Um, as great as that sounds, I already have plans tonight."

"You . . . you already have plans." I do my best to ensure the words don't sound as bitter as they taste, but I'm not sure I succeed.

Eliya's shoulders sink. "I'm meant to be going to my uncle's house for dinner tonight."

"And you can't get out of it?"

She shakes her head, and my heart plummets. "No, I'm sorry. We arranged it weeks ago. I forgot it was your birthday until this morning."

I can't believe what I'm hearing. "You forgot it was my birthday." I turn away from her and squeeze my eyes shut, willing myself not to cry. First, I suffered a horrible defeat at Kaely's hands, and now it appears my best friend forgot my birthday. And she even has the audacity to tell me I should be happy on my birthday, especially my eighteenth one.

Maybe I'm overreacting, but her betrayal cuts deep.

"Please don't be mad at me," Eliya whispers.

"It's fine," I force out, waving my hand and trying to keep my words as steady as I can. "I'm not mad. Not mad at all."

My tone must not be very convincing since she says, "You are cross—I can tell. I'm really so sorry, and I promise I'll make it up to you."

I suppose I should say something, but I can't find the words. I stare at her in disbelief.

She wraps her arms around me in an apologetic hug, but I feel numb. The arena's stone walls loom over us, casting their shadows in every direction.

I manage to place an arm across her back, but that's all. As much as I don't want to hurt her feelings, she forgot my birthday.

She releases me from the hug, and I step back, unable to look at her. "I'll see you later," I say, drawing aether around myself like a blanket.

Eliya wrings her hands together, guilt visibly gnawing on her. At least she knows she has done wrong.

I close my eyes, picturing my home in as much detail as I can: the enormous gates, the luxurious gardens, the glistening stone walls of the manor itself. When the image is fully formed, I release the aether and let it spiral from my grasp.

"*Laxus*!" I say, and the teleportation spell washes over me.

I drift away, leaving behind aether dust to scatter across the empty arena.

CHAPTER 2

THOUGH I HAVE CAST THE spell thousands of times before, a part of me is yet to become accustomed to the way teleportation feels. In one moment you're standing on solid ground, and in the next you're drifting through the folds of time and space. It's as if you're floating through something more liquid than air but lighter than water. That substance is, of course, aether.

When teleporting a few paces away, the spell is over in the blink of an eye and the peculiar sensation is much less noticeable. But when traveling from one side of Nolderan to the other, the teleportation takes far longer, and I am shrouded in darkness for perhaps ten seconds. It isn't the same darkness as night, not even a moonless one. I suppose it's closer to being locked inside a deep cavern. Prior to learning this spell, I never knew absolute darkness.

When my teleportation spell is complete, the first thing I feel is the solidness of the ground beneath my feet and the stability it provides. The second thing I feel is the late summer breeze brushing over my cheeks. Even after fully materializing, I remain in darkness for several heartbeats.

Finally, violet light pierces the void. It sketches the enormous gates guarding our manor, complete with our family crest: a shield featuring two winged lions roaring at each other, their manes fanning out like wildfire. Our family is known for its special affinity to fire spells, earning us the surname Ashbourne. And I won't lie: Fire spells are definitely my favorite sort of magic. Our preference goes back a thousand years, when Nolderan was in its infancy. It's well recorded that an ancestor of mine, Alvord Ashbourne, invented *ignir'alas*, the spell of fiery wings which Kaely hurled at me during our duel. I hate that she has mastered the spell so perfectly, while mine is far from flawless. At least the inferno itself isn't lacking in ferocity.

The light drafts out the gardens beyond the gates and the tall chimneys of our manor. It also outlines the buildings behind me and the street I'm standing on.

When the aether finishes sketching the most intricate details of my surroundings, the darkness dissolves into a world of rich color.

I stride over to the gilded gates, and my attention falls onto the magnificent lion crest. Aether hums across the metallic bars, and the golden highlights shimmer like threads of sunlight. I place my hands on my hips and raise my head. The movement hurts a little less than before. It seems Archmage Gidston's healing elixir is finally starting to kick in.

"Reyna Ashbourne," I announce to the gates, my voice loud and clear.

The aether barrier flashes, and the gates swing wide open, recognizing my voice and permitting my entry. I step through, and once I'm on the other side, the gates clang shut behind me.

Rainbows of bright flowers decorate the gardens. My mother has tried many times to teach me the names of all the species she grows in our gardens, but I never remember any of them. Except for roses, tulips, and pansies—and maybe a few others I can't think of right now.

My mother plants the flowers herself, entirely by hand, and even uses a shovel rather than an earth spell. When I was younger, I sat on the grass and watched her labor and then asked why she didn't use magic since it would complete the task in a fraction of the time. She replied, "If we use magic for everything, then life itself will lose its magic." I didn't understand her words then, and I still don't. Especially since she doesn't even water our gardens by hand.

Enchanted buckets sweep up and down the flower beds, sprinkling droplets of water across the vibrant petals. Unlike the gates, which have their enchantment powered by Nolderan's Aether Tower, these buckets will eventually run out of magic and fall to the grass. The water inside them isn't conjured, either. That comes from the fountain at the center of our gardens.

Once my mother has painstakingly planted the flowers with her own hands, they are maintained by our reptilian servants. In case you're wondering, that isn't a metaphor. Our servants are quite literally reptilian. Though they might be closer to what one calls pets than servants, or perhaps something in between.

These creatures are known as faerie dragons and called the island of Nolderan their home long before my ancestors did. But they aren't like actual dragons. Rather than fire, they spew tiny balls of aether when agitated. They're also the size of a cat, with azure scales and amaranthine butterfly wings. Faerie dragons are easily domesticated since they will do absolutely anything for aether crystals, and conjuring aether crystals is effortless for magi, even for useless adepts like me.

As I walk through the gardens, one of the faerie dragons darts past me and almost knocks me over with the empty bucket it clutches in its tiny talons. I pause and watch as the faerie dragon continues to the fountain to refill its bucket.

The fountain is made from marble and is twice my height, with three tiers from which the water cascades. An ornate pattern is chiseled into the edges and reminds me of frills.

Once the bucket is refilled, the faerie dragon flies back to its colorful flowerbed. I hold out my palm, and though the gesture is small, the faerie dragon immediately takes notice. It lowers the bucket onto the path, and water sloshes out and spills over the sides, but the faerie dragon doesn't care. Its butterfly wings flutter as it swooshes over to me.

The faerie dragon hovers above my palm and lets out an impatient yelp. Greed glints in its jewel-like eyes, and its velvety maw nudges my fingers. Delicate antennae tickle my wrist.

Despite the abysmal day I've had so far, I can't help myself from laughing. "Are you really that hungry, Zephyr? Has my mother not fed you at all today?"

Though faerie dragons are unable to vocalize any syllables, they understand every word of our language. Zephyr bobs his head in the most unconvincing nod I've ever seen. Faerie dragons are notoriously difficult to tell apart since there's little variation in their size and shades, but I've never had any trouble distinguishing Zephyr from the rest of our reptilian helpers. His temperament always gives him away.

I know my mother likely fed our faerie dragons at lunchtime, but I humor him anyway. I draw aether into my palm, and Zephyr's scaly tail trembles with anticipation. Many might say that the magi are addicted to magic, but faerie dragons suffer from a far worse affliction.

"*Crysanthius*," I say, and the aether solidifies.

Zephyr swoops down, and his long pink tongue darts out like a frog's as he snatches all the crystals from my grasp. His tongue is extremely slobbery and leaves a thick layer of saliva coating my palm.

"Ew, that's gross, Zephyr!" I exclaim, wiping my empty hand on my robes. "Have you really no manners?"

He flashes me a toothy grin that reveals his tiny fangs. While I've never been bitten by a faerie dragon, I'm certain it would do more than sting.

Zephyr somersaults through the air as he returns to his bucket.

I roll my eyes. "Show off."

His tail flicks out as if to assure me that he heard the insult. His talons close around the handle of the bucket, and he darts back to his flowerbed, leaving me to continue through the gardens.

Arched windows line the sides of our manor and glitter like diamond panels in the late noon sun. I don't pause to gaze at them as I ascend the steps leading to the large doors of our manor.

They're gilded like the gates, and just as heavy. Since there's no enchantment over them, I have no choice but to heave them open. I would utter *ventrez* and shove them aside with a gale, but my mother would scold me if I ruined the paintwork.

With my injured shoulder, pushing the doors open is a considerable effort. I clumsily burst into the hall and nearly fall face-first onto the tiles.

There are several faerie dragons inside, all busy supervising the enchanted brooms and feather dusters. None turn to look at me. Those we allow to work inside are the most well-behaved. If Zephyr saw me stumble, he would throw me a smirk.

After regaining my balance, I make my way through the hall and pass the portraits of many long dead Ashbournes. Some offer me a cheery wave, while others blatantly ignore me.

I find my mother in the drawing room. She has a paintbrush in her hand, like usual, and is staring down the canvas in front of her. I'm certain she spends more time scrutinizing her artwork than actually painting, but that technique has somehow earned her the reputation of Nolderan's most illustrious artist. That's also how my parents met, apparently.

When my father was crowned the Grandmage of Nolderan, my mother was commissioned to paint his portrait for the Arcanium, and somehow they fell in love. I've never cared to learn more details than that.

Today my mother isn't painting portraits. She's instead painting flowers blooming across a dreamy, twilight landscape, and they rustle in a breeze I can see but not feel. A shooting star whizzes across the shadowy sky.

My mother is so focused on her painting that she doesn't notice me as I enter the room. I collapse on the sapphire chaise opposite her and let out the most dramatic sigh I can muster. That gets her attention.

Her eyes narrow as she takes in my disheveled appearance. "Darling, your robes are singed," she says and then returns to her painting.

My fingers claw into the chaise's velvet. It seems even my own mother has forgotten that today is my birthday. Or maybe she cares as little about me as both my best friend and my boyfriend do.

"Kaely nearly killed me today in the arena!" I blurt.

"Nonsense," she says, her eyes not leaving her painting. "Archmage Gidston would never allow such a thing. Besides, you said the same thing yesterday."

"No, I didn't," I protest. "That was last Friday when she swapped my Blood Mint for Fire Bloom during Alchemy, and the potion exploded in my face."

"And like I said, that was your own fault for not smelling the herbs first. Besides, are you sure Kaely was responsible? I know the two of you have had a strained relationship since starting at the Arcanium, but you can't blame her for your every mistake."

"It's far from a 'strained relationship.' She hates me! And I still don't understand why."

"I've explained this to you before," my mother says, swirling her brush across her palette as she mixes together navy and indigo paint. "Kaely is ambitious, as all adepts should be. Graduating from the Arcanium and becoming a mage isn't easy. She strives to be the best, and as the daughter of the Grandmage of Nolderan, you're her greatest rival. It's natural for you both to have grown apart by this."

That's a ridiculous reason to hate someone, but I keep my opinion to myself. I unfasten the first few buttons of my high collar and slide the cerulean fabric far down enough to reveal my injured shoulder. Even with

Archmage Gidston's healing elixir, it's as bruised as I expected. Burst blood vessels lace my skin like black spider webs.

I thrust my index finger at my bruised shoulder. "Would you also call this a strained relationship?"

My mother's eyes drift over to me. Apparently the injury is severe enough for her to set down her paintbrush and palette on the nearest table. "Oh," she says, peering at my shoulder. "It seems she did try to kill you this time."

The calmness in my mother's voice would concern me, if not for the fact she's always like this. Through all my eighteen years, I can't recall a single instance of my mother raising her voice. I can also safely say that I inherited my volatile temper from my father. I suppose the Ashbourne temperament goes hand in hand with our preference for fiery spells. The other thing I inherited from my father are my spindly legs—though his are as stocky as they are long. When my mother and I are both standing, I dwarf her petite frame.

She perches on the chaise, and her slender fingers splay across my bruised shoulder as she examines it more carefully. My similarities with my father start and end at my height and temper. I seem to have inherited everything else from my mother. Like me, she has hair the color of the midnight sky on her current painting, and her face is long and oval.

"How did this happen?" she asks softly.

"Kaely struck me with a blast of aether," I say. We tend not to use the true names of our spells in conversation, lest the aether in our blood reacts with our words. "If I hadn't been in mid-teleport, I'd be dead."

She frowns at my wounded shoulder and then shakes her head. "I will ask your father to speak to Archmage Gidston. Training should not be this dangerous."

I give her a stiff nod. The reason Archmage Gidston didn't intervene earlier is probably because I'm an Ashbourne and she thinks I can endure more than I can.

My mother leaves the chaise and paces over to the oaken cabinet in the far corner of the room. It features paneled doors and drawers with brass handles and is decorated by floral flourishes carved into the wood. The upper part mostly consists of glass and displays the finest crystalline chalices we own. Most have been in the Ashbourne family for centuries, and my father tells me some are as ancient as Nolderan itself. If that's true, it would make them over a thousand years old. Thanks to the aether imbued in the chalices, they are resistant to shattering. As a child, I once came close to testing their durability, but my father stopped me before I could let the chosen chalice fall onto the hallway's tiles. He was so furious he couldn't bear to look at me for a whole week. If I brought up the incident now, even a decade later, he likely wouldn't speak to me for an entire day. That particular chalice belonged to his grandfather, so it is far from the oldest one we have inside our cabinet, but it is the most precious to him. My great-grandfather was a Grandmage of Nolderan, like my father, and he idolizes him greatly. Sometimes I catch him staring up at my great-grandfather's portrait when he thinks no one is looking.

My mother opens the topmost drawer of the cabinet and rummages through until she finds a round, silver tin. She returns to her spot beside me and unscrews the lid.

The salve inside is so red it looks like hundreds of crushed rubies. While Blood Balm is the name of this regenerative ointment, blood isn't an ingredient, and it's instead made from the leaves of Blood Mint. The balm smells far more pleasant than the potion Archmage Gidston gave me in the arena. Blood Mint is the most prominent note in its fragrance, being the active ingredient, and it makes the ointment smell like something between cool mint and spicy pepper.

She dips her fingers into the ointment and slathers a thick layer of glossy crimson across my shoulder. As vivid as the hue is, it doesn't stain my skin. My pores quickly absorb the balm, and if not for the sting spreading across my shoulder, I would forget it was there.

I hope that with both the healing potion and the regenerative balm, my recovery will be quick. Each time I look at the bruise, I'm reminded of Kaely and the defeat I suffered at her hands.

Once my mother finishes applying the ointment, she screws on the lid and sets the tin onto the nearest counter.

"Does Father still have meetings until late tonight?" I ask. "Or have they been canceled?" The hopeful note to my voice raises it a pitch higher.

To my dismay, my mother shakes her head. "We'll do something at the weekend to celebrate your birthday."

"Even Eliya is busy," I grumble. Apparently all those dearest to me care little about my birthday. At this rate, I'll be left to celebrate it alone with only a bottle of wine for company.

"Have you asked Arluin?"

"He's forgotten, too."

"What do you mean he's forgotten?"

"Last night he didn't mention anything about making plans."

"Well, why don't you find him and see if he's busy?"

"I suppose I'll have to," I say, sliding off the chaise and striding out the room. Though I'm annoyed at him for forgetting that today is my birthday, at least his company is better than none at all.

"Don't forget to change your robes," she calls after me. "And make sure you brush your hair!"

CHAPTER 3

DUSK HAS FALLEN BY THE time I leave my manor. I've swapped my singed robes for a sky-blue sleeveless dress. Blossoms climb the skirts, and a pink ribbon accentuates my waistline. A gossamer shawl drapes my shoulders, and dainty rose-colored slippers cover my feet, but they're hard to see with my skirts brushing the floor.

An illusion conceals the bruise on my shoulder. Other magi will be able to tell I've cast an enchantment over my skin, but they won't see it unless they dispel my illusion. And doing so is regarded as a terrible insult here in the Upper City of Nolderan, where magic is free to flourish.

I don't bother teleporting myself to Arluin's manor, knowing he won't be there. Other than sleeping, he spends little time inside his home. But he can hardly be blamed. If I lived in a big, lonely manor then I would also spend little time in it. He doesn't even keep faerie dragons and insists they are merely pests.

I instead teleport to the archway which marks the Arcanium's entrance. QUEL ESTE VOLU, PODE NONQUES VERA MORIRE is etched into the ancient stone. It's written in Medeicus, the language of aether and translates to: *That which is aether may never truly die.* When saying the phrase out loud, we prefer to use the common tongue, in case we inadvertently activate our magic. All our architecture features the Medeicus translation, however.

Beyond the arch, a lengthy path trails to the Arcanium. Statues of long dead magi tower on either side and cast long shadows over me as I pass beneath. Glittering violet crystals float along the path. They are much like the ones I fed Zephyr, though these are clustered together and housed in decorative silver hemispheres. They glow vibrantly with aether, acting as tiny streetlights.

The end of the path is marked by the statue of Grandmage Delmont Blackwood, Founder of Nolderan and the Magi. The plaque fixed to his podium reads exactly that, but I doubt there's anyone in the entire city who wouldn't recognize him. He has a long beard and bushy brows which the portraits of him inside the Arcanium depict as being the shade of black ink. He wears the magnificent robes that only Grandmagi are permitted to wear and clasps the same crystalline staff my father never goes anywhere without. The weapon is forged from aether, and its surface ripples with magic, though you can't tell that by looking at the statue.

I don't stare up at Grandmage Delmont Blackwood for long before following the flight of stairs which spirals around him.

The Arcanium itself is a sprawling palace of countless spires. Thick pillars form a portico, and illustrations are carved into the pediment atop it. They portray the Primordial Explosion: when aether exploded in the emptiness of time and space, forming the Heavens, the Abyss, and Imyria—the mortal plane of existence. Throughout my first year at the Arcanium, my tutors insisted on drilling the origins of the universe over and over during our classes, even though every child from magi families can already recite the tale by heart.

My footsteps echo through the portico as I pass the rows of pillars. The Arcanium's large doors are spread wide open, allowing the adepts and magi to pass through in a stream of cerulean and indigo robes. Since I've changed out of my adept robes for the evening, I'm a stark contrast to the rest of the crowd. The Arcanium is off limits to the ordinary people of Nolderan, but no one stops to question me. They all know my face, thanks to my father.

The inside of the Arcanium is as grand as its multi-pillared entrance and opens to a large, domed atrium. Thousands of aether crystals form the ceiling, and their dazzling light casts the chamber in a lavender glow. In the day, they shine even brighter with the sunlight reflecting off them.

There are a few faerie dragons inside the Arcanium, but they stay far from the crowds. They flutter across the ceiling, ensuring the sponges cleaning the crystals don't lose their magic and fall on anyone below.

With it being nightfall, most people are leaving, and it's a struggle to squeeze past everyone heading in the opposite direction, eager to return home.

On the other side of the atrium, there's an entrance which looks like a smaller version of the portico outside. When I reach it, I hurry down the plummeting staircase.

It's a long descent into the Grand Library of Nolderan since it was built far beneath the Arcanium itself, shrouding its secrets from the rest of the world. I use the bannister to steady my steps, and my hand skims over the polished whitewood.

The staircase splits near the bottom, and I bear right, mostly because of my shoulder. Otherwise it would make little difference which side I choose, since the stairs arrive at the same part of the library.

Bookcases span every wall and climb toward the high, vaulted ceilings. Their shelves are made from the same wood as the bannisters, and the ornamental flourishes gilded across their edges make them so regal they wouldn't look out of place inside a real palace. An enormous chandelier hangs at the center of the library's main chamber, and dozens of glassy arms spiral from it, but they don't hold candles. Aether crystals instead hang from the ends, and all are chiseled into multifaceted teardrops.

Even work-shy adepts like myself can appreciate the breathtaking beauty of the Grand Library of Nolderan.

My feet reach the last step of the plummeting staircase and meet the tiled floor. Black and white squares run diagonally alongside each other and form a chess board, though there are no playing pieces. With the chandelier's blinding light reflecting off the surface, staring at the tiles is like gazing at an optical illusion. I quickly avert my gaze to avoid being disoriented.

Beneath the chandelier lies a gleaming white desk. Like the other tables and chairs situated around the library, its legs are carved into wooden scrolls. Dusty old tomes are stacked on the desk, their leather covers battered and bruised from centuries of wear and tear.

An elderly woman sits there, binding the pages of each ruined book to new covers. Her round face reminds me of a tortoise's, and the wrinkles across her cheeks and brow are as deep as folded pages. Her snowy white hair forms wispy clouds around her globular face. A pair of too-small, black rimmed circular spectacles perch on her nose. She peers through them as she diligently works to heal each book piled on her desk.

The ancient librarian's name is Erma Darkholme, and fifteen years ago she was the Archmage of Knowledge before handing her title to Lorette Gidston. She's also the most terrifying woman I've ever had the misfortune of meeting and makes Archmage Gidston seem like a saint.

As busy as she is with repairing the Grand Library's most ancient books, she notices me as soon as I set foot upon the checkered tiles. She may be extremely short-sighted, but she has the ears of a bat. Her glassy magenta eyes snap up and narrow at me.

I freeze as if I've been caught in a game of blind man's bluff, and conjure the most amenable smile I can muster. I need no mind-link to read her thoughts. Her gaze is revealing enough. I know she's suspicious as to why one of the Arcanium's most indolent adepts would visit the library past dinnertime. My reputation is also far from clean, but I hold Eliya accountable for most of that. After all, it was her idea to skip our History Finals last year by filling our tutor's goblet with a Draught of Forgetfulness we concocted during Alchemy. We hoped it would cause our History tutor, Professor Rellington, to forget all about our examinations, but we brewed the potion incorrectly. Green boils sprouted across his face, and they lasted an entire month. He has never forgotten the incident, and neither has the rest of the Arcanium.

Erma holds my gaze for a moment longer before returning to her work. I don't doubt she's still watching me out of the corner of her eyes as I scurry across the library.

A few adepts gather around curve-legged tables, meticulously scribbling notes into their journals with fluffy white quills. I pay them no attention as I march toward the library's left wing, where Arluin normally sits.

The aisles sprawl out, displaying archaic books on every topic imagin-able. Their colorful covers form a rainbow which contrasts the gilded white-wood bookcases containing them.

I soon spot Arluin's curly, raven-colored locks at the very back of the left wing and crouch behind one of the bookcases cutting through the chamber. He sits on a crushed velvet armchair, its cushions of a violet hue. His left hand curls around the ornate wooden arm, while his other holds open the current page of the worn tome he's reading.

One by one I withdraw the books sitting on the shelf in front of me, careful not to let their hardened leather covers scrape against the wooden shelves. But I suppose it makes little difference. Whenever Arluin's nose is stuck inside a book, his ears stop working.

A pile of books soon forms beside me, and my view to Arluin is clear. He still wears his cerulean adept robes, having not yet returned home since his lessons ended this afternoon. His uniform looks far more elegant on him than it does on me. His robes emphasize his majestic presence, while mine only serve to drown me.

I lean on the bookshelf, and it creaks under my elbow. I haven't yet forgiven him for forgetting my birthday, but I can't help myself from resting my head in my hands and peering at him.

His face is so serene while studying. Tiny lines of concentration crease his brow. From where I crouch, I have a side profile view of him. His nose is perfectly straight, and his jawline is bold. The black curls nestling atop his head appear even glossier with the glow of aether, and their softness somehow sharpens his features. If I weren't annoyed at him, I might have stared at him for hours.

The corners of my lips tug upward as a plan hastily forms in my mind. It would be unfair to say Eliya is responsible for all of my mischief.

I curl my fist as I draw on the aether buzzing through the air. The tiny particles of raw energy snap to my command, swirling between my fingers. The aether is fueled by that which already flows through my veins.

"*Ventrez*," I whisper quietly enough for only the magic to hear. As the spell-word is spoken, aether warps into air magic. A wind spell forms at my fingertips.

I flick my wrist and unleash the magic upon Arluin.

The conjured breeze swirls forth, growing in strength as it nears him. The wind spell sends his cerulean robes billowing out, and the book he's reading slams shut with a deafening thud.

He looks so astonished as he leaps onto his feet that a laugh escapes me. I remind myself I'm meant to be furious at him.

"Reyna," he calls out, whirling around as he examines the countless aisles. "I know it's you. There's no one else in the whole Arcanium—no, the entire city—who's as silly as you."

The bookshelf groans beneath my elbows. I spring away, but it's too late. The sound is loud enough to condemn me.

His gaze snaps over to my direction. His eyes are purple like all of us who practice aether, but his are among the most vibrant shade of magenta I've ever seen. Only my father, who is the most powerful mage alive, has brighter eyes than him.

"*Ventrez*," Arluin says before I can realize, summoning a wind spell of his own. The gale crashes into the shelf above me, and all the books topple over.

There's little time to leap away and stop them from smacking me in the face. I draw more aether into my fingers and envision the spot a few feet from Arluin.

"*Laxus*," I say, and the magic obeys my command.

In the next breath I'm safely away from the falling books, and they land onto the tiles with a tremendous clamor. I wince at the sound, knowing it won't go unnoticed by Erma.

While my teleportation spell is for the most part successful, I'm not exactly in the spot I intended. Instead, I'm much closer to Arluin.

He glances me up and down, his eyes dancing over the blue flowery dress I wear. Judging by the smile playing on his softly arched lips, he appears to be satisfied with his evaluation. His arm slips around my waist and pulls me nearer.

Now we're so close I can feel the heat of his chest as it presses against mine. Our lips are close enough to touch, separated by the thinnest thread of distance. My stomach flutters.

Though I've kissed Arluin a thousand times before, I long for more. Even if I were to kiss him every day for the rest of my life, it will never be enough.

We are both silent and still, the air around us thick with tension. Our breaths fall to the same rhythm, our gazes fixed on each other.

Arluin is the one to break our stare. He leans closer, his warm breath trailing across my neck. Though I wish it had instead been his lips, I shiver at his closeness.

"Reyna," he whispers into my ear, his lower lip grazing my lobe as he speaks, "have you cast an enchantment over me? Because you look far too bewitching." His arm wraps more tightly around my waist, and with his spare hand, he sweeps a strand of dark hair from my face. My skin tingles as his fingers brush my cheek.

With his words and the way he holds me, I can't help myself from arching into him. Then I remember he forgot my eighteenth birthday, and

I'm supposed to be mad at him for it. Which I still am, of course. Even if he's currently holding me in the most distracting way.

I wrinkle my nose at him, but I must admit it's an effort not to grab his hair and kiss him as if we aren't in Nolderan's Grand Library. "You say that exact same sleazy line every time I make an effort to look pretty!" I definitely don't mention how it has the same effect every time he says it. "If you want to seduce me, you'd better try harder."

His gaze returns to my lips, and I immediately regret my words. Warmth bubbles in my stomach as his hand slides down my neck and traces my collarbone. I wonder whether his hands will slip even lower. "Then what if I tell you about all the indecent ways I'm thinking of kissing you?" he murmurs into my neck, all but kissing the skin there. "Would that seduce you more?"

My body is screaming that yes it would, but I do my best to resist his charming words and teasing touches. Especially because we're in a library.

Clarity descends on me before I can forget my purpose in coming here.

"Do you even know what day it is?" I blurt.

He has the audacity to answer: "Tuesday?"

I slap him across the cheek. Not particularly hard, or else Erma will hear. That is, if the falling books haven't already alerted her to our mischief. I'm surprised she's not yet stormed over. She normally has by now.

"Tuesday?" I exclaim in a vexed whisper. "Tuesday! So, you really have forgotten then!"

I try to wriggle from his grasp, but there's no escaping his arms.

He wears an innocent expression on that captivating face of his. Now I wish I'd slapped him harder, even if it risks inciting Erma's wrath. "I honestly have no idea what you're talking about."

"It's my birthday—my eighteenth birthday! I can't believe you!"

"Oh yes," he says, "of course it is. How could I forget something as important as that?"

"I knew it all along!" I jab my index finger into his chest, but it hurts me more than him. "You really do care more about those books of yours than you care about—"

He silences my accusation with a chaste kiss. It might have tasted sweet if I weren't so furious with him.

Before I can scold him for the stolen kiss, he chuckles. "Don't be so silly. How can I care more about books when they don't look half as lovely as you?"

"So, you only care about me because you think I look lovely?"

He simply smiles at me. "And because you're the silliest person I know."

To anyone else, that might sound like an insult, but I know it's a compliment of deep meaning.

Once, when we were drunk in the dead of night, he confessed to how much he loved my silliness. He said it helps him forget all that has happened.

That he is an exile's son.

Though I very much wish to still be mad at him, his smile disperses the remnants of my rage.

I let out a sigh and sink into his arms, allowing them to support my weight. "You are the most awful boyfriend in all of Imyria."

"And the most dashing."

I roll my eyes at him. "Don't think I'll let you off lightly."

"Oh, I know. I expect to be groveling for weeks."

"I suggest you start groveling tonight."

"In that case, how about I take you to The Violet Tree and buy you all the wine you can drink?"

I flash him a triumphant grin. He knows me so very well—even if he did forget my birthday.

But before I can respond, footsteps thunder from behind. The sound ricochets through the vaulted ceiling.

"What do you two think you're doing inside my library?" Erma snarls, glaring at us through her small, circular spectacles.

If I were not preoccupied with leaping away from Arluin, I might have pointed out that this isn't her library. It isn't even my father's. It belongs to Nolderan.

"N-nothing," I stammer, my cheeks burning a crimson so vivid that my expression alone is evidence enough of the lie.

Arluin is a little less flustered than me. "We were just leaving," he says, hurrying over to the books lying heaped beneath the bookcase.

Erma's temples twitch as she examines him and the fallen books. "Good," she snaps, whirling around. "They had all better be returned to their rightful places, or else I will be informing Archmage Gidston of your insolence."

My shoulders sag with relief as Erma's purple robes disappear around the bookcases. While our position was rather compromising, this isn't the first time Erma has caught us—or other adepts—locked in amorous embraces.

"Come on," Arluin murmurs, gathering the books. "It seems we ought to get going."

CHAPTER 4

HAND IN HAND, WE LEAVE the Grand Library. The Arcanium's atrium is mostly empty now, and we stroll through the large, circular space.

We reach the other side of the chamber and pass the rows of pillars standing sentry outside the Arcanium's entrance. Floating crystals illuminate our path as we follow the staircase around Grandmage Delmont Blackwood.

When we're at the bottom, I turn to Arluin. "So, we're going to The Violet Tree?"

"Indeed, we are."

"And you really meant what you said about buying all the wine I can drink?"

"Of course."

"You know I can easily drink all your wealth in a single night."

"We'll see about that," he says with a laugh.

We continue through the Arcanium's grounds, passing the dozens of towering statues which line the path. Many depict my own ancestors since the Ashbourne family has produced the most Grandmagi throughout history. One day, my father will also likely have a statue erected here in his memory. I can't say the same about myself.

We slip beneath the archway, Arluin's hand still clasping mine, and step out onto the cobbled streets.

The buildings of Nolderan are all made from white granite, and the smooth surfaces appear silver in the dusky purple glow of the floating streetlights. Cobalt tiles ripple across the rooftops like waves, and they peak into perfect triangles. We turn left down Lenwick Street, the main road which winds through the Upper City and connects all the most important structures. It reaches to the very back of Nolderan, where the Aether Tower lies.

Day and night the Aether Tower hums with raw magic, fueling the city with power. It's connected to a network of several smaller spires and ensures the flow of magic through every street to maintain permanent wards such as the one enchanting my manor's gates. Larger wards, like the one covering the entire isle, prevent any foreign sorcerers from teleporting inside.

We turn onto another street and head to Revelry Row, where The Violet Tree is situated. Many of Nolderan's finest establishments can be found here. The Violet Tree itself is the city's most luxurious inn, and the food and wine they serve is exquisite.

The stars twinkle high above, and the shadows dance around us. Our walk is tranquil, or at least it is until we take a shortcut through the quieter streets and pass a faulty streetlight, its crystal flickering on and off. I can't remember the last time I saw one broken and squeeze Arluin's hand. He, however, seems unbothered by the sight of it. Even when we pass another one.

An uneasiness ripples across my skin like tiny shards of ice. Now the shadows are suffocating, and inexplicable dread coils through my stomach.

The air smells like death. Cold, lonely, and rotten.

And I am certain we are being followed. No—stalked like prey.

I stop.

"What is it?" Arluin asks. I feel his gaze on me, but I don't turn to look at him.

I spin around, searching for whatever it is pursuing us, but with many of the crystalline streetlights broken, it's almost impossible to discern anything amid the shadows.

Yet as I train my eyes on a narrow dark corner, I'm certain I can make out the silhouette of a hooded figure.

I tremble at the ominous sight. Arluin grips my hand.

"Something's there. . ." I whisper, not daring to raise my voice in fear of alerting the shadowy figure. "Watching us."

Arluin follows my gaze, squinting at the darkness. When I look back, the silhouette is gone.

"There's nothing there."

"But I saw someone—something."

Arluin pulls me in and kisses the top of my head. Even the caress of his lips doesn't banish the uneasiness crawling across my skin. "You must be imagining things. Don't tell me you've already started drinking."

I press my lips together. Perhaps he's right. There's no one there, nor any trace of them. Maybe the hooded figure was only a figment of my imagination. Yet I can't shake away the realness of the presence. How it felt like death whispering through the shadows.

"Come on," he says gently. "If we stand here all night, staring into the darkness, won't we end up wasting your birthday?"

I manage a small nod, and he leads me farther down the street. After a few paces, I glance back to where I thought I saw the hooded silhouette, but there's still no one there.

Only darkness.

With The Violet Tree being Nolderan's finest inn, it's also the most expensive. That's why I'm pleased Arluin offered to fund my drinking for the night. My adept's stipend is measly, and I've almost spent every penny this month. Arluin also receives a stipend from the Arcanium, though his is greater since he's a fourth-year student and is better able to help with brewing potions and conducting research than a second-year such as myself. But he doesn't need this small salary. After his father was exiled, being the only child, he inherited all his family's assets. That includes the Harstall's manor which is as splendid and ancient as mine, and also various business shares which have ensured him with a steady income during these past five years.

Revelry Row is bursting with life when we arrive. Men wear colorful silk tunics, heavily embroidered with metallic thread, while women wear dresses so extravagant they make my pale blue dress look dull in comparison. Though Arluin is still clad in his cerulean adept robes, he doesn't look too out of place. The few magi strolling the streets are also in their uniforms. Some are so proud of their robes I'm sure they never take them off. My father is one such example.

The Violet Tree is located at the beating heart of Revelry Row and has the same white walls and cobalt roof as any other building along this street. If not for the sign, it would be difficult to tell it apart from all the other inns and restaurants.

In the late summer breeze, the sign lazily swings back and forth from its steel pole. A violet oak is painted on the sign, and it glows against the dark background. The tree's leaves rustle in the wind, and it's enchanted with aether, like my mother's artwork.

The inn's door is a deep shade of mauve, and blossoms are carved into its wood. Arluin holds the door open for me, and I step inside.

For a long moment, everything is silent and still—so unlike the inn I always visit.

Convinced he's somehow taken me to the wrong place, I turn to him. But before I can say anything, a cacophony of voices erupts from the darkness.

"*Surprise!*"

The crystalline lights switch on, revealing the faces of everyone I hold dear. My mother and father both stand there, as do Eliya and the rest of my extended family. All of them are crowded into The Violet Tree's front room.

Aether dust sprinkles over me. I'm so astonished I don't look to see who it comes from. "I . . . I thought no one wanted to spend my birthday with me."

Behind me, Arluin clears his throat but says nothing as Eliya rushes over to me. Her hug is so forceful it irritates my injured shoulder.

"You have no idea how horrible I felt lying to you before! The look of disappointment on your face was so unbearable I almost told you everything."

"And it's a good job you didn't," my mother says with a sigh. "Or else weeks' worth of plans would have been ruined."

Eliya gives my mother a meek look as she releases me.

I turn to my father. He stands a head and shoulder above everyone else, and in his magnificent robes he looks as fearsome as Grandmage Delmont

Blackwood's statue outside the Arcanium. He has also brought his crystalline staff with him. Only my father would bring Nolderan's most deadly weapon to a birthday party.

"What are you doing here, Father?" I ask, my brows knitting together in confusion. "What happened to all the important meetings you have until late tonight?"

The corners of his auburn beard tug up as he smiles. "Since my daughter's birthday is far more important, I canceled them all."

I laugh at that, though I doubt my father would have actually canceled his meetings. Most likely, he's managed to book a rare night off his duties. But if something dire does arise, he'll have no choice but to leave and see to it.

Dozens of tables and chairs are normally scattered through The Violet Tree, but tonight they're replaced by an enormous table which spans the entire length of the room. It's made from polished sandalwood, but you can only tell that by the double twisted legs since the rest of the table is covered with silver plates and crystalline goblets.

It takes me at least ten minutes to make it to the table, thanks to my aunts, uncles, cousins, second cousins, and relatives I'm not even sure are related to me. My father's side of the family is rather small, since he's an only child like me, but my mother more than makes up for it with her expansive family.

When we're all seated, servers bring over countless dishes of more foods than I can imagine—and these are just our appetizers. My parents have hired out The Violet Tree to throw a mighty banquet, most likely through my mother's charms and my father's reputation. And of course, our family's riches.

It seems the inn is still serving other guests this evening, however. A few patrons trickle in through the door, and the servers take them through to the back rooms. All look over at our banquet as they pass, and many stop to speak with my father. My father knows nearly everyone in the Upper City. How he can remember so many names and faces, I'll never know. His acquaintances all come over and wish me a happy birthday. While I suppose it's nice of them, it's also rather annoying since it stops me from eating my food and drinking my moon-blossom wine—an extravagant import from the elven lands which is infused with aether. We only drink it on special occasions.

Eliya sits to my right, and Arluin to my left. He talks about boring things with my father, like the research he's currently involved in. My father is as strange as Arluin in that he enjoys discussing such matters, and the two of them engage in one of the longest and dullest conversations I've ever heard. He doesn't blame Arluin for his father's mistakes, though he personally banished Heston Harstall from Nolderan. But I know he remains wary of Arluin, a part of him wondering whether one day he too will fall down the same path. It's by the slight reservation in his eyes that I can tell, but he's never said anything out loud to me nor has he objected to my relationship with Arluin. I don't doubt that he has many such conversations with my mother, though. It's probably because of her that he holds his tongue.

In between dishes, I chatter with Eliya about our Medeicus and Fire Magic tutors. Apparently several other adepts have spotted them looking incredibly familiar when out and about through the city over the past few weeks. It's a far more riveting topic of conversation than research.

By the time we finish eating, I am certain I've nearly finished an entire bottle of moon-blossom wine all by myself. I'm presented with a mountain of gifts, but unwrapping the colorful paper is an almost impossible task. I end up dropping the present from my mother and father. It falls onto the wooden floor with a thud. In my defense, it is a small box.

My entire family laughs.

"You're already really drunk!" Eliya exclaims beside me, unable to control her giggling.

"No, I'm not," I protest, leaning down to find the box beneath my feet. But it seems she's right since I fall off my chair. More laughter erupts across the table.

I tilt back my head and stare up at the arched ceiling. The walls spin around me in an awful bout of vertigo.

Arluin's face appears above me. Actually, I can see three of him, all his faces blending together where they meet.

"Do you need some help down there?" he asks, raising a brow at me.

His voice echoes in my ears, and it takes me a moment to understand his words.

I lower my gaze. "Maybe . . ."

Arluin kneels beside me and searches the floor for where the box landed. When he finds it, he scoops it up and helps me back onto my chair.

He hands it over, but I slide it back across the table to him.

"Can you open it?" I ask quietly. "I think I will drop it again if I try."

Eliya finds that question hilarious.

Arluin obliges and tears the red paper off the small square box. He opens it and presents me with a pair of diamond earrings. They are shaped like chandeliers, and I'm certain they would reach my shoulders if I put them into my ears.

"They're beautiful," I gasp, my fingers running across one of the diamond swirls.

When I look up, my mother is smiling. "I knew you would like them, darling."

"I do have impeccable taste," my father says. That earns him an annoyed look from my mother.

"These aren't the ones you picked, Telric," she says. "You wanted to buy Reyna the ugly set which looked like spiders."

My father scratches his chin, disturbing the thick auburn hair which sprouts there. "Are you sure?"

She sighs at him and shakes her head.

When at last all my gifts are unwrapped, I take to drinking once more. Arluin's eyes tighten as I lift my goblet to my lips.

"Are you really going to drink more wine?" he asks me.

"Of course. Why wouldn't I?"

"Because you've already drunk so much."

Eliya leans forward, joining the conversation. "Don't worry, Arluin," she says. "Me and Reyna are used to drinking until we pass out."

Arluin runs a hand down his face. "That's exactly what concerns me."

He has little say in the matter, however, and after another bottle of wine, I end up passing out. I'm not sure how long I'm unconscious, but when my eyes reopen, I see my mother and father leaving. The rest of the table is mostly empty now. Eliya hasn't passed out yet, though. I feel her patting my head. Why exactly, I don't know.

"Make sure she doesn't spend the night in a gutter," my father grumbles to Arluin.

"I'll look after her!" Eliya exclaims beside me. Maybe that was the reason for her patting my head.

My father doesn't turn to Eliya. Thanks to her, I have spent the occasional night sleeping in an alleyway.

"I'll help you take her back home," Arluin says. His arm wraps around my waist, preparing to lift me from my seat. I spring to life and shake him off.

"I'm not going home!" I object. "It's my birthday, and I haven't finished celebrating it."

Arluin sighs. I'm surprised he doesn't bother pointing out that I've spent most of it with my head on the table.

"That's the spirit!" Eliya claps her hands together. "Here, Rey-rey, drink some more wine!"

Much to Arluin's dismay, she passes me another goblet.

The moment the wine greets my lips, I black out again.

When I finally return to my senses, Eliya is long gone and Arluin is hauling me off my chair.

"Where's everyone gone?" I demand, this time not resisting as he lifts me. One of his arms is secured under my legs, while the other supports my back. The ground looks a lot farther away than it probably is. "Why did they leave so early?"

Arluin chokes out a laugh. "It's definitely not early."

"Oh," I say, blinking at him. In his arms, I feel like I'm floating. "Can I have more wine?"

"Not a chance."

I pout. "Why not?"

"Because you are very, very drunk right now."

"I'm only a little bit drunk."

Arluin doesn't seem to fall for that lie. He shakes his head and carries me toward the door. I let my head droop back. From this angle, the table is upside down. All the dishes and goblets are gone. And my gifts, too.

"Where are all my presents?"

"Your parents took them home," he says. "They had to make a few trips."

"Oh."

We come to the door. It's shut.

"Can you get that?" Arluin asks, his arms still full with me.

I reach for the door, but my hand is too far away and my fingers only find air. I use my foot instead and give the door a mighty kick. We barge out into the night and almost collide with the couple who are entering the inn. I throw back my head and laugh. I immediately regret doing so. It's more evidence that I'm drunk.

He flashes them an apologetic look, but it does little to soothe their scowls. Their angry expressions make me laugh harder. Arluin hurries away from them before I can add to the insult.

"Hey," I say when he comes to a stop. I prod his chest. "I just remembered something."

He peers down at me. "What did you remember?"

"That you didn't get me a present."

"I did."

Maybe he gave me his present when I blacked out. "Oh yes," I say with a big nod. "I remember now. It was a lovely . . . uh . . ."

His shoulders shake with silent laughter. "Reyna, I haven't given it to you yet. You asked me if I got you a present, not whether I gave it to you."

"Oh. Right. When are you going to give it to me then? You can't wait until tomorrow or it won't be a birthday present, will it?"

"I was intending to give it to you tonight. But now you're too drunk so it'll have to wait until the morning."

"I'm not too drunk."

He shoots me a dubious look.

"Please, Arly," I beg him. "I won't be able to sleep now. Not knowing what my present is will keep me tossing and turning all night."

"You were sleeping just fine on the table before."

I scrunch my nose at him. "I'm not waiting until the morning. Besides, why can't I be drunk for your present?" I don't add that all my other presents were given to me while I was drunk, but I do think it's a strong argument.

"Because," he simply says.

"'Because' isn't a reason."

"Reyna, I'm taking you home."

"No, I don't want to go home. I want to go to yours. I'll be good, I promise."

"You're never good," he says, kissing my cheek.

"If I go home with you, then at least you'll know whether I'm asleep or whether I'm awake drinking more wine."

He breathes a laugh. "All right. Point taken."

"So, that means we're going back to yours?"

"Yes."

"And you're also going to give me your present?"

"We'll see about that part."

I lift my head and commit to being on my best behavior. Perhaps then he'll let me have his present.

He's never made this much of a deal about presents before. Not even when he got me Mr. Waddles for my sixth birthday. Arluin chose him because ducks are my favorite animal and purple is my favorite color. Even twelve years later, Mr. Waddles still sits on top of my chest of drawers. He's not as fluffy as he once was, though.

Arluin has always gotten me the most thoughtful presents. That's why I'm dying to know what this year's will be.

He closes his eyes and draws aether around us.

"*Laxus*," he says, and we leave The Violet Tree behind in a glittering cloud of purple dust.

CHAPTER 5

WE EMERGE OUTSIDE THE GATES of Arluin's manor. Like mine, they're enchanted to prevent others from teleporting inside. The Harstall family crest features a serpent coiled around a sword like vines. Its forked tongue darts out, and I'm sure I can hear it hissing. But that could also be the aether humming across the tall steel bars.

"Arluin Harstall," he announces, and the gates swing open.

Arluin carries me through, and they clang shut when we're on the other side. I could have opened them myself, though perhaps not particularly well in my current state. As the current owner of this manor, Arluin has enchanted the gates to also recognize my voice and my name. But I doubt it would recognize my slurred speech.

While the architecture of his manor is as splendid as ours, the gardens are not comparable. The grass is wild and overgrown with weeds. When I used to visit as a child, the shrubs were perfectly clipped into lions and griffins and stags. Now they have all long lost their magnificent shapes.

The pond is just as neglected. Long ago, it was filled with pink lilies and shimmering fish. And many ducks, too. I always fed them lots of bread, much to his mother's delight. She loved baking.

Once, I accidentally dropped a large crust into the water and tried to fish it out. I leaned too far over and ended up falling into the pond. Arluin had to pull me out. I thought he would laugh at me for it, but he never did.

I return my attention to him. His raven curls shine in the starlight. He's so focused on walking and not dropping me that he doesn't seem to notice me gazing at him.

"You can put me down now if you want," I say, feeling rather guilty that he's doing all the work while I'm doing nothing.

"I don't want to."

Since I'm quite comfortable, I don't argue with that.

He carries me through the rest of the gardens and up the few steps leading to the manor's double doors. Both have brass knockers, and twin serpents coil around each ring. Some of the black lacquer has peeled off the doors, revealing small patches of brown wood. I've pointed this out to Arluin many times, but he hasn't bothered to repaint the doors. There are no servants to do it for him, either. There hasn't been since Arluin's mother died. That was when his father, Heston, started delving into necromancy, though it took six years for him to be caught. It was his gray eyes which finally gave him away, along with the inability to draw upon aether. Dark magic consumed and corrupted it all.

The magi searched their manor and discovered the ancient tomes Heston stole from Nolderan's vaults, where forbidden relics are locked away beneath the Arcanium. It was easy for him to get hold of them, since he was the Archmage of Defense before being exiled and replaced by Kaely's father.

But I shouldn't be thinking about such awful things. Especially not on my birthday.

Arluin's hand shifts beneath my knee as he flicks his wrist.

"*Ventrez*," he says, and the conjured gale blows the doors wide open. This is why much of the paint has chipped off. He often uses his magic instead of pushing them open with his hands.

His grasp tightens around my legs, holding me more securely, and then he carries me through the doors. He doesn't bother shutting them behind us. There's little reason to do so. The enchanted gates ensure no one can trespass on his property. And since it's summer, the weather is mild.

His manor is far tidier inside. The tiles are so well polished that they gleam despite being cast in darkness.

"Can you get the lights?" Arluin asks, angling me toward the switches on the left of the doors.

I lean forward and feel the wall until my fingers locate the circular button. I push it firmly, and the chandelier switches on.

It's like the one hanging inside the Grand Library, but much smaller. Aether crystals droop from the arms. While there are far fewer crystals than the library's chandelier, they're more than bright enough to illuminate the hallway.

A deep blue rug sprawls out before us, and it stretches over to the spiraling staircases on the other side of the hall. Golden thread weaves through the rug, forming a hexagonal pattern. Arluin continues over it and ascends the stairs.

"You'd better not drop me," I warn him when we're halfway up. I glance back and see that it's a long way down. I don't look for long.

A smirk dances on Arluin's lips, and I wonder whether he's considering it. Or at least pretending that he is. But he instead replies, "I promise I won't."

We reach the top of the stairs without him dropping me, and we head straight into his room. The door was left ajar, so we easily burst through.

A mahogany bed takes up most of the space. Its four posters look like oversized candlesticks, and regal swirls are carved into every inch of the wood. White silk hangs from the frame and ripples with the delicate breeze blowing in through the open window.

A crystalline lamp stands on the counter beside the bed, and it looks like a standing chandelier. Zig-zagged wooden panels of assorted shades form the floor, and a crimson square rug featuring a paisley pattern lies in front of the canopy bed. It's set at a diagonal and appears diamond-like as we enter.

This has always been his room, even before Heston was exiled. It's a lot smaller than the master bedroom across the corridor, but Arluin can't bear to enter it, let alone sleep in there.

He sets me down on the bed and heads over to his wardrobe to hang his adept robes. The wardrobe is also crafted from mahogany, and the decoration carved into its panels matches the swirls running across the bed. I normally leave my robes hanging over the armchair in my room, but Arluin is much fussier than me about having wrinkles in his clothes.

I tilt my head over the edge of the bed and watch from upside down as he loosens the metallic buttons of his high collar. If he notices me staring, he doesn't look bothered. He finishes unbuttoning his collar and pulls the cerulean fabric over his head, revealing the hard planes of his torso. If he weren't so far away, I would run my hands over his chest. Maybe I will when he comes closer. Though with how much I drank tonight, he'll probably insist we go straight to sleep.

As he opens the wardrobe to hang his robes, I turn my attention to the grandfather clock standing in the corner. Thanks to the aether imbued in its springs, it perpetually ticks. According to its hands, it's currently quarter to twelve.

My birthday is almost over.

"Arluin," I lament. For dramatic effect, I let my arm flop over the side of the bed. "You need to give me my present before midnight, or else it won't be special anymore."

He shuts the wardrobe and turns around, his breeches still on. I watch him cross the room, and the bed dips as he perches on the edge beside me.

"Very well," he says.

"Really?" I exclaim, having expected him to refuse. I scramble up, but most of my weight is hanging over the bed, and gravity pulls me down. I'm unable to haul myself back up.

With a soft laugh, Arluin grips my waist and helps return me to a sitting position. Our faces are so close they're almost touching, and his warm breath caresses my skin. I would kiss him, if not for the fact I'm dying to know what my present is.

He reaches for my face, and his thumb sweeps across my cheek. "Reyna, I . . ." His shoulders are taut with tension, and hesitance clouds his expression.

The last time I remember him being this nervous was four years ago, when he confessed he no longer saw me as a friend. When he first kissed me.

I rise onto my knees so we're at the same height, wrap my arms around his tense shoulders, and kiss the top of his head. "What's the matter, Arly?" His dark curls muffle my voice. They're as soft as they look.

It occurs to me now that he might be using my drunkenness as an excuse. Whatever the gift is, he's worried about how I will react to it.

He hesitates. Then he draws in a shaky breath and holds out his hand. "*Conparios.*"

A jewelry box emerges from violet light. It's covered by midnight blue velvet and decorated with small flowers. His hands tremble slightly as he opens it.

Inside lies a silver, heart-shaped locket. Delicate roses are etched across its gleaming surface.

My breath catches in the back of my throat.

"Do you like it?" he asks with a frown.

"Of course I like it. Did you think I wouldn't?"

"It wasn't that," he says, lifting the necklace from where it lies. He mutters *evanest*, and the empty box disappears in a cloud of aether.

"Then why were you so nervous to give it to me?"

He lays the locket flat on his palm and glances up at me. "A memory crystal lies inside. I wanted to make a promise to you and have it forever recorded so you know my sincerity."

I sit back on my heels. "What promise?"

Arluin doesn't answer. He waves his hand over the locket, and it springs open to reveal a glittering crystal. *"Incipret."* At his command, the memory crystal fills with a purple glow as it starts to record.

"Reyna," he begins, "I am a man who has nothing, who is nothing. I know I don't deserve you, but you mean everything to me. In this world, I have nothing else left."

I rest my hand on his cheek. "Arluin, please don't speak about yourself like this. You mean everything to me, as well."

He places his finger on my lips, hushing me. "I've loved you for as long as I remember. And it's only when I'm with you that . . . that I forget . . ."

That he is a necromancer's son. That he watched his father commit atrocities in an attempt to resurrect his mother.

Though I silently finish his sentence, he doesn't voice the words. And I don't expect him to. I hate the tortured look in his eyes as he relives his darkest memories. His father's most horrifying experiments.

I pull his finger from my lips and then kiss him, hoping it will banish the nightmares afflicting him.

But Arluin stares at the wardrobe. Even when my lips trail across his jawline and down his neck, he barely reacts to my touch.

Realizing my efforts are in vain, I kiss his nose and say, "Arly, we can't change the past. We can only shape the future."

My words have more effect. He snaps to life and clasps my face so tightly it's as if he fears I will slip away.

"Marry me," he gasps. "Please marry me, Reyna. I can't bear the thought of ever being without you."

My heart makes a giddy flutter. This must be the promise he wished to make.

"Of course I'll marry you," I say. "Who else would put up with my drunken antics?"

The attempt at a joke seems to go unnoticed. His expression remains serious.

"We'll marry each other after you graduate from the Arcanium. By then, I will have been a qualified mage for two years and will hopefully have a good career ahead of me—"

I brush a low hanging curl from his face. "You know I'd marry you tomorrow."

"Reyna, your father will never allow that. It would be too great a distraction from your studies."

"I'm eighteen now," I say with a shrug. "By law, I no longer require parental permission to marry. I'll come and live with you. I spend most of my nights here, anyway."

"I can't do that, Reyna. I'll be lucky if he even lets me marry you." He pauses, chewing on his lip. "Do you think he will?"

"Why wouldn't he?"

His shoulders sink. "Because of my father." His voice is so quiet it's barely audible.

"Arluin, you are not your father."

"Maybe you don't see the shadow of my father when you look at me, but everyone else does. Behind my back they whisper about how I will follow in my father's footsteps, how I too will become a necromancer. Even your father."

"No, he doesn't," I say, and hope he can't see through my lie. I know every time my father gazes upon Arluin, he is reminded of his oldest friend's treachery.

Arluin doesn't argue with me. A brief silence stretches between us. He glances down at the locket and finally says, "Anyway, this is the promise I wanted to make. I will marry you when we've both graduated from the Arcanium. I swear it."

Though I would rather marry him tomorrow than in three years, I don't protest any further. It doesn't matter when we marry, so long as we do.

"Then I will wear this locket every day, as my promise to you," I say. "And we'd better have the most extravagant wedding Nolderan has ever seen."

That brings a smile to his lips,. "If you want an extravagant wedding, then an extravagant wedding we shall have."

I return his smile.

"*Terminir*," he mutters. The memory crystal ceases to glow, and he closes the locket.

Arluin leans behind me and sweeps away my hair. He secures the locket around my neck, and his fingers tickle me as they brush over my skin.

When the necklace is fastened, he turns back to me and takes my hand in his. "I promise," he whispers, "I will marry you—"

I cut him off by pressing my lips to his. He is at first caught off-guard, but he soon reciprocates and kisses me back with as much vigor. Our lips move in time to one another's, and we kiss each other as though we are starved for air.

My fingers knit through his dark curls, and I use them to pull him closer. His hand slides up my waist, reaching higher until it comes to my breast. He kneads the soft flesh through the thin fabric of my dress, and a moan escapes me.

I shove his shoulders, and he falls into the scarlet sheets. I straddle him, my pale blue skirts pooling around us.

"It's late," he says. "And you're drunk."

I run my fingers across his chest, feeling the firm edges of his lean muscles. "You asked to marry me, and now it seems you don't want me," I tease.

"I never said I don't want you," he says, gripping my waist and hauling me off him. He sets me onto the sheets beside him and leans on his elbow, gazing down at me. His fingers trace my shoulder. "Just that it's late and you're drunk. Both of which are facts."

"I don't want to sleep."

"Then we won't sleep," he says, pulling down one of my sleeves and leaving half of my chest exposed to the cool night air.

He kisses me there—and then everywhere else. And as he promises, we spend most of the night making love to each other and very little of it sleeping.

CHAPTER 6

I WAKE WITH MY HEAD resting on Arluin's chest. Crimson brocade blankets spill over us, and our bare legs are tangled together. Sunlight filters through the open window and sharp shadows slice across the room.

His skin is warm beneath my cheek. My fingers trace lazy circles across his chest. One of his arms is tucked around my waist, holding me flush against him. Every now and then he lifts his arm, flicking to the next page of the book he's reading.

I tilt back my head to get a better look at the cover. But my temples scream in protest, and the pain is so piercing my sight blurs. A groggy fog descends over me. While I have experienced many a hangover, this might be the worst one yet.

I must have let out a small whimper of pain since Arluin asks, "Feeling the wine?" His lips twitch with amusement as he looks down at me. If I felt a lot less awful, I would slap him for his smirk.

"Yes," I grunt.

"Do you regret drinking so much?"

"No. Never."

Arluin lets out a gentle laugh and returns to his book.

I close my eyes again, feeling the steady rise and fall of his chest. With my ear pressed against his skin, I can hear the drum of his heartbeat. I try to focus on that rather than the pain shooting across my temples.

"If it's really that bad," Arluin says after a while, "I have a numbing potion in the top drawer." He gestures to the counter on his side of the bed. The crystalline lamp there casts a purple glow over the pages of his book.

"You could have said so sooner!"

"You needed to learn your lesson."

"There's no lesson to be learned."

He arches a brow at me. "You passed out. Several times."

"I only remember the once."

"And you were dancing on the tables with Eliya so loudly the servers were trying to usher you both out."

"I don't remember that."

"You don't believe me?"

"No, I do." Dancing on the tables is something I've done plenty of times before with Eliya, and considering how much my head hurts, it isn't surprising I don't remember it happening.

Arluin shakes his head as he puts down his book and leans over to the counter. He pulls open the top drawer by its birdcage handle and rummages inside until he finds a potion vial. It's as small as the one Archmage Gidston gave me yesterday in the arena, but this one is far more decorative. Gold swirls encase the glass, spiraling up to the top where they form a cap. The liquid within is as thin as water and of a shimmering lapis hue.

He passes it to me. The glass is freezing where the potion touches, but room temperature where it does not. I flip back the metallic lid and drink the entire contents in a single gulp. This numbing potion is called Ice Honey, and it tastes as sweet as its name. The frozen nectar slides down my throat, and I can already feel it working. It's one of the fastest acting potions—and also the most addictive. Small amounts relieve pain, but large quantities can freeze every muscle in your body—including your heart. Overdoses require immediate medical attention, and even then the chances of survival are slim.

"Thanks," I say, returning the empty vial to Arluin.

He places it beneath the crystalline lamp, and the vibrant purple light makes the gold swirls glitter. I lie back on his chest as he picks up his book and continues to read.

The burgundy leather cover is embossed with ornamental flourishes and is entitled '*The Arcane Art of Alchemy.*' I suppose he's reading it as part of his research project. The Arcanium is always trying to improve Nolderan's potions, particularly ones with undesirable side effects such as Ice Honey.

We lie there in a peaceful silence for several minutes. Then a terrible thought occurs to me.

"What day is it today?"

"Wednesday," he says, not glancing away from his book.

"What time?" I ask, bolting upright. The scarlet sheets fall from my shoulders, leaving my back vulnerable to the morning breeze.

He points to the grandfather clock ticking away in the far corner of the room. "One o'clock."

"My morning classes!" I swear under my breath. My tutors will report my absence, and then my father will know I've been skipping classes again.

Arluin chuckles and pulls me back onto his chest. "Don't worry," he says, his free hand brushing away the strands of hair which have fallen in front of my face. "I submitted letters of absence for us both last week."

I let out a sigh of relief and crawl back under the blankets. With my head resting on his chest, I stare at the silk drapes hanging from the bed-frame. They dance back and forth in the light breeze. I listen to them rustling against the wooden floor, as well as the turning of pages as Arluin reads. My eyes drift shut, a heaviness falling over me. The Ice Honey has shifted my headache now, and the gentle sounds are like a lullaby.

But before sleep can claim me, Arluin says, "Reyna?"

My eyes flutter open. "Yes, Arly?"

He clears his throat. I realize he's set his book down on the counter. "I . . ." he begins, but his words falter. "There's something I need to tell you. I should have last night."

"What's the matter?" I ask, sitting up.

"If you change your mind about marrying me, I will understand."

"Arly, what are you talking about? Why would I not want to marry you anymore?"

Arluin leans back into the embroidered pillows and closes his eyes.

I weave my fingers through his and press our conjoined hands to my chest. "We already made a promise to each other. Whatever you feel you must tell me will not change that."

His throat bobs as he swallows hard. "I've never told you about this . . ."

"Is this about your father?"

He manages a slight nod.

"If it's too painful to say, then don't say it." I brush aside a dark curl and kiss the skin beneath.

"But you have a right to know what you'll be marrying." His eyes remain shut.

"Whatever this is, I will love you all the same."

He draws out a deep breath. I hear it shudder as it passes his lips. "Even if I am a monster?"

"You're not a monster, Arluin. I've told you so many times that you're not your father. Nor will you ever be."

Arluin shakes his head. "You don't know what I've done."

My throat dries as my racing mind tries to fill in the blanks. I suspect what he will say next, but I desperately don't want to believe it. Nor do I wish for him to see the resignation in my expression. I'm glad his eyes are still closed.

"Arly," I say softly, not trusting my tongue with anything else.

"I missed her so much, Reyna. I still do."

I know he's talking about his mother. I keep my mouth shut, hoping he will continue talking of his own accord. He does.

"He started studying necromancy the month after she died. At the time, I didn't know exactly what he was doing, only that he would bring her back and that I could never tell anyone, or else she would never return.

"The following year, he forgot to lock the door to the cellar. I followed him inside and I saw . . . I saw him bring a corpse back to life." He grits his teeth. "A human corpse."

I say nothing, barely able to breathe.

"It looked human, but it was closer to a wild, starved animal. My father only realized I was watching when the corpse rolled off the table and charged toward the dark pillar I crouched behind.

"My father incinerated it before it reached me. With the way it screamed, I thought all of Nolderan would hear. I was only ten and didn't understand necromancy was forbidden, but I knew what he had done was wrong. And yet . . ."

Arluin inhales sharply, his nostrils flaring with the force, and he finally opens his eyes. My entire body is frozen, my face included.

"I asked him if I could help. If he brought back my mother, I didn't want her to be like that corpse. He explained to me that wraiths are the most sentient of undead, as the soul is left intact when they are created, whereas the souls of ghouls and wights are fragmented.

"He was aiming to bring her back as a wraith and have her possess her body. Normally undead rot, but if the magic is powerful enough, then they will not. Since my mother was buried in a crystal coffin like all magi, her body would still be intact. The problem he faced was that her soul was long gone, having dispersed into aether upon her death. With his experiments, he was trying to reconstruct the souls of those already long dead.

"He first taught me how to raise ghouls by reanimating dead rats. Did you know, Reyna, that the first spell I ever cast was that of dark magic? Not aether. I learned forbidden magic before I learned ordinary magic. And I didn't just practice on rats, either. Sometimes when I look in the mirror, I fear that dead, gray eyes will gaze back at me."

Then he falls silent. He stares up at me. I know he expects an answer, but I can offer him none.

He lowers his eyes, looking at the blankets around us rather than me. "Do you hate me now, Reyna? Now that you know what I've done? What I truly am?"

Maybe I should hate him, maybe I should fear him. But I feel neither and that's what scares me.

What he has told me . . . If my father knew, he would be exiled just like Heston. And my father was lenient with banishment. The punishment for practicing dark magic is death.

I wish Arluin had confessed none of this. Because now I don't know how I will face my father. I should immediately report all of this to him. Keeping Arluin's secret means betraying my father—betraying Nolderan. But I can't break Arluin's trust. I can't bear to see him exiled.

Or executed.

In that instant, I know my choice.

I rest my head on the pillow beside him. Arluin doesn't move. He stares at the ceiling.

"I don't hate you," I finally manage, my voice but a breath. He doesn't turn to look at me.

"You should," he insists. "I'm a monster."

"If you're a monster, then you'll be my monster."

That gets him to turn and face me. There's a tortured look in his magenta eyes. I reassure myself that if he were still practicing necromancy, they would not glow with such a vivid hue of aether.

I take his hand once more and hold it against my cheek. "You were young, Arly. You can't be blamed for any of it. This is your father's fault, not yours, and he has already been punished for it."

He hangs his head and whispers, "Is it wrong of me to miss him?"

I sit up again and wrap my arms around him. "He's your father," I say, resting my head on his shoulder. "The two of you are bound by blood. All that he has done doesn't change that. It's natural for you to miss him."

Arluin is still at first. Then his fingers find my hair, and he toys with the ends, lost in thought. I wish I could banish his demons, but other than by hugging him, I do not know how.

"Reyna," he says after a moment, "will you still marry me, despite everything?"

"Of course I will," I reply, kissing his cheek. "I promise I will still marry you, no matter what."

CHAPTER 7

EVEN BY THURSDAY AFTERNOON, MY hangover is yet to disappear. I took plenty of Ice Honey this morning, but it's long worn off, and I don't dare take more. Not if I want my heart to keep beating.

At least the nasty bruise on my shoulder has healed, and I no longer need to conceal it with an illusion. Yesterday I returned home at five o'clock, and my mother slathered more Blood Balm over my shoulder. I slept all evening and barely woke on time for my classes this morning. It was only thanks to her I did.

Throughout my History and Medeicus lessons, I sit with my head in my hands. I stare at my tutors as they waffle on, and though my ears hear their words, my mind doesn't register their meaning. My eyes might be open, but my brain is fast asleep. My tutors notice nothing out of the ordinary, however, since I rarely pay attention.

During Alchemy, it's harder to sit and stare into space due to the practical nature of this subject. Luckily, we're allowed to work in pairs, and Eliya brews the potion by herself. She's quite understanding of my current affliction, but I suppose that's because she played a large part in causing it.

"You're not actually still hungover?" she asks in a hushed whisper, leaning over our cauldron. Aqua liquid bubbles within. We're supposed to be making a Potion of Water Breathing, and it looks just like the color of the ocean. While that sounds rather pretty, you probably wouldn't think so if you knew the three key ingredients: jellyfish tentacles, fermented sea kelp, and mackerel gills. The reagents must be boiled slowly before finishing the potion with a splash of water magic.

I don't look up at her and instead watch her wooden spoon stir the frothy mixture. "I don't understand how you're not. Did you even drink any wine yourself, or were you too busy trying to make me drink it?"

"Of course I drank just as much as you," she says, shaking her head at me. "Your parents were paying for the entire banquet, wine included, so I made the most of it."

I can't argue with that and dearly wish I had Eliya's remarkable tolerance for wine.

After Alchemy, we have Illusionary Class, and unlike the rest of today's lessons, I'm unable to sit there and do nothing.

Professor Donatus Nyton has stacked all the chairs and desks at the back of the classroom and has replaced them with dozens of mirrors. We are instructed to conjure an illusion of ourselves—a perfect replica. While we have practiced cloning flowers and food and animals, this is the first time we have ever crafted illusions of ourselves.

And it turns out replicating humans is the most challenging illusion of all.

I'm stationed at a golden, full-length mirror that sits before large, arched windows. They're pulled wide open to allow the summer heat to escape, but I'm sure the breeze is blowing more warmth into the stuffy classroom. I would conjure ice and use it to cool myself, but I'm otherwise preoccupied with sculpting my illusion. It's nearly impossible to concentrate with the heat.

Eliya, who stands before the mirror on my left, lets out a sudden laugh. "Koby!" she exclaims to the adept next to her. He's a cheery, round young man with a mop of brown hair. "Look at your nose!" She points at the illusion he's made of himself.

The clone is nearly perfect—aside from its nose almost being the same size as its hand. Its ankles are also bent at an odd angle. The illusion doesn't twitch and looks more like a life-sized doll than a living person. Even if its nose and ankles weren't strange, no one would be fooled into thinking it's the real Koby.

"As if you're doing a better job, Eliya," he says.

"You just watch," she tells him. Intrigued to know how her next attempt will fare, I stop the illusion I'm conjuring to look at hers.

Eliya draws aether into her fingers and gazes into the mirror opposite her. "*Speculus!*"

The magic swirls out and settles between her and the full-length mirror. The purple cloud swells, forming the silhouette of a person. When the light fades, an image of Eliya remains.

Except it isn't entirely like Eliya. It has the same crimson hair and heart-shaped face. But it's several inches taller, and there's a large discrepancy between its breasts and Eliya's. It's hard not to notice the size difference. I wonder if Eliya is joking with this attempt, since the illusion looks like it will topple over from the front-heavy weight.

"See," Eliya announces, gesturing to the illusion. "Look at how perfect mine is."

Poor Koby doesn't know where to look. His round cheeks immediately flush.

I let out a gentle cough. "Eliya, don't you think—"

She turns to me, placing a hand on her hip. "Don't I think what?"

"Well, the illusion looks rather stretched." I figure that's the safest way to say it's much taller.

"No, it doesn't."

I decide not to press that point.

"And uh . . ." I try to gesture in the direction of the clone's breasts. With how red Koby already looks, it's probably best not to shout that particular word.

She frowns at me. "What?"

"You know . . ."

Apparently she doesn't know. So, I have to be more creative. I nod to my chest and then to the illusion's.

She finally understands. "They are that big!"

I cast her a dubious look.

"You're just jealous," she insists. While I can't deny I'm envious of Eliya's curves, I'm very certain they're not over-exaggerated like her illusion's are.

"All right, I'm just jealous," I say, holding my hands up in defeat. If not for this splitting headache, I wouldn't have surrendered so quickly.

Eliya flashes me a triumphant grin and points to my mirror. "It's your turn, anyway."

I didn't realize we were taking turns and go to explain that I can't concentrate because of the heat and my headache, but then I notice Professor Nyton standing behind us. He's a tall, thin man, and it's a wonder I didn't notice him sooner. His arms are folded across his chest, and he peers at us through his monocle.

I really hope he didn't hear our conversation about Eliya's breasts.

I'm left with no choice but to turn to my mirror and gather aether into my fingers. I focus on my reflection as best I can: the oval shape of my face, my dark brows which pinch together in concentration, and the sunlight reflecting off my long hair. When I'm satisfied that I've captured every detail, I release my magic.

"*Speculus!*"

The aether spills out and forms my illusion. It's identical in every way, like my reflection has sprung from the mirror. The clone's unblinking eyes stare back at me.

A slow clap sounds from behind. "Splendid work, Ashbourne. Truly splendid. Though we should expect no less from the Grandmage's daughter."

Most of my tutors see me as the lazy student I am. A few are somehow convinced I'm a genius. Professor Nyton is one of the latter. But I suppose I am better at Illusionary Class than Alchemy or Medeicus. It isn't as boring, and I spend less time asleep.

Professor Nyton continues his lap of the room and watches the other adepts as they replicate themselves. The twins—Jaron and Braedon Trindell—are doing an especially good job, no doubt because the two boys are used to staring at identical versions of themselves. But Professor Nyton doesn't marvel at their illusions. Not like he did with mine.

When he's out of earshot, Eliya scoffs at me. "Yours is only good because you spend too much time in front of the mirror."

If we weren't in class, I would splash her with a water spell for that. Actually, I'm tempted to do it anyway. Professor Nyton would probably let me off lightly for it, especially if it were just a small splash.

My expression cracks into a wide grin. "Now look who's jealous."

She just wags her tongue at me and waves her hand, dispersing her illusion. Then she sets to work at creating a new image of herself, this time shorter and less voluptuous.

I return my attention to my illusion. It still gazes straight ahead with its unblinking eyes. Though I've succeeded in creating a perfect replica of myself, the next step is to make it mimic my every move.

In the mirror, I catch Kaely glaring at me. Her fists tighten, and so do her clone's. It seems she is ahead of me yet again, having already mastered the next stage of the spell.

Yet when Professor Nyton passes her, he spares her no more than a glance. And that only fuels her rage.

While I don't hate Illusionary Class, I'm glad when it ends. It's our final lesson of the day, and I can't wait to crawl back into bed.

Eliya's arms are linked with mine as we cross the Arcanium's atrium and step through the portico which leads outside. When we pass the rows of pillars, she turns to me and says, "So, did you like the locket?"

With a frown, I glance down. The necklace is hidden beneath the high collar of my robes. "From Arluin? How did you know?"

"He asked me if I thought you'd like it," she replies, as we descend the staircase which spirals around the statue of the Founder of Nolderan, "but I told him it would be too plain for your taste. He looked quite sad when I said that, though, and I felt pretty bad. But I changed my mind when he told me what he planned. Anything too fancy would distract from its purpose."

"Oh," I say. "I didn't know he asked you about it."

She stops in front of Grandmage Delmont Blackwood. It feels like he's scrutinizing our every move, but that's silly since these statues can't move. "So?"

"So what?"

She grabs both my arms. "What did you tell him? He proposed to you as planned, didn't he?"

I scan across all the adepts leaving the Arcanium. First-years and second-years finish at three o'clock, while the upper years have classes until later this afternoon. There's still plenty of people around us, however. Eliya may not shun Arluin for his father's crimes, but many others do. Though I suppose after what he told me yesterday, his father's crimes are also his own.

I don't dwell on that thought.

I give Eliya a pointed look and say, "He didn't propose to me. He promised to marry me."

"Isn't that the same thing?"

"He didn't get down on one knee, so that means he didn't propose."

She looks unconvinced. "Anyway," she continues eagerly, shaking my arms, "what did you say? You promised to marry him too, right? I swear if I'm not your Maid of—"

"Promised to marry who?" Kaely asks, marching down the last step.

I grimace inwardly. This is exactly why I wanted to avoid having this conversation in public.

"That's none of your business," Eliya snaps before I can speak.

"Did you have a nice party the other day?" Kaely asks me, ignoring Eliya. "I was heartbroken to learn I received no invitation."

I tighten my jaw. "And I was just as heartbroken to receive no 'Happy Birthday' from you. All I received was a nasty bruise."

Kaely tugs on her braid, pulling it to the front. "I hope it's healing well." She flashes me a smile that doesn't meet her eyes. "How's that necromancer of yours doing? I wondered what you were both up to yesterday when neither of you showed up for your lessons." I don't want to know how she found out Arluin didn't attend any classes yesterday. It's concerning she would go to such lengths to find out something like that.

"Again," Eliya says with a glare, "that's none of your business, Kaely." She shoots me a pleading look, silently begging me to leave.

Eliya is right that we should go, but I can't tear myself away just yet. "Arluin is no necromancer," I hiss.

Only after I speak do I realize that may no longer be true. Not after what he told me yesterday. But practicing a few dark spells years ago doesn't make him a necromancer, does it? His eyes still glow with aether. That means he's still a mage, or at least one in training.

I hope Kaely doesn't notice my hesitation before I add, "With how frequently you discuss necromancy, I fear you may be the true necromancer here."

Kaely lets out a sharp laugh and shakes her head. "Reyna, it wasn't my father who was banished for practicing necromancy. For digging up coffins and experimenting on corpses. Does your father approve? I mean, Heston was his closest friend, so maybe your relationship with Arluin doesn't disgust him."

"My relationship with Arluin doesn't concern you."

Kaely releases her braid and tosses it over her shoulder. She steps closer to me, malice glinting in her eyes. "I would wager your father doesn't mind that you're a necromancer's lover. After all, he allowed Heston Harstall to walk free when the punishment for such crimes is death."

"Kaely!" Eliya's eyes widen with horror. "You shouldn't speak of the Grandmage like that!" She tugs my wrist. "Come on, Reyna. Let's go."

I let her pull me away, and we start down the path lined by the many towering statues of long dead magi. But we only manage a few strides before Kaely calls, "*Laxus!*"

In the next instant, she appears in front of us, blocking our way. Before either Eliya or I can utter a single word, she continues her taunts. "I've heard you're frequenting the necromancer's manor more often these days."

"You've taken to stalking me now, have you?" I growl back. "What in the Abyss do you want with me, Kaely?"

"You misunderstand me. Are we not friends?"

"We are not friends," I grind out. "Not anymore."

"As saddened as I am to know you feel that way, I've always seen you as otherwise. I'm only looking out for you, Reyna. And with each day that passes, I'm becoming more concerned for you."

I cross my arms. "That's your pitiful excuse for obsessing over me?"

"I simply wanted to remind you to take your contraceptive potions with great care. If you have children with Arluin, then they will surely follow in their father's and grandfather's footsteps."

I stare at Kaely, my mouth hanging agape, unable to believe what I'm hearing.

"How dare you!" I roar when the shock of her words has worn off.

My patience with Kaely is quickly wearing thin. How I long to wipe that smirk off her freckled face.

I lunge for her, but Eliya grabs my shoulders and spins me around. "Ignore her," she pleads. "She's not worth it. If you allow yourself to be riled by her words, then you'll only give her the confrontation she wants."

I close my eyes and exhale deeply. Eliya is right. Kaely isn't worth wasting another moment on. She doesn't deserve even my anger.

I give Eliya a nod, and we pass around Kaely. But she refuses to let us leave so easily.

"Do take care he doesn't impregnate you with an undead fetus, Reyna!"

I halt.

Blood drums in my ears, deafening me. It boils through my body so furiously I think I will burst.

"What's the matter?" she asks me with a delighted laugh. "Scared he already has? Have you found out whether it's a baby ghoul or a baby wraith yet—"

My magic possesses me. Aether sparks in my fingers, and the fury in my veins rises to a crescendo.

"*Ignira.*" As the spell-word escapes my lips, I barely recognize my voice as my own.

The crackling flames are as loud as thunder. A ferocious fireball forms in my hands.

I unleash it upon her.

Other adepts shout, and so does Eliya. But their cries are distant, as though I'm hearing them through a stone wall.

"*Aquir'muriz!*" Kaely calls, conjuring a water shield before the fireball slams into her. The barrier withstands the attack, and droplets splatter across the stone path.

Magi charge forth, grabbing my arms and restraining them behind my back. I struggle to free myself but don't dare use any magic against them.

The corners of Kaely's lips curl into a vicious smile. When I try to breathe, it feels as if steel encases my chest.

I have made a horrible mistake.

Kaely taunted me into lashing out, and I have given her exactly what she sought. Using magic to strike other adepts or magi, unless instructed during classes, is prohibited by Nolderan's laws.

I should have heeded Eliya's warning.

This time, my father will be furious.

CHAPTER 8

ARCHMAGE LORETTE GIDSTON PACES BEFORE her desk. Her footsteps are muffled by the narrow, rectangular rug spread across the wooden floor. The yarns are weaved into a geometric pattern of reds, yellows, oranges, and browns, depicting the colors of fall.

The books lining the back shelves are arranged in alphabetical order, and each spine is perfectly aligned with the next. A small chandelier laden with aether crystals hangs from the ceiling and casts violet light over us all.

I stand to the left of Archmage Gidston's desk, restrained by the two magi either side of me. Even if my arms weren't secured behind my back, I wouldn't try to escape. Running would be futile, and foolish. It would only worsen my inevitable punishment.

Kaely stands across from me. When I lift my head, our gazes lock together. The corners of her mouth curl into a savage smirk, eager to see me punished.

Beside Kaely is her father, Archmage Branvir Calton. He's bald, with a beard the same shade as Kaely's braid. His bushy brows pull together in a deep crease, and his fists are tightened at his side. When his eyes sweep over to Kaely, she swaps her expression to a facade of fear, as though she is the victim.

I don't hide my glare, though I know it will only further condemn me.

In all my eighteen years, I've never known anyone to be more a snake than Kaely.

To think I once called her a friend.

I tear my attention from Kaely and scan across the few other adepts brought here as witnesses. Eliya is among them, as well as Koby.

My best friend's eyes are filled with worry. When Eliya catches my gaze, she presses her lips together in gentle reassurance, as if everything will be fine.

But it won't.

I've broken the city's laws. Adepts who commit such crimes are often expelled from the Arcanium, deemed unfit to become magi because of their volatile temperaments. This is why Archmage Gidston is unwilling to deal with the matter without my father present.

Now I can only hope that my father, despite his fury, won't subject me to such harsh punishment. This is the first time I've used my magic to strike another adept outside of the arena. And it isn't as if Kaely didn't deserve it.

Surely they won't expel me for a single mistake?

"Archmage Gidston," Branvir says after a while, "we've been waiting for almost an hour for the Grandmage to arrive. Perhaps we should begin without him?"

Lorette pauses her pacing. "No," she replies, "we cannot proceed without the Grandmage being present. Even with two Archmagi, this matter is far too delicate."

I can't bear to look at either of the Archmagi. If I were not the Grandmage's daughter, my crimes would be long judged by now. I would already be expelled from the Arcanium.

Branvir doesn't protest again, and so we continue to wait.

My palms are hot and sticky, and my racing mind imagines a thousand different ways this trial could go. Even muffled by the carpet, Archmage Gidston's footsteps drum in my ears to the rhythm of impending doom.

The walls spin around me. I struggle to keep myself upright. I don't know how much longer I can bear this excruciating wait.

But then the doors finally swing open, and my father strides in.

Though the room was quiet before his entry, now it falls completely silent—as if no one dares to even twitch in the Grandmage's presence. His magnificent robes storm around him and gold thread flashes through the indigo fabric like bolts of lightning.

My father comes to a stop before Archmage Gidston. He stands less than an arm's length away from me, but he doesn't turn in my direction. Nor does he glance at me from the corners of his eyes.

It's as if he can't bear to look upon his disgrace of a daughter.

"Archmage Gidston," he says, resting the end of his crystalline staff on the carpet, "if you will explain this matter. And swiftly. I must soon return to Tirith's ambassadors."

"Yes, Grandmage." Lorette folds her hands behind her back and straightens. Her eyes drift between Kaely and me. "This afternoon, shortly after the second-years finished their classes for the day, Reyna Ashbourne was seen attacking Kaely Calton with a fireball spell."

Only now does my father's head snap toward me. "Is this true?" His temples pulse with barely controlled rage. "Or do you dare to deny Archmage Gidston's words?"

"Yes, it's true I struck Kaely with a fireball spell but—"

My father raises his hand before I can explain, wordlessly silencing me.

A lump swells in my throat. I swallow, but it doesn't shift. I stare at the carpet to avoid looking at the disappointment on his face.

"The perpetrator confesses to her crimes," my father says, his tone painfully neutral. "For what reason did you call me here, Archmage Gidston? I believe both you and Archmage Calton should be more than capable of addressing this incident."

"Of course," Lorette replies, bowing her head. Her platinum hair doesn't move with the motion, the bun too tightly bound. "However, as it concerns your daughter, I thought it best to settle this matter with you present."

"While Reyna may be my daughter, she will be treated no differently to any other adept of the Arcanium."

Branvir huffs his agreement, while Lorette's shoulders stiffen with tension.

"Since Reyna is found guilty," Lorette says, "we must agree on the punishment she is to receive for breaking Nolderan's laws by using her magic with the intention to harm another." Her voice reveals little of her thoughts. It almost sounds like hesitation, but I'm not sure whether it's born of reluctance or apprehension.

"Is the punishment for such crimes not expulsion?" Branvir interjects.

Both my father and Lorette turn to face him, their expressions unreadable.

Will my father agree to expel me from the Arcanium? Will he allow me to be the first Ashbourne in generations to fail to graduate as a Mage of Nolderan?

Maybe he will disown me to prevent me from tarnishing our family's legacy.

My breathing is shaky, and my vision blurs. I may not be the most studious adept, but becoming a mage is my destiny.

I bite back the tears welling in my eyes—thick, heavy, and painfully bitter. I can't cry here. Not in front of my father, and certainly not in front of Kaely, who would take much delight in seeing how weak I am.

"The severity of the punishment depends on the specific circumstances of the incident," Archmage Gidston states. "Furthermore, this is the first time Reyna has committed such an offense, and no one was harmed by it."

My lips part. The tears freeze in my eyes before they can spill onto my cheeks.

I think she might be defending me. Though she let Kaely beat me horribly in the arena, she's arguing on my behalf. Even when my own father is not.

Is she doing this because I'm the daughter of Grandmage Telric Ashbourne, or because I'm Reyna?

"No one was harmed?" Branvir exclaims. A few adepts flinch at his shout. Koby is one of them. "My daughter could have been killed!"

"While your concerns are understandable," Lorette replies, her words as cool and precise as ice, "it's unlikely that Kaely would have been killed by a mere fireball. As the Archmage of Knowledge, the Arcanium falls under my jurisdiction. I know the capabilities of every adept in my charge. Kaely is one of the most talented second-years, and that is evident from her performance in the arena."

It seems Archmage Gidston is far more calculating than I realized. Though Branvir was moments away from exploding in a fit of rage, his wrath is pacified by the praise she offers Kaely.

He shifts his weight and scratches his brown beard. "Hm, perhaps that is true. But Reyna Ashbourne should not be let off lightly. It's fortunate my daughter is so talented, or else this incident could have proven disastrous."

"Again," Lorette responds, dipping her head, "your concerns are understandable. I can assure you that she will not escape lightly." She pauses and glances across at my father, her eyes tight with wariness. "I am of the opinion that suspension would be the most fitting punishment."

Hearing her words lifts some of the weight from my shoulders, and my exhalations come out steadier.

Suspension—I can live with that. It doesn't mean expulsion. And hopefully it won't mean disownment, either.

"For how long?" Branvir demands.

"I believe a month would be sufficient. What do you think, Grandmage?"

My father is silent, a contemplative frown etched deep into his brow. Before he can respond, a shout comes from behind.

"This isn't fair!" Eliya exclaims, her fists balled.

Everyone turns to Eliya. My father's expression grows sterner, while Archmage Gidston's fills with irritation.

"Adept Whiteford," she snaps, "you will remain silent. Or else you too shall be disciplined for speaking out of turn, especially while in the presence of the Grandmage of Nolderan."

But Eliya isn't so easily deterred.

"Archmage Gidston," she begins, placing her hands on her hips. "Was I not brought here as a witness? Does that not mean I have the right to recount what I saw with my own eyes and heard with my own ears?"

"Eliya Whiteford, I will not tell you again." Lorette's tone is glacial. "While it is true that you were summoned here as a witness, we no longer require your account since the perpetrator pleads guilty. There is no debate to be had, for this judgment has already been made—"

My father raises his hand. "Archmage Gidston, why don't we see what the girl has to say?"

Eliya bows her head, her crimson hair cascading over her shoulders. "Thank you, Grandmage."

"But be quick about it," he continues. "As I said, I must return to Tirith's ambassadors, and I do not wish to keep them waiting."

"Yes, Grandmage."

"Then speak your piece, Adept Whiteford," Lorette says. "Why is it you believe Reyna is undeserving of this punishment? Do you instead believe she is innocent?"

"No, Archmage Gidston," Eliya replies. "It's true that Reyna struck Kaely with a fireball spell, and I do agree she must receive some punishment for that."

I arch a brow at her, wondering whether she's even on my side. I'm quite content with a month's suspension, and I dearly hope whatever Eliya says won't worsen my punishment. Though I wouldn't be aggrieved if they decide to extend the suspension to three months.

Archmage Gidston folds her arms. She's not a particularly patient woman, and it's clear Eliya is testing her limits. "If you agree that Reyna is guilty and that she should be disciplined for her actions, then what more do you wish to add? As the Grandmage has already said, he has far more pressing matters. We should not waste anymore of his time."

"All I wanted to point out is that no one's bothered to question why Reyna struck Kaely. Like you said, Archmage Gidston, this is the first time Reyna has ever committed such an offence. And I, as the primary witness, can assure everyone in this room it was not without good reason." When Eliya finishes speaking, she glances at me. Determination burns brightly in her eyes.

Determination to see justice be dealt.

I return her expression with a wry smile. If I am to be punished, then Kaely ought to be as well. It's time she learns she can't spout whatever she pleases without fear of retribution.

"And what was that reason, Eliya?" my father presses.

"Kaely insulted Reyna. Several times. She refused to leave us alone."

Branvir turns to Kaely. "Is this true?"

"Of course it's true," Kaely says, her voice unshaken by Eliya's claim. "Reyna and I had a disagreement, and it's inevitable that during an argument, one may say words they later regret." She steps toward me and lowers her head. "If you took offense by what I said, Reyna, then I truly am sorry. I don't wish for ill feelings to fester between us. We have, after all, been friends for so many years."

I grit my teeth. It's almost impossible to hold my tongue. To prevent myself from screaming how much I hate her. How the two of us are not and will never again be friends.

Not after all the unforgivable words she has spoken.

"Such misunderstandings are not uncommon," Archmage Gidston says. "However, this does not justify violence. Regardless of Reyna's reasons for attacking Kaely, I believe the punishment for her offenses remains fitting. And if we are all in agreement, then this incident is also resolved."

I can bite my tongue no longer. I loathe how Archmage Gidston dismisses the incident as petty bickering. How Kaely will emerge unscathed. While I will be punished.

"It wasn't a simple misunderstanding," I seethe. "I did nothing to deserve the way Kaely spoke to me. Should magi be allowed to go around, spouting whatever awful words they please without fear of retribution? Is that the city—"

"Silence!"

The room stills at my father's shout. His attention remains on the tidy bookshelves behind the desk. He doesn't turn to look at me as he speaks.

"Magi should act as model citizens for Nolderan," my father asserts. "Their words should be chosen out of wisdom and not out of malice, and they should certainly not strike down others due to their ill-temper. What Archmage Gidston says is fair. There are no reasons that can justify your actions."

"You weren't there!" I know losing my temper will prove them right, but I can't contain my rage. "You didn't hear what she said! About Arluin, about Heston, about you. She claimed the reason you spared Heston from death is because of your previous friendship with him—"

"I think you remember incorrectly, Reyna," Kaely interrupts, her lips twitching. I can't tell whether it's the hint of a smirk or a snarl. "I never said the Grandmage spared Heston because of their friendship."

I wrestle with the magi still gripping my arms, but they don't relent. If my fists were free, I would use them to shatter Kaely's disgusting expression.

That was my ultimate mistake. I should have struck her with my fists instead of my magic. They probably wouldn't even suspend me for that. Most likely, a stern talking to by Archmage Gidston is all I would receive.

And hitting her would be so much more satisfying.

If only I thought it all through before unleashing my magic.

"You insinuated it," I spit. "Even if you didn't say it outright, you mocked Arluin and my father."

"And also she insulted you, Reyna," Eliya adds, her nose wrinkling. "Kaely, don't think I've forgotten that comment about undead fetuses—"

"That is enough!" my father booms, his voice reverberating through the small room.

It is safe to say I inherited my short-fused temper from my father, and not my mother.

Heston's betrayal plagues his heart even to this day, and his resulting wrath is terrifying.

"Leave us!" he roars. "All of you!"

Everyone is so taken aback by his sudden outburst that no one moves.

"Leave! I will deal with my daughter myself!"

On his second shout, the room springs to life. The doors swing open, and all the adepts brought as witnesses spill out. None wish to face the fury of Grandmage Telric Ashbourne. Even the magi restraining me leave.

With my arms now free, I roll my shoulders. The motion does little to relieve the cramp.

Eliya lingers longer than the rest. Her gaze meets mine, and her brows knit with concern. I know she is reluctant to leave me at my father's mercy, but there's nothing more she can do. She has no choice but to follow the others through the doors.

Though the room has mostly cleared, five of us remain. Aside from my father and me, that includes Lorette, Branvir, and Kaely.

Branvir's eyes narrow at the double doors, and he harrumphs, his disdain thinly veiled. I know he doesn't like my father much. Thirty years ago, when the previous Grandmage retired, Branvir was one of the few candidates in line to take his position. The following decade he also ran for Archmage of Defense, but Heston Harstall was instead appointed. It was five years ago, when Heston was exiled, that Branvir was finally promoted. But I think he would much prefer to be the Grandmage of Nolderan than the Archmage of Defense.

Thanks to all the aether humming through our veins, magi live at least twice as long as normal humans—sometimes even longer. My father will reign over Nolderan for the most part of another century. By then, Branvir will be nearing retirement himself.

Maybe this is another reason Kaely hates me. Because my father outranks hers. And because he will never have the chance to become the Grandmage.

Branvir doesn't dare to directly defy my father, though. That would cause him to lose his position. And being the Archmage of Defense is better than being nothing.

"With all due respect, Grandmage—" Branvir begins.

"I shall deal with my daughter," my father snaps. He turns to Kaely and glares at her, not bothering to hide the flames burning in his magenta eyes. She has the sense to flinch at his fury. "I also suggest you deal with yours. Matters which concern the safety of Nolderan and the magi should not be spoken of so lightly."

Branvir opens his mouth, and I wonder whether he'll argue with my father. Maybe to say that Kaely isn't entirely wrong. That Heston should never have been spared from execution.

Instead, he seems to change his mind and bows his head. "Indeed, such things should not be spoken of so lightly." He glances at Kaely, his eyes sharpening. "I can assure you that the two of us will have a thorough discussion concerning this matter."

My father gives him a curt nod, and Branvir starts over to the door. Kaely trails behind him. She doesn't turn, but I know if she dared, she would shoot me a venomous glare.

Now only Archmage Gidston remains, aside from my father and me.

"Lorette," he says as she too leaves, "I will inform you of Reyna's punishment when it is decided."

"Of course, Grandmage." Without another word, she steps out of her office and closes the doors behind her.

My father and I stand there in silence for a long while. He stares out of the arched windows, clasping his crystalline staff. Archmage Gidston's office is situated inside one of the Arcanium's highest spires. It can't compare to the vastness of the Aether Tower, but you can still see the entire city from up here.

Cobalt tiles ripple across the rooftops below, and Nolderan's walls stand proudly at the edges of the city. Beyond them lies the thick cover of trees, surrounding Nolderan like leafy clouds. They quickly turn into the deadly drop of steep cliffs. Then there are only sapphire waves, stretching on for hundreds of miles. From the docks in the Lower City, however, you can see the coastline of the mainland on the horizon.

I doubt my father is simply gazing out at the sea because he enjoys looking at it. Most likely, he's watching the lull of the waves in an attempt to soothe his rage.

What he's contemplating, I dread to discover. Is he considering worsening the punishment Archmage Gidston suggested? Will it be a longer suspension, or will it be something else entirely?

Maybe he's deliberating over the decision to disown me.

It seems I fidgeted at that awful thought since he finally speaks. "You will no longer see him."

"No longer see who? Archmage Calton?"

He must take my genuine confusion as sarcasm, since he whirls around with a face reddened by anger. "Arluin! You will see him no more!"

"Arluin?" I repeat, leaning on the desk. "What has Arluin got to do with any of this?"

"Your feelings for him have made you lose all sense! Made you stupid enough to strike a fellow adept!"

"Fine," I hiss. "Blame Arluin for this. Even though the reason I lost my temper is because of what she said about both of you."

His temples twitch. He says nothing. It seems he doesn't quite know how to respond to my brazen words.

"Don't think I don't know exactly what you're doing."

"And what is it you think I'm doing?" My father doesn't raise his voice. I've pushed him so far beyond anger that he's lost the ability to shout.

"You're using this as an excuse to stop me from seeing Arluin. And you can try," I sneer, "but it won't work. We're already promised, he and I."

"You're what?" he bellows.

"Promised," I say, my lips curling. "It means we are to marry."

My father whirls back to the window. His breathing is so loud I think all of Nolderan will hear it. If he spends another moment looking at me, he'll probably kill me.

He can lecture me about losing my temper, but he's no better himself.

"You don't care at all, do you?"

"I don't care about what, Father?"

"About our family. About being an Ashbourne. Is becoming a mage another joke to you, Reyna?"

I throw back my head and let out a hysterical laugh. "Now you're saying that because I love Arluin, I don't give a damn about our family? About graduating from the Arcanium? Maybe I will fail on purpose. Just for you."

His shoulders quake with rage, like a volcano moments away from eruption. It's a wonder the entire room hasn't yet exploded into flames. From either of us.

"What did I do to deserve such a disgraceful daughter?" he mutters, asking the waves far beyond that question. Not me.

I answer, anyway.

"Then don't let me disgrace you any longer, Father. Disown me. I know you're considering it, so go ahead and do it."

I don't know why I said any of that. I don't actually want him to disown me. Maybe that's why I said it, because I want to hear him say he won't. That however disgraceful I may be, he won't disown his only daughter.

"Is that . . ." he begins, but the words extinguish in his throat. "Is that what you want, Reyna?"

There's pain in his voice, and I hate hearing it. I already regret my words.

He turns to look at me, but now it is I who cannot face him. My gaze falls to the carpet. "Of course it's not what I want," I mumble.

"Then why would you say it?" he asks, his voice softening.

"Because that's what you want."

He draws out a long sigh. "It isn't what I want."

"It's not?"

"No, it's not."

We descend into silence. Both our tempers no longer blaze, but smolder quietly like embers.

"Then what do you want?" I ask. My voice is hushed, not daring to disturb the tentative peace budding between us.

"I want you to graduate from the Arcanium."

"And you don't want me to marry Arluin?"

"I never said I don't want you to marry him."

"But you don't, do you? You don't want me to marry the son of the man you exiled. Like everyone else, you misjudge him for his father."

Again, I hate what Arluin admitted. I fear it makes me a liar.

But it isn't Arluin's fault his father led him astray. He was young. How can he be blamed?

I will never tell my father the truth. I will take his secret to my grave. Arluin doesn't deserve banishment. Nor death.

"No, Reyna, this has nothing to do with Arluin's father. I would say the same regardless of whom you're planning to marry. You are too young, and marriage will only serve to distract you from your studies."

"I never said that Arluin and I are getting married soon. We might have promised to marry each other, but he insisted we marry after I graduate from the Arcanium."

The last of my father's rage slips away. His shoulders relax, no longer trembling with molten fury. "I see. Good."

"So, does that mean I'm still allowed to see him?"

"He remains a distraction from your studies."

"No, he doesn't. Arluin studies harder than every other adept in the entire Arcanium, just to prove he isn't like his father. That he doesn't deserve the way people fear and shun him. Ask Archmage Gidston if you don't believe me. And if you want to blame someone for distracting me from my studies, then blame Eliya. After all, we spend most of our time laughing and gossiping. But you're not cruel enough to stop me from seeing her, are you? Not that you could, since we have the same classes every day."

My father shakes his head and takes to staring out the window once more. I hope the fact he's lost for words means I won this argument.

"There's also the matter of your punishment," he says after a pause.

"It's fine. A month's suspension is fair. I did launch a fireball at Kaely, after all."

He scoffs. "Not a chance. You will certainly not be receiving a month's suspension from your studies."

"Why not? I'm guilty."

"I know you're guilty."

I frown at him. Not that he can see it. He still faces the arched window.

"Reyna, you forget that I am your father and that I know exactly what you're thinking."

"And what's that?"

"You're looking forward to having a month off from your studies and doing nothing at all."

"No, I'm not."

He turns to me and raises a bushy auburn brow. "If you insist on lying to me, I will worsen your punishment."

"Fine," I huff. "I may have been looking forward to some time off from my studies."

He gives a satisfied nod and then returns to the window. "That is why suspension would be an ill-fitting punishment. Fortunately, the one I have in mind is far more appropriate."

My heart dips. If it isn't expulsion or suspension, I'm scared to imagine what it will be. "What punishment?"

"Community service," he says, his mouth quirking. "At the library."

CHAPTER 9

THOUGH MY FATHER SAID HE must swiftly return to Tirith's ambassadors, he now has no problem with marching me to the Grand Library himself. It's as if he doesn't trust me to deliver myself to Erma Darkholme.

I can't possibly think why that would be.

He leads me out of the office and down the central spire. The winding staircase is so narrow there's not enough room for people to pass simultaneously. Flickering aether crystals are fixed to the walls like sconces, but their pale light fails to illuminate the entire spire.

The steps spiral down so far I can't see their end. The ornate rail is all which prevents me from tripping and plummeting into the unending darkness.

At the sight of the Grandmage, the magi ascending the stairs halt. They step aside, leaning into the walls to make room for us, and bow their heads in deference to my father. If it weren't for his position, I'm sure it would take us far longer to reach the bottom.

The antechamber we arrive in is high-ceilinged and dozens of portraits decorate every inch of the room. Like the paintings of my ancestors inside my manor, they are enchanted with aether, and the magi within the frames seem very much alive. All are dressed in their purple robes. Some wave at us, while others are far too busy reading their tomes.

Many elaborate benches lie beneath the portraits, and a group of adepts sit on the leftmost ones. First-years, I think. When we enter they're giggling and gossiping loudly, but they all fall silent as my father strides past. Apprehension initially clouds their magenta eyes, but it soon changes to intrigue upon noticing me. The entire Arcanium—perhaps even the whole city—will have already heard what I did. How the Grandmage's daughter launched a fireball at the Archmage of Defense's daughter, right in front of the Founder's statue. I don't doubt these first-years will start chattering about it as soon as we're out of earshot.

The antechamber leads to the Arcanium's atrium. Aether crystals glitter high above, twinkling in the late noon sunlight. The faerie dragons assigned to the Arcanium aren't polishing the ceiling today. Instead, they are supervising the enchanted brooms as they sweep across the polished marble floor.

The Grand Library lies opposite us, and my father marches toward it. Like on the stairs, the magi passing through the atrium pause to dip their heads at my father. He returns a brief nod, but his attention doesn't leave the library's entrance.

We descend the long, steep staircase, and bear right as it splits at the bottom.

Like usual, Erma sits at her gleaming white desk. Today she is stamping books and comparing each title to a long list. These tomes are especially old, judging by their torn pages. Most likely, enchanted quills have replicated their text into new copies, and she's marking the old books as being withdrawn from the library.

Erma doesn't look up as we approach. She just continues stamping away at the pile of books. But with her impeccable hearing, I don't doubt she knows we're here. Only Erma Darkholme, who held the title Archmage of Knowledge for almost one hundred and twenty years, is bold enough to ignore my father. After all, it is he who should show her reverence. Erma would have been in charge of the Arcanium when he was studying here.

For a long while, Erma says nothing. She simply dips her stamp into a pot of crimson ink and presses it onto the first page of each book.

My father finally lets out a gentle cough. I suppose it's unfitting for the Grandmage of Nolderan to be ignored by a mere librarian. A few adepts cast us curious looks. But that could also be because they've heard about me attacking Kaely.

"Erma," my father begins, "I have a matter which only you can resolve."

"Yes, yes, what is it?"

"It is regarding my daughter, Reyna."

Erma looks up. Her eyes narrow at me—no doubt recalling the other day when she chased Arluin and me from the library.

I do hope she doesn't start complaining about that in front of my father.

"I have already heard of this matter." She uses her stamp to gesture at the adepts huddled around a table in the far corner. "They all burst into my library as soon as their lessons finished, shouting to each other about how the Grandmage's daughter struck another adept with a fireball. The ruckus I had to deal with because of this incident!" She shakes her head, and strands of wispy white hair drift around her like clouds. "What is it then, Telric, that you require me for?"

"To oversee Reyna's punishment."

"What punishment is she to receive?"

"For the next month, she is to act as your assistant and help with any tasks you require completing. She is expected to help you every day after her lessons until nightfall, and from dawn to dusk on Saturdays and Sundays."

It's all I can do not to groan. I hadn't expected him to be lenient with my punishment, especially not after the argument we just had, but this is going too far. I will be exhausted every day for the next month and have no time to myself.

"If you find she does not arrive promptly at these times, disappears unexpectedly while working, or does not conduct herself in the appropriate manner, then I will see to it the consequences she suffers are far worse."

I'm certain those words are meant for me rather than Erma, though his attention remains on her. I peer at him, but his expression offers no clue as to what my alternative punishment might be.

If I behave inappropriately, will I receive the punishment Archmage Gidston suggested? A month's suspension? That's doubtful, since he knows it wouldn't bother me in the least. But I can't think what else he might have in mind.

I flash Erma a smile. It's probably best to do as she says. And to avoid annoying her too much.

"Leave her to me." Erma's icy glare fixes on me. "I will see to it that she's kept busy."

"Thank you, Erma," my father replies, stepping away from the desk and turning to me. He pauses, examining me carefully, as if he expects me to wreak havoc upon the Grand Library. "Be sure to stick to the times I have outlined. Or else, the consequences will be dire."

"Dire as in suspension? Or expulsion?" I know I risk his wrath for asking, but I can't help it. I need to know what's at stake. In case I accidentally sleep in too late on a Sunday morning. Or something else of the sort.

My father doesn't deign to answer the question. Without another word, he storms up the stairs.

Now I am left at Erma's mercy.

Hopefully she won't make my life too difficult. While she has scolded me plenty of times, she scolds many adepts every day. Surely she doesn't bear a personal grudge against me?

Any hope I had is dashed when she points to an enormous stack of books. It towers so precariously I think it may topple over if I breathe too suddenly. And if that happens, Erma will make me pick them all up. I approach with caution.

"These books have been left out by good-for-nothing adepts like yourself," she says, giving her current tome a particularly forceful stamp. "Each one needs returning to its rightful place."

I do my best not to grimace. Putting them all away will mean countless hours of running around the Grand Library. But if I show any sign of reluctance, she will assign me far worse tasks. Like reorganizing the topmost shelves.

Since resistance will worsen my sentence, I give Erma the most enthusiastic nod I can muster. "Yes, ma'am!" With that, I scoop up the books lying at the top of the towering pile.

"Get to it then," Erma growls.

I don't hesitate and set to work before she can bark out another command.

I glance down at the first book in my arms. *'The Origins of Medeicus, the Arcane Language of Magic, by Alward Brayton'* is scrawled onto its cover in cursive script.

I scurry over to the right wing of the library which contains books concerning the languages of Imyria. Besides Medeicus, the Grand Library is home to books on the different Elvish dialects of Lumaria, Alanor, and Fenyr Forest; the human languages of Selynis, Valka, and Tirith—though the latter's is also known as Common; and the Orcish tongues of both Jektar and Dromgar. Even the holy language of the Selynian Priestesses is featured in our books.

The only language which can't be found inside the Grand Library is Abyssal, the dark tongue of demons.

But long ago, our shelves would have been filled with grimoires of forbidden magic. Over a thousand years ago, when Nolderan was first established, the original magi hadn't shied away from practicing dark magic.

That was until the Lich Lord arose, a former Archmage of Knowledge. His quest to eradicate all life from Imyria almost succeeded.

Since then, Nolderan has strictly forbidden all forms of dark magic.

Or at least, that's what my History tutors have spent the last two years lecturing me about.

I scan across the nearest bookshelves, looking for where this one on Medeicus is supposed to go, but I only find books on Orcish and Elvish here.

My search takes me deeper into the Grand Library's right wing, and I pass a book with beautiful illustrations painted onto its cover. It depicts the shadowy trees and ever twinkling stars of Lumaria, the land of eternal night where the moon elves dwell.

I set aside the three heavy books I'm carrying, and my fingertips trace over the artwork. Even my mother would be jealous of the artist who painted this cover. With how lovely these illustrations are, I can only imagine how breath-taking Lumaria is itself.

Unfortunately, I have yet to visit. The Magi of Nolderan have little to do with the elven continent of Belentra, despite the moon elves having taught the first magi how to wield the aether in the air and in their blood. Our broken relationship with Lumaria is because the Lich Lord was once an Archmage of Nolderan and they blame us for his crusade against the living. My History teachers mentioned that the relationship between Nolderan and Lumaria became strained after that.

While my father receives ambassadors from all over the world, including even a few orcish Stormcallers who come from the lands beyond the three human kingdoms, I have only heard of him meeting one Lumarian ambassador.

It was five years ago, shortly after my father banished Heston for practicing necromancy. I suppose that's what Lumaria wanted to discuss, especially since they distrust us after what happened a thousand years ago.

I sneaked inside the Arcanium—a bold move considering this was long before I became an adept—and waited outside my father's meeting room all day for a glimpse of the Lumarian ambassador. She stood so tall that she dwarfed even my father. Her dusky purple skin shimmered like crystals, and her long silver hair billowed like streams of moonlight.

And her eyes were nothing like ours. Her eyes shone much brighter, her iridescent irises glowing with blues and purples. Her appearance captivated me so greatly that I forgot I was supposed to be hiding. My father scolded me for sneaking into the Arcanium, but I didn't regret it. Glimpsing a moon elf for the first time was more than worth suffering his fury.

Footsteps sound from behind, snapping me from my daydream. I glance back, but I can't tell whose they are. Nonetheless, I retrieve my stack of books from the nearby shelf. Just in case it's Erma, already checking on my progress.

I peer at the books in my arms. The cursive letters of 'The Origins of Medeicus' stare back at me.

I swallow. I've not yet returned a single book, and there are dozens to work through. If I don't hurry, Erma will soon be informing my father of my idleness. And then I will be granted a punishment far worse than assisting Erma or being suspended for a month.

Whatever that might be.

The books on the history of Medeicus, the language of magic which magi speak to invoke their spells, lie at the far end of this aisle.

I tilt back my head and examine the highest shelf. The books are arranged alphabetically, and authors with surnames beginning with 'A' and 'B' can be found at the very top. There's a gap between two tomes which looks the same width as this book's spine. Since I can see no other such gaps, that must be where this book lives.

I lift 'The Origins of Medeicus' in one hand and balance the rest of the books in my other. "Atollo."

Violet light envelops the book and raises it to the very top shelf. The magic fades as the book slots into place.

I watch it for a moment, hoping that my spell was accurate enough and that the book won't lose balance and come tumbling down.

It doesn't.

I turn on my heel and continue on, traveling to the next section of the library.

Though I return the next two books faster than the first, I soon realize a more efficient method is required. Or else it will take until midnight to tidy away all the other books.

I return to the Grand Library's main chamber and set to work with categorizing the stack of books. The steady thud of Erma's stamp sounds behind me. I half expect her to complain that I'm wasting time, but she doesn't.

When I finish organizing the tomes, I gather as many geographical books as I can carry and hurry over to those shelves.

There are now far more adepts inside the library. That must mean the fourth-years, whose lessons run until six o'clock on Thursdays, have finished for the day.

My lips pull into a smile as I weave in and out of the aisles, distributing the books as quickly as I can. Arluin will be here shortly, and at least gazing at him will make this punishment more bearable. Provided that Erma doesn't catch me staring at him.

But it isn't Arluin I first find.

Just as I turn a corner, I almost collide with Kaely. I nearly drop the books I'm carrying, half from surprise and half from fury.

I can't have been here for more than an hour, and yet Kaely has managed to locate me.

Didn't she go home with her father? Wasn't he meant to lecture her about not making light of necromancy?

I suppose I should expect nothing less from Archmage Branvir Calton.

Kaely's lips distort into an ugly sneer. "So, it's true. They've not even suspended you."

"Kaely," I hiss, my fingers clawing into the leather covers of the books. "What are you doing here?"

"I'm also an adept of the Arcanium. Is it a problem if I visit the library after lessons?"

My jaw tenses. She's not planning to continue taunting me, is she? Hasn't she already caused enough disruption today?

"You may go wherever you please," I grind out. "But stay out of my way."

"Or what? You'll strike me with a fireball again?"

While I can't use my magic against Kaely, I can whack her over the head with the heavy tomes I'm holding. That wouldn't break any of the city's laws.

But it would mean Erma reporting my unruly behavior to my father. On the very first day of my sentence.

I can't afford to lose my temper for a second time today.

"Just leave me alone, Kaely," I snap, pushing past her. But like earlier this afternoon, she refuses to let me go so easily.

"You should have been expelled from the Arcanium for your crimes!" Kaely calls after me, daring to raise her voice to a level that will enrage Erma.

I halt and turn back to Kaely. A vicious scowl distorts her freckles.

"You were bold to strike me with your magic in broad daylight," Kaely jeers, "and there were dozens who witnessed it."

"Just as they witnessed the insults you hurled at me."

Her nose wrinkles in disgust. "The reason you were spared is because you're the Grandmage's daughter. It seems I'm the only one who can see this injustice."

"Even now you continue to spew hatred." I cling to the books I carry, not trusting my hands to stray from their leather covers. I can't allow my anger to burst free again. "Kaely, what have I done to deserve the way you treat me?"

"You're the Grandmage's daughter," she blurts, her fists tightening. "You're lazy and useless, and you're not a good sorceress. Yet to everyone else, especially our tutors, you're someone special. But it's only because of your father. He's the Grandmage, not you. Why do you deserve such reverence? You haven't earned the right."

I shake my head in disbelief. "So, this is the reason you hate me? Do you think it was my choice for my father to be the Grandmage of Nolderan? Do you think I can help how others treat me? If it bothers you this much, then the next time anyone praises me, I'll tell them they should instead praise Kaely Calton because she can't control her irrational jealousy. Actually, no. I doubt even that would suffice. How about I ask my father to disown me and take you as his daughter instead, since you can't bear the fact that I'm the daughter of the Grandmage of Nolderan and you're not?"

A deep shade of crimson paints Kaely's face. Fury blazes in her magenta eyes. If she came here to goad me into losing my temper again, then she has failed greatly. If only my mind and my tongue were sharper earlier this afternoon.

"Reyna Ashbourne," she spits, "I have never known anyone to think more highly of themselves. Your arrogance disgusts me."

"My arrogance disgusts *you*? Have you not looked in a mirror lately? I think you'll instead find that your arrogance outshines everyone in the entire city."

"You—"

"That's enough," a male voice calls.

Too focused on Kaely, I didn't hear any footsteps approaching. When I turn, I see Arluin behind us. Frost shrouds his expression. The muscle at his jaw twitches as he meets Kaely's eyes, refusing to give her even an inch of ground as their stares lock together.

"Arluin Harstall," Kaely chides, her stare unrelenting as she speaks, "what a surprise. It seems you have your dog on a tight leash, Reyna."

"Leave us," Arluin hisses through his teeth. While my fury burns like wildfire, his is stone cold.

"You don't scare me, *necromancer*."

Arluin steps closer to her, his expression still frosty. I doubt even Kaely will succeed in melting it. I've never seen him lose his temper.

But there's a darkness in his eyes which makes me tremble. All I can think about is what he confessed to me yesterday. About the magic his father taught him, the crimes he himself has committed, and the secrets I swore to take to my grave.

Kaely's shoulders jerk back as he approaches. She would never admit it, but there's fear in her gaze. Whatever I can see in Arluin's expression, she can see it too.

"What are you going to do?" Her tone doesn't reveal her unease. It's as brash as always. "Kill me and raise me from the dead, just like your father reanimated corpses from graveyards?"

"Yes," Arluin breathes, mere inches from her. His voice is so quiet it's barely a whisper. "That is exactly what I will do. I'll kill you and bring you back from the dead as a mindless ghoul, forced to obey my every command while the very flesh rots upon your walking corpse."

Biles creeps up my throat. Especially as his face twists into an expression so wicked even Kaely's pales in comparison.

He terrifies me.

It's an awful thing to admit. That the boy I love, the boy I will marry, frightens me so much that a chill rattles through my bones.

I shouldn't be thinking this. I shouldn't fear him like everyone else. But I feel only horror.

Kaely stumbles back. A strangled noise escapes her throat as she stifles her fear. She whirls around, searching for witnesses. But aside from the three of us, only the books heard Arluin's terrifying words.

"You . . ." Her voice quivers. "You wouldn't dare. You would be banished. Just like your father. Or worse."

Arluin arches a brow. "What makes you think I fear banishment? Or even death? Do you dare test me?"

Kaely draws in a shaky breath. She opens her mouth, but no sound comes out.

Never have I seen her lost for words.

I should relish in her fear. But I feel only dread.

"You're still standing here?" Arluin sneers. "You wish to become my undead pet?"

Kaely stares at him, her eyes wide with horror, as if she can't believe what he's saying. When Arluin's lips curl into a wicked smile, she turns and flees without hesitation.

I gaze at the empty spot where she stood. I can barely breathe. Fear still imprisons me. I must banish it. Or my reaction will hurt him.

But I don't know how to shake away the dread coiling through my stomach.

Arluin draws closer to me. I try not to shudder as he takes my hand. As his thumb brushes over my cheek.

"I just heard what happened this afternoon," he murmurs. "I'm sorry I didn't come sooner. Are you all right?"

I can only manage a stiff nod.

I am a horrible person. He stepped in to defend me, is worried for my sake, and yet I can barely stand the feel of his touch.

I force myself to meet his eyes. Magenta. They are magenta, and not the color of death.

He must see the fright in my expression since his fingers leave my cheek. His hand releases mine.

"You're scared of me." Arluin takes a step away, his throat bobbing as he swallows. "Aren't you, Reyna?"

A wave of guilt crashes into me, and I shake my head hastily, the gesture likely too forceful to look sincere. "No," I lie, "I'm not scared of you."

Arluin heaves out a breath and runs his fingers through his loose, dark curls. "I didn't mean what I said to Kaely. I heard rumors of what she said this afternoon, and with the way she was talking to you now, I just . . ."

"I know," I say, not meeting his eyes as I reach for his hand. I focus on his fingers and the way they feel against mine. "I know. It's all right, I promise." I hope he can't hear the trepidation in my voice and that my words sound more convincing than they do in my head.

"I'm sorry," he whispers, his shoulders sagging.

And I am sorry, too. But I don't tell him that. Because it would mean admitting my fear.

I close the distance between us and wrap my arm around him. I press my head against his chest, staring down at the hardened leather covers bundled in my other arm.

Arluin returns my hug, and we remain like that for a long while.

He's not a monster. I know he's not. If he were a monster, how could his embrace be so comforting?

His fingers curl around a stray strand of my hair. "What time will you finish working for Erma?"

"By nightfall. But I doubt she'll let me leave until I've finished returning all the books."

"I was going to study for a few hours, so I'll wait until you finish."

"I'll stay at yours tonight," I say, wanting to return the atmosphere to normal.

His lips brush the top of my head in a soft kiss. I give his hand a squeeze before we break away, and I return to the task of tidying away the stack of books.

CHAPTER 10

RETURNING ALL THE BOOKS TAKES me several more hours, and we don't leave the Grand Library until long after nightfall. The Arcanium is mostly empty now, though we pass a few magi as we cross through the atrium.

We step beyond the pillars at the Arcanium's entrance, and the night breeze washes over my cheeks. Having spent far too long inside the library, the cool night air feels refreshing.

Our hands entwined, we wind down the spiraling stairs and continue past the statues lining the path out of the Arcanium. When we reach the archway with the words QUEL ESTE VOLU, PODE NONQUES VERA MORIRE etched into its stone, we come to a stop. Arluin pulls me nearer and closes his eyes, conjuring aether in his fingers.

Before he can finish casting his teleportation spell, I tug his arm.

"Let's walk back," I say.

"Aren't you tired?" he asks. "Erma had you running around the entire library."

"She had me running around so much I can't even feel how tired my legs are. My head is the most tired. Hopefully some fresh air and a gentle stroll will wake me up enough to cook. I can't even remember when I last ate today."

"I'll cook."

I snort. "How? You can't cook."

"I can."

"Your cooking tastes awful."

"It tastes fine to me."

I cast him a dubious look. "Then not only am I worried about your cooking skills but also your taste buds."

"There's nothing wrong with my cooking, nor with my taste buds."

"Fine," I say with a shrug. "I'll cook for myself and you can cook for yourself when we get back. How's that?"

Arluin presses his lips together and hesitates for a terribly long moment.

I flash him a triumphant grin. "See? You prefer my cooking."

"Though I can't deny the fact you're a superior cook, that doesn't mean I'm incapable of cooking."

I shake my head. And he calls me stubborn.

"Come on then," I say, pulling him through the archway. "Tell me what's left in your pantry, and I'll think of something nice to cook us both."

As we continue along the cobblestone road and turn left down Lenwick Street, Arluin tries to remember what he has left in his pantry. His memory is excellent with useless facts such as what years various kings died, but it's awful at holding essential information such as what food he has.

But our conversation is soon cut short.

Halfway back to Arluin's manor, I once again feel the same suffocating presence I felt two nights ago.

I stop, my breaths ragged. I squeeze Arluin's hand tightly, my knuckles whitening with the strain.

"What is it?" he asks as I whirl around, frantically seeking the source of this terrifying presence.

Finally, I find it.

A hooded silhouette stands amid the shadows of a darkened alleyway.

"There!" I hiss, pointing at it. Maybe I should act more cautiously, but this time I'm determined for Arluin to see the figure. To prove it isn't a figment of my imagination.

The shadowy being lingers long enough for Arluin to glimpse it. His shoulders stiffen.

Then the silhouette is gone.

We both stare into the shadows where it disappeared. Neither of us says anything, our minds too wrapped up in our own thoughts.

"Who would be stalking us like this?" I mutter after a long pause. "It can't be Kaely, can it? From what she said earlier this afternoon, it sounded like she's been following us around."

Despite my words, I'm not convinced it's Kaely. She looked petrified of Arluin's threats, and this presence feels like that of dark magic.

I shiver.

Arluin releases my hand and scratches his chin as he thinks. "You could be right. Maybe she seeks retribution for how I threatened her." But I hear the note of doubt in his voice.

"Maybe she's following us around in the hope she'll find something to wield against us?" I say.

I pray that it is Kaely. Because if it isn't her, I dread to think whom it may be.

Arluin's fists tighten.

I know what he might be thinking. And I hope with all my heart he's wrong.

"To determine whether it's Kaely or not," he continues, "we will need to investigate further."

I suck in a sharp breath, staring into the darkened alleyway once more. "You want to follow them?"

Arluin doesn't answer. He clenches his jaw and strides into the shadows. Leaving me alone.

Though he's only a few steps away, the air grows much colder. I pull my cerulean robes tighter around myself and hurry after him.

I know it's foolish to chase phantoms, but I doubt it's wise to remain here by myself. Staying by his side is far safer. He is, after all, one of the most talented adepts in the Arcanium.

His footsteps ring out across the cobblestones. I wince at the sound. If his intentions are to ambush the mysterious figure, he isn't going about it the right way.

The streets grow narrower and darker. We race deeper into the tangle of alleys which sprawls through the Upper City. Too focused on trying to keep up with Arluin's furious pace, I almost fall over a stack of discarded crates. With how weather-worn the wood is, it seems they've been left out for some time. I don't stop to inspect them, though. Arluin is already turning the corner ahead. I sprint faster so he doesn't disappear from my sight.

His furious pace continues until we reach the end of that next street. Our path forks, and he glances around in search of the hooded silhouette.

I open my mouth, wanting to persuade Arluin to cease this pursuit and return to his manor before we're led any deeper into Nolderan's alleyways. But before I can speak, he's already off, running down the street to our right.

"Arluin!" I call. He doesn't seem to hear me.

Grimacing, I hurry after him.

One day he really will be the death of me.

We soon reach a circular sewage grate that has been cast aside. Arluin stands before the dark hole, peering into its depths.

"They wouldn't have gone down there, would they?" I whisper.

Arluin raises his head and examines the dark alley ahead of us. I don't want the shadowy figure to reappear but if it does, I would prefer for it to emerge from behind the corner. I dread the thought of going down into the sewers.

But no matter how much Arluin stares at the dark streets around us, the silhouette does not appear.

His attention returns to the sewage grate, and his expression hardens into steel.

"Please tell me you're not planning on going down there."

If the hooded figure disappeared down there, it can't be Kaely following us. She would never lurk in the sewers.

Going down there would be madness.

"I need to look," Arluin murmurs. "I need to be sure."

"You need to be sure of what, Arly?" I ask, my fear heightening. "We have no idea what's down there. We need to return to the Arcanium now. My father is probably still with the ambassadors. We'll tell him a cloaked figure has been following us. That the presence surrounding them can only belong to a dark sorcerer."

Arluin stares into the sewers, inhaling deeply. Then, before I can stop him, he leaps into the darkness.

I grit my teeth, glancing around at the shadows. If the hooded figure didn't disappear into the sewers, then I don't want to be left standing here. Maybe they're planning to strike me right now, seizing their opportunity while I'm separated from Arluin.

I curse him under my breath.

For such a seemingly clever man, he really is so stupid.

Rather than jumping straight into the hole, I slide over the edge and use the metallic rungs to steady my drop. My feet meet the stone beneath.

A putrid smell fills my nostrils. It's hard not to gag.

"*Iluminos*," Arluin says. A brilliant orb of aether spreads from his fingers. It floats above us, illuminating our surroundings with its dazzling light.

We stand on a narrow platform cut into the stone. It overlooks a canal of water which ensures sewage and rainwater run out to sea.

"There's nothing here," I whisper. Despite how soft my words are, they echo throughout the tunnel. "Come on, please, let's head back to yours."

"Don't you hear it?" Arluin asks, closing his eyes as he listens.

I fall silent and strain my ears as I try to discern anything but the rush of water.

"What—" I begin but stop. Because I too finally hear the noise coming from deeper in the sewers.

It's a rumbling. No, a growling. And it doesn't sound like it comes from only one being.

My pulse quickens. "Please," I beg him. "Please let's just go."

"There's something down here."

"I know. That's why we'll immediately report it to my father. We're adepts, not magi. We should let those who are more experienced deal with this."

But he only ventures farther into the sewers, the floating orb illuminating his path.

I follow him for a few strides, dread growing with every step until it becomes too much. Even if Arluin is a talented sorcerer, I have no idea what lies ahead of us. And whether we will be outmatched.

We must turn back now, before it's too late.

But Arluin refuses to listen to me. I will have to leave him here, though I hate the thought of abandoning him. My father needs to know something dark and rotten dwells within Nolderan's sewers.

I turn and race back to the hole we came through. This part of the tunnel is cast in darkness now that Arluin's orb has drifted away. I glance back, wanting to tell him that I will meet him at his manor. Hoping that he will see sense.

But then, the shadows hiss. They swirl and obstruct my path. From them, the hooded silhouette emerges.

I take a step back.

Darkness pours out, thick and heavy like foul smoke. When I draw in a breath, the air suffocates me.

"Where do you think you're going?" a man demands, his voice frighteningly familiar. Before I can respond, or teleport to safety, he raises his hand. "*Vorikaz*."

Dark magic flings toward me. Obsidian chains wrap around me so tightly I fear they will snap me in half. I struggle beneath the bindings, but my arms are pressed into my sides and I can't move them at all.

Nor can I use any magic.

I can feel aether humming in the surrounding air, but it refuses to answer my call. The obsidian chains sever me from my magic.

"*Laxus*!" Arluin cries, appearing between us. Aether blooms in his palms as he prepares to unleash an attack on the hooded figure. "Release her at once!"

"Or what?" the man taunts. His deep laugh rumbles around us, echoing down the endless, dark tunnel.

Arluin's heels dig into the stone beneath, refusing to yield. But before he can release his magic upon our enemy, the shadows shift, spinning into clouds of darkness.

From them, a dozen more figures appear. Humans, orcs, and elves form their ranks. All are clad in black robes, and the same terrifying presence oozes from them.

Arluin can't defeat them all. Even if I were not bound by these chains, the odds of success would remain impossible.

A group of dark sorcerers lurk in Nolderan's sewers and threaten the safety of our city. My father must be alerted immediately. Before it is too late.

"Go!" I cry to Arluin. "Teleport to the Arcanium. Tell my father. Now!"

Arluin doesn't heed my words. The aether in his hands shines brighter, moments away from unleashing a spell upon our enemies.

But fighting them is futile.

"He looks the spitting image of you, my lord," says an orcish woman. She stands to the right of the hooded figure. Her skin is ashen green, and her white hair is woven into many long braids.

"He does?" the hooded man replies. "I've always seen more of his mother in him."

Horror hits me like a sudden blow to the chest. I can't breathe.

My legs betray me by giving way, and I tumble to the ground. Stone strikes my knees, and sharp pain jolts through them.

I stare up at the hooded figure, praying against all sense that I am wrong.

Shock too slams into Arluin. His eyes widen, and his mouth falls agape. The aether in his hands fizzles out and returns to the dark air. His shoulders tremble as the man strides toward him.

He throws aside his hood. The illumination orb high above shines over his face.

He shares Arluin's dark curls, though silver dusts his hair, and their bold jawlines are identical.

There is no denying their blood relation.

A cruel grin stretches across Heston Harstall's face, and his gray eyes gleam. "You are much taller than I remember, my boy."

CHAPTER 11

"Father," Arluin gasps.

A draft blows through the sewers. It carries with it the stench of death and decay.

"I have waited years for this moment," Heston says. "For our reunion."

The grimy walls sway. Numbness washes over me. I no longer feel the stone slabs digging into my knees.

Heston has returned. And he brings with him a cult of necromancers.

I know not what they plan. Only that they will doom my city.

Dark magic erupts from Heston's hands. "*Vorikaz.*"

Obsidian chains fling at Arluin. They bind him as tightly as they bind me.

"What are you doing?" Arluin exclaims. He writhes against the chains, desperately trying to shake them off, but they constrict. A sharp exhalation shudders through his lips as the chains give his chest a forceful squeeze.

"Taking precautions. Though I have missed you greatly and have thought of you every day, I fear you may not have missed me in return."

Arluin doesn't reply. But I know he missed his father. He told me that much yesterday.

I don't know whether Heston can see through Arluin's expression. His gray eyes rake over Arluin as he tries to discern his thoughts.

A sudden bout of courage ignites in my heart. Before fear can snuff out the small flame, I force myself to confront Heston.

"What do you want?" I demand, hoping my words sound stronger than they do in my head. "Why have you dared to return to Nolderan when my father exiled you? When he made it clear that if you were ever to return, he would execute you on the spot?"

Heston tears his attention from Arluin and scrutinizes me instead. I try to conceal my fear with an icy mask, but it begins to crack as his cruel eyes bore into mine. "To see my son. All fathers share the same grief over being separated from their children. Your father is no different. And this is the greatest weakness of the Grandmage of Nolderan." The edge to his voice tells me he intends to exploit this weakness.

I shrink back, but there's nowhere to run. Not with these heavy chains and the dozen necromancers looming over me.

Blood thrums in my ears, urging me to fight with the only weapon I have left. My words.

"If you so much as lay a finger on me, my father will see to it you die a painful death, Heston." I spit his name with all the disgust I can.

"You already said he would execute me simply for breathing Nolderan's air, girl. What difference does it make if he will kill me, regardless?"

I have no retort. Not that one would improve my current situation.

I am bound with chains and cut off from my magic. So far beneath the streets, no one would hear if I scream. No one but Heston and his necromancers. And Arluin, who is as helpless as me.

If Heston decides to kill me right now, there's nothing I can do to save myself.

I stare up at him, trembling beneath the chains. I wish I could stop. But I can't.

"Don't look at me like that," he chides. "Tonight, you will serve an invaluable purpose?"

"W-what purpose?" I hate how my lower lip quivers. But I'm no longer in control of my body. Fear shackles me more tightly than the obsidian chains.

"You will see," he simply says. The malice in his eyes fills my heart with dread. I don't know how it continues to beat. Especially so frantically.

I pull my gaze from Heston and look across to Arluin. He stares at his father as if he's seeing a ghost. His face is the color of bone.

He fears his father, and what is to come. Just as I do.

We should never have ventured down here. We should have gone straight to my father. If we had, we wouldn't be bound by Heston's chains, our magic cut off from us.

Nausea crashes into me. Have our actions already doomed Nolderan?

"I believe that's enough reunions for one day," Heston declares, turning to his necromancers. "We still have a city to sack and a Grandmage to slay."

My father.

I barely hear the responding sneers. The drum of blood deafens my ears. Saliva tastes like ash in my mouth.

If Heston threatens my father with my life, I fear what choice he will make. And what Nolderan's fate will be.

Heston gestures to his necromancers, and two step forth. They haul me onto my feet and shove me farther through the tunnel. I feel weightless, as though I'm drifting over the stone.

As though I'm no longer here.

We enter deeper into the sewers, toward the growling. I think I know what it belongs to, but I don't dare to admit it—not even in my own mind. Because thinking that thought would make it real.

I edge closer to Arluin, though that's difficult with the necromancers escorting us. But I get close enough.

His head is lowered, his shoulders sagged in defeat. He must feel my gaze on him since he turns to me.

Fear and guilt cloud his magenta eyes. "Reyna," he murmurs so quietly I barely hear him over our footsteps, "I am so sorry."

At first, I don't know how to respond. This is his fault. If we hadn't come down here, we wouldn't be captured by Heston.

But I'm also to blame. I knew what a stupid idea it was, yet I followed him all the same. I should have immediately teleported myself back to the Arcanium. I should have left him. Nothing awful would have happened to him. Heston would never hurt his own son.

Or at least, I think he wouldn't.

Nonetheless, I squeeze my eyes shut and say, "This isn't your fault."

When I dare to reopen my eyes, his shoulders are taut with tension. "I won't let him hurt you."

All I can manage is a small nod. It isn't that I don't trust the sincerity of his words, it's just I know he's speaking from his heart and not his head.

Heston's spell prevents us both from casting magic. And our arms are too tightly bound to wield a knife against him.

There is nothing either of us can do.

The growling becomes louder. As does the rattling of bone against stone.

Finally, we arrive at the source of the noise.

The sewers swarm with hundreds of corpses. Some are skeletal, without even a lick of flesh on their bones. Others are half-decayed, and the rotten smell of death wafts from them. All their eye sockets are empty, aside from the shadows swarming within.

The guttural growls, the clattering of bone—it all proves too much.

I double over and vomit across the stone. The sick splashes onto the robes of the nearest necromancer. His nose wrinkles at the sullied hem. He's a sun elf, evident by his pointed ears and golden hair. His tanned skin is sallow, however, and his eyes aren't bright like the few sun elves I've seen strolling the streets of Nolderan.

The elven necromancer looks at me from above his hooked nose and snarls, "Get a move on." He shoves me forth before I have the chance to compose myself.

Heston comes to a stop before his horde of undead and raises his hand. The rabble falls silent and still at his command. Hundreds of empty sockets stare back at him, awaiting his orders.

"Grizela, Virion," Heston calls. The sun elf who escorted me steps forth, as does the orcish woman with braided white hair. "It is time."

"Yes, my lord," they answer, bowing their heads.

"When you have completed your task, return here."

The two of them disperse into shadows. Dark magic hurls through the sewers swifter than any wind spell I can conjure.

"The rest of you," Heston continues, "take your positions. Wait for the signal and then direct the undead to begin their rampage. Raise all the fallen and rejoin us north of Lenwick Street. We need the numbers to take the city."

The remaining necromancers obey his orders, each taking a portion of their forces with them. Some undead remain behind with Heston.

"Impressive, isn't it?" Heston says to Arluin, when all the necromancers are gone. "I must admit, stealing corpses from graveyards without the magi noticing was no small feat."

I want to tell him that he's monstrous, that his wicked plans will never succeed. But I can't. I can do nothing but stare at the horde of shambling undead.

Arluin says nothing. He too watches the masses of decayed corpses.

Heston's patience quickly thins. "Do you have nothing to say to me, boy?"

Arluin pauses. He inhales sharply. "You left me." His tone isn't accusatory. It's flat and hollow, devoid of emotion.

"I was exiled. What choice did I have?"

"You could have taken me with you. Instead, you left me here to be shunned."

"Is that what you wanted?" Heston asks. "To leave behind everything? Everyone?"

Arluin says nothing. I feel his gaze drift over to me.

"That's what I thought," Heston mutters.

Explosions roar high above. They come from somewhere in the distance. The Lower City.

My stomach churns.

Heston's mouth twists into a cruel grin. "And so it begins."

Before either Arluin or I can demand to know what the necromancers have done, Grizela and Virion emerge from the shadows.

"It is done, my lord," says the orcish woman. "The magi and their guards are rushing to the Lower City to control the fires raging through the streets."

"Then we make our next move." Heston turns to me and sneers. "Time to pay my old friend a visit."

He grabs my shoulder and drags me through the crowd of undead. I try to resist, but he only pulls me more violently.

As we pass the mangled corpses, I keep my eyes lowered to the stone floor. But the rotten toes and skeletal feet are almost enough to make me vomit again.

"What of this one?" Virion calls to Heston.

"Leave my son down here. Bind him to a rock if you must."

"Again you abandon me," Arluin spits.

Heston halts.

"Let me help, Father."

At his words, my blood chills.

Arluin doesn't really want to help his father, does he?

When I turn to him, I hope to see something in his expression which indicates his words are a ploy to earn his father's trust. To enable our escape. But I see nothing. Only tempered ice.

The threat he paid Kaely echoes through my mind. That he would kill her and raise her corpse, just as his father taught him.

What if he meant every word he said?

"Help?" Heston scoffs. "How would you help?"

"You said you need the numbers," Arluin says. His eyes remain cold, not betraying his true thoughts. "You know I can raise the dead. Let me help."

Heston's hand tightens around my shoulder. "Are you prepared to betray the one you love?"

Arluin's gaze meets mine. Silently I beg him not to do this. Not to follow in his father's footsteps. His eyes soften. But only for a heartbeat. Then they freeze once more.

His attention returns to his father. "You are my blood," he says. "This city has shunned me since you left, and I care little for it. Allow me to play a part in its destruction. Don't turn your back on me again."

Heston watches him for a long, careful moment. Arluin stares back at him, unflinching.

"Very well," Heston says. He waves his hand and the obsidian chains around Arluin crumble away, freeing him. Dark magic returns to the shadows. "Do not make me regret this."

"I won't, Father."

CHAPTER 12

HESTON SHOVES ME THROUGH THE sewers. Arluin follows close behind, while Grizela and Virion lead the clamoring undead. Our path is lit by the ghostly white light radiating from Heston's hand. The shadows dance around us as the spell flickers.

We soon reach a sewer grate larger than the one he lured Arluin and me down. Heston comes to a stop and peers at the metallic plate above us. He extinguishes the light, and darkness descends over us.

"*Arisga,*" Heston commands.

A bolt of dark magic slams into the sewer grate and throws it aside. The metallic plate clatters as it shudders into a nearby wall. I examine the steel rungs leading up to the surface. Maybe Heston will release me from the obsidian chains so that I can climb up to the streets. If he does, maybe I can try to run or teleport away.

But Heston grants me no such chance. He grips my arm.

"*Farjud.*"

Shadows consume us. When I glance down, I can no longer make out my physical self beneath the cloud of darkness.

In the next instant, we are rushing through the air.

Solid ground greets my feet. The shadows fade away to reveal Nolderan.

We are deep within the side streets winding through the Upper City. Few lights shine through the windows at this late hour, and most folk will be tucked in their beds, oblivious to the threat looming over them.

Arluin appears from the hole next, the two necromancers behind him. Then the undead scramble out, piling on top of each other as they fight to enter the realm of the living.

"Grizela, you take that road," Heston says, pointing to the street which veers to the left. "Virion, take the other."

The two necromancers wordlessly follow his command and lead the undead through the streets, beginning their destruction of Nolderan. With their dark magic, they tear through the magical enchantments which secure houses. The ghouls are free to pour inside, their ravenous hands out-stretched as they search for the living.

Screams erupt through the night. Grizela and Virion weave in and out of the houses, raising the corpses inside. The undead rampage ahead, leaving a trail of fresh bodies for the necromancers to reanimate.

It doesn't take long for the horde of undead to double in size.

So many lives will be lost tonight. If the undead are not stopped soon, this could mean the end of the magi.

Of Nolderan.

Heston watches his undead storm the streets. When the path has cleared, he urges me onward.

In the distance, fire rages through the Lower City. Smoke billows into the sky and suffocates the stars. Even when Heston drags me down several streets, his undead destroying everything in their path, I find no guards. They must still be focused on containing the destruction sweeping through the Lower City, unaware of the real danger.

By the time they realize, it will be too late. Heston's army will already be of an unimaginable size.

The streets widen as we approach Lenwick Street. The Arcanium's spires peek through the cobalt roofs.

Is my father inside? Or has he too been summoned to the Lower City to deal with the fires?

"*Gelu'tempis!*" a mage cries to our right.

A blizzard of frozen needles rains over us.

"*Ekrad!*"

Heston draws the shadows over us, forming a shield and preventing the blizzard from reaching us. When the mage's attack subsides, he releases the shadowy barrier.

Arluin steps forth. Aether swirls in his fingers. It crackles, spreading into ice.

I can't let him do this. I can't let him condemn himself.

If he chooses this path, he will become as monstrous as his father.

I open my mouth to scream, but no sound comes out. Terror mutes my tongue.

Arluin shapes the ice into a sword. "*Gelu'gladis!*"

He unleashes the frozen blade.

The mage draws aether into his fingers. But it's too late.

Arluin's icy sword strikes him through the chest.

The mage falls onto the street. Blood wells around the chunk of ice lodged inside him. He gurgles and chokes as he desperately tries to tear the frozen blade from his chest.

The life in his eyes soon fades. As does the magenta glow of aether.

The buildings spin around me.

If Heston wasn't gripping my shoulder and holding me in place, I would have collapsed onto the street along with the mage.

Arluin killed him.

Horror strangles me. I choke in its grasp.

When I finally tear my gaze from the corpse and look at Arluin, his face makes my blood curdle.

His expression remains indifferent. He has killed, and yet he does not care.

I can no longer believe this is an act. The Arluin I know is no murderer. He would never kill just to earn his father's trust. How can he stand there with such an icy expression? Has he killed before? Is that another secret he has never confessed to me?

He gathers the shadows into his hands—the same shadows his father wields.

"*Arka-joud,*" he hisses. Dark magic pours over the mage's corpse.

I scream until my voice falters. Until my throat is raw and broken.

Arluin is a necromancer. As wicked as his father.

All along, I was blind to the truth.

The shadows wash over the mage's corpse. They gouge out his eyes and replace them with orbs of darkness.

The mage's fingers twitch first. Then he sits up. His head hangs limply as he stares at the ice piercing his chest. The surrounding blood has dried and blackened.

The corpse stands. He peers at his new master with his unblinking shadowy orbs.

"Go," Arluin commands. "Purge the living from these streets. Do not stop until all are dead."

The fallen mage turns and joins the rest of the undead as they rampage through the streets. He doesn't attack with his hands and teeth like the other ghouls. He conjures bolts of darkness and hurls them at any in his path.

Pride plasters across Heston's expression. "A wight? How impressive. I feared you would fail to raise a mere ghoul, let alone a wight." Heston grins. "You will prove a greater asset to our cause than I expected, my boy."

Arluin dips his head.

I don't look at him again.

Grizela and Virion soon rejoin Heston, and the number of undead with them has tripled. They march down the road and turn onto Lenwick Street.

More necromancers gather here. Together they have turned a hundred ghouls into an army so large I fear Nolderan stands no chance against them.

Many wights now fight the magi alongside the ghouls. They return the bolts of frost and fire with bolts of darkness. And when the magi fall, the necromancers raise them as another wight to fuel their army of the dead.

Heston remains at the rear of his onslaught. As does Arluin, raising so many ghouls and wights that I'm certain his eyes will turn from magenta to gray at any moment.

The magi surround the undead, slowly pushing them back. Hope surges in my chest. Maybe Heston won't win this fight. Maybe Nolderan will stand strong.

But that hope soon falters.

Heston releases my shoulder and strides into the sea of corpses.

"*Arka-kyrat!*" he shouts.

Shadows sweep over the fallen, magi and undead alike. As the dark magic touches them, each rises once more.

Even if the magi defeat a ghoul, Heston and his necromancers reanimate it—unless it was burned to ashes. Attacking the undead is futile. The only way Nolderan will succeed is if the necromancers fall. But the magi concentrate their attacks onto the foes nearest them, not onto the necromancers who remain far behind their undead minions.

Hands grab me, spinning me around.

I lift my head to see Arluin. As I look at him, I can only think of all those he has killed. All those he has risen from the dead.

After what he has done, how can he gaze at me with such softness?

Aether blooms in his hands. He closes his eyes and presses his index finger to the center of my forehead.

"*Mundes.*"

His spell cleanses the dark enchantment Heston cast on me. The obsidian chains wither away, returning to the shadows from which they were made.

I blink, unable to believe that he has freed me. That though he wields dark magic and has killed so many innocents, he has decided to save me.

Was this all an act? Did he resort to these measures so that his father would drop his guard? So that he would have this single chance to free me?

I want to believe that's the case. But I can't shake away the horrors he has committed.

Concern and fear fill his eyes. Fear for me.

Despite all he has done, gratitude blossoms in my chest.

"Go!" he whispers, just as Heston turns and witnesses his betrayal.

His father bellows with rage and merges with the shadows, charging straight for us.

I stumble back, my hands clasping Arluin's tightly.

"Arly," I gasp. I can't let go of him. If I do, I may never again hold his hand.

"*Rivus!*" Heston snarls.

Dark magic surges toward us.

"*Muriz!*" Arluin calls, forming a barrier of aether around us. The shadow bolt slams into the wall. He grits his teeth, desperately holding the shield in place. "Reyna, go!"

I know I must go, but I fear what will happen to Arluin. How his father will punish him for this treachery.

Arluin glances at me from over his shoulder. Desperation strains his brow.

Heston stalks nearer, anger blazing in his gray eyes. If I hesitate for a moment longer, I will be unable to escape. Arluin's efforts will be in vain.

I draw in a shaky breath and turn my back on Arluin, fleeing down the nearest alley. My heart pounds as I run. Blood thunders in my ears.

"After her!" Heston barks.

Shambling footsteps hurry after me. As do guttural growls. I don't look back to see what ghastly creatures Heston has sent. I run as fast as I can, unable to pause long enough to mutter *laxus* and teleport to safety.

I reach the end of the narrow street. But before I turn the corner, I hear a cry of pain.

Arluin.

My pace falters. I glance back. Heston looms over him, shadows encasing them both.

I don't have time to stop and see if he is moving—whether he is alive. The ghouls and wights are almost upon me.

I break into a sprint once more. Tears spill onto my cheeks, blurring the alleyway. I run so hard that breathing burns my nose and my throat.

I can't slow, not unless I wish for Heston to capture me again. To serve as my father's undoing.

Neither can I allow Arluin's sacrifice to be for nothing.

I choke at that last thought and pray that I'm wrong, that Heston would not kill his only child. The reason he turned to necromancy was to revive his wife. Surely a man who can't let go of his loved ones will be incapable of killing his son, no matter how much the betrayal may infuriate him.

I tell myself that over and over as I run. Yet I cannot shake away the fear snaking through my mind, threatening to extinguish any hope for Arluin's survival: The Heston who has returned to Nolderan is not the same Heston who was exiled five years ago, and there's no telling what a man as wicked as him will do.

The footsteps of the undead draw closer. And louder. Fatigue sears through my legs. Though I tire, the restless undead do not. Their strides quicken, gaining on me.

I will not last much longer.

If only there was enough time to teleport away before the ghouls reach me. Maybe I can cast a fireball but in my haste, it would be weak. Then what will I do when they are upon me and I'm unable to cast a second spell as their decaying hands wrap around my neck? As their teeth rip through my flesh?

The street opens to the main road. I suck in a breath. The air scolds my throat. It feels like swallowing venom. Ahead, a crowd of magi fights the undead. If I can reach them before my pursuers catch me, maybe I will stand a chance of survival.

Drawing in air and forcing my legs onward is becoming increasingly difficult. I don't know how many more steps I can take. I glance back to see how close the undead are.

Their gnarled hands are mere inches from me.

I return my attention to the path ahead. But I am too slow. One cobblestone is broken and juts out. When my foot meets it, I am thrown off balance.

I slam into the ground. My shoulder hits it first, the one Kaely injured. It isn't fully healed yet, and the resulting pain is excruciating. Though trying to move is unbearable, I force myself to do so.

But the undead are already upon me. And there is no time left to run.

CHAPTER 13

THE UNDEAD STALK TOWARD ME. Their strangled groans sound almost like sneers.

"*Muriz!*" I cry. Aether wraps around me.

The ghouls crash into the barrier. Ravenous growls echo through my shield. I hug my knees, staring up at the decayed faces.

I am trapped, surrounded by a horde of undead that seeks to return me to Heston. And that's if I'm lucky. Maybe they will misinterpret his command and return my half-eaten corpse to him.

And Arluin . . .

I squeeze my eyes shut, lowering my head.

I fear his fate, and whether I am soon to follow him.

A shadow bolt slams into my shield.

My gaze snaps up. Three wights stand behind the ranks of ghouls. Each utters *rivus* in its unnatural voice, and their calls reverberate off the narrow stone walls. A barrage of shadow bolts hurls at me.

My shield won't hold off their attacks for long. Cracks are already emerging in the crystalline barrier, and it shudders from the bolts of dark magic. Aether dust scatters into the wind.

Then the shield splits apart, falling around me.

And I am left entirely exposed.

I crawl back. The ghouls advance. Scraps of blood and flesh lie between their teeth and under their nails.

I gather more aether, preparing to blast the ghouls nearest me and praying I can also fend off the wights. But before I can, a shout comes from behind.

"*Ignira!*"

Flames surge forth, taking the shape of an enormous fireball. The spell skims over my head, singeing my hair with how close it sweeps. It slams into the ghouls.

The blast gives me enough time to scramble off the ground and return to my feet. I sprint to my savior, my breaths ragged.

It is my mother who stands there. Her long dark hair and magnificent magi robes flutter in the wind. She raises her hands, weaving aether into a wind spell. "*Ventrez!*"

A gale throws the undead back.

"Mother!" I choke out, clasping her hands when I reach her. Fresh tears burst from my eyes.

"Reyna!" She clutches me, pulling me into a hug. "Are you hurt?"

I shake my head. Though I'm not physically hurt, the images of Arluin raising the dead, of him falling at his father's hand, wrack through my heart. And I fear I will never repair.

"Thank the Heavens," my mother mutters, holding me tighter.

Our embrace is short-lived. The undead climb back onto their rotten feet and lumber toward us. Their blood-curdling howls echo through the night.

My mother pushes me behind her. I peer at the undead beyond, feeling more like a helpless child than a second-year of the Arcanium.

"*Gelu'vinclair!*" Frost swirls from her fingers and spreads across the street, covering the ground like a thick blanket. The ice winds upward, wrapping around their legs and freezing them in place. The ghouls snap their yellowed teeth at us, but the frozen shackles prevent them from taking another step closer.

Though my mother's spell renders the ghouls harmless, the wights remain a threat. They call out *rivus* in their guttural voices and launch shadow bolts at us.

"*Tera'muriz!*" The ground obeys my mother's command and rises into a wall of stone. Her earthen shield absorbs the volley of dark magic.

Then she snaps her fingers. *"Tera'quatir!"*

The stone wall shatters. Rock rains over the undead.

The spell crushes many of our enemies, but more close in from behind.

With my mother fending off the wights ahead, I whirl around to deal with the new threat.

"Quatir!" I cry. An explosion of aether rips through the air, slamming into the ghouls. It provides me with enough time to cast my next spell.

"Ignir'alas!" Flames spread from my fingers. They stretch into the scorching wings of a phoenix. The spell sweeps into the night and crackles through the dark air.

Then it descends at a terrifying velocity.

Fire roars. Smoke billows. Ash blows through the evening breeze as the flames obliterate the ghouls.

I glance back at the alley where the undead pursued me. They too burn from my mother's conjured flames. Even the wights.

It seems fire works best against these ghastly creatures.

My mother grabs my hand. She pulls me down the road, toward a large crowd of magi.

But we only manage a few strides before the air hisses to our right.

Heston appears from a cloud of shadows. Fury burns in his gray eyes.

"Ekrad!" he snarls.

Darkness spins from Heston's fingers. It warps into a towering wall and cuts us off from the group of magi.

Heston's mouth curls into a heinous smirk. "Mirelle Ashbourne. It's been a while."

"Heston." Aether dances in my mother's palms, ready to strike. "You will pay for what you have done."

"Will I now?" Heston barks out a laugh. "And who will I answer to? Nolderan has all but fallen, and its Grandmage will soon share the same fate."

"You're gravely underestimating my husband. Your vile magic will never stand a chance against him."

"You put too much faith in one man, my dear. What will he do when the lives of those he cares for most are at stake? I will force his surrender without needing to cast a single spell."

"If only Narla could see you now," my mother says, gritting her teeth, "what a monster you have become."

"Then it's a blessing she can't see me now." He raises his hand. Darkness gathers. "*Rivus.*"

A shadow bolt hurdles toward us. My mother draws aether into her grasp. "*Telum!*"

Her attack meets Heston's. Aether and darkness explode, ripping through the air. The resulting gust almost throws me off-balance. Both spells annihilate each other, and their remnants dissolve into the atmosphere.

Before my mother can conjure her next attack, Heston hisses, "*Gavrik.*"

A murder of crows envelops us. Shadowy birds swoop from all angles. Their caws pierce through my ears. Razor-sharp talons and beaks tear at our robes, seeking blood and flesh.

We use our magic to blast the phantom crows with aether and flames. Until finally, the spell is shattered.

We emerge from the cover of darkness with tattered robes and scratched faces. But the attack inflicted no fatal injuries on either of us.

"*Muriz!*" my mother yells.

Aether encases me. The barrier is as thick as the Arcanium's ancient stone walls.

I press my hand to the shield. Magic hums furiously beneath it. Beyond the barrier, undead stalk toward my mother.

"Your father," she gasps between shouting *ignira* and battling the ghouls nearest her. "You must tell him Heston is here!"

I swallow, the strained note in her voice hard to bear.

She is greatly outmatched. And if my father doesn't arrive soon . . .

I banish the thought. I can't let fear distract me.

I close my eyes and exhale deeply, focusing on my breathing. Aether sparks in my fingers.

Creating a mind-link works similarly to teleportation. The difference is that I must instead imagine the person I wish to communicate with in meticulous detail. I learned this spell recently, and I failed many times during practice.

I can't fail now.

I first imagine my father's magnificent robes and the golden thread running through the indigo fabric. Then I add his auburn hair and beard which ripple around his face like a lion's fiery mane, and also a deep crease in his brow as he frowns at me. Finally, I complete my image of him with the vivid glow of his magenta eyes and the crystalline staff he always clutches.

"*Aminex* Telric Ashbourne," I whisper when I finish painting the mental portrait of my father.

I hold my breath, fearing that maybe my magic hasn't worked. Or that maybe my father hasn't heard my call above the chaos raging through Nolderan.

But after several long heartbeats, he finally replies.

"*Reyna?*" His voice echoes through my mind.

"*Father!*" I exclaim, without the syllables physically leaving my lips. Conversation via a mind-link flows as easily as thoughts, heard only by those it's cast between.

"*Where are you?*" His words are hurried. To answer my call, he would have needed to clear his mind, just as I did. And that means he cannot fight the undead while our mind-link is being channeled.

"*With Mother. Heston—he's here!*"

"*Where is here?*" comes his frantic response.

"*Somewhere along Lenwick Street. North. I came through an alley. I think—*"

Before I can offer more information, a scream shatters my concentration. The mind-link falters.

A shadow bolt pierces my mother's chest. The veins in her neck blacken and throb as the poisonous magic seeps through her blood. Her eyes bulge from their sockets, blood-shot and swollen.

"Mother!" I leap onto my feet and push against the aether shield. But it refuses to move. No matter how desperately I try to rush to my mother's side.

Her hand reaches out for me. Then it falls.

Swollen eyes stare at me. She doesn't blink.

I slide down the aether shield. I don't feel the impact of the ground.

Heston steps over to where my mother lies.

"*Arka-duat.*"

A stream of shadows floods into her nostrils, filling her corpse with dark magic.

My forehead presses into the barrier. My fingers dig into it.

The shadows darken. They swarm upward and form a figure which resembles my mother.

A wraith hovers above my mother's body. Its features are identical to hers, except it is born of shadows and not flesh and blood.

"I only need one of you to render Telric helpless," Heston says. "And this way he will know the consequences of failing to surrender."

I crawl away, my eyes not leaving my mother's spectral form. My back hits the other side of the aether shield, preventing any further retreat as Heston and his undead stalk toward me. The spell my mother cast to protect me now hinders my escape.

I shove my shoulders into the solid wall, hoping it will give way beneath my weight. The energy continues to hum. No cracks show. Panic overwhelms me.

Shadow bolts smash into the shield. They come from Heston and his wights. And my mother too, or at least the wraith of her.

Stiff fingers claw at the aether barrier. Ghouls surround me from every angle.

I conjure what flames I can, knowing fire magic is the most effective against the undead.

My shield shatters.

The ghouls advance. I open my mouth, but there's no chance to speak any spell-words.

"*Ventrez!*" a voice rings out from high above.

A wind sweeps under my feet, lifting me from the ground before the ghouls can reach me.

The gale blows me up onto the cobalt roofs and gently sets me down beside the Grandmage of Nolderan.

My father clenches his crystalline staff with both hands, his knuckles ivory white. The veins in his forehead throb, and his shoulders quake with rage.

His wrath is so ferocious I fear flames will sweep from him without him speaking the spell-words, and that they will be born of a fury so wild, they will obliterate even me.

Though his magical presence is terrifying as he stares down at Heston, the undead and my mother's corpse, I cling to it like a blanket.

"Mother," I choke out, my body wrought with grief.

He places a hand on my shoulder. "Stay here." Then he releases me and raises his staff. "*Muriz.*"

Aether swirls out, covering me with a dense shield. Despite the immense energy humming around me, I know this spell cost my father only a fraction of his strength.

"*Laxus.*"

In the next instant, he appears on the streets below, standing opposite Heston. His teleportation spell is complete before I can blink.

"*Muriz,*" the grandmage mutters again. This time aether sweeps across my mother's body, protecting her from further violation. He swallows hard, staring at her body beneath the aether shield. His hand trembles from both grief and wrath.

"Heston," he growls, "how dare you return to Nolderan."

"I missed my boy," Heston says with a shrug.

I clench my fists. Fresh tears well within my eyes. All I can see is Heston standing over Arluin. I still don't know whether he is dead or alive.

"What you have done . . ." My father inhales sharply. "My wife—your crimes are unforgivable. There's no retribution great enough for your evil. Even the Abyss has no place for one as heinous as you."

Heston laughs. "I really am terrified, oh mighty Grandmage. How do you expect to save your city when you couldn't even save your wife?"

My father lets out a roar of fury, which turns into the word *ignira* halfway through.

Flames rush toward Heston. He raises his hands, and the shadows shift around him in a shield. "*Ekrad,*" he whispers.

His wall of darkness is wide enough to protect himself and the undead nearest him from the scorching flames. But the fireball doesn't collide with Heston's shield. It continues past and slams into my mother's wraith.

Fire rages across its shadowy form, eating away at the darkness. The wraith lets out a piercing shriek. Though the scream is unnatural, I hear the traces of a voice which sounds like my mother.

I squeeze my eyes shut, unable to watch as the fire consumes her and sends dark magic scattering through the air like soot.

When I finally dare to reopen them, the wraith is gone.

My father's jaw tightens. His gaze lingers on my mother's unmoving face.

"I *spared* you," he spits, turning back to Heston. "The punishment for your crimes should have been execution, but I instead exiled you. And this is how you repay me?"

"You expect me to be grateful for what you did?" Heston snarls. "You banished me. You stole everything from me. Tonight you finally tasted the bitterness of loss, and you cannot bear it?" More dark magic gathers in his hands. "*Rivus.*"

A shadow bolt surges toward my father. The wights nearest Heston imitate the attack, and a volley of darkness rushes at him.

"*Ignir'muriz.*" A wall of fire erupts around him, absorbing the attacks. The dark magic shrinks back.

My father drums the end of his staff against the ground. The sound thunders through the street and echoes off every wall.

"*Ignir'quatir.*"

The flames explode, blazing toward the undead.

Heston only has enough time to shout *ekrad* and conjure a shield to defend himself, leaving the rest of his undead exposed to my father's attack. The fire consumes their decaying bodies. Thick smoke blows into the air, as does the smell of charred, rotten flesh.

My father's spell is so fearsome it leaves the cobblestones streaked with charcoal.

Though Heston's shield protects him from the brunt of the blast, it throws him off-balance.

"*Tera'vinclair,*" my father calls before Heston can retaliate. The street rumbles. A shock wave charges forth. When it reaches Heston, the ground lifts and encases him in stone chains.

The necromancer roars with fury as the earthen manacles bind him to the street. He draws the shadows into his fingers, but before he can utter any spell-words, my father unleashes more flames upon him.

"*Ignir'alas.*"

Fiery wings sweep up, gaining velocity in the air. Then they crash down to Heston, who is unable to defend himself.

He screams as the ardent flames engulf him, as they lick the flesh from his bones. Beneath the fervid amber light, his silhouette struggles against the earthen restraints. But the shackles do not relent. Neither does my father.

"Ignira."

An enormous fireball rushes from my father's hands and obliterates whatever remains of Heston.

His dying shrieks ring through the night. I fall to my knees. The hard cobalt roof tiles slam into me.

Though this monster murdered my mother, I can't bear to listen to him burn.

But he soon falls silent. Then there's only the crackling of flames.

And Heston Harstall is dead.

CHAPTER 14

For a long while, I just stand there, gazing down at the streets below. It could be minutes or hours that pass. The firm ridges of the cobalt tiles dig into my knees. But I feel no pain. Numbness spreads over me. Ash whirs around me. The smell of death fills my nostrils.

A vague thought arises in the back of my mind: I'm likely breathing in Heston's incinerated remains. The realization should nauseate me. But I feel nothing. Not disgust. Not rage. Not even grief.

Just emptiness. Like I'm no longer here. Like the images racing through my mind are only ghosts of a nightmare I dreamed.

My father steps toward my mother's unmoving body. He waves his hand, and the aether shield around her disappears. As does the one encasing me.

"*Laxus*," I breathe, my voice coarse and broken.

The teleportation spell washes over me and transports me to the street. My father stands ahead of me, and as I watch him fall to his knees, it feels as though more than a few feet separate us. As though I'm peering at him through a clouded window. I want to step toward him, but my legs refuse to oblige.

His crystalline staff drops from his hand. It falls onto the cobblestones. The clatter rings through the street. And over and over through my mind. Beneath it, I can scarcely hear the death and destruction beyond. Fires simmer in the Lower City. Before, they were raging infernos. Now they are flickering embers, their amber glow streaks the night sky. The unnatural howls of the undead sound in the distance.

But this street is silent and still. Just like my heart, my mind.

"Mirelle!" he chokes, cradling my mother in his arms. Anguish rolls down his cheeks. Somewhere far in the depths of my mind, it occurs to me this is the first time I've seen my father cry. And it only makes me hollower, until I can no longer feel the ash dancing over my face.

Like a statue, I stare at my father as he grieves, the shattered pieces of my heart unable to grieve with him. Unable to even feel guilt for failing to do so.

Dawn pierces the darkness, bringing with it a new day. Golden rays blaze through the sky, igniting the clouds. It's as if the Heavens are enraged by the horrors wrought upon us last night.

Footsteps sound from down the street. My father slowly raises his head as they approach. My neck is too stiff to move, so I turn my eyes in their direction.

Archmage Branvir Calton marches toward us. A dozen magi follow him.

Branvir comes to a stop before my father. Shock flashes across his face as he notices my mother's body.

No one says anything. Not my father, not Branvir, not any of the magi with him. A morning breeze sweeps over us. It brushes through my hair, sullied and knotted by last night's chaos.

Archmage Calton finally breaks the silence. "Grandmage," he says, dipping his head. "We have managed to capture two of the necromancers. They have been secured for questioning."

"And the others?" My father's voice is shaky, far from his usual strength.

Branvir hesitates. "We have so far been unable to locate them."

"Find them," he growls. "Then incinerate them all."

Branvir's gaze turns to me. "And the boy?"

"What boy?" my father demands.

"Heston's boy. It is reported that he raised the dead alongside the necromancers."

Arluin.

Fear penetrates the hollowness like a knife. My heart, which was so frozen it barely beat, now pounds furiously in my chest.

My father looks at me. "Is this true?"

I say nothing, lacking the strength to lie. But I refuse to condemn Arluin with my words. There must be something in my gaze that gives me away, since my father's face turns to stone.

"Kill him too," he grinds out. "Kill every last one of them."

Branvir's eyes return to me. I meet his stare. Our icy gazes lock together.

I must find Arluin before he does. Whether he is dead or alive, I do not know, but I will not let anyone harm him.

He saved me. And yet they would execute him for it.

Branvir's nostrils flare. I know he can see it in my expression, what I intend to do. My father must see it too. He sits upright, horror filling his magenta eyes. Horror that I would seek to save the son of his enemy.

I grit my teeth and pull aether into my grasp. It flickers like purple flames, fueled by my frenzied heart.

"Reyna!" my father shouts, his voice thick with worry. Worry for me or for what I will do, I don't know. Nor do I have time to contemplate it.

I must find the boy I love. The boy I have sworn to marry, no matter what.

"*Laxus!*" I cry.

And before any of them can stop me, I fade into aether.

Blood pounds in my ears like relentless drums of war. But the war upon Nolderan is over. Now only a few undead remain, and magi blast them into smoke and ash with conjured flames.

A sea of bodies stretches before me. They are of varying states of decay and mutilation. A thousand dead faces stare at me.

Everything spins.

I think the ground might be rushing toward me, but I refuse to let it win.

I force myself to remain upright and wade through the depths of death. I try to avoid the bodies, but I still feel the softness of flesh and the brittleness of bone beneath my boots. The sensation threatens to collapse me, but I cannot save Arluin if I allow myself to faint.

I must find him. Quickly, before Branvir and his magi track me here. I must ensure he escapes Nolderan.

And if he is dead . . .

No.

He can't be dead. We made a promise to each other. He wouldn't break it.

I arrive at the alleyway where Heston's undead pursued me. I come to a halt upon the spot where Arluin freed me, where he fell.

I scan across the lifeless faces, but I don't see Arluin's. Nor do I see his raven curls amid the mountain of corpses.

I try farther along the street. But even when I search the street after that, I still find no sign of him. Neither dead, nor alive.

I remain there for a while, staring down into the stream of bodies.

I should feel relief at not finding Arluin's corpse. But I only feel hollow. As hollow as I felt while gazing down at my mother's broken body.

I don't know where he is, and I have no proof of his fate. And it is the not knowing which threatens to break me.

I must find him. Whatever it takes, I must.

With the street swaying around me, I stagger toward the nearest heap of bodies. Then I begin the task of rolling them away. Each and every one. Not caring how their too-cold skin feels against mine. My mind is bursting from the seams with one single thought: that I must find Arluin. No matter what.

I roll aside an elderly lady, her unseeing eyes staring up at the approaching dawn. Beneath her lies a boy, no older than ten. Dried blood trails across his cheek. Bites mangle his arms. Bone glimpses between the torn flesh.

I don't linger on him. Because I next spot dark curls.

"Arluin!" I gasp, reaching for him. I pull with all my strength, willing for him to part from the mass of bodies. He comes loose and rolls to me.

My stomach clenches. I think I may vomit. But I don't. I can't.

I turn his head toward me. The dark curls fall away—

To reveal a face that looks nothing like Arluin's. The man's brown eyes gaze up at me. Unblinking. His nose is too hooked to be Arluin's, and he's at least a decade older.

The tension in my stomach slips away. I slump back onto the bloodied street.

For a moment, I was certain it was him. And now I'm grateful it is not. Even if it means another man lies in his place. Another loved one snatched from someone else.

If he isn't here, amid the stream of corpses flowing through the street, that means he is alive. And if I don't find him before my father, before Branvir, before the Magi, he will be killed.

I squeeze my eyes shut and block out the noises drifting through the street: the guttural howls which grow fainter and fainter, the crackling of flames which now sounds like distant whispers. Aether flutters through the wind, and after all the magic used and the lives lost last night, the air is even more abundant with it. I draw the humming energy into my fingers.

Then in my mind, I paint Arluin in as much detail as I can. His glossy curls that look as though they're carved from onyx, his magenta eyes, his bold brows, his soft chuckle as he laughs at something I said.

When his portrait is achingly vivid, I release my spell.

"*Aminex* Arluin Harstall."

I wait. And then I wait a moment longer. But there is no response.

I try the spell again. And again. Yet no matter how many times I try, the only voice in my mind is my own.

If he's alive, why would he not respond? Why would he let all my frantic calls go unanswered?

Unless his silence means that he's dead. And that the reason I can't find him is because his body has been reduced to ash.

I sit there huddled on the street, surrounded by countless corpses. My entire body trembles. Cold sweat drips from my skin.

The sun rises higher in the morning sky. Its bright rays bask the white walls of Nolderan in a golden glow, and it makes the cobalt roofs ripple like sapphire waves. A new day is upon us, yet I remain chained to the night before. The events play over and over in my mind, an inescapable echo of the past. I watch as Heston murders my mother and raises her as a wraith. I watch as Arluin reanimates the dead before falling himself.

I would give anything to forget it all, to rid my mind of the ghastly images which haunt me.

And then the unbearable truth slams into me. I choke, suffocated by the terrifying realization.

My mother is gone. I will never again watch her paint.

And Arluin is gone, too. I may never know his true fate.

Tears burst from my eyes, bitter and heavy with anguish. It's as though a dam has burst apart. Before, my heart was numb, unable to grieve, unable to feel anything. But now I feel everything all at once.

Pain pierces through my heart like a dagger. My chest feels like it's being torn from the inside out. My breaths come out as sharp gasps as I struggle to breathe.

A part of me considers falling back onto the street with the corpses and letting exhaustion consume me.

I hear footsteps. I think it may be Branvir and his magi, having tracked me down in the hope I will lead them to Arluin.

But Arluin isn't here. I'm not even certain whether he lives.

I don't turn to look as the footsteps continue pacing toward me. As they pound furiously against the street, breaking into a sprint.

"Reyna!"

It is neither Branvir nor my father's voice which calls my name. It is Eliya's.

She shouts my name again. I still don't move. She slides down beside me on the ravaged street. She pulls me close, and blood coats her hands as she clasps me. Grief blurs my sight, but I see the crimson stains blemishing my cerulean adept robes. It isn't my blood. I don't know whose it is.

Eliya says nothing as she hugs me. Though we sit amid this horrifying stream of dead bodies, she doesn't flinch. Last night, she probably witnessed enough terrifying images to haunt her for an entire lifetime. Just as I have.

"They're dead," I croak out. By now, the sun shines upon us with its full radiance. "They're both dead."

Eliya pauses, stroking the back of my head. I can barely feel her fingers. "Who's dead?" Her voice is little more than a whisper, as though she can't bear asking such a terrible question.

I stare down at my blood-stained fingers. At first, words fail me. "My mother," I gasp, my heart thudding as I relive her death. "And Arluin . . . I think he . . ."

Eliya doesn't respond. She hugs me tighter.

We stay there for a while. The summer sun shines gloriously upon the street. I scarcely feel its warmth across my cheeks. The gentle heat begins to bake the bodies around us. Magi and guards soon appear, clearing away the ruins and corpses which litter the streets.

After some time, Eliya helps me to my feet. Her arm secures my balance. If not for her, I would have already fallen back into the stream of bodies. In fact, I wouldn't have stirred at all.

"Come on," she says softly. "Let's get you home and cleaned up. Sitting out here on the street won't do you any good."

I know she's right. Staying here will achieve nothing. I will only get in the way of those who are clearing the streets and trying to return Nolderan to a state of normality.

But I don't want normality. It would mean accepting that my mother, that Arluin, are both gone. I would rather stay out here on the streets, dwelling on what has already passed. Because I can't bear the bitterness of the present and would rather keep on rejecting it.

Despite all this, I let Eliya guide me away—if only because I lack the strength to resist. I am but a fallen leaf flowing down a stream, allowing the water to take me wherever it pleases.

Eliya draws aether into her hand. With her other, she clasps my arm.

"*Laxus*," she says and then we drift into the wind.

We become one with aether, floating through the folds of time and space—through the fabric of reality. But since I already feel weightless, I don't really notice the sensation.

My manor manifests before us. The elaborate gates stand tall, no different from any other day. The two winged lions on my family crest roar at each other as they always do.

I hate how normal everything looks. That my manor is untouched by the destruction which wrought through the city and the darkness which murdered my mother.

"Reyna," Eliya mutters, nudging my shoulder. It's only now I realize that the enchanted gates won't open for her and that we have stood here for some time.

I squeeze my fists. I don't feel the sharpness of my nails against the softness of my palms. I could be drawing blood, and I would not know.

"Reyna Ashbourne," I force out. Each syllable is a tremendous effort. Yet I heave them all out, and the aether shrouding the gates glistens in response. They swing wide open, and Eliya guides me through.

She leads me along the path which winds through our gardens. I hate the colorful flowers blooming everywhere. The pansies, the tulips, the primroses, the marigolds—I hate them all. They are too vibrant, too cheery.

They remind me of my mother.

The faerie dragons sweep up and down the gardens, ensuring the enchanted buckets thoroughly nourish each flower. It's as if nothing has changed—as if my mother is alive.

But she isn't. Heston killed her. He raised her from the dead with his vile magic. My father destroyed her ghost.

A sob wracks through my body. Eliya can urge me no further.

She lets me stand there for a while, as I cover my face with my hands so I don't have to look at my mother's bright and beautiful garden. I weep into them.

Finally she nudges me forth, and I'm so lost my body complies. I vaguely see Zephyr fluttering over to us. His head tilts to one side as he silently asks what's wrong, why tears streak my cheeks.

"Not now, Zephyr," Eliya mutters, waving him away.

But the faerie dragon doesn't leave. He watches as we climb up the manor's stairs. His violet wings beat back and forth.

Eliya opens the doors and helps me inside. Zephyr glides through behind me. Too busy helping me through the hallway, Eliya doesn't shoo him away.

We pass paintings as we ascend the staircase. Many are my mother's, and they depict quaint landscapes and delicate flowers. I can't bear to look at them and keep my gaze fixed on the steps. My fingers curl around the polished bannister, and I use it to haul myself up. Zephyr's wings flap behind us.

She guides me through to my room and sits me down on my bed. Zephyr perches next to me.

Lavish golds and creams decorate my room. The cabinets are all gilded with flourishes, and an embroidered rug stretches across the marble floor. Eliya presses the switch beside the door, and the aether crystals high above flicker on. Their brilliant light makes the threads weaved through the rug shimmer like sunlight.

I stare blankly at the rug.

Eliya says something and then leaves. Since I don't catch her words, I don't know where she's going.

Zephyr nestles into me, his head resting in my lap. His amaranthine eyes stare up at me, quizzical yet concerned.

I tentatively run my fingers across his head, just between his antennae. His azure scales are smooth and cool beneath my skin. The motion is more soothing than I expected, so I stroke him again. Zephyr growls softly, his forked tongue flicking out with contentment.

His eyes shut, and we remain like that until Eliya returns.

She carries a porcelain bowl and sets it onto the counter beside my bed. Her eyes scan across the crimson stains which mar my robes. "Let's get you out of that."

I give her a small nod, but don't rise. I stop stroking Zephyr, however. He lifts his head and peers at me.

"Zephyr, you'll have to move," Eliya says. "Reyna can hardly get changed while you're sitting on her lap, and she can't sleep in those robes, can she?"

He doesn't move. At least not at first.

Eliya glares at him until he slides from my lap and onto the silken sheets beside me. He rests his head in his talons and sulks at her.

She pays him little attention as she helps me out of my robes. Sweat and blood makes the fabric stick to my skin, and removing them takes several minutes. She finds a loose nightgown in my cabinet and helps me change into it. The material is silken like my blankets, but plainer and complete with thin straps.

I try to crawl into bed, but Eliya stops me.

"You'll get blood all over your sheets," she says, lifting my hand and inspecting the dried blood which coats my skin. "Let me help you wash it off."

Eliya leads me to the counter where she placed the porcelain bowl and gathers aether into her hands. "*Aquis*," she says. Water splashes from her fingers. She finds a cloth in the top drawer and dips it into the conjured water. After wringing it out, she sweeps it across my hands and face. The water is lukewarm as it glides over my skin. Some of the blood dissolves quickly. Other patches are so stubborn she has to scrub until my skin is so red and raw I think it may bleed and undo her hard work.

When I'm free of blood and dirt, Eliya lets me climb into bed. I wrap the blankets around myself and shiver. She casts me a pitiful look, but it soon falters as she yawns. I doubt she slept much last night, either. Guilt wrenches through me.

I don't know what she suffered from the attack—who she may have lost. And yet here I am, so weak and pathetic that she has to do everything for me.

"Did . . ." I begin, but my voice breaks. "Did you also lose . . ." Consumed by my own grief, I don't know how to ask such an awful question.

Yet Eliya seems to understand my meaning. To my relief, she shakes her head. "No," she replies. "No one."

A pang of envy plucks at my heart. The emotion vanishes as quickly as it appears. Though it's brief, I feel terrible for feeling it.

It isn't that I wish she lost anyone dear to her. It's just that I wish I were like her: that I hadn't lost both my mother and the boy I love in a single night.

"I'm sorry, Reyna." She scoops me into another hug. Her tears dampen my hair. "I'm so sorry that all this happened to you."

I don't hug her back. I stare at the tall mirror in the far corner of the room. Through it, I watch her hug me and wonder whether she feels guilt over losing nothing while I have lost so much.

I know I should tell her she has no reason to apologize. She didn't steal Arluin and my mother from me. That was Heston. He's the one to blame. But since he's already dead, what use is there in hating him for it?

And maybe my father also holds some of the blame. The punishment for practicing dark magic is execution, yet he spared Heston. If he instead executed him all those years ago, none of this would have happened.

Except Arluin would likely hate him for it. But my mother would be alive.

I let out a deep breath. In the mirror, I can see how broken I look. My skin is deathly white, and the rings around my eyes are so dark they appear bruised.

Eliya finally releases me and steps back, wiping her cheeks with her sleeve. "You should rest. As we all should."

I only nod, still unable to summon words to my lips.

Her gaze trails across to Zephyr, who is crawling up the bed to my side. "And you should come along as well," she says to him. "Reyna needs to sleep."

The faerie dragon buries himself into the blankets next to me. He watches Eliya out of one eye, daring her to move him.

"Don't think I don't know what you're doing."

Zephyr shuts his other eye in response.

"You're just being nice so Reyna feeds you more aether. But she really needs to sleep now, so you'd better not bother her."

His tail twitches.

Eliya pulls the embroidered curtains together, blocking out the sunlight, and she turns off the aether crystals on her way out. "Sleep well, Reyna," she mutters, closing the door behind her.

Then we are cast in complete darkness.

Zephyr nestles deeper into my side. I stare up at the shadowed ceiling, once more watching as Heston murders my mother. As he breaks Arluin with his wicked magic. Each time, I break a little more with him.

Gentle snores come from Zephyr beside me, and while it seems impossible at first, his sounds eventually lull me into a deep sleep.

CHAPTER 15

Fire blazes through the sky, *and thick, black smoke shrouds the moon and stars. The smog clogs my throat as I try to breathe.*

The flames roar through the streets, ravaging all they touch. A large chunk of rock hurls toward me. I dart underneath, just as it comes crashing down. The sound booms through the street and rings through my ears. I don't stop to glance back at the heaped rubble. I just keep running.

My feet are bare, and I wear my thin nightgown. I sprint through bloody puddles. Crimson droplets splash up at me, staining the pale silk of my gown. Even though my feet and my ankles are slick with blood, I don't pause.

Heston—I must find him. Before it is too late.

Rain falls on me. But it isn't water which splatters over my shoulders. It is blood. The blood of all the lives lost tonight—all the lives that will be lost if I don't stop Heston before he claims everything and everyone.

Stiff fingers reach for me. Rotten claws grab my ankles and tangle through my hair. I shake them off and continue running.

I find no one else alive as I hurry through the streets. Only piles and piles of bodies, the undead feasting on their flesh. I almost vomit at the sight of a ghoul gnawing on a severed arm, but I can't stop for even a single heartbeat. I must keep running and running until—

The street opens to the Upper City's square. An enormous fountain lies at the center, as it always does. A mermaid perches on the top tier. Each marble bowl is carved into the shape of a clam. Stone benches are strewn around the fountain.

The square is empty. Except for Heston. He has my mother. He presses an obsidian dagger to her throat. The blade is serrated, and dozens of skulls are etched into the handle.

I halt. I stare at Heston, and my mother. There's a pleading look in her magenta eyes.

"Reyna," she whispers. "Go, please! Leave me."

Heston laughs as he draws the dagger across her skin and slices through her neck.

Blood gushes out like a waterfall. Her eyes widen, watching me until the very last moment when she slams into the ground. Then she doesn't move.

I scream until my throat is raw—until I can scream no more.

When I raise my head, it is no longer Heston who looms over her body and clasps the bloodied blade.

It's Arluin.

"Arly," I gasp, staggering toward him. I've searched all over the city for him, and yet here he is, standing right before me.

He doesn't respond. He grips the obsidian dagger and gazes down at my mother and the puddle of blood spreading around her. A wicked smile curls on his lips. I choke at the sight, but he doesn't turn to me. It's as if I've become invisible in this scene. As if I don't belong.

Then I notice his gray eyes, the same shade as his father's. Cold and dead: the mark of a dark sorcerer.

He is a monster, just like his father.

I shiver with horror and wrap my arms around my chest. My fingers become sticky with the blood coating me—the blood which the Heavens wept.

Footsteps sound from behind. I whirl around. It's my father.

His violet robes billow in the wind. Once magnificent, they are now sullied with blood.

"Father!" I shout, but he doesn't seem to hear me. He marches to Arluin.

"You," he snarls, aether crackling like lightning in his hands. "I will execute you like the vermin you are."

"No!" I scream, racing forth. My heart pounds to the same frantic rhythm as my feet. They slap against the slippery street, and I skid. The balls of my feet burn with the friction from the edges of the jagged stones.

But I don't reach my father in time to stop him.

"Telum!" he cries, unleashing a blast of aether from his fingers. He hurls it at Arluin.

My gut twists.

Arluin will die.

Even if he has become a monster, he is still the boy I've always loved. The boy who betrayed his own father to save me.

"Farjud," Arluin calls before the spell reaches him, melding with the shadows.

He slips through the blast as though it's merely air and not pulsating magic. His cloud of shadows penetrates the aether, and he materializes on the other side, inches away from my father. Now there is but a slither of air between them.

Arluin raises his obsidian dagger. He plunges it through my father's chest.

"This is for my father," he hisses as he twists the blade.

Pain shoots through my heart. It feels as if he has also stabbed me.

I scream loudly enough for Arluin to finally notice me. He turns and smiles. It isn't a smirk or a sneer. Just an ordinary smile.

And that makes it even more terrifying.

"Reyna," he says, stepping toward me. He holds out his bloodied hand.

I stumble back, tripping over my feet. But I don't hit the street.

I fall through the darkness of my grief.

There is no end. I keep tumbling through the emptiness until it finally claims me.

I jolt awake, my murderous heart thundering in my chest. How it does not explode and end my life, I do not know. In that moment, as I am lingering between the state of sleep and wakefulness, I think it will.

My skin is soaked. Not with blood like in the nightmare, but with a cold sweat. My breaths come out like gasps as I desperately suck in all the air I can, my lungs starved from all my screams. The scratchiness of my throat tells me I wasn't only screaming in my dreams.

Zephyr sits up and looks at me with his amaranthine eyes. They glow in the darkness. I stroke his head, and he settles back beside me, nestling in the silken sheets. I steady my breathing to the rhythm of my fingers running over his azure scales.

From across the room Mr. Waddles, the stuffed purple duck Arluin bought me for my sixth birthday, stares back at me. For several beats I glare at it, considering whether I should leap from my bed and throw it out the window. But I don't. The images I just witnessed were nothing more than cruel dreams. Not memories. They weren't real, and they never will be.

Arluin is gone, and I don't know whether I will ever see him again, except for in my dreams. And I hope I never again dream of him, because I hate how my treacherous heart twists him into a monster that he is not.

Instead of hurling Mr. Waddles out the window, I murmur *ventrez* and blow him into my lap. His lilac fur is patchy in many places.

As a child, I took him everywhere with me. That means he suffered much damage over the years, and some of his stitching has come loose. But I will never throw him away. Even when he is threadbare, I will still cherish him. He's one of the few things I have left of Arluin, other than my memories.

And his locket.

I set Mr. Waddles on the pillow beside me and reach for the locket hanging from my neck. Since Arluin gave it to me, I haven't taken it off. That was only three days ago, and yet it already feels like an eternity has passed. In one night, everything has changed. My entire world has been torn asunder.

Now my mother is gone. Never again will I be able to watch her swirl her aether-imbued paints across her palette and bring mystical landscapes to life. Never again will I be able to turn to her when I am hurt. I must spend the rest of my life without her.

That single thought is enough to send fresh tears streaking down my cheeks. Their flow is obstructed by the dried ones from when I wept in my sleep.

My fingers run across the locket, feeling the edges of the silver heart. It is warm from being pressed against my skin. I consider opening the locket and allowing the memory crystal inside to play. But I decide against it, knowing that I will be unable to bear listening to the promise we made to each other only three nights ago. That we would marry when we have graduated from the Arcanium.

Now that seems an impossible thought.

Even if Arluin is alive, he can never return to Nolderan. Not after his father murdered my mother, not after he wielded necromancy against the magi. I'm certain he planned it all along, to ensure Heston lowered his guard long enough to free me. And though he became a monster to save me, my father will never accept that—will never believe it. As soon as he sets foot inside Nolderan, my father will execute him where he stands. He will burn him with the same flames he used to destroy Heston.

And that, all of that, is only if he lives. Because I can't be certain that he does. But if I allow myself to believe he is dead, then I will truly break.

I release the locket, and it falls back into the hollow of my neck. I lift Mr. Waddles and cradle him to my chest, lying my head back onto my pillows. My breaths are slow and steady, and the toy duck rises and falls to the same beat.

I gaze up at the shadowy ceiling, and once more, my nightmares arise. I feel a blade twisting through my heart, and I move Mr. Waddles to check if the phantom knife is there. But there is nothing. My skin is intact beneath my nightgown. It's my grief which causes the sharp ache.

Realizing that my dreams will only further torment me, I slip from beneath the sheets and pace across the room to my cabinet. Zephyr doesn't stir, having already fallen back asleep, and my footfalls are soft. He will probably wake soon and demand aether crystals. Maybe Eliya is right about him, but I appreciate the company.

I return Mr. Waddles to the top of my cabinet and grasp one of the entwined handles, pulling open the middle drawer. I find a satin robe inside, and I wrap the pale fabric around my nightgown, securing it with the thin belt. Then I pad out my room and head downstairs.

My fingers trail across the bannister as I descend the staircase and use it to support my weight. My body is fatigued, and each step is a great effort. It's as though I haven't slept for even an hour, but the waning light filtering through the stain-glass windows tells me it must have been several. And that's assuming it is still Friday.

I find my father downstairs in the hallway. He is gazing up at one of my mother's paintings. This one depicts Nolderan's waves against a midnight sky, and a braided golden frame crowns the seascape. Her brushstrokes form dark waves of varying shades of deep blue and green, and sea foam powders the crests. The full moon shines high above, and the waves reflect the starlight. Like all of my mother's artwork, it's enchanted and appears more like a window than a painting. The sea rises and falls to a steady rhythm, and it laps against the shore. The pebbles stir as the waves meet them.

Judging by how stiff my father's posture is, it seems he has stood here for a long while. He doesn't stir as I come to a stop behind him and stare up at the painting as well. We stay like that for several minutes until he finally speaks.

"This was always her favorite," he murmurs so quietly that at first, I think he's talking to himself.

I give him a feeble nod. Though since his back is turned to me, he won't be able to see the gesture.

I already knew it was her favorite; she told me herself many times. It's why we display it at the very center of our hallway.

"It was the first one she painted after you were born," he continues, his gaze still fixed on the lulling waves. "That's why it was her favorite."

The way he talks about my mother, as if she is already long gone, fills my heart with more pain. I don't know how much more it can take. As I stare into the rolling waves, I watch her die all over again.

My weeping must be loud enough for my father to hear, since he turns and pulls me into a hug. I can count on one hand how many times my father has hugged me. Unlike my mother, he isn't particularly warm. Only his temper is.

Yet now he hugs me all the same, and it's clear in the way he embraces me that he needs the comfort as much as I do. I can also tell from his blood-shot eyes and ashen skin that he feels as broken as me.

"I'm sorry, Reyna," he says after a moment, his voice so laden with regret it sounds breathless. "I'm sorry I couldn't save her." He leaves many words unspoken, but I hear them all: that he is sorry he could not destroy Heston in time, that he is sorry he did not execute him five years ago, that he is sorry his mercy murdered my mother.

I say nothing. I know it isn't truly his fault, yet I can't bring myself to speak. I just stand there crying, my weight resting entirely in my father's arms.

After a while, when my tears stop falling, my eyes drift over to the arched window across from us. The sun slowly sinks into the horizon, casting us all in darkness.

"I'm sorry, too," I say.

My father frowns at me. "For what?"

"I forgot to go to the library and help Erma today. I'll go tomorrow morning and assist her all day. I promise I won't forget again."

To my surprise, my father shakes his head and hugs me tighter. "No, Reyna," he says, the words breaking as they leave his mouth. "You don't need to. You never need to again."

CHAPTER 16

MY MOTHER'S FUNERAL IS HELD on Sunday. Though I slept through all of Saturday, I appear no more well-rested as I stare into my mirror. My oval face appears narrower than usual, my cheeks sunken. Over the past three days, I have eaten nothing. Last night, I tried to eat but the first bite left me nauseated and I ended up returning to bed. My eyes, despite having spent most of this time closed, are puffy and swollen.

I wear a black lace gown that may have been beautiful if I were not wearing it to my mother's funeral. If she were here, she would insist on me using an illusion so I don't walk through Nolderan looking like a hideous wraith. And maybe I should, but I feel too fatigued to cast a single spell.

I leave the mirror as I am—with my long, dark hair barely brushed— and descend the stairs to the hallway. My father is waiting for me, his attention drifting across my mother's paintings as he paces back and forth. This morning, he wears black brocade robes with ornamental silver buttons decorating the high-collar. I can't remember the last time I saw him wearing anything other than his Grandmage's robes.

I've kept him waiting for some time, but he doesn't comment on it. He pushes open the grand doors of our manor, and we wordlessly step outside.

Even though my mother is gone, the faerie dragons still tend to our magnificent gardens. On Friday, I couldn't stand the sight of the brightly colored flowers, but today I stop and stare at them all. I can almost see my mother planting each with her own hands. While the flowers will bloom for a long time, thanks to the faerie dragons, they will eventually wither away.

"I'll plant them," I whisper. My father pauses and turns to the bed of violet pansies I'm staring down at. "Without her, our gardens will soon grow bare. So, I'll plant the new flowers when these ones die."

He is silent for a short while and then nods slowly. "She would like that," he mutters. The rushing fountain almost drowns his soft words. "She would like that very much. If her gardens were to wither away, she would blame us for not taking better care of it."

We stand there for a while longer before continuing to the enchanted gates at the end of our gardens. Since we are approaching from the inside, they swing open without either of us needing to command them.

The gates close behind us and then my father clasps my shoulder. He gathers aether into his other hand, and it's only now I realize he has left our manor without his staff. Today is one of the few occasions he ever has.

"*Laxus*," he says, and the manor fades away.

The pale purple light sketches the Upper City's cathedral. The needle spires stand tall and proud, and the many stained-glass windows depict the gods.

Though we aren't particularly religious here in Nolderan, Grandmage Delmont Blackwood was from the Kingdom of Tirith, where they worship the ten major gods. The magi do acknowledge the existence of the Caelum—beings of pure light energy who originate from the Heavens. Legend says they once walked our world before Meysus the Wise separated Imyria from the Heavens and the Abyss. While we believe in the gods, we do not revere them like we revere aether—the origin of everything in the universe. Including both the Caelum and Malum, since light and dark magic formed from the splitting of aether during the Primordial Explosion.

The cathedral's spires sway above me, and I am thankful for my father's arm as he guides me up the white stone steps and through the arched entrance. Like with the archway at the Arcanium's entrance, the words QUEL ESTE VOLU, PODE NONQUES VERA MORIRE are etched into the otherwise smooth stones.

As I reach the cathedral's final step, I glance back over my shoulder. A low white wall marks the cathedral's perimeter, and beyond that lies a crowd of somber and tearful faces. I don't recognize any of them; they aren't gathered here for my mother. Most likely, they await the funeral which will follow my mother's. I've been so wrapped up in my own grief that I almost forgot my father and I are not the only ones who have lost a loved one. Heston's evil has scarred all of Nolderan.

I turn back to the Cathedral's entrance, my neck stiff and slow with the motion, and then step forward and through.

Inside, the vaulted ceilings reach so high that my breaths seem to echo through them, let alone my footsteps as we walk through the hall. Hundreds of wooden pews stretch before us. Their ends are carved into ornate detailing. All the pews are filled, save for the one at the front where there's still room beside my aunt and my cousins. Beyond the sea of pews, the cathedral opens to a high domed chamber. The gods are painted onto the curved ceiling and are imbued with aether, making them seem as real as all the people gathered on the pews.

Meysus the Wise, God of the Moon, sits on a crescent moon. He has a long white beard which swirls like smoke and wears midnight black robes embroidered with silver thread. He flicks through the thick tome he is reading. It is Meysus which Tirith venerates the most, though they pray to all the ten major Caelum.

On the opposite side of the chamber is Zelene, Goddess of the Sun. Her skin is deep amber, and her hair and eyes shine brilliantly with golden light. The white skirts of the single shoulder dress she wears flutter around her legs. She holds the sun in her hands, high above her head. The Mother Goddess is worshipped fervently by the people of Selynis, and it is said she is the one who shaped humans from clay and breathed life into us.

On the eastern and western sides, Aion the God of Wind and Navis the God of Sea stand opposite each other. A great eagle perches on Aion's shoulder, while Navis clutches an enormous trident. The rest of the chamber's domed ceiling features the remaining ten gods: Iara the Goddess of Music strums a lute, Tyronis the God of Thunder strikes his hammer and calls down lightning, Avris the Goddess of Dreams slumbers on a cloud beside Meysus the Wise, Ranthir the God of Love aims an arrow with a heart-shaped head, Thela the Goddess of Hunt throws her spear at deer, and Vetia the Goddess of Luck jingles her coin purse.

Beneath all the gods lies my mother's coffin. Like the Arcanium's atrium, it is formed from crystallized aether. It's of a pale purple hue, and the surface glimmers as the light reflects across it. The crystal is translucent enough that I can make out my mother's shadow through the sides.

The sight of her, vague though it may be, brings me to a sudden halt. We are halfway through the cathedral now, and everyone turns to look at me, but I barely notice them. All I am aware of is the strained rhythm of my heart.

I stare at her crystal coffin for so long that the cathedral spins around me. My father catches me before I fall, though it's only afterward that I realize I was falling. He helps me to the front right pew, where my aunt and cousins have left room for us.

On our way, we pass Kaely and her father—as well as Eliya and the rest of her family. The other two Archmagi are also gathered here: Lorette Gidston, Archmage of Knowledge, and Krasus Lanord, Archmage of Finance.

I slide down onto the pew beside my father. The wood is cool and smooth beneath me. As solid as the bench is, I feel no more stable than I did on my feet, and I dig my fingers into the edges to prevent myself from teetering over.

For a long while, no one dares to say anything—not so much as a hushed whisper. We all stare at the crystal coffin in the center of the chamber. My sight blurs and then there are three coffins: one for my mother, one for my father, and one for Eliya. And maybe I should imagine one for myself too, because I fear my heart will cease beating at any moment, suffocated by grief.

My gaze trails up to where the Goddess Zelene is holding up the sun. Golden petals scatter around her. It's as though they are made from sunlight.

She created us, and we are supposedly her children, but it's impossible to see her as a loving mother. If she cared for her creations, why would she allow us to suffer? Why would she create humanity with a capacity for such evil?

But Zelene, or at least the enchanted painting of her, doesn't answer my questions. She continues staring up at the sun above her head, her gossamer skirts twirling around her.

There's no afterlife, either. Though Selynis would have you believe otherwise. We magi know better. Upon death, souls disperse into the energies they are made from and return to the atmosphere. Only the most powerful sorcerers can hope for their souls to remain intact enough to become aether spirits drifting through the world. Perhaps some of Selynis's priestesses burn so brightly with light magic that their souls transcend to the Heavens upon death and become immortal saints. But that is merely conjecture, since Nolderan has neither proved nor disproved the fate of Selynis's priestesses after death.

As for my mother, it's unlikely fragments of her spirit remain in the world. Heston warped the aether in her soul into dark magic, and my father obliterated the resulting wraith. All that remains of her now is her paintings and her gardens.

"We gather here today to commemorate the life of Mirelle Ashbourne," a priest begins, pulling my attention from my thoughts. His voice echoes through the grand hall. Light magic radiates from him. He wears white robes decorated with golden thread.

"And to commit her into the hands of the gods," he continues.

The finality sends fresh tears streaming down my face, and I consider shouting that none of the gods care about us mortals. They are locked away in their Heavens. Only for priests and priestesses might they spare a second thought.

They certainly don't care that my mother is gone.

I barely hear his next words, too busy trying to control my weeping so that it doesn't echo through the cathedral's vaulted ceilings and disturb everyone else listening to his speech. I vaguely hear him talking more of the gods, of aether and light, and of how my mother had been a kind and brilliant woman.

My blurred gaze fixes once more on my mother's crystal coffin. In the shimmering surface, I see Heston standing over her body, her veins throbbing as poisonous dark magic chokes the life from her. And I see myself helpless to stop him from murdering her and raising her as a wraith.

If only I weren't so weak. If I were stronger—as powerful as Kaely—then I would have been able to fight Heston with her. We would have held him off long enough for my father to arrive. And then my mother would still be alive.

I can blame Heston for her death, even my father for not executing him five years sooner, but I can't deny that I also had a hand in her death.

If only, if only—there are so many *if onlys*, and yet I cannot change the past. I must accept what I have done. That my weakness killed my mother.

My father rises, and as I feel the shift of his presence, I notice that the priest has finished speaking. My father gives a speech, of how he met my mother when she painted his portrait upon his succession as Grandmage of Nolderan, of how she scolded him so many times to sit still. His words twist the dagger already piercing my heart.

Eventually he falls silent once more, tears streaking his cheeks. I doubt he is aware of them. The Grandmage of Nolderan would never normally allow himself to cry in public, to show that weakness. He is too proud for that. But what use is there for pride when my mother is dead?

The priest continues to speak of gods who care not for us, and he offers more prayers to them and her memory. Only his final words penetrate my ears: "That which is aether may never truly die."

If I were not choking on my tears, I may have laughed at what a half-truth that is. Yes, aether can never be destroyed—that part is not inaccurate. But what Nolderan's favorite maxim fails to mention is that aether can be warped into dark energy, while the reverse is impossible. When my father destroyed my mother's wraith, the dark energies consisting of her soul scattered through the world.

She is dead in every sense of the word. The saying does not apply to her.

That is why when everyone bows their head and mutters it back, I cannot bear to do so. It would be a lie upon my tongue.

Soon my father ushers me from my seat and guides me to the center of the chamber where my mother lies. I feel like a piece of string trailing behind him.

We come to a stop before her crystal coffin. The lid is half open, revealing my mother's pale face and the vibrant flowers she clasps to her chest. Though crystal coffins preserve bodies and my mother's appearance hasn't deteriorated over the past few days, I hardly recognize her face. The expression she wears is too still. She looks more like a doll than a person.

I grip the edges of the crystal coffin, and my tears fall within. Aether vibrates beneath my fingers.

This is my fault. If I were not so weak, I wouldn't be looking down at my mother's corpse.

I don't know how long passes before my father pulls me from the coffin. I stagger back and stare up at the gods and goddesses. Silently I curse them for their cruelty.

The truth is clear. The mighty Caelum care not for us mortals, and there is little use in praying to them for salvation. We can only believe in ourselves and our own abilities. I can pray over and over to them, but the only way I can protect those I love most is with my magic.

And that is why, no matter the cost, I will become the most powerful mage Nolderan has ever known—even more powerful than my father.

Never again will I allow those I love to be stolen from me.

THREE YEARS
LATER...

CHAPTER 17

AETHER RUSHES THROUGH ME. I am deaf to all but the magic singing through my blood, begging for release.

I focus the energy into my fingertips. The storm of aether crackles. With the sheer force pounding through my body, even the arena's towering walls fail to make me feel small.

I am power. I am fury.

"*Folgos*," I hiss.

The aether sparks into lightning. It thunders from my palms and darts across to where Kaely stands.

"*Laxus!*" she calls, teleporting away before the lightning reaches her.

My spell continues onward and collides with the barrier surrounding the arena. The lightning bolt fizzles out. If not for the enchantment, our magic would have long destroyed our audience.

It isn't only our class that watches us; many of the lower years perch on the edges of their stone seats, intently watching our duel. Fifth-years sparring on their final day at the Arcanium makes for a remarkable performance. Next week, we begin our Mage Trials. We are almost magi.

I turn, searching for Kaely's new position. I find her behind me.

"*Speculus!*" she calls.

The aether in her hands spins out into two clones. Now three identical Kaelys conjure magic.

"*Gelus!*" they cry in unison, flinging large shards of ice at me. Each is shaped into a frozen arrowhead.

The two frost bolts conjured by her clones contain only a fraction of her power. But they will still hurt if they strike me.

I weave aether into fire magic. "*Ignir'muriz.*"

Flames roar in my hands. I pull them around myself in a blazing shield.

The three frost bolts crash into the fiery wall. The ice hisses. Water splashes across the stone slabs. Steam billows through the arena.

My shield remains strong. I shape the flames into a mighty fireball.

"*Ignira,*" I snarl.

Three years ago, I was disciplined in Archmage Gidston's office for striking Kaely with this same spell. Now the Archmage watches us through narrowed eyes, her hands folded across her lap, as though she doesn't realize that the two of us are aiming to kill each other.

This fireball might be the most ferocious one I've ever cast. Since my mother died, I have worked tirelessly to hone my skills and master all the spells I know—as well as the advanced magic I've learned more recently. Even my father would be proud of this fireball.

My lips curl. Fear glistens in Kaely's eyes—in the eyes of all three of them. But the fleeting emotion vanishes as swiftly as it appears.

"*Aquis!*" the three Kaelys shout together.

A water blast shoots from their fingers and meets in the middle. Then their attack gains momentum and charges at my fireball.

The two spells collide with each other at the center of the arena. Though water holds a colossal advantage against fire, my fireball is fueled with immense power, and that makes our attacks equal.

Magic roars. The force flings back both Kaely and me. Her mirror images dissolve. The blast is so thunderous I don't hear myself slamming into the ground. Nor do I hear Kaely's thud.

The resulting haze is so thick I can barely see her across the arena. But the hatred in her eyes burns vividly enough to penetrate the dense steam.

In our third-year finals, I scored the same mark as her. And last year, I *beat* her. By ten whole marks across all of our classes. To achieve that, I had to study day and night, and my father was so very pleased by my dedication to my studies. I even scored the highest in our year.

That's why she hates me more than ever. She can no longer say I'm undeserving of our tutors' praise. Now I might actually be better than her.

At least with written examinations. I've yet to beat her in a duel.

That's why I must defeat her today. Once we graduate from the Arcanium and become magi, I may never again have the opportunity to duel her.

And if I can't beat Kaely, how will I ever protect those I love from monsters like Heston?

I scramble back onto my feet. Through the smoke, I scarcely make out her doing the same.

But before either of us can unleash another spell, aether radiates from the center of the arena. Archmage Lorette Gidston emerges from the cloud of violet light.

Our duel is over before the real fight can begin.

"That is enough." The Archmage's crisp voice rings through the arena. "*Ventrez.*" She conjures a wind spell and uses it to blow away all the steam.

With the fog cleared, Kaely glares at me, every ounce of the loathing in her heart unveiled. I glare back at her with as much bile, my own expression as disdainful as hers.

If Archmage Gidston notices our murderous scowls, she doesn't comment on them. "Excellent work, both of you."

Neither of us responds. We continue glowering at each other.

Lorette turns and scans across the other fifth-years sitting in the audience. "Trindell, Varsley—you're both up next."

Koby stands, as does Jaron.

But Archmage Gidston shakes her head at Jaron and says, "Not you. You've already had your turn in the arena." She gestures to the other Trindell twin. "On your feet, Braedon."

The two of them teleport down to the arena.

Kaely and I hold each other's glare for a moment longer. Then she scrunches her nose and murmurs *laxus*, teleporting back up to the stone seats. I do the same, appearing on the stairs at the end of Eliya's row. My fists curl as I stride over to where she sits.

"What's the matter?" she asks as I slump down beside her.

My jaw hardens. "Nothing."

She arches a brow at me. "Really? You don't look mad at all."

I lean back, the stone wall of the row behind digging into my shoulders, and I blow out a breath. "I didn't beat her."

"Your match was a draw."

"Drawing with her isn't the same as winning."

"Why are you so focused on beating her? Three years ago, she was completely wiping the floor with you. Look at how far you've come. Now you're her equal."

"I don't want to be her equal."

"Then what do you want, Reyna?"

I want to be better than her. So much better. Even as an adept, my father would have easily defeated someone like Kaely. And yet I've never come close to beating her.

If I can't defeat even Kaely, how can I become as powerful as my father? Three years ago, I swore to become mightier than him in order to protect those I love. As it stands, how can I ever hope to achieve that?

But I tell Eliya none of this. I turn to where Kaely sits on the opposite side of the arena, and I continue glaring at her. Not that glaring will help me defeat her.

At the end of the day, we gather inside the Arcanium's hall. Three enormous chandeliers hang from elegant ceiling roses, and aether crystals dangle like raindrops from the spiraling arms. Their light has a purple tint and makes the white herringbone tiles of the floor appear lilac.

Natural light filters in through the many arched windows lining the hall, and they are tall enough to reach from the floor to the embellished ceiling. Plum velvet drapes are tucked beside the windows, held in place by tasseled, golden cords.

Since the lower years have spent the past few weeks completing their written examinations, the hall is filled with square drop-leaf tables. They are carved from oak—as are the matching chairs—and all feature twisted legs.

Every adept of the Arcanium is present; there's nearly one-hundred and fifty of us in total. With there being far more adepts than desks and chairs, many are crowded around the walls.

Fortunately, Eliya and I arrived early enough to claim seats next to each other. We sit two rows back from the front, behind the adepts who arrived even earlier. That includes Kaely, who sits on the frontmost row. I glare at her mousy brown braid and the back of her cerulean robes, but it is far less satisfying than glaring at her freckled face.

Archmage Gidston sits on the dais, and her eyes rake across every adept of the Arcanium. Her chair is oaken like ours, but grander. Floral details are etched across its arms and legs. Beside her stands many of our tutors, their hands clasped behind their backs.

When every last adept has arrived, she finally addresses us all.

"Today marks the end of the Arcanium's 1694th Year," she declares, her words carrying to even the furthest corners of the hall. "This year, we have witnessed many outstanding achievements. Such as Quella Hyers, who obtained full marks in every examination she completed last week."

She gestures to a student sitting in the row ahead of me. The girl stands, and everyone claps.

When we fall silent, the girl returns to her seat and Archmage Gidston continues her speech.

"And also, Artus Milford who, despite being only two marks off failing last year, has now emerged as the top of his class."

Another student rises from his chair, and the entire hall showers him with applause. His achievement is quite remarkable. When I put little effort into my studies, I never came close to failing. To now be the top of his class, he must have worked even harder than me. I suppose the fear of almost failing and being thrown out of the Arcanium probably had much to do with that.

He sits back down, and Archmage Gidston continues praising various adepts. A second-year is also commended for their performance during Combat Class, while a fourth-year is applauded for their work with an Alchemy research project. None of us fifth-years are mentioned, however. Not until the end of her speech.

"And now we must applaud our fifth-year students for all their hard work over the last five years."

We fifth-years get to our feet, and the rest of the hall applauses us.

"However, their time as adepts is not yet complete," Archmage Gidston continues when we return to our seats. "Next week, they will begin their Mage Trials. In order to graduate from the Arcanium, they must prove they have the required strength of heart, mind, and magic. We wish them all the luck with their trials and the bright futures ahead of them."

CHAPTER 18

"No more lessons," Eliya sings as we pour out of the hall with all the other adepts, "ever again!"

We come to a stop at the center of the Arcanium's atrium. The aether crystals which form the domed ceiling glisten in the late noon sun.

"You do realize this means you'll have to get a job soon?" I say.

"Why would I need a job? My father's apothecary makes so much money that he doesn't need to work. I'll just inherit his business."

"You'll have to share it with your brother," I point out. Eliya's brother is six years younger than us and is due to start at the Arcanium next year. Which I suppose is next month now, since we're already in December.

"Even if I have to share it with Wynn, there will still be plenty of money for us both—" She cuts herself off as Koby walks past, and she grabs his shoulder, spinning him around. "Hey, Koby! Do you want to come to Flour Power with Reyna and me?"

"Sure—" he begins.

"When did we decide on that?" I interject. "I need to go to the library."

She rolls her eyes at me. "Why do you need to go to the library on a Friday evening?"

"I need to find a book."

"What book?"

As we speak, Koby's head snaps back and forth between the two of us.

"*Concerning Conflagration and Combustion* by Alvord Ashbourne," I reply. "I need to improve my fire wings spell."

"Your fire wings spell is already great," Eliya says. "Besides, don't you have a copy in your manor? What about the original one old Alvord wrote?"

I shake my head. "The original manuscript was taken to the Vault centuries ago for preservation. That's why I need to go to the library and find a copy before our Mage Trials."

"You won't need a fire spell on the Trial of Heart."

"I'll definitely need it for the Trial of Magic."

"The Trial of Magic isn't until Friday."

"I need to study it this weekend. I'll be too tired in between the trials next week."

Since the three of us are stopped in the center of the atrium, many adepts flash us annoyed looks as they wind around us. Eliya pays them no attention and heaves out a sigh at me.

"Can't you go some other time? The library will still be here in the morning. Go and get your book tomorrow."

"And the bakery will also still be there in the morning."

"But it won't be our final day at the Arcanium in the morning, will it?"

I press my lips together, unable to argue with that.

"Lorea! Blake!" Eliya calls over to more adepts in our year. "We're heading to Flour Power now. Do you want to join us?"

Lorea is as tall as me, with dark skin and ebony hair bluntly cut to her shoulders. Blake is almost half her height, and he has short strawberry-blond hair and nearly as many freckles as Kaely.

"Sure," Blake says. Lorea nods. Both of them start over to us.

"Great," Eliya replies. "Now help me convince Reyna not to go to the library and to come with us instead."

"Why do you need to go to the library?" Lorea asks, peering at me.

"To study?" My response comes out sharper than I intended.

"You seem to do a lot of that these days," she says.

Eliya snorts. "Too much."

I turn to Koby for support. He only shrugs.

"Maybe you should take a break," Blake suggests, unhelpfully.

"Fine, fine," I say, throwing my hands up in surrender. "Let's go to the bakery first, and then I'll go to the library later."

Eliya purses her lips, probably deciding whether to tell me to get the book tomorrow, but she leaves it at that.

"All right then!" she says. With that, she bounds out of the Arcanium, and we all trail after her.

When we reach the street beyond the Arcanium's archway, we each mutter *laxus* and teleport ourselves to the bakery.

Like all the buildings of Nolderan, Flour Power has a cobalt roof and walls built from white granite. The door is painted powder blue and has paneled windows. Through them, I see cake stands filled with colorful treats. Lace trim decorates the edges of each tier.

It's only when my teleportation spell is complete and the aether has faded away that I remember which part of the Upper City this bakery belongs to.

Glancing over my shoulder, I see the alley where Heston's undead pursued me—where my mother saved me. And I'm certain I currently stand upon the very spot where Arluin fell. But when I look down, the cobblestones beneath me are no different to any of the others. Since that fateful night, I've visited this part of the city several times. And it always leaves me shaken.

The bakery's gleaming windows spin around me. I barely notice as the others open the door and head inside. The tinkling bell chimes over through my ears.

"Reyna?" Eliya asks. A frigid wind blows over us, and she pulls her cerulean robes tighter around herself. "Are you coming inside?"

"Coming," I murmur. I tear my feet from where they stand and follow her inside with everyone else.

The others have chosen to sit at a circular mahogany table with curved legs. A lacy tablecloth covers its surface. There are only two empty chairs left. Both face the windows and have a clear view of the alley beyond.

For a moment, I consider asking Lorea to swap with me, since her back is to the window. But then I wordlessly slide onto the chair beside Eliya. Explaining why I don't want this seat would mean reliving those horrors. Over the past three years, I've tried to bury the nightmares as deeply as I can. But now, being here, so close to where everything happened, all those terrifying memories are violently bubbling to the surface.

The locket around my neck suddenly feels as heavy as a string of bricks. I clasp at the fabric of my robes, feeling where the locket lies beneath.

Not once have I taken it off. Nor have I opened the locket and watched the memory recorded within. Arluin's promise echoes through my mind. His words are loud enough to drown out the conversation around me.

There has never been any sign of him. To this day, I don't know his fate.

We never found a body but if he's alive, why has he never tried contacting me? I know he can't return. My father and the Archmagi would have him executed the moment he sets foot inside Nolderan. But surely if he's alive, he would try to see me again. Or at least let me know he isn't dead.

After all, we made a promise to each other. The proof of it hangs around my neck.

A sharp nudge pulls me from my thoughts.

I turn to Eliya and blink.

She gestures to Mrs. Baxter who stands before us. "Reyna, what are you having?"

Mrs. Baxter is the owner of Flour Power. She bought this property six months after the necromancers attacked. I can't remember what this building was before she took it over. Perhaps it was a tailor's, or maybe a quill and ink shop.

She's a plump lady who wears the same flowery, pastel apron and bright smile every time I visit her bakery. Her pale blue eyes mark her as being neither a mage nor a descendant of the founding families. She uses no magic in her baking, but her cakes are the most delicious I've ever tasted. My mother would have liked her. Especially since she always went on about how we shouldn't use our magic for everything.

"Um," I begin, chewing on my lip.

As lovely as Mrs. Baxter's cakes are, I've lost my appetite. With the bitter lump swelling in my throat at the thought of Arluin, I don't know how I'll swallow a single bite. And then Mrs. Baxter will think I don't like her cakes. I suppose I could say I'm not hungry, but then Eliya will want to know what's the matter. And I don't feel like explaining to her right now, especially not while the others are around. Though we've been in the same classes for the past five years, I'm not particularly close to any of them. It's Eliya who is friends with them.

"I'll have the same as you," I quickly say to Eliya.

Thankfully, no one comments on my hesitation.

"Would you like cream with it?" Mrs. Baxter asks.

I have no idea what I'm ordering. But I can't say that without revealing how distant I've been.

In the end, I just nod.

"All right," Mrs. Baxter says, turning away. "I'll get everything plated up for you now."

When she leaves, the others carry on talking. I tune them out and stare into the alley across the street.

All the images of that terrible night come rushing back so vividly I can hear the growling of ghouls and smell the putrid stench of their rotting flesh. The mahogany chair wobbles beneath me, and now the thought of eating cakes and cream—or whatever else I ordered—almost makes me vomit all over Mrs. Baxter's floor.

Then, as everything is spinning around me, I'm certain I glimpse Arluin's raven curls amid the alley.

I blink and sit up.

But when I stare into the alley again, I can only see the long shadows that the late noon sun is casting across the street.

Was he there? Or did I imagine him?

Then I'm thrown back to the moment where I was rummaging through all the dead bodies, desperately trying to find him.

My breaths come out as gasps. I bolt from my seat, no longer caring what the others think.

"Reyna!" Eliya shouts after me.

I don't stop. I continue through the bakery and shove open the powder blue door. The bell tinkles overhead. I keep running. All the way across the street, until I reach the alleyway.

The shadows loom over me. Several moments pass.

But Arluin doesn't appear. Not even when I squeeze my eyes shut and will for him to step from the shadows.

It seems he was never here at all.

"Reyna!" Eliya shouts again. Her hurried footsteps chase me.

I glance back to see her racing toward me. Then I return my attention to the shadows and grasp the locket beneath my robes.

She stops behind me. "Reyna, what's the matter?"

"I thought I saw something," I whisper, not turning to her. I don't want her to see my disappointment. "But it seems I was wrong . . ."

"What are you talking about? What did you see?"

If I explain that I thought I saw Arluin, that I think of him every day, then I fear I'll rip open the stitches holding together the broken pieces of my heart.

She reaches for my hand and squeezes it. "Come on, let's go back inside. Mrs. Baxter just brought the cakes over."

With how horribly my stomach is churning, I know I won't be able to eat anything. "I think I'll head home," I say. "I don't feel too good."

"How come?" she asks with a frown. "What's the matter?"

"I've probably caught a cold. It's the season for it, I suppose."

Her frown doesn't abate. I know she doesn't believe me. At least not entirely. "Well, make sure you take a healing potion as soon as you're home."

"I will." I hold out my hand. "*Conparios.*" My coin purse emerges from violet light. It's of a pink and gold satin brocade, complete with a decorative metallic clasp.

Eliya shakes her head before I can open my purse. "Don't worry about that. I'll eat your slice."

"Are you sure?"

"Of course I am," she replies. "Make sure you look after yourself. Our first trial starts on Monday, so don't forget to take that healing potion."

"I won't forget. I promise."

She gives me a wave and then heads back into the bakery, her crimson waves floating behind her.

My gaze returns to the shadows. I stare at them for several minutes more, a question weighing on my mind.

What if I didn't imagine Arluin at all?

CHAPTER 19

WHAT I SAID TO ELIYA was a lie. I don't teleport home. Instead, I teleport back to the Arcanium and head to the library.

The Grand Library of Nolderan is as it has always been. Nothing has changed over these past three years. The enormous crystalline chandelier is as dazzling as ever, and the checkered tiles still disorient me as I reach the last step of the long staircase.

There are few adepts inside the library, which is fortunate because Eliya would be hurt if she found out I lied to her. Guilt gnaws at me, but I shake it away. She is better off with Koby and the others rather than someone who sees ghosts wherever they go.

Erma Darkholme sits at her desk beneath the chandelier. Today, she's flicking through an old tome. I don't stop to look at which it is. Her gaze rises as I pass her desk, and she peers at me through her dark-rimmed spectacles. They sit so far down her nose it's a wonder they don't topple off.

"What are you doing here?" she demands.

"I came to find a book."

"Hm," she simply says. I turn away, but she continues speaking before I can leave. "Haven't you adepts finished for the year?"

It seems even Erma is discouraging me from studying. Maybe Eliya is right to be worried about me. Maybe I am going mad.

I doubt Erma's words are spoken out of concern for me. Her only concern will be whether she has a break from us adepts over Yuletide.

"Yes, Professor Darkholme," I say, dipping my head. "We finished today."

"Then why not wait until January when your studies resume?" Her eyes narrow with suspicion. She hasn't forgotten my mischievous ways during my first two years at the Arcanium.

"My studies won't continue in January, Professor Darkholme. I'm a fifth-year student, so today is my last day as an adept of the Arcanium. My Mage Trials start on Monday."

"Ah," she says, her attention returning to her old tome. "I see."

I continue through the library, and this time Erma doesn't stop me.

The book I seek, *Concerning Conflagration and Combustion*, is located on the Grand Library's second floor, along with the other tomes dedicated to fire magic. During my third year, I studied this book to improve my fireball, but I didn't make many notes on the spell for *ignir'alas*, which Alvord Ashbourne famously invented five hundred years ago.

I take a right turn and ascend the narrow, winding steps. They aren't as numerous as the ones leading into the library, and I soon reach the second floor.

The shelves containing books on fire magic are located at the far end, so I weave through the sprawling aisles until I arrive at that section.

I come to a stop before the bookshelves. Like all the others, their edges are gilded and they stand at five times my height.

Concerning Conflagration and Combustion perches on the highest shelf, exactly where I remember. Its burgundy leather spine sits between two smaller books, and its title and 'Alvord Ashbourne' is scrawled onto it.

I imagine holding the book in painstaking detail: my fingers brushing over the smooth leather cover and the gold leaf ornamentation glistening in the violet light of the nearby aether crystals. When the book is concrete in my mind, I speak the spell-words. "*Vello* Concerning Conflagration and Combustion *per* Alvord Ashbourne."

A glittering cloud swirls up to the topmost shelf. My magic locates the book, secures it, and then drifts down, depositing it in my hands.

I tuck the tome under my arm and return to the winding stairs.

But I only manage a few strides.

From the corner of my eye, I glimpse a flash of cerulean, and I pause, peering down the aisle. Another adept stands at the far end. He has dark curls. And his frame looks so very familiar . . .

My heart skips a beat. I hurry toward him, my frantic footsteps ringing throughout the library.

I go to shout his name, but my lips barely part before he turns.

And when he does, I realize that he isn't Arluin. His face is too round, too soft, and his nose is too pointed. His curls aren't raven black, but deep chestnut. From the other end of the aisle, his hair looked much darker.

"Um," the boy begins, "can I help you?" He looks at me like I've gone mad. Maybe I have.

Wherever I go, I see Arluin. Today isn't the first time I've imagined him, but it has never been this frequent. Maybe it's because our Mage Trials are around the corner, and my mind is haunted by the promise Arluin and I made. That we would marry when I graduated from the Arcanium.

"I . . ." My throat closes around my words, but I force them out as best I can. Or else, I will only make myself look more foolish. "I thought you were someone else."

I'm glad he turned before I could shout Arluin's name, because everyone knows who the traitor's son is. Now I can only hope he doesn't ask who I thought he was. Maybe I could give him Koby's name. He probably doesn't know Koby well enough to know that he looks nothing like him.

Fortunately, the boy doesn't ask.

"Oh," he says. "You're Reyna Ashbourne, right?"

"Yeah."

"That's amazing."

"It is?"

"You're the Grandmage's daughter."

"Yeah," I say again, hoping my voice doesn't sound as bitter as it does in my head. Is my father all people see when they look at me? Will I forever live in his shadow? "I am," I add, in case my initial response sounded as short as I think it did.

"What's it like having the Grandmage as your father?" he blurts and then seems to remember that we're both strangers. "Oh, I shouldn't ask something like that. You don't need to answer if you don't want to."

"It's fine," I reply. It isn't as if other adepts haven't asked me the same question a thousand times before. Though that was mostly in my first year at the Arcanium. "I suppose it's like having any other father," I say with a shrug.

The boy doesn't seem content with that response.

"Maybe he has higher expectations for me than most?"

He appears a little more satisfied with that. "Your Mage Trials are next week, aren't they?"

"They are."

"I bet you're nervous about them."

I smile and try to make it not look like a grimace. "A little. Anyway, I should get going." Most of all, I don't want to get caught by any other adepts. Hopefully, he won't tell anyone he's seen me here and Eliya won't find out I lied to her.

"Oh, of course," he replies. "Good luck with your Mage Trials next week."

"Thanks," I say.

With that, I turn and head back to the winding steps.

When I return to the central chamber, Erma is still reading the same book. She looks up as I place *Concerning Conflagration and Combustion* on her desk.

"I would like to borrow this one for two weeks, please."

Erma scans over the cover and then reaches across her desk for the ledger, opening it to the current page. The current date, Friday 2nd December 1694, is scribbled across the top. The rest of the page is split into a table with five headers: *Title, Author, Name, Duration,* and *Returned.* She dips the nib of her quill into her pot of ink and writes out all the information onto the next empty line in the table. She leaves the cell for *Returned* blank.

"*Concerning Conflagration and Combustion* will be of use in the Trial of Magic," she says as she returns her quill to its golden, bell-shaped holder. Her name is etched into the gleaming surface. "Particularly on the second round."

"That's what I was thinking. I was hoping to improve my fire wings spell before then."

"Best of luck with the trials," Erma says, to my surprise. Until now, I didn't know that she could even manage a single nice sentence.

I retrieve *Concerning Conflagration and Combustion* from her desk and turn to the steep stairs leading out of the library.

"And do remember, there are no second chances. If you fail even one trial, you will never become a Mage of Nolderan."

As if I needed that reminder.

Nonetheless, I force a smile. "Thank you, Professor Darkholme. I will do my best to ensure that I do not fail."

CHAPTER 20

I<small>T'S LATE WHEN MY FATHER</small> comes home. Though for him, ten o'clock on a Friday night is rather early. Some nights he doesn't return at all. He would never admit it, but I'm sure he sometimes falls asleep at his desk. His office is on the highest floor of the Aether Tower.

I'm currently sitting in the drawing room, studying *Concerning Conflagration and Combustion*. Taking notes is difficult thanks to Zephyr, who has mistaken my desk for his bed. I tried to move him, but he started spewing balls of aether at me. In the end, I decided to share the desk and work around him. I don't know why he likes it so much. Surely a hard, wooden surface isn't comfortable?

The only blessing is that he doesn't snore too loudly.

My father peers around the door. "You're home? And . . . studying?"

I don't tell him that he's the third person who has commented on my studying habits today. "Why wouldn't I be home? It's ten o'clock."

"It was your last day at the Arcanium, wasn't it? I thought you and Eliya would be celebrating until the early hours of the morning."

I wonder if Eliya and the others left their celebrations at Flour Power or if they continued inside taverns. Another pang of guilt sweeps over me, but I brush it aside. I wasn't lying when I said I wasn't feeling well. Except I have a sickness of the heart, rather than the body.

"I wasn't in the mood for it."

My father is the last person I want to discuss Arluin with, especially after he ordered Archmage Calton to execute him. Since then, neither of us have mentioned it. I suppose we both know how the other will react, so we seem to have silently agreed it's something best left forgotten.

He gestures to the book lying on my desk. "What are you studying?"

"*Concerning Conflagration and Combustion,*" I say, holding up the burgundy cover. "I want to improve my fire wings spell."

"I passed Archmage Gidston earlier in the Arcanium. She spoke highly of your abilities during Combat Class today."

I shrug as I place the book back onto the desk.

"What's the matter?"

I stare at Zephyr's shimmering scales rather than my father's face. "Nothing."

I wonder whether he will press the matter, but he doesn't.

"Aside from your fire wings spell, are you ready for your trials next week?" he asks after a short pause.

"What choice do I have but to be ready?" If I fail my trials, I will tarnish my family's legacy and shame my ancestors like Alvord Ashbourne, whose book lies on my desk.

"Indeed." Maybe once he would have spoken that word as a sigh, frustrated by my lack of discipline. But now I can't tell what emotion laces his voice.

I feel his gaze on me for a few more minutes. The drawing room would be silent, if not for my flicking of pages and Zephyr's slow, gentle breaths.

"Well," my father finally says, "I'll let you get to it."

"I left you some food in the kitchen," I say. That meal was made with my magic, of course. My mother would be disappointed to know the two of us do nothing by hand these days. My father is too busy working, and I'm too busy studying.

"Excellent, thank you." With that, he steps out the room and leaves me to continue examining *Concerning Conflagration and Combustion.*

I end up falling asleep with my head on the book. I jolt awake and frantically inspect the pages to see whether I've crumpled them. If there's even a single wrinkle, Erma will bill me an extortionate amount to have a new copy bound.

Last year, I spilled a few drops of mulberry juice onto the book I was studying for our midterm examinations. In my defense, the specks were tiny, though they were a vivid shade of purplish-red. She charged me half of my monthly stipend.

Once I'm certain the pages are free from creases, I shut the tome quietly enough not to wake Zephyr and lean back in my chair. My attention drifts over to the brass clock hanging over the fireplace. Its black serpentine hands point to twenty past three.

I almost fall off my chair with surprise. I didn't realize I slept for so long.

I rise and gently push the chair under the desk. Despite my carefulness, Zephyr's eyes flutter open. He yawns, revealing rows of tiny ivory fangs. I leave the drawing room and head upstairs. Zephyr follows me.

I pass my father's room. No light filters through the narrow crack beneath the door, so I do my best to prevent the floorboards from creaking under my weight. My father is a light sleeper, and at three in the morning, I'm in no mood to deal with his crankiness.

When I arrive at my room, I close the door softly behind me. Zephyr darts over to my bed and claims the center.

"You know I'll have to move you," I hiss. "How do you expect me to get into bed with you right there in the middle?"

Zephyr opens an eye and stares at me. I glare at him until he crawls over to the left side of the bed.

I drape my cerulean robes over my golden armchair and pause. I only have one more week of wearing them. If I pass my Mage Trials, I will be bestowed with the violet robes of the magi.

And if I fail, I will wear neither adept nor magi robes for the rest of my life.

I pace over to my cabinet and pull out a nightgown. I change into it, switch off the crystalline chandelier, and slide into bed beside Zephyr. His azure scales are so luminous that they are visible even in the darkness.

The shadows swirl as my vision adjusts to the lack of light. I close my eyes and keep them shut for a long while, but no sleep finds me. Even the softness of my bed doesn't lull me into slumber.

I grasp the locket around my neck and run the silver heart between my fingers.

What if I didn't imagine Arluin standing there in the alleyway?

All my foolish wishes weigh heavily on my heart. The darkness shifts, and I find myself staring up at the ghost of his face.

I reach for the lamp beside my bed and switch on the aether crystals. But there's no one else here. Only Zephyr and me. My cerulean robes stare back at me from where they hang over my armchair.

I don't try to fall asleep again. With all the onerous thoughts playing on my mind, it would be pointless.

I switch off the lamp and climb out of bed. On my way out, I grab the velvet cloak hanging on the back of my door. Zephyr doesn't stir as I leave.

The corridor beyond is dark, and I use the walls to help me navigate back to the stairs. When I near my father's room, I tip-toe past. Not only do I fear his grumpiness at being awoken, but also him demanding to know why I'm creeping out at three in the morning.

Actually, it might now be closer to four o'clock, but I don't peer into any of the rooms downstairs to check the clocks. I continue through the hallway, passing all my mother's paintings, and out the grand doors. I close them behind me carefully.

On the other side, the golden lion knockers stare at me with suspicious, metallic eyes. I turn away from them and start through the gardens.

Moonlight shimmers across the satin petals of the blooming flowers, and the fountain at the center flows to a steady rhythm reminiscent of gentle rain.

My warm breaths form a small cloud as they meet the frigid air. Frost powders the grass and glistens in the starlight. A sharp chill claws over my arms. I clasp my velvet cloak tighter around myself and wish I picked a thicker one. The stones are like ice beneath my bare feet as I traipse over them.

"*Calida,*" I murmur. A flame sparks within, warming me from the inside out. Now when my toes touch the stone, the ground feels no colder than my bedroom floor. Nor do I feel the wintry breeze gliding through my cloak.

The aether enchanting the tall gates glows brightly through the shadowed gardens. When I reach them, they swing open in a shrill, metallic clang, and the sound ricochets through the night.

I wince and glance back at the manor. No light switches on. If my father heard the sound, then he has ignored it, likely thinking it came from someone else's manor farther down the street. Thankfully, the gates close more quietly than they opened.

I step out onto the dark street. There's no one around to wonder what the Grandmage's daughter is doing out in the dead of night, barefoot and dressed in her nightgown. Before anyone can appear from around the corner, I mutter, "*Laxus.*"

A violet cloud enshrouds me, and I fade into the night.

I emerge outside Arluin's manor.

Dark iron gates greet me, as does the serpent coiling around the blade on the Harstall's family crest. The gardens were neglected when Arluin lived here, but now they're entirely out of control. The weeds have grown so tall they strangle the trees.

Though Arluin has distant cousins, none of them have claimed this place. It seems they want no connection at all with Heston or his manor.

After the necromancers and their undead were defeated, Branvir and a group of magi searched the manor. I don't think they found anything, and if they did, I heard nothing about it. The eventual fate of this manor will be demolition, but my father is yet to issue that order. And I don't think he will for a very long time. He can't bear to utter a single word about Heston.

Over the last three years, only I have visited the manor. This isn't the first sleepless night that I've teleported here.

I take another step toward the gates. The protruding edges of the cobblestones dig into the soft undersides of my feet.

"Reyna Ashbourne," I say to the enchanted gates. They remember my name and swing open.

Passing through the wild gardens isn't easy. Overgrown roots jut out, and brambles spiral across the path. A few thorns nick the back of my calves. I stop and curse them under my breath. The brambles are sharp enough to draw blood, and a few drops dribble down to my ankles.

"*Ignira,*" I breathe, launching a fireball at the thorns which dared to attack me.

The brambles crumble into ash as my flames touch them. I turn on my heels and continue to the manor's entrance, trying to avoid being stabbed by more thorns.

The brass twin viper knockers are rusted, and most of the paint has peeled off the doors. Large, wooden patches streak across them. When I push open the doors, they creak so violently I fear they will fling off their hinges and crash into me. Luckily, they don't.

The blue rug spread through the hallway is so filled with dust that it appears gray. Cobwebs hang from the ceiling like enormous fishing nets. I push past them and ascend the spiraling staircase.

The steps groan beneath my weight, no longer used to being walked upon. As I come to the top of the stairs, I pause and stare at the door to the master bedroom. Heston's face and the image of him being burned to death by my father's flames flashes through my mind. His tortured screams ring through my ears.

Clenching my fists, I force myself away and continue toward Arluin's room. The door is still left ajar from the last time I was here.

Musty air chokes me as I enter. For three years, the windows have remained shut, and the room is suffocated. The curtains are tucked away, and moonlight streams through the grimy windows, silvering the edges of all the furniture inside the room.

Ticking comes from the corner where the old grandfather clock stands. Thanks to the abundance of aether imbued inside its springs, it will likely last another fifty years until it falls silent and still.

I pad over the zig-zagged wooden panels forming the floor, and my feet soon meet the crimson square rug lying in front of the canopy bed. My heels sink into the plush threads. I reach for the nearest mahogany bedpost and my fingers curl around it, feeling every peak and valley of the ornate design carved into the wood. My attention settles on the scarlet quilt. Dust motes blanket it like snowflakes. It feels like only yesterday Arluin carried me up here and promised to marry me.

Exhaling deeply, I leave the post and settle onto the edge of the bed. The mattress dips with my weight.

I sit there for a while, my fingers running across the silk brocade sheets and disturbing the dust. My gaze sweeps around the room, taking in every aspect: the aether crystals hanging from the ceiling, the paneled wardrobe still filled with Arluin's clothes, the crimson curtains held beside the arched windows by matching tiebacks.

When I finish absorbing every detail, I reach for the silver locket around my neck. My hands tremble slightly as I unclasp it.

I pinch the delicate chain between my fingers and dangle it. Like a pendulum, the silver heart swings back and forth. It takes several moments to fall still.

I want to believe with all my heart that Arluin lives. That there's hope the two of us will meet again, even if we can never be together. But if he is alive, why wouldn't he try to contact me? Why wouldn't he let me know he survived his father's attack?

I need closure. But I fear I will never find the answers I seek.

The silver heart blurs as tears well in my eyes. I brush them away and place the locket flat on my palm.

I gaze down at it, hearing the echo of the words within. I've never once opened it. I feared doing so would cause our promise to lose its sacredness. To become truly impossible.

But that thought is nearly laughable. It's already impossible. How can Arluin keep his vow when he's not here? When he might be dead?

And so, I do what I've contemplated doing for three years. I open the locket.

Aether pours out. It sketches the scene of the memory it recorded. The two of us are shown in magenta light. The crystal even captured the brocade detailing of the sheets beneath, though the fabric is painted in a purple glow.

"*Reyna,*" Arluin says, "*I am a man who has nothing, who is nothing. I know I don't deserve you, but you mean everything to me. In this world, I have nothing else left.*"

Upon hearing his voice, I choke out a sob. He sounds so distant, but it's still him.

This is another reason I didn't dare to open the locket. I knew I would be unable to bear the sound of his voice. A part of me considers shutting the locket before old wounds are ripped open. But I don't. The wounds are festering, anyway.

In the memory, my hand reaches up and rests on his cheek. "*Arluin, please don't speak about yourself like this. You mean everything to me, as well.*"

He places his finger on my lips. I wish I could feel his touch—for me to be sitting there beside him instead of my ghost. I hardly recognize her as being me. Her eyes are too bright, too filled with hope. She doesn't know that this night will be one of her last with the boy she loves.

Would this memory be any different if I'd known what destiny planned for us?

"*I've loved you for as long as I remember,*" Arluin's voice continues. "*And it's only when I'm with you that . . . that I forget . . .*"

That he is a necromancer's son.

If only he were someone else's son. Then all this wouldn't have happened. Then we might still be together.

The locket weighs heavily in my palm. I don't know how it doesn't slip from my grasp and fall to the floor.

I watch myself kiss him, watch how still he is within my embrace. Maybe he suspected that our time together was reaching an end and that this moment would be one of our last. Maybe that's why he decided to record this memory.

"*Arly,*" I say when I finish kissing him, "*we can't change the past. We can only shape the future.*"

My words sound nothing like my own. All I want is to change the past. To change it so that we can be together, so that my mother is alive. Maybe if I'd immediately reported my suspicions to my father, everything would be different.

Or would it? Would fate still have torn us apart?

"*Marry me,*" Arluin gasps. In the vision, he clasps my face. "*Please marry me, Reyna. I can't bear the thought of ever being without you—*"

I don't wait to hear my response.

I slam the locket shut, and the delicate metal shudders from the force. My shoulders tremble as I stare at the silver heart in my palm. I squeeze my fist shut, and the locket digs into my skin.

I fall into the silk sheets. The mattress reverberates with the impact. Dust fans into the air and swirls in the moonlight. I gaze up at my hand, the locket concealed within. I let out a heavy breath. It leaves my lips hoarse and uneven.

I wish for him to return, even if that's a selfish wish. If he's caught here in Nolderan, no amount of pleading will save him from my father's wrath. But I need to know the truth. I can't spend the rest of my life with a gaping hole ripped through my heart.

I need to know that he's alive. That he didn't die to save me.

I refuse to believe I'm the reason he is dead.

I bring my knees up to my chest and stare at the fine silk drapes hanging from the mahogany bed frame. My breaths reach them and they ripple slightly. I squeeze the locket tighter in my hand and cradle it to my heart in a silent prayer. To whom, I'm not sure. The gods certainly aren't listening.

We swore a promise to one another, and I'm clutching the proof of it in my fist. I can't help the foolish hope that he may come back, as impossible as it may be.

My eyes flutter shut. The ghost of Arluin's face drifts through my mind, gently lulling me to sleep.

That night, I dream of passing my Mage Trials and him returning to Nolderan.

To marry me, just as we promised.

CHAPTER 21

RELENTLESS WINDS WAIL IN MY ears. They tear at my hair, and the strands become long, slender blades which slice across my cheeks. Overhead the Aether Tower's enormous orb of energy hums, powering all of Nolderan's magical needs.

I pause on the very top step leading up to the tower and scan across the city beneath. The cobalt rooftops appear even smaller than they do from Archmage Gidston's office in the highest spire of the Arcanium; the Aether Tower is at least thrice its size. I can see all the waves as they tumble across the sea and the dark silhouette of Talidor's coastline crowning them.

While I've never known myself to have a phobia of heights, a dizzying bout of fear crashes into me. The city below spins. We're so high up that we must be within the clouds.

My breaths are labored from the countless steps leading up here. I'm certain Eliya and I were walking up the spiraling staircase for at least an hour, though it feels an eternity. My legs are numb from fatigue. It's hard to believe ascending the tower isn't part of the trial itself.

And it's even harder to believe that Eliya is undeterred by the strenuous climb. She bounds ahead to the edge of the platform. The way she leans over and points below makes my stomach lurch. All I can hope is that a sudden gust of wind doesn't blow her off before the Trial of Heart begins.

"Look!" she exclaims. "I can see my house from all the way up here. Even the pond in our garden!"

How she can see such details from this height, I have no idea. Even when I squint, I can't make out much more than rippling cobalt roofs and the streets weaving through them like a network of spiderwebs.

I take a step nearer and force a smile. "How wonderful."

She's too busy marveling at the world below to notice the dryness in my tone.

We aren't the first adepts to arrive. The Trindell twins are already present, and they both lean against one of the tower's curved stone spires. Blake is also here, along with a few others.

Koby appears behind me. His cheeks are bright red, and he seems even more out of breath than I was. When he reaches the last step, he doubles over.

"By the gods," he groans. "I didn't think those stairs would ever end."

"Nor did I," I reply. "And we still have an entire trial to complete."

He straightens and wipes his brow. "Don't remind me. Hopefully, I'll manage to catch my breath before Archmage Gidston arrives."

I start to respond, but Eliya calls me.

"I can't see your house, Reyna!" she shouts, leaning dangerously far over the platform. "Maybe it's because yours is on the street right beneath us?"

I take a few strides closer and hesitantly peer at the city below. With the winds battering into me and threatening to blow me over the edge, every instinct screams at me to run back down the stairs. Even if it would take an hour to reach the bottom.

But I don't. If I refuse this trial, I will never become a mage. I only have this one chance to prove my worthiness.

And if I fail, I will shame the Ashbourne legacy and disappoint my father.

I ignore my fear and stay right where I stand.

"Maybe it's that," I say.

"And look at how small the Arcanium is," Eliya continues, pointing at the distant spires. "Isn't it crazy since it's actually so big?"

I follow her gaze across to where the Arcanium lies beneath us. Even the tower containing Archmage Gidston's office seems so low down. The looming statues which guard the entrance are little more than dots.

But my assessment of the Arcanium is cut short. Purposeful footsteps stride toward us. I glance back to see Kaely approaching. The wind tugs on her braid.

She scans over my face, and her lips twist with smugness. Whatever she sees in my expression delights her. "Morning, Reyna," she says, stopping a few paces short of Eliya and me. "You look awfully pale today. It wouldn't be the height getting to you, would it? That would be such a shame, since your father can't help you now, can he?"

At her words, the other adepts gathered atop the Aether Tower fall hushed. Koby's mouth hangs agape. I don't know why everyone is so shocked. Maybe it's bold of her to confront me right before our first trial, but this is Kaely. She probably hopes to work me up into such a fury that I strike her with a fireball the moment Archmage Gidston arrives and disqualify myself from the Mage Trials. She would take great pride in being the reason I failed to graduate from the Arcanium.

Maybe she succeeded three years ago, but I'm no longer that same person. I won't lose my temper. Not when it means putting everything at stake.

The other adepts are silent. They glance between Kaely and me, awaiting my response.

Eliya steps between us, no doubt fearing that I will lose my temper and destroy my entire future.

"Why don't you just mind your own business and leave Reyna alone? Everyone is anxious to begin our first trial. The last thing anyone needs is for you to pick a fight with Reyna."

The other adepts nod their agreement, but none dare to directly oppose Kaely. Only Eliya is willing to involve herself in an argument between the daughters of the Archmage of Defense and the Grandmage of Nolderan.

Kaely's gaze rakes across the other adepts. When she finds no allies, she turns on her heel and storms over to the other side of the tower.

I blow out a breath and run my fingers through my hair. With the fierce winds slamming into us, it does little good in tidying the tangled locks.

"Can you believe she tried that stunt right before our first trial?" Eliya grumbles.

I shake my head. But I'm far from surprised by Kaely's behavior. She will stop at nothing to ensure my failure. If there's an opportunity to sabotage my trials, she will seize it.

Before Kaely can decide to march back over and taunt me again, Archmage Gidston arrives.

She steps from a cloud of violet light. The violent winds blow the aether dust through the air.

I'm not the only adept who stares at her in disbelief. Here she is, teleporting straight to the top, while we all had no such luxury. The wards surrounding the tower prevent anyone but official Magi of Nolderan from teleporting inside. The Aether Tower isn't the only area restricted to adepts. The Vaults are another, where Nolderan's most dangerous artifacts are stored far beneath the Arcanium. Only Nolderan's most senior magi are permitted inside.

"It appears everyone has arrived," Archmage Gidston says, scanning over us all. "Good. Then let us delay no further." She continues to the platform's edge.

Eliya and I step away and line up with the other adepts. She stands to my left, and Koby to my right. His fists clench as he visibly braces himself for the trial. Eliya appears much more relaxed. She looks like she's waiting for an order at Flour Power rather than waiting for the Trial of Heart to begin.

"The past five years of your education at the Arcanium will culminate in these three Mage Trials," Lorette declares. "Making it this far is an achievement itself. Many struggle to complete the grueling years of training as an adept.

"Now, as you should all be aware, the Mage Trials consist of three separate trials: the Trial of Heart, the Trial of Mind, and the Trial of Magic. Today, you are all to undertake the first trial and prove whether you have the courage and faith required of a mage. To prove that you will not waver in the face of any danger. To prove that you will serve Nolderan with the utmost dedication and obey the orders of the three Archmagi, and the Grandmage himself, without hesitation."

She gestures to the city below. Her indigo sleeve ripples in the roaring winds. "As for your first trial, I'm sure you can guess what is expected of you."

I swallow at that.

I've heard rumors of what the Trial of Heart entails. Namely, jumping off the edge of the Aether Tower. I dearly hope my suspicions are wrong, but the glint in her eyes suggests otherwise.

"While the task is simple, it is not for the fainthearted." She holds out her hand. "*Conparios.*" A plain feather appears. It is of a tawny color with white spots along the tip and most likely originates from a quail.

She pinches the feather between her fingers and holds it high for us all to see. "One by one, you will leap from the Aether Tower with nothing but this feather. And I must stress that I mean nothing else, not even your magic. Casting even a single spell is forbidden on this trial. Choosing to use your magic means demonstrating a lack of faith, and you will fail this trial."

I stare out at the sea of cobalt rooftops. My legs feel wobbly. I hope I'm not visibly shaking, or else Kaely will be pleased to see my fear.

Despite the terror snaking up my spine, I have no choice but to place my faith in Archmage Gidston and the Trial of Heart. Because failing this trial means failing to become a mage.

"Are there any questions?" Lorette asks.

Koby fumbles for a moment. Then he hesitantly raises his hand.

"Yes, Adept Varsley?"

"Um," he begins, chewing the inside of his cheek, "if we are forbidden from using our magic, how will we survive the fall?"

Further down the line, some adepts murmur. I suppose they're wondering how we will avoid certain death. That's also what I would like to know.

"Answering that question would defeat the purpose of this trial," Archmage Gidston replies. "However, I can reveal two things. Firstly, that if we allowed all our adepts to fall to their deaths, then Nolderan would be in very short supply of magi. And secondly, that if you ensure you hold the feather at all times, then you will be in no danger. I cannot say more than that, nor can I reveal the specific mechanics of this trial. You must all have faith."

"What if we let go of the feather?" Koby asks. "By accident, I mean."

The Archmage gives him a pointed look. "Don't let go of it."

His throat bobs as he swallows.

"If you would like to forfeit, Adept Varsley, then you are welcome to do so. However, you will fail your Mage Trials and will be unable to graduate from the Arcanium. The same goes for anyone else who lacks the faith to complete the Trial of Heart."

Koby quickly shakes his head. "No, Archmage Gidston. I don't want to forfeit."

"Good," she says, her gaze returning to the rest of us. "Then if there are no further questions, we shall begin. Who would like to go first?"

No one steps forth. Aside from the howling wind, there's only silence. Maybe if nobody volunteers to be the first person to leap, Archmage Gidston will pick someone herself.

Behind my back, I cross my fingers and hope she doesn't choose me. If I see someone else jump and not die, it will go a long way to bolstering my faith in this trial.

Before Lorette can select anyone, Kaely raises her hand. Tension slips from my shoulders. She's only volunteering herself to prove how much better she is than me, but for once I'm grateful for her arrogance. I really didn't want to be the first one to leap off the tower.

"Adept Calton, you wish to go first?"

Kaely's lips pull into a calculating smile. Her expression makes my heart skip a beat. Whatever she is planning, I'm not sure it has anything to do with her going first.

"Actually, Archmage Gidston, I was wondering whether I could make a suggestion?"

"What suggestion do you wish to make?" Lorette asks.

"I was thinking that it would be the most fitting for Reyna to go first, since her father is the Grandmage of Nolderan. I'm sure I'm not the only one who wants to see how it's done."

My stomach sinks with dread. Everyone's eyes are on me. I grit my teeth, willing for my apprehension not to show.

I'm probably not the only one who noticed Koby's fear, but he can afford to show such weakness. His father isn't the Grandmage of Nolderan. He isn't being constantly measured against impossible expectations. And not just the expectations imposed on him by others, but also the ones he imposes on himself.

To my dismay, whispers of agreement ripple through the other adepts. They are almost inaudible over the violent winds, but I hear them anyway. Even Koby nods his head. It's all I can do not to glare at him for hanging me along with everyone else. If I do, I will reveal how much this trial terrifies me. They will all think me weak. And I refuse to ever again be weak.

Because the cost of weakness is death.

Eliya is the only adept who doesn't fervently nod her agreement. Unlike the others, she isn't thinking of how my going first benefits her. She clenches her jaw and doesn't even try to hide the glare she flashes Kaely.

"Adept Ashbourne," Archmage Gidston says to me, "would you like to go first?"

Since she has asked, I suppose I could decline. But that would mean admitting my fear. And maybe she would interpret my refusal as forfeiting this trial.

That's a risk I cannot take.

I paint the most courageous expression I can muster on my face and hope that it convinces me as much as everyone else.

I can do this.

I am the Grandmage's daughter, and a descendant of Nolderan's most powerful family. My heritage must count for something.

And, as Archmage Gidston said, this trial is arguably easy. All I need to do is hold the feather, jump off the tower, and ignore the instinct to save myself from falling with my magic.

I suck in a breath and say, "Of course I would love to, Archmage Gidston. I'm honored that Kaely would request for me to go first."

I must appear calm. Or Kaely will know how much she's riled me.

"Excellent," Lorette says, holding the feather out to me. She gestures for me to come forth.

Eliya squeezes my hand and whispers, "Good luck!"

I return her gesture with a thin smile and start over to Archmage Gidston. When I reach her, I take the feather from her grasp.

The feather itself is unremarkable. I hold it high and examine it with great care, but I detect no magic within the feather—just the residue from when she summoned it.

I'm not certain how an ordinary feather will ensure my survival, but I can only cling to it and maintain my faith in this trial.

"Are you ready to begin?" Archmage Gidston asks.

My gaze drifts beyond the feather to the city below. Soon I will be plummeting toward those cobalt rooftops and pointed spires. My stomach tangles into a thick knot.

I don't look at Archmage Gidston as I nod. The gesture is stiffer than I expect, and I hope no one can see the tension in my neck and shoulders.

"Then you must now jump from the tower," she says. "And do not, under any circumstances, release the feather."

The moisture drains from my mouth at the warning, and my throat is left parched. All I can imagine is the quail feather slipping from my grasp and leaving me to tumble to my death.

I'm glad my back is to all the other adepts. I'm certain the blood has drained from my face, casting me a sickly pale shade. I keep my attention fixed on the city beneath, so that Archmage Gidston can't see the true extent of my horror.

My fingers grip the quail feather. Faith. I just need to have faith that Archmage Gidston won't let me die, that the feather won't slip from my fingers. As long as I keep hold of it, I won't fall to my death.

I hope.

"And if you are having any second thoughts—"

Knowing that I've delayed long enough, I don't let Archmage Gidston finish. Before she can ask me whether I'd like to forfeit the trial, I throw myself off the tower.

The winds are quick to embrace me. They slam into my cheeks. The cobalt rooftops and deadly spires rush toward me. My gut clenches. I think I might be screaming into the wind. But they roar so loudly that they drown out my voice.

A sudden gust shoves me to the right. The impact catches me off-guard, and the quail feather almost slips from my grasp. I clutch it with all the force I can. My survival depends on it.

The wind spins me over and over as I tumble through the air. A painful ache fills my ears from the changing pressure.

Gleaming spires hurdle toward me, threatening to impale me like enormous spears. I'm falling faster than my mind can process it. A moment ago, they seemed so far away. Now they are so close.

One spire draws sickeningly near. I squeeze my eyes shut, unable to watch as it surges up to meet me. I wonder whether I will feel any pain before the spire rips me open.

Panic shoots through me like bursts of lightning. My magic screams at me to save myself. To teleport to safety.

But I ignore every instinct. I can only place my faith in Archmage Gidston. Using my magic means failing.

And I can't fail.

The spire skims past. I open my eyes a heartbeat later. By then, it's already high above. And the street is almost upon me.

People below are going about their daily business, unaware that I'm plummeting toward them. Toward my death.

The ground is only a few feet away.

I'm going to die.

I scream. But no one seems to hear me. I'm too panicked to check if the quail feather is still clutched in my fist, or if I lost it on the way down.

Magic boils in my veins. With death so near, it's almost impossible to ignore its desperate plea. Aether snaps to my fingers. The image of my manor's gates and the lion crest on them flashes through my mind.

But before I can utter *laxus* and teleport away, aether explodes around me. The blinding light swallows me. I no longer feel the wind whipping me. Magic thunders in my ears and makes them ache.

When I next blink, I'm standing at the very top of the Aether Tower, in the exact spot I stood prior to jumping.

My legs buckle beneath me. I don't know how I manage to stay on my feet. I grasp my wobbly knees, willing them to steady, and rapidly breathe in and out. My eyes trail across to the city below. Knowing how close I'd been to death almost makes me vomit. Thankfully, I don't.

"Congratulations, Adept Ashbourne," Archmage Gidston says. With the ringing in my ears, her voice sounds distant, though she stands less than a few feet away. "You have successfully passed the first Mage Trial, the Trial of Heart. Today, you have demonstrated the faith and courage required of a mage."

Right now, I feel anything but courageous. All I want is to teleport home and curl up in my bed. I take a moment to process the rest of her words. That I passed, even though I was so close to using my magic and forfeiting my trial.

With my body in shock from the closeness of death, I'm incapable of feeling triumph. I stay there at the edge for a while, doubled over and gasping for breath. I'm surprised she doesn't usher me away.

At least I'll never again need to jump from the Aether Tower. This is certainly an experience I don't intend to repeat.

When I straighten and force my trembling legs to walk away, Archmage Gidston turns to the rest of the adepts. "Who would like to go next?"

Eliya's hand shoots up. "I'll go!" she exclaims, darting forth and swiping the quail feather from my fingers.

Before Archmage Gidston can say anything, Eliya leaps from the tower. Her crimson hair spills around her.

With widened eyes, I stare down at her descending form. There isn't even a trace of fear inside her eyes.

And that either makes her the most courageous person I know, or the most foolish.

CHAPTER 22

I STUMBLE OUT OF THE Violet Tree, almost tripping over the low step and flying into Eliya. She laughs and grips both my arms, steadying me in place.

The icy evening breeze slams into my cheeks, somewhat sobering me. I tilt back my head and peer up at the darkness veiling the sky. The clouds are as dense as smoke, and specks of snow whir through the wind. Some gather on my lashes, and I blink them away. The crescent moon peeks from the cover of clouds and illuminates the heavens with its silvery rays.

My vision blurs. Then there are two moons staring down at me.

I rub my eyes until my sight returns to normal. Tonight, I drank much more wine than I intended. I was hoping to get up early tomorrow morning and take some more notes on *Concerning Conflagration and Combustion*, but I doubt I'll wake before noon. Coming to The Violet Tree wasn't my idea, though. It was Eliya's.

When we were descending the Aether Tower after the Trial of Heart, Eliya suggested celebrating our success with a few glasses of wine. I declined when she first asked and reminded her that we still have two more trials to complete this week. But she only insisted our next trial isn't until Wednesday and we have all of tomorrow to recover. Having no argument to that, and still feeling awful for leaving her at the bakery on Friday, I ended up agreeing.

The thought of the next trial fills me with dread. Archmage Gidston said the Trial of Heart is arguably the easiest of the three, and that involved a near death experience. Two adepts failed this morning. Each teleported away before Archmage Gidston could summon them back to the top of the tower. Now our class of twenty adepts is down to eighteen.

I'm also not entirely sure what the Trial of Mind involves, aside from it assessing whether we adepts have the cleverness required of magi. It also apparently takes place in a maze far beneath the Arcanium, though I'm uncertain of the accuracy of those rumors. While studying Alvord Ashbourne's old tome probably won't help me pass the next trial, it's better than sitting around and doing nothing while my anxieties gnaw on me.

"What should we do now?" Eliya asks, interrupting my thoughts. She murmurs *conparios* and summons her crimson coin purse. She shakes it, but only the rustling of velvet fills the night. Not the clinking of silver. "That last bottle we ordered emptied my purse."

My own purse is just as empty. With Yule around the corner, I've already spent a lot on buying presents for New Year's Eve. And tonight, I also burned through the last of my stipend.

"Well," I say with a shrug, "I suppose if we're out of money then we'll have to head back for the night."

Eliya pouts. "But it's not even nine o'clock!"

"It's the week of our Mage Trials. We should get an early night so we're well rested for Wednesday. The Trial of Mind will involve more than jumping off a tower."

Eliya grabs my arm and swings it back and forth. "Reyna," she grumbles, drawing out both syllables of my name, "when did you get so old and boring?"

"We *are* twenty-one now, in case you've forgotten."

"Age is just a number, especially when you're a mage who will live until like two-hundred."

"We're not magi yet. We still have two more trials to pass. And drinking so much that we sleep through all of tomorrow and still feel groggy on Wednesday morning certainly won't help with that."

"But we won't feel groggy on Wednesday morning if we sleep through all of tomorrow."

I shake my head at her. "Anyway, we don't have any money left. How are you expecting to get more drinks? By flirting with rich noblemen?"

"That isn't a bad idea." Her lips stretch into a wide grin. "But I have an even better one in mind."

I know I shouldn't ask, since it will only encourage her, but curiosity gets the better of me. And the wine is also likely to blame. "What is it?" I ask, folding my arms and bracing myself for whatever maddened idea Eliya's crazy mind has conjured.

"We'll solve our money problem like old times!"

"What are you talking about?"

"Have you really gotten so old and boring that you don't remember the mischief we got up to as first-years?"

"Oh," I say, now realizing what she means. "Absolutely not."

"Why not?"

"Because we're fifth-years who are soon to become official Magi of Nolderan and should know better than to break the law."

"It's only my uncle we'll be stealing from," Eliya replies. "It isn't illegal if it's from family."

"I'm pretty sure stealing is illegal no matter who you're stealing from. Besides, he's your family—not mine."

"We've never been caught before."

"And what if we're caught this time? We would be in so much trouble that Archmage Gidston will probably disqualify us from the Mage Trials."

"Why would we get caught now? We're better at magic than when we were first-years."

"You never know what may happen."

"Fine, fine," Eliya says, waving her hand dismissively. "Let's go home and miss out on the enormous shipment of moon-blossom wine my uncle just received this evening."

"Moon-blossom wine?"

"Mm," she says and pulls me along the road. "Doesn't matter now though, since we're going home."

"Wait." I tug my arm from her grasp, and she comes to a stop. "Has he really got loads of moon-blossom wine?"

"That's what I just said. An enormous shipment of moon-blossom arrived earlier this evening, and we're going to miss out on it. Think about all the aether swirling inside every sweet, sweet drop. Drinking plenty of moon-blossom wine would ensure our bodies are fueled with magic for Wednesday's trial. It's such a shame we're going home."

"Fine," I say, heaving out a sigh. "You win."

Eliya beams triumphantly at me. "I knew you would eventually come to your senses."

The offer is too tempting to turn down. Moon-blossom wine is like liquid gold poured into a bottle, and certainly costs as much. Only the moon elves of Lumaria brew it, so we have to import it from the elven continent of Belentra.

Long ago the magi tried cultivating moon-berries, the aether-infused fruit which flowers into the precious blossom, but they never had any luck. Lumaria is situated upon more nexuses—clusters of ley line intersections—than Nolderan, and even imbuing the soil with aether isn't enough for the moon-berry trees to grow. Maybe it's because the plant prefers the eternal night of Lumaria. Unfortunately, we don't have our own equivalent aether-filled fruit.

Most people can't afford moon-blossom wine, and those who can only drink it on special occasions. Such as New Year's Eve.

When we started at the Arcanium, Eliya and I regularly drank moon-blossom wine, thanks to Eliya's uncle. We only ceased our exploits when he became suspicious over his mystery thieves and tripled the security of his warehouses.

I hope he's dropped his guard over the past four years.

"To your uncle's warehouse, then?"

Eliya's grin widens. "Let's go."

Eliya's uncle, Garon Whiteford, is unequivocally the richest man in all of Nolderan. While he possesses no aptitude for magic and was never selected for adept training like Eliya's father, he more than makes up for it with his trading expertise. Whatever goods you want from the three kingdoms, or even from Belentra, Garon can get them for you. He holds shares in at least half of all businesses in Nolderan: from taverns to barbers to tailors. Even those he hasn't invested in owe him many favors. And most importantly, he's the key supplier of moon-blossom wine here in Nolderan.

While a merchant as illustrious as Garon lives in the Upper City, his warehouses are situated away from his own residence and lie along the docks: the perfect location for receiving his latest shipments.

Eliya and I emerge from a cloud of violet light. The gentle sea breeze rustles through my hair, and the smell of salt wafts into my nose. Behind us, ships of all sizes sit docked at the many wooden piers traipsing out to sea. There are huge galleons carrying silks from Selynis, and there are also small fishing vessels which have not long returned from their evening haul.

In the shadowed horizon, far beyond the slumbering ships, mountains from the mainland of Talidor rise above the sea's tumultuous surface.

Ahead of us are the vast stone buildings of the Warehouse District. Eliya takes the lead, starting down the street and gesturing for me to follow her. Garon's storehouses are clustered together, and they are some of the largest in Nolderan.

The buildings loom over us, and their towering height blocks out the night sky. No specks of snow are visible down these narrow streets.

Our hurried footsteps sound tremendously loud against the silence. After a few strides, I glance back over my shoulder. I'm not sure why I do, since we are yet to break any laws, but I can't shake away my paranoia. If we are caught, the consequences will be dire.

This is such a stupid idea. Why did I agree to it?

My pace falters. Eliya immediately notices. She frowns at me.

"What's the matter?" she hisses.

"What if we get caught?"

She shoots me an exasperated look. "We've already been through this. It's only my uncle. I promise it'll be fine."

I press my lips together. "You're sure?"

"Very sure."

I hesitate for a moment longer. Before I can change my mind and teleport home, Eliya grabs my arm and pulls me deeper into the Warehouse District.

A few blocks later, Eliya stops behind a corner and peers around it. The warehouse Garon uses to store his liquor is up ahead, but she doesn't take another step forth.

"What is it?" I whisper.

"My uncle," she mouths. "He's here."

"Maybe we should go back."

Eliya continues to stare at the street around the corner. I can't see past her.

"What's he doing?"

"Talking to someone," she says, turning back to me. "And his workers are all carting out moon-blossom wine. Lots and lots of it."

"There will probably be none left for us," I murmur.

"Let's wait until they're gone. Then we'll see how much is left."

Knowing she won't leave without first searching her uncle's warehouse, I don't bother arguing with her. Hopefully, we won't get caught for trespassing a warehouse already emptied of moon-blossom wine.

I close my eyes, straining my ears to make out what the muffled voices are saying.

"Alric!" Garon shouts. "Be careful with that! If even a single bottle is broken, I will have to deduct it from your wage."

"Yes, sir," comes the meek reply. Rickety wheels roll over the cobblestones. I suppose the sound belongs to the carts which Garon's workers are using to distribute the moon-blossom wine.

Minutes stretch into what feels like hours. I lean against the stone wall behind me and fold my arms. It takes an eternity for the voices to quieten and for the footsteps to fade away.

"They just shut the doors," Eliya says. "We should be good to go now."

"Is there anyone left?"

"I can only see one of his workers. But we'll need to be quick. In case they come back."

"And you're sure we won't get caught?"

"Stop worrying so much," she says, shaking her head at me. "Right, let's not waste any more time. You deal with the worker. I'll get the doors open. We'll grab all the bottles we can and then make a run for it."

I only nod.

"*Conparios*," Eliya says. A dark cloak appears from a cloud of aether. She drapes it over her shoulders and pulls the hood over her crimson hair.

I do the same, and when both our identities are concealed, Eliya dashes beyond the safety of our corner. I hang back a few paces and watch as the worker, who is busy tidying a stack of crates, notices Eliya rushing toward Garon's storehouse.

He opens his mouth, either to shout for guards or to demand to know what she's doing, but no words have the chance to escape his lips. Aether swirls in my fingers.

"*Somnus*," I mutter, my words barely brushing the evening breeze. Though I speak quietly, it's loud enough for my magic to answer my call.

Violet light drifts over to the worker. It seeps into his nostrils as he inhales.

He blinks lazily, and his movements slow as my spell tightens its grasp over him. Then his eyes finally close.

In the next breath, he tilts over and falls face-first onto the street, snoring loudly. I pause for a few beats, ensuring he's definitely fast asleep, and then hurry after Eliya.

How long his slumber will last depends on two factors. Firstly, how much aether I used to fuel the spell. Since I cast it quickly, I didn't power it with an awful lot. Secondly, it depends on how much aether flows through his blood. The greater his affinity for magic, the more he will resist my spell.

With some luck, he will remain asleep for several minutes. That should be long enough for us to get in and out of the warehouse.

Up ahead, Eliya fiddles with the warehouse's gigantic lock. She wiggles a thin metal pick inside it. Magic is of no use. The building is heavily fortified with defensive wards, and even the slightest tremor of magic will set off the city's alarms. That means we can only resort to ordinary methods to break into the storehouse.

Fortunately, Eliya is an expert at lock-picking. Her father keeps his most treasured potions inside large chests with similar locks, offering Eliya plenty of opportunity to practice over the years. Somehow, her father has never caught her breaking into his chests and borrowing his potions.

It takes less than a minute for Eliya to burst the lock open. The internal springs click into place. She glances back and flashes me a smug grin. Then she tears the padlock from the wide wooden doors and shoves them open, revealing the contents of Garon's storehouse.

Barrels of ale and crates full of rum line the stone walls. We waste no time rummaging through them and head up to the second floor, where Garon keeps his more expensive liquor. The bottles here are from world-famous breweries, indicated by the fancy script on their labels. Many crates of moonblossom wine lie at the back, and the dusky liquid sparkles in the low light.

"I can't believe how many bottles he has in here!" I exclaim, sifting through for the most expensive wine. The labels are written in Elvish, and while I can't read it fluently, I can recognize their alphabet well enough to identify which are from Twilight Hill—the finest winery in all of Lumaria.

Eliya picks up several bottles with the same labels, filling her arms with wine. "Yule is only a few weeks away. I suppose he's hoping to make a good profit off moon-blossom wine this year."

Once we have gathered all the crystalline bottles we can carry, we hurry back down the wooden steps.

Just as we reach the lower floor, I see another worker kneeling beside the sleeping one, frantically shaking him. Worst of all, he's shouting loudly enough for his voice to echo through the entire street.

I curse and bolt out the warehouse, Eliya close behind. As if on cue, a patrol of guards appears from around the corner. They glance between us and the two workers. The bottles of moon-blossom wine bundled in our arms are incriminating enough.

The guards don't hesitate before charging straight for us.

CHAPTER 23

WE RUN, AND THE GUARDS give chase. I clutch the wine tightly as we flee through the Lower City. We turn street after street, hoping to lose our pursuers. Exhaustion makes our breaths ragged, and rawness burns down my throat and into my chest. But I press on at full speed.

No matter what, we can't get caught. Not when it means being disqualified from the trials and never becoming magi.

We reach a dead end. I grit my teeth, examining the wall. The guards' hurried footsteps sound a few streets away. Maybe we'll have enough time.

"Let's teleport," I say. "Now."

"To the cliffs?"

I give her a hurried nod, already gathering aether into my hands. I visualize the cliffs lying far beyond the city walls, at the very edge of our island. "*Laxus*," I call. As does Eliya.

Just as we unleash our magic, the guards appear at the end of the street.

Fortunately, they are too far away to interrupt our teleportation spells, and we vanish before their eyes.

In the next heartbeat, the blinding light fades into shadowy cliffs. The moon silvers the crests of the waves rolling beneath, and the evening breeze rustles through the surrounding trees. With our arms still full of wine, we continue higher up the grassy mound and collapse at the top.

"Thought they nearly had us there," Eliya gasps, setting her bottles down on the grass and wiping the sweat from her brow.

"That's because they nearly did," I retort. "I thought you promised everything would be fine."

"We weren't caught, were we?"

"We were worryingly close."

"But we weren't actually caught, and that's what matters." She tears the cork off the bottle closest to her and lifts it to her lips.

I watch her for a moment and shake my head, but I don't continue the argument. I reach for a bottle and sip on the moon-blossom wine inside. The elegant sweetness washes over my tongue, every drop oozing with magic.

There really is nothing better than moon-blossom wine. And this stash might be worth almost getting caught.

"Wouldn't it be nice to be a moon elf?" I say, shaking the crystalline bottle either side as I muse over it. The dusky liquid swirls within and glitters in the starlight.

"What makes you say that?"

"Well, moon-blossom wine will be much cheaper in Lumaria since it won't need importing. And if I lived there, I could grow my own moon-berry trees and make my own wine. I could even start up a winery."

Eliya leans forward, her eyes gleaming. Some of her wine splashes out of the bottle. "If I had my own Lumarian winery, I would drink it day and night. I would have so much I could bathe in it."

"You wouldn't be able to sell it if you bathed in it."

"I just wouldn't tell any merchants about that part."

"What if they found bits in it?"

Eliya narrows her eyes. "Are you saying I'm dirty?"

"Maybe," I say with a shrug.

"*Aquis.*" Water splashes from Eliya's fingers. It soaks me from head to toe.

My mouth falls agape. I stare down in disbelief at my drenched dress. A chilling wind rolls over me, far icier now that I'm soaked through. "I can't believe you just did that!"

"And I can't believe you just called me dirty," she says, a smile twitching on her lips. "Serves you—"

Before she can finish, I call out *aquis* and return the favor. My water spell splashes over her, and then she is as drenched as I am.

We both burst into laughter. But it isn't funny for long, because now we're both soaked and shivering. My teeth chatter. If we weren't magi in training, the chill would spoil our evening. Luckily for us, the problem is easily fixed by speaking the spell-word *calida*. Warmth sparks within, and I can no longer feel the chill. The heat radiating from my skin dries the fabric of my clothes.

We soon return to drinking our moon-blossom wine, and it doesn't take long for us each to finish a bottle and crack open another. With each sip, more aether courses through my bloodstream.

"Reyna?" Eliya says after a moment.

I glance up at her. "Yeah?"

Her fingers play around the top of her crystalline bottle, and she chews on her lower lip. She looks stuck for words. Eliya never hesitates to speak.

"Are you sure you're all right?" she finally asks.

"What do you mean?"

"You didn't seem yourself the other day."

My heart skips a beat. I hope she hasn't found out I visited the library after leaving the bakery. "On Friday?"

She nods.

"I had a headache."

"I don't believe you."

I flinch.

"At least, not entirely. I don't think it was just because you had a headache."

I lean back onto the grass. "Then what do you think it is?"

"I don't know," she says with a sigh. "It's just after you went, I remembered that street was where I found you three years ago, when you were . . ."

When I was searching the heaps of bodies for Arluin.

She doesn't say those ghastly words. They linger between us, nonetheless.

She puts down her bottle and takes my hand. "If you want to talk about it, I'm here to listen."

I lower my head, unable to meet her gaze. I know I should probably talk about everything with her. It's been so long, and yet I've not spoken to anyone about what happened that night. I doubt it's healthy to keep such awful things bottled up, but trying to speak about it feels like a monumental task.

"I . . . I never found his body," I whisper. My words are so quiet I don't know whether they reach Eliya over the roaring wind. "I have no idea whether he's dead or alive. And I don't think I'll ever know the truth."

Eliya squeezes my hand. The small gesture grants me a sudden burst of courage. My caged emotions bubble and overflow, spilling from my lips.

"If he's alive, why has he never come back? Why didn't he at least let me know that he isn't dead?"

"Reyna," Eliya says softly, "if he's alive, after the crimes he committed, he can't return. And I think it's best he never does."

"I know," I reply, swallowing down the bitterness swelling in my throat. "My father would have him executed. That night, he ordered Archmage Calton to burn them all. Even Arluin. I know what fate awaits him here, but I miss him so very much."

Eliya releases my hand and presses her lips together. Her reluctance is clear. Whatever she intends to say next, I know I won't like to hear it. But I don't stop her from speaking. "Reyna, he's a necromancer. During the attack, he sided with his father. He murdered innocents and raised them from the dead."

"You weren't there," I grind out, my fingers curling around the neck of my bottle. "Heston captured me and planned to use me against my father. The only way Arluin could save me was by earning his father's trust. And to do that, he had to resort to using necromancy. If he hadn't made those choices, the entire city would have likely fallen."

"You're right, I wasn't there. But how did he know how to wield dark magic?"

"His father taught him," I say, picking at the decorative label of my bottle. I don't look up at her as I speak. I fear what I'll see in her expression.

But I hear the betrayal in her words all the same. "You knew about it?"

"He only admitted it after promising to marry me."

"I can't believe you didn't tell me about his father teaching him necromancy."

I hate the hurt in her voice. "It was Arluin's secret to tell, not mine."

"But you're my best friend."

"If anyone else had found out, Arluin would have been exiled. Or killed."

"You didn't trust me?"

"No, I just didn't want to burden you with such a terrible secret. And he only told me a few days before everything happened."

Eliya gives me a stiff nod. She doesn't press the issue any further and sips on her wine.

I stare down at my bottle instead of drinking from it.

Would things be any different if I had told her Arluin's secret? If I'd told my father?

I shake my head. Telling anyone wouldn't have stopped Heston's attack. It wouldn't have stopped him from murdering my mother. All that would have changed is Arluin being unable to rescue me. Then I probably would be dead, along with my mother. And I don't want to even imagine what Nolderan's current state would be.

"Anyway," Eliya says, "I guess it makes sense."

"What makes sense?"

"Why you've been so down lately. There's a part of you that's wondering whether he will come back, isn't there?"

My shoulders sag. "Is it wrong of me to hope that he will? Even though he is a necromancer? Even though it will mean certain death for him?"

Eliya shifts closer and pulls me into a fierce hug. "It isn't wrong of you to want that," she whispers. "You still love him. And you've loved him for a very long time. But he can't come back. You know that, don't you?"

"I know," I mutter.

We stay like that for some time. The waves crash into the rocks far below, and the frigid wind howls. With the warmth radiating from us both, we don't feel the chill. Snowflakes powder our hair.

"Come on then," Eliya finally says, releasing me from her embrace. "Let's go home."

The crescent moon has drifted far through the sky, still shrouded by the heavy clouds. I'm uncertain what time it is, but I know it must be late for Eliya to suggest returning. Or maybe she suggested it because I'm such awful company tonight.

I gaze at the unopened wine bottles scattered all around us. "What should we do with these? If I take them home, my father will be suspicious as to where I got them from. As will yours."

"We can bury them here," she replies, tapping her chin in thought. "And then after we pass our final Mage Trial, the Trial of Magic, we can come back here to celebrate."

"All right," I say and stagger up onto my feet. The world sways around me. While sitting down, I didn't realize how tipsy I was. But now that I'm standing, I notice the full extent of all the wine I drank this evening.

"*Tera*," Eliya mutters, and green light swirls in her fingers. She directs it to the grass, and her magic carves out a hole. The layers of mud float a few feet above, surrounded by a vivid green glow.

I'm grateful Eliya took charge of digging the hole. If I tried, I would probably carve through the entire cliff. Wine makes magic far less precise. Especially if you slur the spell-words and your magic thinks you mean something else.

While Eliya collects the unopened bottles and deposits them inside the hole, I gather the empty ones and murmur *ventrez*, blowing the evidence off the cliff. I take care to say the spell-word with as much clarity as I can. Thankfully, nothing unexpected happens.

I don't see where the wine bottles land. Since I hear no smashing, the waves must have devoured them.

Eliya lowers the layers of mud back into the hole. When the earth is returned to its rightful place, the emerald glow fades. There is no seam in the grass to show where Eliya dug it up. It looks like it was never disturbed.

"All done," she declares, brushing her hands together. "Time for us to head back, then. Will you be fine teleporting yourself home?"

"You definitely drank more than me tonight. It should be me asking you that question."

"We both know I can handle my wine better than you," she says with a wink. "But anyway, I don't want to leave you here by yourself if you're not feeling well."

"I feel fine."

"You know what I mean."

"It's been three years. I can handle it."

"All right," she says. "Make sure you don't study too much in the morning."

I breathe a laugh. "I promise I won't."

She draws aether into her hands. "Night then, Reyna. Sleep well."

"You too," I reply, just as she mutters *laxus* and disappears into violet light.

Aether dust scatters through the wind and swirls with the snowflakes.

With a deep breath, I gaze up at the crescent moon. My fingers play with the silver locket hanging around my neck.

Eliya is right. If Arluin is alive, it's probably best he never returns. Because I fear I would forsake my future, my father, just to be with him.

I know I must put the past behind me. I can't spend the rest of my life wallowing over what happened three years ago. But I don't know how to banish the grief which haunts my heart.

I draw out a sigh. Standing out here all night will do me no good.

Closing my eyes, I gather aether into my fingers and picture the towering gates outside my manor. I imagine them so clearly that I can almost see the two lions roaring at each other on our family crest.

When the image is concrete, I whisper *laxus* and unleash my magic. I fade away into the night, leaving behind a cloud of glittering purple light.

Yet when I emerge from the teleportation spell, brine wafts into my nose.

I open my eyes. The tall gates of my manor are nowhere to be seen.

I let out a groan and blink several times, praying that I'm not actually looking at the ships anchored in the harbor. But no matter how much I rub my eyes, the piers don't morph into my home.

Fantastic.

I slap my forehead. It seems I mis-targeted my teleportation spell, no doubt because of the wine. The only consolation is that my mistake hasn't meant a trip deep into the sea. That has apparently happened to a few magi before.

Not daring to try teleporting again in case it lands me beneath the waves, I break into a sprint and hurry through the Lower City.

The streets are almost empty at this late hour. A few drunken sailors stumble out of taverns and call over to me. I ignore them all and keep my attention fixed on the road ahead. Fortunately, they don't bother me with anything more than a few slurred shouts.

Since my manor is located at the far end of the Upper City, my journey home is a long one. The streets are shadowed, and only the radiance of the floating aether crystals stops me from tripping over the uneven stones. The buildings seem to sway as I run. I grimace. If only I'd targeted the spell more carefully. I was certain that the image was clear enough in my mind, but apparently not.

It takes me a long while to reach the steps leading up to the Upper City. By then, my pace has slowed to a jog. With everything spinning around me, I'm not sure whether I'll manage the rest of the way home. Not wanting to spend the night sleeping in an alleyway, I force myself onward.

But it seems Vetia, the Goddess of Luck, really isn't on my side tonight.

A force slams into me. It sends me flying back onto the cobblestones. The impact bruises my limbs, and I graze my palms from trying to break my fall.

Wood splinters, and the cart I crashed into topples over. All the bottles inside smash onto the street. Red wine splashes out like blood and soaks me.

Dazed, I stare at the debris.

Footsteps hurry toward me.

"Are you all right?" a low male voice asks, nudging my shoulder.

Still disoriented, I blink a few times until my sight refocuses. I tilt back my head and turn my attention upward.

A very handsome stranger gazes down at me.

CHAPTER 24

WE STARE AT EACH OTHER, neither of us saying anything. The night breeze tugs on the fine, golden strands of his wavy hair. A hint of fair stubble dusts his jawline, and his emerald eyes glisten in the radiance of the surrounding aether crystals. I've never seen such a vibrant shade of green.

His gaze breaks away from mine, and he scans over the rest of me. I follow his eyes as they sweep over my torn sleeves and the grazed skin peeking from beneath.

He seems to remember himself then and jolts back to life. He reaches for my hand, which is scraped from the uneven stones. "Here," he says. "Allow me to help you up."

I don't protest as he takes my hand and guides me back onto my feet. Lightning sparks from our conjoined fingers and surges up my arm. It's as though magic is pounding through my body, but I know this energy isn't aether. Yet it feels like sorcery, nonetheless.

His doublet is of scarlet satin, with a filigree pattern entwining the cuffs and the high collar. Beneath it he wears dark breeches and polished black boots which reach his mid-calves. He appears to be a few years older than me— certainly no more than five—and stands only a few inches taller. His fingers are also callused, which is unexpected since his clothes suggest he is of nobility.

"Have we met before?" I blurt, the words out of my mouth sooner than I can realize. I immediately regret them. He must already think me an idiot for gawking at him, let alone for asking him such a ridiculous question. Of course we have never met before today. How would I forget those striking emerald eyes?

Fortunately, he doesn't mock me for the question. He only blinks at me. His fair lashes are long enough to make even Eliya jealous.

"No," he says. "No, we have never met."

Unable to withstand the intensity of his gaze, I lower mine and focus on the cobblestones beneath. Thousands of tiny glass shards glitter around us like fallen stars. Puddles of blood-red wine streak across the street.

"You're hurt," he says, examining the scrapes on my arm. My eyes drift over the wreckage surrounding us. I notice the labels of his smashed bottles: *Ruberra* and *Sanguilus*. While they are both nowhere near as expensive as moon-blossom wine, they certainly aren't cheap.

"All your wine! I'm so terribly sorry—"

"Don't be," he says, cutting me off. "They're only wine bottles. They don't matter."

"But so many are broken!"

"And you are injured." There's a softness to his voice, which makes me shiver. I do my best to stifle my reaction to him.

"I'm fine," I say, pulling my arm from his grasp. He lets me go.

His perfectly straight brows pinch together. They're as golden as his wavy locks. "Are you sure?"

"They're just shallow scratches. With a bit of Blood Balm, I'll be healed within a few hours."

The handsome stranger says nothing. He continues to stare at me with that piercing gaze of his, making me feel increasingly uncomfortable. I suppose I could bid him good night and continue on my way, but I don't. I could tell myself it's because I feel guilty over smashing so many of his wine bottles, but I would be lying if I said it has nothing to do with the way I feel inexplicably drawn to him.

"Where were you taking your cart?" I ask.

"Oh," he says, scratching the back of his head and disturbing the golden locks which tumble from there. "Back to my tavern."

"You own a tavern?"

"I do," he replies. "The Old Dove."

"Oh, I know that one. Isn't it a few streets away from The Violet Tree?"

"Yeah, on Fairway Avenue."

"So, you must be the new owner who bought the place a couple of weeks ago?"

"That's me."

"My friend and I have been meaning to visit. The last owner was too shrewd to hire enough staff, so you would always have to wait hours to be served."

"I have heard that the previous management left much to be desired," he says. "We're closed tonight, since it's a Monday, but why don't you stop by tomorrow and see what you think of the service under my management?"

His offer almost sounds like a business affair, but there's an edge to his voice which suggests this is more than a friendly invite. Maybe I'm imagining that he's flirting with me.

"Sure," I say, even though tomorrow night will be the night before our second trial. "I would love to visit."

We stand there awkwardly. Then I remember that I was asking about his cart.

"Do you need any help with your cart?"

His gaze sweeps across to it and lingers on the broken wheels. He doesn't look as concerned as I expected him to be, and I'm relieved he isn't too annoyed at the current state of his cart. And his wine, since most of the bottles are smashed.

"I can use my magic to help you bring it back to your tavern."

"Are you sure?"

"It's my fault they're broken," I reply. "It's only right that I help you bring the unbroken ones safely back to The Old Dove."

"It's my fault for not swerving the cart away fast enough."

"It's hard to maneuver carts quickly, so you can hardly be blamed."

"But—"

"Just let me help you."

"All right," he says. "If you insist."

I step closer to the cart. "*Ventrez.*"

A wind spell rushes from my fingers. It blows the cart up from the street and hovers at shoulder height.

"Lead the way," I say.

With a nod, he strides down the street. I follow, blowing the cart in front of me and taking care not to let any more bottles fall and smash.

On the next corner we pass a few people, but no one stops to gawk at our levitating cart. They mostly ignore it and continue their laughter as they stroll past. In a city full of magic, where the streetlights themselves are floating crystals, such a sight is unremarkable.

"You know," I call over to the golden-haired stranger, "I don't think I caught your name?"

His pace falters, and he falls into step beside me. "Nolan." He holds out his hand, but I flash him a strained smile and gesture to the floating cart I'm focused on. He lowers his hand and hastily adds, "Nolan Elmsworth."

"Well, it's lovely to meet you, Nolan Elmsworth. Though I do wish it hadn't been because I broke all your wine."

"You didn't break them all." He points to the remaining bottles in the cart.

I breathe a laugh. "True enough."

Nolan doesn't ask for my name, but I decide to volunteer the information.

"I'm Reyna," I say. "Reyna Ashbourne."

"It's my pleasure to meet you, Reyna."

He doesn't mention my father. I can't remember the last time I introduced myself to someone and they didn't ask about Grandmage Telric Ashbourne. But I'm not complaining. It's a relief to not be in my father's shadow, for once.

"Most people ask about my father when they meet me," I tell him, anyway. "I think you might be the first who hasn't."

"He's the Grandmage of Nolderan, isn't he?"

"Yeah, he is."

"I only moved here a few weeks ago when I bought the tavern. I did have an inkling that you shared his surname, but I wasn't sure if I remembered correctly. I hope I didn't offend you."

"No, not at all," I reply. "I just thought it unusual that you didn't ask me about my father. But it makes sense since you're new here. Where are you from?"

"Tirith."

"Tirith is rather large."

"I'm from Dalry. Does that satisfy your curiosity?"

"For now."

"I suppose that means you will have more questions for me later?"

"Perhaps. Though I have yet to think of them."

He chuckles at that.

Fairway Avenue is the next street along, and The Old Dove lies five doors down on the left. A white dove with a monocle and a walking stick is painted onto its wooden sign.

I slow my pace as we near the tavern, guiding the cart with great care. If I smashed Nolan's windows as well, then that would probably be enough to make him mad. Especially since they're so immaculate. With how gleaming they are, it looks like they were cleaned earlier today.

Nolan pulls out a key and jiggles it inside the lock until it yields. He swings open the door and holds it wide as I direct the cart inside. I set it down at the center where there's plenty of space away from the tables and chairs.

The Old Dove looks much like I remember from when Eliya and I visited last year. Due to how long it would take for our drinks to arrive, we tended to avoid this one.

Wooden beams run along the cream ceiling. Each round table features a small aether crystal. All are switched off, and the room is blanketed in shadows. Moonlight spills in through the polished windows, bright enough that I can discern most of the tavern's interior.

A counter lies at the far end of the room. Behind it, the stone walls are decorated with shelves containing barrels of ale, bottles of wine, and dozens of tankards.

Nolan flicks on the switches beside the door, and the aether crystals hanging from the center of the ceiling ignite, washing us in dazzling purple light. The tabletops glint with the radiance.

"Right then," I say, turning to Nolan. I point to the broken cart heaped at my feet. "What are we doing with all these bottles?"

He gestures to the door next to the counter. "We'll put them all inside the cellar, along with the rest of the wine and ale down there."

"Sure," I say, bundling up several bottles into my arms. Nolan grabs the rest, and I follow him into the cellar.

The wooden door groans as he opens it, and we start down the few stone steps. We enter a small room that is barely large enough to fit the countless barrels strewn around. Two large racks are propped against the back wall, filled with bottles of assorted wine. Nolan begins to fill the gaps with the wine he carries, and I do the same.

Once we're done, we head back up the steps and Nolan shuts the door behind us.

"Well," he says. "Thank you very much for your help tonight."

"It's the least I could do, seeing as it was my fault your cart broke and your bottles got smashed."

"And I am to blame for your injuries," Nolan replies. "So, I think we can conclude we're both equally at fault."

"I'm not that injured."

"You look rather injured to me."

I glance down at my arms. It's my right one which is the most battered, likely because I used it to break my fall. On closer inspection, it's in a worse state than I thought. I suppose all the moon-blossom wine I drank this evening is responsible for numbing the pain. The scratches are deeper than I realized.

"They're just minor wounds," I insist.

"They'll still need cleaning."

"They'll be fine after a bit of Blood Balm."

"And you will manage to clean your injuries and apply the salve to them yourself?"

I hadn't considered that part. If my father is home, he will probably be asleep. While I might manage the task myself, it would take longer than letting someone else do it. And I would likely make a racket loud enough to wake my father. Then he would be furious over being awoken in the middle of the night, and also that I drank so much during the week of my Mage Trials.

On second thought, allowing Nolan to help me with my injuries seems the wisest choice. And he isn't wrong that we are both to blame for our collision. I've repaid my debt—or at least partially—by helping him to carry back the unbroken wine bottles. I suppose it's only fair he repays his debt by assisting me with my injuries.

"Fine," I say, huffing out a sigh. "If you really won't take no for an answer, then I guess there's no harm in letting you help me with them."

"Good." Nolan takes my uninjured arm and guides me to the nearest table. He pulls out a chair and helps me sit. I consider telling him it's my arm which is wounded and not my legs, but I decide against it since he's just trying to be nice.

"Wait here," he says, turning to the stairs. "I'll get the tin of Blood Balm and a bowl of water."

The steps creak as he ascends them, and then I hear his footsteps above the ceiling.

Nolan returns downstairs a few minutes later, with a tin of Blood Balm in his hands, and starts over to the wooden counter at the far end of the tavern. He rummages through the shelves until he locates a clean cloth and a ceramic bowl.

"You don't need to find any water," I call over to him. "I'll use my magic to conjure some."

Nolan nods and carries the items over to me. He sets the bowl and the tin onto the table.

"*Aquis*," I say. Water splashes into the bowl and fills it entirely. Tendrils of steam swirl from the bubbling surface. I hope I didn't make it too hot.

Nolan helps me roll my sleeve up to my shoulder, exposing the wounds. They look worse than they feel. Not that I trust my senses right now. I keep the fabric held in place as he sloshes the cloth inside the bowl and soaks up all the warm water. When enough has absorbed, he wrings out the cloth and glides it across my skin.

I flinch.

"I thought you said the injuries weren't bad," he says, a light smirk playing on his lips. It's only now I realize how close he is. Lightning pulses in the little space between us, and I lean back slightly to avoid it.

"The water's hot."

He dips his finger into the bowl, and the surface ripples. "It's only lukewarm."

"Fine," I say, scrunching my nose. "The scratches might be a little deeper than I thought."

He doesn't dwell on his victory and sets to work with swiping the damp cloth over my wounds and cleaning them.

When he's done, he reaches for the tin of Blood Balm and opens it, revealing the glossy crimson contents. The scent of cool mint and spicy pepper wafts into the air.

He presses his fingers into the balm, leaving an imprint, and smears the substance across my scratches. I jolt as he traces over my skin, and this time I'm glad to have the excuse of the Blood Balm stinging me.

Once all the scrapes are slathered in ointment, I roll down the fabric of my sleeve. Nolan screws the tin's lid back on.

"Thanks," I say.

"No thanks is needed," he replies. "We are both to blame for what happened tonight. It was only right that I helped you with your wounds, since you helped me with my cart."

"I'm sorry again about all your wine."

"Don't be," he simply says.

We fall into a silence. Nolan's attention turns to the window behind me, while mine drifts over to the bowl of warm water. I watch the tendrils of steam wafting out as I try to think of something suitable to say, but my mind has become devoid of words.

"It's very late," Nolan finally says. I suppose commenting on the time is as good as anything, especially since I could think of nothing myself. Pointless conversation is certainly better than tense silence.

"Yeah, it is." I would love to extend my response, but I don't know how. All I can think of is to say it's dark, but I doubt that would further our conversation.

"If you need to stay here for the night, you're more than welcome to do so."

I whirl around, my mouth hanging agape. "You want me to stay for the night?"

Nolan cringes at my expression, his dimpled cheeks tinging with crimson. "I didn't mean it like that. I was just thinking that with your arm being injured and it being so late . . . And there are several spare rooms upstairs."

"Oh."

Now it's my turn to redden. I can't believe I interpreted his words like that.

"I drank a lot of wine tonight," I tell him, though I'm not sure it's a good enough excuse.

He laughs. "It's fine. It's my fault for not realizing how that would sound."

"No, that was definitely my fault."

We pause again. Nolan breaks it before it stretches on for too long.

"Anyway," he says, "the offer stands. But I will completely understand if you would rather not."

I hate how there's a part of me that wants to spend the night with Nolan—

In his tavern, I mean. In one of the guest rooms.

Before I can lose good sense, I swiftly reply, "Thank you for your kind offer, but I will have to decline. My Mage Trials are taking place this week, and I really should head home. If my father learns I've been out drinking all night during such a critical time, then he will be furious."

"I understand."

The chair legs scrape against the tiles as I stand.

"Wait," he says as I turn to leave.

I stop and glance back at him. "Yes?"

"I was wondering when I could see you again."

"You want to see me again?"

His lips tug into a soft smile. "Only if you would also like to see me again."

"Yeah," I say, the words spilling off my tongue before I can realize, "I would like to."

"Then will you come by tomorrow?"

"My second Mage Trial is on Wednesday morning, so I won't be able to stay for too long. But I'm sure I could spare an hour or two."

"Great," he breathes, "then I look forward to seeing you tomorrow."

Dizzying warmth sweeps over me. My knees feel like soft clouds beneath me as I stare into his mesmerizing emerald eyes. The distance between us feels too small, despite us being farther apart than before.

"As do I," I whisper.

Our gazes hold. My heart thumps with anticipation.

Before this moment can last a heartbeat longer, I tear myself from where I stand and hurry out of his tavern. Only when I am outside, with the chilly night air biting my cheeks, do I realize that I didn't bid him good night.

CHAPTER 25

A BARD'S MELODIOUS VOICE CUTS through the busyness of the Upper City's square. Though the crowds are bustling this morning, everyone stops to listen to her lute and her captivating voice. The fountain at the center of the square trickles in the background.

I swing my legs back and forth from the bench I sit upon, watching the bard serenade her audience. The bowl at her feet is already brimming silvers, and I even spot a few gold coins thrown in there.

One gold coin is enough to cover the annual salary of a well-paid dockhand. Or at least, I think it is. Since I've never held that job role myself, I can't be certain of their exact income. But what I do know is that this bard would never receive this kind of money down in the Lower City. Here, we are just a stone's throw from the Arcanium, and plenty of nobles pass by. To those who are as rich as Eliya's uncle, a gold coin is nothing compared to the talent of this bard.

Apparently she only started playing here last week. And according to the murmurs amid the crowd, she worked as a barmaid in the Lower City prior to her newfound fame. Already she must have earned a fortune. I can't deny that I'm envious. Unfortunately, I'm unable to play a single instrument. Nor can I sing. Now I realize what a mistake that is.

Since I'm long out of my monthly adept's stipend, all I can offer the bard is applause between each song. I wish I could offer her more, seeing how her gentle music is doing wonders for my headache.

When I woke up, my temples were filled with excruciating fire. I took a large dose of Ice Honey to numb the pain, but it has worn off. And I don't dare to take any more.

Moon-blossom wine really is strong. And I drank so much of it.

I clasp my head in my hands. Even the thought of alcohol nauseates me. Right now, I don't intend to drink another drop of wine ever again.

All I hope is that I will have recovered by tomorrow morning. Or else raiding Garon Whiteford's warehouse will prove to be a very costly mistake.

Too busy nursing my headache and listening to the bard's silvery voice, I don't notice Eliya sliding onto the bench beside me.

"You look worse for wear," she chirps, startling me.

I look up at her and groan. "Do I honestly look that bad?"

"Oh yes," she replies. "You should have fixed yourself with an illusion before heading out."

I sigh. Compared to me, she looks well-rested. But I suspect that's only due to carefully conjured illusions. With how much Eliya drank last night—which was even more than me—she should look dreadful.

I should have probably done the same and hidden my awful appearance with illusions. But the headache made it impossible to concentrate on casting any spells. Clearly Eliya has a higher pain threshold than me.

"Remind me to never again agree to one of your plans," I grumble, rubbing at my temples.

"Why?" she asks. "Didn't you have fun last night? Isn't the headache worth it?"

"No," I growl. "And neither is it worth the mess I've gotten myself into."

Her magenta eyes sparkle with curiosity. "Mess? What mess?"

"After you left, I miscalculated my teleportation spell."

"You didn't accidentally teleport yourself right into the middle of the sea, did you?" she asks, choking on a laugh.

"No, but nearly. And it was far worse than that."

Eliya taps her chin as she contemplates all the possibilities which might have befallen me. "Did you teleport yourself into the sewers and get covered in waste?"

"No, but that probably would have been far less messy."

"Just tell me," Eliya demands. "I'm already out of ideas."

"I teleported myself to the docks."

"That doesn't sound too bad. Not like teleporting yourself into the sea or the sewers."

"Yes, but when I was sprinting home, I ended up crashing into someone because I wasn't looking where I was going."

Eliya frowns. "That still doesn't sound terrible."

"He was wheeling a cart full of expensive wine back to his tavern, and I smashed most of his bottles."

"Oh, I see," she replies. "You're right, that doesn't sound great. I bet he was furious. Listen, I'll talk to my uncle about it. Nearly everyone owes him a favor. I'm sure he will be able to convince this man to leave you alone. Even if he has to replace the bottles you broke."

"No, no," I say swiftly, "that isn't the problem. He wasn't annoyed about the wine. Not even in the slightest."

"I'm confused. If he isn't angry at you, what is the problem? How have you gotten yourself into such a mess?"

"Because he wants to see me tonight," I mumble. "And I agreed."

"You're still making no sense. If he isn't mad at you, then why would he—" She cuts herself off, realization illuminating her face. "Oh, I get it now. He likes you and asked you out on a date. That's what it is, isn't it?"

"He didn't ask me out on a date."

"Didn't you say he wants to see you again tonight?"

"Yes, but it's not a date."

"It sounds like a date to me."

"No, he just asked if I would stop by his tavern tonight."

"Hm," Eliya says suspiciously, scrutinizing my expression. "Is he handsome?"

"I don't remember. I was drunk, thanks to you."

"Well, he must have been handsome if you agreed to meet him again."

"I miscalculated my teleportation spell, so I wouldn't place too much trust in my judgement last night."

"Do you remember what he looked like?"

"He was around my height with wavy gold hair and very green eyes."

"And when you say *his* tavern, do you mean he owns it?"

"Yeah, he does."

Eliya sucks in a deep breath and fans herself, despite the frigid winter air. It looks like it's trying to snow again, judging by the thick gray clouds swarming in the heavens. "I'll have him if you don't want him."

"You've never even met him."

"He sounds handsome. And he owns a tavern. What more can a girl want?"

I roll my eyes at her.

"And I still don't see why it's such an issue. If you don't want to meet him, then don't."

I stare down at my hands. "Well . . ."

"You're not sure whether you want to go?"

"I don't know," I mumble.

"What do you mean you don't know?"

"It was dark. And I was drunk. Maybe he's hideous."

She narrows her eyes. "I think you're making up excuses."

"Why would I be making up excuses?"

Eliya hesitates. "Because . . ."

"Because of what?"

"Because of Arluin," she whispers.

I swallow and turn away from her. My attention settles onto the bard who is still playing her lute for all those gathered in the square.

I can't deny Eliya's words. Last night, after the tipsiness wore off and I crawled into bed, an overwhelming wave of guilt crashed into me. Guilt over flirting with Nolan, over agreeing to meet him tonight. The emotion is so irrational that I don't know how to explain it to Eliya. Arluin has been gone for three years. He might even be dead. Why can I not let go of him?

Eliya places her hand on mine. I clench the edge of the stone bench so tightly that my knuckles whiten. "Reyna," she says softly. "It's been three years."

"I know," I reply, my words cold and dead.

"Do you think . . ."

"Do I think what?"

She bites her lip. Whatever she intended to say, she seems to have decided against it.

A few tears escape my eyes and trace down my cheeks. I hurriedly wipe them away with the back of my sleeve. "Sorry," I mutter.

"For what?" Eliya asks.

"For this."

She pulls me into a hug. "You never need to apologize for being upset, silly. What sort of best friend would I be if I were mad at you for crying?"

I give her a slight nod but remain silent.

"Why don't you stop by his tavern tonight?" Eliya says after a moment, releasing me from her embrace. She lifts my hand from the stone bench and squeezes it. "Since it isn't a date, what's the harm in meeting him again?"

I can think of no answer to her question, other than betraying Arluin's memory. How can I move on from him so soon? Three years is nothing compared to the eighteen years I knew him.

After our conversation last night, I know exactly what Eliya thinks of him. Like everyone else, she believes him to be wicked. But he freed me. And I refuse to believe that using dark magic to save me makes him monstrous.

"I'll come with you," Eliya says, "and if he's as hideous as you fear he might be, then we'll run straight out. How's that?"

I close my eyes and let out a heavy breath. I wish I could explain to her how all this makes me feel. I wish I could make her understand.

"What if you don't go tonight and you spend the rest of your life wondering you missed because you were too busy holding onto the past?"

I can't argue with her. What she says is the reason I've not entirely ruled out visiting The Old Dove tonight. There was an inexplicable connection between Nolan and me. Gazing at him made my pulse quicken. And he appeared to be as dazed as me.

But all of that could have been down to the moon-blossom wine. To know, I need to meet him again.

And if I don't, will I regret it?

I already knew that I couldn't go on like this, wallowing over Arluin for the rest of my life. Maybe meeting Nolan signifies the start of a new chapter. I think that's what terrifies me the most.

But, as Eliya says, what's the harm in us visiting The Old Dove? It isn't as if I'll be going alone. And if I change my mind, I'm sure Eliya would happily flirt with him and divert his attention from me.

"All right," I finally say. "Like you said, what's the worst that can happen?"

"That's the spirit!" She leaps to her feet and pulls me up with her. "Come on then, let's go! But first we need to get you properly dressed to impress Mr. Handsome-Tavern-Owner!"

CHAPTER 26

GLIMPSING MY GAUDY APPEARANCE IN a nearby window, I turn to Eliya and grimace. "I look ridiculous," I say for what must be the tenth time. At the very least.

For a start, the midnight blue dress is barely thick enough to keep the wintry chill at bay. And the cut is straight across my shoulders, exposing them to the night.

Then there's my hair, which Eliya has weaved into an excessively fancy updo. If only she let me wear it down. I'm still considering pulling out all the pins when she's not looking. But if I do, she will be furious, and Eliya's rage isn't a pretty sight to behold. I definitely don't want to be on the receiving end of it.

So, I press on through the streets in this ridiculous dress, doing my best not to shiver. With how thin the fabric is, I suggested teleporting us both to The Old Dove and avoiding the chill. But Eliya wanted to walk so she can see exactly where Nolan's tavern is located. I tried to explain it's the tavern which had the awful service, but she insisted that she didn't remember. I think she just wanted me to suffer.

"Don't forget we have our second Mage Trial in the morning," I warn as we turn the corner and step onto Fairway Avenue. "We can't stay too late tonight. Nor can we drink more than a few drops of wine."

"I know, I know," Eliya mutters under her breath. "You've already said so five times."

"I mean it. One drink all night. Nothing more."

"Yes, yes," she says, waving her hand dismissively. She won't admit it, but I know she is already scheming to get her hands on more than just one drink. Though we both spent all of our stipend last night at The Violet Tree, Eliya's father was kind enough to top hers up. Mine didn't, however. If my father knew I was heading to a tavern on the night before the Trial of Mind, he would flay me alive.

That's why we need to be back early. And sober.

When we arrive at The Old Dove, Eliya pauses outside the door and peers at the white dove painted onto the swinging sign. Three men burst out, and we step aside to let them pass.

"You know," Eliya says once they're gone, "I haven't been here in years."

"Nor me. Well, at least not until last night."

"Let's hope this handsome new owner knows how to treat his customers properly."

I clamp my hand over Eliya's mouth and glare at her.

"What?" she demands, her voice muffled by my palm. She grabs my wrist and yanks my hand away, freeing her mouth. "It's not like I said you thought he was handsome."

The two people passing by shoot us curious looks.

"You'd better behave."

"I'm always on my best behavior," she says, mischief glinting in her eyes.

I groan. Bringing her here was a terrible idea.

"What's his name, anyway?"

"Nolan Elmsworth," I say, my voice hushed in case anyone overhears.

"Even his name is handsome!" Eliya remarks far too loudly. "Well, let's see whether his face measures up to the rest of him." With that, she shoves the door open and strides inside. I trail after her.

It's busier than I expected, with many of the round tables full. There are six staff in total, including Nolan. He's behind the wooden counter, chatting to a man and pouring ale from a nearby keg.

His hair is fair and tousled like I remember from last night, and his eyes sparkle like vivid emeralds. There is only one thing the moon-blossom wine caused me to forget: He looks far more handsome than I recall.

I lower my head as he passes the filled tankard across to the man and hope he hasn't caught me staring at him. Warmth tinges my cheeks, incriminating me.

My pace must have faltered since Eliya grips my arm and drags me to the empty table in the corner. Last night, every table was gleaming beneath the aether crystals, but now this one is sticky from the ale spilled across it.

When we are sitting down, Eliya leans over the table, careful to avoid dipping her sleeves into the patches of ale. "Don't tell me that's him!" Again, her voice is much louder than I would prefer.

"Which one?"

"The one behind the bar!" she exclaims in a half-whisper. "I can't believe how gorgeous he is. He practically looks like a god walking among us mere mortals. How could you think he might be hideous?"

"I drank a lot of moon-blossom wine."

"Imagine if I hadn't talked you into coming here tonight. Look at what we would have missed out on!"

I raise a brow at her.

"What *you'd* have missed out on, of course," Eliya quickly corrects herself.

"If you're really that interested in him, I can introduce you."

She wags a finger at me. "Not so fast. Don't think I don't know what you're doing."

"And what is it you think I'm doing?"

"Trying to wriggle out of this."

"No, I'm not."

"Go and talk to him then."

"What?" I blanch. "I can't just walk up to him!"

"Of course you can. We're in his tavern, and we're here to drink. So, hurry up and place your order."

"The Trial of Mind is tomorrow, and we aren't here to drink. Why don't we come back another time?"

"Not a chance. I spent hours making you look pretty."

"I look ridiculous."

"Come on, Rey-rey. If you end up marrying him one day, think how grateful you'll be."

"By the gods, Eliya! Marriage? You're getting quite ahead of yourself."

"I'm just being prepared. Who knows what might happen?"

"Definitely not that."

"Fine," she says. "When he gives you the night of your life, then you'll be grateful to me."

"Eliya!"

"What? Now don't tell me that's unlikely to happen. He looks like he would be good in bed, too."

How exactly she's come to that conclusion, I have no idea. Nor do I wish to know.

I bury my head in my hands. If I weren't red before, I certainly am now.

"What's the matter with you?" she asks.

"Your behavior is the matter."

"I never knew you were such a prude."

"I'm not."

"When was the last time you had sex, anyway?"

"We are not having this conversation here!"

"Why not? A tavern is a perfectly good place to discuss such matters."

I bolt up from my seat, fearing she will find a way to worsen this conversation. "Give me the money," I say, holding out my hand. "I'll get the drinks." Right now, I would do anything to shut her up. Even approaching Nolan is preferable to continuing this discussion.

Eliya grins triumphantly at me. "*Conparios.*" Her velvet coin purse appears in her hands. Metal clinks as she chucks it over to me. I catch it clumsily.

"What do you want?"

"Wine. Any will do."

With a deep breath, I head toward Nolan's counter.

Soon I will become a Mage of Nolderan—provided I pass my trials, of course. That means I can order drinks from a bartender. No matter how handsome he may be.

Despite my silent words of encouragement, my hands are shaking by the time I reach him. What if I imagined him asking me to come here tonight? What if he doesn't recognize me?

I clutch Eliya's crimson coin purse tightly and hope he doesn't notice my trembling.

As soon as he finishes serving his current patron, he sweeps over to me. His head tilts to one side as he studies me.

A silence lingers between us. His emerald eyes lock with mine. Everyone else melts away. Even Eliya.

I don't dare breathe, worrying it will come out as a sudden gasp. His gaze is so intense that sparks of lightning pulse through my nerves.

With how potent this energy is, I wonder whether he too can feel it.

I break our stare to glance back over my shoulder. Eliya is watching us. When she catches my eye, she pretends to drink from an imaginary goblet.

That's right. Drinks.

I turn back to Nolan. His eyes haven't strayed from me. My breath catches in the back of my throat. Surely he doesn't gaze at all his customers like this?

"I . . ." Words fail me. I clear my throat and try again, this time with more force. "I was wondering whether I could have two goblets of white wine, please."

"Will it be *Vedemia*, *Jasone*, or *Enti Adega*?" he asks, his eyes remaining fixed on me as he speaks.

"Um, *Vedemia*, please."

"For both of you?"

"Yes, please."

Only now does his gaze leave me. He reaches behind him for two goblets and a bottle of *Vedemia*. He pulls out the cork. Before I can wonder whether he remembers me, he asks, "How's your arm doing?" He tilts the bottle over the goblet nearest him, and the bubbly liquid flows within.

"Better," I reply. "Thanks for asking."

Nolan inclines his head in a slight nod, while I inwardly curse myself. Why can't I think of anything better to say?

He finishes pouring wine into the first goblet and reaches for the other. "Reyna Ashbourne, wasn't it?"

I grin widely at him remembering my name, and probably end up making myself look like a fool. But I suppose I shouldn't be surprised he remembers me, since he was sober. Or at least, I think he was.

"Yes, and it was Nolan, right? Nolan Elmsworth?"

"Indeed, it is," he replies, popping the cork back into the bottle.

He's almost finished serving me, and so far all we've discussed is my arm and our names.

As Nolan turns to place the bottle of *Vedemia* back onto the shelf behind him, I glance over at Eliya. She shoots me a thumbs-up. I'm sure if she actually heard our conversation, it would instead be a thumbs-down.

And if she knew how little progress I've made, she would kill me.

"So," I say as he slides the two goblets toward me, "how much will that be?"

"Nothing," he replies.

"Nothing? How can wine cost nothing?" Unless you steal it from Garon Whiteford's warehouses, that is.

"It's on the house."

I gawk at him, having no idea how my terrible flirting has caused him to buy drinks for us. Well, not exactly to buy drinks since he owns all the alcohol here. But free drinks, nonetheless. "You're sure?"

A smile dances on his lips. It makes my heart flutter. "Why wouldn't I be?"

"Because I already cost you a fortune in wine last night." Eliya would clip me round the ear and tell me I should just graciously smile back, lest he decides to charge us for the drinks.

"I can think of far worse reasons to crash a cart full of wine," he says.

Is he flirting with me? Or am I imagining it? This time I don't have a single drop of wine to blame my imagination on.

A blush spreads across my cheeks, and I dip my head before he can notice. Like a bumbling fool, I almost spill the goblets over as I reach for them. Fortunately, Nolan steadies them in place, preventing a disaster.

"Thank you," I mumble as I turn away. With my words spoken so softly, I don't know whether he hears them.

I start back over to Eliya and my wobbly legs threaten to spill the wine all over my dress. At least it's only white wine. After several strides, I begin to think of better responses. Such as that I can also think of far worse reasons to be crashed into. If I'd said that with a coy smile on my lips, I might have actually gotten somewhere.

But am I even trying to get anywhere at all?

I don't look Eliya in the eye as I sit opposite her. Gingerly, I slide one of the metallic goblets across to her.

"Well?" she demands, drumming her fingers against the table.

"Well, what?" I ask, quickly lifting the goblet to my lips so that it covers most of my face. I keep it there for as long as I reasonably can.

"How did it go?"

I take several long sips of wine before I have no choice but to set it back down and face Eliya. "Um, well. I think?"

Eliya narrows her eyes, clearly unconvinced.

"He gave us free drinks," I say.

She leans back in her chair, folding her arms. Surprisingly, she has not yet touched her wine. "Good. What else?"

"He asked about my arm."

Her eyes narrow a little more. Clearly that wasn't the response she was hoping to hear.

"He remembered my name."

"And?"

"And . . ." I tap my lower lip, which is moist from the wine gathered there. "And that was it."

Eliya's forehead meets the table with a thud. I glance around to see if anyone is staring at us. Luckily, no one is. Not even Nolan.

"You absolute idiot!" she roars. The wooden table thankfully muffles her voice. "By the gods, you're a lost cause."

My shoulders sag, and my fingers toy with the fine details engraved into the bottom of the metallic goblet.

"Right well," Eliya continues, sitting up in her chair and taking a long sip of wine, "since you've ruined tonight's plans, we have no choice but to come back here tomorrow."

"Can't we just brush this off as incompatibility?"

Her temple twitches. "No," she growls into her wine. "I know you like him. Or else you wouldn't have stood there, blushing and gawking at him like a fool."

"Was I really?" I ask with a groan.

"Don't worry," she replies. "He was especially smiley while talking to you, so I can tell he also likes you."

"That wasn't what I was worrying about," I mutter. Still, her words send my stomach somersaulting. And a part of me hopes her assessment is accurate.

"Anyway," I say a moment later, "does this mean we can go now?"

"Fine. But we're coming back here tomorrow night." She gives me a pointed look.

We drink the rest of our wine. Eliya finishes hers in mere minutes. She drinks it as though it's water.

"You're so slow," she complains, gesturing to my goblet. In my defense, only a small amount remains.

I push the goblet over to her. "You drink it then."

She does and finishes it in a single gulp. Then she gets to her feet. "Right then. Let's go."

I stand from my chair and follow her through the tavern. We weave past the surrounding tables as we head to the door. But I only make it halfway across the room before a hand snags my wrist.

I turn to face Nolan.

Now that there isn't a counter between us and his fingers are wrapped around my wrist, the rush of energy is as overwhelming as I remember last night.

"Reyna," he murmurs, "can I borrow you for a moment?"

Enthralled by his emerald eyes, I find myself nodding.

Nolan leads me farther back into the tavern, just behind the stairs. Here, we are out of everyone else's earshot.

I stare at him, losing myself in his mesmerizing gaze. I barely notice as he begins to speak.

"I know you said you needed to leave early because of the Trial of Mind in the morning, but I was hoping you would stay a little longer. We didn't get much of a chance to speak tonight."

I swallow, glancing down at his leather boots.

"If I offended you before, then I do apologize."

"Why would you have offended me?" I ask.

He opens his mouth but then closes it, seeming to have nothing to say. I feel terrible. He's probably worrying about how I abruptly left after he said that he could think of worse reasons to crash a wine cart.

"I wasn't offended," I say quietly. "I just didn't know how to respond."

I suppose when in doubt, honesty is always the best policy.

A light smile twitches on his lips. He takes a step closer. "You weren't sure what to say?"

I try to step back, but the wall behind me prevents me from moving any farther away. Any thoughts of escape die when he closes the distance between us so much that I can feel his warm breath against my cheeks. The air pulses with vigorous energy. With anticipation.

My hands are clammy, and my heart thumps wildly in my chest. I hope it isn't loud enough for him to hear.

"You ran away so quickly," he continues, his eyes tracing over my face, "that I didn't have the chance to ask you something."

At first, my voice fails me. Fortunately, it comes rushing back before I can yet again make myself look like an idiot. "What is it you wish to ask me?"

He pauses. Many heartbeats pass between us. Then he finally asks, "What are you doing on Thursday evening?"

"Nothing," I reply. "Aside from sleeping early so I'll be well rested for my final trial. Why do you ask?"

"I was wondering whether you would like to join me for dinner?"

I blink, momentarily taken aback by his question. It's hard to believe he's asking me this. That this isn't some cruel joke.

"Yes," I breathe, before sense can return to me, "yes, I would love to."

"Great," he says with a smile. "Then meet me here at six o'clock on Thursday evening."

"Won't you be busy working?"

"I have enough staff to handle things for a few hours."

"In that case, thank you."

"For what?" he asks.

"For inviting me to dinner."

"And thank you for accepting my invitation." He steps away, and I suddenly realize how cold it is without him so near. "Best of luck with your trial tomorrow."

I thank him again and start toward the door. Eliya is waiting there, a curious look spreading across her face.

When we burst out of the tavern, she turns to me and exclaims, "You'd better tell me exactly what just happened. Every last detail!"

And so, I tell her everything.

CHAPTER 27

ARCHMAGE GIDSTON LEADS US DOWN a dark, steep staircase. Aether crystals glisten along the walls, illuminating the steps ahead of me. I can see little beyond that, aside from the back of Eliya's head. Everything else is lost to the shadows.

With the passage being so narrow, we're forced to walk in single file. My palms skim across the coarse stone walls as I try to maintain my balance. When we first started down here—the South Western exit of the Arcanium's atrium—there was an ornate metallic banister to guide our way. But now we are so far underground that the smooth steps have turned to jagged rock and I stumble over them.

Thousands of steps lie between us and our trial, just like with the Trial of Heart. At least this time, the stairs are going down.

Eventually, we reach the end.

A vast cave stretches out before us. Aether crystals protrude from the walls, bright enough to illuminate every inch of the chamber.

Archmage Gidston strides to the stone altar at the center. An enormous hourglass floats above it. Instead of sand, aether dust fills the lower bulb, and an ornate golden frame houses the glass.

"Today, you will all undertake your second Mage Trial, the Trial of Mind."

No one dares to breathe as Lorette speaks. Down here, there's no wind. When she pauses, an unnatural silence fills the cave.

"These tunnels form an underground maze beneath the Arcanium," she continues, gesturing around us. Aside from the stairs, there are five exits. Only darkness lies beyond them.

She points ahead at the largest exit, the one directly opposite the stairs. "Though the tunnels are long and winding, they all converge back to this chamber, and you will have an hour to return. If you cannot escape the maze within that time, you will fail your trial. As this is the Trial of Mind, you must use your wits to solve the many magical obstacles which will stand in your way."

If I pass today, I will be one trial away from graduating the Arcanium and becoming a Mage of Nolderan. Though I do not know what obstacles await me inside this maze, I know many adepts fail this second trial. Especially compared to the first. I can't be one of those adepts. I can't fail.

Archmage Gidston's eyes narrow as she scans across us. "Do you all understand what this trial requires?"

We answer her question with nods. Except for Kaely. She raises her hand.

"Yes, Adept Calton?"

"What if we meet other adepts inside the maze?" Kaely asks. "What are the rules for interacting with peers?"

I clench my jaw. I have little doubt she is wondering whether the two of us will cross paths. And if we do, whether she will be permitted to strike me.

A few adepts murmur at Kaely's words. But they're probably more concerned about what it means for their trial, rather than if it allows them to attack their rivals.

"That is a good question," Lorette says. "Though you will each start from different entrances, many of the tunnels overlap, and it is inevitable some of you will meet each other inside the maze. As this is a Mage Trial, the usual rules of the Arcanium do not apply. Whether you choose to see a fellow adept as a friend or as a foe is entirely your discretion."

Wonderful. Not only do I need to worry about the magical obstacles scattered throughout the maze, but also Kaely, who will look for every opportunity to attack me and to ensure I don't pass this trial.

The corners of Kaely's lips curl with vicious satisfaction.

I do my best to ignore her murderous expression, but a terrifying thought snakes through my mind.

If the Arcanium's rules don't apply on this trial, then does that mean Kaely wouldn't be punished if she killed me?

Nausea sweeps over me. Today, failure isn't my only concern, but also death.

"Are there any other questions?"

No one speaks or raises their hand.

"Good," Archmage Gidston says. "Then we will begin."

Her indigo sleeve flutters as she gestures to the exit on the far right. "Reyna Ashbourne, Lorea Bayford, Keion Bridwell, Kaely Calton, and Myron Dalston. The five of you are to follow me to your starting positions. The rest of you are to wait here." With that, she turns and marches into the tunnel.

"Good luck," Eliya whispers.

"You too," I say with a brief smile and then hurry after Archmage Gidston and the other four adepts.

The passage is narrow, like the stairs. Since there are no aether crystals in here, Archmage Gidston murmurs *iluminos* and conjures an orb of dazzling light. Though it's bright enough to light our path, the uneven ground remains shadowed. I take each step with great care, careful not to crash into Myron, who's in front of me.

"Feeling nervous?" Lorea hisses from behind.

"Yeah," I reply, glancing back at her. "A bit. You?"

"Just a little."

We soon arrive at another chamber, this one smaller than the previous. Five more tunnels surround us. All are shielded with aether. The humming barriers are so thick I can't see the path beyond.

"Reyna Ashbourne," Archmage Gidston says, pointing to the first tunnel on our left. "You will start here. Please take your position."

I do as she instructs and make my way over to the first tunnel. The barrier's surface ripples and swirls, bursting with magic. Even this close, the path ahead is obscured.

"Lorea Bayford." Archmage Gidston gestures to the next tunnel, and she continues to work clockwise until she has allocated everyone else's starting positions.

"A thunderclap will mark the start of the trial," she says, once we are all waiting before our designated tunnels, "and the aether barriers will fall.

Your hour will begin at that precise moment. I wish you all the best of luck on this second trial."

With that, she heads back into the main chamber.

"Good luck, Ashbourne," Kaely sneers when Archmage Gidston is gone. "You're going to need it."

More focused on passing the Trial of Mind, I ignore Kaely and don't bother with a retort. As I stare at the aether barrier ahead of me, I feel her glare burning into me, but she says nothing else.

Archmage Gidston's voice echoes from down the tunnel as she leads the next group to their starting locations. I can't decipher the names since she's muffled by the cavernous stone walls, but I know Eliya can't be among them. Her surname is Whiteford, so she will be in the last group, along with Koby.

Another moment passes.

Then I hear Archmage Gidston taking the third group of adepts over to their starting locations. There will only be one more group after this.

Gravel crunches beneath another adept's boots. My nerves are so taut that I spring to action, convinced the trial has begun. But the aether barrier still hums in front of me, barring my path. I place my hand flat against it. The magic vibrates beneath my touch. Its tingling is so intense it feels like tiny needles are pricking my palm. I jolt back.

Archmage Gidston announces the final group. Her voice fades as she leads them away.

Any moment now, the trial will begin.

My heart pounds with anticipation. Adrenaline spikes through my veins. The trial hasn't even begun, and I already feel as though I will burst apart. The wait drags on, and I begin to wonder whether the trial will ever begin, or if we will be waiting forever and—

Thunder booms. It comes from everywhere, ringing out so loudly the cave walls tremble.

A crack follows. The aether barrier shatters. But it doesn't fall like glass. It dissolves into glittering dust and scatters into the shadows.

The Trial of Mind has begun.

I plunge into the darkness. The aether barrier repairs behind me, preventing my retreat. My footsteps drum wildly against the stone path, but I only manage a few strides before I come to a halt, realizing that I can't see anything.

"*Iluminos.*" My magic explodes into a brilliant orb. Its rays penetrate the shadows. The end of this path is just a few yards ahead. If I'd continued much longer, I would have collided with the wall. The tunnel forks into two paths. I glance down each, but both are shrouded with darkness. I can't tell them apart. From where I stand, they look identical.

There is no way to know which path I should take.

With a deep breath, I turn right and pray I made the right decision.

My illumination orb hovers above as I run. It casts a shadow over me, and my silhouette sprints on the wall beside me. This path leads to several more turns, and I choose each at random. Soon I worry I'm heading in circles, blindly charging through this maze of tunnels.

My path splits into three. I halt.

If I am sprinting in circles, I'm wasting precious time. I have only one hour to complete this trial, and I don't know what obstacles will hinder me.

I must think of a better way to navigate this maze. A way to recognize whether I've ventured down each path before.

Frowning, I scan over the bumpy ground, hoping to find something of use. If only I had string, or maybe seeds, to scatter across the stone. Then I could mark my path.

An idea strikes me.

"*Gelu,*" I mutter and press my palm to my boot. Ice swirls over the sole.

I return my foot to the ground. When I stride forth, frost glitters where my boot was. Hopefully, the icy footprints will last long enough for me to navigate the maze.

I continue through the tunnels, now choosing each with more confidence. But I soon run into my frozen footprints, and I curse under my breath. It seems I was definitely going in circles before I covered my boot with ice.

I trace back my tracks until I find the turning which set me into this loop, and I choose an alternative path.

My boots pound against the rocky floor. Too focused on running, I barely notice the flash of fair hair to my right.

I pause, glancing in that direction.

Myron stands there. His magenta eyes fix on me. Recalling Archmage Gidston's words, I swallow.

He isn't one of the best adepts in our year—far from it. But I don't wish to waste time fighting him. Yet if he decides to strike me first, I will have no choice in the matter.

Aether blooms in my fingers. Just in case he makes his move.

Our gazes hold for a moment longer. I wonder whether he will propose another option: to ally together and use our wits to solve the obstacles scattered throughout these tunnels. I've hardly ever spoken to him during our five years at the Arcanium, and he's one of the quieter adepts in our year, but such an alliance would be beneficial for us both.

Deciding he would have struck by now if he intended to fight, I let the aether in my hands fizzle out. I open my mouth to call over to him, but he turns and flees in the opposite direction. His cerulean robes disappear around the corner.

I roll back my shoulders. It isn't as if I needed him. An alliance would have benefited him more than me.

Knowing I've wasted several precious moments, I pick up my pace as I hurry through the tunnels. Though my icy footprints tell me I'm not going in circles, I still worry whether I'm taking the wrong path through the maze.

The stone walls open to a cave. Ornate braziers sit at each corner, and a large one lies at the center. I scan over the metallic structures and then notice the door on the other side. It blends so perfectly with the walls that, if not for the faint lines marking its edges, I wouldn't know it was there.

I stride through the cave and over to the door. Then I shove it with all my might.

To my dismay, the door doesn't so much as creak.

I grit my teeth and try again, but it's still no use.

Realizing brute strength won't work, I murmur *ventrez* and conjure a wind spell, hoping a gale will blow aside the door.

Again, it has no effect.

With a sigh, I turn to the braziers. It was foolish to expect that force alone would open the door.

What I'm meant to do with these braziers, I have no idea.

I study them for a while longer. Braziers are usually filled with fire, so does that mean lighting them will open the door?

While I doubt it's that simple, I suppose there's little harm in trying. And maybe even a failed attempt will lead me closer to figuring out what I need to do. There's no point standing here and staring at the braziers while time is ticking away.

"*Ignis*," I say and send flames into each of the five braziers.

My conjured flames dance in the braziers. I hold my breath, hoping I've somehow overcome this obstacle—unlikely though it may be.

But then the flames surge up, leaving the braziers behind. They gather into a roaring inferno. Fire rushes toward me.

"*Aquis*!" I shriek.

Water blasts from my palms and crashes into the flames. It sends them spilling out into the chamber. The remnants of the fireball collide with the stone walls, charring them.

If I had been a moment slower, I would be nothing but ash right now.

Shock strangles me. I double over and gasp for breath until I recompose myself.

I turn to the braziers again and study them more carefully. Clearly lighting them isn't the solution.

I sigh and lean back against the charred wall behind me. Since this first attempt nearly killed me, I'm hesitant to try again. The next attempt could mean death.

But I also can't waste any more time.

I need to think of something clever. And fast.

I scan over the room, wondering what else I can try. I hope to find a hidden clue somewhere—maybe a riddle—but I find none. Only plain stone walls surround me. The room is empty aside from the five braziers.

Though my last attempt failed miserably, I remain convinced I must somehow light them to unlock the door. But if not fire, what else?

My eyes narrow at the center brazier. It's larger than the rest, indicating its superiority. There must be a reason.

Think, Reyna. Think.

I chew on my lip, desperation clouding my mind, and squeeze my eyes shut. I can hear ticking in my ears. But thinking about the time will only distract me and waste more minutes. I need clear thoughts. Not panicked ones.

My gaze trails across to the door. If only I could blast it open. Though the wind spell failed miserably, what about aether? After all, it's far more powerful than the four elements—

That's it!

The largest brazier must represent aether, while the four smaller ones represent the elements. Maybe that means I must light the center brazier with aether.

I draw on my magic and watch it swirl in my fingers. A part of me fears I will be wrong yet again. That this attempt will fail and the spell will retaliate.

But if I don't try . . .

Before I can change my mind, I whisper, "*Volu.*"

The aether follows my command. Violet light drifts to the center brazier and settles within. My jaw tenses as the aether flickers, and I pray my guess is right.

Several moments pass. More aether whirs in my fingers, ready to conjure a shield in case the magic inside the brazier strikes back at me.

But nothing happens.

The violet light remains within the brazier.

Hope soars within my chest. It worked!

I turn to the other braziers. Fire, water, earth, and air must go inside each. But in which order? Placing the wrong element inside the braziers will cause my magic to retaliate.

Water defeats fire, and fire defeats air. Because of that, I'm certain water and air must go on either side of fire. First, I need to decide which brazier to place fire inside. And if I choose wrongly, I risk my magic striking back.

But if I don't try, I'll never pass this trial. I've already wasted too much time here. I need to open this door as soon as possible. Or I won't make it out of this maze before the hour is up.

At least I will be prepared if my magic retaliates again. Since I'm only lighting one brazier, rather than five, there will be fewer flames to hurl at me if it does.

"*Ignis,*" I say, sending flames toward the nearest brazier.

For a moment, they hover there. Then they charge for me.

But I am prepared and cry out *aquis*, meeting the spell with a blast of water. Since these flames are less potent than the previous ones, my water spell easily douses them. Tendrils of steam pour out. I wave them away, clearing my view.

I try the brazier to my right. This time, the flames stay right where they are. Their amber light flickers inside the brazier.

I grin.

Two down, three to go.

Now I need to decide where to place water and air.

I stop before the flame-filled brazier and glance at the ones in the adjacent corners, unsure of which to pick.

In the end, I choose the left brazier. "*Aquis.*"

Water magic splashes over to the brazier. It hovers there. I ready myself to summon an earthen shield in case I've guessed incorrectly.

But the magic remains within the brazier.

I guessed correctly.

I turn to the brazier on the right. "*Ventrez.*"

Air magic flutters to the brazier. Knowing that the choice must be correct—after all, fire defeats air—I don't bother summoning flames to my fingertips.

White light shines in the brazier. I start over to the final one.

"*Tera.*"

Earth magic springs from my fingers and fills the remaining brazier with emerald light.

Magic hums. Green, red, blue, and white beams fire at the center brazier. The aether inside explodes. Violet light shoots out and strikes the stone door.

Rumbling echoes through the small room. The door rolls upward, revealing my path.

I sprint straight through.

CHAPTER 28

BEYOND THE DOOR, MORE DARK walls greet me. I turn corner after corner, my frozen footsteps indicating whether I'm heading in circles. I don't know how long has passed since the trial began. I'm certain it can't be more than half an hour, but I might be wrong.

My pace is frantic as I navigate through the winding tunnels. My breaths burn my nostrils, and my lungs greedily gasp for air. But I can't slow. If I do, I will fail.

A force crashes into me. It sends me flying into the stone wall behind. I steady myself and spin around, aether humming in my fingers. Whether they're a friend or a foe, I don't know, but I will be ready for either case.

"Ow," whines a female voice. She clutches her shoulder where we collided. Curly red hair sweeps out as she turns to me.

"Eliya!" I exclaim, grabbing her hand. While the backs of my arms hurt from where they slammed into the wall, it appears Eliya took more of the force from our crash. "Thank the gods it's you!" For a moment, I feared it was Kaely.

"Of course it's me." She rubs her shoulder. "Why do you have to hurt so much?"

"Don't run into me, then."

She wrinkles her nose at me. "You're the one who ran into me. Besides, don't you have a streak going for running into people?"

"Technically, I ran into the cart and not Nolan," I correct. "Anyway, we don't have time for idle chit-chat. Not when the clock is ticking away."

"Don't you mean the hourglass?"

I roll my eyes at her.

We hurry through the tunnels. After a few strides, Eliya glances back and gestures to the icy footprints behind us. "What a genius idea," she says in between panting. "Why didn't I think of that?"

"Thanks," I reply.

Eliya's illumination orb hovers over us, as does mine. Both our silhouettes run alongside us. Our furious footsteps and ragged breaths fill the darkness beyond.

Several turns later, we reach our next obstacle.

The path opens to a sitting room, with crimson sofas, oaken shelves filled with books, paintings of wondrous landscapes, and a crackling fireplace. The other half of the room is a perfect reflection of it.

I step toward the mirror and press my hand against it. From its cool touch, it seems to be ice rather than glass. If it is, then maybe fire will work against it.

Hopefully my magic won't retaliate against me, like it did with the braziers. At least I have Eliya here.

"Be ready to conjure a water shield," I tell her.

"What—"

Before she can finish, I weave aether into fire magic and unleash it upon the mirror. "*Ignira!*"

Flames swarm from my hands and slam into the frosty reflection. Fire licks at the ice and drops spill across the wooden floor. A hole emerges, revealing a tunnel that continues through the maze.

Just as I go to step through, the mirror freezes again. The path vanishes.

At least my magic doesn't return with a vengeance.

"Maybe it'll work if we both try?" I suggest, turning to Eliya.

She casts me a dubious look. "Somehow, I doubt it will."

"What's the harm in trying? If it works, we'll have broken through quickly. And if not, we'll just have to put our heads together and figure out how to solve it."

"Fine," Eliya says with a sigh.

The two of us conjure flames and cry out, "*Ignira!*"

Two fireballs slam into the mirror. This time the ice melts quicker, and the resulting hole is larger.

I dive toward it. But as I draw near, the mirror freezes.

"Maybe we shouldn't try that again," Eliya snorts. "In case next time you lose your fingers."

I don't turn to her as she speaks. Instead, I glare at the mirror. Like the door with the braziers, force won't break it, no matter how much magic fuels our spells.

"How do you think we can solve this one, then?" I ask.

Eliya taps her chin as she thinks. "Well, the only other obstacle I've faced so far was a door with a riddle on it."

"What did it say?"

"*What runs around the city, but never moves?*"

"Roads?"

"That's also what I first thought," Eliya replies. "But apparently that's wrong."

"Streets?" I try again.

"Same thing. And don't try guessing paths, either."

"Sewers?"

"Still wrong."

"I give up," I say with a shrug. Besides, we currently have a far more urgent matter to deal with. "What was it?"

"Walls, of course! Because walls run *around* the city, whereas roads and sewers run *through* the city. That's why they don't count!"

"Ah, I see."

Eliya shakes her head at me. "And here I was thinking I was bad at riddles. You're actually awful at them!"

"Thanks." I gesture to the surrounding room. "Now, how about you put your amazing riddle skills to use and figure out how we can solve this puzzle?"

"Right, right," Eliya says, scanning across the room and the mirror.

I take to searching our surroundings. I move aside the books on the shelves and lift the round, embroidered pillows which lounge about on the crimson sofas, hoping to find a clue hidden somewhere. Maybe a scrap of paper with a riddle or instructions written on it. But I find nothing. Not even when I pick up the book resting on the mantelpiece. It's a biography of Nolderan's founder, Delmont Blackwood. The pages are old and dusty.

"Wait," Eliya says as I go to return it to the mantelpiece.

With the book still in my hands, I turn to face her. "What?"

"That's it!"

"What's it?" I ask.

"Look, look!" she exclaims, bouncing up and down. She points to our reflection in the icy mirror.

"Where?"

"Look at the table in the mirror."

I do as she says. My gaze falls onto the reflection of the low table. On it lies the same book as the one in my hands. But in the reflection, I clutch only air.

"I see," I reply. "Since this book differs in the mirror, it must have something to do with how we need to solve this puzzle. But what do you think we're supposed to do with it?"

"Maybe we need to place it on the table, just like it is in the mirror?"

I do as she suggests. Nothing happens.

With a groan, I lift the book. But this time, my reflection is also holding it. I pause, frowning at myself in the mirror.

"I think we did something," I muse, turning back to Eliya. "When I first picked up the book from the mantelpiece, I wasn't carrying it in the mirror. Now after placing it on the table, my reflection is also holding it. So, that means we must have done something right. But what I don't understand is why it's still not letting us pass?"

"Maybe there are other items out of place? What if we need to match them all to the reflection?"

"That could be it."

We search high and low through the rest of the room, comparing every item with its reflection.

I check the shelves again. This time, I notice a few books out of order, so I rearrange them to match the mirror. Meanwhile, Eliya moves the candle on the cabinet to the mantelpiece, just as it appears in the reflection.

A crack rumbles behind us. The mirror shatters.

"*Muriz!*" I cry. Aether encases us both. Shards of ice fling at us. The edges of each are sharp and would tear us to shreds, if not for the aether shield.

When the barrage of frozen shards ceases, I let the aether shield fizzle out. The way is clear, and ice crunches beneath my boots as I stride into the tunnel. Eliya follows me.

The wooden floor returns to coarse stone. After we pass the frozen debris, I notice that the icy magic on my boot has faded away.

"Wait," I call to Eliya, who is sprinting on ahead. "I need to enchant my boot again. The spell has worn off."

"All right," she says, coming to a stop.

I lift my foot and press my palm to the bottom of my boot. "*Gelu.*" At my command, frost envelops the sole. Now when I walk, my footsteps once again mark the stone path with ice.

"Right," I say, jogging over to Eliya. "Let's go."

We hurry through the endless tunnels, retracing our footsteps if we end up doubling back on ourselves. By now, we must be well over halfway through the trial—maybe forty minutes. But it could be more than that. Maybe fifty minutes have passed, leaving us with ten minutes to navigate through the maze. Perhaps only five remain.

And I'm uncertain how far we are through the maze. Maybe we will reach the end at any moment. Or maybe we are heading deeper and deeper into the tunnels.

I do my best to ignore those thoughts of failure and focus on the path ahead. At least I can be certain we aren't going in circles, thanks to my—

"*Ignira!*" a shout booms to my left.

A fireball hurls toward us.

"*Aquir'muriz!*" I hastily throw a water shield in front of Eliya and me. She does the same, reinforcing our defenses.

The fireball slams into our shields. I grit my teeth and channel more magic into the spell so that it holds the relentless flames at bay.

Through our combined efforts, the fireball is extinguished. Steam fills the tunnel.

Through the haze, it's hard to identify who attacked us. I can only see their blurred silhouette and the illumination orb floating above them.

But there is only one adept arrogant enough to attack the two of us together, to risk their own future just to sabotage mine.

"*Ventrez,*" I mutter, waving my hand. A wind blows down the tunnel, dispersing the steam and revealing the adept who stands there.

Kaely.

CHAPTER 29

KAELY'S BRAID FLUTTERS IN MY conjured breeze. Malice burns in her magenta eyes.

She seeks to destroy me once and for all.

"Is now really the time for this?" I spit.

Kaely strides through the tunnel and closes the distance between us. "Now is the only time for this. To settle our debts and ensure that someone as undeserving as you does not become a Mage of Nolderan." Her gaze snaps across to Eliya. "But you may go. Continue through the tunnels, pass this trial. I have no quarrel with you."

Eliya's jaw tightens. "That's a shame. Since I have a quarrel with you."

Kaely snorts an unhumorous laugh. "So be it."

Aether sparks in her fingers. In the next heartbeat, it turns to earth magic, swirling like gaseous emeralds inside her palms.

"*Tera!*" Kaely calls, her voice echoing through the shadows. The green light slams into the ground a few paces ahead of us. It burrows into the stone and digs out an enormous chunk. A chasm is left in its wake. Kaely raises the rock high into the air and hurls it at me.

But aether is already blooming in my fingers. I weave it into air magic. White light whirs in my hands.

"*Tempis!*" I shout.

My wind spell rushes forth to meet the boulder. The violent vortex slashes through the rock like a storm of daggers. Pebbles rain on us as my magic erodes the boulder and reduces it to rubble.

Before Kaely can launch another attack, Eliya takes the offensive. "*Gelu'gladis!*"

Ice shoots out from Eliya's fingers, forming a frozen sword.

"*Ignir'muriz!*" A wall of flames wraps around Kaely, preventing Eliya's icy attack from reaching her. The fire licks the frozen blade until it's nothing but droplets. The remnants spray across the tunnel's walls.

"*Ignir'quatir!*" Kaely roars.

Her fiery wall explodes. The flames spread out in all directions. The inferno scorches the surrounding stone walls and hurdles toward us with as much rage.

I barely have enough time to process the rushing flames, let alone conjure a shield. I cry out *aquir'muriz* and do my best, converting aether to water magic as swiftly as I can.

The resulting defense is paper thin. The flames blaze through it as though it's merely air.

Boiling heat slams into me. I collide with the ground. The back of my head strikes the stone first, and pain jolts through me like white-hot lightning. But that pales in comparison to the flames which threaten to gnaw on me until I am nothing but ash.

"*Aquis! Aquis!*" I scream, desperately trying to extinguish the fire engulfing me.

It takes two blasts of water before the flames die down and I can roll away. The embers at the front of my robes are snuffed out as I press my chest against the cool stone and suffocate them.

Footsteps ring out as Kaely approaches. I struggle to push myself upright. Specks of darkness scatter across my vision. Agony courses through the back of my head.

My cheek presses against the coarse stone as I turn to look at Eliya. She seems to be faring better, probably because Kaely aimed her attack at me. Though Eliya was also flung off her feet, the flames were more merciful to her. Her robes are singed, but she staggers upright and manages to stand. Unlike me. My arms fail to even push me into a sitting position.

Kaely halts before me. Smugness distorts her expression. "And here I thought you might actually put up a fight—"

"*Telum!*" comes Eliya's cry.

A blast of aether flies from her hands.

"*Muriz.*" A powerful shield encases Kaely and absorbs Eliya's blast. "*Quatir.*" The shield erupts.

Aether surges toward Eliya. She cries *tera'muriz* and hastily shapes the ground into a barrier.

But when the explosion slams into her defense, the earthen shield shatters. Pebbles fling out. Some scatter across me.

Eliya stumbles back, unable to defend herself from Kaely's next spell. "*Gelu'vinclair.*"

Frost spreads across the floor, thickening as it reaches Eliya's feet, and shackles her in place. The icy chains spiral up to her knees and then to her chest, rendering her firmly rooted.

All I want is to leap onto my feet. To face Kaely and prove I am not this weak. But my flesh is raw from the flames and my muscles protest at every movement. As does my head, which is rapidly plummeting into oblivion.

Eliya opens her mouth to cry out another spell. But before she can, Kaely calls *laxus* and teleports across the chasm she created. She appears in front of Eliya.

Kaely tears off the violet ribbon securing her braid and wraps it around Eliya's mouth. Her brown hair unravels in thick waves. She knots the ribbon in place. Now all of Eliya's spell-words are muffled. No magic springs to her fingers.

Eliya scowls at her, rage blazing in her expression. Kaely tilts her head as she studies her, amusement glinting in her eyes.

She doesn't spend long staring at Eliya, though. She soon turns to me, a venomous sneer plastered across her face.

"Even two against one, you cannot beat me. You are this weak, and yet you believe you deserve to become a Mage of Nolderan?"

My nails claw against the coarse stone, cracking from the force. A desperate growl escapes from the back of my throat. I barely recognize it as my own. It sounds too pathetic to belong to me.

"Look at you," Kaely continues with a dark laugh. "You're so useless I didn't even need to break a sweat to defeat you and your friend. Yet all of our tutors favor you. Even Archmage Gidston. How can they possibly think someone this weak is better than me?"

I hate that I can't deny her words. I *am* weak.

When Heston attacked Nolderan and murdered my mother, I wasn't strong enough to save her. Over these past three years, I have dedicated myself to becoming the best mage I can, but despite all my hard work, I still stand no chance against Kaely. All those times we dueled inside the arena, when I thought we might be at least equals, I was so terribly wrong. With Archmage Gidston there, she was always holding back the true extent of her murderous intent, but today there was nothing stopping her from unleashing her full power against me. Even with Eliya's help, I was unable to defeat her.

And if I stand no chance against someone like Kaely, how can I protect those I love from the horrors of dark magic?

Fury courses through my veins. My blood boils like wildfire. When I squeeze my eyes shut, I can see Arluin falling at the end of that narrow street—Heston standing over his too-still body. My mother's face turning to me. Life fading from her eyes, along with the magenta glow of aether. Shadows suffocating her, swarming into her mouth and nostrils, chaining her soul to Heston's will and warping her into a wraith.

Before I can realize, aether is brimming within me, flooding from my fingers and renewing my strength.

The pain through my head, my scorched skin—they all become nothing. They are insignificant compared to the anguish scarring my heart. Even after three long years, these torturous wounds have not healed. They have only festered.

Kaely doesn't know pain. She has never watched helplessly as a monster murdered those she loves, unable to save them. And yet she dares to mock me, to stare down at me with that disgusting smugness.

My fists tighten.

Ignira.

My lips don't move as I cast the spell. The words ring through my mind, drowning out every other thought.

Flames spin from my fingers, gathering into an enormous fireball. The inferno roars through the tunnel as it charges at Kaely. Without the restriction of spell-words, the magic is wild and unbridled.

Kaely is caught off-guard. When the fireball reaches her, she has drawn no aether to her fingers.

She is entirely defenseless.

Though she screams *aquis* and fights off the flames which threaten to devour her, I refuse to let her escape so easily. We will settle this once and for all. Never again will I allow her to belittle me.

I weave fire and earth magic together into a fizzling orb of rubies and emeralds. "*Magmus!*" I hiss, flinging the spell into the stone beneath me.

My magic eats away at the rock and melts it into furious lava. I launch the molten earth at Kaely while she is still fending off my fireball.

The lava encases her and cocoons her in fire. I hear her calling out *aquir'muriz*, and then her shouts fall silent. The magma hardens into dark, polished stone.

Dread pools in the pit of my stomach.

What if I took this too far? What if I killed her?

I shake my head. Kaely can't be dead. I only caught her by surprise with my fireball. The reason I can't hear her must be because the wall surrounding her is too thick. When I stop, I'm sure I can hear her muffled shouts. She's probably buried deep beneath the rock, furiously trying to battle her way out. And if I delay, she will burst through and strike me with all her wrath.

I hurry to Eliya, who is still chained in icy shackles. I untie the violet ribbon from her mouth and press my fingers to the center of her forehead. "*Mundes.*"

My spell breaks the enchantment, and the frozen chains shatter. Shards of ice heap around our feet.

Eliya stares at me with widened eyes. "Did you cast that fireball without any spell-words?"

I lift my head in a slight nod.

"Reyna!" she exclaims. "If the spell slipped out of your control, it could have killed us all! Or it could have drained all the aether from your blood!"

"I know the risks," I snap. We all do. Never casting magic without spell-words is a rule taught to every adept on the first day of our enrollment. "What choice did I have? Kaely would have defeated us. We would have both failed this trial."

Which we still might, if we linger here for much longer.

I don't wait to hear Eliya's response. I grab her wrist and pull her down the tunnel.

CHAPTER 30

As WE RUN, EACH STRIDE sends pain ricocheting through my body. Kaely has inflicted many injuries upon me, and my skin is scorched from her attacks. The wounds are worsening with every passing second. The tunnel's stone walls sway around me.

Only the determination of passing this trial and becoming a mage keeps me on my feet. I fear I will collapse at any moment. We need to finish this trial. And fast.

We say nothing as we hurry through the darkness, the glow of Eliya's illumination orb lighting our path. Our labored breaths echo through the shadows.

I don't know how much longer we have, how much farther we must run before we will reach the end of this maze. With every turn we take, I hope to see Archmage Gidston standing there. But no matter how much I will to see her indigo robes and neat platinum hair, she does not appear.

A sudden wave of fatigue crashes into me, threatening to drown me.

I clutch the nearest wall, my palms scraping over the coarse rock.

"Reyna?" Eliya says, shaking my shoulders.

I don't answer her. Patches of void eat into my vision. I feel myself falling. Eliya's hands steady me. I stop falling.

"Reyna? Can you hear me?" Her voice rings through my ears like a relentless drum. My temples throb in response.

I want to say something, but I can't. Everything requires more energy than I can give. Even breathing taxes me.

"*Conparios.*" Through my half-closed eyelids, I see violet light bursting in Eliya's hands. When it fades, a vial of ruby red liquid emerges. She tears out the stopper and presses the cool glass rim to my lips. "You need to drink. Please, Reyna."

My mouth parts. She tips the vial and sends the potion pouring down my throat. It has a metallic, alcoholic taste which fizzes on my tongue. I choke on the liquid. Some of it slides down my chin. Eliya wipes it away with the back of her sleeve.

"*Evanest,*" she says, sending the empty bottle glittering away into a cloud of aether.

The potion slips down my gullet, burning me from the inside out. Where the warmth touches, energy sparks. Adrenaline surges through my veins. Everything still spins around me, but I no longer feel weak. I push myself from the wall. My senses are so heightened that even my own breathing sounds too loud.

The potion I drank was an Elixir of Flurry, and it makes my reflexes sharper than ever. Even my thoughts are unnaturally rapid. But the potion's effects will not persist for long. It might grant me ten minutes, if I am lucky. I hope it will be enough time for us to navigate through the rest of the maze. When the elixir wears off, I am likely to collapse.

"How do you feel?" Eliya asks, peering at me.

"Fine for now," I reply, the words bursting from my mouth so quickly they jumble together into one syllable. "Let's go before it wears off."

We continue racing down the tunnel, desperately seeking the end. Now I feel no fatigue, even though I am sprinting far faster than I normally can. I seem to see the uneven peaks and troughs in the stone before they appear and leap right over them. Eliya, whose reflexes are at a normal speed, begins to fall behind. At each corner, I wait for her to catch up.

The tunnel arrives at another cave, much like the first one I faced inside this underground maze. A stone door lies at the far side, and a golden altar sits in the center. As we draw near, it gleams in the radiance of Eliya's illu-mination orbs. Two candles sit on either side of the altar's polished bowl. Both are lit. The conjured flames flicker, burning for eternity.

We stride past the altar and halt at the stone door. Words are etched into its surface, rippling with aether.

Before you may enter,
Look upon me with great care,
On my words and nothing more.
Only those with courage,
Dare to pay my price.

We both silently read the words and then exchange glances.

"Another riddle," Eliya says with a sigh.

"I thought you were good at them?"

"I never said I was good at them, just that you were bad at them."

I would pull a face at her, but my thoughts are too fast, spiraling out of control. The door's words echo over and over in my mind, forming a rhythm so relentless I can barely think.

Read carefully. Pay the price.

I read the riddle again and again until the shimmering letters blur. Still, I do not know what price the door demands.

"Could it be money?" Eliya muses aloud.

"Maybe," I say with a shrug, having no other suggestions myself. "So, do we just say money to the door, and it will let us pass?"

"With the riddle I faced, I had to write the answer onto the door before it let me through."

"With aether?"

"Yeah, beneath the riddle."

I take a step closer to the door and murmur *volu*. Violet light radiates from my index finger, and I use it to trace each letter of 'money' into the stone. Aether glistens where I mark the stone. But as I write each letter, the previous one disappears and fades into glittering dust.

I glance back at Eliya. "It didn't work."

Her brows furrow.

If we don't break through this door soon . . .

I banish the thought. Thinking like that won't help me solve the riddle.

"Any other ideas?" I ask.

"Maybe this one is different." She holds out her palm and mutters *conparios*. Her coin purse appears, and she hurriedly pulls it open, retrieving a copper coin. She holds it up to me, and it glints in the dazzling light of her illumination orb. An outline of the Aether Tower is pressed into the coin's metallic surface. "Maybe we need to literally pay the door before it will open."

"Maybe."

Eliya tosses the copper coin at the door. It bounces off the stone with a metallic clink, but nothing happens. She swears under her breath.

I gesture to the golden altar behind us. "Surely that wouldn't be here for no reason? Maybe try placing the coin inside there?"

With a nod, Eliya hurries over to the bowl and throws the copper coin inside. The chime of metal sings through the cave.

Again, nothing happens.

Next Eliya tries emptying the entire contents of her purse: countless coppers, several silvers, and a few gold coins. Though her offering would be enough to send the streets of the Lower City into a frenzy, the door is far less impressed. It doesn't budge.

Cursing again, Eliya scoops up all her coins and returns them to her purse.

I whirl back to the door. The aether across the riddle ripples, mocking us. "It isn't money."

"You don't say," Eliya grumbles, staring down at her coin purse. "*Evanest.*" At her command, it disperses into aether.

I glare at the riddle, but it reveals no clue. "Before you may enter," I read out, wondering whether the puzzle will make more sense when spoken aloud, "look upon me with great care, on my words and nothing more. Only those with courage, dare to pay my price." Several moments pass. Despite verbalizing the riddle, I still don't know how to solve it. "What in the Abyss does it want from us?"

Eliya scrunches her face as she racks her mind. "What else would the price be? I suppose it's something we're supposed to place within the altar."

"Something that has nothing to do with wealth." I run my fingers through my hair as I think. The strands are a tangled, matted mess from the fight with Kaely. As my fingers reach the back of my head, they come across something sticky.

I pull my hand toward me, peering at the liquid on my fingers. It seems I must have hit my head hard enough to draw blood in the fight with Kaely. With the Elixir of Flurry pounding through my body, I hardly feel the pain.

The blood trickles down my finger. I stare at the crimson bead, my eyes widening. Realization slams into me.

"Blood!" I cry.

Eliya turns to me. Her expression becomes panicked as she notices the blood on my index finger. "Reyna, you're bleeding!" She clutches my shoulders, examining me carefully. "Are you all right? I didn't know you were this hurt!"

I hold the blood-coated finger up to Eliya, marveling at it. Maybe I should be concerned that I'm bleeding, but I'm far more focused on solving the riddle.

I return my gaze to the door, reading over the words once more. A grin stretches across my face, certain my guess is correct.

"Reyna?" Eliya says. "You're scaring me. Did you really hit your head this hard?"

"Don't you see?" I exclaim. "Look at the first letter of each line: *Before, Look, On, Only, Dare*. The answer is blood!"

Eliya's mouth hangs agape as she stares at the door, seeing the answer for herself. While she's busy examining the riddle, I murmur *gelu'gladis* and conjure a frozen blade. Clutching the icy hilt tightly in my hand, I stride over to the golden altar.

"What are you—"

Before she can finish, I slice the sharp edge of the frozen blade across my palm. Blood wells out from the cut. I squeeze my hand and place it over the altar, allowing several drops to splash into the golden dish.

The door rumbles, rolling upward and revealing our path.

I cast the icy blade aside, and it clatters onto the ground. I wipe my bloodied hand onto my singed cerulean robes and then grab Eliya's wrist, pulling her forth.

We are through the door even before it has fully opened, sprinting down the winding tunnels. We turn right and left, and with every corner I pray it will be the last.

Darkness clouds my vision. Even the illumination orbs behind me cannot keep it at bay. Exhaustion weighs down my legs, and intense pain burns across the back of my head. It feels like a knife is burrowing into my skull.

The Elixir of Flurry is wearing off.

My pace falters. I lean against the nearest wall, using it to support me. "Eliya," I wheeze, "I don't think I can . . ."

Eliya stops and whirls around. She hurries back to my side, clutching my shoulders and helping me to stay on my feet. "Reyna! You can't faint. Not now."

"I feel so tired," I murmur, my eyes shutting.

She grabs either side of my face. My eyes remain closed. "Please," she begs me. "You can't give up now. We have to complete this trial."

I don't respond.

"Reyna!"

When I still say nothing, she hauls me from the wall and wraps my arm around her shoulders. "We don't know whether the trial is over yet. We have to keep on going."

Her words remind me of my purpose. Remind me that if I fail this trial, I will never become a mage.

Determination washes over me, but it is weak compared to the pain. I drag my feet forth and lean my weight into Eliya. With her help, I continue down the tunnel. Our pace is slow. I stumble over the uneven edges of the stone, almost sending us both falling over. My illumination orb fizzles out, leaving only Eliya's. The tunnel is left more shadowed and harder to navigate. Not that I can see much in my current state.

Many turns later, I feel myself slipping from Eliya's shoulders. She grips me more securely, refusing to let me go. "You must keep going."

I try, but it's becoming more difficult with every stride. The urge to rest is nearly impossible to ignore. Soon Eliya is all but carrying me through the maze of tunnels.

My senses dull. Even the intense pain numbs. I'm rapidly sinking into emptiness.

Before the darkness can claim me, Eliya suddenly shouts, "Look!"

Languidly, I lift my head. Through my partially closed eyes, I see a faint light gleaming at the end of the tunnel.

"That must be the end, Reyna! It must be!"

She picks up her pace, or at least tries to. With my weight burdening her shoulders, she doesn't manage more than a brisk walk. I do my best to lighten her load, but sleep has almost claimed me. My steps falter.

"Come on!"

Eliya heaves me down the rest of the tunnel. We burst out into the chamber beyond.

Aether crystals shine brightly. Their radiance blinds me.

When my sight adjusts, I see Archmage Gidston standing there—along with many other adepts. My vision is too blurred to identify them, but I think I see Lorea and Koby among them. The golden hourglass sits at the center of the room. Barely any aether dust is left inside the top glass bulb. I don't want to think how many minutes—seconds even—we were from failing.

"Congratulations, Ashbourne and Whiteford," Archmage Gidston says. "You have both successfully passed the Trial of Mind."

"Reyna," Eliya breathes, turning to me. "We did it. We actually did it!"

I want to rejoice with her, but numbness spreads through my body. I can no longer feel anything, not even her shoulder beneath me. All I manage is a slight smile, and then the last of my consciousness slips away.

I descend into darkness.

CHAPTER 31

WHEN I WAKE, THE COARSE stone walls beneath the Arcanium are gone. Instead, my eyes are greeted by the lavish creams and golds of my room. Mr. Waddles sits on the gilded cabinet opposite me and watches me with his glassy, black eyes.

The Trial of Mind comes rushing back to me: Kaely being consumed by my lava, Eliya hauling me down the dark tunnels. We made it out in time, didn't we? Or did I dream of Archmage Gidston congratulating us on passing the trial?

Fog shrouds my mind. Clutching my temples, I push myself upright.

"Don't move."

I turn to see my father sitting on my cushioned armchair which he has moved beside my bed. Since the curtains are closed, I can't tell what the time is.

"Father? What are you doing here?"

"You need to rest." He stares at me through narrowed eyes until I lie back down. "A healer came to examine your wounds and apply Blood Balm. She said you will be fine, but that you must sleep."

"What time is it?"

"Six o'clock?"

"What?" I exclaim, my heart skipping a beat. Wasn't I supposed to be somewhere at six o'clock? No, wait. That was tomorrow night, wasn't it? Assuming I didn't sleep for longer than I think I did. "Is it still Wednesday?"

My father peers at me suspiciously. "Yes, why?"

"Because if it was Thursday night, then my last trial would be in the morning," I hastily reply. He doesn't need to know about my date with Nolan. I don't think he would mind—and if he does, it would only be because of my Mage Trials being held this week—but I don't feel like telling him. Though we are close, we don't have that kind of relationship. If my mother were still here, I would tell her in a heartbeat. She would laugh at how I ran into Nolan and broke all of his wine bottles. Her absence leaves a gaping hole in my heart, one I doubt will ever heal.

I miss her so very much.

I stare at my hands. My father is silent. His magenta eyes don't leave me, as if he fears I will collapse again. If I do, at least I'm already lying in bed.

"What about Kaely?" I ask. As I await his answer, I chew on my lip. I don't want her to be dead. Not really. If only because it would make me a murderer.

"She was in an even worse state than you," he says with a sigh. "Archmage Calton was beside himself when they found her inside a tomb of cooled magma."

"A tomb?" My lower lip trembles, betraying my emotion. "She . . . She is alive, isn't she?"

"It will be a few days before she will be able to walk. She is lucky to be alive."

I swallow down my guilt. A few tears well in my eyes, but I blink them away and blame them on all the turmoil.

"Did she pass the trial?" I ask, not meeting his gaze.

"No, she did not."

"So, she will never become a mage now?" Once, I thought such knowledge would fill me with glee. But it doesn't. It just makes me feel hollow and heavy.

He shakes his head. "She will not. I suppose that is punishment enough for her actions."

"For her actions? What do you mean? Archmage Gidston said that the usual rules didn't apply on our Mage Trials. That we wouldn't be punished for attacking each other."

"Yes, you are right. She broke no rules. As the Grandmage of Nolderan, I cannot punish her for what she did. But she nearly killed you, Reyna. And as your father, I cannot accept that."

"Well, I also nearly killed her. And I think I did a better job at it, too. I bet Archmage Calton was furious at me, wasn't he?"

"He was," my father replies. "He also tried to have you disqualified from the Mage Trials, but Archmage Gidston reminded him that the trials do not come without risk."

"I definitely passed, didn't I?" I ask, dread knotting my stomach. "I didn't imagine Archmage Gidston telling me I passed the trial?"

"No, you didn't imagine it," he says. "Though I did hear there was little time to spare." There's a sharpness to those words.

Here I am lying wounded in bed, and he's disappointed that I completed the trial too slowly. Even though I defeated Kaely, it's still not enough.

"That wasn't my fault. If Kaely hadn't attacked me, I wouldn't have needed to navigate through the rest of the maze injured and on the brink of collapsing. It was only thanks to Eliya that I made it out."

"That wasn't how I meant it."

"Then how did you mean it?"

"As you said, it wasn't your fault, and I don't believe for a second that you would have instigated the fight."

"If I hadn't passed, would you be angry with me?"

"Of course not," he says, taking my hand in his. "When the healer was examining you, for a moment I thought . . ."

That he might lose me. Just like he lost my mother.

He says none of those words, but I know he means them. I can tell by the way his brows pinch together and his eyes stare down at our hands.

I squeeze his thumb, since his hands are much larger than mine. When I was younger, the size difference was even more astonishing.

"If it's six o'clock," I say, breaking the brief silence, "shouldn't you be working?"

"I was in a meeting when Archmage Gidston called for me, and I immediately teleported over to the Arcanium."

"What happened to your meeting? Did you return to it?"

"No," he says. "I have been here all day."

"Sorry for interrupting the meeting," I mumble. "And that you had to stay here all day because of me."

"Why would you be sorry for that?"

"You probably have far more important things to do."

"I don't have more important things than you, Reyna. But you need to rest. If you don't, you will not be well enough for your final trial on Friday."

"I'll be well enough," I reply. "I promise."

"Good," he says, releasing my hand. "Then sleep."

With the sternness in his voice, I don't argue with him. I close my eyes and sink deeper into my silk sheets and soft mattress. The gentle flicking of pages comes from where my father sits. I didn't see what book it was, but I'm willing to bet it's an exceptionally old and dusty tome. I don't open my eyes to check whether I'm correct. He would scold me for that.

My stomach growls. Apparently it's loud enough for my father to hear since he chuckles.

"You haven't eaten all day," he says. "You must be hungry. I'll go and cook something for us both to eat then."

I can't remember the last time my father cooked—using his magic, of course. He's certainly never cooked anything by hand.

"Thank you," I say.

I hear him place his book onto the window ledge and stride out the room. When the door shuts behind him, I dare to open my eyes and sit up.

After cooking us both dinner, my father resumes his vigil beside my bed. Only when Eliya arrives a few hours later does he finally leave my side. Apparently she came earlier this afternoon, but I was still out cold.

"She needs to rest," my father's voice comes from the other side of the door. "And make sure she doesn't get out of bed. The injuries she has suffered today are not light."

"Yes, I understand. I was also wondering whether you would like me to keep an eye on Reyna tonight, so you can also rest?"

My father pauses.

"You're the Grandmage of Nolderan. The city cannot run without you. I promise I will take good care of her." Eliya can sound incredibly responsible when she tries. Surprisingly.

"She will need to take an Elixir of Rejuvenation on the hour if she is to make a swift recovery ahead of Friday," my father replies after a moment.

"I will make sure she takes it."

"Good. Try not to talk to her for too long, either. She must sleep."

"Yes, of course."

"And don't let that faerie dragon into her room. I don't want it disturbing her."

"I will make sure he doesn't."

With that, my father permits Eliya into my room. She shuts the door softly behind her, and his footsteps fade away down the corridor. When he's safely gone, she flashes me an exasperated look.

"I know," I groan. "He won't even let me open my eyes. I'm only allowed to drink potions and sleep."

"I can't decide whether your father is sweet or terrifying," she says, crossing the room and sitting on the cushioned armchair beside me.

"Definitely terrifying," I reply. Though my eyes are open, I don't sit up in case he suddenly decides to return.

"How are you feeling?" she asks, leaning forward. Her eyes scan over me, lingering on the many bandages wrapped around my arms and my forehead.

"I feel fine."

"Are you sure? You didn't look so good after the trial. I don't know how I managed to get you out of those tunnels."

"Thank you for that." Tears swell in my eyes, and I blink them away before they can escape down my cheeks. "If not for you, I wouldn't have passed the trial. I don't think I can ever repay you for what you did."

"Repay me?" she scoffs. "Don't be silly. You're my best friend. Why would you need to repay me? Though if you are insisting, I certainly wouldn't say no to a bottle of moon-blossom wine. And Mrs. Baxter's finest cakes."

I laugh, and so does she. But then my chest starts to hurt, and we both stop laughing.

"I thought you said you felt fine," she says, giving me a dubious look as I clutch my chest.

"I do," I wheeze. "Or at least I did until I started laughing."

"Then don't laugh. Now I see why your father told me not to talk to you for long."

I roll my eyes.

"He's right. You need to sleep."

"I'm tired of sleeping," I complain. "I've already slept all day. What time is it even?"

"Just past nine o'clock."

"I've slept for at least eleven hours. Must I really sleep more?"

"Yes," she replies, wagging her finger at me. "You absolutely must if you are to complete the last trial on Friday. The Trial of Magic will require a great deal of strength. You know that."

"I know, I know," I huff, slumping into my sheets.

"Oh, that's right," she blurts. "Don't you have a date with Nolan tomorrow night, as well?"

Grumbling, I grab a pillow and bury my face in it. The golden tassel tickles my nose.

Eliya confiscates it. "You'll knock your bandages if you're not careful."

I wrinkle my nose at her and pull the sheets over my head.

"What's the matter? Yesterday, you were excited about it."

"Yesterday, I wasn't injured," I retort. "Nor was I excited about it."

"Were too."

"Was not."

"Come on, Reyna. It'll do you some good to have some fun for once. And that's all it needs to be. If you decide you don't like him, you don't ever need to see him again. I'll even break the bad news to him, if you want. You know I'm an expert at that. But at least see how it goes first before deciding."

"I don't think I'm in any state to have fun right now."

"You've told me twice that you feel fine. And that you're tired of sleeping."

"My father won't let me leave my bed, let alone go on a date with someone I just met."

"We have an entire day until then. And your father normally works until late, doesn't he? I'll convince him to let me look after you all of tomorrow."

I press my lips together, trying to think of an excuse she can't counter. "I'm not like you," I finally settle on saying. "I don't want a long line of broken-hearted boys pining after me."

She cackles. "It is a long line, isn't it? But you won't have a long line. At least, not yet. There would only be Nolan."

It seems nothing I can say will persuade her.

She pulls the sheets from my head and tucks the edges around my shoulders. "Anyway, you have a trial and a date to recover for, so you'd better get back to sleep."

Though I know I will be unable to sleep, I don't protest any further. Eliya glares at me until I close my eyes, and I decide that she might be even more terrifying than my father.

CHAPTER 32

"AND . . . perfect," Eliya says, sliding the final hairpin into my updo. The delicate gems on the end twinkle at me in the mirror.

I glance down at myself. This time, Eliya talked me into wearing a dress even more ridiculous than what I wore to meet Nolan on Tuesday. This one is a deep mauve, with flowers embroidered into the satin. And by the gods, Eliya has pulled the corset tight. My poor breasts look as if they may burst at any moment, and the corset can't be helping my injuries. Though I've mostly healed from the Trial of Mind yesterday, I still feel rather tender. Not that I would admit it out loud.

Eliya convinced my father to attend all of his meetings today. I'm not sure what time he will come home, but I'm hoping it will be late before he does. He'll be furious if he learns that I've gone out, and if he catches me in this ridiculous dress, I will have no excuse to offer him. Eliya said she'll keep watch, but I don't know what we'll do if he arrives back before me. Maybe she'll think of a way to smuggle me into the manor without him noticing. If anyone can pull that off, it's Eliya.

My father wouldn't be wrong to be annoyed, though. I *was* badly injured, and the Trial of Magic is far more important than a date. But I also can't bear to sleep for a moment longer. At least this date gives me a reason to escape my bed.

"Don't you think I'm showing too much skin?" I ask, tearing my gaze from the mirror and turning to Eliya.

"Nonsense!" she replies, glancing over my bare shoulders and arms. Thanks to the copious layers of Blood Balm, my skin is mostly healed now. There are still some raw patches from the flames, but Eliya helped me conceal them all with illusions. The enchantment should last for a few hours. "But if you're worried about being cold, then I'll find you a shawl."

I will need a lot more than a flimsy shawl, since it's the middle of Winter, but I don't protest as Eliya starts over to my chest of drawers and rummages through them. Besides, I can simply murmur *calida* and warm myself from the inside out if I feel chilly.

"There," Eliya says, returning to me and draping a translucent pink shawl over my shoulders. "How does that look? I think it matches quite well."

I give her a hesitant nod, though the shawl doesn't hide the main problem I have with my attire—namely the excessive cleavage I'm currently exposing. "What if the corset bruises me?"

Eliya rolls her eyes. "Heavens, I didn't pull it that tight!"

"What if I can't have a normal conversation with Nolan?" I try instead.

"Why wouldn't you be able to?"

"Because what if he's too busy staring down here"—I point at my chest—"rather than my face?"

Eliya grins wickedly. "That's the entire point."

I slap her shoulder, but her laugh only grows.

"You'll thank me later," she promises me with a wink.

I scoff at her. "Anyway, I'd best get going. It's probably long past six."

"Relax," she says. "You don't want to show up too early, or he'll think you're too keen. And if you decide to break his heart, he'll be even more distraught."

Despite her words, she lets me leave my room. She follows me all the way downstairs and out the door. It's already dark outside, and the stars twinkle high above.

"Good luck," she says as I start down the few stone steps.

My stomach churns. My hands already feel clammy, and I haven't even teleported myself to The Old Dove yet. "Do you think things will go well?"

"Of course they will," she replies. "You look stunning, thanks to me."

"What if I say something stupid and make a fool out of myself?"

"Don't worry, you already made a fool out of yourself on Tuesday."

"Thanks, that really helps."

Eliya shrugs. "He still asked you out on a date, so just be yourself. Apparently he likes that. Besides, it doesn't matter what he thinks about you. What matters most tonight is your opinion of him. You're the one who needs to decide whether you like him or not. So, you have no reason to be nervous."

"Maybe that actually does help."

"Good, now go and have some fun!" She shoves me down the steps, and I almost trip over them. "But remember, we have the Trial of Magic in the morning, so don't let Nolan keep you up *all* night!"

Before I can respond, she slams the door and leaves me no choice but to continue down the steps and through the gardens.

A few faerie dragons are still tending to the flowerbeds, and when Zephyr catches sight of me, he whizzes over. His violet wings beat back and forth, and his amethystine eyes stare up at me.

"Don't look at me like that. I'm busy."

He swoops toward me and nudges my shoulder.

"I really am going to be late."

He blinks lazily at me.

I heave out a sigh and gather magic into my hands. "*Crysanthius*," I say, and the aether solidifies into glittering crystals.

Zephyr doesn't hesitate to gobble them all up, his forked tongue greedily darting out. When he's finished, I wipe my hand on my mauve skirts. Eliya would lecture me about getting faerie dragon spit all over my dress, but at least she isn't here to see. And when I peer down, the patch isn't too noticeable. Hopefully, it will soon dry.

I hurry down the gravelly path winding through our gardens, and Zephyr trails after me. When I reach the gates, I turn and frown at him.

"Zephyr, you can't come with me."

He growls in protest.

"I have a date."

He tilts his head. Though faerie dragons understand our speech perfectly well, I don't think he understands what I mean by 'date.' He probably thinks I mean the calendar kind.

"I'm meeting someone, and we're going for dinner." Only now do I realize that Nolan didn't specify where exactly we would be eating. I hope it's somewhere formal, or else I'll be extremely over-dressed. I run a hand down my face. I really shouldn't have trusted Eliya to dress me.

I'm still unsure whether Zephyr understands what I mean, since he blankly stares at me.

"Oh, and you can't let my father know I've gone out or he'll kill me. If you tell him, I won't ever conjure extra aether crystals for you again."

Zephyr swiftly bobs his head at that, his azure scales glinting in the starlight.

He thankfully doesn't follow me as the enchanted gates swing open and I step out onto the street.

When I teleport to The Old Dove, Nolan is already waiting for me outside. He leans against the paneled windows, and the tavern's wooden sign swings back and forth in the frosty wind.

Tonight he wears a vivid green doublet which matches his eyes. His black boots are as polished as always, without a single speck of dust on them. The wintry breeze tugs on his tousled golden hair.

At the sight of him, my breath catches in the back of my throat. It has only been two days since I last saw him, and yet it seems I've already forgotten how handsome he is.

I know Eliya said that I shouldn't be nervous, that tonight is about me deciding whether I like him, but I forget how to breathe when his mesmerizing emerald eyes meet mine.

"You're here," Nolan says, shattering the silence between us. To his credit, his gaze doesn't linger on my chest for long. He is far more focused on my face. Impressive, since Eliya did her best to make my breasts as prominent as possible.

I lower my eyes. "Sorry if I kept you waiting. Especially with how cold it is outside."

"No, no. Not at all." He holds his arm out to me, and I gingerly slip mine through his, linking us both together. It means that we're standing rather close, and I'm conscious of every part of my arm that touches his.

We begin down the street. A layer of frost sheens the cobblestones, and I take care not to slip. The delicately embroidered slippers on my feet provide little grip against the ice. Fortunately, Nolan's arm prevents me from sliding over the stones.

"Where are we going?" I ask.

"You'll see," he says.

"Is it a surprise?"

He chuckles. "I suppose it is."

We soon reach the end of Fairway Avenue and arrive on Lenwick Street. Nolan guides me farther into the Upper City, closer to where the Aether Tower hums above all the cobalt rooftops.

Though it's dark, it is still rather early, and we pass plenty of people on our way. Some are dressed as extravagantly as me, so no one spares me a second glance. And Nolan himself is also dressed in fine clothes. I hope that means wherever we're heading, I won't look out of place. Then again, Nolan always seems to be well-dressed.

Luckily, our destination proves to be The Shimmering Oyster, which is one of Nolderan's most luxurious restaurants. There is nowhere finer to dine than here. The guests flowing in and out of the restaurant's double doors look as though they have stepped out of a Ball. If anything, I feel underdressed compared to them.

"The Shimmering Oyster?" I exclaim, turning to Nolan as we reach the dozen steps leading up to the restaurant's entrance.

Twin baskets of ivy hang on either side of the carved doorframe. Purple azaleas add a splash of color to the green. The ivy's tendrils sway in the breeze.

"What's the matter?" he asks. "Do you not like it here?"

"No," I swiftly say. "This is my favorite place to dine." What I don't say is that I'm astonished Nolan would bring me here. The prices are incredibly steep. And hasn't he just bought a tavern? Can he really afford to take me to dinner here?

Maybe he thinks because I'm the Grandmage's daughter, I can afford to pay for us both. Maybe that's the real reason he asked me out to dinner. What he doesn't realize is that I've already spent my stipend for this month, meaning I will be unable to offer a single copper coin toward the bill. If Nolan insists on me paying, then I will have to tell the owners that my father will pay on my behalf. And then I will be in so much trouble because I should be in bed, recovering for the Trial of Magic tomorrow.

But Nolan was the one who asked me on this date, so surely he expects to pay? I know it would probably be best to clarify this with him before we sit down and eat, but I don't know how to ask politely. I should have checked on Tuesday before agreeing to come here with him. Now I fear this will end up in disaster.

"Shall we go inside?" Nolan asks, gesturing to the door.

Perhaps now would be the opportune moment to check whether he will be paying tonight, but I lack the courage to ask him. Instead I nod, and Nolan leads me up the stairs and through the open doors.

The Shimmering Oyster's interior is decorated as lavishly as I remember. Glittering chandeliers hang from the ceilings, large enough to rival the Arcanium's magnificent ones. Fine white lace decorates the tables, and small vases sit at the center of each, painted colorfully and filled with fragrant flowers. All the table legs are carved into spirals.

I haven't been here since my mother died. The three of us used to come here often, but my father hasn't suggested it over the past few years. I suppose it would feel strange without my mother with us.

Arluin took me here for dinner on the last Ranthir's Day: a day for lovers to celebrate their affections for one another. Since it was early summer, we sat out on the balcony. Tonight the balcony's doors are shut since it's the middle of winter. Though I can ward off the chill with fire magic, most guests are neither magi nor adepts.

Nolan starts over to the man behind the tall wooden stand, leading me along with him. The waiter looks up as we approach.

"Can I help you?" he asks.

"I reserved a table for six o'clock," Nolan replies.

"What's your name?" the waiter asks, rolling out his scroll and revealing a list of names scribbled across it. He holds it open with one hand and reaches for a quill with the other. He dips the nib into a pot of ink.

"Elmsworth."

The waiter pauses, scanning through his list. When he finds Nolan's surname, he strikes a line through it and returns the quill to his stand.

"Mr. Elmsworth," the waiter says with a stiff bow, "if you would like to follow me to your table."

We follow him through the restaurant. Most of the tables are full, aside from a few at the back, and the waiter escorts us to one near a large, arched window. Through the frost glazed glass, I can see the shadowed street below.

When we are seated, the waiter places a menu on our table. "Do take your time," he says. "I will return when you've had the chance to look through our menu."

With that, he turns and leaves. There's already a line of guests waiting at the entrance.

Nolan picks up the menu and holds it out to me. "Ladies first."

"Thank you," I reply, taking it from him and opening the thick, folded paper.

A variety of dishes are scrawled onto it in letters so cursive I can barely decipher what they say. My fingers drum against the table's lace cloth as I mull over the many choices.

"I really can't choose," I say, breathing a laugh. "Everything sounds so good, and they have so many new things since I last visited."

"Order as much as you want."

I glance up at him. "I can't do that."

"Why not? It's my treat."

"You're much too kind," I reply and scan over the various dishes again. In the end I decide to have clam chowder and rum-glazed salmon and hand over the menu to Nolan.

When the waiter returns, Nolan insists I order more than just a soup and main, but I decline. I don't want to take advantage of his generosity. And I feel awful for worrying that he would take advantage of my status as the Grandmage's daughter.

Another waiter soon appears with red wine and pours it into our glasses. Once he leaves, we are alone again.

Nolan gazes at me with his vivid green eyes. I instinctively reach for the menu but find it has been taken away. With nothing to hide behind, I feel terribly exposed. I wonder whether Nolan even realizes just how intensely he's staring at me.

I reach for my drink as an excuse not to meet his intent gaze. With nerves bubbling furiously through me, I almost knock over my glass. Thankfully, I steady it in time with my other hand and avoid spilling the wine all over the delicate lace tablecloth. But I suppose if I spilled it, it would interrupt Nolan's stare. Then again, I'm not entirely certain I want him to stop, as uncomfortable as it makes me feel.

"I forgot to ask," Nolan says, "how was the Trial of Mind yesterday?"

I set down my drink and fiddle with the frilly edge of the tablecloth. "All right, I suppose."

"All right?"

"Well, I passed."

"You don't look very pleased by it."

I sigh. "I almost failed."

When I dare to glance up, I catch him frowning. "Why? What happened?"

"On the trial, I fought with another adept and was badly wounded. I only made it out in time because my friend carried me through the tunnels."

"You were injured?" he asks.

"I collapsed at the end of the trial and have been in bed since yesterday morning."

"I didn't realize," he said softly. "If I had known, I wouldn't have dragged you here."

"You didn't drag me here. If I hadn't been well enough to come, I would have asked Eliya to let you know. Though you might have then thought I was using my injuries as an excuse."

His frown deepens. "I wouldn't have thought that."

Not knowing how to respond, I continue to fiddle with the tablecloth. Nolan silently watches me.

"Anyway," I say, hoping to alleviate the tension, "tell me about yourself. All I know is that you're from Dalry and own a tavern."

"What would you like to know about me?"

"Hm, maybe about your family. What did they think about you moving to Nolderan and buying a tavern here?"

Nolan pauses. "My family is dead."

"I'm so sorry. I didn't realize."

"It's fine," he replies. "My father died a few months ago, and as the only child, I inherited his entire estate. I decided to sell his property to have a fresh start here."

"Oh," I say, lowering my gaze.

Before he can reveal what happened to the rest of his family, the waiters appear with our soup.

Blue swirls are painted onto the bowls, and they look like waves rippling across the porcelain. The edges are tipped with gold and floral details are etched into the silver spoon.

We talk little as we eat our soup, and soon after we finish, our main dishes arrive. The steaming food arrives on elaborate silver plates, and the rum-glazed salmon I ordered proves to be far more delicious than I expected.

"More wine?" Nolan asks when we've cleared our plates. Less than a quarter of wine remains inside the bottle.

"It's probably best I don't have another glass, since I have my final trial in the morning."

"Of course," he replies.

Nolan doesn't finish the wine and signals to the waiter for the bill. If Eliya was here, she would lecture us about leaving so much wine.

Once Nolan has paid, he leads me back out of the restaurant and into the cool night.

Outside, it's trying to snow, and a few specks dust my hair. We reach the bottom of the steps, and Nolan holds out his arm. I take it, linking us together.

"Where to now?" I ask, my warm breath swirling into the chilly air.

"You know, I didn't think this far ahead."

"If you don't have any other ideas, maybe we could head to the fountain in the square? It'll probably be quiet now. And there are some benches to sit on."

His gaze sweeps over my thin shawl. "Won't you be cold?"

"I can conjure an aether shield around us. That'll stop the wind and the snow."

"All right," he says. "Sounds like a plan."

He begins to walk on ahead, but I pull him back. He raises a brow at me.

"You do remember that I'm a mage in training? I can just teleport us there."

"Right, of course."

With our arms still linked, I close my eyes and visualize the Upper City's square as vividly as I can. Teleporting someone else with me takes more concentration, and a lot more aether. If I'm not careful, I could end up teleporting us somewhere else in the city.

When I'm certain I have thoroughly prepared the spell, I release it. "*Laxus.*"

Magic washes over us, and we disappear into the night. My body becomes weightless, and I can no longer feel Nolan's arm around mine.

The floating sensation lasts for only a heartbeat. Then the darkness opens to the scene of the Upper City's square, sketched in vibrant purple light. Color fills the city's outline, and the buildings materialize around us.

A mermaid sits at the top of the fountain, carved from stone, and the water flows from her raised hands, splashing against each tier. Long, wavy hair covers her bosom.

We sit beside each other on the nearest bench, and there's enough distance that our legs aren't touching, but I still feel his warmth. The snowflakes fall thicker now, and I blink away the few which land on my lashes. Before more can cover us, I encase us both in a bubble of humming light.

"*Muriz.*"

Aether shrouds us and prevents snow from falling on us. Even the frigid wind can't penetrate my magic.

Nolan stares up at the shield with a contemplative expression. I can't tell what he's thinking.

I also tilt back my head and peer at the stars beyond the aether barrier. With the rippling surface, they are almost impossible to distinguish.

It takes me a few moments to realize that Nolan has lowered his gaze and is watching me. When my attention returns to him, heat floods my cheeks.

"Reyna," he murmurs, "you look lovely tonight." He lifts my hand and presses his lips to my skin.

I don't breathe. Neither do I pull away. So taken aback by the gesture, I only watch as he lifts his lips from my hand and lowers it.

But he doesn't let go. His fingers remain wrapped around mine, and we stare at each other, neither one of us blinking.

His other hand reaches for my face. His fingers trail down my cheek, tracing my jawline and then the curve of my neck. I shiver from his touch.

"May I kiss you?" His words are as sacred as a hushed prayer.

I can say nothing. The way he gazes at me—the way he touches me—overwhelms all my senses. I manage a small nod.

Nolan leans closer, leaving only a strand of distance between our lips. His fingers skim across my collarbone and over my neck. His emerald eyes settle onto my lips. He hesitates for so long that I wonder whether he has changed his mind. Whether in the next heartbeat, he will withdraw and leave my lips untouched.

But then he kisses me.

At first I freeze, unsure of the steps to this dance I have not known for so long. His lips are unfamiliar against mine but my uneasiness soon thaws, and I fall into his rhythm, kissing him back with as much certainty.

He pulls me in deeper, his fingers tangling through my hair, and I am lost to the bliss of his fervent touch. All else ceases to exist. There's only the scorch of his lips and the sting of his stubble grazing my skin.

His hand drifts from my neck, gliding over my shoulders and down my arms. My silk shawl falls loose, tumbling to the stone bench beneath us and leaving me exposed. I tremble, and he reaches for my hand, stroking my palm with his thumb. The tingle sends a dizzying rush crashing into me.

I don't know how I felt nervous about Nolan, about kissing him, because in this moment everything feels so achingly right.

When he lifts his lips from mine and ends our kiss, it feels far too soon. My breaths are uneven and heavy. Despite the aether barrier humming around us, sheltering us from the elements, I feel oddly cold. Already I crave the warmth of his lips.

His fingers return to my neck, sweeping over my skin and down my chest. Molten heat floods through me, and I wonder whether his touch will reach lower still. But he comes to a stop at the locket sitting below the hollow of my neck. He toys with it, his gaze fixed onto the silver heart.

I jerk back, pulling the locket from his grasp. The last thing I want is for the magic to pour out and the memory inside to play. For him to hear the promise Arluin made.

A flash of hurt flickers in his eyes. When I blink, the emotion is already long gone. Guilt stabs my gut. But I don't know who I am betraying.

"What's the matter?" he asks.

Maybe he thinks my pulling away means I'm rejecting him. I lower my gaze, focusing on my shawl beneath us. "The necklace was from someone important."

He frowns at me. "From whom?"

I swallow. "My . . . my mother."

I feel awful for deceiving him, but I don't know how else to explain the locket. If I speak about Arluin, I fear he will hear the affection in my voice. And that whatever is blossoming between us will never have the chance to flourish.

At least that's how I justify the lie.

"I see," he says, releasing the necklace.

We say nothing then, and I feel increasingly worse. Eventually, when I can bear it no longer, I reach for his hand. He glances up at me, surprised by the gesture. Maybe he interpreted my withdrawal as rejection.

"Thank you for tonight," I whisper. "I've had such a wonderful time."

His golden brows pinch together. "Are you sure?"

"I am," I reply, but it seems to do little to relieve his uncertainty. "I'm sorry about how I reacted just then. My mother died a few years ago, and her absence is still raw." While that's no lie, it is deceitful. To remedy the situation, I am spinning an even deeper web of dishonesty.

"It's all right. I understand."

"I would like to see you again," I say. "There will be a Ball tomorrow night in the Arcanium. Assuming I pass the Trial of Magic, that is."

"You will pass." He says those words with great certainty. I wish I had as much confidence in myself.

"I know you'll be busy working in your tavern, but it would mean a lot to me if you are able to come."

"I'll be there," he assures me.

I flash him a small smile. "Thank you."

He dips his head.

"Anyway," I say, grabbing my shawl and hauling myself from the bench. My wobbly legs manage to support my weight. "I should probably head home now."

"Of course," he replies. "Good night, Reyna. Thank you for seeing me tonight, especially after all the injuries you have suffered."

"It's not a problem. Thank you for inviting me." I draw aether to my fingers, preparing my teleportation spell. "See you tomorrow night."

With that, I drift away into a cloud of violet light, leaving Nolan and the bench far behind.

CHAPTER 33

THE CROWD ROARS WITH ANTICIPATION. The air crackles with tension.

Every seat inside the arena is filled, from the first tier all the way to the very top. It seems all of Nolderan has gathered to watch our third and final Mage Trial.

I sit on the lowest row, along with the other adepts. On the opposite side lies a raised platform where my father and his Archmagi are seated. Their chairs are so elaborately decorated they look like stone thrones. Though we sit hundreds of yards away, I feel my father's sharp gaze fixing on me, willing me not to fail.

I grip the edge of the bench, my nails scraping against the stone. I cannot fail. If I do, all I've ever worked for will be in vain.

Today, I must succeed. There is no other choice.

Archmage Gidston doesn't sit on the platform with my father and the other two Archmagi. She stands at the center of the arena. When she raises her hand, the crowd falls silent.

"We gather today to watch the remaining fifteen adepts undergo their final Mage Trial. Over the past five years, they have worked tirelessly to develop their abilities at crafting aether into spells and enchantments, preparing themselves to become fully fledged Magi of Nolderan.

"These remaining adepts have thus far proven they possess the required strength of heart and mind to graduate from the Arcanium as magi. Today, we test their proficiency with aether.

"Behold, the Trial of Magic!"

Once more, the crowd clamors with applause. My stomach tightens at the deafening noise.

Many don't gather here just to witness new generations of magi being born. They come because the Trial of Magic can be brutal. My mother forbade me from attending the trial until I joined the Arcanium, and that was only because adepts are required to watch. After all, it's the fate which awaits us all.

The Trial of Magic has the highest failure rate. Death is also not unheard of. We aren't supposed to die, but in the heat of battle, the Arch-mage of Knowledge may intervene a moment too late.

Over the last four years I've watched the Trial of Magic, I've seen only one adept die in the arena. And technically, he died outside the arena from his injuries. All the Blood Balm and healing potions in the world couldn't save him from his mortal wounds.

I pray I will not share his fate. At least the odds are favorable: one in approximately sixty adepts.

Archmage Gidston continues to speak, and the crowd quietens again.

"To pass this trial, each adept must complete a total of three rounds. Failing even one means failing the Trial of Magic, and they will be unable to graduate from the Arcanium. Only the brightest and most talented of our young adepts will join the ranks of the magi.

"For this first round, the adepts shall face a colossal stone structure: a golem. These constructs are bound and animated with aether.

"We now call the first adept to the arena: Reyna Ashbourne!"

I suck in a sharp breath. It's no surprise that I'm the first adept to be called. I am the only one left who has a surname beginning with 'A.'

At my name, cheers explode through the arena. My breakfast starts to come back up. I force it down. The crowd expects a spectacular performance from the Grandmage's daughter. I can only hope I don't disappoint them.

Eliya seems to sense my nerves, and she squeezes my shoulder. "Don't worry," she whispers, her voice nearly inaudible over the booming cheers. "You'll absolutely slay that golem—I know you will!"

Then she releases me, and I stand, drawing aether into my fingers. "*Laxus*," I call, and the crowd seems to quieten at the spell-word.

I glimmer away into violet light and re-emerge beside Archmage Gidston at the center of the arena.

Her narrowed eyes scan over me. I try to stifle the trembling of my hands. With the arena's terrifyingly tall walls looming over me, and the knowledge that failure will cost my entire future, a ferocious wave of nerves threatens to drown me.

"Ready, Adept Ashbourne?"

I don't know whether I'll ever be ready to face failing in front of thousands and losing everything, but I nod all the same.

"Good," she replies. "Then I wish you the very best of luck."

Her words make my gut knot even tighter.

Archmage Gidston teleports herself onto the platform where my father and the other Archmagi sit. There, she watches me for a moment, leaning over the balcony. The crowd falls hushed, eagerly awaiting her next command. It feels like a lifetime passes before she speaks again, and the thousands of faces staring down at me send terror plunging through my heart.

"Let the Trial of Magic begin!"

At her shout, the grinding of steel rumbles behind me. I whirl to see the enormous gate rolling upward. The crowd remains hushed. Everyone stares at the shadowed entrance with bated breaths.

For several beats, nothing happens. The tension is thick and heavy like inescapable fog. My heart hammers at an alarming rate.

Then comes the thundering storm. Hulking footsteps pound toward me.

The golem emerges from the tunnel, and it's so gigantic I briefly wonder whether it will collide with the gate's pointed ends. Unfortunately, it does not. Neither does its pace slow as it charges at me.

The construct is almost humanoid in appearance but is oddly disproportionate. Its square head is far too small for its mammoth body, and its fists and feet consist of monstrously sized boulders. I fear one punch or stomp would be enough to smash through the arena's dense walls. Never mind what it would do to me.

This was what killed that adept three years ago: a titanic blow from a golem's massive fists. I don't remember his name. Nor do I try. Not with the construct rushing forth.

Violet light glows between its joints, holding it together. A glittering crystal pulses in its chest, powering its every movement.

Thanks to the aether imbued within the golem, it is incredibly resistant to magic. Fortunately, its enormous size makes it slow and it's unable to cast any spells of its own. It also has a critical weakness: the very crystal which energizes it.

As the construct stomps across the arena, I prepare my first attack. Since the golem's core is formed from crystalized aether, the other four elements will be ineffective against such concentrated magic.

By the time my spell is ready, the golem is almost upon me.

"Telum!" I cry, unleashing a powerful blast of aether. Against the hush of the audience, my shout sounds far too loud.

My attack is precise. The spell's trajectory is perfectly on target to strike the golem's heart. To defeat it with a single blow. I bet my father accomplished such a feat during his Mage Trials.

But as my magic reaches the construct, it raises its arms and shields its exposed core from my attack. The blast of aether collides with its huge fists. Purple light ripples across the stone as it absorbs my magic. Not even the slightest chunk of rock chips off.

Despite defending itself from my attack, the golem doesn't slow its charge. It continues lumbering toward me.

Panic pounds through me. The stone construct is a few feet away. If I'm not quick enough, I will be crushed beneath its tremendous weight.

The golem swings for me.

"Laxus!"

Before the construct's fists can connect with my body, I fade into aether.

For a moment, everything ceases to exist, and I feel weightless, drifting through time and space. Then the ground returns beneath my feet, and I materialize several paces away from the golem. But not nearly as many as I envisioned.

I gasp for breath, shaken by the nearness of the blow. I need to be more careful. A heartbeat later, and I would have been pulverized. Or Archmage Gidston would have intervened, disqualifying me from the trial and ensuring I never become a Mage of Nolderan.

The golem does not relent. It charges for me again. This time more furiously, as if the failed attack has enraged it.

I don't have time to conjure a fearsome blast of magic or teleport to the other side of the arena. I can only summon an aether shield and leap as far back as I can, praying I will avoid the reach of its fists.

"*Muriz!*" I call, mid-jump.

The barrier spreads around me, just as the golem swings for me again. I am within its reach, but far enough away that the blow glances across my shield. It still tears through my barrier as if it's made from paper, but at least the impact is not fatal. The aether shield fizzles out, and I'm thrown back onto the ground. The collision leaves me winded and momentarily dazed.

The golem shambles forth. I don't even have the chance to scramble upright. Its immense foot comes crashing down, blanketing me with a vast shadow. I roll and barely avoid its thunderous stomp. The ground quakes and reverberates through me.

If I don't return to my feet, I will be crushed.

When I next roll away from its attack, I do so with enough momentum to fling myself upright. The construct's fist swerves toward me.

I duck, diving between its behemoth legs. I fear they will snap together and squish me between them, but this is my only chance of escape.

I emerge unscathed. With all my strength, I sprint as hard and fast as I can, desperate to put enough distance between me and the golem. To gain enough time to conjure an attack. The construct's weighty strides thump behind.

I draw upon aether as I run. When I'm certain there's enough distance, I spin and hurl my magic at the construct. "*Telum!*"

The aether blast isn't as precise as my previous, but I don't have the luxury of time. It will have to be enough.

The spell catches the golem by surprise. It raises its arms to defend itself, but it does so a moment too late.

My magic slams into its chest, meeting the pulsating crystal.

The golem falters. I hold my breath. But the stone construct doesn't come crashing to the ground.

Disoriented, it stumbles back. As the light fades, I see that the core isn't shattered. Only a slight crack pierces its surface.

I clench my fists. But there's no time to bemoan the lost victory. I can only press on, conjuring my next spell before the golem can recover.

"*Laxus!*"

I teleport to the far end of the arena. The stone construct hurtles toward me. This time there's enough distance for me to thoroughly prepare my spell.

Blood drums in my ears. I do my best to clear my mind and focus on the magic I'm weaving together between my fingers.

The golem is mere heartbeats from me now. The air shudders from its powerful momentum. But I hold my ground, knowing it's my only hope of defeating my opponent.

Its fists come crashing down. At that same instant, I seize the opening. Too busy attacking, the construct is unable to defend itself. And with the close distance, there's no risk of my magic missing.

"*Telum!*" I yell.

Aether bursts from my fingers, crackling with the intensity. My blast slams into the golem's heart.

Beneath the fizzle of my magic, I hear the core cracking. Fragments of crystallized aether rain on my face, and I shield my eyes. The glow fades from the golem's joints. It falls still, frozen mid-swing. Its enormous fists are a hair's breadth from me. I flinch at the nearness.

Before I can consider how lucky I was not to be smashed apart, the construct explodes.

I dive away. Rock hurls at me. I duck and cover my head with my arms. They bruise from some of the larger chunks.

When the barrage ceases, I straighten and stand there, gasping.

The arena erupts with applause. The rush of battle still courses through me, and I take a few seconds to realize they are cheering for me.

I succeeded.

"Congratulations, Reyna Ashbourne!" Archmage Gidston's voice rings out. The audience quietens as she speaks, hanging onto her every word. "You have successfully completed the first round of the Trial of Magic. Please now return to your seat. Lorea Bayford, if you will take your place inside the arena."

Before teleporting back to my seat beside Eliya, I stare up at the crowd towering all around me, briefly losing myself to the dizzying height and the sea of faces.

Though I have passed this first round, I must face two more before I can earn my title as a Mage of Nolderan.

CHAPTER 34

"I TOLD YOU THAT YOU'D slay it," Eliya says as I slide back onto my seat beside her.

I pull my lips into a strained smile. "It came awfully close to smashing me apart."

Eliya shakes her head. "You had it perfectly under control."

"I'm not sure I did."

"You at least looked like it."

Magi teleport themselves down to the arena where Lorea waits to begin her battle. They call *ventrez* and blow the remains of the golem out of the arena.

When the area is clear, Archmage Gidston calls, "Begin!"

Once more, the steel gate rumbles open. Lorea stands there at the center of the arena, anxiously waiting for the golem to charge out. She doesn't have to wait long before the stone construct appears.

It lumbers toward her with heavy, purposeful strides. This golem is a perfect replica of the one I faced, with a pulsating crystal powering its every movement.

Like me, Lorea focuses her attention on the construct's exposed core and blasts her magic at it. But her attack misses, and she is forced to teleport out of its reach. She repeats the same cycle over and over, teleporting around the arena and striking the golem with aether, until she eventually succeeds.

Her attack meets its target, and the crystal shatters. The golem explodes, chunks of rock bursting out in all directions. The crowd roars with applause, and then Archmage Gidston calls forth the next adept: Keion Bridwell.

One by one, the remaining adepts teleport down to the arena to fight a golem. Thankfully, no one dies and only one adept fails. Archmage Gidston had to intervene and stop the construct from killing him.

Soon, it's Eliya's turn. When her name is called, I grab her hand and give it a quick squeeze.

"Good luck," I whisper.

Eliya grins at me. "I don't need luck," she declares, lifting her chin and placing her hands on her hips. "But thanks, anyway."

With that, she teleports into the arena. She is the final adept to face the first round of the Trial of Magic.

At Archmage Gidston's shout, the gate rolls open. Eliya doesn't flinch. Nor does she gawk at the entrance, waiting for the golem to thunder out. Instead, she gathers aether into her fingers and calls, "*Speculus*!"

Two clones emerge from a flash of glittering light. Since they are all identical, I lose track of which is the real Eliya.

The construct emerges from the gate.

It pauses. Its glowing eyes scan over the three Eliyas who stand several yards apart from each other. The golem selects the middle Eliya and strides over to her, ignoring the other two.

All three begin casting. In unison, they cry out *telum* and unleash their magic. The golem raises its arms, defending itself from the attack. Its enormous fists absorb her magic. When the barrage subsides, it continues toward its chosen Eliya.

With full force, its fists swing for her. I hold my breath, praying with all my heart it's not the real Eliya. She makes no attempt to evade or defend herself. I fear Archmage Gidston might decide to intervene, disqualifying her from the Mage Trials, because there is no way of distinguishing which Eliya is real. I'm not even sure whether an accomplished mage could tell the difference.

Archmage Gidston doesn't teleport herself down from the platform. She continues to lean over the balcony as she examines the fight below.

The golem's fists slam into Eliya. She disperses into a shimmering cloud of aether.

I let out a sigh, the tension slackening in my shoulders.

I'm still unable to tell which of the remaining two is her. The construct's attention flickers between them both. Then it charges to the one on the left.

Before the golem can reach its chosen Eliya, the two of them release their spells and cry out: "*Tera!*"

Their magic crashes into the ground directly beneath the construct, carving out an enormous ditch. Though it is impervious to magic, it isn't invulnerable to the ground breaking under its feet.

Eliya flings aside the earth, and the golem crashes into the pit. It tries to scramble back out, but with its colossal weight, it is far from agile. Eliya seizes the advantage. Both she and the clone conjure another blast of aether.

By the time the stone construct hauls itself out of the hole, she has finished preparing a mighty spell.

"*Telum!*"

With the golem pulling itself out of the pit, it's left in a vulnerable position. Eliya's magic slams into it, and it's unable to defend itself from the blow.

Her spell pierces the golem's crystalline heart, defeating it. Its remains crumble onto the ground. The crowd cheers, and Eliya murmurs *terminir*. Her remaining clone disappears, and she is left alone at the center of the arena.

The applause is the loudest I've heard today—even more deafening than when Archmage Gidston announced my name. Eliya defeated the construct faster than the rest of us, thanks to her genius strategy. She deserves all the cheers which the crowd shower her with.

Eliya teleports back up into the audience and strides over to me. "Told you I wouldn't need any luck."

"You were amazing!"

She returns to her place beside me and flicks her crimson waves over her shoulder. After the fight with the golem, her hair is even wilder than usual. "I know," she replies with a wink. "I always am."

We have little time to discuss her outstanding performance. Archmage Gidston teleports to the center of the arena. Several magi are already working down there, swiftly mending the ditch that Eliya created and tidying away the golem's remains. Archmage Gidston waits until they have finished before addressing us all.

"Fourteen of our adepts have successfully completed the first round of the Trial of Magic, but they must face two more in order to prove they possess the skill required of the magi.

"We now move to the second round of this trial. Our remaining adepts will each battle four lesser elementals. To emerge victorious, they must carefully select their spells against each opponent and fluently wield all four of the elements.

"The first adept will now take their place inside the arena—Reyna Ashbourne!"

At the Archmage's command, I teleport down to where she stands. This time, she offers me no words of encouragement before returning to the platform which overlooks the arena. Behind her sits my father on his stone throne. He clasps his crystalline staff as he stares down at me. I don't meet his magenta eyes for long, and I soon turn my attention to the steel gates behind me.

"Let the second round commence!"

The gates open.

Blinding lights dart out. There are four colors in total: red, white, green, and blue.

As they rush forth, the spirits manifest into physical forms. The red light becomes a blazing salamander, the white light becomes a gigantic hawk, the green light becomes an elk formed from gnarled vines, and the blue light becomes a stallion with a mane of streaming kelp. Water ripples beneath its hooves.

The four elementals charge at me. The hawk swiftly takes the lead, thanks to its enormous wingspan.

I weave aether into fire magic and unleash the conjured flames upon it. "*Ignira!*"

The resulting fireball isn't my most ferocious, but I lack the time to make it so. I can't afford to spend too long on one enemy, or else the other three will overpower me.

My spell is enough to stop the hawk from swooping toward me and leaves it dazed. The flames feed on the air magic comprising its body. I don't stop to examine how much damage I inflict. The water stallion is already upon me.

It rears. A wave crashes forth, sweeping high over me and threatening to drown me.

"*Tera'muriz*!" I shout.

Just as the water reaches me, I wrap the ground around myself and form an earthen shield. The water slams into the rock, and I hear it churning beyond the safety of my barrier.

The wave falls silent. I shatter my shield. "*Tera'quatir!*"

The rock explodes, hurling out in all directions. It slams into the water stallion, forcing it back several paces. A large chunk also collides with the salamander which was gaining on me, gaining me a few extra moments from its sizzling flames.

When I glance back, I see the elk charging forth. Its hooves slam into the ground. Thunder rings out. The ground shatters. A bolt pierces through the center of the arena.

I fall to the right of the crack. My knees strike the ground first. My gaze briefly drifts over to the chasm. It plummets into the earth, hundreds of feet deep.

Before I can leap up, the hawk swoops at me. Its translucent wings beat back and forth, generating a terrifying force. A howling gale rushes forth, tearing through all the air in its path.

"*Ignir'muriz!*"

Flames ignite around me, and they stop the violent wind from ripping me apart. The fiery wall roars, feeding off the air magic. It grows in size until it snuffs out the gale.

The four elementals charge at me again. They come at me from all directions. I am at the center. Cornered.

I can't let them defeat me.

"*Ignir'quatir!*" I rasp with all the desperation in my heart.

My shield explodes, slamming into all four of my opponents. The hawk takes the brunt of my attack. Thanks to the damage I previously inflicted, and its vulnerability to fire, the air elemental is obliterated.

The hawk bursts apart, disintegrating into tiny fragments. Remnants of air magic descend on me like crushed diamonds. My face tingles as they land on my cheeks, but they cause no harm.

There's no time to relish my victory. Three enemies remain. The water stallion advances.

Its kelp-like tail lashes out, and its nostrils flare. A bolt of pressurized water darts toward me.

"*Tera!*" I call, carving out an enormous boulder from the ground. I launch it at the blast.

Water sprays across the arena, soaking me. The salamander's flames are momentarily doused by the splash.

The elk bows its head. Green light glows between its antlers. A giant onyx thorn springs forth. Its point glistens as it rushes at me.

"*Ventrez!*" Air magic bursts from my fingers. The furious wind tears through the thorn. Dark pieces of bark scatter across the arena.

Flames crackle behind. The salamander spews a fireball. I notice the attack too late.

I swerve back. The flames catch my shoulder, singeing my cerulean robes and scorching my flesh. I let out a sharp cry of pain but have no chance to check the wound.

The elk stomps. Green light spreads over the ground.

The earth rumbles, and vines sprout from beneath the arena. Thorns cover each tendril. They wrap around my ankles, and their needlelike points penetrate the leather of my boots. A sharp stabbing pain tells me the thorns have penetrated far enough to draw blood.

The vines curl tighter, securing their hold around me. They creep higher up my leg and press in deeper. It feels as if thousands of needles are digging into me.

I use the pain to fuel my fury. Aether boils in my blood. I unleash it as a powerful blast of air magic.

"*Tempis!*"

A vortex erupts. The sharp winds slice through the vines, and the severed remains fall in a heap of foliage. The vortex continues forth and crashes into the earth elemental. The violent winds are as sharp as blades and carve through the vines which form its body.

My spell shreds the elemental apart. Earth magic drifts from its remains in a cloud of green light. Now only two enemies are left.

Both the water stallion and the fire salamander charge at me. I stumble back. The pain shooting through my leg, where the thorns ripped through, makes it impossible to leap away.

So, I don't. I draw on my magic and wait for a moment. Then another. When both elementals are upon me, I release my spell.

"*Laxus!*"

I fade into aether. My two enemies crash into each other. The water stallion's enormous wave devours the salamander and destroys its flames. It disperses into red light, and ash scatters through the wind.

Only one enemy remains. The water elemental.

After its collision with the salamander, the water stallion is left disoriented. It takes a few seconds to recover.

I don't hesitate before launching my next attack.

"*Veitis!*"

Emerald light strikes the ground. Vines burst up, reaching for the remaining elemental. They wrap around the water stallion. It struggles beneath the vines, but their grasp tightens.

An anguished whinny pierces the silence of the arena. Then the elemental bursts apart.

Water splashes across the ground. Blue light pours out.

I glance at the puddles, gasping for breath.

The crowd roars with applause.

I've vanquished my enemies. I've passed the second round of the Trial of Magic. Only one battle stands between me becoming a Mage of Nolderan.

"Congratulations, Reyna Ashbourne!" comes Archmage Gidston's shout. "You have completed the second round. Please return to your seat until the third and final round begins."

I do as she says and return to the audience. My injuries make it hard to walk, and I hobble over to where Eliya sits. She jumps to her feet and helps me back onto our stone bench.

"Are you all right?" she whispers as Archmage Gidston calls Lorea's name. Magi teleport down to the arena and use their magic to smooth the ground, ready for her battle to begin.

"They're just small wounds." I hold out my hand and draw aether into my palm. "*Conparios.*" A vial of fluorescent green liquid appears. Even the sight of the potion makes my stomach turn, but I tear off the cork and drain every drop from the small glass bottle. The putrid slime slips down my throat. I gag, but don't let myself cough up any.

With some luck, the healing potion will work long before the third round begins. I'll have at least an hour, seeing as there are thirteen more adepts to complete the second round of the Trial of Magic.

"You only have one more round now!" Eliya exclaims, as if reading my thoughts. Her eyes gleam.

"I know," I say, clenching the empty potion vial. "One more round to go."

I pray I will pass it. Fate would be cruel to snatch away everything after I've come so close to achieving all I've ever wanted.

Lorea soon begins her trial. Magic collides as she battles the four elementals. And when she successfully completes the round, Archmage Gidston calls down the next adept.

By the time Eliya takes her turn, and the second round concludes, two adepts have failed. One girl was nearly immolated, and Archmage Gidston had to douse the flames to save her. Another was almost strangled by barbed thorns. Both required immediate medical attention.

Then the third and final round begins. Archmage Gidston calls me down to the arena. Not once do I look up at my father. I can't bear to.

I train my gaze onto the steel gates, barely breathing as I wait for them to open.

This is it. My final reckoning.

Either I will defeat my opponent and become a Mage of Nolderan, or I will lose everything. This is my only chance. I cannot fail. Not when my future is at stake.

I'm so lost to my fear that when the gate finally rumbles open, I am delayed in noticing it.

Violet light surges out from the darkened entrance and whizzes across the arena. It comes to a halt beside me. The aether spirit swirls. Magic ripples through the air.

The surface shifts, forming a girl's silhouette. It becomes so blinding that I'm forced to shield my eyes from its dazzling radiance.

The girl steps forth, and the light fades. Her features become clearer.

Then I'm staring back at myself. Her eyes are of the same shade of magenta as mine, and her long, dark hair has even the same sheen.

It should come as no shock. I've watched this final trial unfold countless times before. The last round is always facing an aether spirit. And the elemental always clones the adept.

Staring at it is uncanny. When I summon clones of myself, they are an extension of my will. This being is separate entirely, and yet it looks completely identical to myself. It is as though I'm staring into a very real mirror.

Before I can recover from my surprise, the fake me raises her hands and sends a blast of aether hurling forth. She requires no spell-words to control her magic. That's the formidable advantage she has against me.

"*Laxus!*"

When the aether blast reaches me, I am barely fading into my teleport-ation spell.

I am immaterial enough that the attack continues past me. It collides with the barrier on the far side of the arena. I emerge behind my opponent, unscathed.

She spins to face me.

"*Ignira!*" I call, launching a hasty fireball at her. But she teleports away, replicating my movements.

My spell blazes through empty air and is absorbed by the arena's barrier. She reappears on the right.

It is then I realize my grave mistake.

Besides replicating my appearance, the clone can imitate whichever spells I cast. The longer I fight it, the more spells it will learn from me. After watching many other adepts undertake the Trial of Magic, I know the successful ones are always the ones who defeat it the swiftest.

That's because my opponent is a being of pure aether and can instantly restore its strength by absorbing the magic lying in the surrounding air. My power, however, will quickly deplete. I am limited by the amount of aether in my blood. Without it, I can't draw more from the air to fuel my spells. Only resting will replenish the aether coursing through my veins.

My strength is finite. The aether spirit's is not. I must defeat it before it learns too many spells, and before I tire. Only by selecting every move with great care will I achieve this.

The aether spirit conjures a fireball much like mine. Flames rush at me.

Teleportation requires much aether, and it won't inflict any damage onto my enemy. I must conserve all the magic I can.

"*Aquis!*" I instead shout. The aether in my hands turns to water magic. I fling the bolt of pressurized water at the fireball.

The two spells collide. The water extinguishes the flames, and the remaining drops splash across the ground. Puddles glisten beneath us.

I glare at the aether spirit, and it glares back. I can see the calculating look in its eyes—in my eyes—and I know it's already plotting its next attack.

I must strike first.

"*Telum!*" I call, releasing a blast of aether. It's far from a complex spell, but it's better that way. My clone's first attack was also a blast of aether, so there's no risk in it learning a new spell.

But the aether spirit teleports away. When my blast reaches it, only empty space remains. My enemy has no need to worry about the cost of teleportation spells. Thanks to its endless supply of aether, it can cast as many spells as it likes.

Panic jolts through me.

I made a terrible mistake with my first move. I should never have teleported away. Now the aether spirit knows this spell, landing a blow on it will be nearly impossible.

I curse my stupidity. Then I whirl around, searching for where the aether spirit has reappeared. I know my father will be so disappointed with me for this foolish error.

I find the aether spirit behind me, already launching three quick bolts. Not daring to create a shield and teach my opponent yet another spell, I leap aside.

The move is far from graceful. I lose my balance and fall.

The ground slams into my shoulder at an awkward angle. I force myself upright and stagger onto my feet, clutching my shoulder.

Flames crackle. They surge toward me.

Left with no alternative, I hurriedly conjure a water shield. "*Aquis'muriz!*" I shout, drawing a bubble around myself. My haste makes the spell weak. But it's enough to cause the flames to fizzle out when they reach me.

Though the attack saved me, I've now taught it how to counter fire.

Fighting with reservation and choosing simple spells is doing me no favors. While we have only exchanged a few blows, it seems the aether spirit is already beating me.

No.

I can't let it win. Failure isn't an option. Failure means losing everything. Sacrificing my future. Shaming my father.

I must defeat the aether spirit before it defeats me.

Determination rises in my chest. I must strike it down with all the force I can muster. And quickly.

The aether spirit conjures a bolt of water.

I turn my attention to the ground and spread emerald light across the stone.

"*Tera!*"

The spell carves out an enormous boulder. I fling it forth.

The rock smacks into the water blast, and it bursts apart, spraying across the ground. Onward the boulder continues, straight toward the aether spirit's stolen face.

It conjures a water shield: the only shielding spell I have so far taught it. A terrible miscalculation. Any child knows that water is a pitiful defense against earth magic. It should have instead chosen to teleport away.

The chunk of rock tears through the water shield and crashes into the aether spirit. The boulder bursts apart from the impact. Pebbles scatter across the arena.

The blow has left the aether spirit dazed, but I haven't yet defeated it. If I strike again, I just might succeed.

None of the elements are advantageous against aether. Only aether works best against aether.

"*Telum!*" The spell-word is all but a scream as it rips through my throat. If I fail to destroy the aether spirit with this blast, I might never defeat it.

I fuel the attack with every ounce of magic in my blood. The blast of aether is ferocious as it bursts from my fingertips. The air crackles as my spell tears through it.

My magic collides with the aether spirit. Dazzling light explodes, filling the arena with its radiance. Aether dust rains over me, coating me like iridescent glitter.

It is gone. Defeated.

The audience erupts with deafening applause.

I've done it.

I've passed the Trial of Magic. The third and final Mage Trial.

I gaze up at the platform where my father sits. He is out of his seat, and so are Archmage Gidston and Archmage Lanord. My father's magenta eyes are illuminated with pride. He claps more enthusiastically and beams at me more widely than he ever has.

My heart nearly bursts at the sight.

I didn't fail. I didn't humiliate him. I made him proud.

The realization chokes me with tears.

When Archmage Gidston addresses me, I stare up at her through blurred eyes. Despite my hazy vision, I can still make out the broad smile stretching across her face.

"Congratulations, Reyna Ashbourne," she declares. The crowd quietens at her words. "You have successfully passed the Trial of Magic, the third and final Mage Trial. Let it now be known to all that you are officially a Mage of Nolderan!"

CHAPTER 33

I STARE AT THE GIRL who stands in my full-length mirror. She looks nothing like me. Her magenta eyes shine too brightly; her skin is too lustrous. If I were not alone in my room, I would believe the reflection belongs to someone else.

I have achieved all that I've ever wanted, and yet I cannot shake away the hollowness clinging to my heart. For years I imagined completing my Mage Trials, but I never gave much thought as to how passing them would make me feel. I suppose I thought starting a new chapter would rid me of the grief still plaguing my heart to this day, but its chains have only constricted tighter around me.

I believed becoming a mage would make me stronger, would prevent me from ever again being weak. But I still feel like that helpless little girl who was unable to stop Heston from murdering her mother.

Tonight, I'm supposed to be happy. Only once in my life will I graduate from the Arcanium, and I have awaited this for so long, but it feels as though a piece of me is missing—or broken—and that I don't deserve to wear the magnificent indigo robes draped over the back of my golden armchair.

My fingers play with the silver locket around my neck. A part of me considers pulling it open and watching the memory inside. But I don't. If I listen to Arluin's promise, I know I'll be reduced to tears. I must wear a mask and conceal the grief which consumes me.

A knock comes at my door.

I jolt, tearing myself from the mirror and doing my best to shed the torturous thoughts.

"Come in," I call.

The door opens to reveal my father. While I wear the most luxurious gown I can find—a dress made from pearlescent silk—he wears his usual Grandmage's robes.

He leans on his crystalline staff and beams at me with pride. "Look at you—all grown up and already a Mage of Nolderan."

I pull a smile and hope it looks more enthusiastic than it feels.

"Are you ready to leave?" he asks. "It's seven o'clock."

I take one last glance at my reflection, scanning across the delicate aether crystals hanging from my ears and then down to the pale skirts which flutter with my every move. I may not feel it, but I am a victor.

I turn back to my father and give him a nod. "Ready."

We head downstairs and through the hallway. When we pass my mother's favorite painting, he comes to a stop and stares up at it. He is quiet for a moment, contemplating the lull of the dark waves and the twinkle of the glistening stars.

"She would be so very proud of you," he finally murmurs and gives my shoulder a quick squeeze.

The painting blurs with my unshed tears, but I bite them back. I must wear a mask. If I let myself cry, all my powder and illusions will crumble apart.

I freeze my emotions into cold, hard ice and force myself to reply, "I hope so."

We continue through the hallway, and my father holds the grand doors open for me. I step outside, and the frosty evening breeze ripples through my flowing skirts. Shadows darken the blooming flowers, and water trickles from the fountain, preventing our gardens from being blanketed with silence.

My father closes the doors behind us, and we follow the narrow stone path to the enchanted gates. They swing open, allowing us both through, and clang shut once we're on the other side.

My father holds out his arm, and I take it. He draws aether into his crystalline staff, using it as a focus for his magic, and closes his eyes as he concentrates on his spell.

"Laxus!"

At his command, we fade away. Our forms dematerialize, and we float through the darkness until solid ground finally returns beneath my feet.

An archway is sculpted from purple light, and translucent spires rise behind it. The details grow sharper, and color fills the Arcanium's outline as it becomes real.

I let go of my father's arm and trail behind him as he strides through the archway. Many magi, adepts, and nobles flock toward the Arcanium, but all step aside to let the Grandmage of Nolderan pass.

We reach the statue of the city's founder and ascend the winding stairs. The stone walls are decorated with celebratory banners. Thousands of tiny triangular flags dance in the breeze. They are of alternating cerulean and violet hues, representing the transition from adept to mage. The transition that I myself will undergo this night.

We step through the portico, passing the many pillars which stand sentry at the entrance, and into the Arcanium's atrium.

The aether crystals which form its ceiling look even more dazzling tonight, as though they have been painstakingly polished in preparation for the Ball. There are so many people gathered inside, and everyone streams through the circular chamber. My father marches across to the entrance opposite us, and the crowd parts for him. Every head bows in reverence.

All the chairs and tables are cleared from the hall. Only four finely carved oak ones remain on the dais. Archmage Gidston and Archmage Lanord are already seated on the outer two chairs. They look up as my father strides through the wide-open double doors. His heeled boots clatter across the pristine herringbone tiles.

Three enormous chandeliers hang from the ceilings, radiating brilliant purple light through the hall. Heavy plum curtains are tucked beside each of the large windows, revealing the grassy fields at the back of the Arcanium's grounds. The arena's impressive silhouette sits in the distance.

Everyone is dressed in their finery, and the blinding aether crystals make them appear even more magnificent. Silk looks glossier; leather looks sleeker.

My father comes to a halt at the center of the hall. "We will begin when Archmage Calton arrives," he says to me. "For now, I will take my seat with the other Archmagi."

"I'll look for Eliya."

He leaves me and makes his way to the dais where Archmage Gidston and Archmage Lanord sit.

I begin my search for Eliya and carefully examine the lavishly dressed crowds. She manages to find me first.

"Rey-rey!" she exclaims, bounding over to me. "You look so pretty tonight!"

"And you look like a princess," I reply, glancing over the yellow dress that she wears. It's as though the petals of a hundred buttercups are stitched together to form her bright skirts.

"Of course I do," she replies with a grin. "But so do you."

I smile back. She takes both my hands and leans closer.

"Is Nolan coming?" she whispers.

"I invited him last night, but I haven't seen him yet. Have you?"

She shakes her head. "Maybe we should wait for him outside. It's still early, so maybe he hasn't arrived yet."

"Maybe."

We slip through the crowds, heading out the hall and through the atrium. Many more people are pouring into the Arcanium now, and descending the stairs is far from an easy task, since everyone is going in the opposite direction.

When we reach the bottom, we come to a stop before the statue of Grandmage Delmont Blackwood. He stares down at us with his unblinking eyes.

The moonlight silvers the other statues which guard the Arcanium's entrance. Behind us, music echoes from the hall. Hopefully the reason my father has ordered the enchanted instruments to start playing is because there are now so many people, and not because Archmage Calton has arrived.

"How did things go last night, anyway?" Eliya asks far too loudly for my liking. "You hardly told me anything about your date when you got home."

"I was tired."

"So you said."

When I say nothing, she raises a brow at me. "Well, what actually happened? Spit it out."

"Like I told you last night, we went to The Shimmering Oyster."

"Yes, yes, I know. But I want to know the more interesting parts. It obviously went well, since you said you invited him here tonight. So, the reason you're being so close-mouthed about it isn't because things went badly—" She cuts herself off, a devilish smirk curling onto her lips. "You kissed him, didn't you? That's the reason you won't tell me anything!"

I flush. "I didn't kiss him. He kissed me."

"I should have guessed it sooner!" She claps her hands together in delight. "So, tell me about it!"

"Tell you about what?"

"Was he a good kisser? Or was there too much tongue? Too much drool? Or did he have really bad breath? Though I suppose he must be a good kisser if you were willing to see him again."

"No, he was a perfectly acceptable kisser."

"Perfectly acceptable?" Eliya scoffs. "I bet that means he was really good."

"He was quite good," I admit.

"Anyway," she says, waggling her eyebrows, "did the two of you get up to anything else other than kissing?"

"Of course not!"

"I'm not here to judge."

"You know exactly what time I came home, since you were busy keeping watch. How would I have had the chance to do anything but kiss him?"

Eliya opens her mouth to speak, but I interrupt her before she can respond.

"On second thought, please don't answer that question. I don't want any of your stories."

"Are you sure you don't want to hear them?"

"Very sure."

She pulls a face at me but spares me from her answer.

We wait outside the Arcanium for many more minutes, but there's still no sign of Nolan and the music grows louder inside. Maybe Archmage Calton has already arrived. Maybe the Ball has already started without us.

"What if he doesn't come?" I say.

Eliya peers at me. "Why wouldn't he?"

"I don't think things went that well."

"I thought you just said he was a good kisser?"

"That part was fine. I mean after it."

"What happened after it?"

"He started looking at my necklace—"

"The one Arluin got you?"

"Yes, that one."

"He didn't open it, did he? Because if the memory crystal started playing and he heard Arluin proposing to you, then I hate to say it, but I don't think Nolan will be showing up tonight."

"Luckily, he didn't open it."

She lets out a sigh of relief. "Thank the gods for that. Did he ask who it was from?"

"I told him it was from my mother."

"Did he believe you?"

"I'm not sure."

Eliya pauses, watching as the guests ascend the stairs around us. "It doesn't matter if he doesn't show up tonight."

"It doesn't?"

"No, because you're an official Mage of Nolderan now. And that matters more than anything."

"You were the one encouraging me to get to know him in the first place."

"Just to get to know him. I thought a bit of harmless fun would do you some good. And I think it has."

I play with the locket, running my fingers across the edges of the silver heart.

I don't know whether Eliya is right, whether Nolan is helping me to set aside the past. When I think of Arluin, the burden does feel a little lighter—if only marginally so. But there's a part of me which fears closing that door means forgetting him and betraying his memory.

Eliya glances back at the Arcanium.

"It's all right," I say. "You head back inside."

"You're sure?"

"Just come and get me if they start without me."

She breathes a laugh. "Will do."

With that, she ascends the stairs and disappears inside the Arcanium.

There are fewer people outside now. It seems everyone is already in the hall, waiting for the Ball to begin. Since Eliya hasn't hurried back out, it's probably yet to start.

I shiver from the wintry air and consider murmuring *calida* to warm myself. But before I can, I glimpse golden hair emerging from beneath the Arcanium's archway.

"Nolan!" I exclaim, picking up the hem of my pearlescent skirts and hurrying over to him. "You made it!"

We come to a stop in the middle of the path, and the statues of long dead magi tower above us. A frigid wind rolls over us, but I'm too elated to feel its chill.

Tonight Nolan wears a dusky blue doublet, its sleeves finely embroidered with silver thread. His black leather boots are especially polished, and his green eyes are as vibrant as ever. It only occurs to me now how much I was worrying he would not show up. Maybe I like him more than I'm willing to admit.

He scratches the back of his head, ruffling the golden strands of his wavy hair. "I do apologize for my lateness."

"No, no," I quickly say. "You're not late at all."

Nolan scans our surroundings, lingering on the emptiness of the path. "I think I am."

"Well, maybe a little. But the Ball hasn't started, so you're not that—"

Before I can finish, Eliya reappears from the Arcanium's entrance. She sprints so fast that she almost trips over her yellow skirts. "Reyna!" she shouts from atop the stairs. "They're about to begin!"

I turn back to Nolan and shrug. "On second thought, it seems it has. Come on, we'd better hurry."

CHAPTER 36

TOGETHER, NOLAN AND I ENTER the hall. Everyone else is focused on their own conversations, and no one turns to look at us. Except for my father, that is. He stares at us from where he sits on his oaken throne at the far end of the hall, and his sharp gaze fixes on us both from the moment we step through the double doors. I don't doubt he will have many questions for me later regarding Nolan.

We don't even reach halfway through the hall before my father stands. All three Archmagi are present now, and they sit beside him on their own decorative chairs.

"*Terminir,*" he calls, drumming the end of his staff against the tiles. A wave of aether sweeps through the hall, and the enchanted instruments playing in the far corner fall silent. The floating flutes flutter back onto their chairs, and the strings of violins and cellos still.

His spell has a similar effect on the crowd. Everyone stops talking and turns to face him.

"Tonight, we welcome ten adepts into the ranks of the Magi of Nolderan," my father announces, his voice echoing through the hall. "Through successfully completing their Mage Trials, they have proven they possess the required strength of heart, mind, and magic. They have proven themselves worthy of this status.

"We now call forth each successful adept, so that we may congratulate them on their achievements and so that they may be officially granted their new position as a Mage of Nolderan.

"Reyna Ashbourne, if you will step forward."

An even greater hush falls over the crowd.

My fingers slip from Nolan's hand. I lift my chin as I stride through the length of the hall, and even when I reach my father at the dais, I don't lower it.

"Reyna Ashbourne," my father continues, "you have proven you possess the courage, the wisdom, and the power required of the magi. Do you solemnly swear that you will never waver in the face of danger, that you will obey every order issued by the Grandmage and the Archmagi without hesitation, that you will serve the people of Nolderan with all the fervor in your heart?"

"Yes, Grandmage," I reply, dipping my head. It feels strange to address my father by his title, as though he and I are not familiar, but such is tradition. There is no exception for being his daughter. I am a Mage of Nolderan first and foremost. "I, Reyna Ashbourne, do solemnly swear that I will never waver in the face of danger, that I will obey every order issued by the Grandmage and the Archmagi without hesitation, that I will serve the people of Nolderan with all the fervor in my heart."

Aether radiates from my father's fingers. He starts down the steps leading to the dais and presses his thumb to the center of my forehead. "Then from this moment forth, I hereby declare you a Mage of Nolderan."

Magic erupts, flooding through his thumb and into my body. The aether fizzes and bubbles as it reacts with that which flows through my blood. But when the magic fades, I still feel like the same Reyna I was moments before. I expected the mark of the magi to change me somehow—perhaps to make me stronger or wiser—but I feel no different. Maybe if I look in the mirror, I will find that my eyes glow with a brighter shade of magenta.

I have a sudden urge to teleport to the top of the Aether Tower and see the effect of the boon my father has granted me, but I keep my feet fixed to the hall's tiled floor. I can always try that later, after the Ball. Or maybe tomorrow. Eliya will probably want to try it, too.

The crowd showers me with applause, and then my father calls forth the next adept: Lorea.

As I step away from the dais, Archmage Calton's attention lingers on me. Though my back is turned, I can sense all the loathing radiating from him. He blames me for Kaely's failure and is unable to see that his daughter's own arrogance and hatred were her undoing. If she had focused less on destroying me and more on passing the Trial of Mind, she would be here with the rest of us as we transition from adepts to magi. I've heard no more news of her condition since Wednesday, but at least that means she's alive. Despite our feud, I have no desire for her blood to be on my hands.

I slip past the finely dressed guests and make my way back to Nolan. I've lost sight of Eliya, even though her dress is such a striking shade of yellow, but I suppose she will soon reappear when my father calls her name. Some lower year adepts I recognize from passing along the Arcanium's corridors stare at me in awe. It feels strange to no longer count myself as one of them.

"So," Nolan whispers as I come to a stop beside him. He leans toward me, and in the distant background, Lorea speaks her oath. His warm breath brushes over my ear, and every nerve within me shivers. The gesture somehow seems too private with so many people gathered around us, but it probably doesn't look as intimate as it feels. I hope I'm the only one who can tell what effect Nolan's closeness has on me.

"You're an official Mage of Nolderan now," he continues, his voice hushed. "How does it feel?"

I pause, pressing my lips together as I think. "Not quite what I expected."

"How so?"

"I don't know. I just thought I would feel different."

Nolan doesn't question me any further. We watch as my father presses his thumb to Lorea's forehead and a wave of aether rushes over her. When the magic settles, he summons the next adept.

Eliya is the last to be called to the dais, and once all ten of us have sworn our oaths and been marked by his magic, my father bangs the end of his crystalline staff against the floor.

"*Incipiret!*" he booms, and aether surges forth.

The magic swirls through the hall, twinkling like thousands of tiny stars. My father's spell reaches the instruments in the far corner, and their enchantment resumes, strings vibrating of their own accord.

People start to dance at the center of the hall. Their colorful clothes form a rainbow as they spiral and sway across the polished tiles. The chandeliers high above sparkle with violet radiance.

Nolan extends his hand to me and bows slightly. "Would you care to join me for a dance?"

The corners of my lips twitch into a light smile. "Of course. I would love to."

I place my hand on his, and he leads me to the center where everyone else is busy dancing. Nolan's arm slips around my waist, and our fingers weave between each other's, interlocking in an unbreakable embrace. I'm not sure what to do with my spare arm, and trying to decide is difficult with the dizziness sweeping over me. Standing this close to him is always intoxicating, and I'm unsure whether I welcome or fear the way he makes me feel.

In the end, I settle for resting my free hand on his shoulder, but it feels rather limp and useless there.

We step back and forth, flowing in the same gentle rhythm as all the other couples around us. I relinquish my wariness and allow the music to guide my every move.

A flash of crimson hair appears to my right as Eliya waltzes past with Koby. He must have asked her for a dance like usual, though it appears Eliya is taking the lead rather than him.

"You look lovely tonight," Nolan mutters, pulling me from my thoughts of Eliya and Koby.

I arch a brow at him. "You said the same thing last night." I regret the words as soon as they leave my lips. Though I tried to make my tone lighthearted, I worry it comes out a pitch higher than I intended. And far too accusatory.

But it seems my concerns are misplaced since Nolan chuckles, not at all flinching at the unintentional sharpness in my words. "Did I? My mistake. I can't help it that you always look so bewitching."

I flush and have absolutely no way of responding to that. When I dare to tear my attention from my clumsy feet and glance up at him, I notice his emerald eyes are scanning over my face, as if he's trying to soak up every detail.

I recall how his fingers brushed over my cheek. How he kissed me.

Then all I can think of is his lips on mine, and I take a wrong step, almost tripping over his feet. He steadies me and smooths out the movement. I doubt anyone around us will have noticed my misstep.

"Thank you," I breathe.

Nolan smiles, and his eyes continuing to sweep over me in long, lavish strokes. I try not to redden and focus on each next step, rather than the intensity of his gaze.

I'm not sure how long we dance, but I am the one who stops first. We take a break at the edge of the hall and sip on the wine served by floating silver trays. It is red wine—maybe *Sanguilus*—and not moon-blossom wine. The Arcanium could never afford to give out this much moon-blossom wine for free.

"Shall we dance again?" Nolan asks, leaning against the large arched window behind us. Condensation hazes the panels, and I imagine he must feel the glass's icy chill through the fabric of his deep blue doublet.

"What else would we do other than dancing?" I reply, setting my empty goblet on a tray as it drifts past.

Nolan's gaze flickers down to my lips and remains there for many moments. Long enough for my heartbeat to elevate, and then I feel as flustered as I did while we were dancing.

But instead of my lips, he takes my hand and kisses the back, just like he did last night.

"I would very much like to resume where we left off last night," he says softly.

With his fingers curled around my wrist, I wonder whether he can feel the wild tempo of my pulse.

When I don't respond, his shoulders stiffen. "If that was too bold, then I sincerely apologize."

"No, no," I quickly say. "I mean, it was rather bold but . . ."

I hope Nolan will say something, to save me from having to search for the words, but he doesn't. He peers at me expectantly.

"I . . . I have also been thinking about last night."

His fingers tighten around my wrist. "What have you been thinking?"

"That . . ." I lower my gaze, unable to look him in the eye. "That I would like to kiss you again." I wish I could blame my words on the wine, but the goblets are quite small and filled halfway. I've also only drank one so far.

I'm sure I sound as embarrassing as I do in my head, but Nolan smiles. His arm wraps around my waist, pulling me nearer. "I would also like to kiss you again," he whispers into my ear.

Remembering that my father is still somewhere in this hall, no doubt watching me closely, I jolt and withdraw from Nolan. "Not here," I murmur.

He lifts his head in a slight nod and then starts toward the double doors, leading me with him.

We are barely out of the hall before he starts kissing me. Luckily, this corridor is tucked away enough that there's no one around. And it's also shadowed, since all the aether crystals are turned off.

His lips are soft as they glide over mine. The cold stone wall presses into my back like hard ice, but with all the warmth pouring through me, I barely notice the chill.

Nolan's fingers weave through my hair. Then he pauses our kiss, admiring my face. His touch follows his gaze, and he gently traces my cheek, coming to a stop beneath my lower lip.

"Reyna," he murmurs, "you are the most beautiful person I've ever met."

I don't respond with words. I wrap my arms around his shoulders and pull him back to me, kissing him as deeply as I can. When my teeth graze his lips, a groan escapes him.

He pushes me harder against the wall. Now there's no escape, even if I wanted it. His every touch threatens to undo me, and all I know is that I need more of him. I can't kiss him quickly enough.

Nolan's hand slides up my waist, skimming over the pearlescent silk of my dress. He breaks our kiss, but I have no chance to protest. His lips slowly trace my neck, and his hand slips higher up to my chest. He cups the soft flesh through the thin fabric, and I can't stop myself from moaning.

A disgruntled cough sounds to our left. Nolan tears himself from me, and we both glance down the corridor. Two old magi stand there, shaking their heads at us. I suppose with how busy the Arcanium is tonight, it was foolish to think we wouldn't be caught here. Thankfully, they soon continue on their way.

"Perhaps we should go somewhere else," Nolan says when they're gone.

"Like where?" I ask. It's only as I speak that I realize how unsteady my breaths are. At least Nolan's aren't much better. "The Upper City square, like last night?"

He shakes his head. "Somewhere more private. Somewhere we won't be interrupted."

My heart drums with anticipation. I have no chance to recover before his lips are on mine. They are even softer than before.

"You could teleport us somewhere else right now," he murmurs, his fingers tracing my shoulder. I shiver. "We wouldn't even need to walk."

"Do you have somewhere in mind?"

He pauses. "How about the cliffs?"

"The cliffs?" We would be awfully secluded there, and we certainly wouldn't need to worry about anyone finding us.

Both desire and nerves ignite through me. How much further does Nolan intend to take our kiss? I don't know whether I'm ready for this step yet, but I find myself nodding all the same.

Nolan kisses my cheek as I draw aether into my fingers and wrap it around us both, preparing my spell.

"*Laxus.*"

Magic basks us in violet light. We fade away, disappearing from the Arcanium's narrow corridor.

When I next blink, we are standing on the shadowed cliffs. And something cold and sharp presses into my neck.

I freeze.

A dagger.

Nolan's dagger.

CHAPTER 37

"Don't move," Nolan hisses, his voice piercing the wind. Beneath, dark waves crash into the cliffs.

"What—"

He presses the blade more firmly against the soft flesh of my neck, silencing me. "If you wish to live, then do exactly as I say."

Dread claws through my heart. The dagger's sharp edge is so close to drawing blood. If I even twitch too abruptly, the movement will send the blade slicing through my throat.

"Teleport us to the top of the Aether Tower." His voice is tempered into cool steel. "Now."

I say nothing. I only stare up at him.

"Do not make me repeat myself," he grinds out.

My heart pounds frantically against my sternum.

I could teleport us back to the Arcanium, where my father will still be. But Nolan's dagger is pressed so tightly to my throat, and if he realizes I've teleported us to the place, he could kill me sooner than I could scream.

I don't dare to risk my life. I do exactly as he says.

"L-laxus." My brittle voice cracks around the spell-word.

The teleportation spell seizes us both.

As we slip through the emptiness, the pressure of Nolan's dagger fades. The darkness lasts for only a heartbeat, but it's long enough for me to consider blasting him with my magic.

Then we return to the material world. Before I can cry out *telum*, I feel the cool, metallic kiss of his dagger. And all thoughts of escape are banished from my mind.

A gale slams into us and whips across my face. The Aether Tower's enormous orb of magic roars above, blinding me with its violet light.

"Good," Nolan purrs. "Now invoke a mind-link with your father and tell him to come here."

Pressure builds in my chest, squeezing the life from my lungs. I don't know what Nolan intends, just that it must involve my father.

How could I be so foolish? How could I trust Nolan? Especially when I know so little of him.

I promised myself I would never again be weak, but now my own stupidity has made me fall into this trap.

"And . . ." I begin, but my voice sounds frail and broken. Swallowing, I try again. "And if I don't?"

With his spare hand, he traces my cheek. Only minutes ago, that gesture sent warmth pooling through me. Now ice washes through my veins. And when I shiver, it is with fear alone.

"If you choose to defy me, then you will leave me little choice." His thumb sweeps over my lower lip. "And believe me, I would very much prefer not to hurt you."

"What do you want with me?" I snarl.

"Everything, Reyna. I want everything with you."

Bile burns the back of my throat. "And I want nothing to do with you."

He doesn't flinch. His fingers trail lower still, brushing down my neck and past the dagger in painfully long strokes. He comes to a stop at the silver locket and toys with it. Then he looks back up at me and smiles. "Oh, but we both know that's a lie. Why else would you take such good care of this locket? Of our promise?"

"What . . . What are you talking about?"

He lets out a sigh. "Have you really forgotten me during these three long years? Did you never think I would return for you? For us?"

Realization slams into me like a sickening punch to the gut.

"No," I gasp. "It can't be."

"You don't believe me? Let me prove it to you, Reyna. Let me show you who I truly am."

Darkness gathers in his left hand. He rakes his fingers down his face and strips away the shadows.

"*Lokriz.*"

He melts into a cloud of dark magic. A phantom hand remains, keeping the dagger fixed to my throat. The shadows swirl, reshaping. His silhouette grows taller and a little broader. Then color returns to him. His golden waves become raven curls, and his emerald eyes become gray and dead. He wears the same deep blue doublet as before, but now an amulet hangs from his neck: an obsidian skull with an icy stone plummeting from its jawless mouth.

"Have you missed me, Reyna," he says, his hand cupping my cheek, "as much as I have missed you?"

"You . . . I thought you were dead." Tears well in my eyes. They escape and tumble down my cheek.

Arluin sweeps them away with his thumb. "Shh," he murmurs, "don't cry. Of course I'm not dead. I would never leave you."

The tears freeze mid-flow. "No," I blurt, "you can't be him. Arluin . . . he would never hurt me." My attention lowers to the gnarled dagger kissing my neck.

"I don't want to hurt you, Reyna. But I must do what needs to be done—for us both. You will soon understand."

I shake my head, the movement stiff and slow to avoid the blade nicking my skin. "Where's Nolan? What did you do to him?"

My heart constricts with terror. I don't know if he is Nolan or Arluin or someone else entirely.

"There never was a Nolan," he replies. "Or at least not that you knew. I killed him months ago, long before I came to Nolderan. I knew your father would execute me on the spot, so I borrowed his face. I hoped you would still like it, even if it were not my own."

I choke. The strangled noise escapes my throat.

This must be someone else. For him to say such things and so indifferently . . .

This is not the Arluin I remember.

His brows pinch together. "What's the matter? You didn't prefer him to me, did you?"

I don't answer. I just stare at him.

"You must understand, Reyna, it was me all along. Me. Every word, every touch—it was all me."

"It can't be you," I whisper. "It can't be."

"But it is me. Your eyes do not deceive you."

I stare up at him, this man I have loved for so long. He looks just as I remember, except for his gray eyes: the mark of dark magic. I never dreamed we would be reunited like this, with a dagger pressed to my throat—

No. That's a lie. There was a nightmare once, long ago. Where I witnessed him becoming his father. Becoming what he already is today.

Blue light flickers inside the jagged stone of his amulet, momentarily drawing my attention. When I glance back up at him, his eyes glow with the same formidable power.

All emotion vanishes from his face. His lips move, but he says no words.

I wonder whether he is preparing a spell, and I brace myself for whatever magic he will unleash. With the dagger against my throat, there will be no escape.

"Of course I will," he growls, gripping his amulet and glaring at it. "Do you think me stupid?"

After a pause, he releases the amulet. Then he turns back to me, his eyes narrowing. He grips the hilt of the dagger more tightly.

"We are wasting time," he hisses, his lip curling. Whereas before there was a chilling softness to his expression, now it is replaced with vicious cruelty. The icy glow remains in his eyes, turning them from dead gray to ghostly blue. "Tell your father to teleport here now. And tell him that if he does not come alone, then I will kill you before he can stop me."

I hesitate, still trying to make sense of everything that is unfolding. But fog blankets my mind.

He presses the dagger even more firmly against me. The force is enough to penetrate my skin. I feel a bead of blood trickling down. Fear pulses through me.

My fate lies within his hands. If he wants me dead, then I will be dead in mere instants. Long before I can scream for mercy.

"Don't test me again. Do it now."

Though my mind was beginning to suspect this may really be Arluin, now I am far less certain. I don't recognize the murderous glint in his eyes. The longing for blood. For death.

All I can believe is that if I hesitate any longer, he will kill me. The crimson line he has etched across my neck is proof of that.

I close my eyes and imagine my father in as much detail as I can: his fiery hair and beard, his bushy brows of the same auburn hue, his indigo robes with flashes of golden thread, and his glowing magenta eyes.

When my mental image is complete, I release the spell. *"Aminex."*

My father answers immediately. *"Reyna?"* There's an urgency to his tone, or at least his projected thoughts. The last time I contacted him via a mind-link was on the night the necromancers stormed the city. When Heston murdered my mother. *"Where are you?"*

"On . . . on top of the Aether Tower." Even in my thoughts, my words come out shaky.

"Why are you up there?"

"Arluin. He—"

My father doesn't wait for me to finish. He severs our mind-link before I can explain everything to him. Before I can warn him.

When I open my eyes, he's already emerging from a cloud of purple light.

His form becomes corporeal. The violent winds pull at his magnificent robes. His magenta eyes fix upon Arluin, upon the dagger pressed to my neck, and they blaze with uncontrollable fury.

"Take your wretched hands off my daughter," he roars.

Though my father's voice booms across the Aether Tower, disturbing even the relentless winds, Arluin doesn't flinch. He only sneers. "I will do as I please with your daughter. Perhaps I will kill her and raise her from the dead."

My heart stills. I try not to tremble in his grasp, try not to show how terrified I am.

"You would not dare," my father seethes.

"You don't believe I would? Then it seems I must demonstrate my sincerity."

He presses the dagger further into my skin. A cry of pain bubbles in my throat as the scratch deepens. More blood wells out.

My father blanches. "Stop!"

Arluin's hand loosens around the dagger's hilt, removing the pressure he was applying. But the blade doesn't leave my flesh. "What's the matter? Can you not bear the sight of her blood?"

His fingers graze my neck and soak up the blood pooling beneath the dagger. He holds up his hand, inspecting the crimson smear. My blood glitters under the light of the Aether Tower's orb.

"I, for one, think it is quite the remarkable sight. It is almost as radiant as she is." Arluin brings his stained fingers to his nose and inhales deeply. "Wouldn't it be a shame if we allowed all that lovely blood to spill out? What a waste it would be." I barely hear Arluin's words. His voice sounds so distant.

My father's knuckles whiten with strain as he grips his staff. "State your price."

"What I ask for in return is a simple thing."

"Then say it," my father spits.

Arluin tilts back his head, peering up at the thunderous orb of magic above us. "The Aether Tower. I want you to deactivate it. Entirely."

"You will let her go first."

"If I do," Arluin replies, his eyes glinting with the amulet's icy glow, "what reason would you have to fulfill my request?"

My father grits his teeth. "At least lower your blade."

Arluin flashes him a thin-lipped smile. His hand doesn't slacken around the dagger. "I'm growing bored of this. Deactivate the Aether Tower or watch her drown in her own blood. The choice is yours."

"Don't, Father!" I cry. "Please don't do it!"

Disabling the Aether Tower would mean rendering Nolderan defenseless. The enormous orb of magic powers the city's wards, shielding us from any external attacks.

Whatever Arluin intends, deactivating the city's defenses must be the key part of his strategy. He has gone to such lengths to carefully maneuver my father into checkmate.

Something terrible will soon befall us. I can't shake away the shadows snaking through my heart.

"Do it," Arluin urges. "I will not wait any longer."

If Nolderan falls tonight, all the blood will be on my hands. If Arluin hadn't captured me, my father wouldn't be in this impossible situation. He wouldn't be forced to disable the Aether Tower.

I need to escape. Now—before my father deactivates the orb.

Arluin won't expect me to cast magic without spell-words. I succeeded when I fought Kaely. Maybe I can succeed again.

If I harness my grief, my anger, perhaps it will be enough for all the aether in my body to burst free.

But there's no time. My father is already striding to the center of the Aether Tower. He stops directly beneath the enormous orb of magic.

"No, Father!"

He raises his staff. The crystalline surface glistens in the brilliant violet light.

Desperately, I focus my fury. On Arluin deceiving me. On him wielding me as a weapon against my father.

So many nights I cried for him. And yet, he was plotting Nolderan's destruction.

Though I feel magic rushing through me, brimming as furiously as my emotions, it is already too late. When I unleash my explosion of aether, sending Arluin back several paces and freeing myself from his grasp, my father has already uttered the spell-word.

"*Terminir.*"

He drums his staff against the platform. The enormous orb of aether flickers off.

Without its radiance, we are cast in darkness.

The clouds are thick and heavy, suffocating the stars. The crescent moon is pallid against the shadowy haze.

Fearing Arluin will capture me again before I can escape, I break into a sprint. When I reach my father, I clutch his arm. My fingers dig into his sleeve.

"Reyna!" His free hand goes to my neck, examining the wound.

"It doesn't hurt." I wonder whether it should. The scratch is deep enough that blood smears over his fingers. But I feel numb.

Arluin straightens, having recovered from the burst of aether I hurled at him. A smirk curls onto his lips.

The city erupts.

Ghostly beams shoot into the sky, slicing through the dark heavens like sword. There are at least half a dozen, all scattered through the city. Before my father can demand an explanation, blood-curdling howls pierce the night.

The howls of the dead.

CHAPTER 38

UNDEAD SPILL FROM THE PORTALS in a river of decayed flesh. They shamble through the streets, their stiff fingers outstretched like claws as they begin their ravenous search for the living. A horde of ghouls, wights, and wraiths engulfs the city.

This isn't like the night Heston attacked. What Arluin brings to Nolderan is a massacre.

And this is the beginning of the end.

My father's fingers tremble around his staff. Beneath his auburn beard, the veins in his neck pulse to a frantic rhythm. Upon seeing my father's fear, terror shudders through me.

"What have you done?" My father's roar cracks with horror and rage.

"I have done nothing," Arluin replies with cool indifference. "What you have done, however, is to choose your daughter over your city. You are predictable, Telric. It is no secret that Reyna is your greatest weakness."

I clench my fists. I want to shout that I'm not a weakness, nor a liability, but no words leave my tongue. Fear paralyzes me.

And even if I could speak, how could I deny Arluin's words? Nolderan's current state is because of me. I was too stupid to see through Arluin's deceit. If only I hadn't been blind to the signs: how he stared at me, how he kissed me, how he fixated on the locket last night. Now everything seems so painfully obvious. If only it were not too late.

"You will pay for this treachery, boy," my father snarls. "When your father left, I treated you as family. And this is how you show your gratitude? By taking my daughter hostage and unleashing Death Gates across my city?"

"I saved her life," Arluin hisses. "And the cost of saving her was to condemn my father, to my own future. Yet because I used necromancy to save her, you would have executed me. I was there when you murdered my father. I heard each and every one of his dying screams. You offered him no trial."

"I offered him no trial because he deserved none! He sealed his fate when he murdered my wife."

"But I didn't murder your wife. I saved your daughter by betraying my own father. Do you then claim you would have offered me a fair trial, or would you have burned me where I stood?"

My father says nothing. His hand clenches his staff so tightly the wood creaks with the force. His temple throbs.

"That is what I thought. You would blindly kill us all for the magic we practice."

"Your heinous magic threatens the living."

Arluin shakes his head. "Do you know how much I despise you, Telric, and your pathetic self-righteousness?"

Before my father can reply, Arluin raises his obsidian dagger and drags it down his palm in a jagged line. "Tonight, I will avenge the injustice my father and I have suffered at your hands."

A crimson bead wells from the wound. He gathers the shadows, and they merge with his blood.

"*Kravut!*"

Black blood spills across the Aether Tower like ink. The drops swell into an enormous worm thrice my father's height. The worm lets out a ferocious hiss, revealing rows of knifelike teeth.

Adrenaline sears through my nerves, and the numbness dissolves. Lightning energizes me to such an extent I feel as though I've consumed an Elixir of Flurry.

I will not be weak. I will not allow my presence to burden my father. I will prove Arluin wrong.

Aether floods through my veins, bubbling and fizzling as it yearns for release. I force it under my control. I bend it to my will. When my father weaves aether into flames, I do too. Fire is the most effective magic we can wield against the undead and dark magic.

"*Ignir'muriz!*" we call together. Just before the bloodworm descends on us.

Flames erupt.

Maw first, the worm plunges into our blazing wall. Its shriek pierces my eardrums as our flames devour it.

My father and I work in tandem, as though our mind-link was not entirely severed. The aether rushing through our veins is one and the same.

"*Ignir'quatir!*"

The fiery shield explodes. Flames hurl at the bloodworm.

This screech is more horrifying than the last. Even when the worm falls silent, ringing continues in my ears.

"*Ignira,*" my father growls before our enemy can recover. A deadly fire-ball swarms from his fingers. The relentless flames slam into the worm, and it bursts apart.

Black blood splatters over us. Inky blotches stain my pearlescent dress and coat my cheeks. I wipe away the sticky liquid, but it smears further across my face. The substance shares the same abhorrent stench as the decayed flesh of ghouls.

The path to Arluin is cleared. I seize the opportunity. The frenzy of battle guides me from one movement to the next. Before Arluin can unleash his counterattack, I strike.

"*Gelu'tempis!*"

Ice shoots from my fingers. Like a firework, it explodes mid-flight. Frozen needles plunge to Arluin, their glistening points ready to rip him into shreds.

A few icicles find him. They sink into his shoulders and graze his cheeks. Where the shards meet him, they leave crimson stains in their wake.

But before my spell can inflict critical damage, Arluin wraps the shadows around him. "*Ekrad!*"

The frozen needles bounce off his shield like hail. They clatter onto the platform.

Aether swirls in my father's hands. "*Telum!*"

The spell is quick but fierce. So much magic crackles from the blast that it shakes even the violent winds.

The aether collides with Arluin's shield. The shadows intensify into a bubble of viscous ink, concealing his silhouette. I can't tell whether my father's attack dealt him a critical blow.

I pull more aether into my grasp and prepare myself to strike again if Arluin bursts free from his shield.

The shadows ripple. Aside from that, there is no movement. Not for a long moment.

A bolt of darkness spins toward us, formed from the inky shield. The volatile magic is terrifyingly powerful—so much stronger than my father's spell.

Dark magic feeds on aether. Arluin absorbed my father's attack and corrupted it into shadows. For him to accomplish such a feat, his magic must be far greater than my father's.

I don't have time to consider the implications of this realization. The shadow bolt is already upon us.

"*Muriz!*" we both shout.

A barrier of aether forms around us. The shadow bolt pierces our shield, and we are left defenseless.

The attack isn't directed at me. It is intended for my father.

The shadow bolt slams into him, and he is thrown back. He hits the stone with a sickening thud.

"Father!" I call, sprinting toward him.

There is no visible wound, but the dark magic has left him weakened. He struggles to push himself back onto his feet.

Shadows spill from Arluin's hands. The ghastly amulet glints. It must be the source of his unfathomable strength. The skull seems to laugh at me.

Molten fury churns inside my chest. I almost burst from the relentless pressure.

"*Ignir'alas!*" I scream, channeling all my wrath into the spell.

Violent flames sweep from my fingers. They soar upward into the blazing wings of a phoenix.

Though the attack descends on Arluin at a furious velocity, he languidly lifts his head as he regards it.

"*Ekrad,*" he commands. Darkness shields him.

My fiery wings collide with his barrier. They crumble into ash. Sparks fly in the wind.

I stare at him, my eyes widening with horror. I poured all my strength into that attack, and yet he cast it aside so easily.

"*Vorikaz.*"

Arluin flings the remnants of his shield toward me. I have no chance to escape.

Obsidian chains wrap around me. Their grip tightens, squeezing the life from my chest. I can't feel even the slightest trace of magic in the air. Nor can I feel the aether in my blood.

Being cut off from my magic is as jarring as losing my sense of taste or touch.

Arluin paces toward my father, who is barely back on his feet and is significantly weakened from the shadow bolt.

Restrained by these obsidian chains, there is nothing I can do to save him.

"*Ignira,*" my father hisses, fueling his spell with all the magic he can gather. Deep lines of strain contort his brow.

"*Rivus!*"

Arluin meets my father's attack with a bolt of darkness. The two forces of magic collide, and their impact is so great it tears through the air. Wind slams into me. If not for the chains holding me firmly in place, the gale would likely throw me from the Aether Tower.

Both spells annihilate each other. But the attack cost my father much more strength.

He sways in the wind. His energy is so spent he struggles to keep himself upright.

Yet he fights on.

"*Gelu'gladis!*" He spins aether into ice magic and draws it out into a frozen sword. Blade first, he launches it at Arluin.

"*Arisga!*" A force of darkness rushes from Arluin's fingers, and it slings the sword aside. It clatters onto the stone and shatters into tiny fragments of ice.

"*Zadvuk!*"

Dark magic hurls at my father, taking the shape of an enormous hand. Shadowy fingers close around his throat.

My father chokes as the phantom hand lifts him by several feet and squeezes the air from his lungs. He tears at the spectral fingers strangling him and desperately tries to free himself. His eyes bulge from their sockets, and life drains out of him.

Though my father tries to draw on his magic, only tiny wisps of aether form—not enough to interrupt the shadowy hand.

Arluin squeezes his fist tighter. The spell chokes my father more forcefully.

He stalks nearer and raises his dagger. The gnarled blade glistens in the pallid moonlight.

"Father!" I shriek, battling my restraints. But struggling tightens the chains. They dig in so deeply that I fear my ribcage will fracture.

If only I could do something. If only I were not so helpless.

I squeeze my eyes shut and fight the dark magic which suppresses the aether in my blood. No matter how hard I try, I'm unable to sense even the faintest trace of my magic.

"Father!" I cry again. My voice falters, despair suffocating me.

My father's blood-shot eyes flicker toward me. He chokes out something which sounds like my name. His crystalline staff tumbles from his fingers. It rolls across the stone and halts at my feet. If only I could retrieve it. Maybe then I could use it to save him.

But I can't move. I can't do anything. Except watch.

Arluin stops before my father. He regards his dagger and twirls it in his fingers. Scorn contorts his lips. "Enjoy an afterlife of servitude, Telric."

Then he plunges the dagger through my father's heart.

I scream.

I scream so loudly my throat emits no sound.

My tears freeze on my cheeks.

Arluin twists the dagger. Perverted delight gleams in his eyes, still shrouded by the amulet's ghostly glow.

He tears the blade from my father's chest and holds it high. The dagger weeps crimson tears.

"Father," I gasp. "Father!" Though I call him, his head doesn't rise. It hangs lifelessly.

He is gone.

Dead.

Though my eyes witness the sight, my heart contests it as the truth.

He is the Grandmage of Nolderan, one of the most powerful sorcerers in the world. How could he be defeated?

Arluin uses the flat edge of his bloodied dagger to lift my father's limp head, and even when I see his unmoving face, I refuse to believe that he is dead. I tell myself over and over that he is not, desperate to make it true.

Darkness pours from Arluin's hands. He funnels it into my father, who remains suspended in midair by the phantom hand.

"*Arka-joud.*" Arluin's amulet glows brighter as he releases his spell.

Shadowy tendrils plunge into my father's mouth and nostrils. They seize him from within.

Arluin waves his hand. The dark magic forming the phantom hand dissipates. My father is released from its grasp.

He returns to his feet. His fingers twitch.

"Father!" I shout. "Father!"

His head turns. It tilts further over than is natural. His eyes no longer shimmer with magenta. Now the sockets are empty, filled only by the shadows swarming inside.

He snarls at me, his stiff fingers jutting out. He starts to drag his feet across the stone, but Arluin stops him. He places the blunt edge of the obsidian dagger to my father's chest and smears more blood across his robes.

My eyes fix on the wound. I want to look away, but I can't. All I can do is stare at every detail: the way the fabric is unevenly torn, the way black blood continues to seep out like ink.

"Stay," Arluin commands him. "You will not move until I tell you."

My father growls a guttural protest, but he remains still.

I barely notice Arluin lowering his dagger and pacing toward me. Only when he reaches me does my attention leave the gaping wound across my father's chest.

Arluin dismisses the obsidian chains and releases me from their grasp. I stagger. My chest heaves from the removal of the pressure, and air rushes into my lungs at such an alarming rate that my own breaths suffocate me.

The stone platform sways. I offer no resistance as I tumble.

Arluin catches me. His arm slips around my back.

I stare up at him. The icy glow has faded from his eyes. The amulet no longer shines.

"You killed him," I whisper.

The wind howls. It drowns my words.

Arluin strokes my cheek. Where his thumb touches, blood smears across my skin. My father's blood.

I should vomit at the realization—that would be the normal reaction. But I feel nothing.

"Don't worry," he says softly. "You have no reason to fear me. I know I said some hurtful things before, but I meant none of them. Of course I would never hurt you. I only needed you—your father—to believe it, or else he wouldn't have done what was required. But now, everything is nearly over. Without Nolderan, without your father, we can finally be together again."

"Arluin," I breathe, "you killed my father."

"I know you might hate me for it, at least for a while, but this was the only way we could be together. Don't you see?"

I don't blink. I continue gazing into his cold, dead eyes.

He presses his lips to my forehead. "Now that there's nothing in our way, will you marry me, Reyna?"

His kiss shatters my heart.

I am already broken, but I break even harder. Somehow the fragments of me are stronger than my entire self.

An anguished cry rips from my lips. I shove Arluin back with every ounce of my remaining resolve. My palms dig into his chest so deeply that my flesh stings with the force. But I fight through the pain. I push and push until I am freed from the shackles of his arms.

"No," I gasp, my breaths raw and heavy. "Never touch me again."

His dark brows knit together. "You no longer wish to marry me?"

"You killed him! You raised his corpse!"

"You promised you would marry me no matter what," he says quietly.

My nostrils flare. My entire body shakes.

Arluin steps closer. I lunge for the crystalline staff lying at my feet. My fingers close around the shaft. I raise it, holding it out like a ward between us. But the staff doesn't stop Arluin from continuing forth.

I shrink back. My feet meet the edge of the Aether Tower. Winds rush upward, seeking to claim me. I stand my ground. Against them, against Arluin.

"Don't come any closer!"

"All I want is you," he whispers.

I shake my head. Frantically. As if to break free from the chains of this nightmare.

He extends his hand, taking a step forth. And then another. "Come with me, Reyna."

"Never," I snarl, my fingers clenching around the staff. "I would sooner die."

"Reyna—"

There's nowhere left to run. He is almost upon me.

I turn and fling myself off the Aether Tower.

But the gales don't seize me. Arluin's fingers close around my wrist before they can.

"Let go," I growl, clutching the staff. My legs dangle in empty air. But I don't fear the height; I fear Arluin's grasp.

"No," he gasps. "I will never let you go."

Our gazes lock together. His eyes are unyielding. As are mine.

We both reach for our magic. I am first to unleash mine.

"*Ignira!*"

A fireball surges from my hand—the one Arluin holds by my wrist.

"*Okraz,*" he mutters. Darkness pierces my skin.

Only when my fireball reaches him does he release me.

I plummet toward the deadly spires.

CHAPTER 39

AIR CRASHES INTO ME. I cling to the crystalline staff. The relentless winds try to prise it from my grasp, but I refuse to let go.

This is all I have of my father. I will not lose it.

Cobalt rooftops surge up to meet me. As do gleaming spires. But I have no time to fear them.

High above, Arluin melds with the shadows. In a cloud of darkness, he descends toward me.

The distance between us rapidly closes. I can't fall quickly enough.

I must do something. Now. If I do nothing, he will soon reach me.

I gather aether and craft the image of my manor's gilded gates in my mind. *"Laxus!"*

Magic bursts from my fingers. Shadowy tendrils curl around my wrist. But I'm already fading away. The darkness seizes air.

In the next heartbeat, I'm standing outside my manor. Heavy clouds shroud the sky, and the gates glint in the stifled starlight. Now that the Aether Tower is deactivated, the enchantment on the gates is broken, and they are swung wide open.

If Arluin follows me here, the gates will do little to stop him. But with how powerful he is, even if the enchantment remained, it would provide me with little defense.

I don't know why I chose to teleport here. It offers me no advantage. It leaves me cornered.

My breaths come out in sharp bursts, and my pulse beats to a frenzied rhythm. I almost collapse in a heap outside my manor, but I know I can't. I must keep on going.

A cacophony of howls fills the night. The undead are not far. Soon they will reach this street, and I will be overwhelmed by a sea of ghouls and wights. I must escape before they do.

But before I can do anything, a sharp stabbing pain sears across my wrist. It feels as though a knife is piercing my flesh.

I glance down. There is no knife. Only an eye that has been inked across my skin. The mark of dark magic.

"*Reyna*," Arluin calls, his voice echoing through my mind. "*I know where you are. I can see everything.*"

A tracking spell. He must have placed it on me before I fell. Now that he knows where I am, he will be here within moments.

I must run. But to where? No matter where I choose, he will find me. The eye etched into my flesh will make sure of that.

But an eye cannot see if it's blind.

I don't stop to consider whether my theory is too simplistic. I only act.

"*Ventrez!*" A fierce gale blasts from my fingers. It cuts through the thin fabric of my skirts.

The scraps fall to the ground. I grab them and wrap them around my wrist. My fingers are clumsy with desperate haste.

"*I won't lose you. Not ever—*"

I secure the knot with my teeth. Arluin's words are cut off. He doesn't speak again.

Did I succeed? Does his silence mean I blocked his tracking spell?

Even if I did, he knows that I'm here. I can hesitate no longer.

"*Laxus!*"

The gilded gates of my manor vanish. They are replaced by the Arcanium's archway.

QUEL ESTE VOLU, PODE NONQUES VERA MORIRE the carved words read. *That which is aether may never truly die.*

Chaos erupts behind me. I whirl around.

Magi and adepts stand shoulder to shoulder as they battle the rampaging undead. Necromancers are scattered through the horde, their black robes merging with the darkness.

Magic collides everywhere I can see. Ashes of aether scatter through the breeze, falling on Nolderan like glimmering specks of snow.

I push through the masses. No one turns to me. All are focused on their own enemies.

I manage three strides before a ghoul's rotten teeth snap toward me.

Using my father's staff as a focus, I draw upon aether. The crystalline surface gleams with magic, enabling me to rapidly power my spell.

"*Ignira,*" I hiss.

My scorching flames slam into the rotten carcass. It lets out an unearthly shriek as its body disintegrates into ash.

I continue through the havoc, searching for a face I recognize.

I find Archmage Gidston standing several paces ahead. Her violet robes distinguish her from everyone else still dressed in their finery. A few strands of blond hair have come loose from her usually neat bun. They dance around her in the wind.

"Archmage Gidston!" I call, hurrying over to her. Another undead lunges for me. I blast it with flames.

The Archmage finishes her fight with a wraith. Then she glances back at me.

"Reyna!" she exclaims. "Where's your father?"

I don't reply. I can't. Telling her what happened atop the Aether Tower will make it all come rushing back. For now I can only block everything out, focusing on one movement and then the next.

If I stop to think, I fear I may never move again.

Her gaze trails across to my father's staff. She must find her answer there, and in my blood-stricken face, since a shadow descends across her expression. Her lips part. No sound passes them.

This is the end. Of Nolderan. Of the magi.

Archmage Gidston's shock lasts for only a short second. A wight launches a shadow bolt at us.

"*Ignir'muriz!*" she calls, surrounding us with a wall of flames. "*Ignir'quatir!*"

The fiery shield explodes, taking the wight with it.

Ghouls swarm toward us. We stand back-to-back, battling the legions of undead. They do not relent. When one falls, another takes its place. There is no end to this storm.

"Reyna!" a shout comes from ahead.

My aether shield is so dense I can't distinguish the figure racing toward me. All I can tell is that they are among the living.

"*Quatir!*"

The barrier explodes, blasting the surrounding undead. Bone shards rain on me. Their edges graze my cheeks.

"Reyna!"

Now that my shield is gone and the nearest undead are defeated, I have a clear view of the person calling my name. Koby. His cheeks are branded red, and his breaths are labored. He barely manages to stop himself before crashing into Archmage Gidston and me.

"Koby?" I call over the crackling of flames and rattling of bones. "What is it?"

"Eliya!" he wheezes.

A ghoul lunges for him.

"*Ignira!*" I yell.

A fireball surges from my hands and hurls at the undead. It bursts into flames.

I return my attention to Koby. "What about her? Have you seen her?"

He shakes his head. "When the undead started attacking, no one could find you. Or your father. Eliya went looking for you."

My stomach knots. "Where is she? Where did she say she would look?"

"I don't know. Before I could ask, she sprinted out the Arcanium and teleported away. I . . . I hoped she was with you. Or that you had at least seen her."

I grit my teeth. "We need to find her. Now. Before it's too late."

I don't say that it may already be too late. That she may already be dead. I refuse to believe it.

"Would she be at your house?"

"No, I came from there. I didn't see her." I pause. "Flour Power."

"The bakery? Why would she be there?"

I don't explain my reasoning. I grab his arm and draw aether over us both.

"*Laxus.*"

We fade away, leaving the Arcanium behind us.

The street we arrive on is more chaotic. With so few magi here, the undead are free to rampage. Screams of the dying and the dead fill the night.

I break into a run—heading toward the alley opposite us. To our left, a ghoul rips off the limb from a mangled corpse and gnaws on it. The undead wears Mrs. Baxter's face. I don't allow myself to stop and stare.

Koby does.

"T-that's—"

I pull him along before he can finish. He stumbles after me.

We enter the alleyway. The shadows slash across us in bold lines.

There is nothing here. No undead, no Eliya.

I inhale sharply, clenching the staff with one hand and tearing at my hair with the other.

Since she found me here, three years ago, I thought this might be where she came looking for me. But there is no trace of her.

"She isn't here," Koby says.

I scowl at him for the painful reminder.

"Where else do you think she could be?"

"I don't know," I grind out. "Stop talking."

He clamps his mouth shut. I might have felt bad, if not for the white-hot panic pounding through me. My thoughts are jumbled.

I clutch my temple. It throbs manically beneath my fingers. The stone walls spin around me. I think I might fall. But I can't. If I do, Eliya will die.

I must find her.

I break into a sprint. My footsteps thunder against the cobblestones.

"Reyna, wait!" Koby calls after me.

But I don't wait. I hardly hear his words. My blood drums too loudly in my ears.

He hurries after me. His strides are almost as frantic as mine.

I don't know where I'm running to. All I know is that I must save Eliya.

Undead charge at me from all angles. I don't stop. I carve a burning path through their ranks.

"Reyna!"

Koby's shout is drowned by my flames and my gasps. With each corner I turn, I pray I will see Eliya's crimson hair. That it will not be too late.

But it isn't Eliya I first find.

On my next turn, I glimpse a mousy brown braid fluttering in the wind.

"Kaely!" I shout. We might be sworn enemies, but right now we are allies. The fact we are living makes us so.

Except it's not Kaely that turns to me. It's something *else*.

Shadows swarm inside the wight's empty sockets. Loose bandages dangle from its arms. Scorched skin peeks out between the scraps of white cloth.

The freckles across her cheeks might be hers, but this is not her.

Koby comes to a stop beside me. He grips my shoulder. I feel him tremble.

"Reyna—" Koby begins.

I shake him off. I draw on the surrounding aether.

"*Rivus,*" the wight snarls. Its voice almost sounds like Kaely's, but deeper. And the syllables reverberate in its vocal chords.

I thrust out the crystalline staff, both my hands clasping it with strained force. "*Muriz!*" An aether barrier forms around Koby and me. It absorbs the dark magic and has power left to spare. I let it erupt. "*Quatir!*"

A wave of violet light crashes into Kaely. She staggers back.

But I have no chance to launch a subsequent attack. Three ghouls spring at us.

"*Ignir'alas!*" I call. Flaming wings crash into them. Fire devours their rotted skin and their yellowed bones.

I turn back to Kaely. Her shadowy orbs flicker between Koby and me.

"*Telum!*" Koby cries. A blast of aether races toward her.

"*Ekrad,*" she says, drawing the shadows around herself. Koby's attack bounces off her shield. "*Gavrik.*"

A storm of shadows races forth. It splits into hundreds of ravens, all with razor-like beaks.

There's no time to shield us both. I can only shield myself.

"*Ignir'muriz!*"

Flames encase me, preventing the shadowy ravens from reaching me. Their beaks stab into my fiery wall, and one by one they are obliterated.

My shield was hasty, and the attack was powerful. My flames are extinguished before the flurry ceases. The last few ravens break through my defense and tear at my dress and the flesh of my bare arms. But they inflict no fatal damage.

I glance at Koby. I don't know which spell he used to defend himself, but it appears his shield was ineffective. Long gashes mark his cheeks. His fine clothes are shredded into threads. Blood stains the rich fabric.

Kaely raises her hands. Shadows stir once more.

I also reach for my magic and pull aether into my grasp as swiftly as I can. We both unleash our spells.

"*Rivus!*"

"*Ignira!*"

I expect my fireball and her shadow bolt to collide. But they don't. While my attack targets Kaely, hers doesn't target me.

It rushes for Koby.

I shout his name. Aether blooms from my fingers as I race toward him.

He tries to speak spell-words, but it is too late.

The shadow bolt pierces his chest.

Darkness floods through him, choking him from within. The veins in his neck throb and blacken.

My fireball strikes Kaely. She shrieks, but I don't turn to look. My gaze remains on Koby.

A strangled cry comes from his throat. His bulging, blood-shot eyes turn to me.

Then he falls. Dead.

I stare at him. My hand grips the staff so forcefully my fingers ache. I grip it even harder.

Black blood spills from Koby's chest. His unseeing eyes gaze up at the shrouded stars.

I am given no chance to mourn him.

"*Rivus,*" Kaley calls again.

Another shadow bolt surges forth. This one is intended for me.

There is no time to speak spell-words. The darkness will tear through me before the syllables leave my throat.

Like Koby, like my father, I will be dead.

But if I die, how will I save Eliya?

Emotion smashes through the dam of numbness. A wave of fear and fury and grief engulfs me. I am helpless in its tyrannical grasp. I struggle to stay afloat, to not drown.

Magic rips through me—the pressure too great for my mortal body to contain.

An inferno explodes. It seizes everything in its path: Kaely, Koby, the undead nearest me. Stone walls heap around me. The volatile flames don't distinguish between friend or foe. They devour even the people fleeing from ghouls at the end of the street.

When the explosion is spent, I collapse. The cobblestones strike my knees, but I feel no pain.

Only ash and rubble remain. There is no living left, nor any dead. Just me.

Weariness seeps through my mind in blurry black spots. The explosion wasn't restrained by spell-words and almost burned through every drop of magic in my blood. I'm lucky to be alive. If it consumed all my aether, I would be dead.

The staff tumbles from my grasp. A hollow clatter sounds as it hits the ground. Exhaustion claims me. Like the staff, I fall.

No.

Eliya.

I fling out my arms and stop the ground from smashing into my skull.

I must find her. I must save her.

My fingers curl around the staff. I use it to haul myself upright. Once back onto my feet, I sway.

I don't hesitate for long. If I do, I will fall again.

Onward I force myself. My wobbly legs threaten to give way, and my feet are clumsy as they pound against the cobblestones. Once or twice I almost trip on the uneven edges. Determination steadies me. It keeps me from falling.

Two skeletons turn the corner. There's little aether left flowing through my veins, and there won't be more until I rest, but I must fight.

I use the smallest amount of magic possible to control the aether in the air, and I ensure the spell does not take more than I can give.

"*Ignira*," I rasp.

The resulting fireball is far from my fiercest, especially compared to the inferno which raged through the street, but it is enough. One skeleton is destroyed by the blast, while the other is crippled by it. Half its bones crumble to ash. It continues toward me, but I sprint hard and fast, and it fails to outrun me.

On the next street, a wraith turns to me and raises its spectral hands. Shadows rise.

I strike with fire before it can attack. Then I keep running.

My strength is swiftly depleting. I don't know how many more spells I can conjure—or whether my next will falter.

Three corners later, I find Eliya.

She lies slumped at a dead end, her crimson waves cascading over her face. Two ghouls stalk toward her.

"Eliya!" I shout.

The ghouls stop and turn. They race for me, ravenous hands outstretched.

Though my magic is almost spent, fury musters a fierce burst of strength.

"*Ignir'alas!*"

Blazing wings swoop into the night and dive at the undead. Flames consume their decayed flesh.

I don't watch. I continue straight through the embers. My own flames singe my tattered dress.

I lunge for Eliya and skid across the cobblestones.

"Eliya," I call, crouching beside her.

There's no reply. Her chest is so very still. Her fingers do not twitch.

With a trembling hand, I brush aside her crimson locks to reveal her heart-shaped face. Her eyes are closed. A heartbeat passes. They don't open.

I don't breathe as I press my fingers to her neck. I wait for a moment and then another, but I feel no pulse.

"Eliya!" I shriek, shaking her shoulders.

Her limp head lolls with the motion.

"No," I gasp, clutching her cheeks. They are still warm, but I feel them cooling with every passing moment. I cradle her head. "No, no, no. Wake up, Eliya. Please wake up."

No matter how much I shake her, no matter how much I plead, she does not stir.

There's no visible wound. She almost looks asleep. I tell myself that she is. I refuse to face the alternative. That I failed to save her. That I came too late.

The heavens weep. Rain drizzles over us both. Drops splatter onto Eliya's unmoving face, and they flow down her cheeks like tears. A wind blows over us, and it turns my drenched fingers into ice.

"Don't leave me, Eliya," I rasp. "Please don't leave me."

Somewhere in the far distance, chaos rages on. Deep in the back of my mind, I know I should return to Archmage Gidston and help her and the other magi and adepts defend the Arcanium against the hordes of undead, but grief shackles me in place.

All I can do is clasp Eliya and rock us back and forth, whispering her name until my voice breaks. My lips move of their own accord, calling her in an unspoken prayer.

I don't know how long passes. Time ceases to exist. There is only Eliya and me.

Soon the city falls silent and still. The streets become as lifeless as Eliya's body in my arms.

Maybe the undead were defeated. Or maybe Nolderan has fallen. Right now, I don't care which. All I want is for Eliya's eyes to flutter open. For her to laugh and tell me that everything will be fine.

I wait, and I wait. But her eyes never open. She never laughs.

A painful sob racks through my body. I clasp my mouth to stop the sound from escaping.

Footsteps echo from the adjacent street. Voices follow.

His voice.

"Have you searched the Lower City?" Arluin growls.

"Yes, my lord," a man replies in a crisp voice. "There was no sign of her."

"You searched every street?"

"Indeed. We did."

There's a pause.

"I want her found," Arluin says. "Alive."

The footsteps quicken. They grow louder as they draw nearer.

My pulse races.

At any moment, Arluin will turn the corner and find me huddled here at the end of this street. And when he does, he will snatch Eliya from my grasp and desecrate her like he desecrated my father.

He must not find me. Or Eliya.

I could try teleporting away, but I don't know where I can run that he won't find me. And I would leave a trail of aether dust behind. Then he would know that I was here.

I also cannot run. There's only one exit, and it would lead me straight to Arluin.

Instead, I focus on the surrounding stone walls and craft them carefully in my mind. I replicate every bruise and scratch inflicted by time and weather, and when my painting is perfect, I release my magic.

"*Alucinatas,*" I whisper.

A barrier of aether encases me. The wall hums and ripples.

Arluin turns the corner. His black curls are like oiled crow feathers in the dying moonlight.

He marches toward me. My heart hammers in my chest.

With my haste and my fatigue, I worry the illusion won't be powerful enough to fool him. But now, I can do nothing except wait. And pray to gods who never listen.

Each footstep shoves my nerves further over the edge. The tension within me is so taut I fear it will cause my spell to shatter.

He halts three strides from me. His gray eyes scan over the wall and then the floor. Every time his gaze passes over me, my pulse beats at a terrifying tempo. My heart drums so thunderously I fear Arluin will hear it.

Unable to watch, I squeeze my eyes shut.

"I left a corpse here," Arluin says to the necromancer behind him. "Now it is gone."

I dare to open an eye. The other necromancer is built like a stake: tall and thin. Wrinkles weather his face, and the strained light reflects off his bald head.

"Corpses do have a tendency to do that," the necromancer replies. "One of the others must have raised it."

Arluin shakes his head. "No, they couldn't have."

"Then perhaps a ghoul ran off with it and feasted on its flesh."

"Perhaps," Arluin says, his eyes narrowing. "Or perhaps someone else took it."

"The girl you search for?"

Arluin clenches his jaw. "I know she's here somewhere."

"If she is a mage, she could have teleported to anywhere in Imyria. She is likely long gone."

"She has never left Nolderan before, so she couldn't have teleported anywhere off this island."

"You are sure? It has been three years."

Arluin's fists tightens. He doesn't reply.

"We have what we came for, do we not? I understand you have personal reasons for seeking the girl, but you must consider what is at stake. It won't be long before the world learns Nolderan's fate, and when they do, they will be on their guard. Achieving our ambitions will be a far greater challenge. We must strike swiftly, while they are still all unaware."

Arluin exhales deeply, his fingers running through his nest of dark curls. "Very well. Find the others. We will send our undead back through the Death Gates and then we will leave this place."

The tall necromancer bows his head. "*Farjud*," he says, melding into the shadows. He leaves in a heavy cloud of darkness.

Arluin lingers. He stares at the wall behind me. I wonder if he can sense the residue of my magic from when I defeated the undead. Or if he can sense the dark magic which marks my wrist.

I glance down. The knot remains secure and hasn't loosened in battle. I pray it will be enough.

He continues his examination. I hold my breath. A moment passes. Then another. My chest aches from the lack of air.

Finally, with one last look at the wall, he turns and vanishes down the street.

CHAPTER 40

BY THE TIME DAWN ARRIVES, the ghostly beams are extinguished and all the Death Gates are closed. Nolderan descends into an even heavier silence.

I don't know whether the necromancers have left, so I wait longer still.

The sun creeps higher through the clouds, and the heavens bleed with its emerging rays. The rain has dwindled, and wispy drops brush the crown of my head.

Minutes stretch into hours. Arluin does not return, nor do his necromancers.

Only when the sun has long reached its peak do I dare stir. While I've been sitting here, cradling Eliya's lifeless body, a small fraction of my strength has returned. It is enough to craft a teleportation spell and carry us both away.

"*Laxus,*" I breathe. The sound scarcely leaves my lips, but my magic obeys my command.

We leave the narrow street and materialize inside the Upper City's cathedral, on the platform of the circular chamber. The ten major gods stare down at us. With the Aether Tower disabled and the cathedral's power line cut off, the paintings have lost their enchantment and are frozen still.

Once, when my mother's coffin laid inside this chamber, I pledged a silent promise to become powerful enough to prevent anyone I love from ever being snatched away again. Now I realize my foolishness.

Everyone is dead, and I could save no one.

I gently roll Eliya from my arms and kiss her forehead. Her skin is colder than the stone floor beneath us. Her delicate face blurs as a fresh wave of grief crashes into me.

"I'm sorry, Eliya," I choke, my voice raw and cracked. "I'm sorry I couldn't save you."

But she doesn't hear my words. She will never hear them again.

My tears patter across her icy cheeks and trail down into her crimson locks, dampening them.

When my eyes dry and I'm unable to shed any more tears, I lift my head and absently gaze out at the rest of the cathedral. Rows and rows of empty pews stare back at me, framed by the ribcage of the vaulted ceiling high above. A few are knocked over, and blood blemishes the otherwise polished ivory floor. The towering doors at the far end are both swung wide open. The street beyond is deathly quiet, rubble heaped like mounds of snow. Though much debris litters the cobblestones, there isn't a single body in sight. Only a few stains of blood that the rain has yet to erase.

I return my attention to Eliya and clasp her cold cheek. My hoarse breaths echo through the cathedral's hollow walls.

Then I stand and start through the narrow door to my left. I enter an antechamber filled with scrolls and holy relics and continue straight through. Soon I arrive at the stairs which lead beneath the cathedral. It takes longer than I expect to reach the bottom, and I hurry down the last few steps. I think all the necromancers and undead are long gone now—judging by the stillness of the city—but I don't want to leave Eliya for longer than is necessary. I can't bear the thought of her up there all alone, with the callous gods staring down at her.

The room is dark and musty. The faint glow atop the stairs provides enough light for me to make out the crystals lining the walls like sconces. Since they rely on the Aether Tower for their power, I have to draw on the remnants of my magic.

"*Iluminos.*" Though the spell-word is quiet, it shudders through the darkness.

An orb of brilliant light sweeps from my fingers. Its radiance illuminates the entire room.

Dozens of empty crystal coffins lie stacked in rows. Magic ripples across their violet surfaces.

I reach for the nearest coffin and haul it from the top of the stack. But it's heavier than I anticipate and doesn't budge, even when I shove it.

Again, I draw on the dregs of my magic, this time releasing a wind spell.

"*Ventrez.*"

A breeze blows the coffin down to knee height, and I use the spell to guide it back up the stairs.

Eliya lies where I left her. I lower the coffin to the center of the circular chamber and use another wind spell to blow her inside. The vibrant yellow skirts of her dress flutter with the magic. They look as lovely as they did at the Ball, aside from the few specks of dirt which sully them.

The coffin's purple glow reflects onto her skin and paints it with an iridescent luster. Her hair also appears as fine strands of rubies in the glistening light. She looks so beautiful and peaceful in there, and gazing at her feels like stabbing a knife through my chest. But I can't look away. I must soak up every detail and freeze an image of her in my mind so that I never forget her, even if hundreds of years pass.

I clench the side of the coffin, and my knuckles are cast ashen with the strain. Magic pulses beneath my fingers, the same magic that will preserve her until the end of time.

My eyes sting. They're too dry to shed any tears, and it feels as if they instead shed sand. I blink away the grit, but much remains.

Finally, I tear my hands from the coffin. I know I shouldn't waste my magic when I have so little left and still need to bring her down to the crypts, but I draw on the aether in my blood and use it to harness that which surrounds me.

"*Alucinatus,*" I whisper.

A single rose blooms in my fingers. Its thorns glitter in the coffin's radiance, and its silken petals are the same rich ruby red as Eliya's tangled waves.

The rose's thorns don't prick my skin as I lower it into her coffin and close her cold hands around it. The flower is an illusion and would usually wither away with time, but the crystal coffin is crafted from raw aether and will preserve my spell, just as it will preserve Eliya for eternity.

After burying Eliya inside the crypts beneath the cathedral, I return home. Since I used the very last of my magic to blow her coffin through the tunnels, I have none left to teleport back to my manor. Instead, I walk through the empty streets and stumble over the debris. Stone grinds beneath my heels. Several times, I lose my balance and my father's staff escapes my grasp. Every muscle aches as I bend to retrieve it.

I pass no one. Not even at the Arcanium, where so many gathered to battle the undead. There's no sign of anyone. Only blood and ash and streams of rubble.

The necromancers killed everyone, raised them all from the dead. Even the birds are absent. I don't know whether they flew from the horrors of last night, or whether they also fell victim to the hordes of undead.

I barely recognize where I'm walking, but my legs—weary though they are—remember the way and carry me home.

My manor's gates are as I left them, flung aside now that the Aether Tower is disabled and their enchantment is broken. The gardens are ravaged. Flowers are pulled from their roots and half the fountain is smashed apart. Water gushes across the stone path and swamps the surrounding grass.

The doors of my manor are also wide open, and one of the golden lion knockers has fallen off. It lies discarded on the lowermost stone step.

Arluin must have blasted through my manor in search of me, and he might still be here, awaiting my return. I should feel panicked by that thought, but I am too fatigued to feel anything. I stand there, hesitating for a long while, wondering whether I should run or haul myself up the stairs and into bed.

Before I can decide, scratching comes from under one of the large, rectangular planters. The trough is upturned, and mud and flowers are spilled all around it.

I freeze. Instinctively, I try to draw aether, but it fizzles out in my fingers. None remains in my veins to gather the magic in the air.

A low growl rumbles beneath the stone planter. It sounds frail and pained and very much alive. Not undead.

I don't pause. I rush over to it.

Having no magic left, I am forced to shove the heavy trough with all my might until it topples over and reveals its contents.

Azure scales glitter beneath thick layers of mud. Violet wings beat the dirt away, but one moves slower than the other and jerks back and forth, having been battered by the planter's stone rim.

"Zephyr!" I exclaim, scraping away the mud.

He doesn't respond as I lift him from the dirt. His scales are cool beneath my fingers. His usually bright eyes are dull and tired. He blinks once and then lowers his head, sinking into my grasp.

He's alive, and I'm not entirely alone.

I cradle him to my chest, hunched and trembling.

It is a while before I rise, and when I do, I carry Zephyr in my arms. We climb the stone steps and pass through the bruised doors.

Inside, my manor is as devastated as the gardens. Broken vases and ornaments are scattered through the hallway, along with glass from the shattered windows. The small circular table at the center lies helplessly on its side. All around, my mother's paintings have fallen still. I pause and gaze at the midnight seascape opposite me, the one that was always her favorite. Though I stare hard, the deep teal waves do not ripple. Neither does the powdery foam crowning their crests bubble.

I continue through the hallway and up the stairs. Shards of glass and pottery crunch on my way.

When I reach my room, I turn the handle slowly, half fearing Arluin or his necromancers are waiting for me behind the door.

But there's no one inside. The golden brilliance of my rug and curtains and sheets blinds me. I scan my surroundings a second time before fully entering, and I set Zephyr down at the foot of my bed.

He rests his head in his forelegs, and his violet wings fold across his back. The left is crooked and rests at an awkward angle.

"I'll find you some Blood Balm," I say. He doesn't look up at me. I know it isn't pain alone which causes his unresponsiveness. There's no sign of our other faerie dragons. Like the citizens of Nolderan, all are gone without a trace.

I rummage through my cabinets until I find a tin of Blood Balm. I return to Zephyr's side and perch on the edge of the bed, unscrewing the tin's lid. The scarlet substance glistens in the late noon sun. I dig my fingertips through the sticky contents and paste it across Zephyr's left wing in thick layers. At first, he flinches but doesn't shrink away.

When I finish, I screw the lid back on and place the tin onto the square cabinet beside my bed. Zephyr closes his eyes. I turn to the window and stare out at the lifeless streets. The image is distorted by the long crack zigzagging through the glass. None of my windows are smashed, though. Not like downstairs.

I soon grow tired of gazing at the dead city and slump down onto my bed. My eyes fix onto the decorative ceiling above. But they don't stay open for long.

The claws of exhaustion drag me into darkness.

CHAPTER 41

I DREAM OF DEATH AND destruction, of blood and bone, and of aether and ash.

In my restless slumber, I flail and thrash. Sweat pools across my forehead and leaks down my back.

Then, amid the ravage and ruin, a voice calls to me.

Arluin's voice.

I jolt from my sheets and fling them aside as though they are the source of my torment. My wrist throbs. With shuddering breaths, I glance down. The mark is still bound by the scraps of my skirts. I don't loosen the knot to check.

For a moment I consider summoning a frozen blade and using it to gouge the shadows from my skin, but I don't know how deeply the tendrils of dark magic sink into my flesh. And if I do, Arluin will know I am here. Alive.

I haul myself from the mattress, and my bare feet press into the icy floor. My slippers must have loosened during my sleep. I don't search for them and continue through my room. My toes soon reach the plush rug, and I stop at the center.

Mr. Waddles watches me from the opposite cabinet. My fingers curl and my jaw hardens, and then I storm across the room and seize him. My nails claw into him and pierce his seams.

All I can see in its glossy black eyes is Arluin.

Arluin as he kills my father and raises him from the dead. Arluin as he murders Eliya and forever extinguishes her bright light.

My heart blazes with anguish and hatred. Magic, which has recovered from my rest, burns with it.

"*Ignis*," I snarl. Flames burst from my fingers. The stuffed toy duck catches fire. I watch as it withers in my grasp and crumbles across the floor.

And then I fall with it.

My fingers rake through the heaps of ash. I clench my fists, melding the fragile specks together.

From the corner of my eye, I glimpse my reflection in the full-length mirror to the left. Stiffly I turn my head and stare at myself.

My tattered pearlescent gown hangs from me like a tapestry of cobwebs. Dirt and blood smears the delicate fabric. A crusty scarlet line stretches across my neck.

I shove myself onto my feet and stagger. Everything sways.

They are all gone. My father, Eliya, Koby, Archmage Gidston, Kaely, her father, Erma, Mrs. Baxter. Everyone I can think of is dead, or undead. There is no one left but me.

I drag my gaze over to the window. Darkness envelops the city. The streets are as still and silent as before I fell asleep.

The glittering of my father's staff catches my eyes. I start over to it and lift it from where it lies discarded beside my bed. Zephyr's jewel-like eyes watch me as I walk. Until now, I didn't realize he was awake. Perhaps my flames woke him. I don't turn to look at him.

Magic vibrates beneath my fingers as I clench the staff. Across the glimmering surface, I see my father's limp head turning toward me. Shadows convulse in the empty sockets of his eyes. His mouth creases with a ravenous snarl.

I drop the weapon as though it has branded the soft flesh of my palm. It lands on the feathery mattress with a gentle thud.

Frozen in place, I gaze down at the staff, unable to shake away the nightmares which whisper across it.

My father now serves Arluin. His body will never be laid to rest. He will never slumber inside a crystal coffin. His flesh will rot upon his walking corpse until he is reduced to a putrid carcass.

No.

No, no, no.

Tears sting my eyes like acid. They hurt even more when they burst from my eyes in painfully swollen lumps.

I can't allow my father to be defiled like this. I must save him from the shackles of undeath.

My mind numbs. I stop thinking.

I force my clammy feet inside a pair of leather boots and grab the staff. Then I leave the room. Zephyr follows me down the stairs and out the manor. I don't stop him from following me. Though his wing is partially healed from the thick layers of Blood Balm, his flight remains significantly reduced. But he keeps up with me as I enter the darkness. My own pace is slow and heavy.

Shadows shroud the streets, and it's hard to discern my path. I don't summon an illumination orb, though. I let my legs lead me on and on, until they bring me to the Arcanium.

The arch looms over me. Moonlight gleams across the words etched into the stone, mocking me. Because they are all dead. All of Nolderan is dead.

I stumble through the archway. All the statues tower above me. I look none in the eye as I pass beneath them. Zephyr's wings beat behind me, rustling through the air.

I reach the winding steps and ascend them. The portico's tall pillars cast long shadows over me.

The Arcanium's large doors lie wide open. One has broken away from its hinges and leans at an awkward angle.

A crack runs through the length of the atrium's polished floor. But aside from the scorch marks and scratches across the walls, it looks no different from usual. Just deathly still.

The ceiling glows with magenta light. Like the crystals which form the coffins, it was built to eternally store aether.

I don't stare up at it for long. I take a sharp right and follow the dark path deep beneath the Arcanium. Zephyr trails behind me.

While I've never entered the Vaults—only the most senior magi are allowed inside—I know precisely where it lies. Usually the wards hold adepts and inexperienced magi at bay, but now they are broken and I am free to enter.

The heavy doors groan as I push them open.

Chests are overturned, relics spilling out, and old tomes have fallen off shelves. Bookcases lie sprawled on their backs. Like the rest of the Arcanium, the battle has left devastating scars.

I pass through another set of doors. It's within this next vast room that I notice several artifacts missing from their stands. I don't stop to determine what they were. If the necromancers seized them, they must be deadly relics.

I don't know what exactly I seek. All I know is that I will need something dark and terrible to save my father's body and soul from Arluin's clutches.

I halt before an altar with a skull floating above it. Shadows burn in its sockets. I can't tell whose it once was, but it appears to be human. Bony jaws clatter together. Zephyr springs away in fright, his antennae quivering.

As menacing as the skull might appear, it wasn't powerful enough for the necromancers to steal. That means it's of little use to me. I turn and continue through the hall.

At the very end of the Vaults lies a door formed from crystallized aether. It has no handle and when I run my fingers across its surface, I find no ridges where it meets the stone. It's just because of its shape that I suspect it may be a door at all.

I rock back onto my heels and narrow my eyes. My father would surely be able to enter. His staff is linked to Nolderan's Aether Tower, so perhaps it will also share a connection with this door.

I knock the staff against the crystal.

Nothing happens.

With a frown creasing my brow, I draw aether into my fingers and focus all the power into the staff. I weave my magic into an unlocking spell.

"*Aseros.*"

This time when I knock the staff against the door, the smooth surface ripples with energy. Then it swings open, permitting me entry. Zephyr slips through after me, and the crystal door seals behind us both.

We enter a magnificent chamber, every inch of its walls and floors carefully carved from marble. Its ceiling is crystalline like the central atrium's, though remarkably smaller, and magenta light washes over the circular room, keeping it permanently illuminated. Shelves lean against its curved walls, but they aren't just filled by books. Daggers and amulets as cruel as the ones Arluin wielded decorate the gaps between the ancient, leather-bound tomes. There are a few relics which don't exude dark magic, such as the aether-forged sword to my right. And I find a few jagged crystals lying along the shelves. But they don't shine with magenta light. Their glow is tri-coloured, and they are filled with varying shades of purple, gold, and black. I lift one and peer at it. The vibrations through my fingers are not the familiar hum of aether. Rather this stone contains all three energies: aether, light, and dark magic.

I return the strange stone to its shelf and continue my examination of the room. My fingers trail over the dusty book spines, and I lean closer to decipher their titles. There are tomes on advanced spells of the magi—some even from the enchanters of Lumaria. Or at least I think they're on moon elven magic, seeing how they're written in Elvish. I only recognize the letters of their alphabet, and not their language itself.

Other tomes are far less benevolent, and their texts contain the terrible secrets of dark magic: necromancy and demonology. I select a large one entitled *The Origins of Necromancy* and start over to the pillowy armchair in the corner. Zephyr is already curled up in the middle since it's the only chair in this chamber. I lay my father's staff against the wall and lift the faerie dragon onto my lap. He buries his azure head into the withered skirts of my pearlescent dress, licking his wounds with his forked-tongue.

I peel back the tome's leather cover—which is cracked in places—and glance through the pages.

Necromancy was not always forbidden, nor was dark magic, it begins. *In the year 558, the first corpse was successfully reanimated by Nolderan's most senior scholars, and this discovery especially piqued the interest of Korad Banwell who was, at the time, the Archmage of Defense.*

I turn to the next page. The first contains no new information. My tutors at the Arcanium already described how necromancy came to be and why dark magic is forbidden. Their explanations weren't as detailed as this tome, but the dates of experiments and the names of those overseeing them will provide me with no advantage against Arluin.

I scan over several paragraphs and then flip to the middle of the book, but it is evident this book will be of no help. With a sigh, I remove Zephyr from my lap and return the tome to its shelf.

If I am to have any hope of saving my father, I must find a way to become Arluin's equal. And swiftly. I need a weapon which will grant me unfathomable strength, or knowledge of a spell which will act as a bane against necromancy.

I suppose light magic is the greatest power against dark magic, but I'll never be able to wield it. Maybe if I studied for several decades, I would learn to use a small amount, but I would never become proficient with light magic. A fraction of the energy flows through my veins, as it does with all living beings, but my blood is dominated by aether. Those who are exceptional at casting light magic are blessed by the gods and possess souls so radiant they are like living beacons. That is why light magic is out of the question. I must resort to other measures.

Once more I continue to search the shelves. I briefly consider the crystalline sword, but I doubt it's more powerful than my father's staff. And even that failed to defeat Arluin.

No, I require something else. Something more terrible than Arluin.

My fingers stop on the spine of an obsidian tome. Chains wrap around it, binding a dark crystal to its cover. The stone is so black and glossy it looks like pitch. We magi frequently solidify aether into crystals, and it appears this substance is dark magic's equivalent. The shadows oozing from the stone confirm my suspicions.

Despite the chains, the book offers little resistance as I open it, aside from its hefty weight and bulky size.

The words *Grimoire of Demonic Incantation* are scrawled across the first page of parchment. Whoever wrote this book—I can see no name anywhere—was in a great hurry. Either that or their handwriting was awful.

The Abyss is ruled by the Void King, a being as ancient as the gods, and the most powerful Malum were created shortly after the Primordial Explosion of Aether, the splitting of light and dark magic, and the formation of the three planes of existence: the Heavens, the Abyss, and our world of Imyria. The dark energies of the Abyss continue to birth new Malum, and there also exists a second type of demons, formed from the souls of fallen mortals.

On the next page, sketches of demons are etched in black ink. They possess wings, horns, draconic wings, multiple heads and limbs, cloven hooves, claws, forked tongues, and all manner of other ghastly things. Some are tall and thin, others are short and round. Some appear humanoid, others bear resemblance to beasts. Though they are vastly different, each is as horrifying as the next.

I then come to a diagram of multiple circles—eight in total. A large one is featured in the center, and seven more are scattered around it. Some intersect with each other, while all intersect with the middle circle. The diagram almost appears to be a map, though it's unlike any I've ever seen.

My gaze reaches the short paragraph at the bottom of the page.

The Abyss is formed from eight sub-planes, with the largest ruled by the Void King. The other seven are commanded by his lieutenants, who are known as Void Princes. Each realm shares its name with its resident Void Prince, and represents the cardinal sins: Lust, Gluttony, Greed, Sloth, Wrath, Envy, and Pride. Demons value only strength and cunning, and the most powerful command their legions. These seven Void Princes risk being overthrown by rivals at any moment.

This book provides far more detail than any of my tutors ever did. All I knew until now was that the Abyss is home to the most nightmarish horrors one could dream and that it is ruled by an ancient Malum known as the Void King. But I stand against necromancers, not demons. It is doubtful any of this information will help me defeat Arluin and save my father.

Unless . . .

A nefarious idea takes root in my mind. Terrible though it may be, I don't question it. I continue flipping through the pages, until I finally reach the section I seek: *Demonic Summoning.*

These pages contain sketches of ritual circles, filled by pentagrams and triangles and other shapes. Some are complicated, others are simplistic. All are designed to summon and bind demons, though only complex patterns are capable of controlling the most powerful ones.

To summon a lesser demon, one requires three reagents: a soul-gem as payment for the demon to cross the veil separating Imyria from the Abyss, a summoning circle to act as the gate through which it will enter our world, and the blood of the summoner to bind the demon to their will. The summoner also requires the true name of the demon they seek to enslave, and they must use dark magic to invoke the spell 'Kretol'morish,' followed by the demon's name. For example, if one wished to summon a demon named Norrazax, they would use the incantation 'Kretol'morish Norrazax.'

My fingers linger as I turn the page. The instructions are clear and I should in theory be able to follow the directions and summon a demon of my own, but a lesser demon will be of no use against Arluin. The formidable amulet around his neck made him powerful enough to defeat my father. I need a demon so fearsome it eclipses Arluin's strength. Maybe a Void Prince would suffice.

The thought of summoning something so vile and wicked—let alone using dark magic in the first place—chills me to the bone. It is forbidden by all of Nolderan's laws. If I summon a demon, I will break all the teachings of the Arcanium. I will be no better than Arluin and his necromancers.

But if I were only to once use dark magic to summon the demon, and if my intentions were pure, then wouldn't that make me different to them? Wouldn't my reasons make my actions justifiable? Nolderan has fallen, and my father's body and soul are enslaved to Arluin's will. I have been a mage for just one day. Without the strength of a formidable demon, how else will I ever stand a chance?

This is my sole hope, and I am desperate and broken enough to seize it.

Zephyr stirs in my lap. As I glance down at him, bitterness fogs my throat. It feels as if these thoughts are betraying him and all that I am. Despite the heavy tome in my hands, I don't think he yet realizes what I intend. I shouldn't do this, but I also can't do nothing. And if I don't do this, what else can I do?

I turn the page and then the next. The book continues to discuss the process of demonic summoning. Three paragraphs later, I arrive at a section on summoning more powerful demons—including Void Princes.

The greater the demon, the greater the price to summon it from the depths of the Abyss, the book reads. *The summoner must pay with their own blood. In the case of Void Princes, though they are summoned infrequently, the spell requires an additional reagent: the summoner's soul. This price is to be paid upon death, and the soul will be bound to the Void Prince as the Void Prince is bound to the summoner during their life. No matter whether the summoner dies within a day, year, or century of binding the demon, the price remains the same. The Void Prince will be free to do as they please with the soul, for it shall belong to them.*

At that, I close the book with a deafening thud, my breaths heavy in my ears. Zephyr looks at me and then lowers his head back onto the worn fabric of my skirts.

Summoning a Void Prince might be my only hope of freeing my father and defeating Arluin, but it also means eternal damnation. If I choose this path, I will forsake my own soul. Until the end of time, I will belong to whichever monster I summon. I will become a monster myself.

The cost is heavier than I expected. Of course, I never imagined summoning a demon—never mind a Void Prince—would be easy. But damning my own soul? It's a price I don't know whether I'm prepared to pay.

I could leave this chamber now, return the tome to its shelf and pretend I never glimpsed its contents, but where else would I go? What else would I do? Nolderan is gone, and everyone with it.

Though this path may be wicked, it offers me direction—purpose. If I decline, I will wither into nothingness. I must seize it before I lose myself.

I set the tome on the chair's arm and roll Zephyr from my legs. Once more I search the many shelves. Though this book was informative, there are still two more facts I require: the method of channeling dark magic, and the name of a Void Prince so I may call one from the Abyss. If I can learn the true name of the Void Prince of Wrath from these shelves, I am certain that demon would prove the greatest weapon against Arluin.

I find an introduction to conjuring dark magic first. In fact, there are several inside this chamber. I choose the thickest tome, hoping it will provide the most detailed explanation.

The search for a Void Prince's name takes me far longer, though I expected as much. From subsequent books, I learn that the true names of the Malum are known only to them as they come into existence. In the Abyss, names are the greatest currency, and demons may reveal the names of others to the mortals who summon them. For the demons who are not Malum and were once mortals themselves, it is their mortal name which holds power over them.

I suppose this is why I learn the name of the Void Prince of Envy first. A demonologist from a thousand years ago, before dark magic was outlawed in Nolderan, writes about her. She was Lady Eladine Pembelson of Montarra, a land annexed by Tirith long ago, and her sister who was younger and more beautiful married the Crown Prince. Jealous, she used dark magic to kill her. And then when she became the Queen of Montarra, she envied her husband and killed him too and reigned as the sole monarch until her natural death. Her soul was so wicked that the Void King took it for his own.

On the next page, I find a sketch of her. She is depicted as slender with dark curly hair, and her wings and talons and horns make her as deadly as she is beautiful.

I could summon her now, since I know her true name, but I instead continue my search. The Void Prince of Wrath must surely be the most ferocious, and if I am to sell my soul, I must choose the demon which provides me the greatest chance of defeating Arluin and freeing my father.

It takes an entire bookcase before I learn the name of another Void Prince. Though this one is still not Wrath, his description causes me to pause.

Natharius Thalanor was the greatest High Enchanter of Lumaria ever to exist, and the most arrogant. He is the only mortal evil enough to bargain his soul and the souls of his entire city to the Void King in exchange for power. He now resides over the Realm of Pride, as one of the Void King's seven lieutenants.

Unlike the book which mentioned Lady Eladine, this one provides no illustration of the aforementioned Void Prince.

I lean back against the nearby wall and reread the paragraph several times. Though it was the Void Prince of Wrath I sought, there's something about this demon which makes me linger. Perhaps it's because he was once the High Enchanter of Lumaria and wielded aether like us magi, or perhaps it's because his wickedness and ambition greatly overshadow Lady Eladine's. If he was truly that powerful as a mortal, I can only imagine his strength as a demon. Surely a demon this formidable will be enough to destroy Arluin.

"Natharius Thalanor," I whisper. The demon's name is like a prayer, a promise, upon my lips.

My mind already decided, I close the book. I could continue searching this chamber for the Void Prince of Wrath, but if he wasn't previously mortal and has kept his true name well-guarded, I may never find him. And even if I do, he may not be as formidable as the Void Prince of Pride.

I peel myself from the wall and retrieve a tri-colored shard from one of the shelves. The stone hums beneath my fingers. I didn't realize at the time, until I found sketches of the reagent inside the tomes, but this shard is a soul-gem. If my heart was not steeled with cold, hard determination, the thought of holding someone's soul in my hands might have nauseated me. Now, as I gaze at it, I see it only as a weapon.

I have my name; I have my soul-gem. Now to summon my Void Prince, I must first learn to harness dark magic.

CHAPTER 42

For countless hours, I sit at the center of the chamber and practice channeling dark magic. Dozens of tomes surround me in a sea of parchment and ink. In the end, I find that the first one I selected wasn't sufficient. My initial attempts are pitiful, though the subsequent aren't vastly improved. I always imagined that dark magic would come readily, given how corruptive it is, but I discover it requires much concentration.

Since there is little dark magic flowing through my veins, I must use my aether as bait to draw the shadows toward me. At first they are unresponsive, and I am required to manifest even greater quantities of my magic before the darkness is finally lured in.

It snatches the aether from my fingers and corrupts it. Then, before I can realize, the shadows are lost to the air. If I were a dark sorcerer, I would be able to snap all the dark magic back to my command, but I am not and can only use my aether to entice it.

Over and over I try, until I am quick enough to capture the shadows. Though I succeed, the dark magic is merely a faint wisp of black smoke in my fingers—nowhere near enough to summon a Void Prince from the Abyss.

It takes me a long while and hundreds of failed attempts to conjure enough. When plumes of dark energy manifest in my fingers, Zephyr whimpers and cowers into the cushioned armchair. I extinguish the shadows and turn to him.

"I know what I'm doing is wrong," I say, "but this is the only way." Despite the cold look I give him, I find myself yet again doubting this path. But I quickly banish the thought because there is no alternative. I will summon the Void Prince of Pride and bind him to my soul, and I will defeat Arluin and save my father from the shackles of undeath—even if the cost of all that is my own soul.

I can't hesitate. I can't fail.

When I am satisfied with my ability to conjure dark magic, I return all the tomes to their shelves and replace them with pages and pages of summoning circles. I choose the most complex pattern I can find because if my chains aren't strong enough, the Void Prince will burst free and kill me before I can bind him to my soul. This particular summoning circle consists of a seven-pointed star, each of its diagonals crossing through the center and forming smaller triangles. Between each point of the stars lies a circle filled with runes I don't recognize, but I know they must be the letters of Abyssal, the language of demons.

The books state it doesn't matter what substance is used to draw the summoning circles; it may be with dark magic, blood, ink, chalk, or even aether. I choose the latter, not wishing to wield dark magic for longer than is necessary.

"*Volu.*" Violet light blooms in my hands. I kneel and press my glowing fingers to the marble floor and trace the summoning circle with as much precision as I can. A few of the lines aren't straight enough, thanks to my wobbling hand, so I murmur *terminir* and erase them all. I draw them again more carefully, and when I am certain the summoning circle looks identical to the one sketched inside the tomes, I take an obsidian dagger from the nearest shelf.

Everything is prepared. All that remains is blood. My blood.

I press the blade into my palm and hiss as the skin breaks. For a demon as powerful as the Void Prince, much blood will be required. I cut deeply enough to draw plenty and through the pain, I conjure the image of Arluin plunging his dagger through my father's heart, of Eliya lying as lifeless as a doll inside her crystal coffin. My heart hurts so much that my physical pain numbs.

When I remove the dagger and reopen my eyes, blood flows across my palm. I try not to spill any as I grasp a soul-gem and return to the center of my summoning circle.

I tighten both my fists. My left hand stings with the rawness of the wound, while my other aches from where the soul-gem's protruding edges dig into my flesh. But I care not for the pain. What I am about to do will change everything. It will grant me what I seek but cost me all I have left to lose in this world. My soul.

It almost seems a reasonable exchange. Perhaps even that I'm paying too little.

The incantation's letters flash through my mind. I studied them for so long, worried I would forget them in this crucial moment. I'm not sure how accurate my pronunciation will be, since I have never learned Abyssal, but the language forms the spell-words of the magic that necromancers wield and I have heard them speak the dark tongue many times. I hope my imitation will be close enough.

I draw aether into my bloodied hand and use it to summon the shadows. Darkness swirls in my fingers. My heart stills. I stare at the dark magic, a distant part of me questioning how I have ended up here. But I shake away that thought. Doubt will not serve me. I must sharpen my focus into a blade point.

Now that dark magic lies in my grasp, I must begin the ritual.

"Kretol'morish Natharius Thalanor."

I mix the shadows with my blood, and it spills like ink across the summoning circle. It bleeds into the markings of aether and replaces the violet light with thick black oil.

Nothing happens. Long enough passes that I begin to worry I mispronounced the spell-words.

Then the soul-gem disintegrates. Glittering dust falls across the summoning circle and oozes into the pulsating black lines. The markings rise an inch from the floor and spin faster and faster beneath my bare feet until they become nothing but a blur.

Thunder rings through the chamber. Instinctively, I squeeze my eyes shut—only for a heartbeat.

When I open them, the summoning circle has fallen still. A terrifying shadow looms over me. His silhouette is cast across the floor: horns, and wings, and cloven feet.

I stiffly raise my head and look upon the monster I have called forth.

He is even more frightening than his shadow. Too large for this chamber, he stands hunched over and his onyx horns threaten to impale the crystalline ceiling. Draconic wings beat back and forth, powerful enough that I am almost blown from my feet. I dig my heels into the floor and force myself to meet the eyes of this hulking monstrosity.

I can't allow it to think me weak.

His eyes glow an unearthly crimson, as do the markings which wind across the pale skin of his torso. Long, silver hair streams over his shoulders like strands of moonlight. That, and his pointed ears, assure me that I have not summoned the wrong demon. The traces of his heritage are evident beneath his monstrous horns and wings and hooves. Long ago, before demonic corruption seized him, I suspect he was beautiful like the rest of his kin. Now he is a horrifying husk.

"Who dares summon me?" his voice booms, echoing off the walls. His attention sweeps across the floor until he spots my figure far beneath him. Fury blazes in his crimson eyes.

My heart hammers with fear, with desperation. I don't answer him.

The Void Prince steps forth and his cloven hooves almost crack the marble floor. I draw away until I am safely beyond the summoning circle.

He stalks as close as he can but is unable to cross the edge of my markings. I don't know what I would have done if he'd passed through the summoning circle. All I know is that it would have ended in my death. As well as Zephyr's, who cowers behind the armchair. Too focused on the demon, I don't turn to look at him. I quickly shed the guilt which arises from the knowledge of his fear.

A low growl rumbles in the back of the Void Prince's throat. "Little mage, I will tear you limb from limb, carve the flesh from your puny bones and feed you morsel by morsel to my Void Hounds." He grips the hilt of his enormous obsidian sword, and his lips twist into a cruel snarl.

I clasp my hands behind my back to hide their trembling, but it might be in vain. I don't know whether the Void Prince can smell my fear.

Of course I wasn't expecting a Void Prince to be thrilled by being summoned to Imyria, especially not one known as Pride, but I'm paying him with the eternal damnation of my soul. It seems he has little interest in that. Perhaps I should have instead summoned the Void Prince of Envy, or continued my search for Wrath.

But it's too late now. I've already summoned him.

"Natharius Thalanor," I declare, steadying my voice and holding my head as high as I can. "I, Reyna Ashbourne, claim you as my servant, forced to obey my every command until I have freed my father from the shackles of undeath and defeated the necromancy threat which plagues Imyria. In exchange for your service, my soul will be yours for eternity after my final breath."

Unfortunately, those final words are part of the ritual. While scanning through the tomes, I did wonder what would happen if I refused to speak them, but I don't dare to alter the recommended procedure. If I do, the Void Prince could break free and destroy me. It isn't worth the risk. Not when his power is almost in my grasp.

A tendril of darkness rises from the summoning circle. It wraps around us both like thread and knots us together. Then I am as chained to him as he is to me.

The demon howls with rage. But his wrath and the dark flames he conjures are not enough to sever the cord between us.

Our souls are bound.

"I will devour your soul and ensure your suffering lasts a thousand years," he seethes.

Fear coils through me at his curse and the knowledge of what awaits me after death, but the images of my father and Eliya steel me.

I relinquished my soul, and now this demon is mine. I must not fail.

From the ashes of Nolderan, I will rise.

And Arluin pay for his sins with his blood.

EPILOGUE

Juron hated the night shift most of all. The priestess's gentle breathing came from the door behind him: a soft, melodious whisper. Even her breathing was beautiful—torturous.

He leaned against the pillar which stood sentry outside of her chambers, and the grooves etched into the stone dug into his back. When it was only him and the darkness, his imagination always ran amok. It made him imagine a different life, where he was not her sworn protector, where she did not belong to the Mother and to Selynis. Where his sister did not call him soft between the ears for loving one who could never love him back. But he could not help his foolish heart.

Juron shifted his weight and let out a gentle sigh. His fingers played around the elegant hilt of his light-forged sword, and he felt the energy singing within. Slow and steady as a stream, with the soothing kiss of sunlight. Its presence reminded him of the priestess. She was light magic incarnate.

He shook his head and tried to sober himself from his troublesome thoughts. What use was he to the priestess if the mere thought of her distracted him from his purpose? If the only thing he could be was her guard, then he would be the best guard she could ever ask for.

Juron trained his eyes on the blunt shadows ahead and steeled his mind. He wasn't sure what time it was and how long it would be before his sister took over from him, but through the arched window, he glimpsed the ripe moon sitting full and fat like a pearl sewn into the black velvet of night. The unblemished limestone buildings of the city below stood silent and still—

A scream pierced the night.

Taria. It came from Taria's room.

Juron threw himself from the pillar and lunged for the door, shoving it open so desperately that it splintered off its hinges. He charged over the broken door without sparing it a second thought. All that mattered was Taria.

He drew his sword. Steel whispered into the shadows.

But no one else was there. The priestess was sitting up in her bed, the blankets pooled around her. The shoulder of her gossamer nightgown had slipped down, exposing her mahogany skin to the night. The moonlight silvered the soft curve of her shoulder, and he had the sudden urge to trace it. A familiar ache filled his heart.

Her white locks flowed over her other shoulder, so luminous they made the moon look faint. She stared at him with her golden eyes. Light magic poured from her like the aura of dawn. Maybe she was meditating. Though he had never seen her meditating with her eyes wide open.

"Taria?" he said gently.

The priestess did not blink. Juron paced over to her bed and perched on the edge. He nudged her shoulder, the one he'd considered tracing. He tried not to think about the softness of her skin.

She jolted to life then, and Juron almost leaped away with the suddenness. She rose onto her knees and clasped either side of his face, staring at him with unblinking eyes. This close, they blinded him.

"Taria, what's the matter?"

Now she finally answered him, her gaze clouded with the remnants of her divine vision.

"Death," she rasped, her chest heaving with the strain. "Death comes for us all."

Reyna's story will continue in...

STORM OF SHADOWS

To learn more about STORM OF SHADOWS
(Legends of Imyria, #2) and find out how to get a
copy, you can visit here:

www.hollyrosebooks.com/storm-of-shadows

You can also subscribe to my newsletter so that you
never miss out on new releases, giveaways, cover
reveals, or other fun things (like bonus scenes!)

www.hollyrosebooks.com/subscribe

ACKNOWLEDGEMENTS

It's safe to say this book would not be in your hands if not for my sister. Writing *Ashes of Aether* broke a long string of shelved "nearly" finished manuscripts, and until then I had been starting to believe I was incapable of ever completing a first draft again (I wasn't—it was only my mindset). I did almost shelve *Ashes of Aether* twice after the second draft, but my sister convinced me to continue working on it and to bite the bullet and write it from scratch for a third time. So, thank you, Ella, for being my writing counsellor. Thank you for also being my first reader ever. I still remember you always reading my story attempts on scraps of paper when we were kids (usually on holidays, for some reason).

I also owe so much to Aimee, my critique partner. Thank you for helping me to figure out how to turn my messy "draft zero" of *Ashes of Aether* into a story with a coherent structure (oh, the pantser life). Thank you for also letting me spam your inbox with *"OMG HALP!!!"* whenever I'm having a writing emergency and helping me to brainstorm my jumbled ideas into logical plot lines. You are the best C.P. and friend anyone could ever ask for. I can't believe how far we've come over these past six years, and I'm so proud of us both. I can't wait until you also release your work into the world. I know you'll absolutely slay!

Thank you to my mum for being almost as critical as me and for reading through my third rewrite of *Ashes of Aether* when I decided to do a last-minute overhaul. Also, thank you for all your help with my Bookstagram photos! Another thanks goes to my dad for being an even bigger fantasy nerd than me. I certainly wouldn't be writing High Fantasy if not for the fact you let me watch Lord of the Rings and play World of Warcraft at such a young age. Thank you for reading all the Harry Potter and Eragon books to me as a child (even if your voice was rather monotone, haha).

Thank you, Yazzie, for being the best beta reader any writer could ever ask for. Your suggestions are always so on point, and I can't believe how quickly you can read! I am so grateful that you were willing to read *Ashes of Aether* again after I decided to rewrite the story from scratch.

Thank you to Elle and Vanessa and everyone else who beta read for being among my first readers of *Ashes of Aether*. I hope when you read this finished version, you can see how your feedback helped to shape this story from the initial draft you read!

Kolarp Em, you helped me to think more like an artist and this story would never have reached its potential if not for your honesty. You helped me to see the direction I needed to take this story in, and I hope when you read it, you can see the impact you've had on my work. You are an incredibly talented artist, and I still can't believe how you managed to pull my ideas out of my head and illustrate them so beautifully and so accurately. I am so lucky to call you my friend.

And thank you, dear reader, for taking a chance on this story. For that, I will forever be grateful <3

A Serious Man

DAVID
STOREY

A Serious Man

JONATHAN CAPE
LONDON

Published by Jonathan Cape 1998

2 4 6 8 10 9 7 5 3 1

First published in Great Britain in 1998 by
Jonathan Cape
Random House, 20 Vauxhall Bridge Road,
London SWIV 2SA

Random House Australia (Pty) Limited
20 Alfred Street, Milsons Point, Sydney,
New South Wales 2061, Australia

Random House New Zealand Limited
18 Poland Road, Glenfield,
Auckland 10, New Zealand

Random House South Africa (Pty) Limited
Endulini, 5A Jubilee Road, Parktown 2193, South Africa

Random House UK Limited Reg. No. 954009

A CIP catalogue record for this book
is available from the British Library

ISBN 0 224 05158 X

Papers used by Random House UK Limited are natural,
recyclable products made from wood grown in sustainable forests.
The manufacturing processes conform to the environmental
regulations of the country of origin.

Phototypeset by Intype London Ltd

Printed and bound in Great Britain by
Mackays of Chatham PLC

1

HARRIET SAYS I'm going to die.

It's true, she had, moments before she told me, lost her temper (who wouldn't with a man of sixty-five who behaves as if he were approaching ninety?); yet she had been talking to Raynor (was ensconced with him this morning for half an hour and when she came out looked very peaked), and though Raynor has only made the one examination he has, she says, consulted Maidstone, the Sub-Dean of the Medical School and the Longcroft Professor of Psychiatry at the North London Royal, by telephone as well as letter.

Two and a half years in Boady Hall (and the same again at the N.L.R.) have not done me, on the whole, a lot of good. I say 'in', but, to be more accurate, in and out: yet when I was out the threat of re-internment never left me. When, for instance, she said, 'You are going to die,' my immediate response was to say, 'Is that a clinical judgement or merely a comment on the nature of life?' and might have gone on to announce, 'I haven't lived long enough. There's so much still I'd like to do,' but since, moments later, she walked out of the room I was unable to decide precisely what she meant and could only call after her, 'That's what I want. To put an end to all this pain.'

Why she's brought me to this house I've no idea: over the past five years I've come to hate as well as fear the mention of its name. 'I can't leave you in this hovel,' she declared, meaning my home in Taravara Road I shared with Vi, and when I replied, 'I love this place. Vivienne and I were very happy,' she instantly

1

responded, 'Don't talk to me about her. You know how much you despised her.'

'I didn't despise her at all,' I told her, totally confused.

'Why do you think she killed herself?' she asked.

'The pain,' I said, 'became too much. More,' I went on, 'than people like you, with humdrum jobs and humdrum minds (with humdrum feelings and humdrum reflections) can possibly imagine.'

I make her cruel. It's a charge other people have made in the past. 'You make me cruel. Cruel and wicked. I don't know why you do it,' Bea would say.

'Cruel to be kind,' I'd tell her, and, from time to time, might add, 'There's a wicked streak in all of us that's all the better for being out.'

'But why directed at me?' she would ask. 'Someone you've chosen to share things with.'

'I've never had much patience with rectitude,' I'd tell her.

'In that case,' she'd say, 'we shouldn't have married,' and when, later, poor Vi came on the scene, 'Why, for instance, didn't you marry *her*?'

Harriet always loved this house, even as a child, when she skipped about its lawns and through its wood, climbed its trees and dug its garden (rode the neighbours' horses – and one or two of the old shires from Freddie's yard – and held picnics with the neighbours' children by the porch, the steps set out with the contents of a hamper which had been carried by Rosie, the Corcorans' 'woman', around the house, from the kitchen door a distance of no more than twenty-five yards).

'I can't do anything here but die,' I told her when she brought me to the place the other night.

'If that's what you have in mind,' she said.

'Why are you so malevolent?' I asked.

'You make me cruel, Father!' she cried, in much the same way as Bea would cry when, in the last years of our marriage, I told her lies – lies about work, lies about art (lies about God, reality, etc.).

2

'So much of my past is bound up in this place,' I said. 'It was by those trees that I courted your mother. It was by that lawn that I fell in love. It's the worst place you could have chosen. Ask Maidstone. He'll tell you.'

'It was his idea,' she said, 'I should bring you.'

'It wasn't, in that case,' I said, 'from the kindness of your heart.'

'Kindness and heart are not words I care to associate with our relationship,' she told me. 'And haven't done so now for quite some time.'

When we reached the house the other night Charlie had left the gates wide open and the lamps, mounted on their quaint, cast-iron poles, burning in the drive. Only the leafless trees, however, and the lightless hulk of the place itself were visible against the moonlit sky. I shuddered as I stepped out from the car and Harriet, solicitous for me, suddenly enquired, 'Are you all right?' assuming it was the journey and not the place that had suddenly upset me.

'This place,' I said, 'will kill me.'

'It will,' she said, 'if you allow it. You're mad,' she had gone on. 'Why should I listen to anything you say?'

'You told me years ago I had a touch of genius,' I had told her, recalling having lunch in the restaurant at the Tate after supervising the hanging of several of my pictures and, taken aback to see how well they stood up to – or out from – the Picassos and Matisses, she had said, 'You have a touch of genius, Father,' like she might, after half a lifetime, have suddenly announced, 'You have red hair. All these years I took it to be brown.'

'You did have a touch of genius,' she said (her new-found philosophy à la Gurdjieff coming to the fore). 'What difference does it make? You can't take genius with you. Relationships are more important.'

'But don't earn any money.'

She hated me in my mocking mood: as a child, coming home from school with her latest cult which I, in those days,

3

instantly destroyed, she would rush to her room and, slamming the door, stay inside for hours.

'You were brilliant,' she said, 'but your mind,' the biter bit, 'has lost its effervescence.'

I've been ill; how ill I can't recall. Harriet suspects, by bringing me here, she will, as she describes it, 're-animate those areas of your mind that previously existed. Mum says you were at peace,' she had added, 'the times you came up here.'

But can she possibly imagine what my youth in and around this place was like; and, worst of all, could she imagine what life was like twelve miles away, at Onasett, to the north?

When I first came here the valley below the house was full of smoke: a slag heap smouldered from the brow of an adjoining hill; shunting engines chuntered in and out of the village street, hauling lines of trucks to and from the main railway line a mile and a half to the south. The place, morning, noon and night, was full of men with blackened faces and stout, broad-chested women. The school at which, during the war, Bea's mother taught stood at the foot of the colliery heap, its brickwork streaked with soot and smoke, and the marks, or so it seemed, of a million blackened fingers.

I first came to Ardsley late one night in the back of a car, my friend Otterton behind the wheel, the lugubrious Jenny, his girlfriend, beside him, delivering Bea from our last school party – the last time I saw Otterton, or Jenny, and the first time I had escorted B.

I recall drawing up at a green-painted door let into a tall stone wall – its sandstone texture visibly eroded – and, after disabusing me of the notion that she was 'one of those' (girls who allowed intimacies on the first acquaintance), her condescending to a goodnight kiss – a light brushing of her lips on mine – and, with a wave, she was gone – a glimpse, beyond the wall, of a lighted path before a bolt was drawn.

It sits, Ardsley Old Hall, halfway up a wooded hill, a flat-fronted, five-bayed Georgian structure with a central porticoed

4

entrance. A beech hedge, at the front, circumscribes a lawn within which are set rectangular, round and crescent-shaped flowerbeds. Trellises, threaded with roses and, here and there, a fruit tree, run off on either side to where, in one direction, a wicket-gate gives access to an orchard and, in the other, a stone arch, inset in a buttressed wall, opens into an area at one time known as Corcoran's Yard, a cobbled precinct occupied, in the years before my first visit to the house, by Freddie's carts, his stabled horses and, latterly, by his large, tall-sided lorries. Enclosed by terraced, stone-built dwellings, it is known nowadays as Ardsley Close: a pair of recently-erected metal gates, permanently closed, occupy the arch, cutting off Harriet's and Charlie's grounds from this previous heart of Freddie's kingdom.

At the foot of the slope, and all but hidden by the trees, lies Ardsley village. The pit – Old Ardsley Main – has gone: a symmetrically landscaped slope, dotted with trees and shrubs, has replaced the colliery heap – a wedge of uniformly ascending grass which overlooks the terraced streets and, when the trees are bare, as now, the façade and the grounds of the house itself.

2

'I'VE BROUGHT you some tea,' Harriet said, coming into my room this morning. 'What would you like for breakfast?'

It must have been late: Lottie (ten) and Glenda (five) no doubt had gone to school; and Charlie, no doubt, had gone to work (some mornings, Etty has told me – although he only goes to Linfield, twelve miles away to the north – he leaves at seven): the driveway to the house is at the rear and vehicles approaching or leaving are seldom heard.

'I'm not that old. There's still some time to go. I can still get up for breakfast,' I said.

'So you shall. Providing,' she said, 'Mrs Otterman cooks it.'

'Neither Mrs Otterman nor anyone else is needed,' I said. 'I'm quite capable of cooking it myself.'

I watched her open the curtains: 'How she endeavours to indulge me,' I reflected. 'A pavlovian response,' she once remarked: 'I see an old man and my immediate response is to offer to help.'

Turning from the curtains, she said, 'You look older than at any other time I've known you. You even look older than Grandpa,' referring to a photograph of Freddie (Corcoran, the profligate haulage contractor, coal-merchant, insurance agent and landowner, Bea's father) about whom we had been talking the night before ('What youthful spirits!' etc.), the photograph (in a silver frame) standing on the mantelpiece in the living-room below. 'You look more frightened, too,' she went on, never slow, from childhood, to identify my ailments, a sublim-

6

inal form of retribution which gave her, I had always thought, much charm.

'What is madness,' Maidstone had once enquired, his eyes half-shut, flicking the plastic top of his fountain pen, 'but our ability to see other people as they see themselves but not as other people see them?' and though there might have been a facetious truth in this, it has, throughout my life, been my inability to see myself as anything at all that has lain at the root of all my problems.

Etty, of course, has a vested interest in seeing me as not only old but mad.

'I shall have bacon and egg,' I said. 'With sausage and tomato. Toast, marmalade. Fruit juice and coffee.'

'You never eat it,' she complained.

'I shall today,' I said. 'I feel quite well.'

'What are you planning?' she suddenly enquired.

It had been something about the way she had come into the room – moving to the bed and then the curtains, the projection of her arm (after setting down the tea) – that had reminded me of Isabella.

'My life from now on is totally unplanned,' I said.

'That,' she said, 'is what I feared,' dark hair coiled loosely round her head, dark eyes, a thin-lipped mouth (inherited from Bea), a delicate nose, a slender neck: sharp-featured, querulous (Bea, too): nevertheless, I see a great deal of myself in Etty, not least when she contemplates, as she might through the wrong end of a telescope, what, in no other mood but this, she considers to be her blighted ambition. 'You've never gone in want of anything,' I tell her. 'When you and Matt (her elder sister) were young you were seldom out of my sight.'

They spent much of their time, in fact, in my studio, I allowing them, from time to time, to contribute to my pictures: much paint was splashed about (an expressionist phase): 'Just look at it, Mummy!' when Bea came in and globules of red or blue were flicked in her direction.

'What am I doing with my life?' she would ask (like Bea used

7

to ask when they were children: 'What am I *doing* here if you have them all the while?').

'You're happily married. You have two wonderful children. Your husband loves you,' is my reply, followed by, as with Bea, 'But, of course, these things have been devalued. Paranoia, with women, has got the upper hand. The obligation is to go around with a cross strapped on their backs, like the colliers, in the old days, used to haul the waste-trucks to the top of the tip where, fortunately for them, the contents were emptied out. Nowadays, of course . . .' etc., etc.

'What about *me*?' she asks. 'Caring and affection are to do with other people (even if my husband and my children are people that I love).'

'Everything,' I tell her, 'is to do with other people. Isn't Charlie,' I go on, 'as dependent on you?'

'Like you, he,' she says, 'can work.'

'So,' I tell her, 'can you.'

'The centres of research are all in London, Paris and New York,' she says (to mention but a few).

'What centres of research?' My obtuseness, in the old days, drove her mad. 'Isn't life a centre of research? I'm surprised you don't see you're living in such a location now.'

She is the authoress of a single book: *The Caravaggio Papers*. The book, absurdly, despite its scholastic pretensions, was made into a film. Etty, despite my warnings, sold the rights for a single sum. It made, for everyone involved, except the author, a great deal of money. 'I told you not to sell it,' I'd said (rape, sodomy, murder: what more could they want?). 'But if you did,' I'd gone on, 'to guarantee yourself a percentage of the budget. All you said, if you recall, was, "I don't care what they do. The book will last." It has,' I'd added. 'For six months, in paperback, at every airport in the land.'

A tray appears around the door. 'What's put you into such a good mood?' she says.

It is, I have come to the conclusion, the trees, their trunks hidden by the steepness of the slope, that have reminded me

8

not only of waking in this room but of the hours spent sitting or standing by the window splashing or scouring my way across a canvas (attached to an easel set at an angle to distract the southern light), or stooping over a sketchbook scratching with a pen or, more intensely, over a sheaf of paper writing what turned out to be my Onasett poem and the beginning of a novel.

'I've always liked the trees,' I tell her, and add, 'They look much grander (silver birch and chestnut) now they've taken down the elm.'

Laying down the tray, relieved at having something of no consequence to talk about, she says, 'I always regret you can never see the trunks.'

'You see those,' I tell her, 'from the lower windows. In the old days, when the trees had shed their leaves, from up here you could see the pit and hear the panting of the winding-gear and the rattle of the trucks. In the early mornings, too, you could hear the whining of the dynamo and, once the clatter of the miners' clogs had died, came the clatter of the women's as they set off to Moxon's, at Thorncliff. They made cloth for soldiers' uniforms throughout the Second World War.'

'Did you live here long?' she says: affection for the place, though canvassed for, in this case, fills her with unease.

'I only stayed,' I tell her, 'from time to time. Coming here, from Onasett, was like coming to a palace.' I add, 'I was always given this room. I think Corcoran thought he could keep an eye on me in here. Your mother had her bedroom at the back. Her parents, of course, had the one that you and Charlie share.'

Sitting on the edge of the bed she says, 'What about the other rooms?'

'Your grandfather – Grandfather Corcoran – had an office in the one your children have. Your great-grandfather, H.J. Kells, occupied two others. Your great-grandmother Corcoran occupied two more. She and Grandfather Kells were always at each other's throats. Your grandmother, Isabella, also had a room in which she did her thinking.'

9

'What sort of thinking?' Etty asks.

'She was a very peculiar woman.'

'I thought you liked her.'

'Enormously,' I tell her.

I am about to add, 'I loved her deeply. She was the greatest love of my life,' but, recalling Maidstone's injunction, 'Where your children and your wife are concerned I should leave your accounts of that woman alone,' I merely continue,' I didn't expect to have breakfast in bed. I could easily have come down.'

'It won't happen often,' she says and, a moment later, after getting up, adds, 'Are you all right?'

'Perfectly,' I tell her.

'You went quite pale a moment ago.'

'I can't see you,' I tell her, 'against the light,' and, as she moves to one side, continue, 'Most of the time I talk to myself. It's something to do with my illness. Maidstone, whom you never liked, made quite a point of stressing it.'

'I never said I disliked him,' she says.

'Loquaciousness, he suggested, was the indirect result of my spending too much time on my own. "How can I create?" I said. "Don't you realise, before you came here," he said, "creativity had been your downfall?" '

For a while she holds my hand, and neither of us speaks.

The room has little changed: a wallpaper of abstracted shapes has replaced the cubist one of roses: the bed still faces the sky above the village, and though the tang of coal smoke is no longer in the air, and the panting of the pit has gone – the rattle of trucks, the clacking of clogs (the echo, at night, of a whistle on the mainline to the south) – I find myself imagining that the movements below me in the house – Mrs Otterman about her housework, Etty about hers – are those of Isabella, those memorable occasions when – Grandfather Kells on one of his walks (Grandmother Corcoran fast asleep), Bea shopping in the village, Freddie in the yard – she would come up to my room, a cup of tea in one hand, a cake in the other, apologising as I scraped at a canvas or scribbled with a pen (in an old

10

school exercise book stolen from King Edward's), and say, 'I hope I'm not intruding, Richard,' her pale, green-irised eyes alight, a coppery sheen her hair against the southern glow.

'Didn't you love Bea?' Etty enquired when I went down to the kitchen (no sign of Mrs Otterman at all).

'Ours,' I said, 'was a mystical conjunction.'

'All those women that you had,' she said.

'Where are they now?' I might have asked, but merely responded, 'There were scarcely any.'

'They were even in the papers, Dad.'

Her back to me at the sink, she glanced across her shoulder. Outside, in the yard, surrounded by a hedge, her car stood by the garage, a side-window lowered, a child's seat clipped in the back for Glenda.

She was – Mrs Otterman clearly not here – preparing food.

'There were other things,' I said, 'as well.'

'Such as?'

'Why,' I said, 'her own ambition.'

Instead of Etty, however, it was Isabella who was standing there and, in my imagination, I heard her say, 'It's my daughter, my dear, you're supposed to love.'

'I do love her,' I said aloud and, as Etty turned, half-startled, from the sink, I swiftly added, 'She is, they tell me, very good. The Medical Research Council are very pleased. You may have seen it announced. She's on the threshold of discovering, in the anti-coagulant properties of the moorland leech, a possible cure for cancer.'

'Scarcely,' she said, and added, 'Couldn't she have combined research and marriage? After all,' she frowned, 'you say it's what I ought to do.'

'But then,' I said, 'she fell in love.'

'That,' she said, and added, 'Albert.'

'You're talking like the kind of man you say I should despise,' I told her.

'After this wonderful relationship you say you had, it

11

surprises me,' she said, 'she should feel, at the age of fifty-two, the need to go off with another man.'

'Marriage is a morbidity,' I said, and added, 'You sympathised with her at the time. "I hope," you said, "I have the guts to do the same at fifty." '

'I thought she didn't mean it,' Etty said.

'When you discovered that she did,' I said, 'I suppose you changed your mind.'

She smiled (I could see her reflection in the kitchen window): the absurdity of what we were up to struck us both afresh.

'Before I came down,' I gestured overhead, 'I was thinking of a project. I thought it might amuse you. Much of the research you could do from here. I could even,' I went on, 'suggest a title.'

'*The Fenchurch Papers.*'

'Why not?'

'The idea,' she said, 'is quite absurd.'

'If, as you say, I am about to die, you haven't much time. Less,' I added, 'the more you leave it.' When, however, she didn't reply, I hastily continued, 'Science acknowledges that subjectivity is the most valuable tool it has. Who, for instance, would describe Vasari or Lockhart or Boswell as objective? It's not the inscrutability of the observer that qualifies his or her judgements but the warmth, the dedication, the love they bring to their subject.'

At home together, in our early days, Etty both liked and resented me theorising in this manner, fascinated by the conclusions that I drew at the same time as feeling chastened by them. Afterwards I would hear her presenting similar if not identical views (when, for instance, she was at the Courtauld) to her fellow students, Viklund, the accredited authority in her field, describing her as 'the most forward pupil I have', and since he taught me for several terms (evening lectures at the Drayburgh: 'Landscape and the European Mind' – describing me as 'too clever by half') I have been inclined to accept his judgement.

12

'You don't have to go on. I'm perfectly capable,' she said 'of making up my mind.'

I heard her go out later in the morning, once in the car and once on foot. We ate our lunch in silence at the kitchen table, listening to the news. Afterwards I went upstairs to sleep. When I woke she had gone to fetch the children and Mrs Otterman, to my surprise, was busy in the kitchen.

A tall, dark-haired woman, with cadaverous features, she was, like Etty before her, busy at the sink.

'How are you, Mr Fenchurch?' she said.

'I'm well,' I said, in no mood to be patronised.

'Mrs Stott came and fetched me,' she said.

'Did she?'

'In her car.'

'Why should she do that?' I asked.

'She didn't wish,' she turned from the sink, having previously watched me in the reflection in the kitchen window, 'to leave you on your own.'

She was performing, I could see, a needless task – washing-up from lunch – a task, at the time, I'd offered to do myself.

'You can wash those in the machine,' I said, indicating the device adjacent to the sink.

'It's hardly worth the trouble,' she said, her hands, inflamed, plying in the water.

When she withdrew them completely, however, I observed she was wearing rubber gloves.

Whereas Mrs Otterman regarded Charlie as a cut or two above herself – with all the obsequiousness of the northern working class that that implied – she looked on me as something of a rival, she the daughter of a miner, the wife of another, the mother of a third (the last two out of work), I merely the offspring of another: despite differences in sensibility, intelligence, taste and wealth – or almost any other human attribute I might dare to mention – it put us on an equal footing – if not, in my case, having, if not sold out, absented myself, on something less. On the morning after I arrived I heard her

13

talking on the telephone in Charlie's study (assuming I and Etty, no doubt, were out), referring to me as 'Mrs Stott's poor dotty Dad – just like that man in Clatherton Street they took away last night.'

On one occasion, in an attempt to explain the acquiescence of so many of the miners in the village to being out of work, I remarked to Etty, 'So many people in the south, particularly intellectuals, talk of victimisation without realising that true conservatism – the imperviousness to change – lies at the heart of a place like this. What was Ardsley,' I went on, 'before the Wintertons discovered coal, but a dozen farms, as many rows of cottages, a church, a rectory, and Ardsley Hall?'

'It's a commuter village, for that involves work, too,' she said, angered, as the grand-daughter of a miner, by a designation she secretly despised.

'For some,' I said. 'But not for most,' for around the nucleus of the village have been constructed several estates of yellow-brick houses (described on a billboard, at the outskirts of the village, as 'executive-dwellings'): boxes, but for a garage, not much larger than the original miners' cottages themselves. 'Why the theorists go on,' I added, 'looking for change in a place like this, beats me.'

At which, for the first time, she exclaimed, 'It's why those theorists – and not theorists only – despise your work!'

'Why my work?' I enquired.

'Where they might have been looking for an appetite for change – even for revolution – they never find it.'

'In me?' (much feigned surprise).

'If anyone's work has been produced by a place like this – and by these conditions – and from amongst these people,' she further exclaimed, 'it's yours!'

'I think you're a couple of vowels out,' I said. 'Revolution returns any point on a circumference to where it was before. You don't think I'd waste my time on that? It's not revolution,' I went on, 'but revelation you're on about. Unless hypocrisy can be described as a phenomenon with a dynamic all its own, neither religious nor political sentiment affects or has affected

14

anything at all. Both are based on appetites which are unde-clared, and not merely undeclared but dishonestly perceived. I, for one, have always believed in a true revolution – of the individual spirit which prefers not to put its faith in authority, but to disseminate the authority of faith.'

'Feathering your own nest is a better description. Faith,' she went on, 'like love, is only achieved through others.'

'Not through destroying them by political and religious bigotry,' I said.

Taking up a tea-towel, Mrs Otterman, having previously removed her gloves, began to dry the pots.

'Would you like me to dry?' I said.

'No, thank you, Mr Fenchurch.'

'I'm quite capable,' I said (while you could get on with something else).

There was nothing else, however, to get on with: the tea for the children was already prepared (and standing on the table), and the food to be cooked for the evening meal arranged in a variety of bowls and dishes.

'It's quite all right, Mr Fenchurch,' she said.

What she couldn't be sure of, in Etty's absence, was what 'Mrs Stott's poor dotty Dad' might next get up to: not a few of her neighbours, I had heard her explaining one morning to Etty, had in recent years been 'taken off' – to be returned a few weeks later looking, if not changed, markedly subdued: other than that, and the eccentricities, observed or reported, which had preceded their departure (the broken windows, the shattered doors, the peculiar incidents to do with a length of rope or a bottle of pills) she had had, as she had told Etty, 'not a lot to go on'.

It was not, however, Mrs Otterman I was seeing there but Isabella's Mrs Hopkins: the ebullient, broad-bosomed, insolent (high-heeled, broad-hipped – invariably with laddered stockings) 'Rose' – the woman, also a collier's wife, who came and 'did' (stealing a great deal in the process: 'One thing she can't take away: the cheerfulness she leaves behind' – Isabella),

15

and who more than suggested, in her occasional glances, she knew what Isabella and I were up to.

Or did she? And, if so, in the face of so much passion, what could she have done?

'And what are you doing, young Richard?' when she found me in the kitchen, creeping down in the hope the sounds I'd heard were those of Isabella – and not disinclined herself to be hugged, her more than ample figure ill-concealed in a home-made sweater – one of a variety she knitted in a range, as I endeavoured to explain to her on more than one occasion, of uniquely ill-matched colours. 'I suppose you're looking for Bea?' ('The mother *and* the daughter!' she announced coming, one Christmas, upon Isabella and myself kissing under the mistletoe.) 'I wonder what Mrs C is like in bed?' she had whispered to me once having caught me gazing after Bella as she walked off, one evening, down the drive on the way to her weekly meeting of the W.I.

'Why Etty should ask you to come,' I told Mrs Otterman, 'I've no idea. Or did she arrange it earlier? It's a terrible nuisance, I'm sure,' I added.

'Not at all,' she said, putting the pots in the cupboard.

'It's extra income, of course,' I suggested.

'That's part of it,' she said. 'But I'd do it for nothing for Mrs Stott.'

'How are things in the village?' I asked.

'Three-quarters of them,' she said, 'are out of work.'

'I thought the official figure,' I said, 'was a third.'

'If you add to it those who've decided to retire, those who don't bother to sign on, those who are on training schemes, it soon comes up to three-quarters. Seventy per cent, the unions make out.'

'There must be a lot of ill-feeling,' I said.

'And drugs.'

'And drugs.'

'Drugs are the main industry round here,' she added.

'So where does that put us?' I said.

16

'Some of you can get out,' she said. 'As opposed to them that are carried.'

'It must seem odd,' I said, about to take a dish to put away but foiled by her quicker movement, 'seeing someone like me coming to a place like this when everybody else is desperate to leave.'

'In work, or out,' she said, 'it's home.' With a sideways look, she added, 'And where is your home, Mr Fenchurch?'

'I'm not sure where it is,' I told her. 'Another drug-infested street.'

'At least,' she said, 'you have the choice,' and, closing the cupboard door with a bang, added, 'Which is more than most of us can say at present.'

3

MUCH OF the village is visible from my room, the trees, their branches bare, coiled in a familiar frieze against a bifurcated backdrop of land and sky: a characterless scene without the pit. On the lower slopes are the screes of sooty houses, overlooked by the more recently-constructed 'executive-dwellings', each house with its view of Ardsley Dam, a stretch of water divided by a hump-backed bridge (built by the proprietors of Ardsley Hall, the Wintertons, long before coal was discovered on their land), and brought near to collapse in the recent past by the weight of (mainly) Corcoran lorries. On a quiet day, I'm told by Mrs Otterman, the hum of machinery comes over the hill at the back of the house from the outcrop mine at Fernley – another pit which, having been closed, has been replaced by opencast workings.

I've drawn most of the fields and woods, the hedgerows and houses (and, once in London, painted them from memory and sketches). Along most of those lanes I have walked with Bea – and along not many fewer with her mother. I can see the outcrop of rock at Ardsley Edge, an extrusion of fissured sandstone – and recall that amongst its grasses and ferns, and beneath the silver birch (couched by buttercups, anenomes and daisies) that grow in profusion amongst the rock-falls at its base, I have lain for hours, as a youth, with the mother of the girl I was about to marry.

Red hair which, as with Bea, had darkened in later life to magenta: a pallid, lightly-freckled skin, green-irised eyes, an incisive mouth – a robust, slim-waisted, high-breasted figure, the slightest contact with which, whether excised by clothes or not, went through me like a knife.

I met Bea at a Christmas Dance (the boys from King Edward's, the girls from Linfield High: two single-sex schools confronting each other across a city street). Several weeks previously, Harris, an anonymous fellow whose parents owned a shop in town and who lived at Fernley, remarked that he was bringing a girl from a nearby village whom he met from time to time on the train: she would, on the night, be staying in town: 'Ought that might have gone on,' he said, 'on the train back home has gone clean out of the window.' A few days later he pointed her out in the street: amongst the groups of uniformed figures drifting along the pavement hers was indistinguishable. 'She's gone,' he said and, pointing down a sidestreet, departed in the opposite direction towards his parents' shop.

Wandering to the end of the street I glanced along it: a tall coppery-haired figure of slender build, with the mandatory dark blue High School coat stretching to her ankles, was walking away from me. Instantly (inexplicably) the thought came to me, 'This is the girl I shall marry,' and, without glancing back, let alone going after her, I slowly walked away.

On the evening of the party I invited her to dance: even as I held her I was aware of things I would never like: the way, for instance, she did her hair (less to attract than distract, I thought, swept from her brow in the manner of a child), the freckles on her brow, the green-irised eyes, flecked minutely, I observed, with strands of brown: nor did I like – nor could I separate these features from – the sharpness of her glance. Later in the evening, when I invited her again to dance, without any interest, she turned me down.

Six months elapsed before we met again: a party was being held to which several of the boys and an equivalent number of girls who were leaving their respective schools that year had been invited, their numbers supplemented by girls from a lower year: amongst the latter was Bea. As at the dance, she wore a light green dress which complimented the colour of her hair

19

and emphasised, if that's the word, the colour of her eyes and her complexion; gauche, she had little of the assurance of the girls from the year who were leaving, and had come – as, indeed, had I – without a partner.

I had, in fact, come with Otterton, a thin-featured, lugubriously-humoured youth, and his girlfriend, Jenny, the bucktoothed daughter of a dentist whose mother, with some misgivings, had lent Otterton her car.

It was the last Saturday of the last term of our final year at Edward's. Otterton, whose ineptitude at sport had endeared him to me throughout that year, was destined for the army (the Officer Training School at Sandhurst).

I, I had announced, intended to become an artist (more dramatic still, already was one).

The party was held in a garden which stretched along one side and round the back of a (to me) very large house. The sun, as I arrived, was on the point of setting: its light illuminated a greenhouse (incandescent) and an orchard (ethereal), as well as a series of trellised terraces upon which figures were already dancing. Beyond an area of hedged fields and woodland, comprising the lower slopes and the bed of a shallow valley, hills were mistily enclosed in the mellow light. It was an area I'd roamed through as a child: the distant hills, with the bleaker slopes of the moors above, I'd camped in as a youth: the Pennine foothills with their dammed-up streams and rushing falls, their silent ponds and crumbling abbeys.

Chinese lanterns had been strung above a lawn: a gramophone, manipulated by the hostess's sister, in the Fifth Form, played a melancholy tune. It was the one I'd danced to with Bea at the Christmas Party and, looking up, I experienced a secondary shock of recognition, not unmixed with pleasure, to see her chatting with a group of friends.

I invited her to dance.

'Are you cold?' I asked.

'I am, as a matter of fact,' she said. Her hand, as I took it, had trembled.

I drew her closer to me.

20

'Do you come here often?' I enquired.

'You said that the last time,' she replied, to which I instantly responded, 'I'm surprised that you remember.'

'I remember a lot of things,' she said, and when I enquired, 'Such as?' replied, 'About your reputation.'

'For doing what?' I asked.

'Everything, as far as I can make out, that's reprehensible.'

I drew her closer: I felt the tautness of her back and the heat that surged between us, and recalled that this was the girl I was destined to marry. ('Destined by whom?' I mentally enquired, to which, then as now – and particularly on that lantern-lighted evening – came no reply).

We sat the next dance out: prompted by the pastel-coloured lanterns that glowed from the darkening trees, I remarked, 'I know that landscape well: every hill and dell, every beck and pond, every wood and hedge.'

'I live beyond those hills,' she said. She gestured to the south. 'A place called Ardsley.'

'What does your father do?' I asked.

'He owns,' she said, 'a lot of lorries.'

'What do the lorries carry?' I asked.

After a while – not sure, I discovered later, how precisely to describe her father – she said, 'Principally coal.'

'A haulage contractor,' I suggested.

'I suppose he is,' she said, disinclined to discuss it. 'I hear,' she went on, 'from Harris,' (our mutual friend who, I noticed, had not been invited to the party) 'that you're going to be an artist.'

'I am,' I said.

'Why?' Within the constriction of the garden bench, she glanced at me directly. 'There isn't much in it, if,' she went on, 'you wish to earn a living. Particularly,' she paused, 'if you haven't any money.'

'I intend to get a job,' I said.

'And give up,' she said, 'your education.'

'What's education,' I enquired, 'if it hasn't already directed me to art?' A moment later, eliciting no response, I added, 'It's

21

a calling. Like Paul on the Road to Damascus. Three years ago,' I went on, 'I was sitting in the sixth-form classroom when, in the midst of reading Verlaine's "Ode to Autumn", it occurred to me that art is the highest form of human knowledge. I saw the whole of my life before me: a house, a wife, a job, a car: a set of rails that ran as far as I could see. At that instant I decided to dedicate my life to doing something that no one else could do.'

'Weren't you going to university?' she asked.

'I was,' I said. 'I've given it up.' Gesturing at our peers, I added, 'They're going on to something they know and can already see.'

'You'll end up in the gutter,' she suddenly declared. ('Nothing,' she might have said, 'challenges me so much as someone who forsakes their friends, their family, common sense (the destiny chosen for him) in order to pursue what everyone recognises to be an impossible dream'; it was, in short, I suspected, that preliminary lack of faith that brought us both together).

'Do you feel inspired?' she added.

'It's hidden,' I said, 'by other things.'

'What?'

'Practicalities.' I paused. 'Unlike science, industry, or any of the professions, art is useless. You can do it for three hundred and sixty-five days of the year and no one owes you a penny. It's the next best thing,' I was about to add, 'to God,' but, for reasons which only now I am beginning to understand, I substituted, 'love.'

'Are you coming down?'

The sound of Lottie and Glenda came from the living-room below (and of Mrs Otterman from the kitchen: the converging domestic interests of food and television).

When I said, 'Do you remember that party at Allgrave, the last Saturday of the last term of my last year at King Edward's?' I saw my own confusion mirrored in Etty's face – in reality, Bea's face, for, though she had my hair, dark and prematurely greying, she had her mother's features – and added, 'I visited it not long ago and the view was obscured, where not by trees, by speculative building. I used to camp out there. Not at Allgrave, which is on the edge of town, but across the valley at Broughton Wood.'

I was about to continue, 'Broughton Springs was the most magical camp-site in the world,' but suddenly enquired, in order to distract her, 'Don't you use this room?' for she had found me not in my bedroom but in the back upstairs room which Isabella, at one time, had used as a study.

She looked at me, for a moment, as Bea had looked at me on the evening of the Allgrave party: like someone observing an accident which they were not altogether sure had taken place ('Was that a leg? Was that an arm? Was that a *body*?').

'It used to be Gran's. She came in here,' I said, 'to have her thoughts.'

'I suppose, too,' Etty said, 'to write her diaries.'

'Diaries?'

'Mummy has them now, of course.'

'I never knew,' I said, 'she kept a diary.'

'In a lot of Grandpa's ledgers. The ones he used for his trucks. She always had,' she said, 'such terrible writing,' and added, 'She only kept them at the time she married. And when you and Mum were growing up.'

The floor was bare: other than a cupboard, there was no sign that anyone had occupied the room at all: it overlooked the stone-flagged yard at the back of the house – with Charlie's shooting-brake standing by the garage – and, beyond the yard's enclosing hedge, a lawn which, presently unmown, had been given over at one time to a tennis court: a thicker, darker growth of grass showed where the limed white lines had run. A sharply-ascending slope, engulfed by trees, obscured the view on either side, save where, at an angle, the tower of the church – sooty, square, a battlemented crest – and the stone-slabbed roof of the rectory were visible over an intervening wall: tall, buttressed, bowed, its brickwork marked by salt and long, horizontal fissures, it was here, in the time of the Wintertons, allegedly, peaches and apricots grew.

Here, by the presently uncurtained window, Isabella had had her desk: there, by the soot-lined fireplace with its marble surround, she had had her couch and, facing the couch, her chintz-covered chair. On the walls she had had her books – mostly unread, and in glass-fronted cases – and the sketches (which she'd framed) of the house, done by myself.

'She was immensely beautiful,' I said, and added, 'Your mother,' under the absurd illusion I was talking to Bea.

'She'll be glad to hear it,' Etty said. 'Though a bit late in the day, I should think, to tell her,' and, seeing no alternative, took my arm. 'Come down and have some tea,' she added.

With no resemblance to Etty – round, moon-like faces with dark-irised, moon-like eyes ('The epitome of Charlie,' Etty remarked proudly after each of their births), the children were sitting on the couch on which, thirty-five years before, Isabella and I had sat watching the then black-and-white, now coloured television screen.

Although the couch confronted the fireplace, with its marble pilasters and cornice and its iron grate, its black-leaded bars curled upwards like the ends of a moustache, the children were sitting sideways, the unshod feet of the one impressed against the stockinged legs of the other.

'Here's Grandpa,' Etty said, and though the youngest one glanced up and the eldest frowned (and neither spoke) their gazes, dream-like at this intrusion, moved swiftly back to the screen.

'Back to the table,' Etty said, since both of them were chewing, the youngest, Glenda, with the fragments of a bun in her hand and on her knee.

'I've finished, Mummy,' Lottie said.

'No, you haven't,' Etty said, in a manner indistinguishable from that of Isabella.

'I have, Mummy.' Swallowing first, Glenda opened her mouth.

24

'I don't want that chair made sticky,' Etty said.

'It is sticky,' Lottie said. 'It was sticky when I got here.'

Both the children had thick, black hair, with only a hint of brown, or red – the faintest legacy from Bea; they had, however, a pallid skin on which, in certain lights, could be glimpsed a scattering of freckles: in a similarly favourable light I have, from time to time, detected in their eyes a flickering of green amidst the brown – nothing, for instance, that was visible now – and not at all, of course, from a distance. They had, I had always been relieved to see (in light of the taciturnity of their father) something of a temper, an unmistakable Kellsian or Isabellian trait.

With a cry, 'Oh, Mum!' they descended from the couch and scampered to the hall. From the kitchen came Mrs Otterman's, 'Something more to eat, then, loves?' followed by a wail and, in unison, 'We've got to wash our hands!'

'The bathroom would be better,' came the dutiful response, but already the feet were scampering back (followed by, from Mrs Otterman, 'What about the tap!') and, the door slammed back, breathless, red-faced, the two figures once more were sitting on the couch.

'Are those hands dry?'

'Yes, Mum!' (Eyes on the screen.)

'You've scarcely had time to wash them.'

'We have!' (Unison again.)

Etty would sit there, in the old days, on Isabella's knee: Corcoran, who, despite his lorries with their governors which, much to his satisfaction, restricted his otherwise reckless drivers' speeds, had an aversion to 'technological development' (hence his retention of his shire horses and his four-wheeled carts long after everyone else had given them up): he similarly resisted 'the television': '*Everyone* has got one,' Isabella said. 'Then that's all the damn more reason why we shouldn't,' he replied. As for colour, it wasn't, he protested, 'what you see', and when Isabella pointed out – as she was inclined to when her wishes were frustrated – 'everyone's got one' and that colours 'could be seen outside,' he responded, 'Maybe colours

can, but not the ones in theer (I prefer the black and white).'
Even in those days, the second generation of television
watchers, the advisability of watching prompted the same
exhortations to filial or domestic duty.

'Did it do much harm?' I asked.

'Harm?' Etty sat beside me on an adjoining couch. 'I never
watched like these two. If I let them,' she went on, 'they'd be
in front of it all night.'

'We rationed it, at their age, to an hour and a half each
evening,' I said.

'I don't remember that,' she said. 'Why,' she went on, 'they
scarcely look at a book,' and, indicating the younger of the
two, continued, 'I don't even know if Glenda can read.'

Short, white ankle socks on slippered feet, stocky calves and
bulbous thighs, a tiny skirt, a jumpered chest, a pale, broad-
featured, sensitive face: at the mention of her name she turned
in my direction.

'You used to equate it with eating plastic food,' Etty added.

'When you were older,' I replied.

'The arguments we had. Far longer than we used to watch.'
Her eyes, too, were fixed on the screen. 'You and Mum.'

'Look where she is now,' I said.

The curtains on the windows of the room had not been
drawn: visible outside, a frieze of starkly-silhouetted branches
were sheaved against a darkening sky: it was through the second
of the two uncurtained windows, furthest from the door, that
I'd first seen Isabella: sitting where Harriet, her grandchild,
and I were sitting now – sewing, her head bowed, her face
shadowed from the light of an overhead lamp, glancing up as
she heard our step (Bea bringing me home, for the first time,
to the house), and perceiving not so much my face, she told
me later, as a mask, half-lighted, gazing from outside.

'You could look at it,' Etty said, 'the other way around.'
Withdrawing her gaze from the screen, she added, 'What good,
for instance, does it do?'

I was, however, recalling that journey back from the Allgrave
party, stopping in Fernley (where, ironically, Harris lived),

26

Otterton getting out to buy a drink and, finding the off-licence closed, coming back with fish and chips (having, with characteristic generosity, offered to drive both Bea and I home). He, with the toothsome Jenny, sat in front, Bea and I behind, each of us eating what – leaning in the car window to present each of us with a steaming packet – he had presciently described as 'our final meal together'.

I never saw Otterton again: over the years I heard (on the radio) and read (in a newspaper) accounts of him 'on loan' to one of the Arab states (a major in one, a lieutenant-colonel in another).

'You in your attic,' he had said on that final occasion, 'painting pictures, me,' he had added, 'God knows where,' gazing through the windscreen, his and Jenny's heads silhouetted against the light of the village street.

It was, or so it seemed, only moments later that I first saw Ardsley – or, more specifically, the door in the wall – and received, after a rebuke, my first, if peremptory goodnight kiss from Bea.

'Off to your room,' Etty said as the programme came to an end and, getting to her feet, turned off the television. 'You can see a half hour later,' she added, 'when Lottie has done her homework and I've heard Glenda read her book.'

'I haven't any homework!' Lottie cried.

'I'll set you some, in that case,' Etty said.

'Oh, Mummy!' And, climbing on my knee, my daughter's eldest child enquired, 'Will you tell us a story, Grandpa?'

'I want you both,' Etty said, 'to read to yourselves.'

'Glenda can't read, Mummy,' Lottie said.

'She can.'

'I can't,' Glenda said (still ensconced on the couch).

'I've heard her,' Etty said.

'You've just told Grandpa she can't,' Lottie said.

'A lot,' Etty said. 'But she can read some.'

'Oh, do tell us a story, Grandpa!' Lottie placed her arm around my neck: in such a way her great-grandmother, in the most improbable places, would make her first approach.

'Grandpa,' Etty said, 'can tell you one before you go to bed.'

'Will you, Grandpa!' Glenda, crossing the space between us, climbed on my knee as well.

'Whenever your mother says you're ready,' I announced.

'Goody, goody!' Lottie said, removing her arm from around my neck (like Isabella, too, once she'd got what she'd wanted), adding, 'It's got to be one that frightens!'

'It'll be one that sends you to sleep. Up to your room,' their mother said, yet it was Etty who was descending from my knee and it was Isabella who was being beseeched, 'Will you tell us a story, Gran?' and the smile of Bea's mother was turning on me as she informed them, 'If your father lets me.'

'Oh, do, Daddy,' Etty has said and, covertly, two hours later, as Etty and her sister go to bed, I am standing at the bedroom door watching Isabella stoop to kiss their cheeks – as, moments later, outside the door, her head is raised and I stoop to kiss her mouth.

In the car, approaching Ardsley, I had said, 'Do you think I can see you again?' and Bea had replied – her skirt fortuitously drawn above her knee, the consequence of our movements as we cleared the interior of the papers from the fish and chips, 'If you like,' adding, as my hand enclosed the skin above her stockinged thigh, 'I'm not that kind of girl,' drawing down her skirt with – although sitting sideways I couldn't be sure – a great deal of indignation.

'Where shall we meet?' I asked, while Otterton, restricted by his driving, murmured endearments to Jenny in the seat in front.

'I'm going away,' she said.

'Where?' I asked, in some surprise (could someone, I reflected, go away after receiving the sort of confidences I'd confided earlier that night?).

'France,' she said. 'The Riviera. We go there every year.'

An immeasurable gap – we weren't, since her previous rebuke, even holding hands – opened up between us.

'You ought to go,' she added. 'If you ever get the chance.'

I began to suspect she had listened to little if anything I had told her: how could an artist, about to take leave of his friends (his parents, his school, his past) contemplate the expense of going overseas? I hadn't even had the money that evening to pay for the fish and chips. ('On me,' Otterton had announced, leaning in the car knowing I was broke. 'It's our final meal together.')

'How long are you going for?' I asked.

'Six weeks. Sometimes,' she went on, 'it's nearer eight.'

She might, in the light of our predicament, have said, 'Six years': there was little chance, after all that time, and the distractions of the Riviera, that she'd remember who I was.

'I could write to you,' I said.

'That's a good idea,' she said and, with the interior light turned on above our heads, and with a pencil borrowed from Otterton, and a piece of paper from the fish and chips, she wrote down her address.

'Will you write back?' I asked.

'Of course I will,' she said (she hadn't asked for mine).

'Who are you staying with?' I asked.

'Friends.'

'Friends?'

'Of Daddy's. He has lots of friends down there. We sometimes go at Christmas.'

My vision of a future with the daughter of a man who spent both the winter and the summer on the Riviera vanished with the sound of Otterton running the car across the kerb and Bea announcing, 'That doorway over there,' – a green-painted door, like the door to a house, let into a high stone wall.

We kissed, perfunctorily, goodnight.

'I'll write to you,' I said.

'I'll look forward to hearing from you,' she said, and the door was opened and I was given my first glimpse of the path which led, beneath the shadowed mass of trees and through pools of light, to the hidden house above.

4

'KIDS IN?'

Charlie had come in: an ebullient man, he rubbed his hands against the cold and went to the fire, acquainted himself with the fact that it wasn't lit, and, turning, with the same cheeriness to me, went on, 'Had time to find your way about?'

'Etty got in Mrs Otterman when she went to fetch the children,' I said.

'I told her that she should.' His tall, suited figure – a large, square, round-featured head – was turned with its back to the empty grate. 'Now you're up here,' he added, 'we don't want you spending too much time on your own.'

'Most of my life I've been on my own,' I said. 'One way or another.'

'Along with Bea.' He rubbed his ample hands together.

'Without support from anyone.'

'That's right.' His attention drifted to the ceiling: '*I got it first!*' followed by one of the children's cries. 'In their room?'

'That's right.'

A barrister, his practice had, in recent years, confined him principally to the north, briefs of astounding insignificance taking him to Manchester and Leeds, to Liverpool and Hull, Beverley and York (Halifax and Bradford – Wakefield, Castleford, Durham and Shipley): 'Old age,' he had said when I had chided him for this narrowing of his horizons for, as a younger man, before his marriage, he had travelled as far afield as South Africa and South America (the United States and Russia) representing 'causes', a legacy, this, from his years in London, both where he had studied and had met (and married) Etty before, on his father's death, returning north to take on the family practice. 'Why,' I had told him, 'you are still a child,' (he was, I'd estimated, in his middle thirties). 'You don't shut up shop until you're dead, and perhaps,' I'd gone on, 'not even then. The whole of life before you!'

Despite his upbringing, background and profession, he was chairman of the Ardsley and District Labour Party (dominated until recently by the National Union of Mineworkers), succeeding in the task through what I could only describe as (for a lawyer) a uniquely disingenuous nature (as well as the amount of time he was prepared to put in, together with the quality and quantity of legal advice he freely dispensed), his refusal to acknowledge malice in anyone earning him a reputation for what the *Ardsley and District Express* – shown to me by Etty, not him – had described as his 'probitious generosity': 'They even have to invent a word to describe him. Or do you think it's a misprint?' Etty enquired.

'I could sell the house,' he had once remarked when I pointed out the disparity between his own resources and those of the people whom he had chosen to represent. 'At least, Etty could, for it's hers, and I haven't the time. We could live in Second Avenue,' (a row of, at one time, gas-lit cottages, the most notorious street in the village) 'but, taking into account the circumstances, I can't see it would do either us or our critics any good. Those who don't like me living in The People's Palace,' (as the house was now known) 'would only get something worse for their pains, and both the Party and I would be handicapped for the lack of space. Party walls, to coin a phrase, in Second Avenue, aren't that thick, and the amount of work I'm obliged to do at home wouldn't be facilitated by the noise coming through from the other side. When the day comes to hand over our ill-gotten gains they'll get an idea of how much it costs to keep on a roof so that they can come up here most days and sound off as long and as loud as they like.'

When Etty first introduced him to our house in Belsize Park (as if he not I were its rightful owner: 'My genial giant,' she had proudly declared), she had said, 'He is a liberal of the kind which set the Labour Party on its feet: sentimental and, to the degree that it is often mistaken for passion, loyal to his class in ways of which he is unaware. He wouldn't turn a hair,' (indicating, with a swing of her arm – six years out of the Courtauld and still a child – the fourteen rooms of our Victorian mansion) 'at living here if he felt he could put it to good use. Quite a counterblast,' she had concluded, 'to you.'

'I'll give them a shock and go up,' he said. 'Etty's not expecting me back so soon.'

'Why's that?' I said.

'With having you here she's been on tenterhooks,' he said. 'I thought I'd get back early. After all,' he smiled, 'we want to do the best by you.'

A further smile from his brown-eyed, round-featured face – the same expansive look with which he had greeted me when I had first arrived – and he was gone. 'What are you two up to!' came the cry, followed by (a unified), '*Daddy!*'

The sound of a kiss as he greeted Etty, and of several more as, accompanied by the splashing of water (they were evidently in the bathroom), he lifted each of the children.

'What are you going to do?' My father stands in front of the black-leaded range in the living-room of our house at Onasett.

Onasett: Ona's Headland: His Place: a Viking warlord who cleared a space on the crest of the wooded ridge that projected southward to the river – taken over, subsequently, by Dane and Saxon and, previous to all of them, the Romans who built a side-road, west, from Watling Street, into the Pennine hills – passing to the north of Onasett as the road to Manchester still does (isolating, in the process, the between-the-two-world-wars housing estate of three thousand semi-detached houses – a scree of brick and tile, of hedged lawn and field and tarmac that climbs one side of Ona's original Sett to the brick-built school and hospital and the stone-built church that form a crustaceous backbone to the ridge).

Our house, in front of whose living-room fire my father

32

stands, lies halfway up the eastward-facing slope (catching in its principal windows the morning sun – and looking out to the higher ridge on which are poised, in silhouette, the principal buildings of the town: the County Hall dome, the Greek-porticoed entrance to the Courts of Law, the chisel-roofed tower of the French-Renaissance-styled Town Hall, the dog-toothed spire of the Gothic cathedral – a résumé of an architectural heritage poised, in its totality, as a reciprocal spine to this more imposing ridge on which Ona set his original dwelling).

'I've got a job.'

'Where?'

My father is in his fiftieth year: small, broad-shouldered, stocky, his eyes are dark, not unlike my own – darkened further, however, in his case, by the dust that never leaves the lids. In the past few years he has risen from an underground maintenance worker to a coal-face foreman: the responsibility, in charge of thirty-five men, has subdued his once ebullient nature: he comes home now too tired to eat, or, if he has eaten, too tired to undress, falling asleep in front of the fire, his eyes, in his exhaustion, half-open (eerily-gleaming beneath the half-closed lids, the mouth ajar, air roaring through his dust-filled nose).

'At Chamberlains,' I tell him.

'You could have gone theer when you wa're only fifteen,' he tells me.

I've worked, as it is, at Chamberlains for the previous four summers: a contractor and erector of marquees at agricultural shows and weddings.

'After all this time at school. And now,' he goes on, 'you're geving it up.'

The argument is one of several which have taken place over the previous weeks: 'All these years', 'A lifetime of effort', 'What have we done to deserve it?' 'Chucking it away.'

It is the week of my first letter to Bea: I am, amidst scenes of industrial dereliction, imagining her caught up in the distractions of a sun-baked beach, wine-laden tables, palm trees, yachts, a waveless sea: "Here I am, reproached by bickering parents, broke, with no prospects whatsoever, ridiculed for what

33

I intend to be (already am). My form-master has written to say, in giving up university, I have let down King Edward's: 'All these years of teaching' etc., in much the same way as my father says, 'All these years of working down a mine . . .' "

'All these years of working down the pit so you can go to King Edward's and all you do,' his eyes alight with a vehemence which outshines the glow of the fire behind, 'is chuck it in our face.'

'There's a difference between education, as you would define it, and enlightenment,' I tell him (a prick at the age of eighteen as I am at sixty-five).

'Enlightment,' he says, 'is not having to do work like an animal in a cave.'

He coughs: a moment later, he retches.

"You'll be surprised to hear," I go on in my letter, "I've taken a job as a labourer. It won't leave me any time to paint but will give me enough cash, with overtime, to silence the opposition. I've worked at this place over the past four years (since, in fact, the age of thirteen). We travel, seven days a week (double-time on Sundays) to showgrounds across the north of England – and to country houses where, on lawns across which are scattered ancient trees, we erect marquees for society weddings – tents into which the bride and groom occasionally wander and, hand in hand, inspect the coloured awnings, the parquet floor, the boxes and racks arranged with flowers, the metalwork tables and the metalwork chairs, and, once in a while, I hear one or other of the two remark, 'My darling, this is jolly,' and, 'I say, my dear, just look at this,' and imagine turning up one day at Ardsley Hall and setting up a tent in the grounds for the wedding of Miss Beatrice Corcoran to a man who spends in one evening taking you out what it takes me a month to earn with a fourteen-pound hammer."

'I'll never be a teacher,' I tell him. 'I'll never subvert the most precious thing I have – my individuality – to a common interest. Why should I compromise that to become one of a hundred thousand others – a teacher, a hack, a professional?'

'Because,' my father says, 'everybody does, king or miner,

34

teacher or priest. They have to earn a living. Otherwise,' he declares, 'they beg off others.'

'I'll work at Chamberlains,' I tell him.

'Chamberlains,' he tells me, 'employs the riff-raff of the town. They pay a quarter of what you'd earn as a teacher, or in any other job, if it comes to that.'

His face is lined: a file of coal-dust extends laterally beneath the skin where, in the past, a cut has healed.

"The first year I came here, at the age of thirteen, the first to arrive, I sat in the sun. Around me was an ash-filled yard enclosed by low, wooden sheds in which canvas was stored – poles, ropes, stakes, awnings and flooring – and in one of which, on the step of which I was sitting, the canvas was sewn on two rectangular, smooth-surfaced tables, two foot-pedalled sewing-machines attached to the sides. I was joined by a man with a snap-bag on his back who, crouching in the sun beside me, announced that he, too, was applying for a job. He had, he confided, just come out of prison and his application, as a consequence, would be accompanied by one or two lies. He had, in prison, he further confided, acquired a hobby: even as he spoke he was filing at a piece of metal – a 'connecting-rod', he told me, of a model locomotive – looking up as the door to the office was finally opened and the figure of a woman could be seen inside.

To my horror, Bea, when I went in, this woman – sitting at a crowded desk – exclaimed, '*Fenchurch!* What on earth are *you* doing here?' causing me to blush to the soles of my feet. I then realised – which, my dear Bea, you might have done already – that the celebrated (the redoubtable) Mrs Chamberlain, the school secretary at King Edward's, and the terror of the Heads of both that school and the High (not to mention the masters and mistresses) was the wife of one of the Chamberlain brothers (three in number, she the spouse of the eldest and the most retired): unknown to me, during the school holidays, she lent a hand in the Chamberlain office – in front of whose desk I was presently standing. 'Fenchurch!' she exclaimed –

35

much to the puzzlement of the ex-con beside me, 'what on *earth* are you doing *here*? A pupil of King Edward's!'

I have been a renegade, Miss Corcoran, all my life – at home, at work, at school, at play: the last in my year at King Edward's to be made a prefect (a history of beatings lower down the school for misbehaviour), 'a bolshie-headed bastard' in the words of the woodwork-master whom I foolishly confronted at fisticuffs when he discovered me writing in the library one lunch-hour when it was out of bounds – and for which, in my last year, not for the first time, I was threatened with expulsion: 'Don't you realise, Fenchurch,' said the Head (the Oxonian classics scholar P.G. 'Piggy' Norton) 'that Mr Barraclough, like you, *is a former member of the working-class?*'

Dear Bea, with whom I have danced on only one or two occasions and whom, as yet, I have never taken out, to you all this, I know, must sound absurd: reading a letter from someone whom, despite our tête-à-tête at Allgrave, you scarcely know, but – I have to complete this tale in the hope that I may, at the very least, capture your attention when distractions – for you – crowd in on every side. Since you are familiar with the broad-bosomed, tweed-suited Mrs Chamberlain ('Flossie' to her intimates, 'Bloody old Flo' behind her back), who strides between our schools like a policeman on the beat and talks to masters and mistresses – as well as our respective Heads – as ferociously as she does to the boys and girls ('What are you doing in the street, boy/girl, without your cap/hat? I shall report you to Mr Norton/Miss Quartermain!') I feel obliged to complete my account of our interview for, having come upon her in such unfortunate surroundings, I could only confess – as, indeed, I do to you – 'I've come for a job, Mrs Chamberlain,' to which, on this first occasion, she instantly responded, 'You've been a trouble-maker, Fenchurch, from the start,' while, to my equally instantaneous response, 'I have to get a job,' she roared, 'Have you taken leave of your senses! Are you aware of the sort of people who work down here?' gesturing to the sun-lit yard where I could see a group of men assembling, not a minority of whom, in my father's and no doubt Mrs Chamberlain's

36

terminology, would have come under the generic heading of riff-raff. Indeed, attracted by her voice (it could, I discovered later, be heard in the street outside) the whole of this group, with their snap-bags and their morning papers, their disreputable and dishevelled dress, turned in our direction.

'How old are you, Fenchurch?' she enquired.

'Thirteen,' I said.

'Thirteen what?'

'Thirteen years,' I responded.

'Thirteen years what?' she further demanded.

'Thirteen years, Mrs Chamberlain,' I was reminded.

'How can you be thirteen, *Fenchurch*,' (made to sound like an ecclesiastical sewer) 'when last year you were in 5b and next year you'll be in 5 Upper?' (encyclopaedic recall).

'I passed the eleven-plus entrance exam when I was only nine,' I said.

'It's not usually taken until you are twelve,' (further evidence of dissemblement, trouble-making, mischief).

'They closed the loop-hole,' I said, 'the following year. It's to do with my birthday, and the time of the year, and that I was moved up two classes by mistake at primary school,' (further evidence of chicanery).

'We don't employ boys,' she said, 'who are only thirteen. Furthermore, we don't employ people whose minds will be polluted by all they hear from the workmen, let alone by what they are obliged to see. Wait until Mr Norton hears about this.'

'Hears about what?' said a voice behind my back.

Turning, I was confronted by a massive figure: a rock-shaped, square-featured, close-cropped head beamed down at me from the office door.

'This, Harry,' Mrs Chamberlain said, 'is a pupil from King Edward's who, believe it or not, is applying for a job.'

The square, ruddy-cheeked, blue-eyed face beamed at me more broadly.

'I was a pupil theer,' it said, 'myself.'

'That is hardly a comparison, Harry,' Mrs Chamberlain said.

'I'll shove him in my gang, Mother,' the figure replied. 'What

37

d'ost think to that, then, young 'un? If you find it too rough you'll be out on your ear. I on'y have rough 'uns in my lot.'

'This is my son,' Mrs Chamberlain said. 'If you're not up to scratch you'll be out on your ear,' showing, in my experience, not only a surprising deference but a not any the less surprising command of colloquialism.

'What's thy first name, young 'un?' the son enquired.

'Richard,' I replied.

'Richard.' His blue-eyed look went up to the window and the row of curious faces outside. He gave a laugh – not the last I was to hear that day. 'I'll call you college-boy,' he said. 'Come outside and load a lorry.'

On this last occasion, when I arrived this summer, Mrs Chamberlain said, 'Do you mean to say, Fenchurch, you're giving up *varsity* to work down here? The Wainscliff Prize for English Verse, the Atterton Prize for Art, the Athletics' Team Representative in the 880 yards, and the *First Fifteen at Rugger.*'

'I have to get a job,' I said.

'Perversity in your life,' she said, 'I have to admit, has never known its limit.' "

'You've given up all we've done for you,' my father says and, as my mother intervenes ('He takes it all for granted. We've worked our fingers to the bone'), he adds, 'They'll be laughing fit to burst round here. All the neighbours' lads at fifteen were i' the mill or down the pit and he ends up at Chamberlains. Nowt but the bloody riff-raff theer.'

Facing me, his back to the fireplace – a glimpse, through the uncurtained windows, of the darkening trees – is Charlie, a figure whom I have, I believe, already addressed as 'Dad' – and then, more confusedly, as 'Harry'. 'I have to get a job,' I say, to which he replies, 'Your royalties are enough to cover your cost of living. On top of which,' he goes on, 'you have the Public Lending Right.'

'I never joined,' I tell him. 'I've never been a lackey. I've never had a penny from anyone I didn't earn. Have you seen the people who apply? Have you seen the *forms* you have to fill in?' I ramble on ('What's individuality and independence mean if you're subsumed by a bureaucratic function?') to find, or so it seems, the television turned on and Glenda sitting on Charlie's knee and Etty sitting with her arm around Lottie while I, assuming they had gone to bed, enquire, 'Have they had their bath?'

'Charlie wanted to bath them,' Etty says. 'He seldom gets the chance.'

'I could have bathed them both,' I tell her.

'Yes,' she says in a tone which suggests that, no matter how convenient to Charlie and herself, something as controversial as this will not be allowed.

'I used to bath all four of you,' I tell her.

'I remember,' Etty says while, to my astonishment, Lottie says, 'Do hush, Grandpa. We'll never hear.'

Maidstone, when the intensity of my illness began to abate, suggested I went on lithium. 'It won't suppress depression,' he said, 'but once you come out of it it will make its re-occurrence less severe.'

'How long do I have to take it?' I enquired.

'A lifetime,' he said. 'You don't, after all, want to go on living like this. I don't think anyone could stand it.'

When I said, 'I like my life the way it is,' he immediately responded, 'There's more than you, of course, involved.'

I liked him: a prematurely greying, portly figure with uniquely mobile features which he could flex at will into all manner of expressions: grim, kind, despairing and – most frequently – fatigued.

'Being on anti-depressants is bad enough. As for tranquillisers,' I said, 'I've given them up.'

The fact was, I was taking nothing: 'No human being can survive what you are going through. Everyone,' he told me, 'has to take something. In the old days it was Shepherd's Balm, but whether it was opiates, alcohol or, later still, barbiturates, this kind of illness demanded treatment by something.'

I was unhappier than I'd ever been: lying to those who

wanted to help ('You are taking them, I take it?' – the drugs prescribed: 'Of course I am,' I told him), which intensified, in turn, the desolation I felt each morning (noon and night): when I had taken the drugs I had merely lain on the bed and cried, 'Help!' no other formulation of thought or expression of feeling coming to mind.

'The fact is, without lithium, once this spell is ended, I don't think you could carry on.' His eyes examined mine.

'With what?' I said.

'Living,' he said, 'an adequate life.'

'What, by your definition, is adequate?' I said.

He smiled. 'Doing the things you've done before. Like you,' he went on, 'many of my patients are creative people. As a group, they are, like you, more susceptible to this illness than any other, and though they might, temporarily, come off lithium, under supervision – while, for instance, they complete a book, or perform in a concert, or mount an exhibition, they would be in no shape to do any of these things if they hadn't been on it in the first place. It's preferable to analysis, which is inclined to formalise your instinctual life. It's a disability, after all, like any other – an arthritic hip, an impediment of speech, a diabetic condition.'

'I'd describe none of those as an experiential illness,' I replied.

'In that case,' he said, 'you're mistaken. Over ninety per cent of the people in this hospital are here for what I would describe as psychological reasons. All illnesses are injuries to the body, and all injuries to the body are injuries incurred in the mind. Who's to know why a woman broke her leg, or a man has cancer, or a youth gonorrhoea? Yet when each patient comes in it's not for a "psychological" cure. All I'm offering you,' he went on, 'is practical support. I don't know anyone who doesn't have something unsatisfactory in their background, but the problem, as I see it, isn't "when?" and "how?" but "what?" and "which?" If, for instance, you had a broken hip, the remedy I'd apply would have nothing to do with when and how you came to do it. "When?" and "how?" are what the analysts go in for, with a clear-up rate consistent with not having intruded on the patient at all.'

'I don't think, if I had a broken hip, I'd think about the nature of God and have visions of hell that defy description,' I said.

'The effect of the anaesthetic, if the break had been severe, or the discomfort of the break itself, might induce you to think of any number of things, amongst which presentiments of hell would not be the least to be considered. Chemical activity synonymous with depression is not all that different from the effects, let's say, of acid in the stomach. Both can give you a disagreeable night and, despite the current mythologising of mental illness, the principle is much the same. The mind hallucinates, for instance, during fever. When we are over the worst, however, we don't look at the wallpaper and say, "Those roses are human faces. I saw them during my illness and I know them now to be real." '

'You discount,' I said, 'the experiences I'm having?'

'I examine them,' he said, 'to see how far you are past the worst.'

'I've tried to save you from working on your belly eight hours of the day or night, with two hundred yards of rock above your head, smelling like an animal, looking like an animal, thinking like an animal.'

My father's eyes are incandescent, like the fire behind his back.

'All you have done for me,' I tell him, 'I am putting to better use.' ('A use which,' I might have gone on, 'if all goes well, might well transcend our lives').

'What on earth is he talking about?' He turns to my mother, a half-startled, half-apprehensive figure, standing by his side, round-cheeked, round-faced, pale-eyed behind her reflecting glasses.

'Ask him,' she says, 'how he's going to get the money.'

'To do what?' I ask.

'To paint your pictures,' she says, 'and write your poems.

41

Your father can't go on providing for you. He's provided long enough.'

That night I write, "I wonder, with the objectivity that separation from this place must give you (even if it is the Riviera), what, if you were here, you would advise me to do . . ."

'A story, Grandpa!' Having left her father's knee, Glenda, clutching at my leg, waits to be lifted – like, for the better part of twelve years, I hoisted up her mother (even at the age of thirteen, Etty would say, 'Tell me a story! Oh, do!' sitting in my lap).

'Tell us a story, Grandpa.' Her sister sidles up (the television, the programme at an end, turned off).

'About?'

'Scouts.'

'Scouts?'

'The one you told us the other night.'

'We used to camp,' I tell her, 'at Broughton Woods, not many miles from here. It stood, the camp-site, at the edge of a wood, and was approached from the foot of a steep embankment. (You know what a steep embankment is?)'

'A steep rise in the ground,' says Lottie, who has heard the description before.

'We had to carry everything up in bits and pieces but, at the top, we came onto an area of grass in the shape of a horseshoe on which we pitched our tents, built our kitchen, erected our marquee and our flagpole. At the back of the camp-site was a dry stone wall, to one side of which stood a ruined game-keeper's stone-built cottage in which we made use of the old earth closet, a lavatory,' I add to Glenda, 'where you don't have to pull the chain.'

'Oh,' she says and, grimacing, adds, 'Go on.'

'Across a meadow at the foot of the embankment ran a stream. Beyond it rose an area of spoil-heaps where the monks in the old days dug for coal. The whole area was overgrown, with only a herd of cows sent, from time to time, across it. The

42

stream, in places, was very deep and, in one of the deepest pools, below a weir, where a line of stepping-stones led over to the farm where we got our milk, the newcomers to the camp, which, on the first occasion, of course, included me, were tossed in, in a ceremony known as "duffing". Two of the older scouts got hold of your arms and legs and, chanting, threw you in. Whereupon you scrambled out the other side and joined the other "duffers" who, after that, had to sing a song.'

'What song, Grandpa?' Lottie asks.

'The Scout Song, written by the first vicar of St Michael's Church at Onasett, which was built from the stone of a nearby mill, beam on beam and stone on stone, and which to this day looks not unlike a mill – thrust out on the slope above the valley but where, through its mullioned, clear-glass windows, I got my first glimpse of – do you know what a glimpse is, Glen?' I am about to add, 'Of God,' but, without waiting for an answer, add, ' "The Peewit Song" which, because I was a peewit, went, as Lottie knows, as follows:

I used to be a Peewit,
A jolly Peewit, too,
But now I've given up Pee-witting
I don't know what to do:
I'm growing old and weary
And I can Peewit no more,
So I'm going to work my passage if I can:

Back to Ona-sett,
Happy Land!
I'm going to work my passage if I can!
Of course, if you were a Swift, or an Owl, or a Cuckoo . . .'

'A cuckoo!' Lottie and Glenda laugh.

'You sang the appropriate word.'

'Back to Ona-sett!' sings Lottie.

'Happy Land!' we sing together.

'I'm going to work my passage if I can,' sings Glenda.

'Now we're all peewits,' I tell them. 'And when you're as old as I am you, too, will know what you have to do.'

43

'Work our passage,' Lottie says.

'Back to Onasett!' I cry.

'Don't get Grandpa upset,' says Etty, while Charlie says, 'Bedtime, I think, for one of these.'

'What happened then?' asks Lottie.

'Then we went about our usual duties.' I dry my eyes. 'Those who were the cooks, cooked, those who were responsible for fuel went into the wood and brought back branches, which we then chopped up, and those who had to fetch the water took dixies downstream to Broughton Springs. Finally, when we had had our competitions – to do with making implements, keeping the camp tidy and learning how to track and to read the weather and to tie knots and to do first-aid – we played our games.'

'What sort of games?' Glenda, with the threat of bed, snuggles closer to my chest.

'The ones I liked were where half the camp had to go to a rendezvous and retrieve a message hidden earlier in the day by one of the scouters and bring it back to camp, which the other half were obliged to defend. We each wore a coloured ribbon on our arm or around our chest which, if someone succeeded in removing it, made you their prisoner or, in some of the games, meant you were dead. Those were fights! Especially when we played at night, somebody dropping from a tree or rising from the ferns. And the stars and the moon, and the owls and the doves, and the shouts and the cries. Or,' I go on, 'we rode the woodcutters' trolley, a truck which ran on a rail and which, if you pushed it to the top of the wood, took you back, rattling, to the cutting-shed at the foot of the slope where the trees were sawn into planks. The smell of the dust and the wood and the oil from the cutter! For the place was deserted most of the time. There we'd be, hurtling down, the branches clipping by on either side, cowboys or brigands trying to stop us . . .'

'Go on,' says Glenda, her dark eyes shut against my chest, her thumb in her mouth.

'At night, when the last of the attackers had come into the

camp, and we'd counted up the tally of coloured ribbons, we'd make a dixie of cocoa and sing.'

'Your Peewit Song?' says Lottie, her eyes shut, too, against my chest.

'Like "Goodnight, Ladies"! and "Old MacDonald"! and "Michael Finnegan"!, and then we'd have a prayer and go back to our tents and get into our blankets and start telling stories all over again, like "The Ghost with the Golden Arm" while, outside, the moon shone, the dew dropped on the grass, the owls fluttered in the trees, the firelight glowed, lighting up the circle of tents in each of which six sleeping heads finally fell back against their make-shift pillows. Like Glenda's and Lottie's, you see, are falling now . . .'

"Dear Bea, I've been thinking of that incident I told you about some time ago. Do you recall? I was fourteen and twenty or thirty of us were coming home one sunny afternoon from our summer camp on the North Yorkshire Moors, singing songs on the back of a lorry. Ahead I heard a sound which, by its persistency and harshness, I judged to be that of a rusty machine. One corroded flange of metal rasped against another until, as if arrested by the sound itself, the lorry stopped.

The traffic on the opposite side of the road had disappeared – until that moment a steady stream of cars and coaches heading for the North Sea coast – and one of the three scouters who, in the absence of our scoutmaster-vicar, had been in charge of the camp, climbed onto our equipment and, leaning forward, looked over the cab. He was there for only a moment, climbing back down, pale beneath his tan and the reflected light of his glasses (a clerk in a local bank). 'No one look forward,' he said, at which, the troop's principal rabble-rouser, I immediately climbed over the equipment and looked.

Directly in front of the lorry lay the figure of a boy not much younger than myself: in particular I noticed the neatness of his woollen stockings folded beneath his knees, the cleanness of his brown-strap sandals, and the way his grey, short-legged trousers were matched by a light grey shirt. A tie, with an

45

alternately red and blue diagonal stripe was fastened around his collar. Over his shirt he wore a checkered jumper with a similarly diagonal pattern, pale blue and grey. Where his head should have been was a pool of matter, light-grey, in which were scattered fragments of bone. The word 'matter' came to me as a way of explaining what, in those first few moments, my senses refused to acknowledge. A man, standing astride this figure, was endeavouring, unsuccessfully, to direct the traffic which, I now noticed, on both sides of the road, had come to a halt.

In the centre of the road, kneeling, was a second man. With a peculiarly rhythmical gesture he was beating his forehead against the tarmac: it, and the rest of his face, was covered in blood, a mask of blood from within which his tortured eyes gazed out.

Across the road, on the pavement, stood a woman, the source of the screeching sound I had earlier heard: retching, she produced the sound each time she exhaled, stooping, bent forward from the waist, keeping bizarrely in time to the similar movements of the man beating his head against the tarmac.

At the doors of several houses which overlooked the scene – large, detached, with driveways running down to the road – a man was enquiring, ineffectually, for something to cover the body. Finally, having watched his efforts, the man astride the body took off his jacket and covered the upper half with that. Beneath its lower edge its neatly-sandalled legs stretched out.

From a bystander we discovered that the woman screeching on the pavement was the victim's mother, and the man beating his head against the road her husband. They had, we discovered later, been driving in a car to the coast, the boy in the back, despite warnings, fiddling with the door catch. He fell out: a bus, full of holidaymakers, travelling immediately behind, despite swerving, ran over his head.

What I recall most vividly afterwards was the sense of outrage which, amongst other things, inclined me to the view that all vehicles should be destroyed, a feeling which was followed,

46

when our lorry finally moved off, by one of relief – growing, when our speed increased, into something little short of exhilaration. I hadn't, after all, been run over by a bus; and although I could vividly imagine those terrible last seconds – the fall, the cry, the approaching tyre – and share in the mother's grief and the father's anguish, I hadn't been – perhaps never would be – the one to suffer: war and famine, disease and disaster, madness and death had, with a peculiar consistency, passed me by. I hadn't, metaphorically, been obliged to step down from the lorry. Life – destiny – had sanctioned my existence in a way that nothing else quite could.

As I talked to the children tonight, in words though not with feelings far above their heads (and Etty has given me instructions never to get in touch with you again without seeking your permission – something of a contradiction), I couldn't help sitting down in this room where I have sat on so many previous occasions, a reading-lamp lit on the table beside me, the window looking through the trees to the lights of the village, and set down what might be described as a postscript to all the letters I have sent before, a declaration which, at this first effort, reads, 'I am kneeling in the road, beating my head against the tarmac, looking at all we have left of our life together in the hope (not terror but anticipation) that, at the end of another day, despite your marriage to a man whom you knew, when you chose him, I would only despise (the antithesis of all we ever fought for), you might (despite all that has happened to us, Bea) come home to me again . . ."

5

'THY'LL TAKE some stick,' Chamberlain said. 'Riding with me, tha knows, i' the cab.'

'Why?' I said, squashed up beside him, with two other workmen, squashed slightly less, on my other side.

'Dalton usually rides in here. He's up on top o' the load at present. When tha gets out thy'd better stay clear.' He swung the lorry's wheel beneath his hand. 'He's a reet good puncher, is Dolly.'

He laughed: the two men beside him – 'Dolly's pals, are these two,' – laughed as well.

'I'll go on the back, in that case,' I said.

'Nay, thy'll bloody well get blown off, thy's far too light. I asked you in,' he paused at a traffic light, then, with the ramming of the gear beside my leg, set the vehicle once more in motion, adding, 'for an intellectual conversation.'

The men beside me laughed again.

'Thick as planks, these two,' Chamberlain said.

'That's right, Mr Chamberlain,' the two men said.

'Do Latin, do you?' Chamberlain said.

'That's right,' I said.

'Amo, amas, amat. These two won't know what that adds up to.'

'Love,' I said.

'Does Battersby hit you with his stick?'

'That's right.'

The two men laughed again.

'How long were you there?' I asked.

'Not long.' Chamberlain's arm was raised from the wheel. 'My faither yanked me out. "Thy'll learn more about ought i' Chamberlains," he said, "than you'll learn i' theer," and though the old lady put up a fight he had me in the yard at sixteen wi' this bloody lot. Isn't that right, you lads?' he added.

'That's right, Mr Chamberlain,' the two men said.

'They leave it all to me, my faither and my uncles. Teks a man wi' brains to do the setting-up. Isn't that right, then, lads?'

'That's right, Mr Chamberlain,' the two men said.

'Bloody champions, these two,' Chamberlain said.

"The men, after four years at Chamberlains, are used to me, and Harry (the owner, now his uncles and father have retired) sets me off with a gang on my own to put up the smaller marquees. I've a feeling, in a week or so, he'll let me loose on a larger one. The other day I couldn't help contrasting this with the first day I came here: we'd arrived at a house on the outskirts of Linfield with a view to putting up a wedding marquee. The garden was enormous and the tent had to be carried down several flights of steps to a lawn at the back. Because of the weight of the pieces the men grew fractious. One of them, Dalton – a foul-mouthed character of enormous proportions whose place I'd taken in the cab – took objection to the, in his view, minimal amount I carried and picked a quarrel. 'I don't like college-boys,' he said. 'Do you know what I do with them?' at which he picked me up with one arm and dropped me in a bed of nettles. Pulling out a garden stake I ran at him. Hearing me coming, he swung aside and – laughing as he'd walked away with two of his chums – hit me such a blow I fell into a hole at the side of the path which, fortunately, full of compost, softened my fall.

I stank like a sewer and screamed like a child but quickly climbed out and ran at him again. He fought me then as he might a man, picking his blows (holding me, at one point, with one hand and beating me round the head with the other). It was only when Chamberlain came across – he'd watched the incident from a distance – and said, 'Hit him again, Dolly, and

49

thy'll be hitting me,' (he had arms like pit-props and legs to match), 'and you hit Dolly, college-boy, and you'll have to tek me on.'

The next fight I had I was more prepared, and though I was given something of a beating, I gave as much of a beating back, and the man who picked the fight is working with me now and asks me occasionally for the spelling (and meaning) of 'difficult words', not because, he says, he 'wants to know' but because 'he likes to hear my voice',

The place we're in is a municipal park in a town you've never heard of. The ground is rock solid. In groups of six we stand in a circle to drive in the stakes, our hammers, each with a fourteen-pound head, striking up a rhythm, each hammer-head no sooner on the stake and lifted than the next in line descends. The canvas is laid out, secured to the principal poles by metal rings, raised slightly from the ground, then laced together. Finally, in groups of four, we secure the guys and haul the canvas up, insert the side-poles and hang the walls. As darkness falls the tents loom like animals around what, before we arrived, had been a featureless arena.

Things at home are much the same. I hand in a wage which, with overtime, is the same, after deductions, as my father's. How are things on the Riviera?"

Bea gives place to Isabella (*née* Kells), her father the embryologist turned Government dietician who, during the Second World War, created the infamous Kell Cake which, according to my father (who, between 1943, when they were introduced, and 1946, when they finally disappeared, must have fried up several thousand), was comprised of granulated coal, senna pods and a sprinkling of vitamins A and D (the latter, it was subsequently discovered, an antidote to certain types of depression).

A tall, rangey man, with a tongue of white hair that flicked to and fro across his brow, his original claim to fame had been his publication in the 1920s of *The Life of the African Locust: the study of a central nervous system*, in which, digressing from his

50

theme – that there was, in each cell, an imprint of its previous existence – he had offered the suggestion that golf was the one activity in life that would unite the middle and the working classes: 'on the links and in the club-house are where true spirits meet.' The son of a Dorsetshire labourer – the son himself of an Irish navvy – he had worked his way to Oxford and, from there, during the war, to the Ministry of Health – returning to post-war academic life to discover that his proposition that change was exclusive of environment had grown increasingly out of fashion and from where he retired, finally, to the home of his daughter and son-in-law, the 'Ardsley Ubiquitarian', as he described him, and where, in addition to playing golf, he spent much of his time teaching science to Bea – the principle influence, apart from myself, on Bea's life.

'Mum, initially, was against you coming.' Etty offers me a drink (which I refuse), Charlie upstairs seeing Lottie to bed ('He tells her a story, just like you, but is not so long about it'). The curtains are drawn, the fire lit – something which, while the children are being put to bed, I've been inclined to do myself (fetching logs from the yard at the back, or, since that supply is now depleted, from beneath the trees themselves). 'She doesn't like you coming,' (facing me across the hearth, curiously on edge whenever she and I are together and Charlie is around). 'Ever since your illness.'

'I wasn't aware of that.' I add, 'She loved this place. Especially as a child.'

'You ought to let Ardsley go,' she says. 'Don't think you have to hold on to it because of her.'

'I don't,' I tell her, and continue, 'Her father was a labourer's son, of Irish descent who won his way to Oxford and, believe it or not, into insect physiology. During the Second World War he was drafted into the Ministry of Health and became a dietician. He invented Kell Cakes, "the working-man's Yorkshire Pudding".'

'I thought Yorkshire Pudding was the working-man's Yorkshire Pudding,' she says, and laughs, having heard this story a thousand times, and adds, 'In any case, you're talking about Gran's father, not Mum's.'

'Bed-time, Lottie!' Charlie commands, halfway down the stairs, his feet returning to the children's door.

'In the first years of our marriage we came here every month. Certainly every summer,' I tell her.

' "He was always begging to come up," Mum says. "To see his mother-in-law," ' Etty tells me, imitating less Bea's voice than her tone.

'What mother-in-law?'

' "His beloved Isabella. It embarrassed all of us at times. She, of course, pretended not to notice. Father, of course, was always in the yard, or out driving on a lorry." '

'In addition to being a quarter Irish,' I lean back in my chair, 'your mother is Lebanese.'

'An eighth Sardinian,' Etty says.

'Her grandfather was Irish, her mother the daughter of a Lebanese tart.'

'The daughter of a Lebanese who, as was the custom at the time, happened to have had three wives. His daughter by his second marriage, to a Sardinian, she came over here to study science – for the daughter of a Lebanese merchant, far ahead of her time.'

'Corcoran met Isabella on the Riviera between the First and Second World Wars,' I tell her, 'and seduced her beneath a palm tree. As a child he took her back there and said, "That's where you were born," the tree itself still standing. At least, after one of her post-war holidays there, that's what your mother told me. It's what,' I go on, 'induces her moods, that mixture of the Mediterranean and the bogs of Connemara.' My eyes fixed on a space above Etty's head, I suddenly declare, 'It's what drove her back to science. Once she's discovered a cure for cancer in the non-coagulant properties of the moorland leech she'll turn to something else. Her and that bloody Albert, "the people's friend". Has she asked you to go and see him?'

'On several occasions,' Etty says.

'Before he met your mother he lived with another woman.'

'Rose.'

'She came to see me and asked me, would you believe it, if "I couldn't control my wife".'

She sips her drink, disinclined to talk about her mother 'behind', as she once told me, 'Mummy's back'.

'We used to sit in here for hours, Kells and I,' I tell her. 'I told you about his idea that golf was potentially the greatest unifier of mankind since time began. Something to do with the limitation, at any given time, on the numbers who could play it, the space required, and the utter fatuity of the exercise. He was, in my view, locusts apart, completely off his head. It's only now, in the last few years, that I've come to appreciate what a remarkable man he was. He never got on with your Grandfather Corcoran's mother. "Nan", as everyone was obliged to call her. A local woman with a ravaged face who lived to be nearly a hundred. The two of them shared a bathroom. The one you never use at the back. And used to call to each other through the door whenever they found it locked. "Are you going to be in there all day, woman?" and she'd shout back, "Go and eat your Kell Cakes!" Corcoran and Isabella and your mother would sit down here, laughing by the hour.'

As Charlie takes a drink already poured for him by Etty from a table behind the door, I add, 'I was telling Etty how Isabella's Lebanese and Celtic background may well have affected her blood. The sands of Araby.'

'Freddie's still talked about,' Charlie says, 'in the village. I don't think a meeting goes by without his name, in one form or another, coming up. "I wonder what he'd think now if he could see The People's Palace?" as they come grinning through the door.'

'I always liked Grandpa,' Etty says. More than any of our children (who, on the whole, responded more warmly to my father), she would cling to the burly, large-fisted man who, with his lorries and his yard (and, for relaxation, his 'Liberal Club'), had scarcely any time for her at all.

'Fighting his drivers,' Charlie says, 'if they offered him abuse.'

'He was driven,' Etty says, 'by the poverty he came from.'

'Like his son-in-law,' I tell her.

'His background,' Etty says, 'was a great deal worse than yours. He started out with a horse and cart as a youth and worked up,' she goes on, 'to a place like this. If anything, *his* father-in-law despised him.'

'Your Great-Grandfather Kells,' Charlie says, 'fell out with a fellow-Mick. Didn't Freddie's father have a horse and cart, and didn't Freddie himself take over? When he came from Linfield to Ardsley he moved into lorries.'

'I've a letter I ought to write,' I suddenly announce. 'And notes I ought to make. If Etty is going to write her book I intend to give her every help.'

'I'm writing nothing of the sort,' she says.

'I keep telling her,' says Charlie. 'She ought to write something. You know what they say about Ardsley? "First thy frizzles, then thy fries, then, if thy still hast nowt, thy dies." '

'That's when the pit was closed,' she says. 'We're not in that situation, my dear, ourselves.'

'I've a meeting at the Club,' he says, 'at nine.' (The Labour Club, ironically, is next door to the former Liberal Club in the village).

'What about this time?' Etty says.

'Do we oppose the Regional Health Board in the closing down of the Fever and Isolation at Sneighton or the Maternity and Lying-In at Swanley?'

'The Fever and Isolation. Life before death,' Etty tells him.

'Wait till we have the fever and need the isolation,' Charlie says, stooping to embrace her.

I see a bulky figure stooping over Isabella before he goes off with her father to golf (the old man was playing at the age of eighty-seven, 'determined,' as he put it, 'to outlive that bloody Nan'), kissing her not on the mouth but the top of her head, nestling his black moustache in her coppery hair, while Isabella's eyes, unfathomed, gaze at me: 'Will you be long?'

'Just give it a knock-about, Bella,' Corcoran says, calling, 'Are

54

you ready, Father?' as Kells, dragging his bag ('That bloody woman's in the bathroom'), comes grumbling down the stairs.

'I liked him,' Etty says. 'Everything about Grandpa was larger than life, and therefore, of course,' she goes on, 'more real. Whatever we disliked about his views, unlike some he earned them.'

"You won't believe this, of course, as you float on your lilo (is it called?) and pedal your pedallo (is it called?) and drink in the sun (is it called?), along with the young men's looks (are they called?), but most evenings now I'm working on a novel – about a woman longing to escape from industrial confinement – a surrogate, no doubt, you'll say, for me. Since the house is crowded with brothers, parents and me, I write it on the toilet (the only place to sit in the bathroom, and the only place I can be alone). In addition, I am painting (when everyone has gone to bed) on pieces of tenting canvas purloined from Chamberlains. Everyone, of course, complains of the smell, just as they complain of the time I spend in the bathroom (of my giving up my 'career', of my consorting with 'riff-raff') – of, in short, as I'm told every day, 'ruining my life'.

P.S. I have forfeited a paragraph of *The Fox and the Hounds* to write all this – not, I'm sure, a promising title, but I'm sure you will appreciate how far, for you, I am prepared to go."

'I don't know what you've to complain about,' I tell her. 'He's on the Regional Health Board. He's Chairman of the Constituency Labour Party. He's on the parents' committee at Lottie's school, is about to become a governor, and has been asked to stand for parliament when the present member retires, or they've even offered to kick him out and put Charlie in at the next election.'

Her face is flushed: my presence in the house, where I notice so much, oppresses her. 'Get rid of me,' I tell her, 'in a book,' to which she replies, 'All it would do is tie me closer,' at which, to my surprise, she dashes from the room.

*

55

When I go to her room I find her lying on her bed (as I used to in the old days, after one of our 'discussions' to do with school or work or friends or, more potently – and acrimoniously – with 'ideas'): on this occasion, however, it's not face down.

'Would you like me to leave?' I ask, and when she doesn't reply, I add, 'I'd welcome going back. Taravara will be lost without me. The street's full of burglars, prostitutes and drug-dealers. As far as the council's concerned I'm the only one who gives it respectability.'

'You're not supposed,' she says, 'to live on your own.'

'Who says?'

'Bryan.'

'Who's Bryan?'

'Our G.P.' She turns, her red-flushed cheeks half-hidden by the bed. 'The doctor who examined you.'

'All he knows of me,' I tell her, 'is from the one examination.'

'He's been briefed on the phone. And Maidstone,' she says, 'has faxed him your notes.'

'I'm stronger,' I tell her, 'than Maidstone makes out. He's simply using comparable models. Such-and-such had symptoms like you and look what happened to him.'

'If you leave me alone,' she says, 'I'll be all right.'

'What about a book on Donatello? Viklund said your doctoral thesis was the best he'd ever read. Or Fra Angelico. Or della Francesca who, like Rossini several centuries later, inexplicably gave up at the height of his career. Or Domenchino, whose gentility aroused the wrath of everyone who knew him. Not unlike one or two I could mention today. Or the Perfect Draughtsman, Andrea del Sarto. Fra Lippo Lippi. Or Signorelli.'

To each, however, she shakes her head.

'I know what I can do, and I'm doing it to the best of my ability,' she says.

In this room lay Isabella, married for forty-five years to a man whom, though she loved, she considered a 'privateer' ('my brigadoon, my monster').

'Alternatively, your whole career leads up,' I tell her, 'to the illumination you can throw on your mercurial and much-gifted Dad.'

'If your work's failed,' she says, 'to achieve the recognition it deserved, what will mine be worth in fifty years?'

Sitting on the bed I say, 'You can't judge things like that.'

'You have in the past. You still do,' she tells me.

'Failure of that sort,' I tell her, 'doesn't count.'

We can hear Glenda and Lottie stir in their sleep, and the passing of a car in the road below the house. 'In those years,' I add, 'I was showing off. In the past five years,' I go on, 'I've had to pay the price.'

Something in my voice causes her, after a while, to turn her head: she looks at me directly. She wipes her wrist against her cheek and, reluctant to give her the handkerchief from my pocket, unwashed for several weeks, I pull out a corner of the sheet and give her that.

'Price?'

'There is no greater crime,' I tell her. 'All religions are based on it.'

She shakes her head, with the same dark, liquefacient eyes she had, as a child, when she listened to my stories.

'You children are the most positive thing that has happened in my life. I can't bear to see you unhappy,' I add.

She bites her lip – an habitual gesture – whitening the skin beneath her mouth.

'I'm not clinging on,' I tell her. 'I'm all for you standing on your own two feet. It's merely the impatience of the shipwright, wishing to see his vessel afloat. I was exactly the same with plays and novels, paintings and drawings. You've read the last poems of Buonarroti? "Evil has prevailed," he came to the conclusion, despite the Dying Slave, despite the Sistine Chapel. Despite the Dead Christ and His Mother.'

She lay back on the bed.

'That sounds very much,' she says, 'like God.'

'Freewill is a very big thing in my book, Etty. For years I went round as if the price exacted had been too much. "The train to Buchenwald," I said. Now, of course, I shake my head.'

An owl hoots from the Rectory roof (across the old wall against which, in the old days, peaches grew). Down in the village, at the Labour Club, Charlie, I presume, is chairing his meeting.

'I'm very proud of you,' I tell her. 'I'm very proud of Charlie.'

'He's everything, at one time, you used to despise,' she interrupts. ' "The socialiser," you described him.'

'The outsider,' I tell her, 'isn't outside by choice. He's longing, if not to be asked, to find a way back in. Because the everyday world was never for me, I could see the value it had for other people. Charlie is enhanced by fitting in. He brings an expansiveness to it which is normally associated only with those who don't, or can't fit in at all. He's unique. Just as,' I conclude, 'you used to think I was.'

"It's very cold, as a matter of fact," [Bea had written], "and I don't spend every day sitting on the beach. I'm doing, you'll be pleased to hear, a great deal of swotting. Father says I'm not here solely to enjoy myself – something with which, incidentally, I wholeheartedly agree. I've got reams and reams of schoolwork and am currently writing an essay entitled, 'The Starving Third of the World'. Plenty, or even a sufficiency, is not something I shall ever take for granted. I thought your description of sitting on the toilet, writing, was a form of childishness which characterises everything you've written. I hope the same quality is not evident in your novel. Don't you have a bedroom? Don't tell me you paint your pictures sitting there as well. The sun has *not* been hot. It has rained for several days, while the people with whom we are staying are often drunk (though Daddy, who gets drunk as well, merely describes them as 'merry'). They sit for hours at meal-times telling the most incomprehensible stories (in French) which Daddy pretends to understand (largely because he knows that Mummy does). Most of them are to do with the Second World War which, if you lived here, you'd think was still going on. Monsieur Duffon is Mayor of this village and it appears to give him rights to do almost anything he wants. I am longing to get back. Sally, my

58

horse at the stables at Monk Bryston where I ride, has given birth to a foal. It's going to be named after me – Beattie – and apparently is most beautiful to look at. (Not like me, of course, at all.)

Mummy is having a wonderful time. The men ogle her, not least our host. Daddy says it's flattering and the way men are down here, which is where she came from, but if I were a man I wouldn't stand for my wife to be ogled at as brazenly as that. She says, of course, she doesn't notice. Isn't it awful? That men only see one thing in a woman. Despite Mummy's age she has, I can see, a wonderful figure. Her bosom, though not large, is very compact, her waist very slim, and her hips still slim enough to fit inside my costume. I've come to admire her very much, largely because she doesn't care what anyone says or thinks. She wears clothes, for instance, quite old and worn and, in one or two instances, belonging to my Aunt Veronica, her older sister, and Aunt Clare, her younger one, who *lent* them to her before we left.

I shall write again if I've time. Hope everything is well with you. Aren't you making too much of living on a council estate and being an 'artist'? Are you sure, in giving up your university career, and turning your back on 'society', you're not acting, to some extent, from spite? Since you see yourself as an artist and, as you put it, only concerned with the 'truth', I thought I ought to mention it.

Yours sincerely,
Beatrice Corcoran."

'What time is Charlie coming back?' I ask as, having antagonised Etty back to life, I help her out in the kitchen.

She wipes her wrist beneath each eye – onions: the only item that afternoon she hasn't troubled to prepare. 'Any time,' she says, and adds, 'I said we'd have a meal.'

'You don't have to be an outsider,' I tell her. ' "You can't all be like your father." ' I laugh, for this was Bea's most frequent complaint when, in their 'teens, the children 'revolted'.

'I am not,' she says. 'Nor was I ever.'

'Nor feel,' I go on, 'that my illness is infectious. There's no evidence of it in you, nor,' I go on, 'in any of the others.'

'Don't fight me back to life,' she says.

'You make me sound,' I say, 'quite healthy.'

'Only you can tell me that.' Standing at the stove she stirs a pan with a wooden spoon.

Isabella, with her capacity to absorb herself in tasks of little importance – sewing, gardening, playing with the children – the grass set out with cups and saucers, a jug of water standing in for tea – would often look the same: the same pose, and much the same expression.

'Charlie and I were thinking of having another child. One never seemed enough. Three has an imbalance which I prefer to the symmetry of two.'

'If it doesn't stop you writing.'

'I can hardly do research up here.'

Not for the first time I have the suspicion she has not invited me up here for my sake but to formulate something within herself. That, too, I reflect, is like the old days.

'Why not?'

'Your work,' she says, 'is out of fashion.'

'It was never in. I've never been an author in the way the middle class would understand, nor working-class in the way a popular audience would listen to. A humanist in an age of neurosis and romance is bound to go unnoticed.'

She laughs, turning from the pan and brushing back her hair. 'An author who writes books which no one reads, who produces plays which no one troubles to revive. A painter who paints pictures which are plagiarised by others.'

'Much of the work I did as a student became de rigueur with aficionados of the art world two decades after I was kicked out of the Drayburgh for doing it,' I tell her.

'Were you kicked out?'

'I was never invited back for my final year. When I enquired why not they said I had "matured beyond their expectations".'

"Dear Bea, I don't have a bedroom to work in because I share

60

it with my younger brother who, when I should be in there writing, is using it to study, or to sleep. Having explained to you why I've gone the way I have, and refused to be railroaded into a conventional life, I thought you at least would understand. It's easy to make fun of what I've done, particularly from the perspective of where you are at present, but I don't think you can be aware of what it feels like to have a father who works in the conditions that mine does throw his 'sacrifice' at you. Art is my life, whether you like it or not. I don't put any 'value' on it, no more than I would on the bloom of a rose, or the song of a bird. Because it has no political or commercial or, in this context, social worth, it's all the more valuable to me. Perhaps it's better we don't write. I have enough to put up with already. Furthermore, I don't believe the Riviera is as wet or as cold as you make out. As for your pony: I suggest you change its name, unless you wish to condemn it to a life of supercilious self-regard.

Yours,

R. Fenchurch."

'You must have been a handful,' she says, flinging over her shoulder another disparaging look.

The suggestion, I can see, has entered her head that by pretending to an interest in my work she'll be doing me a favour.

'A favour' is Maidstone's phrase – or so she tells me. Asking him, by telephone, if taking me back would be 'a positive step', he'd declared, 'It will do your father a favour. He will go to pieces living on his own, particularly in that house in Taravara Road. Isn't the place infested with drugs?'

She has taken me with her, whatever her other motives, out of love, and because, or so she says, she can't bear to see me 'a second time going mad'.

She is hoping to retrieve me single-handed: I can feel, already, a certain calm returning. I like, for instance, seeing her cook: I like seeing Charlie come in from work: I like his avuncular commitment to everything he does – big-hearted,

61

generous, unthinking; I like seeing the children rush in from school – and rush out again to play with their friends – into the same garden that their mother rushed out to with her sister and brothers.

What I hate are the shadows I can't arrest and, where not the fear, the terror.

'I have always been in trouble,' I tell her. 'My damascene conversion to art at the age of fifteen not only made me enemies but lost me most of my friends. I felt indisposed to the world in which I found myself to a degree which, nowadays, it's impossible to describe. Particularly now the dangers we are faced with loom so large and safety, even in opposition, is only found in numbers. Being alone in opposition was, to me, a positive step. Because I was alone I knew I must be right. If someone, for instance, has to stick it out, it might as well be me.'

'Hubris.' Etty moves across the kitchen to collect a bowl, emptying the contents of the pan inside then turning off the gas.

'That wasn't freedom, of course,' I tell her, 'merely the use I made of it.'

'The renegade,' she says.

'The renegade,' I tell her, 'is all there is, for the world I would have wished to live in has now completely vanished.'

6

SHE IS standing in the evening light outside the Army and Navy stores, the shutters of which the proprietor – conscious of her standing there – is putting up: her coppery hair and her turquoise suit attract not only his but everyone's attention: the stockinged legs, the high-heeled shoes, the knee-length skirt.

'You're looking very well,' I tell her.

She smiles: her teeth, against the Riviera tan, are starkly white. 'So are you,' she says.

'You'd better ignore my letters,' I tell her. 'I had no one else to talk to.'

She laughs.

'It's too nice an evening,' I add, 'to spend inside.'

'Sure.' A handbag on her wrist, she places her hands in the pockets of her suit.

'You're more changed,' I tell her, 'than I'd expected.'

'So are you,' she says again. 'You've lost,' she goes on, 'the schoolboy look.'

'I'm beginning to feel,' I tell her, 'I shouldn't have come.'

'That's all right,' she says, and adds, 'My mind, I'm afraid, is somewhere else. I'm not really, mentally, here at all.' A moment later she goes on, 'I met someone on the Riviera. He's coming up to see me. He lives in Reading.' With the same aimlessness she continues, 'He has a car. What I told him about the place intrigued him. It doesn't stop me, of course, from seeing you,' and, since we are now strolling through the central streets of the town, she enquires, 'Have you decided where to go?'

'I've no idea,' I tell her. The cinema had been our intended goal.

'You're not despondent?'

'No.' I shake my head.

We walk towards the municipal park, away from the central hill of the town: the park where, over the years, I have met more girls than I remember: something of an earlier, carefree self returns. I talk of the past – anything, I reflect, to avoid the dilemma I am facing now.

'Is Otterton still around?' she asks.

'In the army.'

'And Jenny?'

'She went abroad.'

The treed slopes of the park's central, castle hill confront us.

'I'm back at school next week. I can't wait,' she says, 'to get it over. I can't wait,' she goes on, 'to get to college.'

'To do what?' I ask.

'Save life. My grandfather did the same when he was young. During the war he developed a food to supplement the diet.'

'Not Kell Cakes?' I enquire.

'They were named after him,' she says, and adds, 'He's living with us now. My mother's father.'

'They came out like rubber mats,' I tell her. ' "Any fool can make them," someone once wrote on the packet. "And most of the bloody idiots do." My father fried up thousands.'

'Did Mum react to your ideas of the renegade?' Etty asks.

'The first time I met her for a date I took her to Thrallstone Park. The sun was setting. She'd just come back from the Riviera. It was the first time she'd been courted by someone like me. We sat on the grass. Before us lay a view of the river, reflecting gold in the setting sun – not unlike the colour of her hair: so potent an image I fell in love. I wanted, in that instant, to paint a picture, to set her in it, behind her a blaze of red and gold. We talked – until, that is, the cold got to me. I'd put my jacket on the grass in order not to spoil her suit.

"Are you all right?" she said, and touched my arm. It wasn't until we'd left the park – by a hole in the wall I knew, for the gates were closed – that I kissed her – formally – as we waited for her bus. I was reluctant, for an instant, to let her go. "She'll be mobbed," I thought, "at the other end." I sat in the bathroom half the night, the only place in the house I could be alone, my mother saying, after I'd vacated it, "That seat is very hot," to which I replied, "I've got diarrhoea," to which, amazingly, she said, "Just like those Kell Cakes during the war," I unable, for reasons even now I don't wholly understand, to tell her that Kells and I were, that evening, through Bea, sensationally related.'

Do you remember that night lying on the hill in the Park with the strand of the river reflecting the setting sun – silhouetting, when it finally descended, the contour of the Pennine hills – while all around the trees grew dark, the rooks grew quiet, the grass grew damp and my excitement, as much as the chilling of the air, caused me, as you observed, to shiver?

I find – I'm not sure how it happens – I'm talking to myself, Etty in the dining-room, setting the table. When I go through and offer to lay out the knives and forks she says, not having listened to a word I've said, 'Eating so late will give you indigestion.'

'What about you?' I ask for she has, since my arrival, complained of the same.

'I'm used to it. Charlie and I often eat late,' she says, leaving me to arrange the table while she goes back to the kitchen, calling, 'What were you saying?'

'She didn't respond to what you'd describe as my bolshieness. She was all for the world as it might become. She never succumbed to my vision that progress is illusory. Our worst quarrels were to do with what she described as my "negative nature" and when I used to say, "But why do you think I paint these pictures, write these books, put on these plays if I didn't think at heart that life is worth it?" she'd cry, "It *has* to be improved!

65

We don't have any choice but to try and do it!" And I – I, in those days, would say, "That *is* genuine despair, my dear." '

'What did she say to you working as a labourer?' She brings into the room a bottle of wine – one of Charlie's exemptions from their otherwise ascetic life – the wood-panelled room in which, with 'Nan' and Grandfather Kells, and Bella and Freddie – and Bea – I have shared so many meals in the past.

'She refused to understand it.'

'But came to accept it.'

The room, too, in which the redoubtable Rose caught Isabella and I kissing beneath the mistletoe – with a recklessness that left all three of us embarrassed.

'We only met on one subsequent occasion after that evening in the park. For Kells,' I tell her, 'was taken ill and nearly died and the family was in turmoil for over a month, during which this youth in his motor-car came up – the son of a biscuit-manufacturer near Reading – and knowing they occasionally came to town, for we still communicated by telephone as well as letter, I hung around one evening at the cross-roads which, coming in from Ardsley, they would have to pass and, as if by telepathy, that Saturday night, this youth drove by, your mother beside him – looking more radiant, I thought, than ever – and, glancing out, though they didn't stop, she saw me. Years later she confided that that was the moment she fell in love. "Like," she said, "your conversion to art: the difference, I suppose, between 'want' and 'need'." '

'She fell in love from another man's car. Destiny was in it, after all,' she says.

'Like you and the book,' I tell her. '*The Fenchurch File.* Generations will be grateful for what you did.'

'Oh, that.'

'How could something,' I enquire, 'that began like that, end up in the way it did? The Parliamentary Private Secretary to the Minister of Health: that youth from Reading all over again. Class. Conformity. Wealth.'

'She's seen how,' Etty says, 'all you set out to do has ended.

In the psychiatric ward of the North London Royal, and in the long-term residential unit at Boady Hall.'

'I was driven there,' I tell her.

Having placed the food in the oven, she closes the door. 'Were you?' she enquires and, turning, declares, 'You drove yourself.'

I sleep little, if at all, that night: perhaps it's the food, however well prepared; or perhaps it is the house and the silence of the village, a place of perpetual noise in the time of Isabella; or perhaps it's the conversation which, at the end of the meal, concludes with Etty declaring, 'I'm not sure it's a good thing to start dragging up the past. What we must do is look to the future.'

'Not to acknowledge the past is not something,' I tell her, 'I can easily do. We go into the past, not to be detained, but to bring it into the present. It's only when it retrieves us, and not us it, that it's never any use. Moving forward in the way you've described is entirely out of the question.'

'You've got past loving Mother,' Etty says as she sees me up to bed, not sure, I suspect, whether her remark is a statement or a question.

When I say, 'Do you get "past" loving anyone?' she replies, 'I'd say so,' and adds, 'As soon as it becomes a habit, as it did with you and Mum.'

'Or a need,' I tell her, suspecting this idea comes not from her but Bea.

'We're all in need of love,' she says, 'but not in love with need,' and, intent on cheering me up, one platitude following another (one more liability of family life), she adds, 'It's what you saw in Mum. She saw her need in you, not, as you've been led to believe, the other way around.'

After she has gone I begin to fret that the pills I have brought with me are under lock and key in her and Charlie's bedroom.

Then, once more, the thought comes to me: they have brought me here to die.

7

'My mother would like to meet you,' Bea said at the end of our first encounter after the youth and his car had gone back to Reading.

'How about your father?' I asked.

'He leaves these things,' she said, 'to Mum. If she approves,' she added, 'he invariably approves as well.'

'Did they,' I enquired, 'approve of Keith?' (the name of the youth with the car).

'Father did. Mother thought him nice.'

'Nice?'

'She thinks he could do with growing-up.'

'What, in that case,' I said, 'is she going to think of me?'

'It's mandatory,' she said (a peremptoriness in her nature of which I was only slowly becoming aware: we were sitting in a café, eating food I couldn't afford, despite it being the cheapest on the menu: when I hesitated in replying she suddenly went on, 'They won't let me come again until you and she have met.').

I went the following Saturday. It was dusk: for the first time in my life I came through the garden door at which we'd dropped off Bea on the night of the Allgrave party.

We walked, at her prompting, hand in hand, the path flanked, beneath the trees, by knee-length grass amongst which grew cowslips, buttercups and daisies. The silence was intense and evoked in both of us a sudden apprehension.

We approached a flight of balustraded steps leading to a stone-built terrace: a path, dividing from our own, led to a wicket-gate: beyond lay an area of unmown grass across which were scattered several trees, their branches bowed – and in one or two instances broken – with unpicked fruit. Pears and apples, glowing, caught by the evening light, lay scattered in the grass.

Glancing back I saw how the place itself was like a wood: the garden door, the winding path and, beyond the trees, the lights of the village: the sound of the colliery dynamo was audible from below.

The house, a low, stone-built structure with a balustraded roof and tall, square chimneys, was visible beyond an intervening hedge, our path, consisting of irregular paving-stones, leading directly to a lawn into which had been set innumerable irregularly shaped beds of flowers: their scent was discernible in the darkening air along with the dampness of a suddenly descending dew.

One of several gravelled paths led to a pedimented porch, itself approached by a shallow flight of steps. A light shone in two of the downstairs windows, its beams illuminating, in two broad swatches, the ground immediately in front of the house and, attached to the dark façade, fronds of yellow roses.

I caught a glimpse, in the first of the windows, of a wood-panelled room and then, in the second, of a woman: she appeared to be sewing, her head bowed, her shoulders stooped. A needle came up, her head, in profile, drawn up as well. Magenta-coloured hair was secured in a coiled plait above her ear, her neck, arched forward, delicate and thin.

The light, suspended in a tasselled shade above her head, obscured her features until, hearing our steps on the gravel, she glanced up.

Her look was one of such benignity – green eyes made dark by the angle of the shade – that, caught by Bea's hand, I stood transfixed. I had never seen anything so beautiful: the slender boning of the face, the tautened cheeks, the broadening mouth: the gentleness, the candour.

'Come on.'

Bea's feet dragged at the gravel.

'There's Mum.'

The woman must have risen: as we approached the door it was unlocked inside and, a double-featured design, one half of it drawn open.

'You're late.' Her hand extended, Bea's mother came to greet us.

'The bus,' Bea said.

'Of course,' she said. 'You haven't the car.'

She took my arm and when she enquired, 'Are you all right?' glancing, as she did so, at my face, I found I couldn't speak.

I heard Bea exclaim, 'He's shy!' at which, leading us into the room in which we had glimpsed her, with a not dissimilar exclamation, her mother declared, 'But I wouldn't frighten anyone!'

'Mum's very *odd*,' Bea said later, as she walked me to the bus. 'It's to do with being foreign.'

'Foreign?' I said.

'Less Irish, of course, than Middle East. She doesn't know what effect she has.'

'Effect,' I said, less in enquiry than exclamation.

'She's oblivious of her beauty. Curious when, normally, she's so tuned in to men.'

'Is she beautiful?' I said.

'But you couldn't keep your eyes off her!' she said. 'And she, for entirely different reasons,' she went on, 'could scarcely keep her eyes off you. We shouldn't,' she concluded, 'have any trouble now.'

'I suppose,' I suggested, 'she's old.'

'Yes,' she said. 'But very handsome.'

'In you,' I said, 'it's something else.'

'What?'

We waited at the bus-stop, her arm in mine, a sudden and, on my part, a heartening confederacy between us.

'You're younger,' I said, 'and more unspoilt.'

'Am I unspoilt?' She paused. 'Keith said that.'

'He's right.'

I no longer felt challenged by the other youth: all I chose

70

to recall of the evening was the touch of her mother's hand when, on parting, she'd said, 'I hope we'll meet again.'

We had sat and talked in that lamp-shaded, wood-panelled room, and had had a meal. 'What do you mean by art?' she had said after listening to one of my self-proclamatory confessions and when, immediately, Bea had responded, her mother's look, turned from me to her, had calmly suggested, 'You don't have to impress me, my dear. I am impressed enough, as it is, already. If he has to be turned away it won't, I can assure you, be because of me.'

'How old do you think she is?' Bea said.

'I've no idea,' I said, her age, calculated in this fashion, of no interest to me, either then or later.

'She's fifty-two.'

'As old as that?'

'Lots of men still fall for her.'

'I see.'

'Lots.' The mystery of her mother endlessly eluded her: a lifelong antagonism, a lifelong complaint. 'I'm sure she'll speak glowingly to Dad.'

'You think so?'

'She told me as much before we came out, and you went into the hall to fetch your coat. She's not put off,' she added, 'by your being poor.'

'Am I poor?' I said.

'You will be!' She laughed, the bus plunging down the hill towards us and lighting up the queue, the majority of whom, I noticed for the first time, were, where not almost, completely drunk.

From the first-floor window I gaze out at the moonlit garden: many of the fruit trees, closer to the house, have been replaced, their staked stems invisible in the darkness – a darkness where, on summer evenings, Isabella and I would pick the fruit, careless or so it seemed, on her part, whether we could be seen from the house or not, giving vent to those feelings which, in me, had been provoked by the sight of her upward-straining figure – the tautness of her blouse, her skirt, the delicacy of her hand as, first, she fingered, then unloosed the fruit.

Bea's father, the redoubtable 'Freddie', I met on my second visit: a stocky, broad-shouldered, balding man, with dark, thick-set features, he reminded me of Harry Chamberlain, my equally redoubtable employer: as I came in the room he clasped my hand, enquiring, 'Are you the artist?' as if Bea's admirers were both too numerous and too confusing either to identify or to count.

In loving Isabella I came, of course, to love him, too: at a different time, and if not exactly in his prime, he also had fallen for this woman. I observed how, whenever he passed her in the house, he touched her hair – her arm, her hand, her back, her thigh – as a man, in passing, might make obeisance in church, a desire not only to express but to invoke a feeling which otherwise could not be conveyed.

'Come out to the yard,' he said on that first occasion, as much a desire for something to do as a wish to test or examine me, leading me to the, in those days, muddy enclosure at the side of the house where, for the better part of two hours, we hoisted hundredweight sacks of coal from the back of one lorry, which had broken down, onto the back of another.

'What about this art?' he said when we finished and he invited me into a shed he used as an office.

'What about it?' I asked, the invitation accompanied by a request I 'look at this'.

The 'this' he showed me – all the while examining me (something restricted on the back of the lorry) – was a picture he had bought – at, I discovered later, Bea's instigation – with a view to presenting it to Isabella on her birthday.

The colours, such as they were, had been put on with a palette knife, the overall effect, where not 'expressionistic', effusive: nothing in it, as I was quick to tell him, 'added up': the excrescences of paint, at a distance, suggested a line of orange rocks about to be engulfed by cream-topped waves (intimations, I suspected, of the 'Mediterranean'); recognising

72

a look, not unfamiliar where 'art' and 'artists' were concerned, if not of disappointment, outright rage ('short-changed' was the phrase he used when subsequently describing his 'final feelings' to Bea), I added, 'I'm sure Mrs Corcoran will agree, it'll add a touch of colour.'

'I can add a touch of colour mesen,' he said. 'And at a tenth the price of this,' adding, 'You go in for this art, then, do you?' sitting further back behind his desk, the shed, apart from a cabinet and a second chair, on which the picture was propped, furnished with little else: his 'work-office', apart from his 'yard-office', unknown to me at that point, was located in the house.

'It's like,' I told him, 'the calling of a priest.'

'A priest.' Pulling himself forward, he propped his elbows on the desk before him, his hands, clenched together, held in front of his mouth, a gesture – uncharacteristic of him, I was to discover – of uncertainty in anyone else. 'A priest is paid a salary. He has,' he paused before deploying the word, 'a job.'

'I don't mean painting pictures but anything creative,' I said.

'Creative.' The word roamed in his mouth, it seemed, for several seconds: not only tasteless but indigestible.

'Like writing.'

'Writing.' Another serving of the same.

'Or . . .' I might have added, 'Music,' realised, under his scrutiny – a darkening of his expression – I was steadily digging my grave and, unable to think of anything else, slowly waved my hand.

Black, I discovered, like his, with coal-dust (a smear across his mouth).

'We can all be creative,' he suddenly announced, 'if some other bastard pays for it,' adding, with an unconvincing hint of propriety, 'Excuse my language. You've heard worse, I'm sure, at Chamberlains.'

'Much,' I said in the hope that, like the unloading and re-loading of the lorries, this suggestion of confederacy might draw us closer together.

'I could give you a job in the yard.'

He indicated the black-painted lorries with their metal-lined

73

insides ('Corcoran & Co. Contractors' inscribed in yellow paint above the cabs).

'You wouldn't be doing much different to what you're doing now.'

His hands, coal-black and massive, were lowered to the desk: there, fisted, they lay side by side as if, curiously, divested of his body. 'We each lay down our lives for you,' they appeared sensationally to announce – fingers, thumbs, knuckles – white-bared – prominent through the dust.

There was no intention, I realised, I should take the job, merely a desire to point out the incongruity of what I was doing – of his life and mine and, by inference, of my life and Bea's.

'I'm happy as I am,' I said.

'I know Harry Chamberlain. Funny firm to work for.'

'It is.'

His eyes examined mine.

'You won't have much time for painting pictures.'

'No.'

'Nor for writing books.'

'No.'

'He works them very hard.'

'He does.' I paused. 'I intend to find the time,' I added.

'He lays them off each winter. There's nought going on until the spring. Apart from his bunch of regulars. Not much to show for all those years at King Edward's.'

'No.'

'Beattie's going to college,' he suddenly declared. 'She wants to take up where her grandfather left off. You've heard of Kell Cakes? She wants,' he concluded, 'to save the world.'

He returned his hands to his chin.

'What do your parents think?' he enquired.

Later Bea told me he had been 'pumping' me to see if, as he'd expressed it, 'this boyfriend of yours is off his head.' 'He thought you might have been,' she said, 'because of something in your eye.' When I asked her, 'What?' she answered – her eyebrows lowered, her hands thrust up in front of her mouth (her father's expression transmogrified), 'He said, when you

74

talked about art, your eyelids never fluttered, something which he's read is an infallible sign of madness.'

'He thinks I'm after your money.'

'Not a bit of it.' She smiled. 'When he dies, he always says, his debts will equal his credit.'

'They're not very pleased,' I told him.

'I bet they're not,' he said. 'Your father, Bea tells me, is down the pit.'

'He has been,' I said, 'for thirty years.'

'Thirty years,' he said, 'is the time I've been in business. Me and commonsense. You've heard of commonsense? Common-sense is a gentleman few of us can do without.'

'I mentioned thirty years,' I said, 'to indicate he started work long before I gave up what you would describe as my education.'

Something in my expression – whether 'mad' or not – appeared to reassure him: in a curious voice – so inconsequential that, hadn't I been watching him, I might have assumed it to have come from someone else – he said, 'I'm not usually wrong about men. Women, of course, are a different matter,' a suggestion in it of a vulnerability both surprising and endearing.

I liked him; I liked him, above all, for loving Isabella, but also, I suspected, for his careless way with things: in his business, Bea once informed me, he was as likely to change his mind as hours in the day, being convinced he ought to sell in the morning, buy at midday, and do nothing by the evening. 'His evening thoughts,' she said, 'invariably prevail.'

From that first interview onwards he paid me little if any attention. I visited the Old Hall from time to time but princi-pally Bea came to town for our weekend meetings. 'Daddy says I ought to be meeting other boys,' she said on one occasion. 'Of course,' she added, 'there's always Keith. And once I get to college,' she concluded, 'there's bound to be lots of others.'

Whenever I dream of the Hall and Ardsley it is Isabella, however, not Bea, who comes to mind: I see her stooping in

the garden, her figure poised, half-balanced, leaning to a plant
– her arm outstretched, her head half-bowed: the straightening
of her back as, conscious of my approach, she finally turns:
the smiling, green, half-questioning eyes – and my enquiry,
misleadingly uninvolved, 'Is Bea around?'

'She's in the house. Give a shout. I'm sure she's there,' Bea
observing us on one occasion and afterwards remarking, 'You
go together, in a curious way: the way your heads come down
when you're not quite sure what the other one has said. As if,'
she paused, 'you've known her,' she paused again, 'longer even
than I have.'

I spent most of my time, when not at Chamberlains, writing
and painting, the former in an exercise book (one of several
which, on leaving, I'd stolen from school), the latter on pieces
of Chamberlain canvas subtracted from the sheds. 'You mean
you'll earn a living painting fucking pictures?' a fellow-
employee asked me returning one evening to Linfield on the
back of a Chamberlain truck.

'I don't have to, necessarily,' I said. 'I can carry on doing
this.'

'And write a fucking book?'

'Why not?'

'About this place!' He gestured round: the pits, the slag-
heaps, the terrace streets, the railway arches, the advertising
hoardings, and the barge-laden canal by which, at that moment,
we happened to be passing. 'I can't see anybody buying a
fucking picture or reading a fucking book based on a dump
like this!'

He laughed, encouraging our comrades to join him.

'Shouldn't it be about London?'

'London?'

'Or some fucking place like that!'

It was but one of several low-key exchanges which characterised the summer. My only response was to re-apply myself to
writing, to painting – and to seeing or visiting Bea (the last a
pretext, carefully disguised, for seeing Isabella: her smile, the

76

inconsequential touch, the drawing of my arm to hers as she pointed out her roses).

The summer shows – agricultural, horticultural, industrial – were coming to an end as, with the first signs of autumn, were most of the weddings. The summer 'casuals', amongst whom, initially, I'd counted myself, began, one by one, and then in groups, to disappear: we'd see them, as we went off on the backs of the Chamberlain lorries to the last of the jobs, drifting aimlessly around the centre of the town: we'd wave: they'd wave in return, at first cheerily, than, later, offering scarcely any acknowledgement at all. Between Bea and I something, too, began to fade: her schoolwork now was making demands and, as my first rejecting notices began to arrive, a certain disillusion-ment was evident in me: was the species of self-expression I was involved with worth the isolation that, I could see now, inevitably came with it? In addition to which, Bea was being courted – 'passionately', as she described it – by the Head Boy at King Edward's: a boarder (one of a privileged group of twenty-three) and always on hand (much fancied – she much envied by her friends). He had a car; his father arrived to watch him play in the First Fifteen and the First Eleven, and compete in the Athletics Team, in a chauffeur-driven limousine, with a fur-clad wife who led, in turn, a coiffeured poodle on a jewelled lead – Bea much flattered by their and the boy's attention.

It was against this background that the turning-point came in my relationship with Isabella ('Of your life,' Maidstone remarked when I first described it). She and Freddie were dressed up one evening to go out to a dinner of the Inner Wheel at which Freddie, who was visibly nervous, was to give a speech. Uneasy at the prospect of Bea and I spending the whole of the evening in the house together, he had suggested that Rose might be asked to stay behind, 'In case there was anything you might need,' and when the absurdity of this was pointed out by Bea ('I can easily make a cup of tea') he offered, uniquely, to pay for us to go to the Ardsley Essoldo, a flea-pit of a cinema in the terminal stages of decay – and to which he had forbidden her to go on every previous occasion.

It was at this point ('smiling her Gioconda smile,' as Bea put it) that Isabella declared, 'Surely, Freddie, we can trust the two of them together,' stooping, as she did so, to kiss Bea on the cheek and, crossing directly to the chair, beside the fire, where I was sitting, stooping to kiss my cheek as well.

I saw her shoulders, bare within the low-cut velvet collar; I felt her lips: I watched her turn across the room – joining Corcoran at the door where, her arm on his, she called good-night. I watched her hips, I watched her thighs, I watched her ankles: I watched the high-heeled shoes which gave so much shape to her calves. I trembled. Years later, when I asked her if she had been aware of the effect she had had that evening – I had, for instance, never seen her dressed formally before, her shoulders bare, her breasts – fuller than I had imagined – visible, sensationally, as she stooped, within the looseness of her collar – she was, astonishingly, offended: 'You don't honestly think I'd lead you on?' her displeasure at the interpretation I'd put on the incident so profound that it blighted our relationship for months. Long afterwards she would bring it up and when I sullenly enquired, 'What distresses you so much?' she'd cry, obscurely, 'You seeing me like that!'

'But I loved that moment more,' I often told her, 'than life itself. You don't realise,' I'd go on, 'how beautiful you are. More beautiful than anyone I've ever known. Sensationally, organically, ethereally,' brought to tears on more than one occasion when, unbeknown to her, I'd glimpsed her in the street, or across a room, or, at one of our later rendezvous, standing at a window. 'Those are the most important moments of my life when I'm aware how much I love you.'

'I hate it,' she'd say. 'It's voyeuristic. I wish that evening had never happened.'

'To me,' I told her on one occasion, 'there's never been another like it.'

'Not even,' she paused, 'when you first made love to B.'

I may have misheard her: conversely, she may have intended to say 'me' but, during that pause, retracted.

'Not even then,' I told her.

'When was that moment?' she asked.

'That's something,' I said, 'between Bea and I.'

'Why?' she said, increasingly obtuse.

'Just as it is between you and Freddie.'

'Freddie is my husband.'

'Bea is my wife.'

The irony struck her, too – not to say, the wickedness and, as at all such moments, faced incontrovertibly with what we'd done, we instinctively retreated.

'Bella sees you as her son,' Freddie said on more than one occasion, seeking to explain, if only to himself, what, if he didn't suspect, he might, if a more imaginative man, have sensed was going on. He liked, perhaps because of this explanation, to see the two of us together. 'Freddie doesn't mind!' she said on one occasion, laughing, when she'd pointed out Freddie watching us from the living-room window. 'He likes to see us holding hands!' – something she did, and not only with me, without a second thought, as impetuous in this respect as she was in so much else. 'Tell me how much you love me,' she would say in later years when Bea and I came up with the children, adding, in the same loud voice, 'I'm taking Richard for a walk. He looks so pale. The air up here will do him good. It's what, after all, he's used to.'

It had not been long after that 'memorable' evening that the second incident occurred that drew us, in retrospect, if not closer, irretrievably together.

I had gone over to the house one afternoon to find Bea swotting for an examination: Isabella, who was busy in the kitchen, and hating to see anyone idle, said, 'Come and look at our new neighbour. It's in the *Ardsley Express*,' adding, as she got on her coat and put on a woolly hat (it was autumn), 'As an artist you can tell me what you think!'

She called to Bea, 'I'm taking Richard to look at the Swansons',' closing the back door and leading the way across the yard. A backward glance revealed Bea at her bedroom window, waving and, assured of my attention, levelling her palm and blowing me a kiss.

We passed along a footpath enclosed on one side by a hedge and on the other by a quarry. Holding back the branches, I went ahead. At one point, where the path divided, I took the broader of the two and heard her call, 'This one, Richard!' turning to find her close behind me, her cheeks aflame, her eyes alight (our breaths rising in the chilly air). With the same impetuosity which characterised so many of her actions, she took my hand – at one point, pretending an obstruction, I grasping hers more firmly.

With the subtlest – and, because the subtlest, the most sensual pressure, she responded, our bodies stooped, our heads bowed and, because of the encroaching branches, almost touching.

We emerged, finally, at the foot of a steep embankment. The soil was loose, its surface pitted with rabbit holes: I scrambled up, reached the summit and, as she followed, took both her hands.

I drew her to me.

How long we stood there I've no idea, our arms around each other's waists.

'Are you all right?' she finally enquired.

'I'm fine,' I said. 'And you?'

'I wouldn't have got here,' she said, 'without your help. It's just as well you came.'

We drew apart.

'That's the Swansons' house,' she added.

Almost as an afterthought, or so it seemed, her hand slipped back in mine.

Immediately below us, at the foot of the slope, a concrete structure had been erected, into the sides of which had been inserted several rectangular and oval holes intended, I assumed, to serve as windows: the site was encroached upon by builders' debris – stacks of bricks and piles of sand and mounds of ochre-coloured timber – themselves encroached upon by the woods which came up the slope from the back of the Hall and over the crest of the embankment on which we were standing. A brick wall was in the process of construction to separate the two.

Hand in hand, her head imperceptibly but, as far as I was concerned, unmistakably inclined to mine, we stood side by side discussing the impropriety of someone building a concrete edifice in a landscape which, where it was not characterised by woods and fields and hedges, was only distantly encroached upon by the encircling pits.

The coat she wore had a brown fur collar, the coat itself a bottle green – one she invariably slipped on when she went to the village, shopping: the texture of the fur (I allowed her remarks to turn her to me) highlighted the colour of her cheek – a pinkness which extended to her brow where, deepening, it was absorbed within the magenta of her hair.

'He's an architect,' she suddenly declared. 'It's been in all the papers. Though which ones, apart from the *Express*, I can't recall.'

She turned.

'Are you all right?' she added.

'I feel,' I said, 'a little dizzy.'

'I thought you were,' she said. 'It's to do with all that bending.'

'I'll be all right,' I said, 'in a minute.'

'Have you had these spells before?' she asked.

'I have,' I said, 'since adolescence. They very soon pass,' on the verge of confessing to something else entirely, and hastily concluding, 'I feel much better already.'

'What do you think to the house?' she said, intending to distract me.

'It looks more like an office,' I said.

'That's what I thought!' The exclamation drew us closer: linking her arm in mine, she added, 'The view, I suppose, will be nice.'

'It will,' I said.

'Looking the other way!' She laughed: the purpose of the brick wall – to prevent the house from being overlooked from the grounds of the Hall – was obvious to both of us. 'In addition to which,' she went on, 'he's installing central-heating.' (An unheard-of luxury in Ardsley at that time.) 'By oil.'

The logistics of this enterprise – quantities of oil transported to a private dwelling at least twelve miles distant from the nearest town – provoked a second burst of laughter.

As far as I was concerned, the conversation, as, indeed, the view of the concrete house itself, was merely a distraction from what Maidstone was to describe, years later, as my 'principal perception': the realisation I had fallen in love with a woman thirty-four years older than myself.

The first time I described this incident to him I had produced a photograph, creased, from an inside pocket – over which he had stooped, frowning, for several minutes, the photograph itself (he invariably sat in a chair set, incongruously, in the corner of the room, between a filing cabinet and his desk) laid on my file which, in turn, was propped on his crossed legs. 'She is,' he said, after a while, 'a beautiful woman,' a clinical assessment, or so it seemed, to which he appended, glancing up, 'What would you say were her imperfections?'

'It was, incongruously,' I said, 'the accumulation of imperfections that rendered in her, uniquely, the possibility of perfection. In his *Journal*, Delacroix observes that it is the imperfections of a work of art which give it its vitality. Poe, echoing Byron, says much the same about men and women.'

After the second burst of laughter, for several seconds, neither of us spoke, gazing down at the windowless hulk: it was as if that side of my body had been ignited, her cheek so close to mine I could feel its heat.

I moved.

'Looking out, from the inside, you won't be able to see the house at all,' she added, 'and, if the wall weren't too high, you could see up to our wood.'

She indicated, with her head, the trees below.

'But if the wall is too high,' she went on, 'you'll have the view the other side, of Fernley Pit.'

As I listened to her laughing she took my hand, her fingers enclosing mine without, it seemed, a second thought; perhaps,

I reflected, she was used to the importuning demands of men other than her husband, accommodating them in such a manner that it seemed, to the importuning agent, she had scarcely noticed them at all: a graciousness, I further reflected, that only added to her charm.

'We ought, I suppose,' she continued, 'to be getting back,' as if the propriety of our coming here had not yet been settled in her mind and the immediacy of returning, therefore, still in doubt.

She drew her coat about her.

'At least you've seen it now. And your opinion, I can see,' she concluded, 'agrees with mine.'

Her hand now clenched in mine, she began to descend the slope behind us.

Our return along the path was conducted in silence. I watched her back, her feet, her calves (the woollen hat which covered scarcely half her head and from beneath which her hair, unplaited, tumbled out), her head, her hands (her delicate neck): 'Are you all right?' she asked as we reached the yard, using this enquiry to release my hand yet, moments later, when, having turned to me, she had watched me nod my head, she took my arm and led me to the porch where, with a peculiar excitement, she suddenly exclaimed, 'That was a grand adventure!'

A moment later, her coat off, she had returned to her chores in the kitchen – her hat, forgotten, still on her head – while, from overhead, came Bea's shout, 'I shan't be long!' to which Isabella, absorbed already in her tasks, called, 'Don't rush that work, young woman!' glancing up, abstracted, to where, half-stunned, I stood against the wall and, with a smile, announcing, 'Richard and I can wait!'

"Dear Bea, my mind wanders these days from the subject in hand; in hand, literally, on this occasion as I held your mother's on Sugden's Bank (as I later came to know it), my arm, folded in hers, cushioned, moments later, against her breast – the breast which, as she turned to make a remark, moved from me

83

and then, as she listened to my response, came softly back; the breast which, months later, I enclosed within my hand as we sheltered one evening beneath a tree – hidden by its shadow – in the cul-de-sac at the back of your school. I'd met her from a meeting in town – 'by accident,' I told her. 'I happened to be passing,' offering to walk her to her stop (it was before she acquired a licence to drive your father's car and, later, the absurd sports model he went and bought her: he enjoyed seeing her as a flighty figure, seeing it, I suppose, as flattering him). I said I wanted to talk about you and we strolled, not in the direction of the stop, in the centre of town, but up the footpaths that led to your school: a married woman (someone who, in the ensuing years, was not infrequently mistaken for my mother). I can't, no matter how hard I try, remember how 'the moment', as I described it to Maidstone, came about. 'I am a perverse and wicked fellow,' I said. 'I am devious in all things and seldom to be trusted.' Yet I remember Sugden's Bank so clearly – my arm enclosed within your mother's, the turning of her face to mine, our returning to the house, the descent of the bank, our going indoors, your call from the stairs and, 'What did you think to the Swansons'?' when you finally came down. And what I recall most clearly is her face as, once in the kitchen, removing her coat, she turned to me and, for an instant, as I held its collar and helped her to withdraw her arms, I felt convinced, if I had lowered my head, she would, sensationally, have raised hers – as involuntarily as, finally, she did on the evening I met her and we strolled up the cul-de-sac at the back of your school – discussing you (initially) and then, absurdly, prompted by the darkness, her. I say 'involuntarily' for I don't recall any precipitating gesture, merely passing into the shadows between the lamps until, in the midst of one such shadow (the quietness of the evening, the singing of a bird), I turned – as fortuitously, it must have seemed, as she to me and, for reasons neither of us, either at that moment or later, could understand, she raised her face to mine and when, after the closest scrutiny, she closed her eyes, I took that as her signal . . .

84

Why I did what I did I can't make out. Something indecent – against a brick wall – white with salt and bevelled from age – shaking so violently I could scarcely stand . . ."

The moon shines in the garden below: the garden in which the ghost of Isabella wanders, tending her roses (waiting for me): the garden in which the four of us – Bea and I, Corcoran and Isabella – would, in the summer months, often talk for hours: art as opposed to business, pragmatism and empiricism (the meaning of love), Corcoran bored by such discussions but bemused by the animation they aroused in his daughter and his wife, a broad, phlegmatic smile on his otherwise sombre features: 'What does it add up to? You end with what you began!'
'What's that?' (from a sulky Bea).
'Work!' (inexplicably) 'is the only thing that counts!'
The garden is much neglected – by comparison with the care lavished on it by Isabella. She had, in those days, the assistance of a man who came in several days a week, an enthusiast, if not an eccentric, known both for his gardening skills and an idiosyncratic selection of gardens in which he chose to work: Isabella, not the garden – its soil or the disposition of its vegetation – was the principal influence in his choice of the Hall. He loved, like I did – he covertly – to see her red-haired figure move amongst the flowers, raising his head from his digging or raking, his weeding or pruning, his tying back or staking, to watch the juxtaposition of coppery red, or fiery magenta, with lilac, lemon, a reciprocal red, a glowing purple – with the crimson and pink, the yellow and orange of the climbing roses which hung in festoons across the front of the house (drowning the windows, drenching the porch). Once, coming upon Isabella and myself in the garden shed at the back where, our heads together, we were examining the dahlia roots, wrapped in newspaper, stored for the winter, he had hastily stepped outside, aware – despite the fact that no intimacy was taking place – that there was an unseen quality – an unseen presence – which, while not evoked separately by

85

either one of us, was immediately apparent the moment the two of us came together – a vibrancy which he, Mr Rawlston, was by no means the only one to notice and which, over the years, was commented upon openly by Bea as much as by Corcoran himself – a 'peculiarity', as the latter described it, 'as if you were Bella's child.'

I've a feeling Etty looks after the garden herself, with the help of a man who, as the mood takes him (a retired miner), comes in once a week: periodically a firm of contractors appears and lops the trees and cuts back the hedges and gives a perfunctory mowing to the lawns, and hoes the more accessible beds, but, as her grandmother did before her, Etty, at odd moments, dressed in a smock, cuts at the plants and ties back the branches and, whenever they accompany her, allows the children to dig and run about almost anywhere.

It's cold; I'm cold, yet disinclined to return to bed: a cry, from the back of the house, echoing along the landing, comes from one of the children: each night one, or perhaps both of them, calls out, disturbed by dreams which, evidently, never wake them. Once I went along to their room, startled by the sound, but both dark-haired figures were asleep, Glenda snorting (like Etty) with her thumb stuck in her mouth. As with her mother, when I drew it out, it immediately went back in.

I take a chair; I pull a blanket around myself – drawn, after much exertion, from under the heavy quilted cover of the bed – and sit in the window: the lights of the village show beyond the trees and I half-envisage in the darkness the contours of the pit – the steam, the crepitation of distant feet, the whistle, the occasional siren, the murmur of a forgotten village life.

'You hated the place,' Maidstone would tell me, at which I would explain, 'It's in my blood. It's part of me. It's not merely a perversion that impels me to love it. It's the way – perhaps the only way – I can come to love myself.'

At which our talk of Ardsley would deteriorate into one of our endless discussions about 'reclamation': was it, as I frequently declared, a hubristic impulse and therefore self-

86

defeating, or was the desire to retrieve the past and bring it into the present a 'condition for living' – living, as opposed to the 'morassic ingenitive' which was how Maidstone identified existence for the majority today. When, after his third or fourth use of the phrase, I informed him that it was taken from *To Die with the Philistines* (the first play I'd written), and much bandied about in the press at the time, our relationship took on a new dimension ('I thought I'd heard it somewhere': he was, after all, he confided, writing a book himself, of which the provisional title was, indeed, *The Morassic Ingenitive: the inevitable dissolution of the human race*) and, for the better part of a year, if I recall, we talked of little else.

8

"I HAVE A problem. From time to time I am engulfed by terror . . ."

I have picked up a school exercise book ("King Edward VI Grammar School for Boys" imprinted on the cover) which is lying on the window ledge, and which I must have placed there with a view to showing Etty. Numbed, if not bemused by re-invoking the colliery scene outside – all that is actually visible, beyond the trees, are rows of lights, irregular and inter-laced, marking the roads of the commuter estates – I turn on the lamp which stands on the nearby table (the one on which Etty is convinced I should do some work) and read the entry, written in a post-schoolboy scrawl (I was, after all, writing a novel at the time).

" . . . or something akin to terror which not only I can't describe but am driven to hide. Am I alone in this, or is it something that goes on and, by a hidden or implicit imperative – conceivably a subliminal understanding – no one mentions? In which case, to have mentioned it, if only here, makes me a coward . . ."

I re-align the book.

"Where it comes from I've no idea. I thought, at first, it was induced by things I saw. Now I've discovered that what I see is merely coincidental with what I feel (but afterwards becomes irredeemably associated with it: a face, a person, a place: a tree, the shape of a leaf, a branch). The attacks come most fre-quently when I am on my own, or away from familiar surroundings; but they also come in the night – and, most

88

violently of all, when I wake in the morning. Nothing specifically appears to arouse them – the unfamiliarity of a place, for instance, can often raise my spirits – as can the sight of a tree, or a face, or a person, or a place not associated with a previous attack. I am afraid. What I am afraid of I have no idea. As a test of my courage I force myself into situations where the fear is bound to erupt – such a test, of course, is Chamberlains, but the greatest test of all . . ."

I pause: after all these years I recall the reluctance to write it down – not simply fear, but prudence. Below, in a formal script, is inscribed, "The Linfield College of Art" and, at the foot of the page, as if in code, "is a bell a challenge superseding all."

The art school stood near the centre of the town, separated from the High School (and King Edward's) by an area of unpaved private lanes flanked by large, detached, brick-built houses, the lanes interspersed with cul-de-sacs and narrow, gas-lit alleys. I would meet Bea here, occasionally, from school for, the summer over at Chamberlains, I had saved enough money to take time off to write and paint and, over the autumn, attend classes at the college.

The place had been constructed in the previous century – from funds raised by an 'industry and crafts' exhibition when the town – a former river port, trading with Russia (the Czar's armies clad in Linfield worsted) – was at the height of its prosperity. The school reflected the aspirations of the local burghers: two large rooms on the first floor, with windows looking to the north, provided the facilities for, in one room, drawing and painting from the model, in the other for drawing from the antique. Smaller rooms provided facilities for lithography, etching, pottery and printing, and what was euphemistically described as 'industrial design': there was a section for carving in wood and casting in metal, for dyeing cloth, and for baking pots. Over the years, at the rear of the premises, a technical college had been constructed – not in the original stone, but brick – its function gradually superseding that of the original college: its students, on most days (the majority on day-release from local industry) would pass through the original, sienna-tiled entrance hall – flanked by Greek caryatids and figures symbolising the ascendancy of arts and crafts – to the classrooms and workshops at the rear from where, throughout the remainder of the day, came the whine of machinery and the banging of metal.

The art-students, conspicuous by their appearance if nothing else (a raffish bohemianism as parochial as it was absurd) slunk in and out of the building, subdued by the more numerous and invariably younger students who, demonstrably, had a purpose to their labour: out of their studies would come the electricians, the engineers, the mechanics, the plumbers, the carpenters, the machine-operators, the miners, the factory technicians – the inheritors, in short, of a post-nineteenth-century ideal: out of the art school came nothing but art; or, at least, the provincial, twentieth-century substitute for it. Painting and sculpture were largely 'out' – adjunct studies to the more relevant pursuit (cf. the technical college) of industrial design: posters, record-sleeves and advertising were much discussed, along with the prospect of teaching teachers to teach prospective teachers like those teaching there themselves.

Into this atmosphere of purposive endeavour stepped – or latterly intruded – Richard Fenchurch, a self-confessed apostle of non-purposive creativity – a youth who, on his road to Damascus, had seen art as the salvation not only of his own but of 'purposive' existence in general: this mentor of his own and other people's ills – the involuntary offspring of mines and mills, of factories, of waste-heaps – polluted streams, pestilential rivers, odorous lakes and ponds and becks – stepped through the door of the Linfield College of Arts and Crafts and proceeded to lay about him with a spiritual stick – a stick which, if it didn't break (hardened on Keats, Dostoyevsky, Tolstoy, Flaubert, Wordsworth, Dickens – Van Gogh, Mendelssohn, Sibelius, Prokofiev – Beethoven, Shakespeare, Kafka, Lawrence) became, nevertheless, a little twisted – opposed by sticks hardened by more accessible (and immediate) fervours (like

90

earning a living, supporting a wife, educating children, financing a house). 'So what are you going to do in your attic,' Wormald, the teacher of industrial design (record-sleeve covers, food packages, saloon motor-cars and domestic irons) would ingenuously enquire, 'while others labour in coal-mines, mills and factories to supply you with heat and food and light – direct or indirect, I have to add – not to mention adequate transport, armed services to defend your freedom to express yourself in any way you like, and one or two other irrelevances, like a health and dental service, which you may have overlooked? While we all work, what value, *Harry*,' (a nickname he bestowed on me to indicate the fly nature of my enterprise) 'would you bestow on the products of your labour? You're not' (gesturing to the guffawing room in general) 'suggesting you're a *genius*!'

'Yes,' – to more guffaws, for who is the first to know of genius but the genius himself – the first mark of paint, the first paragraph, the first sentence: the sensational effect of the unpredictable coming from nowhere but within oneself?

'Harry,' was Wormald's only response (a provincial boor, a provincial berk, apotheosised as provincial jerk).

Wormald, poor Wormald, was not alone: Bairstow, the Principal, Dawlish, his acolyte, a phalanx of subsidiary teachers (Cass, who taught drawing from life and modelling in clay, whose metropolitan artistic ambitions had foundered in the inertia of the Linfield College of Art – ambitions bred in a similarly shallow stream whose water ran away as soon as not, disappearing into God knows where but, most probably, a hole in the ground) – and not least of all the students themselves – guffawers to a man (and woman) – proclaiming that 'Harry' was, to say the least, an affected fellow – proclaiming 'art' and 'self-expression', not to mention 'spirituality', have precedence over, if not industry, commerce and doing-what-you-can, life itself.

'Have you slept, Father?' Etty coming in the door, having knocked and entered with scarcely a pause between. 'I didn't hear you moving about,' (suspecting, no doubt, I'd died in the night).

The light has come up behind the trees – as on the morning Bea came in the room – this selfsame room – and said she'd been to bed with a fellow student. The news, at the time, had cut me in two: we'd gone into the wood: I'd lit a fire: over the smouldering flames she told me, at my insistence, the details of the incident (the ejaculation which, I could sense, had caught her by surprise, the swallowing of his semen): the sickness that came to me as I rose from the fire (the wood was wet, the fire half out, the drift of its odorous smoke amongst the trees: the distant glimpse of Ardsley Dam). 'Didn't I deserve it?' I asked myself, yet all I felt was – how should I describe it? – a spread of blood from a wound which, after all this time, has never healed.

'I was awake,' I tell her yet realise, from my dishevelment, and the unobserved intrusion of the light in the room, I must have been sitting here for hours. 'It was the most terrible moment of my life,' I add, and when, perplexed, Etty enquires (her housecoat loosely wrapped around her, a cup of tea, I notice, in her hand), 'What was?' I merely shake my head and remark, 'The day your mother came in here, when we were up, as students, one Easter break and confessed something which even now I can't acknowledge,' covering my face and, to my surprise, involuntarily weeping.

'You've been sitting there too long,' she says. 'You've been told,' she goes on, 'not to dwell on the past.'

'How can I fail to,' I tell her, 'in a place like this? It comes back without any warning.'

'I thought you'd got over Bea,' she says, identifying her less as her mother than my wife.

'Long ago,' I tell her. 'But how do you get over so much pain?'

'What did she tell you?' she enquires.

'Nothing,' I tell her behind my hands: tears – at least, the coldness from them – fall from my cheeks and dampen my chest.

92

'You're cold,' she said. 'You ought to be in bed,' and then, 'At least you've started writing,' for, on the table, before me, in front of the window, and only inches from where I'm sitting, are my glasses and my fountain pen and the sheets of paper which Etty, thoughtfully, had provided, and, written on the topmost sheet, a blur which I assume to be the beginning of a sentence.

'I can't remember writing anything,' I tell her and, instinctively, cover it up; then, confused – realising this has been a device merely to get me to lower my hands – I add, 'It's how I started my first novel, the first, at least, to get into print, sitting at a table, like this, in my student lodgings in London, a fountain pen – no glasses – an old school exercise book, its pages numbered,' while, in the process of telling Etty this, I put on my glasses and to my surprise discover I have written, "His mind was in pieces: the normal flow of associations was no longer available to him."

That's all there is left to write: the process of the mind, for the cinema and television have taken over the province of appearance. Actuality is the beginning of appearance, and appearance stands merely on the threshold of reality – the threshold, without the capacity to look inside. 'If Bea were here she'd despise me,' I tell her, rising, taking off my glasses – and, to my dismay, in putting them on the table, placing them in the space beside it and dropping them on the floor.

Etty stoops to pick them up; fresh tears obscure my vision.

'If only you knew how often, and not only in dreams, Bea has come to me in this room,' I tell her. 'Slim, as when I first knew her, dressed in her blue dress with its turned-down, round-winged collar, a rim of white against her neck, the buttons down the front, the line of which, in the most erotic way imaginable, divided her breasts, a thin blue belt outlining her waist. Gone. Without the least compunction. Innocence,' I pause, 'destroyed,' and add, 'Nothing to replace it.'

I am sitting sideways on the bed, reluctant to get in or be put inside.

'This room,' I tell her, 'is like a coffin. Once in, I fear, I'll never be let out.'

'You're free to go wherever you like,' she says, endeavouring to lift my legs (clearly beyond her) at which I get into bed without her assistance.

'Back to London?' I enquire.

'Raynor doesn't advise it. Neither,' she goes on, 'does Maidstone.'

'Maidstone's retired. To write the definitive life of Rossini. Have you,' I enquire, 'heard anything more ridiculous?' aware, once inside the blankets and covered by their weight, how cold I really am. I immediately begin to shiver. 'Why he gave up at the height of his career. Piero della Francesco, of course, was the same. Rimbaud, too, another,' and, anticipating her look of boredom (the children, I can hear, are stirring – with one or two yells – at the back of the house), I add, 'In your case it would have a definitive edge. I'm prepared to spill the beans on everything.'

'Everything?' she asks, more in provocation than with interest, I conclude, for she knows how notorious I am for covering my tracks, or, more nearly, leaving totally misleading signals.

'After all, what have I to hide?' I tell her.

'A great deal, I would have thought,' she says, and adds, 'A child, after all, shouldn't know everything about its parents.'

'Even when it's grown?' I ask.

'Are we ever grown?' she says, with a look in my direction: she is tucking in the blankets and the sheet. Before I can respond, she adds, 'What is knowledge but a half-truth, and often, at best, not even that?'

'If I don't talk, and you don't write, how will we know anything?' I ask. 'Isn't knowing something better than knowing a little?'

'It depends what you mean by "know",' she says. 'Knowledge is rarely matched by a facility for expression.'

Sullen with early waking, her face, her eyes half-closed, her cheeks bloated, is turned away: she is anxious, after all, to see

94

what I have written (it's five years since I wrote anything at all). Moving across the foot of the bed, she tucks in the blankets on the other side, passing closer by the table.

'I could write a great deal,' I tell her, 'if I had an inducement.'

'What?'

'An audience.'

'You have.'

'Inattentive.'

'Not at all.'

'Not always applauding, either,' I go on. 'Nor necessarily appreciative. All I want, after all,' I conclude, 'is to turn subject into object.'

'Those whom we love remain subjects for as long as we are here to love them,' she says.

'And be loved by them.'

'And be loved by them,' she says. 'Though that, in the past, has often been difficult to detect.'

'Did Boswell love his subject less for turning him into the subject that we know today?' I ask.

She hasn't glanced at the paper for, turning to the table, she picks up the cup of tea she's brought.

'Do you want this, Dad?' she says, so unaffectedly that, to hide my distress, I turn away.

'You can put it by the bed,' I tell her, not wishing to be left alone and, as she re-approaches the bedside table on which she has already placed my glasses, I add, 'The past isn't that bad. Think of the illustrations, the paintings and drawings, the shots from films and plays. None of the trivia of domestic life,' at which, unexpectedly, she laughs and, lightened by her mood, I enquire, 'Did you say I could go to London?'

'There's nothing to stop you,' she says. 'Charlie isn't inclined to, and Raynor is unlikely to section you in the way that Maidstone did.'

'What can be disposed of so easily by someone like that leaves a great deal to be questioned,' I tell her, 'regarding his judgement.'

'Maidstone wasn't a fool,' she says and, having placed the tea beside me, retreats to the door.

'He was tired,' I tell her, 'and overworked. The psychiatric department of a National Health hospital is not the best place,' I add, 'to form definitive judgements. No wonder,' I go on, 'he took early retirement. No doubt he's sitting on a terrace in Majorca writing something to the effect that it was depression conjoined with anxiety neurosis that obliged the greatest composer of his age – renowned above Beethoven, in his time – to give up his extraordinary creativity at the height of his career, whereas, as I told him, it was nothing of the kind. He was granted a bursary by the French Government on the sole proviso he spent a certain part of each year in Paris. Money, Etty. Money.'

'Is that,' she says, 'the same with you?' while, 'Mummy! Mummy!' comes from the landing from where Lottie and Glenda have heard her as they dash to the bathroom.

'Hello, Grandpa!' they exclaim as, round-eyed, they cling to her housecoat.

'Money was not my downfall,' I tell her. 'Even though I earned a lot. After all,' I go on, 'there was no one who wasn't, to some degree, rewarded. There are painters in London who never earned a penny to whom I handed cash I never even had. As for the family . . .'

She is, however, already outside the door: 'Grandpa is resting. Now go to your room.'

She has, before departing, drawn the curtains and now, with a perfunctory, 'I'll see you later, Father,' from beyond the door, she closes it behind her: her voice and those of the children, still clamouring, fade to the back of the house.

The moment they have gone I get out of bed and stare at the sheet of paper and, beside it, the school exercise book. "What am I? Who am I?" I have written in the latter. "Isn't what I am doing counter-productive to what I intend to be? Sometimes, walking from Onasett to the art school – a distance of two miles – I pretend to be blind, stepping along the pavement, panicking after a while, glancing down, continuing again, my ears attuned to the traffic, to the sound of approaching feet, inducing – my head bowed, seemingly downcast – a state of mind from which, in a curious way, I feel I'll never be released . . ."

I am standing by the window, looking down the slope, beyond the garden, the trees, the intervening wall, to the village – a smear in the morning light against the mist-drenched hills – and recall Etty remarking on the morning after my arrival, 'The past, I'm afraid, didn't do you any good.'

'Yet we're standing here,' I'd told her.

'We are,' she'd said, without expression.

'What I'm looking for,' I'd said, 'is a way to carry on. To disinter the past has become less of a prerequisite,' I'd added.

'Look at the way,' she'd said, 'your work is written off, or, worse,' she had gone on, 'not even mentioned,' and, suspecting she might have gone too far, she added, 'It should be enough to rouse you to composing something else,' and then, her gaze returning to the window, 'I envisaged you going out with easel and paints and starting again from scratch.'

'The peculiar thing,' I told her, 'about the village is I drew it very often. The number of paintings I have of the pit. Not to mention sketches. Of a place,' I continued, 'that doesn't exist. I put it into novels, descriptions of the streets, the houses, the appearance of the people, the twin winding-gears above the roofs, the colliery engine hauling trucks, the engine hidden in the cutting, visible only as a cloud of smoke, of steam . . .'

And am sitting in Maidstone's room at the North London Royal, he confiding, 'You're written out. It's better to acknowledge that than go on tormenting yourself with dreams that in the future your material and gift will come flooding back. Why don't you teach? It's better than sitting on your own, with or without Vivienne, endeavouring to recapture a fame and a fortune which, let's face it, have gone for good.'

'I don't believe,' I'd told him, 'I've even touched on the things I intended to touch on when I first set out,' and when he enquired, half-smiling, 'What are those?' I replied, 'The malevolence of the family I came from, not to mention, of course, the world around,' and, in that instant, recall walking the lanes and alleyways at the back of Bea's school, her summer dress, her sun-flecked features, the patches of shadow beneath the copper beeches (each garden of each house possessing at least one), the entanglement of their coiling branches, smooth, grey-sheened, flecked with cicatricial scars of rotting wood: the dust stirs at her heels – her white-socked ankles, her thin-strapped, low-heeled shoes which nevertheless enhance the slimness of her calves. Tall, she has her mother's grace but not the fulness of her figure (the same porcelain-delicacy around her cheeks – her eyes, her nose): much of our time we spend avoiding teachers from her school: 'That boy isn't doing you any good,' which, years later, she pointed out, came close to coinciding with the truth: 'A girl's education is more important than a boy's, for he acquires his by the volition of his sex whereas a girl's, in those days, at least, had to be prescribed.'

We are walking, hand in hand, along Cliff Lane, a winding, narrow track, formerly a drovers' back-route into town, above us the sooted sandstone of the town's principal buildings – towered, steepled, domed, irregular and daunting – and come to a gap in a tall brick wall which allows us a glimpse of the hill below the town on which I have lived the previous eighteen years, a scree, as it appears, of red-tiled roofs. 'That, at least,' I announce, 'will soon be gone.' It is the summer of our escape to London, she to college, I to the Drayburgh: applications have gone in the previous spring and, in both our cases, been accepted, she to a college in Regent's Park, I to one off the Euston Road . . .

'You haven't got dressed.' Moving from the door, Etty pulls back the covers from the bed. 'What's that you're writing?' plumping up the pillows, constraining herself from looking, while, seated at the table, the pen falls from my hand.

'I can't cope,' I tell her, 'with interruptions,' and add, 'I thought I'd take a trip.'

'Where?'

'Onasett.'

'Why?'

'See how the old place is.'

'Do you want a lift?' (more alarmed by this, I believe, than anything previously I might have said).

'I'll go on the bus. I haven't been back for years. I wonder if it's changed.'

An ache, beginning in the region of my stomach, rises, like an outstretched hand, to grip my heart – to squeeze then wrench it from its vascular mountings.

'For the worse.' Etty pounds the pillow. 'We passed by it, not long ago. It looks run down. The motorway comes out above it. It's not like it was in the old days.'

'You didn't know it in its prime,' I tell her – and am back inside this house with the rattle of carts and wagons and the revving of trucks from the yard next door, and Corcoran calling from the hall, 'I'll be over in the office, Bella,' she, moments later, appearing in the door, a cup of tea or coffee in her hand, her ingenuous, 'I thought you were going out to paint . . .'

'In those days,' I tell her, 'it was full of life,' yet wonder if, in reality, it was or, retrospectively, I am provisioning it with certainties which were lacking at the time – and which, in reality, are lacking now. 'The people, of course, were innocent. They'd come up from the river – the streets and alleyways around the docks, with the outside toilets, the periodic floodings when the polluted water came over the banks, the stench from the malt-kilns. You've no idea how oppressive a smell like that can be. The odour, too, from the mills, the effluent from the factories,' and, before I know what I'm doing, I'm standing in the door, forbidding her departure, declaring, 'Onasett was freshly built, the contractors' lorries still moving up the slope, the piles of bricks and the stacks of timber, the lorry loads of tiles, the houses interspersed amongst the grey ash spoil-heaps of the ancient pits – gin-pits, themselves overgrown with silver birch and occasional sycamore and alder, like tumuli scattered up the steepening slope, strewn with its coiling crescents, avenues and roads, the brick-built school and the stone-built church bastions at its summit,' breathless, 'to the south, the

99

river, coiling across its formerly lake-bedded valley floor, the gorge to the west silhouetted, at sunset, like a cavernous eye. The great days, Ett, the people stunted dwarfs creeping from the alleys, the mud-flats and wasteland by the river, breathing, reaching out – in effect, new people entirely, the residue of the industrial revolution re-born. At one time I had a photograph: my father, in waistcoat, shirt-sleeves and trousers, in the field at the back of the house – the houses behind him half-completed – Raymond, my eldest brother, in his arms, the gardens unfenced, the moorland, long-grassed and criss-crossed by the tracks of the builders' lorries, running to the back doors and low living-room windows . . .'

'Shouldn't I come with you?' Etty shoulders past. 'We could drive there and back within the hour. Give it two,' she says, 'to look around. The bus,' she is about to go on, 'isn't regular,' but when I declare, 'It wouldn't be the same with another person (no matter,' I add, in parenthesis, 'how loving and caring, and even indulgent she may be'), she slips out to the landing and without a word (other than, 'Your breakfast's been ready for over an hour'), descends to the hall from where comes the sound of Mrs Otterman singing (having foolishly been persuaded by Etty she has a pleasant voice: 'I like to hear *something* going on in the house' – in this instance a song recently made popular, on television, by an (alleged) castrato, and improved in no discernible way by Mrs Otterman's interpretation) – an indication that, in her irredeemably casual way, she has started 'dusting'. 'He'll be down in a minute,' I hear Etty call out (everyone, of course, equal in this house: formal address always in front of the servants – except, curiously, where I am concerned, 'Richard' and 'Grandpa' disseminated like the name of a dog), '*Mrs Otterman.*'

'What I don't understand,' I tell her when I finally get down, 'is where the miners have got to. Some, I know, are in the new drift mine at Wharnley, and some have gone east to the deep mine at Thornton, but where are those who sat on their haunches in front of the Miners' Welfare, and the Labour Club and the Ardsley bus-stop waiting to go out to that ghastly estate they built at Ashworth? They were the salt of the earth. At least, at the very least, the grit in the oyster from which the pearl of enlightenment was supposed to come – the enlightenment, I might add, of industrial progress,' only, of course, she doesn't answer for, moments before, I have heard her call Raynor (and having difficulty locating or being allowed to speak to him), enquiring, finally, 'Is it safe to allow him out alone?'

'Not to mention,' I tell her, 'social justice, for the fact of the matter is the third Industrial Revolution took place without our being aware of it, except, of course, by omission,' (she is peeling potatoes at the sink when, in reality, she ought to be in her study preparing notes for *The Life and Times of Richard Fenchurch*, the life and times of a modern saint). 'Places, not only pits, are disappearing, their entire surface workings with them, so that all we are left with is the residue of a pre-industrial landscape across which is scattered a post-industrial fenestration of streets and houses which have, apparently, no industrial, commercial or – how should I describe it? – onto-logical support. The landscape is bereft – bereft of all but the people living on it. No one,' I go on, 'appears to work.'

'Are you going to Onasett?' she asks and when I enquire, 'What did Raynor say?' she replies, 'He insists I go with you.'

'In that case,' I tell her, 'there's no point in going. It begins to sound as if he's inclined to section me already.'

'Nothing of the sort!' she cries and turns to add, 'Why do you look for the worst interpretation? The best is close enough!'

Tears, and not only recently, I can see, have sprung to her eyes.

'I'm not sure why I'm here,' I tell her. 'Is it because I should have been locked up and it's something Bea couldn't bear to see? Am I to be treated as a prisoner, not for my sake, but the benefit of others? After all,' I tell her, 'I'm not quite mad. I never was, despite what Bea and others might have said. It's the world out there that has gone quite wrong while I, a freak of nature, have remained, throughout this maelstrom, Bea, untouched.'

'My name isn't Bea,' she says.

101

'Etty.'

'Doesn't it come to something,' she goes on, 'when you confuse me with your former wife?'

She isn't, after all, peeling vegetables but potting plants: something with which she has become increasingly preoccupied, according to Charlie, since I arrived in the house: they stand, their stems green-leafed and largely flowerless, in tiny plastic bowls and urns along the window ledge before her, on the draining-board and, I further notice, the kitchen table. 'They remind me of your mother. It must,' I tell her, 'have confused me. She was always preoccupied with plants.'

'Instead of you.' Back stooped, head bowed, fingers blackened to the knuckles. 'I don't think you're even half-aware of how much concern has gone into looking after you. Raynor says Maidstone gave you priority over all his other patients, and Raynor, no doubt, will do the same.'

'I don't believe he did,' I tell her. 'On one occasion, when I arrived, as per appointment, he was nowhere to be found. I was at the time, in an abject state. You've no idea . . .'

'And Mum.'

'Mum?'

She transfers several potted seedlings to a fibre tray.

'All the care she gave you.'

'Was directed to her leeches. Have you seen her in her lab?'

'Often.'

'You never told me.'

'You never asked. I've seen a great deal of her the last two years.' Her next words are obscured by the sound of running water.

'While all the while I was going mad.'

'You've been recovering the past two years,' she says.

'Maidstone wrote me off completely.'

'He did not.'

' "Lithium, Fenchurch," he said, "or nothing." I refused to take it. What you see behind you, for you refuse to look me in the face, is someone who defies, and has defied, the laws of

102

science. Defined, I might add, by medical knowledge which sees chemicals as the solution to all our ills.'

'As it happens,' her back still to me, 'the subject doesn't seem half as important to me as it did before.'

'Why come and rescue me?' I ask.

A feeling of lightness – invariably preceding a delirious attack – absorbs me entirely: instead of sitting down I stand by the sink, gaze into the discoloured water collected there, and at the welter of uprooted, thread-like seedlings – like the whitened nerve-endings of the mind itself – and add, 'Or were you worried about the money?'

'Money?'

'Mine.'

'You gave it all away, you said.'

'Which didn't stop Bea from asking for half. She has a harebrained scheme, when her Medical Research Council grant runs out, of financing her own laboratory. "The proceeds from one of your plays," she said, "will be enough. All the equipment I need I can get into a shed." "What shed?" I asked. "The one on the farm I intend to buy. Didn't Etty tell you? I've thought of a scheme for marketing leeches. Apart from the research demand, they're back in fashion." When I made the inevitable response, "Leeches are the one thing you and I have in common," she threw the electric fire at me.'

'Fire?'

'I'm surprised she didn't tell you. It cut my head from above one eye to behind my ear. I had to have thirteen stitches.'

'Liar.'

She lays down a potting-tool – a wooden spatula – and kneads in the soil around a root.

'What are these going to be?' I ask.

'Sunflowers.'

'From seed.'

'What alternative is there?' she enquires, brushing, as she does so, the back of her wrist against her brow – ironically, in the same spot that the first of the thirteen stitches was inserted when I ducked into the fire which, rather than hurled, was tossed at me by Bea.

'I'm surprised she hasn't told you. On the many occasions,' I go on, 'you've been to see her.'

'She's been up here more often,' she says.

'She doesn't like the place,' I tell her.

'She's getting to hate it less now that she and Albert are married,' she says.

'You can imagine the field-day the cartoonists had with a wife who grew leeches. "Political Leech" was hardly in it.'

The fibre tray, beside the sink, is full: she carries it to the door and, moments later, is visible in the yard, crossing to the recently-constructed greenhouse – erected on what, in the old days, was the tennis-court and is now an area of tussocky grass. I follow – seeing not Etty but Isabella striding there: her tennis dress and tennis hat (she discoloured disagreeably in the sun), standing with Corcoran on their side of the net (he in white flannels and a short-sleeved shirt) while Kells, like an emaciated stick, sat by the net on a chair to keep the score, Bea and I – she attired in a pleated skirt, I in my paint-stained trousers – knocking the ball back with the sole intention of not, by winning, driving Corcoran to distraction.

'Is that the reason she suggested I come here? To get to hate my past?'

'It was one idea,' she says.

The musty air of the greenhouse has a deleterious effect: seeing an upturned box, I remove a pair of gloves and sit – more heavily than I intended.

'Are you all right?' she asks.

'Perfectly,' I tell her, and add, 'As for the care expended on me, I don't suppose you've seen her staining her leeches, her eyes pressed to her microscope more intently than they were ever focused on me. Did she *tell* you about the times we spent up here?'

She is running water from a tap into a watering-can with a preternaturally long spout to which is attached a, proportionately, even larger rose.

'What she didn't tell me, you have,' she says, and adds, 'Apart from your relationship with Gran.'

'Oh, Gran.' I dismiss it with a wave of my hand. 'In the last years of our relationship the whole of her time and energy were spent in re-learning the art of staining cells. Cancer cure or not – and I have my doubts – there was more in her absorption than meets the eye. To have been fifteen years away from research and to go back in with, as she described it, an open mind and a facility she inherited from Kells – his cakes aside – to discover what she has, reputedly, discovered, speaks for itself. She had no time for anything else. Not even Albert when he arrived. She only got her hooks on him when she thought her grant might be running out and the publicity and celebration went to her head.'

'Mother is a remarkable woman,' Etty says and, if briefly, I glimpse something of her own discontent: 'If my mother can achieve all this, what challenge is there left for me?' she must have asked. 'Another treatise on Renaissance art transposed, let's say, to an artist of today? Even with two children, and Charlie as a husband, how does that compare with the achievements of my mother, with her menopausal research, her ten years' younger lover and a husband who, if divorced, was once described as the leading writer of his generation?'

'She's one of a team,' I tell her, reading – or so I think – her mind, but she adds, 'I've been growing these all winter, but the heating went for a time and I doubt if they'll recover,' pouring the water from the can over a row of withered stems which, alone amongst the trays and boxes, appear in need of her attention.

Try as I may, however, I can't keep the objects near me in focus: I look through the distorting panes of glass and see Mrs Otterman hoovering in the children's bedroom, passing to and fro, her head stooped, her arm thrust at an angle, and am reminded again of Isabella, for there is scarcely a door or a window of this house in which I can't or haven't pictured her – as I was, for instance, moments before, watching her agile figure alongside Corcoran's immobile one: her excited laugh

105

as, running in front of her stationary husband, she flicks the ball past Bea and calls, 'Our game, darling!'

The water hisses against the plants, drums on the wood planking of the shelves and on the plastic rims of the pots.

'What has she done when she's been here?' I ask.

'Walked. Gone into the village.'

'To do what?'

'See people.'

'Who?'

'From the old days. There are still one or two. She brought a few back for tea, one day. Rose, who used to clean and who, when I was here, looked after me.'

'Did she bring Albert?'

'Once or twice. She wanted him to see it. "The place," she told him, "where I grew up." '

'And fell in love.'

'With a man from Reading whose parents manufactured biscuits.'

'Boasting.'

'She said she gave him up, not because she didn't love him, but because she thought you needed her more.'

In endeavouring to rise I miss my step, clutch at a seed-tray (intending to clutch at the plank shelf itself) and find myself a moment later lying on the brick-lined floor; more pertinently, with my head immersed in a mound of compost: "potting compost" – the words on a plastic bag pass, in a series of horizontal hieroglyphics, in front of my eyes.

'You seemed to do it,' she says, 'on purpose,' but I realise this is a response she conjures up whenever she foresees an incident occurring, involving the two of us, over which she suspects she will exercise little if any control.

'You don't think I'm lying here for fun?' I ask her and, without her assistance, attempt to rise. My head falls back against an unseen wooden batten holding up the banks of plants.

'Are you all right?' her figure stooping by me, the pressure of her hand beneath my arm.

106

'Ever since I got up I've felt a little strange,' I tell her.

'Not your tachycardia?' she says. 'You haven't taken any of the pills since you arrived.'

'My blood pressure, by all accounts,' I tell her, 'is coming down. I don't need medication for anything.'

I am – should anyone come upon us – on my knees in a position not altogther indistinguishable from that of praying, my hands together, my fingers intertwined: a feeling of alarming despondency overwhelms me: is this, I mentally enquire, how Richard Fenchurch is going to end?

'I swam, you know, each morning, at the Kentish Town baths, eight o'clock, a dozen lengths, which isn't bad for someone who, unlike you, the family swimmer, sinks like a brick unless he's lifted out. I *struggled*, Etty, for every stroke.' Invigorated by this thought I add, getting to my feet, 'Why your mother should say that I've no idea. She idolised me in those early years, if not for a few years after.'

I am standing in a sea of glass: a greenish haze intercedes between me and everything around.

'It's not the past she came here to hate,' I suddenly conclude. 'But me.'

'I'm sure you were included,' Etty says, leading me, within the confines of the greenhouse, to the door.

'You don't accommodate the past by attempting to re-write it. The only past you have is the present,' I announce. 'Though syllogistic exercises of that nature,' I further pronounce, 'are quite beyond her,' she leading me, my hands still clenched, to the yard outside. 'It was the smell of that manure,' I tell her. 'I'm not very good at confined spaces. I recall flying to Los Angeles for the first time – a mad scheme by a producer to film one of my books – and they had to carry me from the aircraft. The moment it moved at Heathrow, knowing I was to be enclosed inside it for the next thirteen hours, I had the most appalling attack of nerves, something which, until that time – I was twenty-seven – I had never had before. Not precisely in those terms. Something no doubt was telling me that a journey of that length, with a purpose of the sort I have just described, represented an unacceptable compromise with the standards I'd pursued with such integrity throughout my life. "This is wrong", my mind announced, and endeavoured, in the most sensational manner, to take leave of the issue in the only way it could. I feel that now, or, rather,' breathing in more deeply, 'did until a moment ago,' at which Etty says, 'These attacks of verbiage are part of the pattern, I take it?'

We are standing, her arm around me, in the yard while, from overhead, I have no doubt, Mrs Otterman is gazing down, the vacuum cleaner still in her hand (more refuse to dispose of).

'This compulsive talking. I've noticed, and so has Charlie, you do it increasingly. Even Lottie and Glenda have mentioned it.'

"Dear Bea, how could I describe those moments when I met you after school without re-writing the past and bringing it into the present with the most disreputable credentials?"

'It's something to do,' I tell her, 'with being on my own. All my previous associates, for whom, in one way or another, I did so much, where not dead, will have nothing to do with me. "Failure", after all, is the most frightful thing to happen to someone who is geared, as I was, to "success". Of a kind, I might add, I prayed for, for, in all those early years, when your mother was living here and I at Onasett, I prayed each night, "Dear God, may it be Thy will I become an artist, for what is the purpose of suffering to leave even part of it unexpressed?" to which I had an immediate response: "You are an artist. Isn't it evident in your susceptibility to love?" I watched my hand acquire a skill in drawing – something which, until that moment, I'd scarcely had at all.'

'You talk as if your life is over,' she says, leading me to the house but, disengaging myself, I announce, 'I've had that impressed upon me in no uncertain manner. *She* says it is, she with her much publicised research and even more publicised – if I have anything to do with it – lover. It's far from true she

108

loved that youth from Reading. It was me – me alone. She told me at the time.'

We are standing face to face: what anyone, observing us, might have assumed we were discussing, is beyond my imagination: the state of the nation, the merits of one plant food over another: compost is scattered about my clothes and, in an aimless manner, she begins to brush me down.

'I'll walk about the grounds,' I tell her. 'I feel much better for saying that.'

'You've only got your slippers on,' she says.

'You water your geraniums,' I tell her. 'I'll get my shoes.'

'And put on a coat.'

'I'll put on a coat,' I tell her. 'You unwrap your dahlias. They ought to be planted by now.'

9

I LOVE THIS house: it stretches forty-five feet exactly from its front façade, forming, at the rear, a kitchen/scullery wing – enclosing, in the process, the stone-flagged yard. In its sunny half, secluded by a privet hedge – one of the few vegetal survivors from the old days – stands the greenhouse on the remnants of the tennis lawn – catching the morning and, in the summer, the midday as well as afternoon sun, a bank of baize-like calmness against the darkness of the stone.

The back of the house is stained where the drainpipes and the guttering in recent years have leaked (the place, for two decades, let to – on the whole – uncaring tenants); and where the accretion of soot was unchecked by the prevailing wind and rain, the yellow sandstone acquiring a greenish tinge. The windows are mis-aligned, the subsidence irregular: one end of the L-shaped façade – that furthest from the scullery wing – declines towards that side of the garden where the old stone arch, with its pitted keystone, surmounted by a painted stork, opens into what, in the old days, was the stable yard and, later, the parking bays for Corcoran's lorries. In the days before I knew him he kept horses here for hauling carts – square, high-sided, two-wheeled creations, as well as low-sided, rectangular, four-wheeled ones – the teams of horses hauling, not in pairs, but single file. The old harnesses, when I first knew Bea, were still hanging in one of the mouldering buildings, and several of the old two-wheeled and several of the four- (and one curious six-) wheeled ones were parked, rotting, in the field, and former grazing pasture, behind the stable wing itself. Now

110

houses occupy 'Ardsley Close', small, three-bedroomed terrace dwellings bought by professional couples whose children often come into the grounds to play with Lottie and Glenda, but whose school, a private one, in Linfield, they don't attend.

The sale of the stable wing and the construction of the houses was one of Corcoran's final 'investments': not many years after Bea and I were married he re-leased the Hall, sold off his business and – in the manner he had foreseen, and prepared for, the nationalisation of coal and its transport – moved his capital into land. On most of it he built 'executive' dwellings: having started off as a colliery stable-lad, his final creation, via horse-drawn transport, motor transport, property and land (he was, for a while, in the insurance business), was the industrial estate which, hidden from Ardsley, dominates the vista of rolling fields and woods that lie between the village and Linfield. 'I've come,' he told me, 'a full revolution. From towing up muck from a hole in the ground I've filled it up and levelled it off and put buildings o'er the top of it. Now, that's what I call *creative*,' (a glint in the eye which as much as said, 'I don't know what an *artist* would think of it,' not much caring, with this as with other things, whether I responded).

The grounds at the back of the house are much overgrown: the old tennis-court apart, the once meticulously maintained woodland, with its ancient quarry – shaped over the years into a smooth-lawned, shrubby dell (a rock-strewn pool, festooned with lily-pads, at its centre) – is indistinguishable from the woodland which, owned by a neighbouring farmer, and much neglected, adjoins it further along the slope. As for the Swansons' flat-roofed house (known as 'The Pillbox' to the villagers), it has been joined, beyond the summit of the slope, by a number of imitations, none of them as austere, and the majority built in brick and stone, or an injudicious blend of both, a string of such creations, each tree-enclosed and garden-walled, standing on the edge of a recently broadened road and acquiring, because of their common size and close location, the district name of 'Ardsley End' – a southern sobriquet which is echoed, perhaps evoked, by their suburbanised appearance.

111

The grounds I walk in, therefore, are somewhat circumscribed and the route through them obscured, where not by fallen trees or untrained hedges, by weeds and grasses and occasional mounds of refuse – most of it of domestic origin – carried here at night and dumped by trespassers from the village: probably, Charlie has declared, relatives of those miners whom he allowed into 'The Wood' to cut timber for burning during the final miners' strike and most of which was used not by the wives for cooking but burning in the braziers at the colliery gates. 'I may have been mistaken, but one lorryload was used to block a lane at Winnington Pit when half a dozen scabs went back to work. The police came here to check it. Contrary to popular belief an "evolutionist's" life is not a simple one.'

It was here that I often wandered with Bea – and, more often still, with Isabella; for it was easier – it appeared a natural and casual extension of domestic life – while I waited for Bea to complete her 'prep', as Corcoran called it, for her to offer to show me a recently discovered nest (she was uniquely fond of birds), a hitherto unknown flower (we bought a book to discover their names), or the latest change to the 'choreography' of the wood or garden – achieved with the help of the gardener, but more often on her own, by cutting back a hedge, removing a bush, or planting something new and, invariably, exotic. Little evidence of her efforts remains: here and there I recognise a shrub, a hedge, a declivity or hollow (the site of an ambitious excavation to uproot a tree), but most, if not all, are overgrown: animals – rats – scurry away in the undergrowth, and in one particular spot where we often embraced – a patch of grass screened by rhododendron – someone, recently, has lit a fire: smoke from a clump of ashy twigs, and, on the flattened ground, the ends of several cigarettes, drifts among the trees.

It was Isabella, after all, I loved: a woman turned fifty – a woman reconciled (it seemed, at the time, supremely) to the kind of life she led: the kind of life she had always led. Much to my surprise, years later, I discovered that what she had told

112

me at the beginning – that this was the only infidelity, on her part, in her marriage – happened to be true: what, I asked myself, ecstatically, each night, could a woman of her age – almost three times my own – want with someone like myself; someone who, uniquely, presented so much danger and could offer her so little, unless our short embraces, our hurried kisses, the frenetic caressing that took place not only in this wood but in alleyways and shop doorways and at street corners in town could be described as 'wanted' – tokens of a love which, at that time, and often later, I told her went deeper than anything I had ever known.

When she complained of being old – 'So old, at times, I daren't think,' – I would cry, 'I love you old! I like you old!' and, 'I wouldn't have you any other way! You're sacred to me: when I'm on my own and think of you my hands, would you believe it, begin to shake. My legs, at times, won't hold me up,' for, on occasion, when we met – particularly after an interval of several days (and once, torturedly, after she'd been abroad, on holiday, with Corcoran, after an interval of several weeks) – I would shake so violently she would grow afraid, holding me at arm's length, while I – I struggled only to draw her to me.

Everything about her – her clothes, her hair, her gestures, her expressions, her appearance – her voice, her manners – entranced me: 'It's not me at all you love,' she would say – she did say – lying on the ground on which I'm standing now: a fifty-four-year-old woman and a twenty-year-old youth. 'It's a fantasy you have of me. And I, of course,' she had gone on, 'must have about you.'

'Is that different,' I'd asked, 'from anyone else?' adding, '*Anyone* else,' caressing her intently. 'What do we have, after all, but projections – *elucidations* of how we feel which we see reflected in other people, and which, in my case, I see so deeply and profoundly reflected in you?'

'But what *am* I?' she would ask, her eyes darkened by a fear I seldom saw on any other occasion. 'A wife, a mother, a woman old enough to have given birth to you – a woman who has given birth to a girl you say you love and who, I haven't any

113

doubt, is in love with you. This would *shatter* Bea if she knew. It would shatter me. It would shatter all of us, even an inkling of what was going on.'

Her stupefaction would drive her to despair – and to almost unapproachable silences: we got in touch, for instance, by the most tortuous arrangement. I would ring Ardsley at a particular time – one she had chosen when, she assumed, Corcoran and Rosie (Mrs Hopkins) would be out, Kells and Nan otherwise engaged. Sometimes – more often than not – it didn't work, so that I would find myself holding a conversation with Mrs Hopkins or, disengagingly, with Nan, or, confusedly, with Kells – or even Corcoran himself, enquiring about a pen or a book or a drawing I may (deliberately) have left behind, Isabella summoned finally to offer her suggestions – a whispered time and place between more loudly-offered phrases, or a vehement, but still whispered (and frightening) 'No!'

I never lost my nerve: not even when Corcoran, on one occasion, in the darkness, came blundering down the garden path and Isabella, whom I had met, moments before, by arrangement, by the garden gate, was caught in my embrace, the shadow of the hedge alone concealing us.

Oh, Bella!

10

SHE WORE a flowered dress: blue-patterned, the flowers, broad-petalled, within a green enclosure; white buttons secured the lapelled collar, the declivity between her breasts incisively pronounced. Her legs bare, she lay back in the grass, the skirt of the dress unbuttoned, the petticoat beneath it raised above her thighs. We had spent the afternoon by the side of Winnington Pond, a reservoir, enclosed by woods, from which a stream wound down, through a rock-strewn, narrow valley, to a smaller, shallower pond beneath. Children – we could hear their voices – played in the stream while on the pond itself a man, throughout the afternoon, motionless, had sat in a boat, fishing, glancing – as far as we were aware – only once in our direction. The bed of the pond was muddied, laced through by a network of weeds and grasses amongst which shoals of tiny, silver-coloured fish darted to and fro. Isabella, allegedly, had been in Linfield, shopping and now, having followed the path down by the playing children, we were lying on a bank beside the lower, deserted pond. A mist, as the afternoon passed and the first chill of the evening came across the unruffled water, caused her to shiver and, as I drew out her dress, to push down her hand and fasten it.

'Let me do it for you,' I said.

I slid each button into its hole more slowly than I had, earlier that afternoon, removed it.

'We can't go on like this,' she said, I, ignoring this threat, as I always did, proceeding with my task.

'How much I love you,' I said, lowering my head to kiss her.

She presented me her cheek.

'Ever since I've met you,' she said as, after several seconds, I withdrew, 'I've lived in two worlds. Heaven, like this afternoon, and misery the rest of the time. My hair is grey, my figure unattractive, my skin has "gone", my breasts have sunk, my thighs, I know, are flecked with veins. When you aren't there, I long – I can't tell you how much I long – for you to touch me. And when you do, I go to pieces. I cry – sometimes when I'm on my own, sometimes with other people. I don't know why. Like this afternoon, you lying there, asleep, so peaceful. It's as if I didn't mind that anyone might see. You know how weak I am, how naive in many ways. No woman I know would have responded in the way I did when I first saw you. I didn't even know myself until long after it was over.'

'I don't think you're like you describe at all,' I said. 'There's not a day goes by when I don't set off for college, walking, without an image of you in mind. I love your breasts, your face, your thighs. There's nothing about you I don't love to touch. Like now. Like this,' until, with a sigh, she arrests my hand. 'You shouldn't diminish yourself in the way you do. My whole life,' I tell her, 'is geared towards you . . .' repeating these words as, walking in the wood at the back of Ardsley Hall, I look up at the spring-bared starkness of the trees, reminded of the times, at dusk, or on a summer afternoon, on the pretext of there being something, to do with her gardening, I ought to see, we embraced beneath these trees, on this now litter-strewn slope, her head couched against the grass, her hand arresting mine before, with a groan, often with a cry, she solemnly yielded (her dark eyes watching mine as, in the depths, she imagined – preternaturally evoked – what, in the next few moments, was going to happen).

The afternoon by Winnington Pond and, later, by the lower pond, was something of a revelation: we stayed until dark; then, in the dusk, as we undressed and, having undressed, slid in the water – swimming out to a raft, made of metal, moored at the centre – we talked, peculiarly, of getting married, me insisting, she, with a tearful vehemence, declining; and then,

116

having reached the raft, and hoisting her beside me, her naked-ness gleaming in the light of a newly-risen moon, I suggested we ran away; that we didn't go back – she to Ardsley, I to Onasett; with whatever money we had, with whatever clothes we had, we set off 'hitching' to the south. 'The south, full,' I misquoted, 'of the blissful sun. We'll find a cottage. You can grow plants. I'll paint. I'll write. Pictures no one's dreamed of. Novels no one has even imagined . . .' lying there for hours until, shivering, the moon, like a baleful presence, reflected in the surface of the pond, we slid back in the water and returned to the bank.

I dressed her; I dried her – I consumed her in that following hour, and yet, towards midnight, as we stumbled through the moonlit wood, she cried, leaning against a tree, her head cradled in her hand. 'How could this have happened?' she said. 'I was a happily married woman. I was,' she told me, 'so content. I loved my husband. I loved my child. I feel like a killer of both of them.'

Later, she described that day as 'our honeymoon'. It was the early hours of the morning when she got home; strangely, I never asked her what she'd told Corcoran, or Bea, to explain her absence. It was in reference to an altogether different incident that Bea mentioned 'the night my mother came home delirious. My father said drunk. He'd phoned the police twice before going to bed, and had driven round the village more times than I remember and even, would you believe it, to Linfield and back, the buses having, by that time, finished running, then to the railway station thinking she'd be waiting there. Then, singing to herself, he said, she came up the garden. She'd met a friend, she told him, in Linfield, whom she hadn't seen for years. "Not since school," she told him. They'd talked, of course, forgotten the time, and when they remembered the friend had driven her back. As I saw when I got up, she was deliriously happy, and when I suggested she'd been out with a man, Daddy laughed. "You don't know much about women," he said. "Which is just as well. As for your mother," – she'd kissed him quite passionately on the lips as

117

he told me – with a directness I'd never seen before, and which, I have to confess, I've never seen since, "she'd be behaving quite differently if she had." '

'The Harem?' I couldn't help reflecting at the time: the legacy, not so much of Connemara as the Lebanon, the Sardinic fringe. For it was true, because of the irregular and vehement nature of our love-making, it affected, in a positive and, to her, bewildering way, Isabella's relationship with Corcoran, he overwhelmed by the passion which, he assumed, he had aroused in her himself. 'Mummy,' Bea told me on one occasion, 'for the past few weeks, has been hanging round Daddy's neck. He gets irritated by her stroking his hair, particularly in the evening when he sits by the fire and smokes a cigarette and tries to listen to the wireless or read a paper. And I get embarrassed, I can tell you, by the number of times she goes up to him, even when Mrs Hopkins is present, let alone me, and says, brazenly, "I love you!" or, "Darling Freddie!" looking into his eyes like those awful girls at the back wall at school look over at the boys from King Edward's.'

When I mentioned this to Isabella she said, smiling, 'How can I help the way I am?' and then, 'I have duties as a wife. They preceded the feelings – which don't amount to duties – that I have for you.'

'How can you love two people at once?' I asked, and when she said, 'Isn't it the same as you and Bea?' I added, 'Physically. How can you allow him in you?'

She cried (allowing me, after that, intimacies in places which, previously, she had proscribed: in trains, in doorways, in buses, even in cafés: I became exacting about the way she sat, her legs, whether stockinged or bare, displaced towards me, allowing, with as little impediment as possible, access to my hand – recalling an occasion, even, when I required her to wear a particular dress – fastened at the side and providing entry to her underclothes and breast).

She grew disturbed at my audacity. 'Aren't you putting your mark on me?' she said after one disagreeable incident on the back seat of a bus, and when I asked her to explain, she added,

118

'Making me submit to indecencies in places where genuine intimacy is out of the question. I don't like that side of it. It's brought out something cruel.'

'Because,' I said, 'you wouldn't go away with me?' at which, to my surprise (we were standing in a bus queue), she slapped my face – so hard I felt the force of it long after the bus itself (she on it) had departed and I was walking home.

Late teens, approaching twenty, childish in thought as well as need: it was shortly after this I suggested she allow me to draw her ('for posterity,' I reasoned, 'if nothing else'), and hired a 'studio' – a room above a barber's, near the centre of the town, full of discarded boxes – an attic used by a fellow-student who had ambitions, misplaced, to be a painter. One afternoon a week I absconded from college and drew her – first in the dresses that she chose then, after much persuasion, without them. I'm not sure why none of these drawings – and, with one exception, paintings – succeeded: the intention was to use them in my application to the Drayburgh, which had a reputation for drawing and painting from life – even (an unspoken codicil) it would provide the means by which I could give full expression – not to my love (on that, to say the least, both of us could count) – but to a talent, if not a genius which hitherto had been proscribed by the regime of the college. She would lie – at first with decorum – on a mattress on the floor; at an intermediate stage with her dress and perhaps one under-garment removed (her beautiful stockinged thighs), but finally, after infinite persuasion, with nothing on.

She would turn her head and watch, anxious at being exposed, the ambiguity of her purpose affecting, or so it seemed, the movement of my pen (later on, my brush): need-less to say, at some point, I would divest myself of my own clothes and, drawing down the blind (for, though in the corner where she posed she couldn't be seen, the room was overlooked by a departmental store across the road) I would cross to the mattress and lie beside her – or beneath her as, by her choice, was frequently the case.

*

119

A bird flies from the shrub ahead: I recognise a chaffinch (another debt unpaid). 'Chaffinches,' Bea once told me – she, too, indebted to Isabella for her fascination with birds – 'acquire a regional accent, so much so that one taken, as an egg, from the Orkneys, sings a different tune when it's hatched in Essex. Like you and me,' she concluded, 'are children of the north, and Mum,' she'd paused, 'the child of somewhere else,' my interest in the bird re-igniting my memory of standing at the window of our house in Belsize Park and watching a firecrest which I had never seen before darting around the root of a rhododendron bush, a minuscule bird, mistaken for a wren (and then a goldcrest) until I identified the strand of orange dashed along its head.

It was the window at which I would stand when I couldn't work, gazing at the old-world garden – the buttressed wall, an ancient fig tree coiled against it, its sinuous, light grey branches masked by the dark green plates of its leaves, the grey-green fronds of the buddleia with its tentacles of purple flowers in June, the roses – ancient and modern – variegatedly coloured against the darkness of the creepers (the numerous shrubs and plants whose names – despite Isabella's teaching – I never retained), the japonica in spring, the lilac in the summer, the 'chrysanthemum shrub' in autumn – and the birds (my bird-book and binoculars – presents from Isabella – by the window), the rare glimpses of a fieldfare (twice), the firecrest (once), a spotted woodpecker (three times), the finches, redpolls, siskins and linnets; the flycatchers, nesting by that selfsame window, the chiffchaffs (perhaps, more nearly, chiff-willows), the tits (willow, blue, great, coal, long-tailed and – once – bearded), the magpies, rooks, the perpetual pigeons, the dunnocks, wrens and starlings; the house-martins, swifts and swallows; the wag-tails, blackcaps and the regular winter redwing – the tawny owl – the thrushes (song and mistle), the blackbirds and, throughout one summer, the (presumably escaped) perpetually mimicking myna bird that perched on the chimney and whistled alternately like a blackbird and a telephone bell.

'Birds are my recreation,' I would say – without conviction –

120

to Bea; and when, years later, I would, in parenthesis, add, 'Like leeches are with you,' she would laugh, eyes querulous (startled, too, at times), her mouth flung open as if, even in the middle of her laugh, she still held back, half-confused by her own amusement. 'Leeches are my work, like writing is with you. Is recreation quite the word?' she'd ask and, if I were in the mood (which, in truth, I seldom was) to pursue the subject, her penultimate response would be, 'It's more a reaction, wouldn't you say ('to Mum', I was always tempted to say) to life,' her ultimate and invariably unanswered rejoinder, 'Birds, when they're frightened, fly away.'

It was the beginning of my 'loneliness', as Etty once described it. 'I've never seen anyone so lonely,' she said at one of my first nights – she in her 'teens. 'The author of the piece, and no one speaks to you, nor you to them. It's to Liam,' (the director), 'that they flock. Haven't you anything to tell them?' While others, too, would come up and complain, Vivienne – the turbulent Vivienne – at the height of her fame, too, at that time, her dyed hair blended seamlessly with that of her cascading wig (bedecked with ribbon and tiny flowers), announcing, in her dressing-room, backstage at the Globe (champagne glass in one hand, bottle in the other), 'I've never seen a sadder man,' leaning forward, her tempestuous, tortured, turbulent blue eyes narrowed with their particular pain, 'What are you *afraid* of?'

It's true: more afraid than I dare express: the wringing of hands, the endless weeping (the cowering on the floor, the involuntary spasms).

Vivienne terrified me more than any person – let alone woman – I had ever known: fiendish, electric – sensational when (as was not unusual) treated with contempt. A robust, venal, undiscriminating woman, besotted by her love for Melvyn, the neophyte actor who rose to stardom, so she alleged, while in her hands, Melvyn Zygorski, an out of work (out of trousers) hustler she seduced into notoriety – one which, to her chagrin, outshone her own (a pedlar of drugs on his way

121

to the top, a free dispenser – tragically, for Vivienne – when he finally got there).

Smaller in stature though larger in presence than Bea (or Isabella), with a peculiar skin which varied, alarmingly, according to her mood (foul-mouthed, loose-tongued), the daughter of a minister of the Scottish Free Presbyterian Church, she might, had she stayed in Glasgow, have survived the vicissitudes of her middle life ('my beauty and my lovers gone, what else is there to live for?') holding up the bottle (of her native drink) that played as much a part in her decline as her 'Hollywood diets', her mystic chums, her free-loading psychiatrist: 'Now there is a man, if you want one, Richard: a genius from the Gorbals,' a fellow-Scot and alcoholic.

The path winds off to the left: I recognise the contour of the land – the layout of the bushes, much overgrown, and crushed, dramatically, close to the summit of the slope, by a fallen tree. An attempt has been made to saw off its branches: scatterings of white dust lie at intervals beside the trunk: no doubt the work of intruders. Skirting it, along a track recently worn, I come to the foot of Sugden's Bank up which, over forty years ago, I scrambled on that memorable day with Isabella.

On all fours, I scramble up again: the rabbit holes, the tufts of grass, the decimated shrubs and bushes. A wire fence, just beyond its summit, divides the grounds of 'The People's Palace' from the still-cultivated farmer's field beyond. The slope, at the foot of the field, is lined by the recently-constructed houses which form the self-enclosed enclave of Ardsley End, the Swansons' original concrete structure obscured not only by the tall brick wall but by trees: the severity of its façade, overlooking a flourishing garden, has been ameliorated by covering it with, if not synthetic, symmetrically-featured stone.

'I am here to make amends. Not,' I add the codicil, 'to hate the past (to bring that hatred into the present).' Amends for what? Being what I was: what biological determinism has made me (demonstrated, alas, for all to see)? To make amends with Etty – the child who, in a sense, is older than myself (wiser,

122

more contained), the last love of my life, perhaps – the inspiration, conceivably essential, to make me move again.

11

HAND IN HAND, walking, finally, past Thrallstone Park – the Chamberlain tents put up for a summer feast – passing beneath a railway bridge, over the canal (a barge locked in the basin beneath, smoke rising from its metal chimney, a line of washing from stem to stern) and over the adjoining river. Beside this second, larger bridge lay a crumbling, cliff-like excrescence, covered in shrubs and, where its grey surface was not exposed, by a smooth, round-bladed moorland grass: the waste-heap, not from a local pit but a soapworks. Perhaps it had been the prospect of London – departure, new worlds, destiny – which induced her to 'vouchsafe' me – as, once, Isabella described a similar if not identical occasion ('the final sacrifice a woman can give': in reality, of course, the first): the warmth of the day, the softness of the grass, the enclosure of the artificially-constructed, crag-like slopes, the shelter of the shrubs, the murmur of insects on the clover and daisies by our heads: the feeling we were embarked on a course from which, foresee-ably, there was no return: those physical, moral, if not artistic considerations (not to mention psychological) induced by a recklessness which nothing in our natures, at that juncture of our lives, was in the least way inclined to discourage. Perhaps the precedent set by her mother persuaded me to pursue a course with Bea which had already been prescribed – she, her mother, an experienced woman: physically, the demands made on her, she told me on one occasion, had been extreme: 'Three times a night he would climb on top,' (weeping into her hand and adding, 'I don't know why I tell you this,') – my own efforts, on more than one occasion, having been greeted with a laugh – unique for her at such a delicate moment: 'You don't know much about it, love,' guiding my hand to a particular spot where, teeth bared, eyes fluttering, she carefully deployed it.

With Bea it was my first experience of – as I tentatively explained it – 'God': the greenness of the grass (the blueness of the sky): the bees, the roar – over a shoal of rocks – of the hidden river (the unblemished thigh, the pubescent breast).

'I had a feeling,' I said, 'of Christ.'

'Christ?' (her dress drawn up above her thigh).

'For the first time in my life,' I said, 'I feel in touch with God.'

'I didn't feel that at all,' she said, and added, 'I'm so glad you enjoyed it.'

With Isabella it happened, invariably, at night – and, on one of the earliest occasions, beneath the trees at the back of the house. Which trees, and precisely in which spot I never found out: we had gone, absurdly, to look for an owl – heard hooting from the wood and since, I declared, I'd never seen one, she had said, 'I must show you, Richard. We see it here quite often,' pulling on her coat, Bea – and Corcoran – if not contemptuous, disinclined to join us. 'Off you go, Bell,' Corcoran had said. 'If *we* come out we'll frighten it,' adding, 'Once you've seen one you've seen them all.'

We had stumbled in the dark, she finding my hand, a peculiar perversity gripping both of us. Without a word she lowered me to the ground and moments later allowed what she described as 'our vouchsafing': the pallor of her face against the grass – featureless, alarmingly, in the dark – the enclosure of her arms – the guidance as her hand reached down – the speed, the brevity: moments later we were returning down the slope, she dusting down her coat, I, bemused, some distance behind (not only bemused, I thought, but mad) – sceptical that Corcoran wouldn't deduce what, in the darkness, had taken place (three times a night, I thought, for him) – he, as it was, glancing up (smoking his pipe beside the fire), enquiring, 'Did you see it?' to which Isabella, shaking out her

125

hair from a headscarf, had said, lightly, 'For a second, Freddie. Nothing else.'

With Bea, paradise, or so it seemed, was in the grass, in the murmur of the insects, in the sheltering shrubs (in the warmth of the sun), in the enclosure of the cliff-like crag, in the roar of the river, in the depths of the sky – in the peculiar opacity of the blue itself.

With Isabella, that summer, it happened most frequently in the wood behind the house where, 'for peace of mind', as she told Corcoran at the time, she strolled each evening, the 'reflection', she assured him, 'did her good', while he, after several weeks, according to Bea, had enquired, jokingly, one evening, 'You're not meeting a lover, Bell?' and had even, still jokingly, offered to accompany her. 'I should meet him,' he told her. 'We might have a lot in common.'

'What do you do out there, Mummy?' Bea had asked.

'Think my thoughts, dear,' her mother replied.

We moved, on some occasions, further afield, meeting on afternoons I took off from college, discovering a wood on the bus route between Ardsley and Linfield where, in the fields fringing it, we would lie with my paint-flecked raincoat beneath us. There was a perfunctory quality to these, as to all our encounters, not least on account of my 'inexperience', as she described it (ejaculating, on one occasion, merely at the sight of her waiting at the stop, I subsequently to be coaxed by the – then unique – deployment of her mouth. When I enquired, 'Do you do that with Freddie?' she had cried, 'Don't ask me anything about him again!').

She was, as she told me frequently – and sincerely believed – 'happily married'. 'I wouldn't change Freddie for anyone,' she often announced. 'Not even for me?' I finally enquired. 'Not even you,' she said, 'for you'll leave me in the end.'

'Never,' I said.

'My dear,' she said. 'You know nothing.'

'Why don't you take a sketchbook?' Etty had said as I came out

126

of the house and, standing on the embankment, I find it and a pencil in my hand. I sit by a rabbit hole and, opening the book, begin to draw. My nerve, over the past five years, has gone, the feeling for line, the feeling for feeling, disappeared: there is nothing but dizziness, palpitation, dispiritation – and, worse than all these combined, dread.

'What is dread?' Maidstone would enquire.

'Fear and dispiritation,' I'd tell him, 'combined.'

'Where do you feel it?' (without a smile).

'In the heart,' I'd tell him.

'The heart, dear boy,' he'd tell me, 'is in the head, and – the great discovery of the century – the head is merely a physiological entity. Which is why lithium, in your case, is indispensable. If you don't agree to it now you'll be obliged to do so later. When,' he'd pause, his features quizzically distorted, 'you'll be much worse. Much, much,' he'd pause again, growing paler, continuing, finally, with the softest exhalation, '*worse.*'

The houses take shape: the line of the field; the trees which have much engulfed the scene in the past ten years, the saplings in the gardens tinged with buds, if not with blossom. Beyond: the pattern of fields and copses and, like Giza without the pyramids, Aswan without the temple, those quaint omissions where the collieries stood – and can see, in the distance, the declivity of Winnington Pond, though not the pale disc of its water, lost in the darkness of the woods where, on alternate evenings, hand in hand, I had walked with Bea and her mother.

I queried five years ago why I drew or wrote: the pictures (even the sculptures), the books, the plays (the poems, the novels), the notes, the diary – 'why?' displaced by the question 'how?' (What was the point in going on?). 'Would you be happy,' Maidstone had ingenuously enquired, 'doing anything else?'

'I'd be happy doing anything,' I equally ingenuously responded, 'that made me happy.'

'A mechanical job?'

'Anything which, at the end of the day, left me with myself.'

A quiet afternoon – an interregnum between visits to the

127

wards or the demands – announced directly by a hammering on the door: 'Are you in there, Professor?'

'Go away. I'm busy.'

'I want to ask you one thing!'

'Go away!'

'*One thing!*'

'*Go away!*'

The pin-striped suit (creased at the back from hours of sitting), the starched shirt collar, the college tie (Balliol: a likeable conceit), the small, square, short-fingered hands, the fountain pen held quaintly between his middle fingers: the 'thousands and thousands of pictures and millions and millions of books' to which I was adding. 'For what? What,' I enquired, 'is the point of it all?'

'Isn't the point of the point,' he ingenuously persisted, 'that the point of the point is a circle?'

Diagonal strokes of the carbon from top right-hand to bottom left: with parallel lines of varying length I shade in the woods and Winnerton Pond (shade in Bea and Isabella); shade in where Fernley and Dorrington collieries stood; shade in the furthest line of hills which, beneath a grey-hulked sky, loom above the streets, the yellow sandstone buildings – the towers, the domes, the steeples (the housing blocks, the polluted Lin) – of the invisible city of Linfield – its presence suggested by a drift of smoke from its soon-to-be-disassembled coal-fired power-station.

'An abundance of riches. Gifted,' Maidstone says, 'in so many ways. Yet all it amounts to is self-referral.'

'A romanticist,' I tell him. 'A layman. Can't you see that art has led me to the psychiatric department of the North London Royal and the delusion to which I wake each morning that I am about, not to be sentenced, but executed for a crime I didn't commit or which, even though I don't know what it is, I know I have committed?'

'Art is a physiological phenomenon, too,' Maidstone says.

128

'Perhaps you ought to see your friend, the maverick Mackendrick.'

'The two great M's in my life,' I declare.

'How about a third?' he says. 'How about your mother?'

'Mother's been very odd,' Bea says.

We are walking, hand in hand, down through the town, from school, to the station.

'In what way?' I ask.

'Oh,' she tells me, 'very *strange*. She says I need a holiday.'

'Perhaps you do,' I tell her.

'Not just me but her. She's invited Veronica and Clare, her two incredible sisters.' (Both widowed, one with a son, the other a daughter – both married – living overseas.)

She paused.

'She's invited you as well.'

'Me?'

'Daddy isn't going.'

'Why?'

'He says he's too much work.' She clasped my hand more firmly. 'In the old days, when Daddy was very busy, particularly during the war, we often went away – Veronica and Clare and my two cousins. Their husbands, during the war, were both called up. It'll be like the old days. It was always jolly. On holiday,' she concluded, 'Mum is such a wheeze.'

I am drawing a copper beech. Where? Not on the slope above the house. I have vacated the spot on Sugden's Bank (Swanson, Etty has told me, after being imprisoned for corruption – paying backhanders to Council officials for municipal contracts – is currently out on parole) and must, I conclude, be at the far corner of Charlie's and Etty's 'kingdom': a gate, behind my back, leads between familiar old stone buildings, the one-time yard of Oldroyd's farm (from where Etty, in the old days, when we were up here on a visit, used to go round with old Oldroyd's father, delivering milk): an architect, however, has transformed the yard (but for the buildings themselves) out of recognition: a Mercedes shooting-brake stands there now and, beside it, a sports car whose make, like most makes nowadays, I fail to recognise – me a one-time Mercedes-Jaguar-Alvis owner – all sold, as a (failed) means of enticing Bea (back) with the prospect of a laboratory at the bottom of our Belsize Park garden. The grey, coiling branches of the copper beech are not unlike those of the fig tree – statelier, stiffer – an arthritic articulation of ageing wood, bowed where the weight of a branch and the swaying of the equinoctial winds have brought the branch itself against the ground: pale filigrees of lemon mark the beginning of the early leaves, spiked, irregular, pointing into and outwards from the dome-like head.

'I am visited by a vacuity of mind,' I explain to Maidstone, 'which I can never explain nor wholly describe. The whole self-system comes apart and in its place a vacuum conveys its presence by a feeling I can only describe as terror. Indefinitely prolonged, it creases the body – the victim stoops, his arms across his stomach, and bows to ease the pain. Your other patients, though less articulate, must surely describe identical symptoms. It gives an insight, on the other hand, into the structure of the mind. How, under stress, it comes apart. *The Quinary or Pentadic Theory.* When I've written the book I'll ask you to check it. Once published, assimilated, and understood, it will revolutionise psychiatry.'

Two evenings before Bea had told me of her mother's invitation I had come out of the art school to find Isabella waiting in much the same fashion as I had waited for her outside the City Women's Institute on the evening of our first intimate embrace. Her face was tense, her habitual tenderness displaced by apprehension, a look which announced, 'There's nothing left for either of us if you don't give me what I want.' 'I had a meeting in town. I happened to be passing. Perhaps,' she said, 'you could come to the house.'

A luminous light in the windows of the offices and shops, and the less prepossessing windows of the college, etherealised, or so it seemed, the street – less a place, I thought, than a vision.

'When?'

'Tomorrow.'

'I'll be at college.'

'Take the afternoon off.' She added, 'You've done it often before.'

'They're beginning to notice,' I said, and asked, 'What's it about?'

'Bea will be at school. Freddie away. Rose I've given the afternoon off. I'd like,' she said, 'to see you in private. Not,' she went on, 'a place like this.'

'Why?'

'There's something,' she said, 'I'd like to ask.' She paused, her look more direct – and curious – than on any previous occasion. 'You're not afraid of coming?'

More than a challenge, I reflected, was implicit in her look: a right was being asserted – one she had earned and to which I'd acceded. 'I'll take the afternoon off,' I said.

I am standing at the Linfield stop: one or two people are waiting with me: it is the middle, I assess, of the afternoon, and realise I have eaten nothing since breakfast (hadn't Etty, moments before, been standing at the sink, peeling potatoes, potting plants?) and concluded it must have been mid-morning. It is warm: traffic comes down the steep slope of the hill, past the church, to the cross-roads at the bottom: here five roads meet around what, at one time, would have been the village green, a rectangular tarmacked area dominated by the employment exchange (housed in a former primary school building) and a piece of cultivated ground equally divided between grass (denuded) and flowerbeds. Here Bea and I have met on numerous occasions, getting off buses, getting on; here, in the past, Etty, her sister and her brothers, have bought ice-creams; here, in the dark I have quarrelled with and subsequently consoled Isabella. Immediately ahead is the principal road leading through the village – and the declivity, some distance away, where the railway crossed from the colliery yard: the ghosts of steam engines whistle in my ear

131

and, in my otherwise vacuous head, the winding gear and slag heap rise, once more, above the roofs: boots shuffle in a cobbled yard; carts, pulled by horses ('Corcoran & Co Contractors' inscribed, yellow paint on black, along the side), come groaning down the hill, the ejaculations of the drivers, the cracking of a whip, the steam from the horses' backs and mouths, the rasp of the metal-rimmed wheels against the tarmac, of the brake blocks against the wheels themselves (the rattle of chains as the blocks are deployed). 'Her father, they say, went off his head.' I hear the words quite clearly. 'He was certified for over a year, believed he'd been condemned to death and woke each morning expecting the sentence to be carried out. Nothing would console him.'

'If I have gone out of my mind it's quite all right by me,' I said. 'Who wouldn't go nuts in a place like this?' to which a woman beside me says, 'It's alus late.'

'Late?'

'The bus to Linfield.'

'Linfield.'

'Aren't you Mrs Stott's father?' she suddenly enquires.

'I was,' I tell her, 'but left, in fact, some time ago.'

'I've seen you on television.'

'Television?'

'Years ago. I don't get much time,' she adds, 'for reading. I go to my daughter's to look after the children. She works. Her husband,' she goes on, 'is unemployed but has no flair with the kiddies. Sits and mopes, when he's not on drugs. Ten years ago he was down the pit, drunk each night and happy as a lord.'

'Not much to choose between the two,' I tell her.

'Give me drunk every time,' she says. 'At least when he was he wa're alus singing.'

The woman is old: her hair, beneath a headscarf, is fastened in pins: a scarf wrapped beneath a bright check coat: stout, double-chinned, rouged cheeks: between two vivid streaks of lipstick she smiles: teeth more vivid than the lipstick itself, eyes brighter, more vivid than the teeth.

'Children keep you going,' to the others in the queue beyond her.

I am on my way to Onasett (via Linfield): o happy land!

Lunch is laid on the table when I arrive; and has been waiting I assume, for several hours (I'm late) – a table at which I've eaten with her husband and her daughter, talking of war, politics, art and religion, on none of which Corcoran has any views other than those conjured up in opposition to Isabella's (and Bea's): called up during the war he was offered an immediate commission, because of his 'transport experience', in the Army Ordnance Corps.

The day is chill (it is raining as I walk from the bus to the house): she wears a suit – a loosely-cut jacket and a pleated skirt: dove grey, it is relieved at the throat by the lace collar of a high-necked blouse: I have never seen her look more lovely. Her colour is high.

I have seen her setting and re-setting the table as I've come up the path through the garden: the neatness of her hair, the squareness of her shoulders, the trimmed-in waist, the flaring hips. 'I don't feel hungry,' I tell her, she, having departed to the kitchen, returning with food she's kept hot in the oven.

'I thought you'd have an appetite,' she says. 'Working,' she goes on, 'all morning.'

'I don't feel hungry,' I tell her again, not sure that my arrival has gone unnoticed: from the yard, through the archway, it's possible to see the house and the garden: any amount of men are working there, lorries being backed, loaded, fuelled.

She shrugs: her hair is brightly ribboned: it has, as on most occasions when I see her, been fastened in a bun (she intoxicates me with her dress, her make-up, her preparation – above all, with her circumspection: so she might prepare, a headmistress, to interview a parent about a child).

'I thought it was better,' she says, 'to talk like this, not like we always do, in a side-street doorway, or on the back seat of a bus, or in a café, or beneath a hedge.'

'I like those places,' I tell her. 'I can't tell you how much those doorways and buses and cafés and hedges mean. I sometimes go by them and, prompted by what went on there, think of you all day.'

'At no expense,' she says, 'to yourself,' and adds, before I can respond, 'At least, in here, we're not overlooked. At least,' she goes on, 'we can talk in private,' (gesturing to the window – the murmur of engines, the cawing of rooks, the panting of the pit, the rattle of the sorting plant, the whistle of the engine – the shuffle – the shuffle of thousands of feet).

She smiles (sitting sideways at the table herself).

'Won't you sit down?'

Fenchurch is what people assume he isn't: malevolent, uncaring, demonic, unkind: the graffitist of the notorious Benedict Ward at the North London Royal, named after a benefactor who came to no good (not unlike the clothing manufacturer who gave his name to Boady Hall, the even more notorious rehabilitation centre in North London).

I, too, sit sideways at the table: hungry I might have been – it is three-quarters of an hour by bus from Linfield – but apprehension – an awful apprehension – grips not only my stomach but my intestines; and not only my intestines but, finally, my heart: I am here, I have concluded on my three-quarters of an hour journey on the bus, to be cast off.

'In many respects, all I want to do,' she says, suddenly, 'is to see you sitting there.' (I can gaze at her for hours, entranced, besotted, entwined.) 'Like an artist,' she continues, 'sits for an indefinite time, or so you tell me, before his subject. I imagine,' she goes on, gazing at me with glistening eyes – enigmatic, in the extreme, 'you've done that lots of times yourself.'

'A few.'

'You're my model.' She smiles again. 'But,' she continues, 'in a different art entirely.'

'Which art is that?' my voice disappearing, huskily, halfway down my throat.

'The art – would you call it? – of growing old.'

'You don't look old, in the least,' I tell her.

'I'm sure.' She laughs. 'Which is why I've spent the best part

134

of the morning getting ready.' She glances at the food, her arm laid on the table beside her: my gaze – her fingers, slightly raised, are tapping at the cloth – is directed to her ring.

Her knee, her legs crossed, gleams beneath the hem of her pleated skirt: her foremost shoe, high-heeled, has drifted from her foot.

'I've given you,' she adds, 'a terrible weapon.'

'How?'

We sit at adjacent sides of the table: by reaching out, I speculate, I could touch her hand.

'By competing with my daughter. You could destroy both of us,' she adds.

'I love you both,' I tell her.

'Do you?'

She waits to be convinced.

'I love you more than Bea.'

'More?'

'Much.'

'How much?'

'In ways I can't express.'

'It's those ways I'd like to hear about,' she says, revealing a ruthlessness which, until this moment, I have scarcely if ever glimpsed. She sees me as an opportunist, I suddenly reflect, dissuaded only from this view by what she suspects may be my talent.

'If I can't express them I don't see how I can describe them,' I tell her. 'I like to love you in ways that neither you nor I can understand. That,' I pause, 'is the heart of it.'

The colour deepens round her eyes – around her eyes and despite her make-up.

'I was never aware of anything,' she repeats '*anything!* – until I touched your hand.'

'When?'

'When you went the wrong way up Sugden's Bank.' Gesturing to the grounds at the back of the house, she adds, 'It was all so wrong.'

'Wrong?'

135

'Terribly.'

The word, used in isolation, brings out a smile.

The ring: nothing entrances me so much as when – its thin gold strand – I persuade her (refusing to touch it myself) to take it off: more erotic, for instance, than her removing her clothes (the mechanical way she draws off her blouse, or, half-twisting, first unfastens then lowers her skirt, unclips her stockings, releases her breasts: the nonchalant way she introduces, with a casual raising of her hips, the 'vouchsafing' which, afterwards, she confesses means more to her than she suspects (incorrectly) it does to me. 'There is,' I always tell her, 'no condescension in it. I'm sure not on your part and certainly not on mine.').

Re-crossing her legs, she says, 'I don't know where we go from here,' while, her own gaze fixed on mine, mine seeks the wall behind her back (a photograph of Kells standing beside a war-time bomber: a visit to a nearby aerodrome arranged by a colleague engaged, he subsequently told me, on radar research).

'Unless,' I tell her, 'we call a halt.'

'A woman old enough,' she smiles (a familiar refrain), 'to be your mother. Certainly,' she continues, 'twice your age.' Her hand reaches out and covers mine. 'And yet,' she smiles again, 'a whole day goes by and, at the end of it, all I have thought about is you.'

She stands.

'Don't you ever wear a hat?'

'Never.'

'I suppose you did at school.'

'A cap.'

'A cap.' She caresses my head. I smell her scent. 'The whole thing,' she says, 'is quite ridiculous.'

'My ring as well?' she says. 'I feel quite naked already,' retaining her skirt as well as her stockings until unbuttoning her blouse ('I chose high-necked, my dear, on purpose') I persuade her to remove them. 'I'll take off what you like. All I wanted,' she goes on, 'is just one time in bed,' recalling each incident as I return home on the bus. 'A betrayal of Bea as well as Corcoran,' I announce. 'Not to mention Kells and Nan.'

'I beg your pardon?' the man beside me says and I am gazing at the curve of a hedge, the shape of a tree familiar from almost forty years before – glimpsed like this, fleetingly, from the window of a passing bus.

'Not at all.' I ease my feet – absurdly, I discover, in my slippers – aware of the draught from the bus's open door.

The hulk of Ardsley Priory appears – a black, stone building, tall and square, and surmounted by a balustrade whose silhouette is pierced by chimneys: beyond a battlemented gatehouse a drive winds off across a tree-strewn park. A wall, bowed and buttressed, its brickwork less dark than the house itself, obliterates the view: we cross a hump-backed bridge: a lake, enclosed by trees, appears.

Lying on her bed, her ring removed, the curtains drawn: 'O, my dearest love,' she said.

I walked this road – the familiar fields, the familiar hedges, the hidden declivities, the sudden promontories – grey-heaped and silver-birched – that marked the medieval gin-pits: walked the twelve miles from Onasett to Ardsley (I was running out of money, that summer before our move to London). At the end of the journey I limped to the door and spent the best part of the following hour sitting in the kitchen, talking to Isabella (occasionally to Bea as she darted to her room, to study, and darted back), my foot in a bucket of water. Periodically Isabella would take the foot and massage the swollen ankle (her ringed finger passing to and fro across the tendon). 'You do too much,' she said. 'That's half your trouble.'

'I need experience,' I told her.

'Of what?'

'All sorts of things you can't imagine.'

'Such as?'

'Love. Hatred. A tent erector,' I told her, 'is nothing to be sneezed at.'

'You and your tents!' (in much the same manner as she might have said, 'You and your kisses!').

'Are you two fraternising?' Bea said, coming in, unaware, as always, of what, in reality, was going on.

'If I am going mad,' I said, 'at least I am going mad in style,' at which the man beside me, turning further round, enquires again, 'I beg your pardon?'

'I spend my days and nights in what I can only describe,' I tell him, 'as a maelstrom of despair,' while at the art school, leaning over my design for a record sleeve for Haydn's 'Creation', the graphics teacher and vintage car enthusiast observes, 'It's too much like a painting.'

'That's what I like,' (a vortex of swirls and whirls in variegated colours).

'This is graphics,' Wormald declares. 'Painting is finished,' he goes on. 'I had a friend at college who now earns his living like everyone else, and who, whenever he wanted to paint a picture, closed his eyes and painted it in his head. Not only does it save money and paint and canvas but time.' He waves his leather-elbowed, tweed-jacketed arm.

But what, after all, I mentally enquire, drew me to self-expression? A feeling – as grave, as inspiriting, as falling in love: as predictable – and as simple – as reading aloud, 'Who is the happy warrior, who is he, whom every man in arms would wish to be?' gained momentum with, 'How oft, on moonlit nights,' and reached a climax with, 'The violin sobs of the autumn wound my heart with a monotonous languor . . .'

Or wasn't it, I reflected (sitting upstairs on the bus on which, downstairs, I am sitting now), my gazing at the familiar landscape of field and wood and hill and dell – the rolling countryside between Ardsley and Linfield – and specifically at the colliery tracks leading from the massive Culloden Pit (a phalanx of coke ovens along one side) endeavouring, beneath the industrial dereliction, to identify the contour of the original fields; or those early mornings in camp at Broughton Woods, looking out from our tree-enclosed clearing (approached, up the slope, like a castle mound) with its view of the iron-workings

138

of the medieval monks on the opposite valley side, and the mounds of the more recent gin-pits covered in moor grass and silver birch; the grandeur of that mist-strewn valley that formed a boundary to Broughton Springs (the sun gilding the trees still wet with dew and, in the furthest distance, the Pennine hills: where the limestone uplands meet the sandstone valleys), the wood-smoke rising from the roped-off fire, the smell of bacon and mushroom frying, the sound of the earliest risers washing in the stream below, the towel-draped figures emerging from the game keeper's cottage which, ruined, provided us with our alternative earth-closet?

Or singing round the fire at night, the moon pinioned to the branches overhead; or those afternoons when, shrieking, we mounted the truck on the tiny, narrow-gauged timber-merchant's rails and rattled and swayed to the wood-shed below (the draped shape of the circular saw: the scoured texture of its metal sides, the angularity of its savage teeth: the smell of wood and the sensuous mounds of resinous dust): that sensation of release, evoked in the bowels, that came with those feelings of beauty and peace?

'Aren't you a romantic?' Wormald enquires, leaning over my 'Creation' design – the lettering of 'Haydn' not all that grand: couldn't I have chosen an orchestra shorter than the 'Phil-harmonic'?

'What's romantic?' I enquire.

'Do you mean, what is the romantic comprised of, *Harry*, or what is romantic in you?'

'In me.'

'By definition,' he says, 'they're both the same. Take, for instance, your addiction to *art*,' (pronounced with a scarcely silent prefix 'f' and an indefinite extension of the vowel). '*Aaaart* has been superseded by life. Who, for instance, is the most significant painter of our time?' voice raised to reach my fellow students scattered, on stools, around the design-room tables, each listening with an interest verging on obsession to this putting down of 'Harry': 'Picasso!' comes up their single cry.

139

'Who is a parodist,' Wormald says. 'Who, half a century before you did, Harry, got the message. When the philistine public – condemned by people like yourself – say that modern art is rubbish, they are, in reality, speaking the truth. Why paint a landscape or a figure when a camera can do it for you, in a matter of seconds, and, further, if required, can make it *move?*'

Discussions of this nature are 'rationalisations', as Maidstone would put it, of Wormald's antipathy to me as a person, viz: 'Your determination to turn every student exercise into a work of art, to eschew not only propriety but common sense, will condemn you to obscurity for the rest of your life. Or do you extol the virtue of living in a garret? Have you ever *known* an artist in a garret? I knew one in London who used to speak like you – until he ended up having to eat his candle.'

Wormald is my antagonist: blue-eyed, fair-haired, axe-wielding (philistine): a Saxon type. His attitude, if more perniciously expressed, is endorsed by the pipe-toting Principal, Bairstow, who not only talks but looks like a miner: short, stocky, with bowed legs. 'What dost think thy's doing, Pisschapel?' on a painting I've stuck on a wall. 'Thy's only here to study,' (not, he was about to go on, to paint bloody pictures).

'My name's Fenchurch,' I tell him.

'Fenchurch, Pisschapel, thy's only here for one thing,' adding to Dawlish, his second-in-command, 'They all look alike to me.' Balding, with a head like a boulder lying, centuries-smoothed, in a Pennine stream, he stalks the rooms of his cultural outpost as might a Roman his beleaguered fort on the outermost fringes of his northern empire: the barbarian hosts have worn him down (assimilated him into their barbarian culture – 'culture', as he might otherwise have known it, a pernicious reminder of all he has left behind in the sun-drenched streets of Rome: days of love and wine and roses – refinement, taste, and self-expression). Much of the beleaguered man of action is evident in his attitude to me: the look which declares, 'You think you're destined for the capital, do you? (Afternoons in the Colosseum, nights at the Baths of Caracalla). I'll be buggered if you'll get away, my friend

140

(Pisschapel or Fenchurch), while I'm condemned to stay in this benighted fucking hole. You'll stick it out like I do. As for *art*...'). He comes into the design-room and, reminded of who I am, remarks, 'You're the artist, are you?' adding to the much-tried Dawlish as he walks away, 'We'll knock that bloody nonsense out. We don't want a place of pussy-footing pansies here.'

My philosophy takes root in opposition.

'I beg your pardon?' the man beside me says again.

I find relief in Isabella: I meet her sometimes once a week: the cost of the 'studio', when it becomes too much (refusing her offer to finance it), obliges us, once more, to resort to a field outside the town – lying beside the road along which the Linfield–Ardsley bus comes twice within the hour: we meet in wind and sun and rain, something monstrous – insatiable, demonic, malign – in everything we do.

'I'm not sure,' she had said on the day I had visited her at Ardsley, 'that it means as much to me as it does to you. That is to say,' she suddenly declared, lying against the pillow as she watched me dress, 'I could go on seeing you without this happening. I do it,' she went on, 'because it means so much to you. To see you so moved and raptured, raptures and moves me, too.'

We are, as it happens, mistaken more and more often for mother and son ('Would your son like another cup of tea?' in the café: 'Your son got your ticket for you, missis,' if we are separated on the bus). She is terrified of being recognised by one of Corcoran's drivers (or, indeed, by anyone from the village: 'I'd like to tell everyone how I feel. There's so much I'd like to confess. But there is, of course,' she'd go on, 'no one.').

On one occasion she didn't turn up.

'Has your mother been ill?' I asked Bea the next time we met.

She shook her head. 'She's been quite perky recently,' she said. 'Over and above her usual self. I've never seen her quite so loud. I suppose,' she went on, 'it's the middle-age crisis, but she's happier than I've known her all my life. She's always asking, of course, after you. "You must look after Richard," she says. As if you were an invalid. "He has," she often says, "a very hard life." '

'She's not been ill?'

'Far from it.'

'I thought I saw her in town the other day. It must,' I tell her, 'have been someone else.'

'If she was looking ill,' she smiles, 'it must have been someone else.'

'In any case,' I tell her, 'you must give her my love.'

'Oh, I shall,' she says. 'She knows how much you admire her.'

'How?' I ask.

'A woman's instinct, Richard!' She laughs. 'As for she and I,' she laughs again, 'one woman to another.'

I didn't see her, nor did I hear from her for several days: I kept away from Ardsley, meeting Bea at the weekend and most schooldays in town. I felt, alternately, relief and alarm – relief that, at last, the relationship was coming to an end (had conceivably, already ended), alarm that, if not the whole of it, something of what had been going on had been discovered – and if not by Corcoran, someone else (Bea still in the dark). It was, I reflected, so unlike her not to keep in touch; although I wrote to her each day – 'I miss you' (platitudinously) 'more than I can say' – re-discovering, in her absence, she meant more to me than often she did when the two of us were together – I tore each letter up. I wrote appraisals of her figure – her eyes, her nose her mouth: her waist, her hips: I imagined her, as Wormald would have recommended, in my head, then drew her naked as I had many times before (several of which drawings I placed in my folder to take to the Drayburgh). 'If I've nothing else to show for it, I might as well,' I thought, 'keep these.'

Then came Bea's message, as I saw her off to Ardsley one evening, 'Mummy leaves for Clare's and Veronica's tomorrow,' (the two widows living together). 'I'm to follow at the weekend.

So are you. She's already bought, she says, the tickets'. I astonished the following day to find a message at the college, a ticket attached, 'I've gone ahead with Mummy. Come as soon as you can. I'm sure we'll have a wonderful time, all five of us together. I'll meet you if you ring,' a telephone number and an address scrawled beneath with, 'Mummy sends her love.' In brackets: 'Not as much as I.'

12

THE TRAIN moves steadily to the south: I sit by a window, hemmed in by a boisterous family, their suitcases piled with my hold-all in the rack above my head. A sense of desolation (arguments at home about my leaving, arguments about the cost, set against my Chamberlains earnings) is lightened by the prospect of meeting Bea but, more potently, being re-united with Isabella (what, I am endlessly reflecting, is she up to: are we, in future, only to meet in the company of other people?). A branch line (the sun is setting); shadows come down from a range of unfamiliar hills (a chilling of the air inside the carriage). I imagine, as the shadows lengthen – coalesce and deepen – I am going beyond the unknown village where Bea and her mother and her aunts are waiting – beyond the south coast where (evidently) our holiday is booked, beyond the English Channel, beyond the coast of France – to a world of art and self-expression.

'I beg your pardon?' the man beside me says again and, shuffling my feet inside my slippers, I gaze at a landscape of ploughed fields and copses, and the unreclaimed, perpetual gin-pits standing up like tumuli from the cultivated ground: we breast a rise: overhung by cloud are the steeples, the domes and the towers of Linfield – in silhouette, not unlike the profile of a castle.

'I was recalling,' I tell him, 'the time I came this way before and saw, as I'm seeing now, the town of Linfield, laid out like a ghost.'

'A ghost?' The man has a pouting lower lip: saliva occupies

each corner of his mouth. His nose is long, his eyes – how much, I idly reflect, have I told him? – inquisitive and strong: his nails – his adjacent hand gripping the seat in front, the barrier of his arm between us – need cleaning.

'Visited by Defoe, Doctor Johnson and – when he caught the wrong train from London – Wordsworth,' the buildings caught in the midday light with, on the slope beyond them, the dull, red glow of Onasett (tiled roofs, brick and pebble-dashed walls) with, at the summit, the short, square tower of Onasett church, the pyramidal roof of the church hall beside it, the long, low structure of Onasett school and, at the highest point of all, the forbidding walls and block-like structures of the isolation hospital. (O happy land!)

'I lived there as a child, a youth.' Beyond the cathedral spire, the County Hall dome, the Town Hall tower – in the shadow of which resided the Linfield College of Art (now closed, its site occupied by a college of technology) – beyond, too, the gothic turrets that marked the site of the former Parochial School and which is now occupied by the renowned King Edward's. 'I am an Old Edwardian, of course, myself and yearly receive the *Edwardian* magazine in which some of my more celebrated feats have been set down, amongst the other sensations of Edwardian life, like the redoubtable feat, last season, of the First Fifteen and the First Eleven having never lost a match – a precedent which was created when I played in the First Fifteen myself. It's not for nothing that my name is Fenchurch, though my books are never on sale in the town, nor have my plays been performed in the theatre, nor my paintings exhibited in the gallery. I have often reflected that a Freeman of Linfield is the very least I might have expected – a golden key to a golden city – but, I'm afraid, apart from an occasional demand for money on behalf of a charity, not a tinkle. I was telling Maidstone, a man of not immodest achievement himself, Sub-Dean of the medical school and Professor of Psychiatry at the North London Royal – the largest teaching hospital in Europe, second only to the Konecki Foundation in New York for the progressive treatment of, amongst many other

145

animadversions, anxiety neurosis conjoined with clinical depression – that, despite a lifetime of artistic endeavour, most of it centred on, if not inspired by this very town and my experiences in it, it has failed to raise a cloud in anything that might be discerned as my direction: not one hand raised to a furrowed brow to give this returning son of home a signal of approbation.'

'Are you,' the man asks me, 'mad?' (more statement, I reflect, than speculation).

'No,' I tell him. 'I am going to Linfield.'

For there, not one hundred yards from the side of the road, where the bus has pulled up to allow a figure not unlike Isabella to ascend, is the wood – or remains of it – where, on many a weekday afternoon and on an occasional summer evening, she and I – hidden from the road yet able to see, through a barricade of leaves, the approach of this, the Ardsley bus – had lain, if not on my familiar, paint-flecked raincoat, on a bed of cushioning leaves. By a curious coincidence the woman coming into the bus – easing her way between the seats – is of the same age as Isabella (of those days): greying at the temples, her face lined, her hands (the backs) marked by tiny blotches, her breasts subsiding above the belted waist of her coat (her abdomen no doubt flecked with post-natal creases, her legs with varicose veins – scarcely, of course, like Bella at all), she takes her seat, as the bus moves off, diagonally across from where I am sitting and, prompted by a desire to re-acquaint myself with those distant times, I smile, and feel an involuntary lurch (an alarming spasm as, without any prevarication, she smiles directly back): a pleasant, rotund face, unlike the austere sanguinity of Bella's, but nevertheless, in that instance, the embodiment of a love that, no sooner had I won, I lost. By the same extraordinary coincidence, outside, on the road, stands a youth – of nineteen, perhaps twenty years – who waves and she, as the bus departs, having acknowledged me, waves back, her head ducked down in that inimitable fashion (love! love!). 'Linfield,' the man beside me says.

'Not much to write home about,' I tell him, for the familiar

146

headgears, waste-heaps and coal-black ponds which stood like sentinels on either side of the road have been displaced by uniformly cambered slopes on which, asymmetrically (deceiving no one as to their spontaneity), have been planted tiny, posted trees and shrubs, the equally anonymously distributed grass sprinkled with daffodils and tulips.

'It's not a bad place,' the man replies, and adds, 'Particularly the market,' I distracted by the woman, her body (her body!) twisted to wave to the youth in the road behind (no doubt, her son) – reminding me less and less of Isabella than of the feelings she inspired.

The station is lit by a single lamp: I take down my hold-all and clamber out – stiff, aching (the confinement of the carriage), scarcely able to stand. In the shadow of a hut, beyond a tiny barrier – the shadow cast by the single lamp – not Isabella but Bea is waiting: a summer dress, a summer coat: white ankle socks and flat-heeled shoes.

We kiss.

'Are you all right?' She takes my hand (my hold-all in the other).

'How far do we have to go?'

'Not far,' darkness all around, the train, a string of lights, tracing its course along, it appears, the bed of a valley. Disparate lights, scattered across a slope, blend, imperceptibly, into the darkness overhead. 'Are you all right?' she says again.

'I think so.'

A country lane gives way to a residential road: as if on stilts, the tallness of the houses heightens the effect of the steepness of the climb: driveways run up past terraced lawns: flowerbeds cascade with shadowed blooms.

Her aunts – one small and slender (Clare), the other short and stout ('Venny') – are waiting at the door.

'How are you, Richard?' Each shakes my hand.

Bea's mother comes out from a room at the rear (a coal-lit fire, a shaded lamp). 'We wondered where you'd got to.'

'The train was late,' Bea tells them.

147

'Full of holiday crowds,' I add, Isabella clad not in a summer but a woollen dress: sweetness, as I kiss her cheek, is in her breath (restraint, however, in her manner).

A tray of food is laid by the hearth.

'We've got your supper ready.'

We sit by the fire: a slender woman, a less slender one, a less slender one still – and Bea. We talk about the journey ('longer than I expected': we are in the Derbyshire hills) and move on to the arrangements the two aunts and Isabella have made for the following day: a taxi has been booked: breakfast will be early: chores are assigned for making beds, preparing breakfast, washing-up: the room grows warm after the relative chill outside: four women all of whom, because of their inter-action with the one, I love.

I am shown upstairs: an attic window looks out to the roof and the unlit windows of an adjoining house (to a starlit sky, to the flank of a hill, to the silhouette of trees ascending precipitously a steepening slope). I fall asleep, tossed, at intervals, into wakefulness by the strangeness of the bed. I am wakened finally by Bea ('Don't stay in the bedroom, pet,' from one of the aunts on the landing outside): she has brought me a cup of tea and, with a kiss to my cheek, departs.

The taxi arrives: having made the beds, breakfasted, cleaned the house, I carry the cases out with Bea. Her mother (I have never seen Isabella so early in the day – as, on the previous evening, rarely seen her so late at night) is radiant beyond belief (what, I reflect, has she in mind?). My heart leaps as she hands me her case (the softness of her fingers, the harshness of her ring) and, with an impetuosity comprised of foolishness as much as love, I kiss her cheek, she drawing back and saying, 'We'll still be together this evening, dear,' as much bewildered as startled by the gesture.

A genial companionship continues throughout the day, Bea and I opposite each other beside the window, the three women chatting to one another across the carriage, I in love (in love!) with two of them, enamoured of the third (the doe-eyed Clare), infatuated with the fourth (the placid if curious

Veronica: what on earth, her look suggests, does she suspect is going on?).

We reach the coast: a taxi takes us to our two hotels – one earmarked for me (modest), the other (family Edwardian) for the rest. My room is small, filled day and night by the sound of running water. I move the following day, at Bea's suggestion, to one around the corner ('Mummy will pay the difference,' which I refuse): a view of the sea, the fold of a cliff, a clump of pine, the room adjacent occupied by a honeymoon couple, their activities, and conversation, scarcely filtered by a thin partition.

We venture, one morning, into the sea: the sky is clear, the breeze warm: a ball is thrown: much spray and screaming: my arm on Bella's: 'Are you all right?' 'Much, Richard, thank you,' while, from Venny, 'Leave that man alone!'

Evenings walking on the front, trips along the coast in the afternoons (mornings on the beach): breakfasts alone (watching the honeymoon couple kiss, hold hands beneath the table, whisper, head to head, over a newspaper or the menu): dinner (my solitary table immediately beside the dining-room door), a copy of *Don Quixote* propped on the salt cellar before me (six hundred and sixty-eight pages still to go), the problems of the amorous knight infinitesimal beside my own: nights spent listening to the sounds – much laughter – and attempting not to imagine the activities of the honeymoon couple next door: 'You haven't tried it!' 'When?' ('What?') 'Is it bigger than you thought?'

And evenings ('Back at nine, Bea,' Bella. 'I don't want you starting any habits,' and, 'We've been in love, you know, before,' her aunts), lying on a pine-strewn slope, the sea below us, rising and falling: 'What does it matter? I can't stand life being so prescribed. (We'll go to Paris. I'll become an artist.)'

We picnic on the sand, play croquet on the Edwardian lawn (waiters in the hall and on the terrace, squirrels in the pine trees, parasols and tennis, shaded tables: teas carried out on white-linened trays): 'We've got to know one another, Richard,

149

on this holiday, so well,' (Venny). 'It's been, apart from one or two anxieties which, I'm sure, when you grow older, you'll understand, an enormous pleasure to have you with us,' (Clare).

'Perhaps I will see you later?' (Isabella).

'Where?' (as I am leaving).

'The gate of our hotel.'

'When?'

'Say, ten?'

She comes down the driveway between the rhododendrons and the pine trees and takes my hand: I've been gazing up for half an hour at the lighted windows, endeavouring, in the darkness, to work out which is her room and which the aunts'.

'There you are,' she says, and adds, 'I hope you've missed me,' her look both matter-of-fact and full of mischief.

'I've waited for this moment,' I tell her, 'since we arrived.'

'And all those afternoons and evenings with Bea.'

'Only,' I lie, 'as a substitute for you.'

'I've seen how much you look at her. So have Venny and Clare,' she adds.

We walk along the chine: the trees, from the moon above the sea, throw shadows up the slope.

'Why haven't you been in touch?' I ask.

She waves her arm. 'It had to come to an end,' she says. 'The whole thing,' she goes on, 'was quite absurd.'

'I don't see why.' She is, I see now, throwing me at Bea, the whole thing – the holiday, the aunts – a device.

'Divesting me,' I say aloud, and as she adds, 'Of what?' I announce, 'There's not one day gone by when I haven't been tempted to get on a bus and come and see you, Freddie or no Freddie, Bea or not.'

'Oh, that.' She waves her arm again. 'It wasn't real. Coming here, with Clare and Venny, seeing me with women as old or older than myself, I thought, at the very least, would help. That's why,' she adds, 'I had to see you. To make it clear it's at an end. Given time, we'll both relate to one another,' she concludes, 'as we should have done from the start.'

At the summit of the chine I turn her to me: I trace the contour of her cheek, her nose: I press my hand against her mouth.

It must have been midnight when I took her back: after ringing the night porter's bell, I stepped back in the shadows and watched her let into the lighted hall: her legs were bare, her coat, I could see now, stained with grass: a last look round, followed by a smile, blinded by the light.

13

'I WORKED AT that pit' the man declares.

'So did my father.'

'What years were that?' The saliva re-appears at the corner of his mouth: coal-dust darkens the tissue above each eye: like the bark of a silver birch, scars, horizontally, cross his brow.

'Until,' I tell him, 'the end of the Second World War. After that he taught D.P.s – Estonians, Latvians, Lithuanians, Poles. Then he came home and got a job at Onasett.'

'Fenchurch?'

'Right.'

'I never knew him.' Shakes his head. 'That hill they have yonder wa're a pit heap ten year ago. That little lake you see down theer, wi' boats on, were the pithead baths.'

'Vivienne, of course, when I brought her here, enthused about the place,' I tell him, 'no end. As for my father – he was still alive and living in a house at Notton End – he couldn't understand a word she said. She had this accent which came out in private whenever she wished to make an impression. On stage, however, as clear as a bell. "What the bloody hell is she talking about?" he said. "I thought you were married to somebody called Bea." '

'Bea?' the man says.

'I said, "This is Vivienne Wylder, the actress that I wrote you about and, if all goes well, I hope to marry. The second," I told him, "Mrs Fenchurch."

' "Mrs Fenchurch," my father says, "is dead," adding to the putative Mrs Fenchurch, "She died before I did." '

152

' "He's talking about my mother," I said.
' "The finest woman that ever lived!" '

The finest woman, I might have concurred, had it been a mother I could write home about. She took him to live in the south of England, away from the millstone grit and the pits and the valleys and he faded like a flower. You wouldn't think of this place as light, but in his case the light up here was the light he was used to. Today, with the coal-dust gone, the manufactories reduced to rubble, with service facilities littering the place, there's nothing to come back to. Except a present-iment of what this place was like.'

'Like,' says the man, the bus cresting a rise at the top of the Common, before us, on an opposing hill, a view which, from a different direction, I knew as a child, coming down the hill from church (on Sundays), school (on weekdays): a rampart of buildings, black with soot: the dog-toothed spire of All Saints church, the chisel-shaped profile of the Town Hall tower, the rotundity of the County Hall dome – a cornucopia of cornices and pediments, friezes and roofs – as, for instance, we see them now, from a different perspective though a similar distance: 'A softer profile, I have always thought, when viewed,' I tell him, 'from the top of the Common,' the bus speedily descending. 'Nevertheless, one which, at this late stage in my career, returning as an Old Linfieldian ("Floreat Linfieldia! Floreat Edwardia!"), a proselytiser of this indentured place, I very much appreciate. To the extent, as you can see, that this view of my native heath – this Common on which I have won and lost (if only at the Easter Feast) much of what I cherish most in life – brings tears to my eyes. Tears that remind me not only of the women I have loved, the men I most admired, the parents who, having borne me, tore me apart, but, specifically, of my wife, of Isabella, who was not my wife, of Vivienne who, to put it mildly, was the revelation of my later years, an amalgam of Bea and Isabella whom if I'd met – for these things do occasionally happen – as a younger man I would have married, if only to my cost, unable to accommodate her ferocities which,

153

unique to her, were antagonistic to my own. I loved and lost –
and lost. And lost.'

'Are you all right?' the man enquires.

'Perfectly,' I tell him, for my voice has carried to the front
of the bus (we are sitting – a precaution one always takes on
public transport these days – at the rear) and heads have turned
(shoulders raised, I further notice, to the conductor). 'I have
never felt better,' I go on, 'even if, between ourselves, if the
truth were known,' I lower my voice, 'I have been in and out
of a certain institution which – again, between ourselves – I
wouldn't recommend to anyone. Boady Hall,' I breathe the
name, 'is not a place to write home about. It contains people
who destroy themselves, and though Vivienne and I had that
in common – she a genius of gigantic proportions (the greatest
Mrs Macbeth in years), with flaming hair – admittedly, the
effect of dye – and ludicrous make-up – though scarcely any in
later years – we struggled – separately as well as jointly – to
overcome the ravages wreaked upon those who travel, whether
by vocation or not, across what is euphemistically referred to
as "inner space" – a maelstrom of a place, without form or
purpose, the black hole into which the mind descends, transcending all laws and known experience, superseding hope
(and joy and love), and for which the human imagination has
yet to provide a word. I've been there, pal!' I slap his arm. 'I've
got to admit that Vi – Vivienne, as I previously described her
– got to me in ways that no one else quite has. She – like I was
– should have been confined. She went to a private clinic in
the south of London, visited, fatefully, a similar place outside
New York, a third in the suburbs of Los Angeles, a fourth in
San Francisco, and came here, finally, would you believe it, and
begged me to minister to her myself. I – like Our Lord – who
could not save himself. One evening, returning to the house,
I found her gone. Along with her luggage and a bottle of
bleach. An innocuous-looking liquid which I didn't miss for
days. Until, one morning, I went out to the yard. Stoned, she
might have been, before she took it. "How," you are beginning
to ask, "could a man, nurtured in these parts, loved by the

154

mother, as it happened, of his future wife, who made his fortune from books and plays, and, latterly, pictures, incur the hatred of his children and the contempt of his wife?" Reason is one thing, existence another. In reality, of course, they are both the same. You have, without your being aware of it, been sitting next to a man who, in the halls of misfortune, is virtually unique.'

'Are you going to Linfield?' the man enquires and, by way of answering, I reply, 'So you worked at that pit?'

'For twenty-five years.'

'Twenty-five.'

'Fifteen afore that at New Rawlston.'

'Weren't twenty-five men killed there in the nineteen-fifties?'

'Eighteen.'

'Eighteen.'

'My cousin, by marriage, was one of them.'

'My uncle, on my father's side, the youngest one I had, was killed at Arnhem. The largest parachute drop in recorded history. I had a photograph of him, years ago, on Linfield Station, standing with a group of men who were painting the wrought ironwork above the platform. A doughty, good-natured, adventurous fellow who was turned into something little short of a bandit. Times, of course, have changed since then. Qualities like those are not required. His nephew, who inherited from him, if you like, his appetite for painting – not railway stations, I might add, but pictures – for not dissimilar reasons, acquired not dissimilar characteristics. In struggling against, if you like, a not dissimilar opposition he became something of a *bandito* himself, dropping out of the skies onto something little short of a cultural desert, a plain of middle-class sentiment, virtue and ambition. My uncle did it as one of ten thousand, I as one of four or five, most of whom expired on landing or, if not on landing, shortly after. The heat and dryness burnt them up, the peculiar desolation, not to mention isolation, in which, surrounded by good intentions, they found themselves. Unlike them, however, or even my uncle, I had a more peculiar training. Enigmatic . . .'

155

'Linfield,' the man says as we pass over the river, visible above the parapet of the concrete bridge: barges were once drawn up above the concrete weir, moored in ranks, the river front, with its cobbled wharf, overlooked by warehouse buildings, malt kilns, cranes and derricks, dockside offices and chandlers' stores (boat-builders' yards and the hulks of barges). The shiny black coal slip and the rusted metal gantries on the coal-wharf, which stood closest to the bridge (on the site of Much the Miller's mill in the legendary accounts of Robin Hood), have gone: a tree-lined walk, relieved by rockeries and stone embankments (a children's playground) and by stone-paved footpaths, following the contour of the river, winds off in the direction of the one remaining mill. The tang of the river is still the same, as is the view on the opposite side of the bridge: an expanse of sky where the valley of the Lin, taking leave of its stone embankments and its gorge-like exit below the town, winds across the shoals of Ferry Ford where the Romans made their earliest crossing.

Beyond the bridge, the bus enters the narrowing streets of the town.

'I get off here.' The man gets up beside me (I feel the warmth of his body). 'Is anybody looking after you?' he adds.

'Lots,' I tell him. 'There'll be a queue.'

'You're going to the bus station, are you?' signalling to the conductor.

'If I don't get off before.'

The bus pulls up: several passengers, preceding the man, descend.

'He's getting off at the bus station,' he says to the conductor. 'You may need the help of a bobby.'

He disappears; at least, I lose sight of him as he steps down to the pavement: more people than I might reasonably have anticipated are milling about outside.

I nod at the woman across the aisle. 'A friend of mine. He worked,' I tell her, 'at New Rawlston, but is presently un-employed.'

'He looks old enough to be retired,' she says.

156

'That as well,' I tell her, and add, 'Your name isn't Isabella, by any chance?'

'It isn't,' she says, refraining from informing me what it is.

'You look like a Mrs Corcoran,' I tell her, 'whose maiden name was Kells.'

· 'Not me.' She smiles.

'You have the same eyes, if not the same mouth. Your hair,' I go on, 'is different. Hers was red, or, to be precise, a curious magenta, a mixture of the celt and the latin. She had, when I knew her, a striking warmth, of personality, that is, as well as manner, which your eyes and your mouth remind me of. In addition,' I indicate these features by pointing at a spot beneath my eye, 'a high, arched nose and glancing cheekbones which, in her daughter's face, was characterised by convergent brows, indicating, in their obtrusiveness, a predisposition, I've been told, to paranoia. That wasn't your son, by any chance, who saw you off at the bus-stop?'

'My nephew.'

'Nephew.'

I am about to add, 'A new one on me,' when she continues, 'My sister's son. They live at Wrainthorpe,' (a village close to the stop where the bus picked her up: how often had Isabella said, 'The Wrainthorpe stop,' on her journeys from Ardsley to me).

'Linfield,' I tell her, 'is a curious place. On the site of the cathedral, for instance, which we're passing now,' (its cleaned sandstone façade visible through the windows on her side of the bus), 'was a sacred grove, in pre-historic times, and, subsequent to that, in Roman times, a temple to Diana. That wouldn't, by any chance, be your name?'

The woman has dark hair: it obtrudes upon her collar in a way which, once I had released it, Isabella's did, cascading down in shiny bright waves; her features, like Bella's, are set widely apart (she may, in effect, be not much older than myself), creating an impression of openness and candour, and – not to be sneezed at in a woman – humour.

'No,' she says.

'And it isn't Isabella.'

'I'm a housewife,' she says (the bus coming to a halt, passengers, with glances in our direction, getting off).

'That's the greatest calling on earth,' I tell her. 'Like "miner" is for men. Where would we be,' I go on, 'without you?' she, however, already rising (the bus in the Bull Ring and, having circuited Queen Victoria's statue on its central island, entering the bus station). 'My friend, the one I mentioned, Isabella, and I haunted this place. A veritable companion,' I tell her, 'in my hour of need. There were thirty years or more between us,' calling over the shoulders of the passengers between us, she already some distance down the aisle. 'More an obstacle in her eyes than it was, of course, in mine, age, inevitably, a preoccupation when appearances are all that count. Yet age, in her case,' raising my voice, 'was her one credential. It informed not only her appearance but her thoughts. Everything she said was imbued with grandeur, with the ineffable mystery of – how otherwise could I describe it – *being in love*.'

I am talking – as far as I can discern – to the concrete pavement onto which – the final passenger to leave the bus – I have now descended. Only the conductor – and, with the conductor, his attention having been attracted, the driver – contemplate my struggle for, in descending, having lost one slipper, I am searching for it in the gutter between the side of the bus and the exceptionally high kerb of the bus station's pavement.

'Perhaps,' I tell the conductor, 'I have lost it inside,' and having re-entered the vehicle, discover it, as I'd anticipated, beneath my seat (so anxious to engage my fellow-passenger's interest: what more, I reflect, have I to lose?). On the seat itself are my sketchbook and pencil. 'Good job I came back,' I add. 'Bringing the great indoors outdoors is invariably, I've discovered, the corollary of wearing one's indoor footwear in the street. Normally, to move at all, I require a stick. As it is, from the moment I got up this morning I felt my hour had come. I must do today what I cannot put off any longer. "I will go outside," I said, "and draw a tree." '

Across the bus station I see the woman.

'That's not the Onasett stop she's waiting at?' I ask, to which the conductor replies, 'The opposite end,' and then, 'Do you want me to put you back on the one to Ardsley?'

'My family live at Onasett,' I tell him. 'Or did. Previous to that, of course, myself.'

The bus doors hiss to behind my back.

I cross to the queue where the woman is waiting and, with a geniality which had, I assume, characterised my previous remarks, enquire, 'Would you like a cup of tea?'

'No, thank you,' she says.

'Coffee?'

'No, thank you.'

'I have the money.'

'So have I,' she says, 'but my bus will be here any minute.'

'The cafeteria,' I tell her, 'is directly opposite the bus station entrance. We can, once we spot it, be back in no time at all.'

'No, thank you,' she says a third time at which a man standing in the queue beside her enquires, 'Is this man bothering you in any way?'

'He is,' she says, 'as a matter of fact,' to which I reply, 'She is like a very old friend of mine. Someone to whom I was devoted. A woman of infinite charm,' to which the man – of no great height – responds by placing himself between the two of us. 'I'd advise you to clear off before I have you taken off,' he says.

'She spoke to me on the bus,' I tell him, 'and smiled at me in a way which, if it hadn't been broken already, would have seriously incommoded my heart. She doesn't know what power she's got. What wonder. What grace. Like Isabella. Like Bea. (Bea stands for Beatrice, by the way),' I add. 'If only you knew how hard it is, not only to focus my thoughts on what, specifically, is happening now, but, out of the memories and feelings associated with this place – the majority to do, if not with love, a state of mind conducive to it – to extract a phrase, an appropriate noun, an adjective which describes what it is I would wish to say, you wouldn't feel obliged, as, evidently, from

159

the pressure of your hand against my chest, you are feeling now, to disengage me from this woman,' peering round to find a woman, not unlike her, standing in her place. 'All I wish to confess,' I confirm to this second figure, 'is that, while I may not be compos mentis, I am nevertheless mentis par dessous, which is another way of announcing that Maidstone and the present Raynor and, before that, the renowned Mackendrick, the transcendentalist Russo-Scottish psychoanalyst whose mother and father were born in the Ukraine, pronounced me "rational", in the latter's phrase, "this side of God", the line a quotation from one of my plays, for want of a better appellation, *A Better Man*, which drew Mackendrick's attention to me in the first place,' concluding, 'Could you direct me to the Onasett stop? I merely wished to ask.'

'This, with one or two exceptions, is the most familiar place on earth,' I tell the man who is waiting there. 'I have endured more, waiting on this spot, than I have on any other. I know this place like the back of my hand. Or, better still, the palm.'

I hold it out.

'A simian line, the heart and head line combined in a single furrow, not unlike an ape's. A sign,' I add, 'of criminality – two out of three condemnees, in a famous survey, possessed this characteristic – or of high, exceptionally high artistic endeavour. Michelangelo, Leonardo, as well as Shakespeare, are often quoted as examples. Which latter case applies to me, the line between crime and art, as that between sadness and madness, not to mention badness, being very thin indeed.'

Bowed down by a bag of shopping, after glancing at my hand, the man announces, 'Mad!' to a figure standing on his other side (a woman) who, in turn, stands at the head of a very large queue.

'It is the Onasett stop,' the woman says, 'but you have to join the other end.'

'I shall,' I tell her and peruse the faces as I move along the line: not once, in my youth, could I have walked along this queue and not seen a dozen, if not half a dozen, if not two or three familiar faces: here Bea would queue (to come and see

160

me); here I would queue after seeing her off; here my mother waited with a weekend's shopping; here my brothers and I on our way from school (the redoubtable King Edward's); here our father on his trips from town; our neighbours, now deceased, from a multitude of errands.

'It's all too much,' I tell a child, the last figure in the queue – and who, with a violent tug, is propelled towards its mother – as I, with similar alacrity (if by invisible strands), was propelled to mine. 'Is this the Onasett stop?' I ask her.

'It is,' she says, and turns aside.

'I too stood here,' I tell her, 'as a child,' and add, 'Or, rather, in the Bull Ring. This place wasn't built until after the Second World War, an area of derelict streets and houses which were bulldozed to the ground before the war began and remained like that until five years after when pre-stressed concrete came to the fore. It's why,' I add, 'it's dropping to pieces. How is Onasett?' I enquire.

Her head turned from me, she remarks, 'Not bad,' as she might, I reflect, of a dog or a husband.

'Not good,' I might have said, but respond, 'That place was paradise on earth. Bricks from Chalkley's Quarry. I suppose that's gone as well. A hole in the ground directly opposite the first road they cut across Onasett Common, a buttress of land, crossed and criss-crossed by dry stone walls, rising to the peak of Onasett Moor, in turn looking out to the Pennine uplands where we, the Onasettians, camped as boys, leaders of the tribe, despatched, in later years, to the four corners of the earth.'

The war went on for a very long time: in some instances, my dear, it never stopped; stepping, as I did, at the age of six, into the field at the back of the house to see reality re-valued: overhead the enemy lurked (about to descend at any moment): nothing after that could be the same, the brick no longer brick, the grass no longer grass, the sky no longer sky, embodiments, merely, of a soon-to-be-unleashed propensity for destruction.

And, secondly, of course, the films of Buchenwald, Auschwitz, Dachau and Belsen: figures that walked into and out of the mind, their ingress and egress continuing for ever.

161

'That man,' the child says, 'is wearing his slippers.'

'Don't point.' The mother draws the child's arm in the opposite direction. 'It's crude.'

Conversely, would I recognise the youth who, thirty-five years ago, came to this stop: the dark-eyed look, the shadowed frown (two vertical creases incising his brow), the drawn-in cheeks – robosity itself, and yet constrained: braced like an animal before a jump which it, and it alone can see (the impediment of his years ahead, the liabilities of temperament)? I doubt, looking round, I would know him at all. Would he, for instance, be disguised as that long-haired, broad-shouldered figure over there who, while maintaining the appearance of having succumbed to the proprieties of everyday life (job, home, wife, car), has preserved a sense of indecorum: the wide-legged stance, the unshaven jaw, a wild-eyed look beneath a furrowed brow? Or – council house, unemployment cheque (disassociation) – is he a plumber on his way from one job to another, the bag at his feet containing, if not his tools, his week-long washing? Or the youth over there with a close-cropped head, jeaned and denim-jacketed (arms thrust to his elbows in his pouch-like pockets), he the embodiment of what I, dark-eyed and shadow-browed, embodied then: an indisposition to take yes or no for an answer, recalcitrant, obtuse, inapposite, grand?

'I lived at Onasett for twenty years,' I tell the mother. 'The first twenty years, of course, are supposed to be the best, the first five being the most important. Quite a sentence when, at that age, there is no redress. Sentenced, I'd say, without a hearing. It was only when I published my own *Theory of the Mind* that this scheme of things had to be revised. You must have heard of *New Mind Theory*, or *The Narrative or Pentadic Theory of the Mind* (attributed exclusively,' I tell her, 'to myself).'

By 'mind', of course, I mean the psyche.

'It may not be commonly known, for instance, that I made much of my recent reputation by re-writing a tripartite theory of the same, replacing it with a more clinically exact one of five recognisable selves.'

162

Viz:

the primal self,

common to us all, described as the reservoir of primal appetites;

the intrinsic self,

the unique conjunction of two equally unique parental systems;

the construct self,

the interaction of the primal and the intrinsic selves with everything around them;

and the preceptorial self,

which was the validating system that emerged from the conjunction of the previous three.

'My extra-curricular discovery was of the fifth self, a super-authorial presence which, while independent of the previous four, was nevertheless integral to them. The impersonal element we become aware of when we sleep, the still, small voice of poetical inspiration – '

'Are you all right?'

'A totality I named "the composite self".'

A policeman – I am aware, merely, of the darkness of his sleeve, and of a silver button which secures a flap (of his pocket) above his heart – and of his finger and his thumb as he takes (perhaps has taken now for quite some time) my elbow.

'Perfectly,' I tell him.

'Where are you going?' (he enquires).

'Onasett,' I tell him.

'The bus,' he says, 'has left.'

He is – I glance up at his face – younger than his voice suggests: a moustache – a low, triangular shape, bifurcated, curiously, by a bare, scar-like patch – lies above a juvenile and singularly ill-formed mouth: sallow cheeks but not unfriendly eyes – immaturity bolstered by authority (constrained, temperamentally, by a lack of style).

He might, on the other hand – not unusual in his profession – have been in an accident.

'I am,' I tell him, 'waiting for the next.'

163

'You live at Onasett?' (Definitely an impediment in speaking, brevity a tool).

'I did. Presently,' I add, 'I live in London. Are you an inspector?'

'No, sir.'

'Nor, I suspect, an Old Edwardian.'

'No, sir.'

'You have a ring of the comprehensive.'

'Yes, sir.'

'All my children went to comprehensive. On principle. It did none of them more than adequate harm. "Education is a right, not a privilege," I told them. "Not a commodity," I expanded, "to be bought. Anyone who thinks it is confounds the first principle of a democracy. No democracy can exist that compounds within its system private education. Privilege abrogates demos." '

'Do you need any help?' he enquires.

'None,' I tell him, 'I can think of. Unless you have, secreted upon your person, a means of redressing pain.'

'Pain, sir?'

'Synonymous with "mind", a physiological phenomenon not contingent upon environment. Indeed, not contingent on anything discernible at all. Were you aware, for instance, that the incidence of psychosis in the rural communities of East Africa – a region beset by natural disasters of every type – is precisely the same as it is in the English home counties? It makes a nonsense of the current superstition that form determines content, or, indeed, determines anything at all. Whereas odium theologicum characterised the previous century, odium psychologicum characterises the present. Odium politicum, I haven't a doubt, will follow.'

'Are you a school teacher?' An impulse to take out a notebook is replaced by a gesture which involves the unhitching of a two-way radio from the region of his waist.

'I was. In some of the worst schools in the United Kingdom. Whitechapel, Dalston, Islington, Hackney. Seventeen, three of them described at the time, in a report from Her Majesty's

164

Inspectorate, as amongst the four worst schools in Great Britain. You name it: I've seen it. Latterly, I have decided art and didacticism do not mix, unlike sentiment and religion, lunacy and charm, except, of course, in the subtlest sense, that the former may serve a moral purpose. For instance – '

'Are you staying in town?'

'With my daughter. Her husband, Charles, is the principal partner in Stott, Stevens and Hopcroft, barristers at large. The final epithet, of course, applying to their fees. Though Charlie, to be fair, is the chairman of the local constituency Labour Party which returns a member to parliament at each election with the second largest majority in the United Kingdom. Or did until the pit was closed.'

'Ardsley?' he enquires.

'Fenchurch is her maiden name, which happens to be mine. Perhaps you've heard of it?'

He shakes his head.

'What sort of education did you have? Apart from one who died a hundred years ago, I'm the only author – not to mention artist – this town has ever had.'

'My father was a policeman and couldn't afford to keep me in school,' he says.

'Mine was a miner and thought he could. First at Callwood Pit and then at Onasett. Both gone. I passed the former, coming into town. Not a sign it ever existed. Ground smooth as silk stretching to the summit of a slope which, in the old days, was decorated solely by a gantry from which the waste-trucks used to tip their load, leaving a plume, on windy days, blowing across the fields, invariably in the direction of Ardsley. I suppose he's still alive.'

'Alive?' He shifts his weight from one foot to the other.

'Your father.'

'Retired.'

'Not much older than I am.'

'No, sir,' he says, and adds, 'younger, I should think.'

At which a shadow falls upon us. 'Onasett,' I tell him, as a bus pulls up by the kerb. 'I might see you,' I go on, 'when I return,' clambering inside – at the head of a queue, formed behind my back, unnoticed.

He watches me take my seat inside (to one side of the driver, anxious, in this instance, to see ahead). I nod my head, point at the sky, mouth, 'Fair,' and nod again. The vehicle sways: people clamber overhead: with one or two groans the vehicle subsides. 'No standing,' I announce, 'on the upper deck. No smoking on the lower. No spitting, of course, on upper or lower!'

The policeman's head appears at the door.

'All right, conductor?' addressing the man who, with something of a smile, has listened to my comments.

'It's all right by me, officer,' the man declares.

'Something of a comic,' the policeman says.

'So I see,' the conductor replies.

Soon to be made redundant (I have heard from Etty): driver-only buses, abandoned because of vandalism, about to be reprieved.

The bus drives out: I see a perspective of the cathedral above the roofs of the nearby shops, the pilastered, tall-windowed façade of the old Mechanics' Institute, subsequently the Music Saloon and now the City Museum, the Town Hall tower – the municipal proponents of a bygone age, the bus passing the end of North Parade so quickly that this vista is curtailed, allowing a glimpse only of the placarded site of the ancient Butter Cross in Cross Square before, with an accelerating roar, we reach the broader expanse of once tree-lined Westgate.

Directly ahead, beyond the driver's bulky figure, across, at the foot of our descending slope, a shallow valley, lies the more precipitous hill at Onasett – framed, in this instance, by the distant, smooth-featured profile of the misted Pennine hills.

'I used to be a Peewit, a jolly Peewit, too, but now I've given up Pee-witting I don't know what to do, I'm growing old and weary and I can Peewit no more, so I'm going to work my passage if I can. Back to Ona-sett, happy land! I'm going to work my passage if I can!'

*

Within himself the putative Richard Fenchurch feels diminished (indisposed, withdrawn) out of his depth, bewildered by his situation – the circumstances which enclose him on every side (and the feelings they evoke). He considers the part of him he and his parents haven't spent, writes (somewhere in his diary – 'Any more fares?' the conductor enquires), "What I am attempting to do appears impossible, reconciling a reflective life with one which is active. There is something in the atmosphere which inhibits me from making contact – unless the willingness to listen is all the contact I require. My invalidity is as absurd as it is oppressive. ('Who wants to be an artist? Our budding Fenchurch here!')"

Fenchurch, the indomitable Fenchurch, his feet, divested of his slippers, shuffling in the debris on the floor of the bus, consults his parents: 'Which stop do you want?' the conductor enquires.

'Is Spinney Moor still there?'

'It is.'

'Spinney Moor,' I tell him, across a gap of forty years. He slides the ticket out, hands me the change.

'Soon to be dispensed with, conductors and the like.'

'They are.'

'Me, too,' I am about to tell him.

'Any more?' without listening: sets off to the stairs.

Onasett, a phalanx of red-tiled houses, rises up ahead.

'On the other hand,' I tell the woman beside me, 'I have, subsequent to the experiences of the past few months, if not the past five years, acquired a tendency to fall in love with every woman I meet.'

She smiles, loaded down with shopping (no view of the way ahead).

'Her physical appearance, for instance, is infused with what I can only describe as the elemental, something little short, I would say, of the irresistibly divine, a quality unimpeded by what, normally, where female beauty is concerned, might be considered a liability, age. Or even insanity, in one or two

167

instances, hence my preoccupation, verging on obsession, with Vi.'

Such a woman is seated by me now: middle-aged, wearied (by circumstance – class, temperament, geographical location – as well as shopping): dark eyes, with folded skin beneath each one, the cheeks drawn in, the mouth crudely fashioned by the indelicate use of make-up: yet, despite the corrugation of skin beneath her chin, despite the amplitude of her waist and bosom – exceeding the demands, the latter, of any reasonable requirement – despite her smile (as much an expression of pain as pleasure) she is everything I love: 'I am,' I tell her, 'from Onasett myself, eulogised by the Reverend Swanson in his memorable creation, "Happy Land!", the first vicar of St Michael's, a song we sang, invariably, on the backs of lorries when returning home from camp. *O happy land!*'

Teeth regular and artificial: she smiles again – I recalling, in that instant, Bella's habit, while talking by the fire, seated across the hearth from Corcoran, of tracing then arranging then re-arranging, the folds of her skirt across her lap – revealing, inadvertently, her stockinged thighs – and further recall the way she lowers her voice – then lightens it – recounting, first with censure, then with humour, an incident witnessed in the village.

She laughed, with me, like a woman who had been restrained from laughing all her life – revealing, in the process, something of the girl she might have been (she *was*, years later showing me – our children, her grandchildren (Etty on her knee) – photographs taken by Kells shortly after the First World War, she in a long skirt and (for those days, I suspected) provocative blouse standing amidst a group of chums: the lean-back of her body – her hands on her hips, her fingers spread-eagled across her stomach – laughing at the father who was taking the picture, her sisters, Venny and Clare, beside her).

I hear a piece of music (played, in reality, at the back of the bus), and am standing at the window of our house in Belsize Park – the fourteen-roomed mansion bought at the height of my career – our youngest daughter, Rebecca, in my arms: I have been living alone in the house for the previous year: Bea, on this particular occasion – a weekend – is in a hotel, in Brighton, with her lover, Albert. Normally, she and Rebecca live in their flat, close to the Medical Research Centre at Barnet. An airship is passing overhead – an aluminium-coloured capsule with the name of a beverage inscribed along one side: a tiny sliver of rope dangles from its prow (a low murmur, its engines, like a vacuum cleaner being pushed across the sky).

A constant occupation of mine over the previous year, I am standing at the window, looking out: a tiny cabin is slung beneath the vehicle overhead (swaying and rearing, ducking and bowing) and behind its square-shaped windows we imagine we can see pale faces gazing down. Five hundred feet, perhaps, above our heads, the airship gives the impression (Beckie flinching unconsciously, as she glances up) of being close enough to step inside (an involuntary lurch, we might find it dangling in the garden). Below us, in the street a cyclist slows and raises his head: arrested, one foot on the ground, he shields his eyes. Clouds unsheathe the sun.

'I'd like to be up there,' Rebecca says.

She grasps my arm more tightly (forty feet above the ground ourselves: the upstairs front bedroom that, years ago, was occupied by Etty).

Meanwhile, to the south, in a hotel bedroom, at Brighton, her mother: the airship is proceeding in that direction.

'Will it crash?'

I shake my head.

'I think it will.'

'I doubt it.' (She flinches once again.)

'Is Benjie coming?' (our youngest son).

'I shouldn't think so, Beckie.' (Arm aching at her weight.)

'Kenneth?' (our other son).

'Kenneth is abroad,' I tell her.

'Where is that?' (head ducked again).

'The United States. Studying,' I tell her, 'the philosophy of science.' ('Has science a philosophy?' his mother ingenuously enquired when, bright-eyed, dark-haired – her colouring, my features – our eldest son declared his intention of studying at Berkeley. 'Hasn't it, Mum?' he asked, wise, at this stage of her life, to, if not her malignancy, her mischief).

Beckie, as it is, more nearly sees her brothers as uncles, her sisters more nearly as aunts: 'What is a sister?' she enquired, examining Matt dressed for a visit to 10 Downing Street (a species of businesswoman approved of at the time: her own management consultancy at twenty-seven).

'Just the two of us?' she enquires (this last child of our marriage, aged nine).

'What shall we do?'

'Dance?'

I put on a record: we dance to a tune much loved by Benjie (before he left for college) – a whining lyric, drowned by its accompaniment: "Would you leave me? Would you love me? Would you leave me here alone?" an incredulity echoed in my mind as I recall this record being played when – like a storm erupting from a cloudless sky – Bea announced, at breakfast, over a cup of tea, 'A most extraordinary thing has happened. I've fallen in love!'

'Love?' ("Would you leave me? Would you love me? Would you leave me here alone?" whined from Benjie's (then occupied) bedroom – the one in which we are now dancing, at the top of the house).

'Isn't it odd?' (The coincidence, I reflect, of the music, or the state of mind itself?). And then, a second cup of tea to follow the first ('Would you like one, darling?'), 'It's never happened before.'

'Never?'

'No.'

'What about us?'

'Never *in* love.'

'I thought it was.' (I thought I was. I thought we were.)

She shakes her head.

'I was intrigued.'

'Intrigued?'

'By your attempt to reconcile God and Mammon.'

170

'God?'

'Art.' (The working class and everything else.) 'How old was I?' she went on. 'Sixteen? Now, of course, I'm . . .' (she's about to tell me 'fifty-two').

'The same age as your mother when you and I first met.'

'There you are!' She gestures. 'The prime,' she goes on, 'of life.'

Had she, I reflected, ever suspected? She had come across Bella, on one occasion, sneaking a kiss and, unable to explain what was clearly a sensual embrace, I had said, 'Your mother was about to scold me. I was thinking too much of you.'

'Oh, Mum,' she had said, 'can keep you in line,' adding, 'He's like that with all the women, Mum, just as all the men are like that with you.'

'Do you fancy her, sometimes?' she had later enquired.

'As a matter of fact,' I said, but added nothing further for, a moment later, she went on, 'The two of you are often spikey.'

'Spikey?'

'Both Dad and I have noticed. He, after all,' she had gone on, 'was very lucky.'

'Lucky?'

'To have attracted Mum. She could have married any number of men. She still could,' she went on, 'as a matter of fact. She married, as it was, the most handsome one of her time.'

It was in Kells, however – 'Grandpa Kells' – that Bea recognised a challenge (as potent as the challenge – of an altogether different nature – I recognised in her mother). 'To continue,' as she expressed it, 'where Grandpa Kells left off. The war, and the awful Kell Cakes – the uniting of science to a social good – appealed to him in a furtive way as much as it appalled him. I, on the other hand, can see it more clearly: science *and* the social good. The two are indivisible. He, for instance, once the war was over, drifted into supervising the research of others: one of the walking wounded, the ones who were killed but never found out.'

It explained – I always felt – once our children were off our hands, the nights as well as the days spent, in a pool of light, stooped over her microscope – staining her slides, those slivers of cells which came up, under magnification, in a range of colours – lemon, yellow, orange, red – like the pitted surface of a hitherto undiscovered planet. 'I always liked,' she said on one occasion, 'to see you and Mum together. That photograph at the wedding, "like the bride and groom", someone said. Her eyes! I've never seen anything like it! You know her ancestors were pirates and most of the women whores!'

'Supernumerary wives,' I said.

'In a harem.'

'It was described as a private house.'

'In Istanbul?'

'Constantinople.'

'Whores.'

'Concubines.'

'Whores!'

On one occasion, lying in bed, shortly after our honeymoon (spent in a room above a sweet-shop in Camden Town), Bea had said, 'There's something about you which isn't right.'

'What?' I'd asked.

'Something twisted. Even indecent.'

'I wonder what it is,' I said.

'I always felt it,' she said. 'All that innocence,' she went on.

'The first time on the soap-works?' I said.

'The first time you kissed me,' she suddenly confided, 'and, to my surprise, you missed my mouth.'

When I asked her to be more specific, she said, 'Father sensed it. So did mother. They couldn't, at an intuitive level, make you out.'

'Have you never loved me?' I asked her when, in the kitchen, over breakfast (drinking tea), she announced, with characteristic candour, she had 'fallen in love'.

With her mother's gentle smile – that amoral, unassuming smile, the legatee of whores and pirates – she responded, 'I've always loved you, as, indeed,' she'd smilingly continued, 'I love you now, but never,' she had gone on, 'have I been in love. Slightly, perhaps, with that youth from Reading. But not

172

like this. Not really,' she'd concluded, 'like a flame in the bowel.'

'Isn't that uncomfortable?' I'd said, but she'd merely responded, 'Like staining a cell and catching, for the first time, not only the pattern but the purpose of its development.'

'Love and work,' I said, 'in that case, are curiously combined.'

'Yes,' she said, 'I suppose they are,' adding, after pouring another cup, 'It's different for a girl to be in love as opposed to a woman of fifty.'

'Two,' I said, 'to be exact.'

'Over fifty,' she replied.

('Would you leave me? Would you love me? Would you leave me here alone?' whined from the bedroom overhead.)

A tortuous year, that first year of our involvement, her mother and I, one evening, 'caught' by a neighbour in the grounds of the house – a trespasser taking a short-cut from the Ardsley Arms, perhaps, to one of the outlying farms (quicker over the fields) and who, coming across us, late at night, lying on the ground (our 'position' unmistakable) had, Bella suspected, refused to believe his senses: ('I saw his face: I can only conclude he must have seen mine'). A few days later, however, she saw him in the village and he had merely raised his hat in, she confessed, a non-committal manner.

She was seldom, if ever, out of my thoughts: I saw her, or thought I saw her in, if not almost, every middle-aged woman I caught sight of walking in the street, or gazing from a window, or seated in a bus. The risks we took only drove us on (managing, on one occasion, to perform the impossible on the back seat of a bus (how easily one unconsidered act leads to another), she sitting astride my lap, the novelty of the situation – there was one man sitting on his own at the front, the conductor chatting to a chum downstairs, the bus rattling along through the countryside with no one waiting to be picked up – heightened my performance). I had nothing to gauge my actions by: everything was possible (therefore anything was allowed).

'Would you leave me here for ever? Would you leave me here alone?'

I danced with Bella's grandchild. Albert's lover's daughter (the parliamentary private secretary to the Minister of Health: why should he get the benefits of thirty years of marriage?), with H.J. Kells' great-grandchild, the seed of Bea's womb, her magenta hair shining in a swathe the length of her slender back ('I didn't want to come, but Mummy made me!' within minutes of her arrival, jumping on the bed: how like a Kells or a Corcoran to know abandonment when she saw it). 'Is Harriet not coming?' (preferring her brothers to her sisters).

'No.'

'Is Matt?'

'No.'

'Is there anyone to play with?'

'Me.'

'Can we go out?'

'We might.'

'When?'

'You've only just arrived.'

'Daddy Albert takes me out.'

'Where?'

'All over.'

'So do I.'

'You don't.'

'I do.'

'You don't,' (her movements unabating).

While, in a sunlit bedroom, looking out to the English Channel, the possibility, in two or three hours' time, of an airship overhead . . .

A policewoman is standing by my shoulder: she has got on, I am told, at the previous stop (on her way home, I suspect, from duty), her cap at an angle on her coiffured head (the conductor standing behind her): a jowelled jaw, a smear of colouring on each high-boned cheek. 'Your noise is disturbing

174

the passengers,' she says (from 'Happy Land!' to 'Do you love me?').

The engine of the bus, the driver gazing backwards, his head craned down as might a child's in looking through its legs, indicates, with its idling speed, that we are standing at a stop: Thrallstone Park, adjacent to the tinier enclave of Onasett Park, its gates, removed at the beginning of the war, represented by no more than a pair of decapitated pillars (entrance to the architecturally venerated and historically renowned – eighteenth-century 'grand domestic' – Thrallstone House: burnt down and replaced by a comprehensive school – 'impersonal puberty' – erection): beyond, undulating furrowed slopes, scattered here and there with ancient trees, rise to the prominence of Scone Hill, a castle mound, obscured by shrubs which, in their outline against a low, cloud-suspended sky, indicate its man-made profile. 'I've done some of my best pictures,' I indicate the motte, 'from there.'

'As well,' she adds, 'as the dishevelment of your dress.'

'Dress.' I pause. 'I'm wearing trousers.'

'Precisely.'

The woman in the adjoining seat has disappeared.

'A fit,' I announce, 'of absent-mindedness, which,' I go on, 'is the consequence,' (perhaps unwisely revealing this to her), 'of recent medical attention, supervised, I hasten to add, by one of the most resourceful practitioners of mental welfare in the land, not merely the youngest ever to hold the prestigious post of Longcroft Professor at the North London Royal, but a doctor chosen by the wife of H. L. Richards when the poet came over from America to escape the pressures of recognition symptomatic of the insecurities of, and therefore endemic to, that land where – and this, at the time, was widely known – he had been what, in this country, we describe as "sectioned" for behaviour which might, legitimately, be described as manic – and therefore, in my view, he *and* his wife – albeit his fourth – to be respected.'

In parenthesis I add, 'I am,' and proceed to make adjustments. 'The medical treatment, to which I referred a moment ago, has, I'm afraid, left me what, in the old days, was described as absent-minded, to a degree,' I continue, 'not normally associated with a man of my years, in the full flow of his manhood, so to speak, and at the very peak – or would be – of his sexual powers, transposed, in my case – from circumstance, I hasten to add, should you be free, rather than disposition – from the libidinal to the creative. I have come,' I produce my sketch-book, 'to draw.'

'Where are you getting off?' she enquires.

'Spinney Moor.'

'The stop after this,' the conductor declares at her shoulder. The bus is rung off.

Subliminally, I must have been aware of it for some time: we are passing between two hills, the one on the left crowned by the vegetated summit of Scone Hill, the one on the right characterised by the red brick and red-tiled roofs of Onasett itself: between the two, the bus cresting a conjunctive ridge, is revealed a vista of the River Lin; specifically, its upper valley, a tree- and grass-strewn fissure, irregularly obtruded upon by industrial and domestic buildings (the fistulaed intrusion of mill chimneys, the darkened profile of a village) which, against the lowering sky, is sombrely enclosed by wooded hills, their arhythmic undulations fractured further by the profile of a cliff, a ragged edge of blackened rock known as Walton Top.

Houses – the estate is flanked by private dwellings – converge upon the road: hidden, halfway up the slope to my right, is the house in Manor Road where I spent, other than for a few weeks, the first two decades of my life.

'Spinney Moor,' the policewoman says, stepping aside to let me pass.

Nothing is lost: everything is forgiven: 'I have made,' I tell her, 'restitution. I have given up my health, wealth and creativity for those I love.'

'It's not a difficult decision,' Maidstone says, 'disassembling your life. What was characterised by dissonance will be done away with, in all likelihood, for good.' ('And by "good",' he had gone on to announce, 'I infer a moral imperative, not

176

merely an infinitude of time.') 'A wholly felicitous re-arrangement will have been achieved which will astonish as much as it will enhance, facilitate as much as be a cause for wonder.'

The bus comes to a halt and the uniformed figure (a smell of perfume evident at the door) waits, having stepped aside as, encumbered by my slippers as much as by the sketchbook, I descend to the pavement.

'I have stepped down here,' I tell her, 'on many occasions, not least in my childhood, returning from school and, subsequent to that, in my youth, from college. The Linfield School of Art, though "art", in my case, at that time, was something of a misnomer. "Applied technology", in this instance, might have been better: printing, pottery, lithography, etching, as well as a cursory stab at carving. If that's the metaphor. I have, as a consequence of, rather than despite a lifetime of effort, disabused myself of the idea that I could equal the passion, the vigour and the dexterity of – let's choose a minor figure – Cellini – and have reconciled myself to the pleasure of doing what I can, as opposed to what I can't but hope to.'

'Which way,' she says, 'are you going?'

'There is, I take it, no law that prohibits me from walking along this road and talking to you, for instance, about things that count. Experience, after all, without exclusion, is tantamount to the religious, and returns us, if unaware, to the source from which we came.'

The bus has departed: two other figures, having descended, are glancing back as they cross the road to the eponymously named Spinney Moor Avenue to see what conclusions the uniformed figure beside me might have drawn, and what actions will flow as a consequence.

'I was going to see the old homestead,' I suddenly confide, 'and draw, on the way, a couple of sketches,' opening my book at a random page: blank. 'I drew a tree this morning,' I add, finding the image (a trunk, bereft of leaves as well as branches) which, on closer inspection, looks like a mutilated penis. 'Then again, I thought I'd walk to the golf-course which has a hill at the centre from where there is a view of Onasett to the north and the Lin to the south, winding into, or, rather, out of the Pennine hills, from where, via the Aire and Calder valleys, it finds its way to the Humber and, from there, of course, the North Sea.'

She is in two minds: one inclines her (her eyes stark behind a pair of glasses – unnoticed, previously, on the bus) to take me with her, across the road, and wait for a bus in the opposite direction which will take me back to town (there to be lost: out of her jurisdiction); the other inclines her, since she is homeward bound – at the end, presumably, of an exhausting shift – to leave me where I am and hope a passing vehicle – conceivably the returning bus – will knock me down.

'Where is the old homestead?' she enquires.

'Manor Road,' I say. 'Or was.'

'I'm going to Manor Road.' She takes my arm.

'I should say, the golf-course, in that case,' I tell her. 'Nothing personal,' I go on, 'merely a desire to re-acquaint myself with the totality of the landscape before, as it were, I descend to detail, you, no doubt, identifying "home" as a place to return to as opposed to one from which to depart.'

The day is bright (as if in response to my arrival, the clouds have broken): it is not unlike other days in the past when I have alighted at this spot, an invigorating breeze blowing from the north (from, in reality, the direction of the estate itself, rising up the slope before us) and which a smell of coal smoke in no way invalidates – the smoke, I recall, of the fires of home. Leaving the wall of the park, the road winds off along the southern fringe of the estate itself while, directly opposite, stands the hulk, like a chapel, of the Carlton Cinema – now given over, I noticed, to 'Bowls' (the word 'Cancelled' plastered over it, the more challenging, 'Scheduled for Demolition' in its place).

A line of shops (their windows blown out by a land-mine during the war) stand adjacent to the bus-stop on the other side – at which, I notice, a number of people have gathered, curious as to the outcome of this encounter.

'I've often thought, since the advent of women in the Force, in numbers large enough to be noticed, that a trouser-suit would be both more appropriate and more prudent. Police-women's legs, in my view,' her hand still on my arm, 'are no match for the black-stockinged calves – and occasional thighs – of the Salvation Army, whose members are conceivably attracted to the movement by this feature alone.'

I know no other way of explaining it, for it enables them, with the greatest possible decorum, and seemingly the highest motives, to display themselves in a way which, otherwise, would be vulgarly attractive to the opposite sex. Perhaps it is a bonus, if not an appropriate reward for the otherwise thankless task of being a salvationist in an age when their function is largely duplicated by the social services, if not by the wider echelons of the welfare state itself. I could have added – a certain stockiness evident in her build – that criticism of this nature did not apply to someone as attractive as herself, more a rule pertinent to the Force as a whole. If, for instance, there were a suggestion box, it might have been brought to the notice of her superin-tendent. It might influence not only the direction but the vigour of any subsequent recruitment drive and, as a result, have a beneficial effect not only on public support but the alacrity with which she and members of her sex were able to pursue and detain criminals.

'I offer the suggestion, of course,' I add, 'as a tentative outsider, one whose days of impropriety, to say the least, where women are concerned, are long since over. My wife is married to a man who, having served as a parliamentary private sec-retary in the Ministry of Health, is destined, so I am told, to be promoted to the very highest echelons of the Home Office. Thank you,' I conclude, 'for your advice, and thank you, too, for all your help,' setting off, having disengaged my arm, not up Spinney Moor Avenue (to the home I have left), but along the road, bounded by private houses – detached and semi-detached – flanking the estate (red roofs glowing in the light of a setting sun, or magenta in a rising one) – following, in effect, the route of the bus, to my left the houses replaced by a stretch of grass across which stands a Wesleyan chapel – of contemporary construction halfway between domestic-func-tional institutional-informal, and beside which a pair of gates opens on to a tarmac drive (motor-cars a precedent to worship) which runs in a direct line to a clump of coniferous and deciduous trees: amongst their foliage and beyond their sil-houette can be seen the Georgian roofs and chimneys of Onasett Hall – built by and lived in by the (celebrated) first member of parliament for Linfield, 'Jack the Democrat' Thornton, a man whose library was said to be 'the most inclusive in the North of England' (and who drowned in the Lin – which runs a few hundred yards behind the house – endeavouring, during a winter flood, to rescue his son, who drowned with him, a child of seven). 'Jack' had witnessed – and participated in – the storming of the Bastille and had brought back with him a handkerchief soaked in the blood of Marie Antoinette, a dark-stained item of cloth which, on view for many years in his library, was now in the town museum – the old Mechanics' Institute in North Parade – a testament – yet one more (along with myself) – to the longevity of the egalitarian aspirations of this industrial town.

The Hall is currently the headquarters of the Onasett Golf Club (a populist stronghold, vide Jack, as opposed to the more selective Cawthorne Club on the opposite edge of town), whose course extends around but principally to the rear of the house itself, retaining much of its original park – oak and beech and chestnut – and which falls, in an irregularly descending slope, not only to the banks of the Lin but to the parallel canal and railway (traversing the Pennines to Liverpool): a broad perspective of the hills is visible from the Georgian windows, along with the V-shaped gorge through which the Lin descends to its flat, alluvial valley.

I enter between the permanently open gates – for the fences and the walls on either side have been removed, the former for scrap during the Second World War, and never replaced, the latter having succumbed to wind and weather, and the said democratisation of the club which – principle apart – having fallen on hard times in recent years, has reduced its membership requirements, in the shape of its fees, to a level compatible with the economic resources, not of the freeholders whose houses flank the rolling, smooth green acres of its course, but of the not always employed, or employable, denizens of the estate: the house through which Bentham, Gladstone and Disraeli, Wordsworth, Turner, Dickens and Shaftesbury were said, from time to time, to have strolled, echoes now to the weekend carousing of 'the lads from Onasett' – snatches of whose refrains, I am told, can be heard as far away as the fifteenth tee, not to mention the nearest houses.

A path, to my left, leads around the rear of the Wesleyan chapel – a buff-coloured structure with pale 'Onasett' sandstone inset around its tall, leaded windows – and follows the line of the back gardens of the houses flanking the road: hawthorn and elderberry shrubs and a variety of fruit trees divide the gardens from the uniformly-furrowed slope of the course itself whose steeply-ascending central hill – my slippers soaked with dew if not overnight rain – I slowly climb.

A solitary figure, wielding a golf club, traverses the slope: with a distant cry of 'Fore!', a ball, a luminescent yellow, bounces across my path. Behind me, the gardens and the houses bordering the road come fully into view, a bus, like the one from which I have descended, visible above the roofs: ahead, a fringe of trees outlines the summit of the hill – beech, hornbeam, conifer, sycamore and lime – their branches silhouetted against an increasingly lightening sky.

As well as the uppers, the soles of my slippers take in the damp: I am, after all, still in my 'house', the interior that the exterior of my existence has now become, no less a room, the hill, than Etty's kitchen, or the scullery of the house whose roof – I glance behind me once again – must surely be coming into view on the opposing slope: a phalanx of inverted v-shaped wedges.

'Does God exist?' I ask Etty on the morning of the day she arrives to drive me up from London – from our house, mine and Vivienne's in Taravara Road, adding, 'I mean for you and Charlie?' and when, suspecting this merely to be a device to

181

distract her (she is packing my case on the bed), she doesn't respond, I recklessly plunge on, 'Does the question still exist or, in this age of molecular obsession, is it not so much done away with as superseded? Is the real, for your generation, only that which can come apart?'

'I don't know what you mean,' she blithely replies and it is, to say the least, a truism of the time I've lived in that 'God' and 'eternity' have become 'definitions' that 'beg the question', inviting derision to the same degree they parody a good intention.

'There is no such thing, of course, as objectivity,' I tell her. 'It's part of the apparatus with which, through insecurity, we seek to surround ourselves. Is the whole of our existence to be shorn of purpose? How can we arrest it? If two thousand years of appealing to a divine presence has failed, to whom may we appeal? Why,' I tell her, 'ourselves! *We* will be objective, even if that objectivity is threatened by all those things which seek to do it down!'

'Isn't that your illness?' she (calmly) enquires, securing the strap of the suitcase (the sound of our neighbours comes through the party wall of this pokey room at the back of the house). When I don't reply, she quietly continues, 'After all, your illness, as Maidstone and others have often said, has a spiritual, not to say a moral dimension, as well as,' she goes on, 'a medical one. Each of which,' (trying the weight of the case), 'has its relevance yet, at the end of the day,' (testing the weight of the case again), 'I thought you attached more importance to the chemical. I thought,' she concluded, 'you thought it was a biological problem.'

The house is small: the homogeneous appearance of the district – one-storeyed terraced dwellings with rarely more than four or five rooms – each with a correspondingly tiny yard at the back – is reinforced not merely by the common source of the street-names: Corunna, Blenheim, Trafalgar, Taravara (a corruption of Talavera) – but by the convergence of several railway lines which, with their arches and brick embankments, create the impression, as Vivienne remarked, when she first

182

arrived, 'of living inside a castle' (an effect enhanced by the numerous bridges – low, brick-built, round-arched – lacking only, it appears, a portcullis).

'I like living in a castle,' I told her, for the area, unlike most I have lived in in London, did have an air – if a peculiar one – of containment – conveyed not merely by the mellow, ochreish brick and large-windowed façades (relieved here and there by stucco – invariably painted cream or white) and the 'butterfly' roofs, the gutter running centrally down the middle, but by the nature and ancestry of the people who lived there. Though the houses were not infrequently described, in house agents' literature, as 'artisan dwellings' – which may have been true of some – the majority, clearly, were of working-class origin, the domesticated working class of the middle and late nineteenth century: service workers as much as labourers: clerks, drivers, bus and coach attendants, shop assistants and what might have been described as 'the lower commercial orders', the owners of the small businesses located in the yards and alleyways fringing the parapet-like railway embankments across which the steam locomotives hauled their trucks and coaches day and night. Even now, in the early hours, the house shuddered to the diesel locomotives drawing long lines of oil-containers, cement trucks or gantried wagons containing cars, as well as the isolated, single-trucked cargoes of atomic waste. It was the descendants of this nineteenth-century labouring class who still occupied many of the houses – now council-owned – half of them only private dwellings.

'Your attention,' Etty would say, 'moves from one thing to another, seemingly without purpose. I suppose you'd say,' she'd go on, '*you* are the purpose,' and if, in this instance, a description of the district I live in – when, in her own phrase she comes 'to rescue me' – appears to have little connection with the purpose of human existence, it has in my mind, if only in the sudden and vivid evocation of that moment when, packing the case in the bedroom which Vivienne and I had occupied, on and off, for the better part of five years – and in which, unknown to me, she had finally packed her cases before taking them down to the yard below (visible through the uncleaned window) – I recall not only Etty's dismissal of my five years' spiritual progress but the moment when, drawing open the garden shed door – curiously ajar when, unused, it was always shut – I had caught the first glimpse of the cases themselves then, grotesquely, of her cruelly distorted body (the blood and bleached tissue around her mouth).

'You must have misunderstood what I meant by "biological",' I tell her. 'Isn't the physical an embodiment of what I, in my illness, no doubt, would call the divine? Aren't the bricks and mortar of this house, not to mention the cracking plaster, the crumbling ceilings, the tiles and stucco, the splintered front door, as much an expression of the divine as anything more portentous you may care to mention? His church, His people, His ministers, His priests, the infrastructure of religion which is as much to do with belief as your scepticism of my motives is to do with me?'

I follow her down the stairs (the case on the bed) into the tiny hall that runs the length of the house: her own suitcase, packed from her overnight stay, is waiting behind the front door. I follow her into the kitchen which runs out as an annexe at the back – facilitating, through a side window, a view of our neighbour's yard. The female of the couple who live on the ground floor (the house divided into two flats) is hanging out her washing: an elderly woman, of a nervous disposition – a legacy of war-time bombing when a section of the street was reduced to rubble (a council tenement occupies the site) – she glances over the low partition wall aware, if not welcoming, my scrutiny from the other side ('I'm glad you're keeping an eye on us, Mr Fenchurch,' she has said on a previous occasion. 'Our kiddies, now we're getting on, never come and see us.').
She nods: behind my back (washing up tea-cups at the sink) Etty says, 'Let's keep it at a practical level. Everyone, including Maidstone, says you can't or shouldn't live alone,' adding (no ceremony intended), 'No one else will have you. You have to come to Ardsley. You know it. You've lived there. God, and metaphysics, have no part in it at all.'

When, turning from the window, I interrupt, she swiftly continues, 'Your incapacity to relate to anything around you in a way meaningful to anyone else is the only relevant factor. If Matt can't have you – which she clearly can't – and the boys aren't in a position to – then it's up to Charlie and me. The only alternative,' she concludes, 'is Boady Hall.'

'Provided by the estate of F. K. Boady who went mad on these premises,' someone had written on the wall while I was there, to which a subsequent hand had appended, in a larger – and significantly neater script, 'Who wouldn't?' Similarly, a poster starkly declaring, 'Apathy is the greatest sin' across which someone had scrawled, 'Who cares?' Boady, in reality, a clothing manufacturer whose wife had benefited, in his view, if dying, from the medical treatment she had received at the North London Royal of which this was the residential psychiatric wing – and where, a significant number of years later, I had taken up residence myself (on and off, for the better part of five years), an indirect consequence, it could have been said, of Boady over-charging for clothes (sold to people like Mrs Laski next door whose husband, injured in an industrial accident – insufficient provision made for safety – is confined, in his premature retirement, to a wheelchair – the ineffable consequence of the means by which Sir Frederick Boady produced the wealth which in turn takes care of the people driven mad producing it). 'Don't you see the connection which, other than by my asserting there is one, you tell me isn't there?'

'Sentimentality,' she responds, drying the pots and – the last of our washing-up – placing them in the cupboard beside the (still) victorian (black-leaded) cooking range. ('How quaint,' poor Vi had said, 'my parents had one in Scotland': it was in the oven – I discovered too late – she hid not only her drugs but her booze.)

'I live,' I tell her, 'in another world, which is just as real as this one.'

'Which one?' she enquires.

'This!' I tell her. 'This!'

14

I HAVE REACHED the top of the hill: the fringe of trees is interspersed with several rhododendron shrubs, beyond – a vista of the valley: the parkland of the old estate running down towards the river (invisible from this distance other than in the form of the raised, dyked bank of its parallel canal and the embankment of the railway). Only in the upper reaches does a silver-like expanse, shadowed by enclosing trees and buildings, and the shoulder of the valley, indicate where the Lin winds out in a broadening, placid curve from its turbulent course through the Pennine hills – a bulwark of darkness against the lightening clouds.

Directly across the valley is Harlstone, its colliery, too, with its familiar elongated waste-heap, gone, the village no more than a crescent of houses scattered across the brow of a hill: above, looms the shoulder of Walton Top, the soot-blackened outcrop of yellow sandstone, its rain-eroded scars visible at this distance, marked at its base by the sombre fringe of Cornthorpe Wood – a place, in the past, where I have courted Bea and – on one sensational occasion – her mother.

The breeze behind me is brisk and sharp: turning to confront it I am met by a view I have drawn and painted innumerable times: Onasett, a scree of red-tiled roofs rising in a series of interlocking planes like the ill-arranged stones on the wall of a castle, its parapet surmounted by the mill-like church of St Michael's, a pale, low, rectangular structure with a stub of a tower, scarcely more than a chimney, and surmounted, in its turn, by the red brick structure of Onasett School – a one-storeyed building which lies along the crest of what, from this perspective, can be seen to be a protuberant headland, projecting like a cliff from the northern flank of the valley: Ona's Headland; His Place; Ona's Sett (Fenchurch's Folly).

Fenchurch examined the scene before him as he might, on this headland, the embers of a fire, or a scene in a forest: was it here he intended to rest; was it here he had rested before; was it here he had hoped to meet a friend (a companion, a guide) or, as in his youth, had he come to this hilltop to view his home, his native heath, with an impervious if not a God-like eye (his God, his Saviour – the spirit of the place, that numinous presence of which, from his earliest years, he had been aware – essence not only of the place itself but of all who lived and had lived there – the neolithic hunters who had crouched at the foot of the Onasett hill and fished in the waters of the lake left by the retreating ice cap; the Celts, the Britons – the Roman centurion who, two millennia ago, had built his villa and farmed his fields, clearing the woodland long before Ona himself had appeared; the invading armies, the marauding hordes, the civilising Normans (killing everyone north of the river, the land desolate for years – other than for Cawthorne Castle, a visible stump on the southern horizon); himself; his father (first tenant of that house whose roof was indistinguishable amongst so many others) who had tunnelled beneath the hill itself)? The spirit of the place was what? Within himself: God, if he only knew it.

'It's immaterial to me,' he had said to Etty as she placed the last of the pots inside the cupboard. ' "Acknowledge" is an indefinite word, perceivable to some and not to others.'

'I am a humanist,' she had, early on in her college life, declared, and he had said, with something of a laugh, 'someone who sees God within him or herself and, pride inverted, then denies it.'

Now I tell her, 'I see the presence in your hand, the way, for instance, it holds that pot. A pot which, in its turn, has been held by me, *was* held by Vi – and has been, on occasion, by your mother on her infrequent and invariably recriminating visits. It becomes,' I tell her, 'axiomatic and, to the degree of having to point it out, of no interest to me any longer.'

'In that case,' closing the cupboard door, 'why bother?'

'I am,' I tell her, 'sowing seeds and, at this point of my life, interested only in doing that. Through my work I go on living. Through my work, of course, and you. Not the "I" with which I came into this world and which, within myself, will go out of it, but the "I",' I hastily conclude, 'beyond it.'

'What about the child-molester?' she suddenly exclaimed (I could see her protest coming, she much exercised at this time by an incident with Lottie when a man in the village had not only exposed himself but endeavoured to entice her into his car: 'What if she had gone?' she had said, her face buried in her hands).

'This isn't,' I tell her, 'the God of Good. This is the God of Nagasaki, of Buchenwald, of Dachau. This,' I tell her, 'is the God of War. We are no more innocent than He is.'

For over an hour.

'Like God to his daughter,' she finally declared. 'Don't look for your salvation, Father, in me.'

A residue of ashes, I reflect, examining the flame-red roofs before me: evidence of what was there before but which can never be re-ignited.

The breeze blows freshly in my face: with it comes the smell of smoke: Onasett coal, from the Onasett seam, a shaky, friable substance that leaves an orange ash – less 'heat co-efficient' than the denser coals from the deeper seams where time and weight have hardened their texture (burning with a whitish flame).

I begin to draw: two golfers cross the slope: a club is swung: invisible at first, a ball – white, in this instance – bounds across the furrowed grass. I am, as I told myself on those occasions I came here as a youth, in tune with tunefulness itself: praise Him Whose praise we sing below: the graphite smears and smudges.

'Don't tell me,' Etty says, 'you want to drive,' getting in,

188

nevertheless, behind the wheel, while all I can enquire (and complain) about as we drive through the maze of littered streets is, 'Are you sure you locked the door? There are so many papers I've left behind. (So many pictures, too.) I'd hate to find it looted.'

'Matt has said she'll look in. And Mum,' she reminds me, 'has said so, too. They can easily collect anything you want and send it on. Though what you have brought,' signalling behind (a cardboard carton tied with string), 'looks quite enough. After all,' she continues, 'you've written nothing for the past five years. What makes you think you'll be starting now? You're getting away,' she concludes, 'to rest.'

'From what?' I ask.

'From resting,' she says, 'that did you no good.'

'I told Maidstone I wanted to discover how real I am, without the aid,' I go on, 'of medication. "Lithium up your arse," I said, "no longer, love, up mine." I wanted, I told him, to get close to God.'

'Mania,' she told me, in a motorway cafeteria, halfway through our drive to Ardsley, 'strikes you, Father, when I least expect it.' ('Father' denotes irony, 'Dad' affection, silence intimacy – or so I reflect). 'You don't mind me speaking frankly,' she adds (more injunction than enquiry). 'Otherwise,' she goes on, 'with the kids and Charlie, the future will be impossible. I'm taking a risk,' she concludes, 'after all.' One hundred and seventy miles from London, the familiar hills and woodland, the valleys and the rivers coming into view, she suddenly enquires, 'You do love Glenda and Lottie?'

'More,' I tell her, 'than life itself,' and add, 'You don't set a very high premium on it, I know, at present, but, for as much as it's worth, or you're able to judge, as much as I loved yourself.'

'I have never doubted you loved me,' she says, stooping to the wheel, gazing with a peculiar intensity (not far short of serenity) at the road ahead.

'Which isn't quite as strong as saying you were always aware that I did,' I tell her.

'No,' she says, 'but then, I was,' adding, 'Do many people travel along this road, I wonder, discussing the nature of God?'

'I don't think,' I tell her, gazing at the vacuous faces in both the oncoming and the overtaking traffic, 'they think of anything I'd care to mention.'

My hand, I notice, has begun to tremble: I have come all this way, I reflect, searching for someone, or something, that doesn't exist: I am, as I told Maidstone, finished.

'You're not much older than I am,' he said. (He was, he'd already told me, fifty-five). 'I expect, when I'm your age, to be in my prime. As you are,' he hastened to add, 'at present. This is merely a reversal before the next prodigal leap.'

'I've made all the leaps I'm going to,' I told him. 'If what I have done is not sufficient I have nothing further to add.'

A pensive man (with a heavy face: a pendulous jaw and soulful eyes) who has said in the past, 'I have no personal experience of what you are going through but, not least from a lifetime's knowledge, I can imagine what it's like,' reflecting, 'There, but for the grace of God,' as he watches each departing lunatic figure (which doesn't obviate his alarm as he watches each subsequent one approach).

The graphite directs my mind to the horizontal line which crosses the paper and which is crossed, in turn, by several shaded patches: I perceive a landscape which, rather than generating awe, precipitates fear – of a magnitude and intensity I can't describe. I shiver: prayers, comprised of the one injunction, 'Help!' alternate with images of Bella – even, absurdly, of Vi: seated at a table in her test for *Hero of Our Time* ('Hoot,' as she described it): the protopsic condition of her eye (swelling at the height of any emotion) for which she saw a specialist in Devonshire Street ('Nothing we can do, I'm afraid,' charging her two hundred guineas).

Figures cross the scene below (I am glancing back towards the river): in pairs, in groups of four: how, I reflect, do they find the time: growers of wheat, hewers of wood, tillers of soil (diggers of coal), builders of houses – those newer structures,

I can see now, impinging upon the golf-course, at the furthest end of the slope? 'A collusion of disasters,' as Bea described it, I first seeing Vivienne, on a screen, in a viewing theatre at Boreham Wood, an intensity, not only about her face but, elusively, her figure (the sharpness of her voice – even her smiles: something forbidding and yet, despite the rapacity, forbearing).

'What do you think?' Liam says as, in the darkness, he leans across (her protagonist in the scene Macauley – a fair-haired Scot who became, via the subsequent film, an even bigger star than Vi).

'How I imagined her,' I tell him, adding, 'The character when I wrote it.'

Liam is short and stocky: Irish – O'Donnell: one of the post-war generation of film (and theatre) directors who have had an education: Caius, via Dublin ('Which has done me, I'm afraid, no good at all, merely inbred, in my case, the vice of patience'). He still preserves a light, inconsequential, hope-lessly deceptive, native accent: blue-eyed, broad-browed – white skin, wide-boned – round-shouldered, gutted already with too much drink (which, rather than lightening his nature, leaves him curiously phlegmatic): his hands are short-fingered – clumsy (round and smooth) – pale, like fish, his fingers as they dangle, subtended at the end of a dimpled arm, round the back of the seat beside me – he sitting one seat away (much shading in as the clouds descend and, returning to the Onasett side, I fashion in the road).

'Intense,' Warren, our producer, says in the seat behind. 'And possibly short on glamour.'

'Glamour?' The word, in Liam's throat, is swallowed like a pebble.

'Sexuality she has in abundance,' Warren goes on: dour (Scot), red-haired, verging to ginger (pallid face – like Liam), sharp-featured, eyes, pale-blue, like those of someone under water: tall, when he stands, and thin: gawkiness not so much a trait as a weapon.

'She is,' Macauley says, 'like a boxer. Never lets you off the hook, and is light on her fucking toes.'

Warren is young: five years older than myself just as Liam is five years older than Warren: twenty-seven years old, myself, on the occasion Warren rings up and says, 'My name is Warren De'ath ('Day-ath'). I've just been reading your *Hero of Our Time*. I'd like you to meet a man called Liam O'Donnell,' the call not unexpected for De'ath has directed a film himself (from which he has made a fortune, its actors, author and himself in and out of the papers), while, 'Liam is directing a play and could meet us after rehearsals.'

'A catholic, a presbyterian and an anglican,' he once described us: 'a Mick, a Jock and – how would you describe yourself?'

Yet O'Donnell, whose mother's maiden name is Cary, is one of those Anglo-Irish 'presbyterian pederasts who have crawled out of the mother church and fornicated across the border': a religious man whose religiosity is sophomorically expressed by telling God to fuck Himself.

We meet in a pub at the back of the Cambridge Theatre – in a bar which, at that early hour of the evening (half-past six), is full of actors from the play Liam is rehearsing – myself an unknown, post-pubescent author, Warren, red-haired, pale, sharp-nosed, broad-mouthed, his brow and cheekbones lightly freckled ('Liam and I have more than presbyterianism in common, more, even, than the catholic church'), Liam with a leather jacket that, in its tightness, exaggerates the rotundity of his figure, his open-necked shirt with its broad-winged collar framing his head – disproportionately large – as a dish might frame a piece of fruit, a stand a piece of sculpture, a frame envelop a picture ('a highbrow, by any definition,' Warren says): broad-browed, a narrow chin, a thin-lipped and slightly upward-curving mouth – creased by dimples the moment (not often) he smiles ('like,' Warren later says, 'a man might bite on a nerve'). Engaging, cantankerous: 'She has no glamour.'

'Anima,' Warren says.

'Anima.'

'Unlike Miles.'

'Miles.'

'Macauley.'

'Surely,' Liam says, 'that's animus.'

Solace (lead on paper): the interminability of the roofs rising to the scarcely tarnished stone of the church, to the red brick of the school, to the high-walled grounds of the isolation hospital (built on the site of a Roman villa, its fractured mosaic pavement destroyed in the building): the shout of 'Fore!' from the slope, the crinkling of last year's leaves against the rhododendron.

Liam's flaw (his fatal error): 'Wouldn't you like to play the part yourself? No experience as an actor? I think you'd do it well,' his predilection to doomed careers: 'I suppose Viv Wylder was another,' (see his own decline: booze – followed by depression: 'She's good,' he said. 'She's fine: ignore Warren,' on the occasion that we watched her test).

I didn't see Vi again until the novel-as-a-film had started shooting and I heard her say. 'He never thought I loved him, but, Jesus, how I tried,' her back to the camera, while I thought, 'Princess of Lost Causes.'

'Meet Richard,' Liam says, 'who wrote it,' bringing her across the floor, and Vivienne says, 'I was so nervous, hearing you were coming,' her face unreal, or so I thought, with make-up, an apologist for Stratford East, the Royal Court: 'I was a star! In L.A.' (in Capri, Hollywood, New York) 'and now I'm in a house in the back streets of a town I never want to hear about,' saying, years earlier, on the studio floor, 'Don't tell me what you think.'

'Which means she's waiting,' Liam says. 'Which means,' his arm around her waist, 'you'll have to. Say: "Even better than your test",' and laughs.

'There's so much more I can do with it,' she says.

Her eyes expand behind her lashes.

'So much. I've scarcely come to grips with it,' I thinking, 'So we're doomed (such spaces we must plunge to).'

Thirty years elapse before I see poor Vi again (but for one

193

or two meetings when the film comes out: the start of my career), she coming in, not drunk ('intoxicated, merely') to enquire about a part in *Cage* at the Beaumont Theatre (my last West End production), she the six-years-dispensed-with wife of Zygorski (currently on film posters throughout the town): dark glasses beneath which, absurdly, are a second pair (attached to the upper frame of which are a pair of swivel lenses): honed, her figure, like a fighter's, stripped to a minimum weight, from hours of solitude, booze and weeping.

Her features 'travel' (Liam says – there for this audition), handsome, curiously attractive – full of grace ('no doubt, from all she's been through' (Liam): two publicised abortions, three interim marriages between the two to Zygorski). Her fingers, as she takes the playscript, tremble: 'I don't read well, I'm afraid,' and then, having cleared her throat – returning the playscript to the desk behind and alongside which, respectively, Liam and I are sitting – she declares, 'On principle I never do. My agent, for one thing, doesn't allow it.'

'Too proud,' Liam says, 'to read for friends.'

Turning to me, she says, 'It's no reflection on your play, which, incidentally, I admire immensely. I wouldn't have come if I didn't.'

'How are you, Vivienne?' Liam says.

'I believe,' she says, 'I'm very well. I merely came,' she crosses her legs, 'because I'd been invited.'

'Don't be ridiculous, Vivienne,' Liam says, 'you can read as well as anyone.'

'As long as I can keep in a vertical position, and, when necessary, sustain a horizontal one, I don't see why I should,' she says.

'Why didn't I get the part?' she asked (years later). 'Because you thought I'd never learn the lines? I'd learnt half of them, I might tell you, the night before. Until five a.m., when I snatched an hour of sleep, then had a shower, then walked the streets waiting to come up to that crummy office and be offered the part. Not asked, God damn it, to audition. I made that man's career. And yours. And Miracle Miles Macauley.'

'We made yours, too,' I told her.

'With *Hero*? Before that, all Liam was known for was making documentaries. You thought,' she went on, 'I was on the bottle.'

'More than thought,' I said.

'I hadn't touched a drop for hours. *Hours!*'

'How many pairs of glasses did she have?' the casting director asks after Vivienne has gone (she herself a former actress).

'Two pairs,' Liam says, 'three lenses.'

'She had a glass-case in her hand, with another pair inside,' the woman says.

'Three pairs, four lenses, which shows,' Liam says, 'she came to read.'

'I would never,' the woman says, 'as a *woman*, get into a state like that.'

'Like what?' Liam says.

'I'd have,' she says, 'more pride.'

'Pride, I'm afraid,' Liam says (he to go down that road himself), 'is all that Viv has left.'

'That's not pride,' the woman declares. 'That, I'm afraid, is subjugation.'

'I was never too humble to be proud,' Vivienne said later. 'The last time was in that office at the top of that crummy theatre. The lift didn't work. I walked the stairs, and didn't even get the crummy part. Which is just as well. I'd never have kept it. How long was the run? Two months? Two weeks would have been my limit.'

'Three pairs of glasses, four lenses!' Liam says, laughing (foreshadowing his own disasters: all of my friends and most of my contemporaries dead).

'I fell down the stairs when I left that office and – what you didn't know – I had to be taken home in a cab,' she ringing me a few days later: 'I liked your face. You looked as though you've been through much the same as I have, booze apart, of course, and three or four husbands.'

'Two moths,' Liam said, 'and a single flame: no wonder you both got burned.'

*

195

I brought Bea to this hilltop – twice: once to see the view, the other to make love – and Bella once (the motive much the same). 'It's a sacred place,' I said to Bella when, winded from the climb, she stood panting in the darkness of the trees: the absurdity of requesting her to climb, her vulnerability (humility) in accepting. 'It must have been an island in the neolithic lake. The signs of a settlement have been found at the southern end. Perhaps you'd like to see it?' the lights strewn out beyond the links (the pressure of her hand in mine: 'How much I love you,' I declared. 'I wish that we were married').

'Hence the difference between us,' Vivienne – who was my age – said when I told her about my earlier life. 'You really need a mother. Was she as lovely as you describe? We must have a lot in common.' When I asked her, 'What?' she laughed. 'Women,' she said, 'who were never loved.'

'I loved her more than any other woman I know,' I said.

'Until she grew too old.'

'Not once,' I told her, 'was she ever too old.'

To see her sitting there, or working in the garden, or merely standing at the door when we departed was more than I could bear: I longed to take her in my arms. I would, when we moved to London, lie awake for hours, aching for her touch. She totally possessed me. 'After I was married, after I had children, after I had been with other women, one encounter merely the presage to another. More to me,' I tell Vivienne, 'than life itself,' recalling the occasion when, in the darkness, she had stood here with me, her hand in mine, gazing at the scree of lights before us (Onasett and, behind us, those of Harlstone, across the valley), the swaying presence of the trees (the softness of her touch). 'Making love was a disappointment. It always led to something else. Disquiet. The fact that she was married. The disparity between our ages. The frustration of never knowing in what circumstances we might meet. The longing to be with her was more than I could bear. I would creep into the grounds at Ardsley and wait amongst the trees, hoping I might glimpse her passing by a window. One evening, when I did, she at an upstairs window, gazing out, speculating,

I imagined, what she would do, or merely feel like if, glancing out, she saw me, it was more than I could bear. I stepped out from the shadows. She never saw me. All she could see, she said, was the dark. It was to appease this indiscretion of mine that she took to walking in the grounds in the evening. "To take the air," as she described it, prompting her husband jocularly to remark she must be meeting a lover.'

'I don't know what it was,' I said to Vi. 'The sight of her alone was enough to set me off. I'd be engulfed by feelings which convinced me I was mad. I'd tremble. Her sounds of gratification, the removal of her clothes, the elevation of her hips, the paleness of the garment which, despite my efforts, still concealed her breast, drove me to distraction. "Don't be so wild," she'd tell me (after all, her tone implied, you're getting what you want), and, "Don't be so clumsy," would be her other plea, the final consummation, even now, after all these years, impossible to describe.'

'It's not me you love,' Vivienne, on one sultry evening, casually announced ('I should never have come here to live or had anything to do with you at all,' she added), 'but that woman you see in me. I'm about the age that she was. It's me you're launching into when you come on top. It's her you're making love to,' requesting (something she'd resisted until that moment) I find a photograph amongst the papers I'd brought from Belsize Park to Taravara Road (no search required at all), showing her the most precious – taken in a woodland clearing (with a camera – at my insistence – she'd brought herself), she sitting on the ground, the hem of a summer frock demurely above her knee, her eyes half-closed, her lips parted, the dimples evident in her unlined cheeks. My coat and her own are on the ground, revealing clearly the impress of our bodies (her hair in disarray): sunlight – we are on our memorable visit to Broughton Woods, close to my boyhood camp-site – sprinkles a patina of shadow across her frock, the outline of her thigh, one leg curled beneath her. She smiles as, years later, Bea would smile at the first of our children – bewildered, perplexed (subliminally entranced).

197

'She's very beautiful,' Vi said, searching, indubitably, for a vestige of herself. 'She must have loved you very much. Incontinently,' she added, stammering (a full glass in her hand). 'To have risked not only her husband's but her daughter's love. You said he idolised her, didn't you?' raising her head to examine the kitchen-cum-living-room of that tiny dwelling (no vestige in the photograph, after all, only the residue of where we are now). 'To have risked all that for a boy of – how old were you at the time? Nineteen? It doesn't make sense, and yet, to me, all the sense,' she belched, 'in the world. I idolised my father in a similar way and have been looking for a surrogate ever since. An awful cheat. Zygorski. An awful fucking creep. Twenty-five years younger and the mind of a child of seven.'

She kept the photograph by our bed: 'How beautiful she looks and – worst of all – how innocent. Isn't the key, my darling, she was really much younger than you? What, I wonder, does her daughter think? That inimitable genius who, sooner or later, will come up for the Nobel Prize.'

'She never knew,' I told her.

'Never?'

I shook my head.

'I thought that's why you split.'

I shook my head again.

'Never?'

'Never.'

In two minds, I could see (a handy weapon), to tell her now herself.

'The only person who knows, apart from yourself, is Maidstone,' I said. 'He thought it was something Bea could sense but not define.'

'Which, in any case, came between you,' she said.

'It might.'

She sat in silence for a while: what, she must have reflected, could I do with that? Damage, she must have concluded, commensurate with her own.

Isabella's collar: her arm, her sleeve, the abrasiveness of the

198

material of the coat itself: the extraordinary effect of her perfume in the dark: her smile: 'Is this what you do with Bea?'

'No,' I tell her, and add, 'You'd decided you'd never ask.'

'Nevertheless,' her hair flung back against the grass. 'It must be desperation that makes me.' ('It's more,' she has said on one occasion, 'than flesh and blood can stand.') And adds – or I think she adds – recollection inhibited by aversion, 'This *instrument* that goes in and out of me, goes in and out of my daughter. Does she, I wonder, feel the same? If she found out, is there only disillusionment for both of us?' (Isn't her gratification, she might have gone on, identical to mine – achieved after all, in an identical way?). 'What, I wonder,' she concluded, 'is so different?'

While on the South Coast, in a sunlit room, an airship passing overhead, her daughter is experiencing what she, her mother, experienced then – on the banks of streams, in sunlit woods, on the back seat of a bus (in moonlit copses): 'I seldom feel afterwards I haven't been raped. Odd, when I invite it.'

My dear. My dear! My love!

Or on the bed, when Corcoran is out: in the guest-room where I am staying at present (the view to the trees and the pit-less village); in my lodgings at the Drayburgh when she came to London – which, only moments before, her daughter had left . . .

199

15

'ARE YOU all right?' the jerseyed (a roll-top collar) zip-jacketed figure enquires: panting from his climb, a golf-club in his hand, a companion – female, skirted – some distance down the slope behind: 'My wife,' he gestures with his club, 'saw you lying down. She thought,' glancing down the slope, 'you'd fallen.' He calls, 'I think he looks all right,' vigorous – thick-calved, broad-chested, face flushed from his exertions: a native, undoubtedly, of Onasett itself.

'Are you a native of these parts?' I enquiring, aware of sitting on the ground, my back against a tree, leaning, my elbow supporting me, over to one side (a dizzy attack or a reflexive action).

'Linfield.' He names a distant suburb. 'The Cawthorne Club is difficult to get into. Onasett isn't so choosey.'

'Onasett,' I tell him, 'never was,' conscious of the damp beneath my thigh: though covered with decaying leaves, the ground is wet. I can feel further evidence through my jacket sleeve. 'It took all the people living by the river, in those streets around the Linfield dock, my parents, as it happened, amongst them,' half a century or more ago, I might have added but he is gazing at my sketchbook which, together with my pencil, is lying on the ground.

'You've got the appearance of it well,' he says.

'I have,' I say, 'and more.'

'Is he all right?' calls a voice from down the slope and, 'He is an artist,' is offered in reply. 'Would you like me,' turning back, 'to help you from the ground?'

200

I take his hand; for the first time – as he takes mine in return – he is aware of my carpet slippers.

'I came out,' I tell him, 'in a hurry.'

'From Onasett?' he enquires.

'Home,' I say, 'is where the heart is.'

'Dougie?' from the slope below: two trolleys parked along the fairway.

'Coming,' he calls, adding, 'Are you sure you'll be all right?'

'Perfectly,' I tell him, he setting off, soliciting a signal, with his golf-club, to which, however, I don't reply.

The etymology of grief is the epistemology of madness, viz:

Grief (*pace* grievance) = injury.

Injury = not right (wrong).

Wrong = unjust (related to wring, awry).

Wring = squeeze, twist (distress, torture).

Awry = crooked (related to wry).

Wry = distort, turned to one side (contort).

(Contort = twist).

Distort (similarly).

Twist = double (twin, twine).

(Double = two).

Two = division:

injury, injustice, torture, distortion: duality – madness, it is conjectured, the logic of grief, its antecedents to be found in injury, injustice, torture, distortion – duality – and self-division.

'Bea,' Maidstone says, 'is no longer a woman,' she is, he is about to tell me, a state of mind, but adds, misjudging my look, 'well known at the Ministry.'

'Ministry?'

'Of Health. Where do you think she gets her money?'

I was about to say, 'Myself,' but go on, 'We separated, would you believe it, after coming to London, and met up again at a college dance: a room full of streamers, played to by a jazz band led by a man with a stammer, his announcements, over a faulty mike, variations on an extemporary theme, she a radiant figure – "Beattie" to her pals, principal amongst them her college tutor who, a molecular physicist, was subsequently fired

201

for screwing a student: magenta hair, green-irised eyes, green-coloured dress.'

'Aren't you a student here?' she says.

'The Drayburgh,' I tell her, 'is affiliated to the university.'

'Oh,' she says, and little else, except, as we spin and whirl – she spiralling politely beneath my hand (has she heard, I reflect, about her *mother*?) she adds, 'The Drayburgh, by the way, is known as "The Drain", on account of the people, of course, who go there.'

'Haven't we met before?' I ask.

'Isn't it reprehensible,' she says, 'the way a reputation like that can get around?'

'Take me,' I say. 'I'm known as licentious,' she waiting – our acquaintance once renewed – in her college room dressed in suspenders, stockings, little else (a dressing-gown half-belted), saying, 'Aren't you early? I thought we said half-seven,' the spry, 'My dear!' as I come inside, a Christmas dance, thrown at the Student Union in Malet Street where I'd hoped (intended) to meet her again – and not a week later, of course, her mother ('I thought you and Bea had drifted apart'), she waiting in my room in much the same fashion as Bea in hers, the spry, 'Oh, Richard!' and then, 'My dear!'

'I was studying painting at the time and a student at the Drayburgh was quite a catch. As for her mother: "I really came down, of course to see Bea." '

'Are you a member?' the man enquires.

Unlike the majority of the men who occupy the room he wears a collar and tie: a square moustache, a pale blue eye buttoned either side of a fleshy, mottled nose.

'I'm looking,' I tell him, 'for Mr O'Donnell.'

'O'Donnell?'

'A member here in nineteen forty-five. He lived two doors away in Manor Road, spent more of his time on the tees than he did with his wife.'

'I don't know Mr O'Donnell,' the man replies.

'This would be where Wordsworth, Turner, Castlereagh, on two occasions, Gladstone and Disraeli, at varying times,' I tell

202

him, 'were entertained. You must know Turner's sketch of Onasett Hall, set against the slope, poetically exaggerated, of Onasett itself, the setting sun, the pink eminence of the house in the middle distance.'

'If you're not a member, or invited by a member, you're not allowed in the bar,' he says.

'Any time, he told me, I happened to be around. "You'll be assured," he said, "of a welcome." '

'If you're not a member, nor an invited guest, I have a statutory obligation,' he says, 'to ask you to leave.'

'My father came down here during the Second World War. The Onasett Home Guard occupied premises in what was the gardeners' hut at the back. A unique structure, circular, brick-built, and probably still there, comprised of two rooms, one on top of the other.'

'Nostalgia,' Maidstone says, 'classified as a medical condition, was first noted amongst mercenaries in the European armies in the eighteenth-century wars: stout-hearted men who suddenly acquired the symptoms of depression, not merely a disinclination but an inability to eat, sitting for hours in a stooped or crouched position: men who, when they first left home, had been, where not relieved, jubilant to do so – escaping from marital or parental discord, lack of food or unemployment – only, once away, to curl up and die. Though discarded nowadays as a clinical diagnosis, nosomania is, in my view, under-rated. A longing for one's home is, in many respects, inseparable from a longing for the past: not merely a sentimental aspiration to return to a familiar place and time, but a passionate regard for experiences which may, in reality, never have occurred, a diffusing of experience to which the victim helplessly clings, like a martyr to a cross or a drowning man to a plank of wood, the recollection, in short, of a place or places without which a person, mistakenly, believes he can't exist.'

'As for Maidstone's reference,' I tell the man, 'to my clinging to the past, I only have to refer him to what actually took place, the material set down in black and white.'

'I'll be obliged, if you won't leave, sir, to call on someone to take you out. We have two policemen here as members,' calling, 'Bryan!' to a figure whom, with several others, reflected in a mirror, I see standing at the bar.

'O'Donnell died,' I tell him, 'in 1955, scarcely ten days short of his sixty-fifth birthday. A rent and rates clerk at the County Hall, I saw him, believe it or not, the day preceding the event, walking past our house swaying, as he did so, not merely from side to side but forwards and backwards.'

'He's come here looking for a man who died in 1955.'

'O'Donnell was his name,' I tell the policeman: in civvies, fair-haired, not disinclined, I suspect, to be moved. 'His namesake, not dissimilar in several respects, directed one of my films and a not inconsiderable number of my plays,' I add.

'I'm afraid,' Bryan says, 'this is not a public bar. I shall have to ask you, if you aren't a member, or haven't been invited as a guest, to leave.'

'Jack the Democrat,' I tell him, 'would not be pleased. A populist when populism had more than a pejorative meaning. As for O'Donnell . . .'

The off-duty constable – perhaps sergeant (or, considering the youth of today, conceivably inspector) – takes my arm. 'There's no reason why you shouldn't, on the other hand, invite me as a friend. I am, after all,' I tell him, 'native bred, a son of the Devonian sandstone, the millstone grit – along with the glacial marls and shales, the sands and gravels, the deltaic deposits. Between you and I,' I go on, 'there is no between. That which comprises the between between me and other people has, in the past few years, been set aside. Certainly by me, if no one else. I am almost too free,' I conclude, 'to be alive. Which is why, if the truth were known, I was sectioned by my wife, working in conjunction with a live wire at the North London Royal. Maidstone by name, if rarely by practice . . .'

We are at the door: it looks directly to a smoothly-cut lawn ('Like a bowling-green,' I tell him. 'It is a bowling-green,' he says) bordered in turn by a balustraded wall through a gap in which (decorated on either side by urns in which spring flowers are already blooming: daffodil, crocus, and the like) the first tee of the golf-course can be seen and, in the furthest distance, across a diagonal view of the valley, the pudding-like profile of Cawthorne Castle, the river – hidden by its low embankments and the parallel canal and railway embankments – somewhere in between.

'Which is not unlike being sent outside with the integument of one's skull removed, the abrasiveness of the air so intense a pain as to be,' I tell him, 'impossible to describe.'

'I advise you to leave by the drive,' he says.

The first of my interlocutors – he of the square moustache and collar and tie – points the opposite way to the one I'm going. 'There is no public access across the course,' he adds.

Vivienne, poor Vi, was ensconced at the N.L.R. herself (a different time to me: 'Would you say,' she enquired, 'we're taking it in turns?'), but, unlike me, was never sectioned (no family nor lover to do it for her): subsequently, she joined her chums in L.A.: "mystical analysis", "rational diets", endless hours of driving the freeways, going nowhere, coming back: between her and I there is no between – I bringing her here on one occasion (her incapacity to disengage the seat-belt alone preventing her from falling out).

'I want you,' I tell her, 'to find a root. This is where I started. This,' I tell her, 'is where I belong.'

'Another fucking place to me. Never a one,' she cries, 'to call my own!'

'You left this behind,' the policeman says, handing me the sketchbook.

'That's kind of you,' I tell him. 'I'm on my way home,' the driveway, however, already empty, no one but myself, he a disappearing figure: no curiosity about the present. None, presumably, about the past.

'When you get into these states,' Maidstone says, 'select an image. Preserve it. Concentrate on one thing and nothing else.'

'What I always choose,' I say, 'is Bella.'

'Vi is Isabella,' he says, 'bereft of prohibition.'

"Thanks for everything," Vivienne wrote in her last letter –

205

leaving it, curiously, with her wedding-ring on the draining-board (where the bleach had stood) beside the sink, I waiting for a call to say she had arrived (conceivably, she'd missed me) – three days, God help me, before I found her (her finger nails filled with garden soil – perhaps, not inconceivably, evidence she'd changed her mind, intending to crawl to the kitchen door, calling me or, God help her, Melvyn.)

A bus goes past: I am once more on the curving, roller-coaster strip of tarmac, rising and falling over ancient, overgrown moraines, which circuits the foot of the estate: an aperture in the façade of red brick and pebble-dash indicates the opening to Manor Road: the familiar verges have been replaced by tarmac, the trees little more than hacked-at stumps: cars, the majority in a dilapidated if not irretrievable condition, are parked amidst pools of coagulating oil: hedges as well as gardens are overgrown and, where the soil has been tarmacked too, vehicles are parked between the houses. The doors and windows have been replaced with inappropriate frames and mountings: out of scale, out of sympathy (out of everything): plebeian exigencies: what was graceful (small and neat) a distortion of the planners' earliest intention: the burgeoning trees, the fresh-cut verges (the smell of grass), the flowered gardens . . .

   "*Thanks for everything. Love. V.*"

An overcast sky, the tarmac flanked by the intermittently-tarmacked-over verges (of the trees, where not missing, only one or two are fully grown), the mutilated (or absent) hedges – gaps hacked in to allow access to cars – the decimated gardens, the air of adventitious debilitation: a drive carved out of the soil by tyres; windows punched in inappropriate walls: 'Nosomania,' Maidstone says, 'is cured by a return to the place – or the past – imagined.'

   'Only,' I tell him, 'nothing, from being observed, is what it was before.'

   Some distance ahead, where the road rises up a gentler slope (never steep enough to sledge down), the front of the house appears: the green paint, inset with yellow, of its window frames and doors is now a uniform brown: the roof is disfigured with wedge-shaped tiles. The front door has changed (a uniform, unmoulded expanse of wood: no relief to its tedious surface), the hedge at the front hacked to waist-height: the gate has gone, replaced by a pair of wooden hurdles which, wedged apart, are already broken. A dilapidated car stands in the gap between the houses (scarcely space to open the door), a make-shift garage blocking the view to the field and – from the enclosing weeds – the overgrown garden behind. The windows are uncurtained, strips of cloth attached on either side.

"Here," Vi had written obscurely in her last letter, "you will find me. We had, did we not, a hell of a time, you fucked up from the inside, I from the outside. 'A woman's work is never done,' ran an advert in my childhood – beside, as it happened, a bottle of bleach. How true! 'Take this cup from me,' Christ prayed in the garden. How, since he prayed alone, did anyone know? When, as a child, I asked my father, all he said was, 'Inspiration!' All I can say to him now, as I say to you. Thanks for everything. Love. V."

In her diary, its writing so small I had to use a magnifying glass to decipher the scrawl: "A sense of obsolescence has preoccupied me all my life: the laughing child, the beautiful daughter, the blushing bride (the fucked-up wife), on each occasion the still, small voice, 'This isn't meant to last.' Nailed to his cross he must have felt the same: 'Don't take it at any-thing other than face value,' the nails, the hammer, the spear, the sponge – the lament of every woman on earth – and Him: *why hast thou deserted me!*"

My father, pushing his upright-handled bicycle, comes up the path: dark (imprinted, his face, with coal-dust round his eyes and mouth, the cracked lines that retain it beside his lids, the crevices beneath his chin), a short, broad-shouldered, smould-ering figure, still at the coal-face at sixty-one – the handlebars grasped in either hand, the querulous, 'It's you?'

207

'How are you?' I enquire – to which he doesn't reply, laying the bike against the hedge (no longer there) which hides the back garden from the road, stamps his feet on the mat in the porch, ducks his head as he pulls off his cap, stoops, removes his clips, before he thrusts his way inside.

'What did Grandpa do?' the children enquire, years later, as they watch his stumpy, white-haired figure recline in a deck-chair on the lawn of our Belsize Park house – solemn, silent, gazing at the air (rasping in the London pollution), their incredulous looks as they listen to his tales of tunnels, pitprops and collapsing roofs (runaway trucks and crashing engines, floods and falls and fire and dying men).

Taking off his jacket, he washes at the sink, turning, hands wet, to the frayed-edge towel: his boots, coal-dusted, are thrust beneath the mangle: lifting the lid on the plate laid across the top of a pan of simmering water, his head is immersed in a cloud of steam: too tired to eat, he allows my mother, who has come through from the living-room, to take the plate from him. He sits, answering briefly my mother's questions, at the living-room table, the food carried to his mouth unseen: 'The roof half-buried the machine this morning,' eating, two-fisted, like a boxer, the gravy streaked across his lips, eyes like a dog's, hungered from exhaustion, submitting to an appetite his body cannot feel.

'Would you mind telling me what you are doing here?' the woman asks.

'I live here,' I say, and add, 'or used to,' aware I have wandered between our old house and our neighbour's and am standing at the side of a makeshift garage: where once stood a lawn, a rockery and, between the rockery and the field, a vegetable patch, are the accumulated remains of several motor cars: clothes, hung for drying, are suspended above them, while the porch, its coal-house door broken, has its brickwork smeared with the imprint of what appear to be innumerable oil-stained hands.

'You're not, by any chance, called Fenchurch?' she says.

'I am,' I say, 'as it happens,' (a commemorative plaque, it's been suggested, should be attached to the front of the house?).

'Someone was looking for you.'

She gestures to the road.

'Who?' I immediately respond.

'A woman.'

Small and stout – a stoutness which, to some degree, belies her age, for she can't, I imagine, be more than in her middle twenties (servile to a savage husband, the mother of more children than she can count: the sound of squawking comes from inside the scullery door: the door through which, for forty-five years, my father daily entered).

'What did she look like?'

'She came in a car. Said, "Has a gentleman been here?" Said you walked with a shuffle, and may even be in your slippers.'

She gazes at my feet.

'Where is she now?'

Gesturing to the road again, she says, 'She drove off when I told her I hadn't.'

'A fan of mine,' I tell her.

'She said she was your daughter.'

'They all say that,' I tell her. I shift my sketchbook to my other hand, recall I may have lost my pencil, and add, 'You have a beautiful dress.'

She looks down at her skirt – stained, ill-fitting, torn at the seam.

'On the line,' I tell her.

'That's a nightdress,' she declares.

'I would love,' I say, 'to see you in it.'

'So would I,' she says. 'I put the wrong heat on and it's gone and shrunk.'

'You're a rough and ready woman, I can see,' I tell her. 'Quite used to your environment, I imagine, and to the rough treatment that you get, no doubt, from your husband.'

'It's a good job he isn't here,' she says. 'Do you want me to ring the police?'

'I merely came,' I tell her, 'to look at the house. I painted

209

my first picture behind that door, composed my first poem, wrote my first novel. For the first twenty years of my life I slept here almost every night, sometimes in the bedroom at the back, more often in the second bedroom at the front. You will hardly credit it,' I go on, 'but I was once put up for the New Year's Honours, until my private life came under closer scrutiny, by which time my reputation, unfortunately, had declined, if not disappeared entirely. Previous to that, several plays of mine had been seen by President Johnson, at the instigation of his wife, Lady Bird – who became, I could almost say, an intimate acquaintance – she arriving at the theatre with her usual guards who not only occupied the best seats in the stalls, the Royal and Dress Circles, but the gallery, each of them armed with an automatic weapon which, on one memorable evening, misinterpreting a line of the play as an attack on her, they drew, pointing them in a variety of directions but principally at the seat in which was sitting the director of the play. I was, for several years, the toast of Broadway and won, for several years running, its principal awards.'

She has turned her attention to a child behind her back, her broad figure stooping to its bare-legged frame which, with a sigh, she hauls to her shoulder.

'Do you mind,' I enquire, 'if I step in the field?' and clambering between the miscellaneous piles of rusted metal, reach the area where normally there might have been a fence and, an instant later, am standing in wasteland (where previously, I remind myself, there had been only grass): here neighbours danced and ate and drank to the music of a wind-up gramophone to celebrate the end of the Second World War and, years later, the coronation of the Queen; here the subsidence that marks the hole where we built our final den, marked itself, like a grave, by weeds; there the cricket-pitch, more pitted than ever; there the slope behind the goal down which the ball invariably rolled after scoring; here – last of all – the level stretch of ground – adjacent to the cricket-pitch – where the tables were set in a single line for the parties to celebrate peace and the coronation – where the women, in their Sunday dresses

210

(overhung with aprons) danced with their waist-coated, shirt-sleeved men, the latter shy to be seen embracing their wives in public, the bolder dancing with their more adventurous neighbours: Mr Clinton (of the large moustache) with Mrs Russell (of the prominent bosom); Mr Walton (with the protuberant waist) with the much animated Mrs Swanson; Mr Wade (bow-legged) with Mrs Braine (from Ireland); my father with my mother, before finding an excuse – the children's demands at the table – to disengage; the golfing Mr O'Donnell with the tennising Mrs Crawshaw, the religious Mr Walls with the irreligious Mrs Shay, the unmarried Peter Waterton (about to be demobbed) with the widowed Mrs Preston, myself an idle youth, leaning on the fence, grimacing at this display of communality . . .

Burnt, the grass, in one or two places: missing, the fences, behind my back: the desultory windows no longer recall the personalities inside: the Davidsons, the Clarkes, the Petersons, the Smiths.

Dereliction.

Almost idly, Fenchurch takes out a pencil (in his pocket all the while) and, the grass too wet to sit, begins to draw: the line of the field, the inappropriately adapted houses – the battlemented crest formed by the silhouetted roofs – identifying, as he does so, the pattern of the windows – alternating double and single – the alcoves of the porches, the scattered trails of smoke – and decides he is too tired, fatigued (worn-out, defeated): how on earth did Etty know? the woman, he observes, still watching, the child, half-naked, in her arms.

Other figures, too, are watching (other windows, other doors).

'Would you like a cup of tea?' she calls, and disappears inside her porch.

Glancing round, once more, at the familiar façades, I complete the sketch – the lowering excrescences of greyish vapour beyond which, at one time, lurked German bombers (the remainder of my life a remoter threat) – and return, with difficulty – negotiating the rusting metal obstacles – down the

211

remnants of the garden path to the oil-stained entrance to the at-one-time Fenchurch porch.

I tap on the grease-marked door ('Come in,' says a voice immediately inside) and step into a scullery smaller in size than the one retained in memory, the cracked concrete floor covered in linoleum, across which has been laid a tattered mat: a motor-cycle, its engine disassembled, leans against the wall against which, in inclement weather, we propped our bikes. A cooker replaces the gas-fired, green-painted copper, the sink in the corner much the same: beneath the window, looking out to the road, a washing-machine is piled high with washing.

'Come in,' she says again (a kettle plugged to the wall). 'Go through to the living-room, I'll bring the tea through,' she adds, 'in a minute,' the child still in her arms.

Crossing the hall, scarcely broad enough to take two figures standing together, I enter the living-room the other side – a vast interior, in memory, of familial warmth – reduced, in reality, to something not much larger than my Taravara Road kitchen: the closeness of the walls, the lowness of the ceiling, the confinement of the view to the field and road outside – the dereliction of the disassembled cars at the back, the asphalt verge, the overgrown and trampled remnants of the lawn at the front: a decaying, grease-stained settee and two similarly disfigured easy chairs, together with a crockery-encumbered wooden table, take up much of the available space; a television set, turned on, stands adjacent to a fireplace which, tiled, unlike the black-leaded stove of previous years, is occupied by cans of beer, which, on closer inspection, prove to have been opened.

Laying down my sketchbook and pencil I hear a voice behind me call, 'Tea or coffee?'

'Tea.'

The chairs are small.

'Make yourself at home, I shan't be a minute.'

Springs protrude beneath the much-stained fabric. My feet are wet: I clench my toes inside my socks, feel the dampness against the slippers and, having sat, remove them.

Taking off my socks, I put them in my pocket.

Here, on many a solitary evening, I have read *Lord Jim*, *Hamlet*, *A Midsummer Night's Dream*: Dostoyevsky: 'procrastination common to Lord Jim and Hamlet: discuss.'

The paper on the wall, distempered, is marked at a uniform height by children's hands: dark patches enclose the light-switch: a smell of beer is obfuscated, to some degree, by that of rotting meat, the air not only chill but damp: so many evenings have I sat behind a barricade of drying clothes, the dampness permeating the furniture and curtains: the glow of the fire through the different thicknesses of cloth, the chink of flame between adjacent garments, the creak of the leather thongs on the supporting wooden frame echoing that of the table where, on a sheet laid on newspaper, my mother irons.

'Sugar and milk?'

'Milk,' I tell her and, a moment later, the child still in her arms, she brings in a steaming pot.

'Would you like a biscuit?'

'No, thanks,' I tell her.

'A piece of cake?'

I shake my head (uncertain where she keeps it). 'Excuse my feet,' I tell her. 'I wet them in the grass,' and add, 'I came out in my slippers.'

'That's all right,' she says, 'by me.'

She sits, the child, its head averted, twisting in her arms.

'You notice any changes?' she enquires.

A feeling of dispiritation, bordering on despair, and not unmixed with apprehension, absorbs me for a while. 'It seems much smaller,' I finally reply. 'I can't imagine how we all got in.'

'How many were there of you?' she enquires.

'Five. Two parents and three brothers.'

'Where are your brothers now?' she asks.

'Abroad.' I add, 'Since our parents' deaths I rarely see them.' (Nor, I reflect, would they want to see me: disparity of purpose, for one thing; disparity of content, for another).

'I suppose, if you lived here before, you could say,' she says, 'we have something in common,' the child wriggling in her

213

lap. 'Mam! Can I have summat t'eat?' it says (surprisingly: I'd assumed it to be dumb). 'I'd better be getting her clothes on,' she adds. 'She's alus wetting herself at present,' (the vestiges, I assess, of an education – brought to a premature end by marriage: fewer colloquialisms in her speech, for instance, than might reasonably have been expected). 'How many children do you have?' turning to a cupboard by her chair.

'Five,' I tell her, noticing, for the first time, a telephone on a stand behind the door. 'Three grandchildren,' I go on, 'at present.'

A mist comes in, within which the house itself has vanished.

'It's not at all like it was,' I add, enquiring, 'How many other children do you have?'

'Two more at school,' she says, 'though this 'un's nearly ready,' the child's eyes unblinking as, turned in its mother's hands, its final garment is removed and dry ones pulled on.

'It looks much younger,' I suggest, and am about to describe the antics of Lottie and Glenda (of Mathilda, Harriet, Kenneth, Benjamin and Rebecca) but, having got to my feet, intemperately announce, 'I ought to be going. There's so much still I have to do. Your husband'll be at work, I haven't a doubt, and you'll have a great deal to do yourself,' adding, 'I have a house of my own in London. An area to the north of the Euston Road, much frequented by the uprooted and the lost,' making for the door only, with a cry, to return for my slippers.

'Mrs Stott said she'd be here,' she says, 'in a very short while.'

'When did she say that?' I ask.

'When you were in the field I phoned her,' she says. 'She gave me her number and told me to call. She said she'd be here in no time at all.'

'She's a very slow driver, and the road from Ardsley to Linfield,' I tell her, 'is full of bends. She's enough on her hands, as it is, at present, not least of which should have been a definitive study of her father, a singularly neglected figure at the best of times but, in my not unprejudiced view, unlikely to be so in the future. Give her a ring. Tell her,' I pause, a car passing in the road, 'I'll come back on the bus.'

'She says you shouldn't be out,' she says, following me to the door.

'I've been on my own,' I tell her, 'for a very long time. Far longer,' I go on, 'than I recall,' returning to the room to pick up my sketchbook and pencil. 'I have,' I continue, 'never felt better. No day passes,' I tap my head, 'but I wake to a feeling commensurate with being hanged. Hanged, I might add, within the hour. An inordinate sense of guilt masks an indescribable sense of dread. Somewhere along the road, assuming I ever had it, I appear to have lost myself. And yet . . .'

I am looking up the stairs: those tiny stairs, scarcely wider than a ladder.

'I hope you won't mind if I leave behind some money,' emptying my pockets of all the coins I have, laying them on the stairs before me, re-entering the scullery while, behind my back, 'I feel very worried at letting you go,' and, 'Is that man going, Mam?'

'Tell her,' I tell her, 'I went into town. I shall be back home,' I add, 'in no time at all. As quick as a flick,' I call to the child, the walls, I notice, of the scullery, as in my time, damp with condensation. 'I suppose your husband,' I continue, 'is unemployed.'

'No,' she says, 'he drives a taxi.'

'In that case,' I tell her, 'he'll not disapprove of me leaving a tip. I could, if I'd had one on me, have written a cheque. I still can, of course, the moment I get back. I know the address,' I add, 'by heart. The old, old home.' I tap the walls (even damper than I'd thought). 'Things being equal,' I go on, 'I'd have looked upstairs, seen the old bedroom,' turning in the door: in another place, in another time – not bowed down by domesticity, debt and propaganda – she might have been another Vi. But then – this, I reflect, or a garden shed? 'I escaped from this place with an alacrity even now I can't recall. I hated its squalor, its aridity, its lack of scale, its denigration of everything I considered fine.' I shake my head. 'Yet here I am. Looking, would you believe it, for what I lost, hoping for

215

a fire amongst the ashes,' yet all I get, I might have told her, is the smell of beer, the scent of oil, the sight of rusting metal.

'Wouldn't you say,' says Maidstone at one of our meetings in his tiny office (the walnut-fascia desk, the plastic chairs, the postcards from abroad and English sea-side places, pinned to the wall above his head: 'Thank you, Professor Maidstone, for all your help'), 'that life is a deeply depressing experience?' adding, 'Mishima, the Japanese writer, described it as the only definitive view of reality we ever have, and although I have never suffered in the way the majority of my patients have I'm not disinclined to agree with him. As you yourself have remarked, we have been given the means to resolve a mystery which, of its nature, eludes definition. Our tragedy is not only that our minds have outgrown our bodies but that our bodies have outgrown their reason to exist.'

Will this unfortunate woman, I mentally enquire, repeat to Etty what I have told her: tell her, in short, I have returned to town (am returning home: shall be back in Ardsley in no time)? 'His taxi isn't here, by any chance?' I ask, at which, standing in the porch, she shakes her head.

'That's not one of his cars,' I ask her, 'in the back?' and indicate the metal wreckage, at least three models evident amongst the rubbish.

'He hires his car,' she says, 'from a man in town and once he's covered that,' she shifts the child to her other arm, 'everything is profit.'

'Not a great deal of trade, I imagine, with so many out of work, and those in work not earning all they might: industry run down and not,' I tell her, 'being replaced.'

'There's quite a bit,' she says, 'at the station,' and, to clarify this, adds, 'The railway station. There are quite a lot of people go up and down from London.'

Already I am walking down the path, between the houses – the path – obstructed by the dilapidated parked vehicle, and all but obliterated by tyre tracks – down which I have walked too many times to count, the wedged-apart hurdles standing

216

in for gates before me – and fail to recognise the figure getting out of Etty's car drawn up in the road outside.

A man in a corduroy zip-jacket and jeans – an open-necked shirt, the collar of which could do with washing – enquires, 'You're leaving, are you?' and (not unpleasant features: fresh-faced, blue-eyed), glancing to the woman and the child who have now appeared at the top of the path behind me, he adds, 'I can give you a lift, if you like.' (Not Etty's car after all.)

'I haven't any money,' I tell him.

The car, though large – its front wheel drawn up on the tarmacked verge – is old.

'It must cost,' I tell him, 'a lot to run,' and add, 'Did your wife call you, by the way, as well as my daughter?' continuing, as he steps aside to let me pass (determination written in my features, I haven't a doubt, as well as implicit in my figure) 'I have an important appointment. One I've been looking forward to for quite some time,' uncertain still he might not delay me, he clearly in two minds. 'The principal characteristics of someone like myself,' I hastily continue, 'are slyness, self-containment, selfishness, aggression – directed against others as well as oneself: manipulative behaviour, an aversion, overtly as well as covertly expressed, to being influenced by others, an unwillingness, if not an incapacity to give gratification, a basic sense of hostility, the whole suffused by an ineradicable and unappeasable feeling of anxiety, manifesting itself, in my case, throughout my life, in unsolicited and unmotivated attacks of terror. These symptoms are caused, exclusively, by a malfunction of the brain – or by what might even be described as a "colouration" of the brain – like I was born with dark hair, you with light – and can't be altered, except by "dyeing". That is, by chemical infusion, of a kind which, on principle, I eschew. Psychotherapy, I'm afraid, of which I am a connoisseur, is out and, except for the psychotherapist, a waste of money, the only exception to this rule being that to have someone listen to one's tribulations is not an altogether disagreeable way of spending the time when time, with this particular syndrome, lies heavy on one's hands. Taking all in all,' having proceeded through the gate, 'it may be just as well to let me pass. I take it you haven't read *A New Theory of the Mind* which, in the last two years, has become a best seller, having sold a quarter of a million copies in the United States alone, that land of the ill- or the half-digested, the proceeds of which have been frozen by the bank in lieu of the many creditors who quite outpace my capacity to give it to more worthy causes.'

I am halfway down the road, the taxi-driver and his wife (with child) standing at the gate, the former uncertain – on foot or in his vehicle – whether (promises from Etty) he ought not to follow.

I turn up Hasledean Road.

Hasledean: a former benefactor of the town – one of the four co-founders of the Free Grammar School of Edward VI, a man who, in his time, poked fun at Rayburn, the Free Church preacher who, on a single day, converted five hundred people by offering to walk across the River Lin (above the site of the present weir) and who, being assured by them that he could, desisted on the principle (cf. Christ's mountain-top encounter with the Devil) that a gratuitous indulgence in divine providence was not to their credit. 'Credulity and the English lower orders' Hasledean was alleged to have said, 'are synonymous.' A mill-owner, pre-dating Owens, yet virtually unheard of in his time, he was also alleged to have said, 'If you look after the workers, they'll look after you,' a system he described as 'the reciprocating system of social welfare: what goes up won't go up again unless it first comes down.'

Hasledean: up which I walked each schoolday between the ages of five and ten, occasionally three times, invariably twice on Sundays (morning service, Sunday school, evensong) talking, most of the time, of war: the numbers of Germans and Italians killed, the number taken prisoner, the number of miles advanced (tanks destroyed, planes shot down): the paraphernalia of killing: life extrapolated – (as it turned out) for ever – by what could be done away with (fear, in the form of anxiety,

218

exonerated as social duty: memory, imagination, perception formulated by terror.)

From Hasledean Road into Horsfall Crescent: another co-founder of the Grammar School – plus the Horsfall Hospital (founded 1553 on the road between Linfield and Ardsley – and two fellowships at St Edmund's, still competed for by the pupils of King Edward's, and 'twenty-four quarters of corn yearly for ever to the great town of Linfield' – the houses here, like all those on Onasett, semi-detached, one or two – where the land rises and the air sweeps in unhindered from the Pennine hills – up for sale: if Etty or Matt would release my money, or Bea give me some of hers, I could buy an Onasett home myself, the one, perhaps, in Manor Road. I could even, with hindsight, have brought Vivienne here.

Yet what would a woman who was used to living in Cannes, with an apartment in Manhattan overlooking Central Park, with a home in Beverly Hills (for most of her married lives) have made of living on an industrial housing estate in the industrial north, a place in which she had no roots, neither religious nor artistic nor familial, a sojourner on the jetstreams of this world, from the age of nineteen (her first appearance on the London stage) to her death in a garden shed at the age of fifty-seven? Oh, Vi!

And would Hasledean and Horsfall have recognised their legacy in or on the road and crescent respectively bearing their names: those educators, philanthropists, benefactors whose enterprise saved the sixteenth-century equivalent of the derelict inner cities, those parochial connoisseurs of ignorance, poverty: fear – endowers of Bone (the ecclesiastical scholar), Taplow, the nineteenth-century divine, Foster, the inventor of the 'mechanical jenny' (which revolutionised the manufacture of worsted wool), Freestone and Morton, designers of the 'Free-stone Car', the first 'people's car' in Europe, Simpson, the lexicographer, who institutionalised the teaching of Latin in schools, Stansfield, the scholar, who re-interpreted the Greek Bible, Simmons, 'the poet of the Somme' whose *Letters to Linfield* is still in print, Garside, the cricketer, Monkton, the footballer, Weston, the politician (a pre-war Minister of State), Henderson, the D'Oyly Carte singer, Featherstone, the actor, Hawks, Wentworth and Ripley (producers and directors) and lastly, if not least, Fenchurch, writer, painter, madman (lunatic at large): anxious, humorous, selfish – duplicitous: strong?

I come out of Horsfall Crescent on to Alceston Road (no associations other than a village of that name further up the valley) which, like a backbone, runs along the crest of Ona's headland: geodynamic definition displaces the philanthropic: sandstone, limestone and millstone grit, scoured by river, ice and weather, ameliorated by river, pond and stream (by apathy and despoliation) dissolve into a mist of hill and valley: directly opposite me, behind a six-foot privet hedge (the shrubbery beyond it overgrown) is the brick-built hall of St Michael's church: humouresque in style – lancet (leaded) windows, nail-studded doors, dormer intrusions into its tall, steep-sloping, low-eaved roof – a place of intimacy combined with informal exaltation: scouts, crusaders, Sunday school, youth club: dances, discussions, concerts, shows – its polished parquet floor and blue-curtained stage, its dark-varnished chairs, its domestically-smelling kitchen, its loft where we stored our camp equipment, its posters depicting disabled soldiers, people suffering from loneliness, disease (leprosy and blindness), children, black or yellow, in a variety of clothes. The shrubbery, which shelters the mellow-bricked edifice from the road, is strewn with refuse: paper, plastic cups, cans – a piece of cloth, a tattered shirt: miscellaneous bricks and pieces of stone: the front forks of a bicycle – an itinerary like the contents of a pocket, forgotten, unemptied, ingenuously added to each day. 'Here I have come,' I reflect, 'to do what?' and walk round the hall on a loosely-stoned path to the church.

St Michael's was constructed from a mill: stone by stone and beam by beam, the industrial structure transposed to a terrace dug out of the southern slope of the Onasett headland: a clay-lined, clay-backed, hacked-out trench into which the church was inserted like a ship into a dock: low-roofed, square-structured: its plain glass windows let in an undiluted light.

"His life had been destroyed by a principle (he wrote), though what that principle was he had no idea: from the very beginning to now, as he rounded the corner of the brick-built hall and contemplated the sandstone structure of the church (its mullioned, horizontally-leaded windows more familiar to him than those of any other building on earth) he had been guided by a voice which said, 'For reasons peculiar to your birth you have ascribed to art a significance which is not that which normally exists between an artefact and its creator' (you have taken to yourself, he might have said, a graven image): he had, as the psychologists would now term it, objectified a process, reified his life."

'What's the first thing?' Mackendrick said, 'that you remember?'

I sitting in the celebrated psychologist's consulting room in Belsize Square (the whole house recently purchased from the sales of *The Phenomenology of Experience* (POE, for short), and transformed from separate flats, apartments and bed-sits into a single unit, with Mackendrick's consulting-room and study in the former basement): a view through the recently-installed french windows onto the recently-planted lawn (enclosed on three sides by plants purchased on the final public-viewing day of the previous year's Chelsea Flower Show), overhead the stamping feet of Mackendrick's son (aged three) and his inter-mittent calls (amounting to screams), of 'Selda! Selda!' to the Mackendricks' former East German nanny, the rosy-cheeked, blonde-haired, ample-bottomed Griselda (Mackendrick's wife was also a psychiatrist, but worked away from home).

'My first memory,' Fenchurch said, 'is of being pushed in a pram beneath a bridge.'

My first memory, dear B, is of being pushed in a pram beneath the railway bridge that runs directly out – across Westgate – from Linfield Station:

directly above me are the rusted, corrugated metal sheets which underlie the bridge and across which, at the time, a train is rumbling; water drips from between the metal sheets and falls on the black, gaberdine cover of the pram – one

221

drop, at its source, high overhead, glistening in the light and descending onto the shoulder of my mother's coat.

A second figure walks beside the pram: I merely have the impression of his darkness, of the sobriety of his dress, and of the movement of his arm as he walks adjacent to the handle.

The stain on my mother's coat expands, darkening the reddish fabric as we pass into the light beyond the bridge.

I am bored; I have outgrown the distractions of the field at the back of the house: the world is circumscribed by the garden, the gardens on either side, by the field, by the houses that enclose it. Other roads lead off from our own: they branch out in every direction – to the town, to the park, to the fields (to the golf-course), but, most directly, to the school which, together with a stone-built church and a brick-built hospital, stands at the summit of a hill.

I bore my mother with my summer complaints: 'Go out and play. When you get to school you'll find you haven't the time,' until, when the day arrives, afflicted by apprehension, the portent, merely, of things to come, I become concerned about my bladder. 'Go before you go in. Go,' she says, 'as soon as you come out.'

The torment of not being able to contain himself dominates his other feelings ('You've been asking to go to school for months'), the vacancy of the previous weeks infinitely preferable to the terror which afflicts him now: on the morning that he leaves – clean socks, clean shirt, clean trousers, shoes (clean handkerchief inside his pocket) – five years old and two months exactly – he sets out from the scullery door. At the corner of the road he turns: from the top of the slope he can hear the raucous sound of children's voices.

He goes back to the house, raises the back door sneck and goes inside: his uncle, his father's younger brother, who lives across the field, has come in through the garden. 'Home already?' he says, and laughs.

They have seen him from the scullery window.

'Anything the matter?' his mother enquires.

'Is my cap on straight?' he asks.

'Of course it is,' she says.

She sets it on his head more firmly.

He turns to the door: 'Laugh and be happy!' his uncle says, years later, giving him lifts in his post office van: Bea on his knee in the tiny cab: down to the station or the Ardsley stop.

Re-setting his cap, he sets off once again.

At some point in the day he cries: a Miss Arnold calls him to her desk (his gaze through the window to the stone of the church: its clear-glass windows, its horizontally-leaded lights, its short, square bell-tower like a chimney, the bell visible inside): the confusion of teacherly commands: don't talk, don't stand, don't turn (sit, listen, learn: fold arms). She presses Fenchurch's head against her breast (his first embrace by a woman): there's the smell of chalk-dust and, before he leans against it – before his head is drawn against it – the softness of her breast. 'Against that softness,' he reflects, 'I have been pressing all my life.'

His crying stops and, as far as he recalls, he never cries again.

"The difference between writing a diary," Fenchurch writes in his as he recalls the incidents of his first morning at school, he sitting at his desk in his back-room study in his gigantic house in Belsize Park, "and writing fiction, is that, with the latter (his diary is full of "latters" and "formers", "comparisons between" and "on the other hands") the context within which it exists has to be set down, whereas with the former that element is given (full, too, of incidents witnessed in the street, out-mayhewing Mayhew). The blank page upon which a created world has to be set down is not the blank page upon which the events and the reflections of everyday life can be recorded: the energy as well as the intensity are different; the evocation of a created character within a created context dissipates casualness and even (in me, at least) reflectiveness. I wish it were different (he underlined the last phrase in his mind), that the effortlessness of setting down a thought or feeling, invariably uncorrected, on a page like this could be transposed directly to a novel. It doesn't work (he underlined that, too). It never has, and no amount of effort is going to make it."

"Bea: beatitude," he doodled: "beatific. Beat. Beattie. Beatrice (Beat*rix* – 'Tricks' – to our children who adopted first the suffix then the nickname at an early age). Mackendrick suggesting today that instead of visiting him in the afternoons at four, when I'm feeling sleepy, I ought to come in at six a.m. When I expressed surprise he informed me it was not unusual for him to see patients at five a.m."

'Who?' I asked.

'A doctor,' he said. 'A civil-servant. A poet who sleeps all day and writes at night. A solicitor. A therapist' (to my surprise).

A portly, genial, black-haired man, dressed in a pin-stripe suit (which I, for one, appreciate immensely), he leans back in his chair (the feet of his demented son across the bare-wood floor overhead: 'Selda! Selda!' the put-upon fascist nanny).

'I thought,' I said, 'you weren't allowed to talk about your clients.'

'What clients?' his hands behind his head: he feels sleepy this time, too, himself.

'Your other clients.'

'I can,' he declares, 'do anything I like.'

"Dear Mrs Fenchurch," I read in a letter Bea received (though no longer living with me at the time), "your husband is seeing another woman. Her name is O'Farrell, though she often goes under her maiden name of O'Connor. Ask him where he was last Wednesday evening. She has been married twice and has four children by three different men."

'Do you think I'm out of my mind?' I ask Maidstone, who has recommended Mackendrick 'as a friend'. 'I often think I'm in it whereas,' I go on, 'to be out of it would be a blessing.'

"Dear Bea, the paint is peeling in the kitchen; mouse-droppings, overnight, appear around the sink. At night there is an owl. I walk in the garden excited by your letter: 'Dear Mrs

Fenchurch (you won't know me but I know you).' Enclosed: someone, it appears, still thinks we're married. (I believe she's referring to Vaughan)."

Bea, Beatrice: Beattie Kells (uses Bella's maiden name in her research).

Must relate to something: Kells, her mother? She is not a PhD for nothing (she is searching at the moment for 'the secret of life'). Her lover, too, is a brilliant man, the parliamentary private secretary to the Minister of Health – divorced and living with a lover who is the picture editor of an international magazine ("such complexity," I wrote, "such singleness of purpose"). Adrian Morley (she calls him by his second name, Albert) is, by any call, a fastidious seducer – in addition to which he has only one arm (a handicap which professionally – certainly politically – has done him a deal of good: he can only write with one hand). His picture-editing lover, too, is something of a charmer: coppery hair, green eyes, a pendulous chin which, not undisagreeably, evokes – misleadingly, I'm told – an air of lasciviousness and languor. B: hair of a lustrous, dark magenta, her colour rich

rich

a northern childhood

her maternal grandfather the one-time syndicalist and latter-day 'democratic communist' H. J. Kells, his *The Locust and the Meaning of Life* being instrumental in the founding not only of his and Bea's careers but of six university embryology departments (three in America, three over here)

overhung, her brows, by that lustrous hair (from beneath which her dark, green-irised eyes gaze out: flecked with brown), the colour, the bloody suffusion of her cheeks

blooming

like the fruit in her father's Ardsley garden (the trees that encroach it on every side).

Her nose is arched: her mother's mother's Sardinian parent, 'the sea,' so she told me, 'in her blood' – evident only, in later

225

years, in the wave-like fervour with which she overlooks her husband's life, smiling

smiling

'no bolts or catches, for instance,' Corcoran tells me, 'on their lavatory door so that, on the occasion of my first visit – when I was courting Bea's mother – *her* mother steps in to clean her teeth, turns on the tap, chatting between scrubs to her daughter's suitor sitting, flushed, on the lavatory seat, caught in the midst of what *my* mother – who was not a primitive woman – was not disinclined to call "my morning ablutions". It's why she and Kells have never got on.'

Mediterranean whore (Bea's mother) mixed with nutty celt (Kells meets Mlle Rievers in Ajaccio, on holiday, in 1912): oriental mixed with occidental: live, dishonest: strong.

"Bea," he wrote about this time, "who has beaten me so badly;

whose pride, after having had five children, has taken a fall;

whose intelligence has been honed by having children;

whose strength has been added to by each mucused streak of bone and gristle deposited on the midwife's table:

Bea: B!"

'Apropos our previous conversation,' Mackendrick says, 'what is revealed in the ideology of confrontation is a shift in the instrumentation of power: behind the nineteenth-century pragmatic idealism is a movement to wrest power from money and invest it in a more expendable commodity: people.'

'People,' I rejoin.

'Note their preoccupation,' he goes on, 'with the "proletariat", a body to be "led", a body "external to the ideology itself" – just as capital is external to the proletariat which, allegedly, it endeavours to exploit.'

'My family name,' he said this morning (not, I might say, at 6 a.m.), his suit uncreased as he lay back in his leather-upholstered chair (how I admire his neatness, a source, to me, of reassurance, providing, as it does, a contrast to my own dishevelment: all the contortions, distortions, dissemblement

226

of the human psyche contained in a pin-striped suit) 'is not Mackendrick.'

'What is it?' (I enquired).

'Butalowski,' (I think he said).

'Butalowski,' (he didn't correct the pronunciation).

'My father came from Russia.'

'When?'

'In 1905.'

'And changed his name.'

'He changed his name,' he confirmed.

'Why did he choose Mackendrick?' I asked.

'He always admired the Scots.'

'In Russia?'

'He was a great admirer of Sir Walter Scott.'

'I thought, in Russia, it was Robbie Burns.'

'This,' he smiled, 'is before the Revolution. He spent his first few years in England in SE 29. After he married he moved to Clapham.'

'What was his christian name?' I enquired.

He smiles again. 'His given name was Yuval.'

'Yuval Mackendrick.'

'He changed that, too, of course to Walter.'

'Apropos Marx,' I said, 'that sounds like the reaction of someone whose family were driven out of their native land and whose father arrived at the London Docks in 1905 and who lived – would it be in West Ham? – before he married.'

'The defensive note in Marx,' he said, 'isn't that of someone defending an ideology against an opponent but that of someone defending a faith against themselves.'

'I, too, have read *Postscript to a Revolution*,' I said.

'In Russian?'

'Paperback.'

Yesterday afternoon he told me that the roots of fascism are to be found in Hegel: the secularisation of the Divine Will: 'It's no coincidence that Stalin and Hitler signed a non-aggression pact in 1939, and the Russians another with the Japanese only a year or two before that.'

Now I ask him, 'What about my wife?'

He is – I am convinced – in love with her himself: after all, we are almost neighbours.

'Bea is making plans to marry Albert if he can get rid of the picture-editing Rose.'

'I thought you weren't divorced,' he says.

'A technicality, in her view, despite our having five children.'

'Your children are all grown up,' he says.

'The youngest,' I tell him, 'is nine.'

'Nine?'

He is about to say, 'Are you sure?' but adds, 'Apart from lovely Rebecca.'

'There is also lovely Benjamin, who is twenty-one, lovely Kenneth, who is twenty-three, lovely Harriet, who is twenty-six, and lovely Mathilda, who is twenty-seven.'

'You can't hang on for ever!' About to laugh, he adds, 'And who is Rose?'

'Rose is Albert's girl-friend, who is six years younger than Albert, and considerably younger than Bea.'

'Rose.' An unself-conscious habit, swivelling in his chair, he slowly picks his teeth: Russian teeth but Clapham-bred.

'Horowitz, neé Schlegel.'

'I don't know the name.' (Cardo, Mackendrick's son, stabs, with his foot, the ceiling overhead).

'Her former husband – Horowitz – is an interior designer.'

'Horowitz.' Listening to Ricardo's voice, he adds,

' "The law protects the ideology of those who have it against the attacks of those who don't and who, possessing no ideology, grow steadily submissive, until, having nothing to define them except their submissiveness, they become," ' his chair comes to a halt, ' "the revolutionary mass themselves." Romanticism, would you say, or faithlessness, or,' avoiding eye contact altogether, 'both?'

The class divides: a few of my (brighter) contemporaries and I, in my second year at Onasett Primary, are joined by others: we enter a room dominated by the tiny Miss Batty: dark hair, dark-eyed, protuberantly featured: on her blackboard are intimidating signs and figures, identified, by her – after a perusal round the class – as mathematical tables: on the top right-hand corner of the blackboard is written the date: a figure in this is changed each morning.

Each morning we inscribe this in our diaries.

Today the sun is out. I ate my dinner,

maturing, years later, into,

'Is Albert very attached?'

'I scarcely know him,' I reply.

'He has been married,' Mackendrick remarks, 'unless I am mistaken, once before.'

'He has,' I reassure him.

'In that case,' Mackendrick observes, 'he's scarcely likely to marry again.'

'Why?' I instantly reply.

'He has two women already (what man,' he is about to add, 'could ask for anything more?' but says), 'The enfranchised proletariat, after all, *are* the bourgeoisie, and where society isn't bourgeois,' he concludes, 'it struggles to become so.'

I am sitting on a slope: a hen has captured my attention: it runs round the back of my mother and, as my father reaches out, the hen runs off. For the first time in my life I stand.

I press my feet against the grass.

I hear my mother's voice call out.

Yet all I am aware of is the thought, 'If I had wished, I could have walked like this before,' and, 'I have walked like this on many previous occasions,' and, like reflections reflected endlessly in opposing mirrors, am conscious of my previous existences stretching out before me.

As, seated in a pew to the rear of the nave, the interior of St Michael's stretches out to the clear-glass, five-lancet window above the altar.

'Surely,' I tell Mackendrick, 'you have removed that from my book,' (*The Logic of Grief*: in reality, a pamphlet – of lectures given at the ICA at the height of my notoriety: "the working classes are the bourgeoisie bereft of their possessions").

It was this pamphlet that brought us together, Mackendrick alluding to it in his introduction to *The Phenomenology of Experience* as well as – and more generously – if equally plagiaristically (Mackendrick is a great synthesiser or, what is referred to benignly as a 'great anthologiser' of other people's work, invariably – after token acknowledgement – subsumed under his own name) – to *A New Theory of the Mind.* In LOG, as it became known, I divide experience into actuality – our awareness of what is happening now – and reality, which includes actuality, but also everything beyond it: actuality is Mackendrick seeing me and me seeing him in his subterranean study in Belsize Park (with intermittent incursions from Cardo and Griselda overhead), and reality, including that, is what is happening in the rest of the house, in all the houses, in all the streets, in the universe as a whole, to the outermost reaches of time, not excluding its potential to go on for ever. Mackendrick's book, not unindebted to my contributions, has become a cult (hence the house) and has been followed by a sequel, *Six Studies in Dementia* which, in the words of one notable reviewer, 'has given psychiatry not so much a new as a novel life', its colloquial style and subsequent accessibility, offensive only to clinicians, contributing in no small degree to the impression created in the mind of the reader that he or she is irretrievably insane.

I dream; I dream quite often in Mackendrick's chair, never sure whether, as was the original case, he was consulting me or I am consulting him: 'Come along and listen to my tapes,' he suggested after the second of our meetings (sure of me at last). 'They're so much like the plays you've written,' tapes which turned out to be of his patients talking of their wives, their husbands, their children, their friends (their mothers, their fathers, themselves). 'What strikes you most?' he genially enquired. And when I said, 'Their exclusivity,' he said, 'Precisely. No one, they are convinced, has suffered like themselves. The subject of comedy, don't you think, as in so much of what you've written.'

"I am lost: I dream of people I have not seen for thirty years:

230

a teacher at school who taught us tables; a boy I feared; another I admired; a neighbour who died and who had only lived for a year in the house next door. I live," I go on, "in a delirium of terror. I wake: I perspire: my eyes frighten me with what they throw back each day in the mirror. I pray, 'Our Father,' followed by the one injunction, 'Help!' "

Fenchurch, prefixed Richard, regarding, in church, the back of the knees of the boy in front, the profile of his head silhouetted against the southerly-orientated clear-glass (five-lancet) window above the altar: the Crusaders' banners, each with its emblem, at the end of the pews (boys on one side, girls on the other): the Marys and Matthews, the Hildas and Johns: the peculiar scales on St Peter's fish, painted in a luminous silver: 'Give us this day our daily . . .'

"Classes in society are only superficially identified by wealth and possessions: what identifies them more profoundly is expectancy: what each class holds itself in anticipation of – a mental or even spiritual condition which identifies different cadres in society in relationship to what each cadre anticipates drawing to itself. A 'classless' society segregates itself into layers of expectancy each of which, in turn, becomes identified as a class itself." (LOG).

Between my praying hands, Allcock, the vicar, his cassock corded like a monk's, tassels hanging from his waist. Our Father: (the yorkstone paving of the aisle, the columns of sandstone: octagonal shape) walnut pews: hassocks, green on one side, blue on the other: church of St Michael (angel of light).

On the way home (my parents in bed) the buttered-once-a-week-only bread.

'Why Maidstone said he'd found a therapist,' I tell the boy in front, 'who might unearth a hitherto unknown source of anxiety, I've no idea. "I sent a poet to him some years ago," he said, "and though he committed suicide two years later I thought Mackendrick's insights at the time remarkable. He's somewhat softened that existentialist-phenomenologist approach and, in my view, is very much open to new ideas. I've written him a letter. Not mentioning you by name, of course, but enquiring if he'd take on a case not dissimilar to that of the poet. His suicide, by the way, as Mackendrick pointed out, was due to him not keeping to the treatment. He was found hanging from a beam in a lodging house in Kilburn. At the age, I might add, of twenty-one. His poetry had a Dantesque intensity. A remarkable fellow. Mackendrick, I mean. The poet, I guess you could say, was promising." '

'I thought I'd find you here.'

Etty is sitting across the aisle: cheeks glowing, eyes bright, wrapped against the weather (a headscarf disarranged, or perhaps hastily put on): she has taken a look at my sodden clothes, at my sockless feet (my mud-stained slippers) and, with a gesture of indifference, sinks further back in the walnut pew.

'I've been all over,' she adds.

'I don't see why.'

She is gazing at the altar, her profile alone sufficient to convey the gravity (depth, range, complexity) of her feelings.

'When you disappeared from the garden I searched the grounds. I searched the village. Your shoes,' she goes on, 'were in the hall. I didn't think you could have gone far. Then I met someone in one of the shops who recalled seeing you waiting at the Linfield stop. I got in the car and searched the town. Then I thought of Onasett. I called at the house where I thought you'd lived. The woman there must have thought I was mad. Nevertheless, I gave her my number and asked her to call me should you turn up.' Tears glisten in her eye. 'You're worse,' she concludes, 'than one of the children.'

'It wasn't a good idea,' I tell her, 'bringing me up. I'll only be the burden to you that I was to your mother. She, if you recall, absented herself. Her instinct, Etty, is one you ought to follow. Just look at it,' I add, and gesture at the pillars: to each is attached a placard: 'Love,' reads one, 'is what unites.' 'They've even taken down the donated copy of Rubens' "Descent from the Cross" and put it against a window, blocking the light and, because it's silhouetted, obscuring the picture. Can any goodness be left when art is in decline? In the old days, shields, symbolising the saints, of either sex, were hung in profusion at the end of the pews. I was in St Matthew's which had, appropriately, a picture of a book . . .'

She has blown her nose: she wipes her eyes: the coldness of the interior – conceivably, the intensity of her feelings – causes her to tremble.

'Considering my career, something portentous in that, don't you think,' and when she doesn't answer, I add, 'Although, at times, I'm not altogether certain where I am, or what I'm doing – or what, for instance, I set out to do – or whether I'm talking or thinking aloud – I am quite capable, Etty, of looking after myself. At least . . .'

She isn't listening: footsteps echo inside the door from which, in earlier days, the choir and the clergy would emerge: a man in shirt sleeves appears, carrying a bucket.

He turns, aware of our presence and, having lowered the bucket, retrieves it and returns inside the door.

'I came here,' I tell her, 'to confess,' and add, 'I don't suppose it'll do much good.'

'I've got the car outside,' she says. 'Do you want me to wait, or are you coming out? I have to get back as soon as I can.'

'I rather wanted,' I tell her, 'a moment to myself,' at which, blowing her nose again, she rises. 'There's no need,' I go on, 'to take me back. If you give me the bus fare I'll be all right. I gave what I had to that woman at the house. The place, though it's where I used to live, is little more than a rabbit hutch.'

'Perhaps,' she says, 'it was before,' startled by my reaction.

'It saddened me,' I say, 'no end. Or would have done. I've got past being saddened by anything,' and add, 'I gave her the money because I don't believe her husband, once he's paid for the car – he rents it from a man in town – makes enough to live on.'

'I'll wait outside,' she says, and adds, 'I'd like to leave as soon as we can.'

'I wanted to look in the classroom windows. Miss Arnold's and Miss Batty's,' I tell her. 'The one considerate, the other

233

alarming. One three is three. One four is four. Evil is the seat of goodness.'

'Will you be long?'

'Not at all.'

She is, moments later, I am aware, watching me through the glass panes of the door which opens to the porch. She is afraid I might get up and leave by the vestry.

The (blue underpainted) body of Christ, strung, pale, a long, descending diagonal from the arms of the man who has drawn out the nails (standing on a ladder) to those of the women who, weeping, kneel by his feet: I saw such looks in Boady Hall and in my outpatient days at the North London Royal: 'I am sorry and ashamed of my love for Isabella. And yet, dear Lord, I love her now. I disavow . . .' the blue underpainting of the flesh, the rattle of the bucket (the greenness of the paint where the flesh has putrefied): the fleck of red around each hole, ravaged at the edges: the pair of pincers in the workman's hand, the upraised fingers of the praying mother, the half-closed eyes shadowed from a light which, glowing on the face, inspires the question, 'Is he still alive?' ' . . . nothing!'

'Your stratagem,' I tell her, when I get outside, 'was to leave me in there, knowing I had nowhere else to go and would therefore be all the more obliged to come out and join you,' while, inside, before I'd left, I'd perused, from a distance, the T-shaped cross, the centre piece of a triptych, on the wings of which, fore and aft, were depicted four scenes from the lives of the saints (Mark, Luke, Matthew, John) which might well have been appended to those witnessed, daily, in Boady Hall, where 'The Prince of Peace' and 'The King of Love' mingled in the dining-hall, the art therapy room, the corridors, offices and wards (though not the padded cells: much reported on but non-existent) with Napoleon, the Primal Visitor from Space, the Martian Dayman and the Man Who Came From Nowhere.

She is sitting on the wall across the stone-flagged terrace, drawing my attention to the view (south, across the valley, to Ardsley: hedged fields and copses, the silver-lit surface of the winding river: the pitless village of Harlstone, a serrated ridge

234

of silhouetted houses), I gesturing, however, to the low, one-storeyed school visible, across a lane, in the opposite direction (to the north).

'I need to take you back,' she says ('Where are your socks? Look at your slippers!') yet takes my arm (her thoughts, I reflect, on something else) allowing me to escort her up the ramp to the narrow lane which divides the school playground from the church itself.

'That's the first classroom I was in.' I indicate the square-paned window yet, having arrived there, don't glance in. She, for her part, releases my arm, cups her hands and gazes inside.

'I suppose it's not much changed,' she says, and when I reply, 'I can't remember,' adds, 'One classroom, I imagine, is much like another,' a score of tiny heads and one adult one turned in our direction. 'In any case,' she concludes, 'they're coming out.'

'We should have a look at the crypt,' I tell her. 'It's where I attended scouts, Sunday school and the youth club and, in my sixteenth year, painted my "Crucifixion", one which, when exhibited, was described in the *Linfield Express* as "a modernist view of Christ". I painted him surrounded, not by people, but robots,' directing her, her hand, this time, on mine, the way we have come, voices already behind our back.

Something not so much about my voice, nor my manner, but my appearance has alarmed her: 'We'll have to be going. Glenda and Lottie will be home from school. You've led us,' she tells me, 'far enough.'

'The crypt,' I tell her. 'The parquet floor, the row of windows looking out to the valley (the Pennine hills, the sweep of the river, the marching column of smoke that indicates a train hauling its way to or from the Pennine gorge).'

'I shall be *quite* glad to get home,' Vivienne said, pale-faced (stuffed with drugs from a recent stay at a clinic in Blackheath), slouched, her head thrust back, in front of the imitation coal-fire (gas flames flickering around synthetic – unburnable – fuel) in our Taravara Road back kitchen. 'I've been feeling, at last, there's a place to go back to,' her bare feet protruding beneath her winceyette nightie, her hands, short-fingered, clasped around a pot of undrunk tea. 'I don't know what I'm doing here. I don't even know where I am. It can't be in a back street in London. Isn't it true' (a glance to me for the first time since she'd got up that morning) 'I'm dragging you down? Isn't it true we're no good for one another? Your preoccupation is with your dreadful wife and her dreadful mother and all your children who hate the sight of me, and mine,' she concluded, 'is still with Mel, a bigger shit than all of them.'

Her bloodless lips, her acned skin ('never cleared up from childhood, dear: one reason, of course, I'm not a *star*'), her bitten-down nails, her vacuous look, her tousled hair – thick-textured, curled ('my hair and my legs – though not above the knee – were considered my best features, pal!').

'She is, to my mind, the greatest actress of her generation,' Maidstone said after I had brought her to see him (the window-less room at the North London Royal). What a tragedy, he might have said, to see her in the state she's in at present. 'I'm sure we might do something for her,' he declared but, although he tried, no improvement was discernible to anyone. 'Her problems are intractable,' he announced after – at the end of six months (without any warning) – she took herself off on holiday. 'Has she,' he asked me, 'gone for good?'

'Those awful diets,' I told her (those awful drives she took alone): 'Nowhere is everywhere,' she said, 'when you're looking for somewhere,' and when I told her she had read that in my pamphlet (LOG), she said, 'I knew that a long time, Richard, before you wrote it. Anywhere is better than nowhere. That's why I drive the freeways. Going from nowhere to nowhere has anywhere between.'

'What?' Etty enquires for, assured we are not to be pursued, I have turned once more in the direction of the school, walking parallel to it, along the lane – marking off, as I do so, the classrooms: 'Miss Schofield's, Miss Setchell's – a teacher in that one whose name I don't recall. I learnt my first poem, by Wordsworth, in that room: such simplicity and directness evoking such complexity of feeling. There never was a writer who came so nakedly to the point. And all before his thirtieth

236

year. After his marriage it turned to dross,' recalling how – was it earlier that day? – I had watched my pen making marks on a sheet of paper – scrawls of ink comprised of lines and whirls – an intermittent dash or dot – as might a machine perform a task – the dark excrescence, a residue of vegetable matter, a coagulation – and wonder: where am I – not Fenchurch, prefixed Richard – but the nameless part of me that searches the San Bernardino and/or the Hollywood Freeway (at the same time as it does so calling out a name, 'Vi!'): what is the 'one' that the 'self' is true to? (what is the 'one' that is lost at birth?).

"Dear Mackendrick, the notion that all experience has a particular locale (and its own dynamic) – 'intrinsic referral', you describe it (another lift from me) – begs the question when you go on to assert that, vis à vis the world in general – 'society', loyalties, and the like – 'intolerable consequences' occur if such experience is ignored, a 'malfeasance', you describe it, of the spirit (yet another lift from me: have you ever had such an uncomplaining plagiaree?): the 'degenerative imperative' (ibid) which envelops – in my view (if unacknowledged by you) – the whole of our life and finally destroys it. My immediate wish to go along with this is dissipated by my inevitable enquiry: what about Ricardo? Shouldn't his *mother* be looking after her son?"

'Over here, where the playing-field forms a small enclosure, surrounded by hawthorn hedge, and the ground, here and there, has uneven swellings, stood a searchlight and anti-aircraft gun emplacement during the war: here, adjoining the school gate, stood a guard-house where the soldiers, at playtime, would pass sweets across the fence: there was one called Lofty who was the butt of the other men: they would get him to dance, drill him with his rifle, get him, even though unloaded, to fire it. Once they lit a newspaper he was reading while sitting at the guard-house door and, using the occasion as a pretext, tipped a bucket of water over his head. It gave to the war a feeling of lightness, the guns, when they fired at night, like giant dustbin lids clanging at the top of the estate, and then, the next day, all clean and shiny, the barrels gleaming, the searchlights like

237

dwarfs hunched up on the ground, and we over here, reciting our poems, endeavouring, in my last year, to link, with a horizontal line, the individual letters in each word (the excrescence of ink – a watery blue mixed from a dark blue powder – which years later I came to recognise as less a vegetable or mineral dye than the matter of the mind itself).'

The novel is dead; at least, in its humanist tradition – and I have died with it. I wouldn't wish to argue: my relationships, the few I have managed to sustain, have all but foundered: I maintain, as Vi described it, the residual passions of the morgue. If someone loves me, as I thought she did (though not as obsessively as Mel), I offer them a helping hand: I love – again, as Vi put it – the poor fuckers in return: an engagement which, in my mind at least, evokes the image of a muddy pool: observations on its nature elicit such remarks as, 'It's opaque. It's dark. It appears to contain no life at all.' Yet, as with most dark pools, a great deal goes on beneath the surface: what the surface reflects the depths conceal. Similarly, what the depressive experiences, by second nature – as freshly and as directly as he sleeps and breathes – is the energised negativity which convinces him he doesn't exist in any of the ways accredited to a normal human being: absence, rather than a passive, is an active definition, and 'self' a misnomer for all he experiences as 'self': he is, in short, dehumanised: he doesn't exist: he experiences his non-existence as active.

"Dear Maidstone, is the reality, that the depressive is allegedly out of touch with, reality at all, or merely the bourgeois world of good intentions (providence: doing the best you can)? Hell, presumably, is as real as heaven, if not a great deal more closely related to everyday life. The reality which 'the greatest poet of the twentieth century' has suggested we can only partake of in very small doses is scarcely the reality to which the psychiatrist would wish us to return – whether by pills, psychotherapy, E.C.T., physical exercise or a change of diet. It might, alternatively, be argued that health for the insane, and for the psychiatrist (therapist, analyst) consists merely of the restoration of that thick skin of which the illness has apparently deprived the luckless patient.

In other words, is Eliot's 'reality' a misanthropic fiction?

Or is it the baseline to which no one in their right senses would wish to return? To be capable of relating positively to people (my constant endeavour) might, in this sense, be as shallow an interpretation of reality as Eliot's perception of it was, allegedly, profound."

'Do you,' Etty enquires, 'often talk aloud, irrespective of where you are or who you're with?' and when I reply, 'Each day and each night I go through extremes of emotion which, even after all these years, I find impossible to describe – a sense of loss, for instance, in which the words "sense" and "loss" are inadequate to convey the degree of awareness, in the first instance and the degree of absence, in the second,' she hastily responds, 'It's a good job I brought you up when I did. Leaving you alone in Taravara Road has done you, as Maidstone suggested, no good at all.'

'I was happy in Taravara Road,' I tell her, glancing not at the school, nor any longer at the playing-field – stretching beyond farm fields to the isolation hospital above – but at the church. 'As happy as I was, for instance, sitting in the crypt, in an afternoon daze, the sunlight streaming through the windows, imagining the tribulations and the ecstasies of the saints, men and women caught up in a vision to which,' I concluded, 'I intended to belong,' to which, not listening, she replies, 'You were living in squalor. The place was filthy. You hadn't washed up in months.'

'What's washing-up,' I ask her, 'when you're coming alive? When I was dead,' I went on, 'I was always clean. Despite all I appear to have done in my life, I have, in reality,' I go on, 'done nothing. Nothing at all,' I conclude, 'until now.'

'Have you done any sketches?' she enquires, glancing at the book beneath my arm (glad, at least, I suspect, that I've retained it).

'A tree at Ardsley, a view of Onasett – from the golf-course, one of a hundred, I should think, of that – another of the

239

houses at the back of Manor Road.' I add, 'The characteristics of dementia are not to be taken as peculiar to the sufferer but merely to the illness. Characteristics which the sufferer him or herself would like to do away with.'

'The car,' she says, 'is over here,' for, even while she grasps my arm, I have led her back across the lane and re-entered the yard at the back of the church and although, plainly enough, her car is there – parked, I observe, with the engine running ('I have difficulty starting it,' she tells me later) – I am leading her to the slope at the side of the church and indicating the square, metal-framed windows which offer a view of the parquet floor of the crypt.

'On that floor we played our games, learned our knots, communed with nature, learned first-aid, chanted our oaths, swore our allegiance (dedicated our lives,' I conclude, 'to God),' but, having scarcely glanced in at the room – a fraction of the size of the one I recall – she leads me back up the grassy slope. 'We constructed an overhead railway here, each year, when they held the church bazaar and made more money than the Men's Fellowship, or the Women's Meeting, or,' I tell her, 'both combined.'

'You're getting more childish by the hour,' she says. 'Leaving you in Taravara Road was a foolish step. My mother shouldn't have considered it.'

'Your mother,' I tell her, 'is happy with Albert. And I,' I go on, 'am happy for her. I did her a disservice. One,' I continue, 'I can never repay. (The biggest mistake of my life),' to which she responds, 'In which case, Father, I wouldn't be here. Neither would Matt, nor Ken, nor Benjie, nor Bec.'

'You were all,' I tell her, 'deeply loved,' and, moments later, 'You'll be getting your car stolen, leaving it unattended with the engine running. An open invitation. You can assume, in effect, it's been stolen already. I suppose you've brought no money with you. In which case, we'll be stranded, stuck up here with no means of getting back. I can't walk,' I add, 'much further in my slippers. "The wise man lives in the house of mourning," wrote Solomon. The most important book, I might add, in the Bible (the book to end all books, etc.). Talk about the death of the novel: not another word, I might tell you, was needed after that. Whereas I have followed that advice by instinct, not by choice. "The house of mourning," I told Maidstone, "has been, and still is, my natural abode." '

'Perhaps,' I go on, 'we should have gone down and that man with the bucket might have allowed us to look in the crypt. I know every knot-hole in that wood. The surface of a piece of polished wood is almost as evocative to me as a woman's skin. Did I tell you when *Philistines* was revived in New York one of the actors in the company bought me, as a present, a session with a Hollywood astrologist? I sat for an hour in a borrowed apartment in Greenwich village, just off Washington Square, and, having previously given her the three facts of time, place and date of birth, I listened to an account of my life as accurate as I might have given if I'd had three or four years to set it down.'

I am sitting in the car: how I have got there I have no idea (I don't recall climbing in or closing the door – an elision that characterises much if not most of my present life), the car turning out of the lane that divides the church from the school and into Alceston Road.

'I might come back to that again, the conjunction of Pluto with the sun at the time of my birth: the god of the underworld (the dead and the dying): a peculiar coincidence when you consider that, during her pregnancy, death dominated my mother's life and left its imprint on me for ever (her first child dying, at the age of six, six months before I was born – after a sojourn, I might add, in that isolation hospital at the top of the road). God of the underworld as well as the afterworld, this woman described it: a colourful character with a flowery gown and streaming blonde hair and a lascivious way of saying, "Sweetheart" as she extrapolated from a column of figures – her only points of reference – a psychoramic account of my previous life, down to specific incidents to do with Bea, your Grandma, and even Vi. None of them specifically named, of course. "Being born," she announced, "under the influence

241

of Pluto endows you with the ability to see in the dark. It gives you," she concluded, "the qualities of a shrink." "To probe the unconscious," I told her, "has always been my line. To go where no man (or woman) has been before, or from where, at least, if they have, they have never returned. Only me," I told her, "me alone." (Sole denizen of a world only I can know).'

'Isn't that what astrology is for?' she says, and I recall she has, in fact – before we set out from Taravara Road – listened to the tape (the murmur of traffic from Fifth Avenue, a police siren, the barking of a dog, the slamming of a door announcing the presence of someone else – unintroduced – in the flat).

'I live my life,' I tell her, 'like Penelope with her knitting. It's the way,' I continue, 'I've always worked,' aware, in the warmth of the car, how cold I am – how mania takes a grip without my being aware.

As for the death of the novel – a printer's error: a missing 'r' from the word in question.

A drunken poet in a London street, raising his hand as he sees me pass: 'Hello, there, famous author! Would you lend me a quid?' his less drunken companion (definitely not a poet) calling, 'A fiver would be better!'

Leading to (his last years with Vi) the sequestration of his funds by the more responsible members of his family:

'He gave it to people in the street,' (Etty).

'How much?' the Judge at the enquiry enquired.

'Five hundred pounds in a single day. (Probably more on occasions we never heard about).'

' "The degenerative imperative",' had been the defendant's only reply (by which time, for much of his time, a privileged internee at Boady Hall).

'It's not the disappearing,' she says, 'nor the aggravation you cause to me and Charlie, nor the inconvenience of dropping whatever I have to do to come and find you, as what you might do if one of us who doesn't know you isn't around. That woman at your former home, if I hadn't have been there previously, would have called the police. She must have thought, as it happened, I was mad myself. "If my father shows up," I said, "will you ring me?" as if I were giving instructions about a missing dog.'

' "Madness" has "sane" in it somewhere,' I tell her. 'In my first group therapy at Boady Hall we played, would you believe it, "Twenty Questions", the most extraordinary version of the game you've ever seen. I'd gone, prepared, as per instructions, with an analysis of my state of mind – causes, symptoms, prognosis, et cetera – a mental index with referential points, together with accessible accounts of alternative interpretations – breaking into tears, at one point, as a demonstration of my willingness to involve others. The therapist, however – too young, unfortunately, to know blood from stone – said, the moment we were settled – telling me, incidentally, to blow my nose: "We don't want cry-babies here," she told me – announced, "The first object is mineral with a vegetable attachment," and when someone said, "What is a mineral?" – no great intellectuals on the panel, I have to add – only Isaiah and the Virgin Mary – someone replied, "You buy it in a bottle," and a third young woman announced – who was there after seven attempts at suicide, "I can get three hundred words out of madness, and one of them is sane."

' "That's good," said the therapist, totally confused.'

No one rang me in Taravara Road, other than my children, Liam (once), with whom I immediately quarrelled, and Bea twice ('How are you?' she asked, and added, 'That's good,' without waiting for an answer) in all of six months.

I have never told anyone how I feel without regretting it. ('Why don't you shut your mouth?' I say each day to myself in the mirror.)

'Would you like Bryan to come and look at you?' she says.

'Who?'

'Raynor.'

'I can't see that he'll see much that he hasn't seen already,' I tell her, the Park appearing to our right, Onasett disappearing to our left. 'What did you mean, the other day,' I suddenly enquire, 'when you said, "You are going to die"? It sent a chill right through me.'

243

'I thought you weren't afraid of death,' she says.

'Curiously,' I say, 'since Vivienne went, I am. Terrified,' and add, 'Was it something that Raynor said?'

'It was,' she says, 'my own conclusion. If you hadn't riled me I would have added, "if you go on as you are." '

Strung up on the x-ray table with a barium enema plugged up my arse while, to help the under-assisted operator, I examine my intestines on the monitor screen and adjust the reflecting plate to his instructions. 'Are you *the* Richard Fenchurch?' one of the group of trainee technicians enquires (boots, jeans and sandals visible beneath their smocks, acned, suppurating foreheads, cheeks and chins) to which I reply (a definitive), 'No.'

'Has Maidstone said I'm about to expire?' gazing at the profile of the town, directly ahead, from the bottom of Westgate as I enquire.

'I only know what Bryan tells me. I haven't seen your notes,' she says.

'He's afraid I'll go the same way as Vi.'

'That's not what he says at all,' she says.

'I should have been warned. I did my best. All Vivienne wanted was an audience.'

Turning the car towards the centre of the town, she says, 'That's not what you said at the time.'

'I admired her. I admire her still. There were times, sitting there, her feet together, gazing out of the window at the tiny yard, that I thought she'd achieved something little short of sainthood. All she'd been through, her body, as she described it, "gone", her looks ravaged, her hands shaking and, involuntarily, just watching her, I wept. I've never seen anyone look so . . . blessed. I never guessed. I thought she'd have an easier passage. Easier than the one she chose. And yet, would you believe it? I have to forgive her. It's why,' I suddenly conclude, 'she won't succeed.'

'In what?' We have reached the centre of the town and she turns down, past the cathedral, towards the river.

'In taking me with her.'

As if detached from her as well as I, the car careers along a

244

one-way system: down the Springs, around the market, past a newly covered-in section: the cathedral about to be enclosed by a pedestrian precinct.

'I've brought you back,' she says, 'to get you better. When you are,' she adds, 'you can go back to Taravara Road,' and then, bleakly, 'I hate to see you in that place. Those streets and that house are not for you. All those brutalised faces. Every other one you meet, brutalised or brutalising.'

'Those,' I tell her, 'are the working class.'

'So,' she says, 'are the inhabitants of Ardsley. Yet their faces have dignity, tolerance, strength. Not the mangled features of the London cockney.'

'Why don't we talk,' I suggest, 'of something else. My head,' I tell her, 'has begun to spin.'

'Those characterless eyes, that pasty complexion, those thin-lipped mouths, the scrawny necks, that bow-legged walk that comes, I suppose,' she says, 'from rickets.'

Whereas it is true I have seen more domestic violence in the street than I have throughout the rest of my life, it is still a place where, if only for the briefest time, Vivienne and I were happy.

We cross the river, beyond it, moments later, a hump-backed bridge, the canal visible below us: past the street where one of my father's uncles lived, a colliery sinker with an invalid wife: an only son who was killed on the Somme: 'a street that hides its dead,' my father declared, once, as I sat with him, passing on a bus, adding, as if of something he admired, 'a man who never showed his feeling.'

'So what became of it?' I said.

'Like all feeling, shown or not shown,' he said, a bleakness in his life which, if rarely glimpsed, I always knew was there.

'Why don't you stay up here? You can,' she tells me, 'write and paint,' and when I reply, 'There was a time when I envisaged doing that, painting amongst the fields around Linfield,' she suddenly calls out, 'You're not old enough to give up!' as if, directly ahead, a door has opened. 'Even if you're out of fashion.'

'It's certainly,' I tell her, 'a philistine age, and we can only assume,' I go on, 'it has to get worse,' pausing, startled, at her laughter.

'A joke at last,' she simply says.

16

IN HIS mind's eye his wife and, with his wife, now someone else's, her mother, the coppery gold of their two heads, darkening to magenta, like the heads of two gigantic nails pinioning the palms of the crucified Christ: the green-tinted eye of Isabella: the grey-tinted eye of H. J. Kells, leaping, lithe, from his celtic ocean: 'I wouldn't say I was a marxist,' he says to Fenchurch when, in old age, the locust specialist spends his summer days filling in football pools on the lawn, in the sun, at the front of The People's Palace. 'I'd say, more nearly, I was marx*ian*,' putting down his crosses.

'What would you spend the money on?' I ask. 'Should you win.'

'People,' was all he simply replies, and adds – wisps of unshaven hair around his chin – 'Wouldn't you say,' he watches his daughter pruning roses across the lawn, 'that art, unless it expresses the will of the people, is a waste of time?'

'What is the will of the people?' I enquire.

'Why,' he says, 'you must have noticed, even at a football match, that the crowd is greater than that which congregates for an exhibition of your paintings, or even of the latest prodigal talent on show, shall we say, at the Linfield College of Art.'

'They generate different interests,' I observe, remarking the angle of Isabella's back, her waist, the protrusion of her hips (the position of more intimate features within the suspended folds of her blouse), the placing of one foot before the hem of her skirt which subtly reveals the shape of her calf.

'Other than by numbers, which always count,' (chuckles at the joke himself), 'who is to judge whether a popular entertainment is inferior or superior to the interests of an esoteric cult?'

His teeth are brown (if artificial) and his jacket, which he always wears, stained by the food he, at each meal, invariably drops down it: from the third button of his waistcoat to its top left-hand pocket (the folds of the garment, when he sits, enclosing his shrivelled chest) stretch the thin gold links of a watch chain, the watch itself rarely, if ever, lifted out – and wound, curiously, while still inside his pocket, his forefinger and thumb disappearing for minutes at a time.

'Otherwise,' he goes on, 'we are merely left with contempt for the popular judgement. The mass, despite what Shakespeare says, is never, and never has been wrong, particularly,' he concludes, 'when its deepest feelings are aroused.'

'Is this senility,' I ask Isabella, 'or mischief?' when, moments later, disengaging myself from the old man – his long, thin thigh flung, with a booted foot, across the other as he studies the list of football teams again – I cross the lawn, and she – who, her back to us, has listened, I discover, with a smile – smiles again and says, 'The product of experience, Richard. He has lived, after all, a very long time.'

Does he, I reflect, know more about us than, say, Isabella's husband or her daughter: does he suspect, with a father's lifetime's perception of his daughter, that the relationship between us is more than appears at first sight; or, *is* what appears at first sight?

'More means better.'

'Better means most.'

'Where does that leave us?' while she, glancing at her father – a pair of glasses, wire-framed, suspended halfway down his nose – declares, 'I found roses, would you believe it, in the wood?' adding, 'I'm showing Richard the roses, Father,' taking my hand, about the wrist – as she might, in school, encourage a pupil.

'I'm afraid I've told him,' she says, 'about us,' and adds, 'He's quite indifferent,' and when, amongst the trees, I ask

248

her, 'Why?' she laughs and, having released my hand, declares, 'Haven't you been in love and wanted to tell someone all about it?'

'I have,' I say, 'but not him.'

'It's quite all right,' she says (the heavy laugh – guttural – like, or so I'm told, her mother's: the high colour of the cheeks, the incandescence of her eye). 'He was quite pleased,' she goes on, 'to hear it. He was always unprincipled,' she adds, 'with my mother. Or, at least, communality was his principle and my mother, with her background, half-believed it. His interest in people, in any case,' she continues, 'transcends any he has in individuals. He sees life, after all, as a generic whole. Hence the pools: it's the figures, Richard, not the money. The greatest mystery of all,' and, with something of Kells' own expression – but more greatly, I suspect, that of her mother's, whispers, half-smiling, '*chance!*'

Later, returning to the lawn, Kells studies me above his glasses. 'Art,' he says, 'in the way you practise it, is a philosophy of despair, the legacy of an already, in most respects, discarded past. If, in your judgement, you are against the people, you can't be for them. If you can't be for them, you are condemned to a life of isolation. Man is a social animal and if, in society, you are alone, you can't and never will be happy. And,' he laughs, 'are we here to be miserable, do you think?'

'Who is this homo serioso?' he would enquire when, appearing on the lawn, ostensibly to call on Bea, I would cross to where he and, not infrequently, his daughter were sitting. 'Your homo serioso, Bella, is here again! Are you to take him for a walk in the wood?' adding, on one occasion – for when, so prompted, we seldom followed his suggestion, 'Two innocents at large.'

'Wouldn't you say,' he asked me on another occasion, 'that my daughter, your would-be-mother-in-law, is very naive?' adding, 'So was her mother. She gets it from her. So was I, in an underhand way: danced rings round by the anglo-saxonic scientific élite – until, that is, I set my marxian cat amongst the pigeons. A good cat is that, related to the Manx but far more

249

clever – and not only for its transformation, at a stroke, by a single letter.'

'A marxian,' I told him, 'without a cause.'

'Not at all. I did it to confound the English, and much more effectively than those apeists from the public schools who were always confounded by their education.'

'Do you,' he said on a further occasion, leaning forward from his chair (as if to examine something close to his feet) 'make love to both mother *and* daughter?' waiting, head stooped (inspecting the grass) until, assured I would not, perhaps could not offer a reply, he raised his lean-jawed head and laughed – his brown teeth loosened from his gums – gazing at the sky.

Rooks, I recall, rose slowly from the trees: they had – disturbing as it was – heard, I assumed, the sound before.

'He wouldn't tell Freddie, or, indeed, anyone,' Isabella said when, on going into the house, I told her of this conversation. When I enquired, 'Why not?' she said, 'It's not important, though, as a scientist, he sees its relevance to other people. He was always discreet with his indiscretions. This, at least, he feels he owes me.'

'For what?' I asked.

'For all he did to my mother and which she, through her good-nature, forgave. "I made your mother unhappy," he said just after she died. "I shall never – I feel it a bounden duty – do the same to you." Why,' she suddenly went on, 'I can tell my father everything. Everything!' adding, with something of his slyness – the sideways look of the long-lashed eyes, 'But, of course, my dear, I don't have the obligation to tell him anything.'

He feared the old man: he feared what he knew: he feared his life of principle (communality, detachment: amoral): 'You do right,' he told him, 'to fear the Irish,' – the long-angled jaw, the far-from-supplicating eye turned, over the top of the wire-framed glasses ('the glasses that have seen everything!' Bea) in

250

his direction, 'the apostate Irish,' he added as homo serioso approached.

Ah, serious man!

'I wish,' Isabella said, 'you had met my mother,' (one autumn day in the kitchen, waiting for Bea, swotting, in her bedroom overhead). From the mantelshelf above the kitchen range she took down a sepia photograph: a woman sitting sideways, on a bench, her dress short-sleeved, her long, bare arms extended to her knee (her fingers clasped together), a compassionate, warm-hearted, broad-featured face, dark-eyed, broad-lipped. 'Father always called her "Gypsy" ': slim calves, feet, delicately poised in high-heeled shoes, demurely held together. ' "Gave nothing away but love," he said.'

In my head, the Sardinian wife: 'Isabella's mother's background was the bordello,' Kells once said – leaning back, head raised, to laugh (scattering the rooks again in the trees). 'You know what a bordello is, I take it?'

He went into hospital, after I and Bea had moved to London, with a broken hip, caught pneumonia and, with 'Cleo' (a more intimate name for 'Gypsy') on his lips, he died: 'Love personalised, after all,' I said, fearing, for the first time, no rejoinder.

'I never missed anyone,' Isabella said, 'as much as I miss him. Not even you.'

He was tired: he couldn't sleep (the noises of the house, once familiar: no longer so): he had come across the subject in a book of Bea's, propping up the missing castor of their double bed (looking out to their Belsize Park garden) shortly after she had left, with Beckie, and taken the flat in Barnet: Harrison's and Schaadt's experiments, at Berkeley, with pregnant mice, twelve of which had been kept, on fertilisation, in a cage in which the conditions were arranged to cause them maximum discomfort: tilting floors, electric bells, flashing lights, irregular food and – cumulatively – electric shocks: in no time at all, Harrison and Schaadt observed, the mice were subject to 'involuntary trembling', subsequently 'fits and spasms' and, finally, 'catatonic withdrawal' – symptoms which, they further observed, 'disapeared without trace' when, at the birth of their offspring, they were removed to 'a normal environment'.

Except (Fenchurch noted) in their offspring: though only foetal witnesses to the events in the previous cage, they, from birth, exhibited those symptoms which had characterised their mothers' earlier behaviour – involuntary trembling, fits and spasms, catatonic withdrawal – and continued to do so until they died.

'You're not,' Maidstone said, 'making a connection between yourself and a traumatised mouse?' to which, at the time, he replied, 'If smoking can affect a pregnant woman, how about the death of a previous child – precisely at the moment when the central nervous system of the unborn foetus comes on tap, namely, the twelfth or thirteenth week of gestation?'

O homo serioso.

'The more you go into it,' Mackendrick says, 'the crankier it becomes. The prognosis, for instance, in its stress on material functions, is not merely derivative but self-protective: someone whose background impels him to disregard the complexities of any situation other than those he can relate to external events. Idealism extends itself first to define and then to embrace the whole.'

'Hole?'

'The Hegelian whole.' He leans back in his chair: the leather creaks: the patter of his son's feet above our heads and the demented cry of, 'Selda!' – the put-upon East German nanny who came through the Berlin Wall in a van driven by a young admirer: Schnabel, subsequently a journalist on *Die Welt.* ' "If the material causes of greed are removed cupidity will disappear." None of this, of course, is true.'

True.

Like Marx, Mackendrick: a pharisaical tradition ('*my* father did not forsake his religion and turn it into a secular joke'): bohemian (despite his pin-stripe suit: a joke on the world he will never join), theoretical, zealous (a charming plagiarist, to boot): firm, Ukrainian peasant legs inside his trousers: dark-eyed, flat-browed – overtopped, his cunning face, by a frieze of curls – tight-sprung, wiry, greying from each core to an outer fringe of black: an attractive, Panic personality merely bereft of the cloven hoof, the five-barred flute: short, square hands – more used to spade or shovel: 'Who, in a "fulfilled" society would work in the kitchen – wash the floors, superintend the laundry, dig the coal – while we, my friend, are hunting and riding (shooting and fishing), walking in the country, painting and writing, communing, if not with nature, with our fellow men? What, for instance, is the individual going to think who has the floor to wash, the fields to till, the street to sweep, the train to drive, the recalcitrant children to teach when there are others who do not have to do these things because of "different gifts"? Who, in short, Herr Fenchurch, is going to shovel shit?'

Charlie says, 'Why did you run away, then, Father?' sitting on the bed: enquiry rather than reproof, perplexity rather than castigation.

The bed creaks, in the semi-darkness, beneath his weight: the children, I conclude, are both in bed (where I have been since my return), Etty, hopefully, writing up her diary: "This morning/afternoon my father ran away. He had gone back to his childhood home in order, so he said, 'to meet his Maker'."

'The tribulations of the creative life are not to be dealt with lightly,' I tell him, 'nor explained, or dismissed in a conventional way. I am not, after all, a clerk in an office.'

'I never said you were,' his face shadowed by the bedside lamp which, casually, he has turned on while I am speaking. 'It's because you aren't that we're so concerned,' (an unlikely snobbery in Charlie). 'We want, above all, to see you better,' his ample hands spread out across his knees, 'and, if possible, living in London.'

'Doing what?'

'Work.'

'What work?'

'Writing.'

He makes the suggestion with a shake of his head.

'My writing days,' I say, 'are over. Such as they were.'

'Painting.'

'What?'

'The drawings,' he says, 'you did today.'

'Negligible. Bea,' I tell him, 'saw to that.'

The arguments we had, first to persuade her to go back to science then, once she was back, not to overlook almost everything else.

'Careers, I'm afraid, are toys to women. Freedom,' I tell him, 'went to her head. One look down her microscope and she had no time for anything else. The bric-à-brac she left, assembled by her friend Constanza, the absolutely frightful South American (Columbian) interior decorator she got in to desecrate our house.'

'Otherwise,' not listening to this, 'it's back,' he says, 'to the North London Royal.'

'Maidstone has retired. Something to do with his pension. They have a new man in now,' I tell him. 'Waddle. Or Coddle. Or Straddle. In my view, it was exhaustion: Maidstone. That and wanting to write a book about Rossini, Rimbaud, and Piero della Francesca. He had a theory they all suffered from unipolar depression. Unmistakable signs he was cracking up. As for my theory about pregnant mice, not to mention New Mind Theory, further and further evidence he was falling behind the times.'

'Harriet cannot devote the whole of her time to looking after you,' he says.

'I've no wish that she should,' I tell him. Far rather, I am about to add, I'd prefer the reverse, only he swiftly looks up at a sound from outside and, reassured we are not to be disturbed, declares, 'So long as you persist in neglecting yourself,' and is about to continue, 'you leave us no choice,' but, to get the gentle giant off the hook, I announce, 'I might as well specialise in something. Neglect is something I ought to be good at. I've had unlimited training. Indeed, if there is one subject I am familiar with it's the very one, Charlie, you've chosen. I ought to be grateful – indeed, I am – at your offering me not only a

254

lifeline but the prospect of a promising way ahead. Certainly,'
I thank him, 'something to rely on.'

'Wouldn't you say,' Maidstone says, 'that your preoccupation
with your brother is a sign that that preoccupation is doing
you no good at all?'

'No,' I tell him.

'He died six months before you were born.'

'My mother's grief is endemic to my nature. There is no
morning when I wake that I am not aware of his dying. (Despite
every effort to beat it down.) I (even) dream of demands I
become more cheerful – demands which, when I turn round
to see who has made them, I find coming from myself.'

'What Harrison and Schaadt have achieved with mice is not
necessarily applicable,' he says, 'to human beings.'

'Why not?' I ask.

'Why,' he says, and laughs, 'they're mice!'

'We shall have to have a rule. If and when you go out one
of us will have to go with you. Or, at least,' Charlie says, 'be
told precisely where you are.'

How long I've been prattling on I've no idea – evidently
some time, I conclude, for he now announces – i.e., threatens
– more sternly than I have previously heard him, 'It's not, at
least, like Boady Hall, nor the closed ward at the North London
Royal. Other than accounting for where you are going, you
have all the freedom you want.'

'People used to defer to me,' I tell him. 'I had great actors
at my beck and call. I talked, occasionally, to princes. Statesmen
called me on the phone. I could, had I wished, have travelled
round the world simply in answer to invitations, and still have
had enough left over to start again. I was,' I tell him, 'in
demand. Not a night went by but that somewhere in the world
a play of mine was being performed: for every hour of every
day, for every hour of every night, people were watching a play
by Richard Fenchurch, a colliery worker's son brought up on
Onasett estate, near Linfield. Now look where I am,' I
conclude.

'Those days are over, Father,' he says, easing his frame against

255

the bed, his figure more sombre for being beyond the pool of yellowish light. 'I always liked,' I say, 'a greenish shade, yet here I am with a yellow one. (Over,' I tell him, 'and long since gone').

'Will you agree,' he says, 'to what we ask? It'll make Etty's job much easier.'

'When the miners come up the path to the door you have a similar manner,' I tell him. 'Those stalwarts of the Ardsley Constituency Labour Party. Why they agree to being patronised I have no idea. I'm sure they talk behind your back. The good-natured Charlie. We are still a class apart,' I add. 'You and your father, me with mine. Despite the absurdity of what, in a life of absurdity, I've tried to do, the absurdity of what, for a time, I almost achieved – the sums of money, the distinguished friends, the awards, distinctions, honours and prizes, I'm still at heart, unchanged from what I was forty years ago on Onasett estate: gauche, inept, untried, lacking in grace, in faith, in love – bereft, by temperament as well as background, of all that might enhance – all that might, you could say, make life worth while.'

I am even, Charlie, going to fat: when I glimpsed, in a window, a reflection of myself today (in a pane of glass when I descended from the Ardsley bus at Linfield) I didn't recognise – in fact, on first sight, ignored – the figure standing there: grey-haired, obesity at that stage where, on a stocky figure, it might easily be confused with muscle.

Etty – at first I thought Bea, then her mother – has, I've noticed, for several seconds, been standing in the door (the sound which, earlier, had caused Charlie to raise his head): the sleeves of her dress are rolled from having bathed the children or, conceivably, from clearing up her room further along the landing – about to get down (at last) to *The Private Papers of Richard Fenchurch* – or, perhaps, more simply: *A Life*. Charlie, unaware of her, goes on, 'It makes Etty's task more difficult if we can't come to an agreement, Father. All you have to say is, "I'll be in the garden," or, "I'm going out to paint." '

'I haven't the energy,' I tell him, and when he asks, 'To

paint? Or tell us where you're going?' I add, 'I took up art as a means of killing fear. I thought, "When I become an artist it will go away": a sense of loss, a sense of isolation, a sense of being alone so fearful at times I couldn't move. Yet the irony is, of course, it goes the other way.'

Etty, stepping into the room, creaking a floorboard, momentarily distracts Charlie's attention: after all, as a socialist, a humanist, he wants to understand.

'Fear is, in reality, a symptom – of an isolation which was generated before I was born. The use to which I put it, or it put me, exacerbated it in a peculiar way. For nothing quite motivates the artist as the desire for recognition, and yet, the moment that recognition is achieved, his isolation is complete. The longing, would you believe it, Charlie? – the most absurd of all our appetites – a longing to be saved! Vivienne, at the height of her fame, when she discovered *that* – not unlike many in her predicament – despite struggling for years against the inclination – found the realisation too much to bear and, after taking a bottle of sleeping pills, swallowed, for good measure, a bottle of bleach. I will never forgive myself for not going in the yard. I, who suffered in that way, too. Nothing can beat that kind of pain: a sense that all you have struggled for has not only failed, but disappeared. Gone: all your efforts inappropriate.'

I pause, Charlie and Etty now standing together. 'When I came in from the yard I sat on a chair and thought, what effect will this have on Bea, then, more pertinently, on Mathilda, Harriet – on Kenneth, Benjamin, Rebecca? What effect does it have on me? An attempt to obviate the shock – of a sight which, even now, I resist describing: the figure reclining on a pile of compost, the snarl which, with rigor mortis, had stiffened into a ravaged grin: teeth flecked with blood, a fly alighting between her lips, her tongue: the smell. A peculiar codicil, Charlie, to what I've done. A peculiar way to end existence.'

'Let's look to the future,' Charlie says. Subsiding on the bed again, he adds, 'That, and the present, is all we've got. The

257

best thing you can do for Vivienne is to draw and paint, to write.'

'Yet the past,' I tell him, 'is where I am,' (the shadow of Etty, who has come closer, now upon me). 'The past, after all,' I add, 'is here. Bea and her mother sat there, too.' I indicate the bed. 'They, too,' I continue, 'sketched out a future. Into the distance (the long flight I followed, the journey I took). Yet here I am, where I started.'

'You appreciate,' Charlie stands, the bed springing up at the removal of his weight, 'we can't proceed from this point unless we have a plan.' (How the constituency devotees – more the men than the women – admire him.)

'What sort of plan?'

'Of action.'

'I shan't come,' I tell him, 'to any harm. Nor do I intend to harm man, woman, child or animal.'

'It's the damage, Father,' he says, his figure looming above me, 'to yourself. Etty, for instance, has other things to do. She can't confine her life exclusively to looking after you.'

'Nor should I wish her to,' I tell him. 'I have already confided to her a course of action. She could, for instance, write a book. The material, I've pointed out, is close at hand.'

His thick, broad-featured face drives outwards in a smile.

'It might, despite Etty's reservations, solve both our problems,' I go on. 'It would, in a constructive way, employ her skills and gifts – which I, incidentally, hold in very high esteem – and I would be obliged to be here with her, if not in close attendance, while the book is finished. An incidental benefit,' I continue, 'would be, not further notoriety for her, but approbation and the possibility, girded by such praise, that I might return to the work which, as you have pointed out, I have, in middle age, despairingly abandoned.'

'I've asked Bryan to look in,' Etty says, taking, as far as I am aware, not the slightest notice of what I have said. 'He says he'll come tomorrow. You'll stay in, I take it, until he comes?'

'Indubitably,' I tell her. 'No doubt,' I go on, 'there'll be a subsequent consultation behind my back.'

'He'll have his own views on the subject, Father,' Charlie says. 'After all, it's for your good,' he adds, 'that he's coming.'

I'm not sure whether this final remark is directed at me or Etty, or both: he looms for a moment at the foot of the bed, then – a flash of his shirtsleeves – he's gone.

'His torso was dark,' I tell Etty, 'with his wearing a waistcoat, but, for several moments, he reminded me of Corcoran. He, too, would come in here – particularly in the mornings, when I was painting, or writing, there, on a chair, by the window – and make a remark about, for instance, the dignity of manual labour – remarks which, I hadn't a doubt, were intended to point out the strenuous nature of his own employment, and the dependency of so many others on it as well as the irrelevance, if not indulgence of mine.

> So that's today, so desperately begun:
> so much endeavoured, so little done,

I'd quote him – but one of the many poems I wrote at the time,

> so much attempted, so little done:
> so much abandoned, so little won,

another version, he striding off to his yard and his lorries – his men, his coal, his steel, his oil – and I would re-immerse myself in my self-appointed task to show up humanity for what it was.'

As Etty sighs, I add, 'I apologise to Charlie but, most of all, to you, for all the trouble I've caused you. In earlier times, someone like myself would simply walk off, at night, into the trees, or the river. Perhaps, in my own way, that's what I intended to do. Different times, different places. I shall not leave the grounds, or the house, without informing you, or Mrs Otterman, or Charlie, or all three. As for Raynor, he can tell you as much about me as he likes. I doubt, after all this time, there'll be much that is new. Having fouled up my life

259

the last thing I want is to foul up someone else's. After all, if I can do anything at all I can at least set a bad example.'

'After all,' I tell Maidstone, 'the strong may cherish their vulnerability: all those elements which in their lives have previously distracted them, are, by their susceptibilities, brought into focus – and swept aside. Their perceptions are extended: they are obliged to move beyond themselves (they are obliged to move they know not where). In reaching the end of things they arrive at their beginnings.'

Hell has no optimum condition.

The unimaginable is realised and precedes the unimaginable again.

While all Harriet says is, 'We don't want you to feel imprisoned.'

'I don't feel that at all,' I tell her. 'This house is how it was four decades ago, at least. I was just turned eighteen when I first saw it and, while I was a student, I stayed here several times a year – on holidays, at weekends. This room,' I go on, 'is haunted, not least,' I continue, 'by the women that I loved. Principally by two of them, and now, of course, by you. It's no wonder I confuse Corcoran with Charlie: large men, both avuncular, both, in their differing ways, good sports. Your grandfather, of course, was a rabid Tory – the only one in the district at the time – and Charlie is one of your middle-class dreamers, promoting a world which, should it ever come about, would do away with people like himself.'

She has gone.

Fenchurch, I reflect – sketching her introduction – is a complex man: too sensitive to be political, too fair-minded to be partisan, too intelligent to submit the variety of life to a dogma: an amazing conjunction of hypocrisy and ambition, of irresolution and certitude, of absurdity and good sense (of baseness and magnanimity): morbidly introspective, revolutionarily inclined, indisposed to expressions of affection.

Momentously, at the height of his success, he arrived at the conclusion that his life – as he had envisaged it from his youth, if not his childhood – pursuing his goals with an energy bordering on venom – had been based on a misconception. His sense of humiliation in his childhood but, more specifically, in his youth, had indisposed him to society in general, and to certain all-too-clearly identifiable aspects of it in particular: his pessimism – deriving from a source beyond his control – inclined him to an anarchic view of his own existence (one which only belatedly he had come to realise teetered on the threshold of despair). His only antidote, a vitalist belief in self, inclined him to use circumstances and people to increase his power (the product of his insecurity) and to dominate his environment: 'isn't domination,' he conjectured, 'in reality, what life is all about? Didn't Christ dominate the Devil (the priests, the pharisees, his parents, the Romans)? didn't he seek, as a child, to over-rule his mother? (What did his father make of that? What, come to that, did his father make of his Father?)'

Night: his daughter and her husband sleeping: their daughters – with odd cries and shouts which characterise their dreams – asleep as well. 'I might, quite easily,' he reflected, 'be in our home in Belsize Park, the night, for instance, Bea tells me – not the confirmation merely the beginning of his crack-up. And Constanza, the South American brood-mare, as Bea described her, with that psychopathic father who had killed – how many people was it? – three hundred in a day ('almost as many as days in the year'), the Minister of Justice. What about Bea: her drawings, her photographs, the stone (breeding) trough in the boiler-room beneath the front door steps? What about – tears flooding his eyes – the years they'd spent inside that building, in partnership, in comradeship, bringing up their children? 'Our children!' (the only revolution they had witnessed in their lives).

The owls, the mice, the rumble of the trains – the sudden rush, as opposed to the vibration, as they passed a vent, brick-lined and grated, between his and his neighbour's house.

The beginning of what he called his 'grand dispersal'.

He gave away his money: first to charities (who wrote grate-ful, personalised, incredulous replies), then to organisations whose activities he wasn't sure about, then to a variety of individuals, from artists whose work he disapproved of ('I might be wrong') to people whose faces or appearances he didn't like ('they might be beautiful to their husbands/wives' – or, conversely, getting his own back: indebtedness, materialism – all the things he sensed had brought him down). Much, of course, he gave to Bea and, a larger sum, shared amongst the children. It was in response to a letter to Bea from his bank that his affairs, finally, were transferred to her control: he was – in proceedings which he didn't attend – judged to be no longer responsible for his actions. 'I have never been more responsible,' he complained – without acrimony or resentment – the first time she visited him, coming to the end of his first month at the North London Royal. 'I have never, as far as I am aware, been so clear-headed. I have done away with everything,' he told her, gazing from the cupboard – empty, but for his night-clothes and wash things – by his bed to the disillusioned faces which filled the rows of chairs in the television and recreation lounge immediately outside his door. 'People queue up to come in here. My bed is very popular.'

He watched her – as he watched her on most occasions – cry; or, if not cry, endeavour not to. 'I used to know you,' she told him, 'as a child,' and when he answered, 'Surely, Bea, it was after that,' she said, 'I was taken in: all that childishness to do with art.'

('This place,' he told her at the time, 'is a paradox: you can say but not do anything you like.').

He introduced her to Walter: 'Walter,' he first warned her, 'is known as the King of Peace,' his head enclosed in a turban (knotted handkerchiefs) and held permanently to one side. 'It keeps it,' he told Bea with a beatific smile, 'from falling off my shoulders.' Then to Oskar, an Austro-Hungarian avionics, electrical and civil engineer: 'I am civil,' he told her with a bow, 'I have electricity within my system and I have, at night, the capacity to fly,' a sturdy, square-shouldered (bald-headed) man who, Bea declared, looked a smaller version of me. '*Was* he bald-headed?' she said when I pointed this out ('They all look alike to me'). 'This is paradise on earth,' I told her. 'Only a genius could live here, and only a genius, Bea, describe it.'

Then to Daphne (ancient at the age of thirty-five, wizened) who, terrified, dug her nails, behind her, in the wall.

Fenchurch, in his letters – why did he write them? – described what he called 'the improvidence of God': the abandonment with which a caring deity dispenses wretchedness, senility, lunacy, disease and pain – even children, even animals – nothing, not even the smallest microbe, is exempt: 'even babies, minutes old'. In the face of the profligacy of God's disasters, he enquired, why, if he cares so little for us, should we, his creations, care for him: did he, frankly, think twenty-four hours on a cross would be enough? If he, for instance, were subject to the laws of man, he would be in prison – for eternity – for child-neglect: an artist takes more care of his creations, a father of his offspring, than God, in his profligacy, takes care of us.

She listened – Albert waiting in his car outside – with patience to her (then still) husband: 'the ravings of a lunatic,' I heard her once describe them to a colleague when, as a surprise, without warning – my first day 'off' – I visited her in her lab.

"How I love to see you," I wrote to her at this time, "with your lovely hair – as deep and as thick as your mother's – piled on top of your head, stooped, and yet erect, sitting on your stool – square-shouldered – peering (with the intensity, I might tell you, of a child) into the binocular lenses of your microscope, your right hand drawing with a pencil, your left adjusting the focus. How proud your mother would have been! How prouder still your dad! The grandchild, would you believe it, of H. J. Kells!"

'It's not the romance of lunacy,' I told her, 'that makes me warm to a place like this, but a cinquetential structure of the mind I'm sure I have discovered. It will revolutionise psychiatry,' and then, 'There's one thing you can say about madness, it gets you out and about!'

263

17

'I DON'T THINK I told you,' I said to Etty the following morning,
'the first occasion I saw your mother not as I'd always seen her
but as she is, sitting on a stool in her lab at the MRC, her hair
piled high on the top of her head. She wore a jacket cut square
at the shoulders, with epaulettes and pleated pockets. Her
colour was high: she was on the threshold, if I'd known it, of
making a discovery she sensed was there but hadn't realised.
Her head was bowed, her right hand drawing. Her left hand
held the focus. A beam of light lit up her brow. At first – I'd
been directed to the room by a colleague – I failed to recognise
her. Her eyes, when she looked up, were out of focus.

"Bea?" I enquired.

Perhaps, at that moment, too, she failed to recognise her
husband.

"Yes?" She waited.

"It's your husband," I announced.

The fact of the matter was (I didn't know it) she was waiting
for Albert and the sight of me, I discovered later, filled her
with alarm.'

She wore, in addition to her jacket, a long, blue denim skirt:
not denim. Wool. Beneath its generous folds a pair of boots.
Soft leather. Wrinkled horizontally across her instep. Sitting on
a stool. Flushed. Loved. On the threshold. In reality, expecting
Albert. Good old Al!

'I rang her up the following day and said, "I have never seen
you so absorbed." "Like you," she said, "when you started

writing. Or when I came into the studio in the middle of a picture, for all practicalities your attention on the moon." '

It's dark. The curtains closed, Etty – so clear in the dream – not there at all. 'The fact of the matter is, independence, self-reliance, to the point of self-contentment (the one man pitted against the rest) was the one quality I prized above all others. Without it,' I informed Isabella, for want of anyone else to talk to, 'I wouldn't be where I am today,' – here in the bedroom where, for the remainder of his teenage years, she had, on all his visits, brought him a cup of tea each morning – her figure arced, diagonally, as she drew the curtain, the sunlight flooding from the south: the warmth, the glow, the preparations she had made (invariably wearing lipstick), the removal, if the moment were propitious, of all her clothes.

O my dear, my love.

Prized, that is, above all others, a singular, he thought at that time, human virtue: in reality a symptom – his independence – of an illness which, perceivable with hindsight, had, from the beginning, engulfed his life.

Hand in hand, as symptom, went reliance – on one other person who, because of his dependency, he despised.

"Nothing," he wrote to Vivienne in her absence (she lying in the shed outside), "will ever be the same again. All the old virtues – independence, single-mindedness, self-reliance – those, that is, I saw as virtues, are, it turns out in middle age, not virtues after all: self-reliance (self-containment); single-mindedness (isolation); courage (an inability to relate warmly, movingly, entrancingly, effectively to others)."

"It was all," he wrote to all of them, "coming to an end."

All the old virtues, Bella, tested, strong and true!

'What happens after that,' he said to Maidstone, 'I've no idea.'

For the first, and the last time, at the edge of existence.

"When we met in the producer's office at the top of the Beaumont theatre the first thing I noticed were your glasses and, the second thing, your legs. 'She is famous for her legs,' the casting director remarked at the time (something of a feminist: in her office a poster of a men's urinal, men back to camera, the centre of the five figures, urinating, a woman). And, 'I would have more pride,' the moment you departed. 'No man,' she announced (or woman), 'would reduce me to the state she's in.' "

Gibbering Vi: no man would reduce you to the state you're in: no man would know that much of love. Paul's Second Letter to the Philippians recommends not a closer walk with God but the acquisition of neurotic symptoms: fear and trembling of an involitional nature: 'Go mad,' he might have said, 'with Jesus (see if he comes if you don't come back).'

'Pour ne désespérer Billancourt,' wrote Sartre for and to the working class (lying to himself).

Collect his thoughts (like kittens placed in a bag by a neighbour and dropped into a river: 'Is this,' they must have thought, in those dying seconds, 'what life is all about?').

No fire to light in Taravara Road (gas: together with the central heating).

In his youth were many mansions (principally the Corcorans').

He wasn't a poet for nothing.

Domestic bleach is indispensable in every kitchen, said an advertisement at the time. 'Am I a housewife?' Vivienne said.

His father lying on the bed where, hours before, he had almost died, saying, 'Would you do something for me?' in a whisper, Fenchurch stooping closer (to hear his father's dying words): 'Would you cut my toe nails. They've been bothering me for hours.'

Going mad: 'not as easy,' he told Maidstone (in the land of the blind there's no premium on light bulbs): 'a bicycle for two,' he complained, 'with only one set of pedals.'

A tautologous effect: I love you.

Naked ways.

I mean more to me than life itself.

"I no longer have an appetite for writing – of the sort that Etty – and Charlie, would you believe it – recommend."

Plays.

Novels.

Are you there?

Bea?

Bella?

Vi.

Treasures.

"Not treasures, dear, but footprints."

She would sit each morning on or by the bed, hair tied with a ribbon, and say, 'What shall we do today?' he, wondering what Corcoran would think should he come in, replying, 'I hope to go out drawing,' resentful of being asked ('Don't ask an artist what he's doing').

Flogging a dead horse.

Dreamed (borrowing, as it happened, Bea's scissors: would she mind, his father's nails? she insisting, 'for old time's sake' in coming with him).

Linfield Municipal Hospital standing halfway between the King Edward VI Grammar School and the High School, his father's room (provided by Bea, who supervised his money) overlooking an expanse of depleted lawn on which, years before, entranced, he'd first seen a reclining figure: a neo-Aztec configuration set, incongruously, in the heart of a coalfield: Moore.

"Things have not turned out exactly as we planned. It is time," he wrote, "we wrote our memoirs. Etty says I'm going to die. She had, she told me, lost her temper. Who wouldn't with a man of fifty-five? (How about sixty?)"

How about – God help me – sixty-five?

St Paul.

An acute, or sub-acute anxiety neurosis.

"The resemblance," he wrote, "of things to come."

Jupiter.

'The lineaments,' on a phone call to Bea at her Brighton hotel (her weekend away while he looked after Beckie), 'of gratuitous desire.' ('Will you not ring me here,' she said, 'unless it's something important.')

What kind of shit is it who cares if his wife is fucked by someone else?

'The bare-headed Fenchurch,' he read in a review, writing, perplexed to the reviewer who swiftly responded: 'A misprint: for "ar" read "on".'

"O, my dear," he wrote, "two things make a right."

This night: strikes each hour, as then: awake in the old days (imagining Isabella with Corcoran in the other room) to realise two hours had passed without hearing a chime and conclude he had, after all, been sleeping.

The classification of visitors (written at the time): those who were interested in seeing what he looked like; those who came because they thought they had to; those who thought they'd better stay clear and this was the necessary inducement to do so; those who felt flattered they had been and survived; those who were curious about what a lunatic asylum looked like; those who thought they might write about him in their diaries (memoirs, columns in the press); those – the one person – who thought they loved him; and his wife and children whose motives came under the generic heading which, after a great deal of reflection, and much rubbing-out, he identified as 'love'. All of them, he concluded, acquired a relish for their own existence together with a disinclination to endorse the one they were leaving behind.

"My mind," he wrote at this time, "is in the region of – by my calculation (rough at the best of times) – two hundred and fifty thousand years old: more images flow through it in one night's sleep (and one day's reflections) than pass through a normal brain in three or four years. Since my discovery that the mind, in sleep, disintegrates into a psychotic state – the five cellular structures which comprise the composite self distinguishable, uniquely, one from the other – the significance of my dreaming has vividly increased. I can elucidate dreams like no one's business: indeed, no one's business is what dreaming is all about."

He understood it clearly: in sleep, as in breakdown, the

psyche devolved into its constituent parts. Dreams were the dramatisation of the process.

"Dear Maidstone, odd how we never got to first names – despite the informalities, despite the intimacy, the delicacy – indeed, the outrageousness of much of what was revealed. There we are: doctor and patient; emeritus professor and psychotic – acute or sub-acute anxiety neurosee. Maybe, in retirement, you have discovered that what goes on in the psyche goes on in the universe as a whole (we are plugged in to eternity): systems are elaborated, patterns evolve, processes reveal themselves – everything is in motion. If the black holes of astronomical speculation are one of the wonders of the universe, entities a billion times more powerful than the sun, switching themselves on and off in a time interval equivalent to two earthly days, then so, in my view, is the black hole of depression into which all matter seemingly descends and where the organism ceaselessly absorbs itself."

The waste, he was about to write, that characterises space – all those galaxies going on for ever, matter evolving and dissolving without purpose – was echoed by the wastefulness of the human brain (see Fenchurch: its unused resources, its neural profligacy unmatched by a proportionate function).

"Dear Mackendrick, I wasn't at all convinced by your performance on television the other night: 'Politics and Madness: are the two irretrievably combined?' No one, for instance, attending courses for training in the practice of counselling or psychotherapy can have failed to have noticed, let alone to have been affected by, the party games or group disciplines involved, where insights are encouraged to appear and manifest themselves, and are accredited, by the deployment of mechanistic verbal and/or non-verbal techniques: neutralised personalities are both attracted by and vulnerable to these neural engagements, and non-neutralised personalities to controlling them.

Yet the rationalisations engendered in and by this form of play, harmful or harmless as it may seem, can just as efficaciously be assigned to the same category of empirical observation as the Virgin Birth, the bodily ascension of Christ, or the service of ritualised cannibalism which lies at the heart of Christian worship. Or – and I come to the point I am making (and you undoubtedly will steal) – the tracts of any political theory."

No light shows beneath the curtains.

Four must have passed without his hearing.

Conversely, regarding his temperature, he might have been asleep.

There is hope for everything, he concluded.

There were those who came to clarify what they thought about themselves; there were those who thought they felt the same and wondered if it mattered: there were those, of course, who didn't come at all.

Those, the latter, he saw little of.

In my mind, I reflect, I see them all the time.

She sat on a log, her legs astride: 'When I am eighty, you, my dear, will be forty-five.' ('Forty-six,' he told her).

Coming to the point when, once again, he would take up drawing.

I have lost, in order of importance: Bella, Bea, our children, Vi, recognition, my vocation: an avalanche before that: Liam, Mackendrick . . .

Here, in the room, I recall, where the mischief started.

The equilibrium he found in dementia towards the end of a faithful life.

"Fenchurch's discovery of the process of dreaming is the logical result of his discovery of the structure of the mind, essentially an n-dimensional concept allied to his observations on the radial nature of perception and its lateral suffusion, or association, throughout the system: the mind perceives radially (he asserts), translating its perceptions through lateral connections which have acquired as well as intrinsic characteristics transfigurations which determine not only what is perceived but how it will be perceived in the future."

Consider the nasturtiums in the garden, they strangulate the lesser plants, yet they weep not, neither do they labour.

'What, in my youth,' he told Mackendrick, 'was of interest no longer is: personality, idiosyncracies, *character*. Do you occupy the same hinterland of terror?'

The tertiary way of doing things (testing, he thought, the lateral extensions).

'What is mind?' Mackendrick said: 'the dirty sheet on which society writes its incorrigible message.'

'What is my mind the window on if not its own reflection?' Fenchurch said.

Vivienne said, 'You have given me such a happy time. Do you remember the day we spent by the river – was it Maidenhead or Marlow? – even if you can't otherwise bear the sight of me.'

'I never said,' he said, 'I would.'

The physiognomy of love: 'Just look at my nose!' (as she examined it in the mirror).

The night: how long the night is when you're on your own: how swiftly it goes in the company of another.

Who was the one that the other lay close to?

He heard the children scamper down the stairs: scrape chairs and clatter cups and open doors: 'I am closer to Isabella's great-grandchildren than I am to my own: there I can see the separation, whereas the my that the self is close to is invisible to me.'

Homo serioso.

'I engineer,' he told Maidstone, 'the engine of the mind,' (selling off the spare components).

'I can't cope with children,' the child psychotherapist said as the secretary led in the next child patient (unaware that the therapist's sole aim is to subsume his or her irrationalities in those of other people), her husband, a celebrated paediatrician – 'killing two birds with one stone', he described it – explaining how the extraordinary size of his fees facilitated his purchasing of our house in Belsize Park, intended to be turned by the pair of them into 'a mecca for child care: cure the parents with very large bills: it is, after all, an open market.'

Rising from the floor, he saw – in the morning light – the ghost of Isabella.

Kells and Corcoran: Irish priests (two men to be relied on).

'Nothing,' Kells says, 'is what it seems,' following, in the sunny garden, the movements of his daughter (stooping, in her middle years, to the flowered beds).

Then Etty got up.

Two selves: what price, he thought, in staying one?

What a lot to be taken for granted, not least the room provided by his daughter, the company that she provided.

'My daughter,' Kells said, 'is a happy woman. She would be happy if she wasn't married. She would be happy if she didn't know you. She is, by nature, a happy woman, in the same way as, by nature, her mother was: a child of God,' a daughter, Fenchurch took it to be, of H. J. Kells.

'My close relatives,' he told Mackendrick, 'are powerful people (how powerful, he went on, you'd be surprised).'

In the night: 'instead of writing a radial novel (which all novels, until now, have been) I shall write a diametric one, which traverses rather than travels in and out.'

('That,' Bea said, 'is good enough for me.').

He dreamed.

Overhead, scratching on the tiles, a rook, he conjectured, or a pigeon.

He no longer cared whether he wrote at all: what came to hand was dispirited, de-energised – unrepresentative of what he was himself.

'Between Linfield and Ardsley: somewhere on that road,' he said, measuring the distance, 'is a quotient of myself.'

He would rise, go down to the shop, owned and staffed by Pakistanis, in Sebastopol Street – hardly more than a converted front room in one of those narrow, one-hundred-and-fifty-year-old houses – and buy a paper and two cartons of milk. Vivienne, meanwhile, would be in bed: the endless charade with her glasses, her compulsive buying of several more, together with a variety of clip-on lenses – until he persuaded her to give them up ('they will not change the nature of what you see,' he said): 'our naked selves,' as she described it – regarding herself, eyes almost closed, as she did each morning in the mirror.

It's cold: despite the introduction of central heating since the days, in Isabella's time, when the inside of the panes, in winter, invariably were frozen up, the room does not retain its heat for long: at night, when the boiler switches off, the warmth disappears in seconds. Charlie is always threatening to improve it: 'These old houses,' he complains, as if his being here is Etty's fault entirely, 'are not designed for easy living: their level of comfort, at the time of their construction, was determined by that prevailing in a cave.' Yet, despite his threats, the windows, for instance, have not been double-glazed: there is no insulation in the roof and draughts whistle in not only from beneath the doors (and from around the windows) but from underneath the floor itself – one vacated knot-hole being a favourite where a stream of air, as if from a bellows, is, on windy days, as undiminished in its velocity as it was when Isabella used to stand there, dressed in a housecoat, and complain, as I do now, about the fact that, despite her protestations, Corcoran, in those days, Charlie now, did, or has done, nothing about it. 'I am,' she would tell Corcoran, 'a Mediterranean woman with a passion for the sun.'

I would see her, on occasion, walking amongst the stalls in Linfield market – held beneath the northern walls of the, at that time, coal-black cathedral – her unmistakable head of hair (around which a green silk scarf would occasionally – strikingly – be fastened) conspicuous amongst the drab-coloured awnings and the colourless figures of the colliers' wives. I would delay, for instance, going up to her, merely for the pleasure of observing her from a distance – as might a devotee of wildlife observe a creature he had long admired but, in its native habitat, never glimpsed. I would follow her amongst the stalls, deriving pleasure of an ecstatic nature from contemplating the inclination, at one stall, of her head, from the extension of her arm at another, from the sway of her body at a third. All the while I would be aware of the glances of the other shoppers, not least the fixated gaze of the men – contrasting sharply with the sideways but nevertheless all-consuming gazes of the women – and the often bizarre effect her face and figure and her

273

manner (her clothes, that is, and her manner of address) had on the stall-holders themselves – invariably resulting in her being offered a bargain rather than, as might have been expected, her being exploited because of the exoticism of her dress). 'Look at this,' she would say, like a child, smiling, when I finally came up – and, with the greatest propriety, she had offered her cheek. '*Half* the price I would have to pay in Ardsley, and for something twice as fresh,' showing me a savoy (a savoy: her 'favourite' vegetable, she more than once announced), a piece of fruit, or – one of Corcoran's favourites – a veal and ham meat pie.

Laden with her shopping we would make our way to the semi-derelict room I occupied over the barber's shop in Southgate, on the opposite side of the cathedral's coal-black hulk, and there, having made a cup of tea, we would, as she, on occasion, described it, 'endeavour to amuse ourselves'. 'Isn't this innocent?' she asked, with surprise, when I remarked, if we were conscious of (the implication of) what we were about, it couldn't be innocent any longer, adding, 'After all, my dear, I see you as a child.'

She was more duplicitous than I imagined, or, rather, wished to acknowledge: was she as unaware, for instance, of being observed as I, in my innocence, or seeming innocence, imagined? Was she oblivious of the effect our relationship would have on Bea had she, either before our marriage or after, been aware of what was going on? Was she as unaware of her attractiveness to me – the, at times, mesmeric effect she had – as she, from time to time, bemusedly made out? 'I don't see what you see in me,' she would protest. 'I am a woman, as far as I can see, without an attraction in the world,' affecting reluctance, when she posed, not only to remove her clothes (which she did willingly enough on other occasions) but to pose at all. 'You'll see how much is wrong,' she'd happily complain, coaxed into submission with gestures which, with hindsight, I see she was soliciting all the time.

Perhaps she was mad. Perhaps she didn't believe in Bea. Perhaps she didn't believe in anything: unquestioning, unasking, untormented – except on those occasions when she identified – or thought she did – something morosely none of these things in me. Perhaps she was an exotic, brought back, unwittingly, by Kells from the Middle East (caught up in his baggage) – something founded in thousands of years of desert life, as unreal, as unlived, as inauthentic in this northern clime as the exotic plants she cherished.

'Not one of Kells' locusts?' Maidstone wryly enquired, while I protested, 'I re-live my life at that time over and over again, as if, after all this time, it will never come into focus. I not only seem to see but need to see something in it which eludes me all the while. An embodiment of a faith in something which I know to be there but which, other than in her, I shall never recognise,' he crossing his legs, inscribing his notes, propped on his knee, murmuring through pursed lips, 'I wonder what that is?'

'Eyes that can see that,' I tell him, 'have not yet been invented.'

'Nothing,' I told her at this time, 'is clear. (Everything, of its nature, is bound to be confused.)' Except, of course, his pictures – and his drawings (principally of her): sitting, for instance, in the third-class compartment in Linfield Station the day he left for the Drayburgh – Bea, whose term started later, coming on behind (with, he understood, a new friend: a pupil from King Edward's who, the same subject, had enrolled at the same college) – his paints, in a tin, above his head, on the rack, buried inside a suitcase: 'My passport,' he'd told his parents – and there, framed in the window, suddenly, her face which, after this date – despite their holiday with Clare and 'Venny' – and Bea (perhaps because of it) – he'd assumed he'd rarely if ever see again.

'How are you?' she enquired, and when he asked, startled, 'But Bella, my love, are you coming to London?' (abandon everything: come with me), she had merely responded, 'I am seeing you off.'

'I live, and let live,' he told Maidstone, 'and fail to come alive,' and he, fatigued (having, that day, announced his

275

coming retirement), had responded, 'You don't let live long enough. You don't, when it comes down to it, give anyone a chance.'

When he replied, 'But I give everyone a chance,' Maidstone wearily rejoined, 'Only a chance with chance. Not, I'm afraid, a chance with you.'

It was the turning-point, he'd thought, in his recovery. 'He thinks,' he'd reflected, 'I'm holding something back. After all this time. I wonder what it is? Something solid, something elusive: something, in the light of his condemnation, I can grasp at last.'

'We have the chance, now that Bea may well be embarked,' I tell her, 'with someone else. Come with me.'

'Permanently?' she says, half-smiling. 'Or for a while?'

'Forever,' I tell her. 'I would like to have you with me.'

'This argument,' she says, 'goes on for ever,' (I have, by this time, stepped out from the train).

'Why not run away for good?' (my arm around her waist).

'I only came,' she says, 'to see you off. This,' she goes on, 'is as good a time as any,' and when, my lips against her cheek, she adds, 'to break away for good,' I whisper in her ear, 'My love! My love! Just step into the train. We'll send a letter. I'll telephone. Your father, I know, will understand. Corcoran, too, no doubt, in time. I can't exist,' I go on, 'without you!'

'This break,' she says, 'will do you good. You,' she continues, 'must go ahead, and I,' she concludes, 'must stay behind.'

She allows me for a while to kiss her lips (months before I had the chance to kiss her again – at King's Cross Station, meeting her with Bea after she and I are re-united: 'on a maturer basis, after each of us has had a "fling",' as Bea described it, Isabella there to visit her daughter). "In her lips," I wrote that night in my room in a hotel in Cartwright Gardens, "I felt the distance that has come between us: the force – for the first time – of those thirty-two years: 'half a lifetime', she described it. Goodbye, my dear, my dear, my love," without, to my surprise, the slightest regret.

That night, sitting in a window of a café in the Euston Road, a stone's throw from my lodgings, I watched the crowds flood by and realised that, for the first time since we had met, my thoughts had moved on to something else: the noise, the surge, the grip of something which, I knew, could only be ambition. 'It is,' I concluded, 'to justify her (all my achievements to justify Bella).'

I watched the dull red glow of the lamps which, spread at intervals along the street, slowly increased in incandescence, changing imperceptibly to a transfiguring orange then finally to a translucent gold. "I wouldn't change my being here for anything," I further wrote that evening.

"Dear God, tolerate my worst excesses for my best are meant for you alone," I might have written at the time, for my decline began the moment that my fortunes rose, the path downwards never, from that instant, more clearly defined.

All I recall is the steam of the engine, the metalwork structure above the platform, the look of relief as we said goodbye.

I hadn't left, after all, but arrived.

18

First, there is the room, twenty feet in height, glazed panels on the upper walls, supplemented, in darker weather, by neon lights. A model, reclining on a cushion, is positioned on a platform: around her, sitting on donkeys, or standing at easels, are a variety of students, tall, short, fat, thin, old, young: male – the women's life-room occupies a similar interior on the opposite side of this ancient, neo-classical, Greek portico-fronted building. The light, on an early winter's afternoon, is fading: the neon strips, an hour earlier, have been switched on: the clock on the wall is approaching five. The model, who has been posing, with rests and an interval for lunch, for the previous eight hours, eases her weight against her arm: her shoulder stirs; a hand is raised, the fingers shaken. Someone, at one of the easels, and two others, seated on donkeys, begin, after glancing, head-sideways, at their drawings or paintings, to pack their things.

Feet stir: there's a distant hum of traffic: the college, its main entrance off, nevertheless backs onto the Euston Road, its presence obscured by a façade of shops, a restaurant, and an amusement parlour.

Someone looks up: the minute hand on a clock set high on the wall approaches twelve, quivers, reaches its zenith and, after coming to a halt, quivers once again.

'Rest.'

'Thanks,' come up on every side.

Groaning, despite her recumbent posture, the model stretches.

278

One of the students – a stocky, well-built figure (dark-haired and of a saturnine expression) – cleans his brushes and packs his equipment and, taking down his painting from an easel, leaves the room with a briskness which marks him out from the others. Depositing his work in a rack outside, he passes along a corridor which runs underneath the centre of the building (with its antique-room and studios overhead), past the student common-room where a sideways look of regret animates his features as he glances at the students congregating in groups and making plans for excursions to the West End that evening, and reaches a back door of the building from where, down a narrow alley, he emerges into the lamp-lit glow of the Euston Road. He walks, increasing his pace, eastwards until, opposite St Pancras Station, he enters a narrow street and, from there, the door of a terraced building, set at the corner of a crescent and, in several rapid bounds, climbs a winding flight of stairs.

He enters an attic room: the walls are lined with pictures (others, of varying sizes, propped against the walls themselves) and on the floor of which are stacked piles of (mostly) second-hand books. An easel, holding a painting, stands beside the window, the uncurtained panes of which look down to a tennis court set in the centre of the crescent's gardens.

Drawing to him a sheaf of papers, he takes out a pen and, sitting at a table immediately beneath the window, a light beside him, begins to write.

A political view of his life was coming to the surface: 'It isn't me,' he reflected, 'but the life I lead which creates the impression of a divided world, dissonance and vulgarity on one side, refinement and perspicuity on the other,' his life, indeed, fragmented, at that time, in more ways than he imagined, Bea (and her mother) on the one hand, the girls he was attracted to, on the other: the working and the (largely) middle classes which, separately, absorbed his artistic and his social lives, providing, the one, the dynamic which, he suspected, energised his work, the other the impetus necessary to his ambition.

Each morning he got up, wrote, walked briskly to the college, entered his name in the Drayburgh register (lying on a shelf of one of the rotunda windows which illuminated the spiral-staircased entrance), descended to the locker-room to retrieve his materials, then made his way to the life-room to which he had been assigned or, if he were working on a composition, to the antique-room where, amidst the casts, the plants and the multitude of easels, he set up his hardboard (cheaper than canvas) and, for the remainder of the day worked as steadily as distractions (too numerous to mention) in such a large interior might allow – not excluding an occasional break for coffee and one for lunch and for earnest chats about 'art' with the men and about 'life and love' with the women.

At some point he went home and wrote, steadily, for several hours: in the evenings, if he didn't draw (or write) or paint, he visited Bea in her room or she came to visit him, or, if he were deceiving her, he visited or entertained someone else.

He was a 'card'; on the other hand, a bundle of conflicting yet nevertheless dogmatic views (he had opinions about every-thing, a compendium of the most divergent and contentious elements in the world he lived in, a synthesis – and the principal protagonist of – the same within himself: 'A liver and lover,' he said to Bea, 'if only because the extremes I live at are common to no one else.')

Even after the pipes start ticking beneath the floor – the expan-sion from the heat as, at intervals, audibly, in the basement of the house, the boiler fires – it is cold: 'These old houses,' I reflect, 'and this one in particular, the one in which I have loved and which has brought me to this pass (unloved by anyone at present), are not for me.'

The girls are romping in their room, sent up, I assume, after breakfast, to prepare themselves for school: Charlie, having come out from the bathroom into his bedroom, is whistling (as, no doubt, he fastens on his tie beneath his triplicated chin), examining, with equanimity, warmth and candour those

280

eyes which, reflected in the mirror, convey nothing but the same in return).

'Breakfast, Charlie!' (from Etty, below).

I've been awake for hours, absorbed in the persona of a twenty-year-old youth (a child, his body and his mind divided, his heart, like his soul, in two).

I used to wake like this at camp: the other sleeping figures, the muggy air, the pigeons in the wood and, at Broughton Springs, the distant sound of the sawmill: the dew, as I crawled out beneath the brailing, first on hands and then on feet (the cool, sharp shock abrasive), the clarity of the air, the shadowed humps across the valley of the medieval mine works, the cows standing in or browsing by the stream, or drifting in a line to or from the dairy on the opposite valley slope: the visit to the toilet, already thick with flies, the smell of the damp, the dust and stone in the decaying game keeper's cottage: the stillness of the wood which, hours before, in the darkness, lit by the flickering camp-fire flames, had sent me to bed with a pang of fear – to be infinitely extended in future years – a deeper darkness, untouched by the flames, lying dauntingly beyond them.

'I thought, this morning, I might go to Broughton Springs,' I say to Etty as she comes in carrying not, as I'd thought, a pot of tea (or my breakfast) but several buff-coloured letters. 'What are those?' I ask to which, seeing me awake, she says, 'Charlie's,' drawing back the curtains.

'Does it require you,' I ask, 'to bring him up his letters? Won't he get them the moment he goes down to the hall (to find,' I am about to add, 'unlike myself, his breakfast waiting)?'

'I thought you'd be asleep,' she says, turning with a smile, and adds, 'If I don't put them in his hand he forgets them. I've brought them to put in his briefcase,'

'Nothing, I suppose for me?' I enquire.

'No one knows,' she says, 'you're here. As for Taravara Road, Matt has said she'll keep an eye on things and post anything that comes.'

'I used to get ten, sometimes twenty, occasionally thirty or forty letters a day,' I tell her, 'at the height of my notoriety,' and add, 'I've been lucky, in the recent past, to get as many as that in a year. Sometimes, in Taravara Road, nothing comes for over a month. That,' I go on, 'despite forty-five years as a writer. And a few other activities as well.'

'They must think you dead.' She smiles.

'Irrelevant,' I tell her.

'Are you getting up, or shall I bring you something?' still smiling in the door.

'What's got into you?' I ask her.

'I have decided,' she declares, 'to make a fresh start.'

'Does that include the first draft of *The Private Papers of Richard Fenchurch*?' I enquire.

'It doesn't.' She smiles again.

'I hesitate to call it a revolution, but what,' I enquire, 'has caused this change?'

'Nothing I can think of,' she says, 'except when I was driving you home, after picking you up at the church, I realised there was nothing more I could do. It took a great weight,' she adds, 'off my mind. No longer do I need to care, slippers or no slippers, sketching or not. You are not my responsibility any longer.'

'I never said I was,' I tell her.

'No,' she says, 'but the whole of yesterday, after you'd disappeared, I'd begun to think you were.'

'You sound,' I tell her, 'like your mother.'

'Exactly.'

Having closed the door behind her, she opens it again.

'As for Broughton Springs, that's up to you,' she says. 'I wouldn't recommend it. And I shan't,' she adds, 'if you fail to come back here, come all that way to fetch you.'

'Then, again, there's Ardsley Edge.'

'There is.'

'And Cawthorne Castle.'

'That, too.'

'Places which, in the past, have inspired, some would say, my better work.'

'You are as free,' she tells me, 'as a bird.'

But I can see, apart from discussing me with Charlie – during the dark hours of the night, or perhaps the previous evening – she is saying this not merely to keep her spirits up but to put me on my guard – not against her, but against my own misgivings. She is doing it to alarm me: I have no one, she is saying, but Charlie and herself: biology alone, she might have said (taking a leaf from my book) is the cause of your distress, and not the conditions you were born in.

The embolismic structure of – let us choose a mind at random – that of a once well-known author, playwright, painter and draughtsman, is exacerbated by circumstance, or what the theorists describe as nature, and that, too – though discounted by his second daughter – may be taken into account when assessing how responsible or otherwise he or other people are for his unprecedented actions.

Verbosity was his greatest sin, she might have said, not least at the moment that he suspected that, against the odds (and the prognosis of his doctors) he might recover his peace of mind (never there to be recovered, he'd omitted to tell them, in the first place).

'I've been tormented,' I tell her, 'the whole night long by the thought of mediocrity: all those practitioners of the same who comprise virtually the whole of those engaged on those activities I have been so busily engaged upon myself and who, by self-definition, come under the sobriquet of "failure".'

Her feet come from the stairs: 'I've got your correspondence, dear. I've put it in your briefcase,' and, 'Glenda! Lottie! Time for school! We're leaving in a minute!'

Charlie, I assume, is late, or is delaying his departure in order, as is his not unusual custom, to give me the benefit of his advice sans wife and children in the background: 'You are an old phoney,' he told me, on one occasion, in Taravara Road, on a London visit, before he realised – or had it from Maidstone – I was already mad.

'What is madness,' I can see his much-chinned face enquire, 'if not a cop-out we could all subscribe to?' revising his view, alarmingly (and, incidentally, to my disappointment), on his first visit to Boady Hall: I'd been counting on cop-out, at the time, myself: that innocent, socialist vision that included all things but the view that life intrinsically is bad.

'The final page,' I tell Etty when I go down, 'should have a single drawing – of the one woman who – I might as well admit it – dominated and still dominates my life, namely,' I am about to tell her, 'Isabella,' only, with a suffusion of alarm (a shock of recognition) she declares, 'You've come down without your clothes,' for, in the mirror of the kitchen I can see, my upper (and I presume my lower) body is as naked as the day when, traumatised by an earlier death, it came soundlessly from between my mother's thighs.

"This is the man I gave birth to: heredity in action, a close-up of death, a foetal spasm at the graveside of his eldest brother:" there, with the grace of God, go I.

As the children arrive she offers me a towel and I say, 'I'm on the way to the bathroom,' with something of a laugh, at which, the moment I have gone, they begin to giggle.

'Has Grandpa come down,' I hear them say, '*like that?*' and later, to Charlie, before she takes them off to school, Etty says, 'He came down like that to shock us.'

'We shall have to send you back,' says Charlie when he comes up to my room (Mrs Otterman already flushing a vacuum outside the door) and when I say, 'To where?' he says, 'To a place that Raynor recommends.'

'Private,' I ask him, 'or National Health?'

'The latter,' he says, and adds, 'knowing your appetite for social justice.'

'I never sent my children to a private doctor – except, of course, in emergency (which happened twice) – nor to a private school,' I tell him (as, no doubt I have, many times before), and when he replies, 'Hypocrisy was always a dominant feature of your life,' (does he talk like that to the local constituency Labour Party?), I respond, 'Even when my wealth was sufficient to buy up a private school (one such became available, while

284

we were living there, at the back of our home in Belsize Park – an area given over, almost exclusively, to private and therefore privileged education) I never had a second thought about sending any of our children to a state school, all of which, with one exception, gave them an education which you would have to travel for ever to find an equivalent in paucity of imagination, enterprise, credibility, professionalism and moral strength. I fought for years to raise their standards, entirely on my own, and for most of that time without success, only in the final years, having taken several years off my own life in the process, and when most other middle-class parents had removed their children to the private sector, did I finally come up trumps.'

He has left the room – yet only to fetch his briefcase, for, returning to the door, he stands there, at my declaration, 'come up trumps', fastening the catch (the old-fashioned type, characterised by a flap, and not the miniature suitcase variety popular today), and adds, as if a postcript to his final remark, 'The choice is yours.'

'The choice was mine,' I tell him, 'a long time ago (and see where I am now,' I add).

'You can button up,' he says, fastening, head stooped, the middle button on his pin-striped jacket – a rotundity below the waist the only blemish on a not unyouthful figure, 'or,' raising his head, 'be buttoned down. The choice is yours,' he says again.

'You are kicking,' I tell him, 'against the pricks, a euphemism, in biblical times, for a genetic disability manifesting itself in the form of a disingenuous indisposition to fulfil the expectations of others,' he already turning from the door, something in his pocket absorbing his attention, his briefcase now beneath his arm. 'This came, by the way,' he says, handing me an envelope. 'The writing looks familiar,' he continues as he lays it on the bed.

'In that case,' I tell him, 'it must be from Bea. Bea,' I continue, 'and the private parliamentary secretary to the Minister of Health, the ubiquitous one-armed bandit who is never off the news-screens at present, much, I might add, to Etty's pleasure. *All* our children appear to delight in their mother's choice of husband – her first not being a choice, she says, and therefore doesn't count,' and when, picking up the envelope (without a second glance), I conclude, 'Their father, I'm afraid, they've no time for at all,' he declares, 'At least he makes a go of things,' turning once more so that his final phrase he gives to the stairs – and Mrs Otterman, not oblivious, despite her vacuum, on the landing, 'from a background, I might add, as unpromising as yours.'

'One arm versus half a mind,' I tell him, at which he is about to add, 'She must have a penchant for cripples,' at least, I do my best to imagine so, only, glancing at his watch, I hear a strangulated, 'I'm late, Mrs Otterman. Mrs Stott isn't back yet. Could you keep an eye on Father?' – the sixty-nine-year-old proletarian fake with his faded if once-pristine reputation for being the only outstanding depicter of working-class life since that androgynous aesthete Lawrence, the one compounded of the elements of earth and water (phlegm), the other of air and fire (bathos).

I hear his car a moment later and the (pregnant) silence from the landing as Mrs Otterman, switching off her vacuum, contemplates, in the absence of her mistress (let alone her master), the possibility of being – it must have crossed her mind – assaulted by the mindless mogul in the bedroom who was once described in a national journal as 'the only writer who, in his depiction of the *material* of English working-class life, illuminates *ideas.*'

'Are you all right, Mr Fenchurch?' comes from the heart of Yorkshire: guttural in its strength: no thoughts of anything other than combativeness promised there.

'I'm well,' I tell her, and when she calls, 'Anything I can get you?' immediately respond, 'No, thank you, Mrs Otterman. I shall, in a moment, be getting dressed,' (an invitation to the picnic, the dissolute old devil whom even a potential Nobel-Prize-winning wife could not constrain) at which, after a pause, the vacuuming begins again.

How much I should have liked the previous mistress of the house, as she did on so many occasions, to have come in the door and enquire, 'Where are you going to draw today? If you'll tell me where you'll be (when I've done the shopping, chores, housework, lunch) I'll come out and join you. I fancy a walk in Ardsley Wood,' I choosing a suitable rendezvous in which to sketch, and pleasurably anticipate her arrival: the reeded stream, the leaf-strewn grass, her summer dress, the sheen of her stockings.

There were times, on these occasions, when I suspected that Corcoran might be, contrary to appearances, a patron of the arts; that, having come to a judgement about my potential, he had decided to contribute his wife, a testimony to and an encouragement of my talent. 'You walk in the woods, if you like!' I heard him – in moments of reverie – exclaim. 'Never mind the neighbours. For the sake of his art, which I know is buried in him somewhere, allow him to take with you, as well as your reputation (for housewifeliness, domesticity, fidelity, etc.) whatever liberties he likes. Go with him! Give the genius what he wants!' I endeavouring, on our next encounter to identify in his smiles and frowns, his gestures and appearance, if not an endorsement a hint of a contributory fervour which might, in the name of inspiration, betray a complicity in his handing over his wife.

How I loved her! When, on one occasion, lying beside me in Ardsley Wood, the sunlight in the ferns above her head, she enquired, tracing my lips beneath her finger, 'Would you give up writing and painting if it threatened to come between us?' I responded, without a second's thought, 'Of course!' at which she laughed and, not for the first or last time, exclaimed, 'You're such a rotten liar! Let's hope you never have to make the choice,' nestling her deliciously smelling hair against my cheek as, side by side, we gazed up at the ferns together.

Sometimes in the wood we lit a fire, a bundle of twigs, a rotted log, and, with a pleasure derived from domesticity as much as anything else, watched the flames flicker beneath the trees, the smoke drifting up against the darkness. 'How nice it would be,' I'd say, 'if we could be married. I'd never have to paint, or write again: just to wake to you each morning,' to which, invariably, she'd reply, 'When I am eighty, my dear, you will be forty-five.' ('Forty-six,' I would correct her.) 'Beauty of your sort,' I'd tell her, 'doesn't fade. (It deepens and increases.)' 'So speaks,' she'd say, 'a young and, if I may say so, not only inexperienced but dishonest man.'

The writing is my own: "Dear Richard Fenchurch, this is written in case (when your daughter arrives to take you 'home' – to that damned house which (nowadays) brings you no pleasure – because in the past it brought you so much) you find, once there you are out of your mind. Recall how much peace, despite loathing it, your Taravara home brought Vi: 'I want to be a star!' and, 'I am the legend that dreams are made of: when I am dead there will be films about my life played by actresses who couldn't hold a candle to me. I call that irony: you, I believe, a suitable reward.'

No doubt this finds you as it's leaving me: confused (terrified), waiting for relief from the tribulations that have plagued my life in general but specifically the last five years when not one morning has there been when I have not woken to a degree of fear and dispiritation that would drive any normal person mad (and this abnormal one also).

"No other writer in his time" is crossed out and replaced by, "No other woman (I am speaking of Bella) ever did me so much good. 'Isn't it strange,' she told me one day in the wood, 'you're the only man I know on whom to gaze has been enough.' What Christ was to the author of the Philippian letters she has been to me: an illumination that transfigures (the radiance of her looks – and, let's face it, the dexterity of her touch).

Now you're in that room you've thought so much about; now you're in that bed; now you're gazing, each morning, at the village – bereft of its pit, headgears and slag heap, now the whole place has returned to something not indistinguishable from its medieval past – its one or two burghers, the 'big man' in the manor, endowed with the debilitating accoutrements of

288

a post-socialist existence – you'll know what it's like to be out of touch – in a way you never were, and never will be, in Taravara Road with its brutalised and brutalising neighbours, its graffiti, its dereliction, its public squalor and its private – how would you describe it? – indolence."

'All right?' A pink-cheeked face around the door: breathlessness within the aproned bosom (head of vacuum in her hand). 'Had a letter?'

Speaking to an idiot: but then, of course, I reflect, I am.

'From myself.'

'Yourself?'

'Addressed to me at this address. Written before I came here.'

More redolent of masculine assertiveness than receptivity, her bosom.

'Keep you up to date?'

'It does. If not,' I tell her, 'a little in advance.'

'On your way to the bathroom?' Indicates the towel. 'Why don't you get dressed?'

'I thought,' I tell her, 'I'd have a rest,' and then, 'I'm about to do some writing.'

'In the buff?'

'I often write like this.' I let the towel drop, and recall that she has seen more naked men in the bath-tub by the fire than I have had hot dinners, as companionable, and as discounted, Mrs Otterman, as any domestic pet.

'Best not let Mrs Stott know about it!' with something of a laugh.

'Or,' I tell her, 'Doctor Raynor.'

'Nor Doctor Raynor!' Another laugh. 'He'll have you locked up in no time,' a threat which, casually delivered, has an immediate effect.

'Think I'll get dressed,' I tell her, at which she leaves the room.

"This is from a chum of yours whom you may have forgotten, the one who lived, disguised as you, in Taravara Road the week before Etty was due to arrive: the one who butters your bread

289

and toasts your toast and goes to bed as you at night in that Vi-less room at the back of the house where the sounds from the neighbours are least intrusive – and the sounds of Vivienne, when she lived there, less extreme: 'I'll never be a star!' "

'No point,' she tells me, 'reading that letter if you've written it yourself,' leaning in the door.

I woke this morning to the rhyme in my head, 'Reason and its guide: reason and its pride,' and thought, 'That presages a return to painting,' and later came the thought which never troubled me years ago but which now troubles me almost daily: 'How could a woman fall in love with her daughter's lover without the slightest guilt, remorse or, as far as I could discern it, (not simply unease but) anguish? At the time I took her to be naive, then I took her to be cunning, then, after talking to her father, that it was due to 'genes' – the sea, the sand, the sub-tropical beaches, the whore-house ridden coast of that almost-inland sea: yet all these, I considered later, were excuses to pacify a sense of fear which, on all those occasions I waited at a bus-stop, approached the house, sauntered up and down a road, sat on a log, preceded our encounters – until I saw the turn of her head, the swing of her skirt: her high-heeled shoes, her low-heeled sandals, her blouse (her jumper, her scarf, her coat).

'Naivety,' I thought, 'must be the answer,' as if, in reality, Bea were not her daughter ('Don't you need a coat? Have you put away your books/clothes/things upstairs?' as she might enquire, not of her own but anyone's child). 'She is of a race with which the Anglo-Saxons have never come to terms,' I thought – the one from the shores of a turquoise sea, the other from pitch blackness: the mine, the cauldron, the pit.

'Naivety,' I said, 'of course,' and add, 'Of which I took advantage. Bea idolised her mother,' and when Mrs Otterman says, 'Who?' the vacuum cleaner in her hand, its orifice directed at me, I continue, 'My wife. She thought her mother a remarkable woman. "A child of nature," she being a scientist and not a poet. "It's why my father married her. *Her* mother, too, was

290

much the same, with the reputation, rumoured in the family, of being a Turkish prostitute." '

In Taravara Road, from my workroom window, I see, each morning in an adjoining garden, the wife of a neighbour: in a benign and wholly passive way, even when Vivienne was alive, I fell in love with her stocky figure, stooping to the plants (another horticulturist), only to discover that she is Greek by birth – and then, not even Greek, but Turkish (a cross-border liaison in a war-torn land) and, God help me, the same age as Isabella when we first met – that fateful glance, open and accepting, through the living-room window to the evening-lit figure in the garden outside. 'How I loved her,' I announce, but the termagant Yorkshire miner's wife, the vacuum turned on behind her, is already thrusting at the floor and, above the wailing, calls, 'I want to do in here.'

'Alki', I discover, is her name, the neighbour's wife, and though her beauty is of the sort that can, with discretion, only be admired from a distance, her smile and her composure (a garden-to-window wave) are enough to reassure me.

Etty is back: 'Sorry I'm late, Mrs Otterman,' the lowered tone, 'Is he all right?' and the breathless, flushed-cheeked face, 'Mrs Otterman says you're dressing.'

'So I am,' I tell her.

'Magnificent,' I announce and when she asks, 'What is?' reply, 'All that life entails.'

She is sitting at her desk, the window of her study looking out to the trees at the back of the house – a room which, in my youth, was Bea's bedroom and from the window of which she waved on the memorable day Bella and I climbed Sugden's Bank, lying immediately before us, to look at the Swansons' house.

'What,' I ask her, 'are you writing?'

'I am tinkering,' she says, 'with a life of Cotman. It comes,' she goes on, 'as some relief.'

'A self-effacing fellow, whose personality,' I tell her, 'had little

291

appeal but whose work can only be matched with that of Girtin and, with reservations, Peter de Wint. A genius,' I continue, 'before his time, the progenitor of much in twentieth-century art, not excluding Cézanne and Picasso, and prone to depression at the end of his life, caused, to some degree, I haven't a doubt, by neglect and the consequent cultural isolation,' adding, 'Why don't you choose a living model? No one else will have the chance. If it turns out you've picked a dud – another Haydon, say, rather than a Christopher Wood – you can, when I'm gone, turn back, if not to Cotman – a worthy subject – someone else. Constable, of course, I've never liked. I can't stand the coarseness of his textures, the paint put on as if with a trowel, and Turner is far too literary for my taste. Except, of course, for the first decade of his century, when he painted like a dream. But whores: his life has whores, and misogyny,' I go on, 'in plenty. If you follow my advice on this occasion you'd make a killing. As for myself, I'm astonished that someone hasn't tried already. A film,' I conclude, 'would be the least of your worries.'

Removing her glasses she massages the bridge of her nose. She frowns.

'Cotman wasn't *prone*,' she says, with surprising intensity, 'he was *ill.*'

'He suffered,' I tell her, 'from timidity and a lack of resolution. Timidity of execution and irresolute ambition. A parochial English figure. Or do you, unlike with Caravaggio, see much of him in me?'

The frown intensifies between her puckered eyes: the spontaneity – the turning over of a new leaf – of earlier that day has gone.

'I can't stand these English mediocrities,' I add. 'They dominate the scene but when I'm gone we'll see who's been the master.'

Her gaze, like mine, is on the trees: the bare oak and beech and poplar: I am, rather than defining a position, digging my own grave.

'What's so wrong,' I ask, 'in writing not about something

you've studied but something you've observed? You can incorporate that part of my life before you even knew me. You have, before you,' I conclude, 'a seminal source.'

'Perhaps,' she says, 'his reticence is inseparable from the quality of his work.'

('A quality,' she might have concluded, 'I very much admire.')

'When he should have ventured all he plumped for patronage,' I tell her, 'of a particularly unenlightened sort. What originality he did possess, to, as I've said, no small degree, he meticulously squandered. If only Girtin had had his life span. Dead at twenty-seven.'

It rains: or is the wind flailing dust, from the gutter and the roofs, against the panes?

In the rain, one evening, Isabella and I lay beneath the ferns in Ardsley Wood: 'Pretend this is a house,' she said, while the drops – she laughing – fell across her face.

'I am,' she says, 'too close to the subject,' and returns her gaze to the paper strewn across her desk. 'If,' she adds, her head still bowed, her glasses replaced, 'you're such an interesting subject, why not try yourself?'

I am in this house with Isabella: we embrace: the windows are blacked out with tar – sprayed on by a figure in overalls outside. I crawl out from a crashed and burning car and find my glasses frosted: 'I shall never,' I tell Bella, 'see you again. (I shall never write and paint)': a dream the night before I heard she'd died (Bea, but not Corcoran, with her).

'If you're going out let's keep to the arrangement we've worked out already,' she says, 'and let me or Mrs Otterman know.'

Meanwhile, at the back of Fenchurch's mind, spring, like feathers, *wings*.

"The writer, painter, raconteur, plagiarist, poseur and charlatan (he raised charlatanism to the heights of a respectable profession) was born in the city of Linfield in 1934 (or was it five – or '33?), date, as yet, to be decided: he had no education other than the one normally available to the majority of

293

children at that time: drilled in spelling, writing and arithmetic (a spouter of mathematical tables backward by the time he was seven), he advanced from one educational peak to another with a dexterity which was the envy of his peers and aroused much pride in his family (if enmity amongst his brothers)."

'I thought I might go to Cawthorne Castle.'

'Isn't it far?' without looking up.

'No further than yesterday,' I tell her. (And yesterday no further than the day before). 'I would like,' I go on, 'to sum up my life (draw a line beneath the account; find out, for instance, how much I owe, how much I am in debt, how much, if anything, is left over.')

'What has that to do with Cawthorne Castle?'

Not that there's much castle, to speak of, there at all.

'I drew up sums in the past while standing there.' Many a sunset watched with Bea: many a sunset watched on my own: the path across the fields, for instance, which led, via a footbridge across the Lin, across the golf-course to a back-garden ginnel leading, through someone's garden (a fretted look from the scullery window), to Manor Road itself. 'It is time,' I say, 'to make amends, to come to a judgement, to recognise all I've been through in the hope I shall not have to go through it all again.'

He heard Alki, from time to time, busy with her pots (preparing her husband's lunch) in Taravara Road, welcoming the sound (all domestic sounds audible in that tiny London back-street house) as evidence of a life other than his own.

'I sacrificed everything,' I tell her, 'for art,' while she, above Cotman's 'Greta Bridge', adjusts her glasses on her nose.

If I released the nude I painted of her, in the room above the barber's, in Southgate, all those years ago, no one would recognise, I'm sure, anything other than another female.

'Many people make the mistake of equating madness with irresponsibility. It's nothing of the kind,' I tell her. Bea, for instance, and that woman in the neighbour's garden who came out each day to tend her plants, and whose appearance, from a distance of twenty-five feet, I mistook for that of Isabella, she and Isabella two figures in one, a definitive form of femininity, the possibilities of which I saw no end. 'The first thing a madman discovers is his obligation to duties which he not only had never responded to before but had never even recognised. First and foremost,' I add, 'his duty to God. Not to his wife, not to his children, not to his vocation, but, above all else ("above all else" a phrase not chosen lightly) to . . .'

She has, that morning, plaited her hair (it must have taken quite a while: up early after a night spent talking to Charlie) and has coiled a plait above each ear – in a manner that reminds me, with a shock – a sensational spasm of recognition – of her grandmother sitting in the same room on her daughter's bed, where I have found her as if by chance – allowing me to stroke her neck, which led moments later to her lying back, the vibrations of the floor beneath us echoed on the kitchen ceiling, Mrs Hopkins (Rose) enquiring, 'What on earth was going on up there?' when we went down, Bella, calm as a dove on a summer evening, responding, 'Richard was helping me to move Bea's bed: there's so much dust collects beneath.'

' . . . higher things. Madness, after all, devolves from grief, and grief, in turn, devolves from loss,' and when she says, 'There's so much, this morning, I'd like to do,' stooping closer to her desk, 'A View of Richmond, Yorkshire' absorbing her attention, I respond, 'If you don't take note of what I tell you there's no way for either of us to look ahead. Charlie's aspirations to a general good are no more realisable than they were two thousand years ago when the first theologian of the Christian religion enjoined us to seek our salvation in fear and trembling, that is, within the parameters, clinically defined, of a sub-acute anxiety neurosis.'

'If you're going to Cawthorne Castle,' raising her head, 'put on your shoes and winter coat. We bought them, if you recall, expressly for this weather. And take enough money to get you there and back and, if you are going to be late, have the courtesy to ring us. I'll give you the number.'

'I know this number,' I tell her, 'by heart.'

'It's changed.'

'Changed?' I am, without intending to, pausing in the door.

She is writing – has been writing on a piece of paper which, getting up, she places in my trouser pocket.

'Remember where I've put it.'

'You look so much like,' I tell her, 'Isabella. Is it one of her photographs you've been looking at?' to which, ignoring the enquiry, she adds, 'Bryan Raynor will be here in half an hour. Don't even go into the grounds until then.'

'This higher responsibility,' I tell her, 'is all that it's cracked up to be. The physiological implications of which I don't even have to go on about.'

So that one morning, in the garden, looking down – the heat of the summer (a July afternoon) – the humid heat that strikes these airless back-street yards – I see her in a low-cut blouse, stooping to her roses (in no way as effulgent as those of Bella) and, from this angle, glimpse her breasts, shadowed, within the collar of her blouse, and recall a not dissimilar occasion when, stooping, Bella too, inadvertently, had disclosed her breasts, stooping to me in her evening gown (twin fruits of femininity transcending transcendentity itself).

'In half an hour?'

'I'll come down,' she says, 'and see him with you.'

'No doubt he will see you without me as well.'

When, after returning to her desk, she doesn't look up, I announce, 'If you look like that in seven years' time, when Lottie brings her first boyfriend home – conceivably from King Edward's – you will find yourself in an impossible situation. You will fall in love with an eighteen-year-old youth and neither the grounds nor Ardsley Wood, nor the entire fields and surrounding copses will be sufficient to contain what it is you are endeavouring to hide, not even the railway line, or the motorway from here to London. Wherefore, I ask you, where will you hide that which years later, you will find, there is no confessing?'

For the first time since I have come into the room she glances up directly: she examines my gaze for several seconds – and I see that Etty is, by no stretch of the imagination –

296

despite the plaits – an Isabella: she is not her grandmother's grandchild so much as the daughter of the opportunist, subvertionist, duplicitous Richard Fenchurch – as inclined to betray his class as he is his family: 'all for art!' he might have said as vehemently as now he cries, 'all that I can gather unto myself!'

Raynor is a small man: at our previous meeting – a week, ten days, a month before? – he has told me in his youth he wished to be a jockey: 'Until I saw the horses: I've never looked at another since.' Slight, with sharply fashioned features: 'Like a bird of prey,' I told Etty on that occasion the moment he had left, with no interest in the past ('The past, Mr Fenchurch, is only a fiction'), he comes into the sitting-room, distinct from the living-room (the children largely excluded) and says, 'So you've been running off again. We'll have a rope around your ankles, like Corcoran's horses had, they tell me, when he hobbled them in the yard.'

'I take it I'm to be seen as something other than a dumb animal?' I enquire.

'Far from it!' cheerily, as he looks round for a chair, selecting a straight-backed one as if to signal he has more important things to see to (and far more important on his mind).

'I have dispensed with pills,' I tell him. 'And I have not caught a fever. No chills or sneezes or pains in the chest. I am, in short, in tip-top condition.'

His pale blue eyes, veiled by light, thin lashes even lighter than his thin, fine hair: auburn ('He is,' Etty explains, previous to our first encounter, 'a shy and self-effacing man.'

'We have, in that case,' I rejoined, 'much in common.').

Bares my arm, takes my blood pressure: makes no comment. 'The worst moment of all,' I tell him, 'in the maze is to discover that the minotaur is preferable to any other choice. That one is the minotaur and there is no better offer.'

'Mrs Stott has asked me to recommend a doctor,' he says.

'I thought you were a doctor,' I tell him.

A window looks out to the front of the house: the descending slope, the remnants of the beech hedge, the crescent beds of roses (pruned) inset at each corner of the lawn – and a window at the side of the room, framed, to its right, by the massive fireplace, looks out to the iron-gated arch which, in the old days, led to Corcoran's yard: nothing but neatly-tiled roofs is visible above the old stone wall.

'A psychiatrist,' he says.

He sits, as might a petitioner, on his hard-backed chair, I, for my part, reclining on a couch (as close to the confessional as, I imagine, will set him at his ease).

'I've seen all the psychiatrists I intend to,' I tell him. 'Many, in fact, have followed my example, having moved on to, or homed in on my discovery of the super-authorial self, a multi-dimensional phenomenon and the closest thing we know to God. Indeed, it's more than my contention that it is the God in all of us, unique, articulate, all-comprehending, our miraculous window on paradise.'

'Doctor Robeson is an admirer of your work,' he says.

'If we know enough,' I say, 'already, why on earth should we need to know more?'

'Another view,' he says, 'is helpful,' in no way swayed, I observe, by my beneficent smile.

'Are you a native of these parts?' I ask.

'As a matter of fact,' easing his trousers around his knees, 'my father was a local doctor.'

'In Ardsley?'

He shakes his head. 'Several miles away.' He adds, 'I was always interested in the mines.'

'After horses.'

'Oh, horses came much earlier,' he says. 'I had ambitions, at one time, to be a vet, but the examination requirements were more demanding than those for medical school, so I followed the family practice. My uncles and brother are doctors, too.'

'In these parts?'

'In London. One of them,' he adds, 'was a former colleague of Professor Maidstone.'

'Oh, Maidstone,' I reflect, inwardly comparing his avuncular frame with the ascetic one before me.

'He, too, has a high opinion of your work.'

'But, then,' I tell him, 'he's retired. The fate, I'm afraid, of all those who have had a high opinion of me. Or my work. It appears to be a pre-condition, a high opinion of Richard Fenchurch and retirement going,' I continue, 'hand in hand.'

'He refers, in his notes, to your habit of giving subjective reactions an air of objectivity,' he says, adding, 'Maidstone,' as I frown.

'He never mentioned that,' I tell him.

'I'm sure he did.' He bows his head (leaning forward, his hands clasped loosely between his thighs).

'I'd have remembered if he had.'

'You may, on the other hand,' he says, 'have chosen to forget.'

'And forgotten,' I tell him. 'I've forgotten.'

'Precisely.'

'I'm far too clever,' I tell him, 'for that.'

'None of us are, I'm afraid,' he says. 'Which brings me back to why I would like you to see my colleague.'

'Not Donny Robeson?' I ask.

'His name is Donald Robeson,' he says.

'I knew him at school, if it's the same Donald Robeson,' I tell him.

'He never mentioned that,' he says.

'I'll run rings round him,' I tell him. 'What new observations will he have to make that I and others haven't made already?'

'It's not so much a question of something new as merely to have an outside view. And one up to date, of course,' he adds.

'To date?'

'Something,' he says, 'to bounce things off.'

'I've bounced a few things off Robeson in the past, a few more,' I tell him, 'shouldn't do him any harm.'

'Having known you in the past might,' he tells me, 'be of assistance now. Particularly,' he goes on, 'at a time of your life when none of your other advisers knew you.'

299

'Is he tall and thin?' I ask.

He nods.

'Red hair?'

'Balding.'

'Oxford.'

'He was.'

'One of the school's great scholars,' I tell him.

'Was he?' Getting up he re-opens his bag. 'I thought,' he says, 'I might look at your chest.'

'Heart?'

'If you wouldn't mind,' he says.

When, a little later, he re-packs his bag, he says, 'I'd like to prescribe some pills. See what effect they have over the next few months.'

'You might prescribe,' I tell him, 'but I'm afraid, even with Donny on your back, I shall not be inclined to take them.'

'They're a precaution, rather than a cure,' he says. 'Rather like lithium in the past, they'll help you to live a fuller life.'

'I live a full enough life,' I tell him, 'already. When the time comes to go you'll find me,' I add, 'at the head of the queue.'

'What if you only half go?' he says. 'The life of an invalid, after a cardiac attack, isn't something, I'm sure, that you'd welcome.'

'I've had these pills,' I tell him, 'before. They didn't do me any good then. They won't do me any good now,' and, at a knock on the door, Etty pausing on the threshold a moment before entering, I add, 'See what your chum is up to. Prescribing pills he knows I won't take. From now on, Etty, it's mind over matter.'

'Mind devolves from matter,' Raynor says (portentously, in my view: not the sort of statement either welcome or expected from a village doctor), 'not the other way around.'

'I shall get well,' I tell him, 'in my own good time, and by good,' I go on, 'I mean good of my own prescription.'

"Nothing," Fenchurch wrote, "was resolved by this meeting with the doctor, in his liveried pin-stripe suit (light grey in (vivid) contrast to Maidstone's charcoal), but," he paused, "the

300

prospect of running rings round Donny Robeson after all these years (he beat me in the mile and got a scholarship – after special coaching – to St Edmund's College) brings me – more than the threat of partial paralysis – back to life."

'He says your pulse is high ("fevered", he describes it), your blood pressure is no better, if not slightly worse, than it was before, and he says your mood is too volatile to be allowed to go out on your own. He's concerned,' she adds, 'you're taking no medication.'

'I am not,' I tell her, 'a chemical bin,' (though I have been, even more than Vivienne, in the past), she having spoken to Raynor in the hall for several minutes – then several minutes (considerably) longer in the yard outside – even stooping to his car door after he's got inside: 'He's doing us a favour coming to the house: most patients, other than the terminally ill, have to go to him.'

'He doesn't consider that a favour, he feels flattered,' I tell her. 'Called out, in this provincial backwater, Etty, to see the scribe, plagiarist, grovelist and playwrong, friend of the grate and the gourd, novelless, playless, plagueless, friendless: good God, he'll make a fortune with his memoirs.'

'Will you see Robeson?' she says.

'Once I've run Donny,' I tell her, 'round this provincial patch I shall be fit and ready, my dear, for anything!'

19

CAWTHORNE CASTLE overlooks the upper reaches of the Lin: a bend of the river skirts it to the north, flowing along a broad, alluvial bed, while to the south, the east and the west, lies the wooded hill-land of the lower Pennine slopes. On an opposing hill, beyond the river, stands the Onasett headland.

I am too tired, I am tempted to tell Etty, to go out, having discovered, after sixty years (doesn't do to be precise), that my body isn't my own, merely the property of an artificer who has little, if anything, to do with what's inside (the facility, Etty, of everything I've done), leaving the house, however, in Charlie's boots (stronger than my own) and my winter coat, with (as if I needed them) precise instructions ('they have moved the stop') where to catch the bus, for, if I go the 'back' way to Linfield, through the lesser mining villages to the west (a favourite route in the past, but now awash with drugs), instead of the more familiar route to the north-north-west, I can get off close to the castle where, at the zenith of my powers, I wrote, 'Meditations Standing on a Hilltop at Cawthorne' – yet minutes later see Raynor leave his car, parked at the kerb, and enter a shop and come out carrying a bag (the shop's a chemist's). Having glanced in my direction he shakes his head (face flushed above his light grey suit: no overcoat for him), gets in his car, adjusts his mirror (a reflection of myself) and, re-adjusting it, drives off.

A stiff breeze is blowing on Cawthorne hill: the town lies in a haze across the valley: to the west, obscured by cloud, is the fissure in the Pennine wall through which the upper river flows (cascading through a limestone gorge: sandstone at a lower level, its ochre boulders strewn in its bed).

I enjoy the bus ride more than (an unfinished sentence is, if frequently repeated, an invariable sign, Maidstone says, of a schizoid condition).

The disassociated frame of mind.

The disassembly of his head.

I am still at the stop (the other side of the road to the direct-to-Linfield stop) waiting for the 'back way' bus.

After a moment of reflection, Fenchurch bows his head, contemplates the footpath by his feet (the eroded flags) and returns, past the church and the rectory, to the door in the old stone wall and makes his way, up the steepening slope, beneath the trees, to a recently-installed wicket-gate in the beech hedge (Charlie's idea, matching the one that leads to the orchard), entering the front garden of his daughter's house, his wife's childhood home and, glancing in the window of the living-room with the hope of glimpsing the love and longing of his life, the woman without whom his existence has no meaning, re-enters the front door which, by his estimation, he has left only moments before.

'The inclination never to complete a sentence is invariably a sign of,' Maidstone pauses to illustrate, unwittingly, the state of mind in question.

'Back?' the vacuuming, at least in the hallway, finished, Mrs Otterman popping out from the kitchen.

'Back?' Etty coming out, spectacles raised above her head, from her study (once Bea's bedroom).

'I have,' I tell her, 'changed my mind. My mind,' and such a mind, tuned, I reflect, to molecular phases, 'is susceptible to change,' I add.

I mount the stairs, still in Charlie's boots and my winter coat. 'I had envisaged taking the back way bus, through those villages which, now the pits have gone, are seldom seen – domestic scree, the grey and crumbled houses amidst the fields and copses, the little streams and dells, the unexpected ponds and lakes, the whole awash, I am told, with drugs, theft,

303

burglary, violence to obtain the same – a sea which will finally engulf this village, this house – everything we have known and loved – you see them now, waiting at the stop, behind the houses, in windows and doors, unemployed miners, their wives, their children, waiting, watching every move – "What," they are asking, "did we dig all that fucking coal for, to be cast on the waste-tip with everything else?" but found that a discontinued course of action is as relevant, in this instance, as a discontinued sentence. Stop.'

'Maidstone said,' however, I go on, 'that a cyclonic depression of the sort I've got is invariably the preamble to something worse. I had such visions, Etty, of the castle, the town spread out below, Onasett across the valley, its ridge poking up beyond the trees.'

He couldn't write,
nor could he right
the wrong
that writing of his wrongs
had done.

The thought occurred, 'I don't feel well,' (decide to tell her), lying there, moments later, boots still on, 'I'll go to bed.'

'Are you all right?'

She coming in.

'That doctor.' Said, 'I think I'll rest. (Think I'll go to sleep). Even though I've just got up.' Shouldn't have dressed. Threats from Charlie. Best behaviour. Found a place not far from here. 'Greater responsibility to greater things unseen when not insane,' et cetera. One thought is always back of brain. Has no one found a master?

Two:

'Caught a chill,' flu (from walking in his slippers).

All day he lay there.

Bells.

Church.

Midday: rhetoric was his strongest suit.

If writing didn't work he could always paint; if painting didn't work – he didn't recall the score exactly: hydrochloric acid mixed with amphetamines.

Well, then, Fenchurch, what sort of person am I? Strong, as a youth; stronger as a man: dependent, despite that, on women as vulnerable as himself: picture entitled by others, not himself – Maidstone, Mackendrick, Raynor, et al, *always looking for the bottom line*: inverted paranoia.

Last night he had had a peculiar dream: he had brought an old steam engine up from London and parked it – to people's amusement – in the field at the back of the house at Manor Road: crowds had collected – figures from his past, contemporaries who, as the saying goes, he had left behind: doltards, thickheads, provincial oafs. He joined in, along with his engine, a 'festival of art': films and pictures (poems and books: songs and dancing) ending, anachronistically, in a football match of the kind he had played at school but involving, rather than a team, these figures (and many more) from his past. At the end of the dream the field, flattened by the festivity, was deserted: the engine stood alone, gigantic and absurd in its garish colours, with its giant metal wheels and its smoking funnel. He set off, directing it from behind, on the long road back to London: no one, other than a policeman, came to shake his hand: no one, he observed, was there to see him off. He had one last ambition – to park the engine in front of his house and allow his parents to see it: that ambition, too, he set aside – for he was, he reminded himself, already on the road and, once started, he knew from experience there was no turning back.

He woke with a clear view of his past: he woke, he recalled later, not to a familiar sense of terror – fearfulness, apprehension – but to a peculiar sense of calm: he and Bea, he reflected, had never lived: they had been joined, throughout their adult lives, in a common venture: the steam engine, with its gargantuan wheels, its hissing valves, its gigantic funnel, its superfluous power, was a symbol of his writing and painting: he had worked to achieve, not so much fame as recognition and she to raise a family of – as it turned out – five vividly

305

contrasted children. He had failed, she succeeded: 'Bea,' he said, on waking, aloud, and then, curiously, in the same loud voice, he had added, without the thought having, until that moment, been in his head, 'That's why she took everything I had: the house, my writing, my money – even our children: she knew about her mother, and this, she felt, is what she deserved – what she was owed by the man who had betrayed her in a way that could, even if explained, or understood, never be forgiven.'

She has come to success by climbing on my back, the Nobel Prize acquired, he reflected, at my expense. And I thought last night I had never slept!

I am ill, unwell, as a consequence of Raynor's visit, that putative jockey (doctorial vet: diminutive build and threat of confinement) and the most absurd suggestion of all I should see a contemporary of mine with whom I was in competition throughout my school career.

And then, she knows: 'Are you going mad?' she would, ingenuously, at the time, enquire as she might, 'Is this the right way to stain a cell?' This – he clutched his heart – is a consequence of that. 'That's why, of course, she instantly agreed,' aloud, 'to my coming here: "*You* go *there*": to rub it in ("Meet my Nemesis" the title of the picture).'

Bereft of wife (possessions) God: she wishes me to be confronted by what I am (defined by my omissions). 'If this is her way of telling me she knows then I have nothing left to fear,' he told her: he was, he reflected – with a peculiar calmness, considering his position – about to fall.

She knows.

I know she knows.

I know she knows I know she knows.

"Dear Bea, not only have I discovered that your theory that the stream that runs (a polluted beck) through the middle of Ardsley, and which, you suspected, was flanked by reeds in medieval times, and thereby gave its name to the house built on this site previous to The People's Palace, is wrong, but that this original house derived its name from the colour of the

sandstone of which it was built: red (hence, Rede House).
Which brings me to a lesser point, namely," I made a pact with
fate (read 'fete', the subject of my dream last night), the lore of
self-expression. I lost my art to Beatrice Kells (her professional
name) but really to her mother, "the doctor came today and
wants to place me in the hands of a quack – a putative quack
when I knew him at school. Didn't you go out with Robeson
(D.), he wanting to put one over on me, you wanting to get
back at me also? Tall, thin, sporty, but not as good as he
thought, and with parents who had a chauffeured limousine?

Etty is convinced I'm out of remission.

P.S. Mrs Otterman says the principal industry in the village
is the procurement and the sale of drugs which makes it surprising that the Hall, unlike most houses in the village, hasn't
been broken into more often (twice: nothing of interest taken),
but it does suggest – despite Charlie's New Labour Line –
conceivably because of it – they won't (we won't) be here for
long: a more modest dwelling closer to Linfield – or even in
London (though never mentioned) – is on the cards, Charlie
champing to get his hands on *global* abuses of humanity again,
the local ones too horrible to mention: debilitation of a class,
almost of a race, certainly a species, that proud, autocratic
(conservative), *humanist* fervour associated with what, at one
time, was a necessary profession ('a rat in a hole,' my father
described it).

P.P.S. I am better than I've ever been."

'Do you want,' she says, 'to take your pills?' (She has been to
the chemist to get them: holds them out).

'I caught a chill,' I tell her. 'I shall stay in bed. Nothing to
write home about – apart,' I go on, 'from a note to your
mother.'

'Are you taking to heart what Raynor said?' glasses pushed
to the top of her head – a mannerism I never liked (two
supernumerary eyes, etc.).

'I've decided,' I tell her, 'to stay in bed.'

'I ought to call Raynor back,' she says.

307

'Carry on with Cotman,' I tell her. 'I,' I assure her, 'will be all right.'

The etymology of grief, the epistemology of madness.

The plight of the middling asses.

'I shall,' I further reassure her, 'draw the line (beneath all these armless jesters). Is your father farther from the truth than your father's father ever was? What's it like,' I further enquire, 'to be embraced by a single arm? Does he use it to support himself or embrace where others have embraced before?' adding, 'I saw Raynor shopping in the village and felt so ill I came back home to bed. All those hours of introspection on which,' I conclude, 'there's been no return,' (a terror of being re-interned).

Neurones and syntases.

'One other thing,' I interrupt, 'I weigh too much. I shall have to slim.'

He went, in the end, in Charlie's car, though it was Etty who came with him. 'Charlie, I suppose, has gone to work?' I enquire as we drive into the grounds of the North London Royal and when I observe we are parking in the forecourt of Eastley Hall, the former Linfield Municipal Lunatic Asylum – passed by, on numerous occasions, on the way to school (its grey brick, mullion-windowed, gothic façade) – having driven all the way in silence – she says, 'He has,' manoeuvring the car into a vacant parking bay.

'It's not,' I tell her, 'so different from Boady Hall.'

'Pleasanter,' she says.

'Worse.'

'Some things get better, Father,' she says, and might have added, 'and some get worse,' but continues, 'It has greatly improved in recent years.'

'Little that I can see,' I tell her.

'But then, you've seen it so little,' she says. 'At least coming out has done some good. I hope you're not going to show Robeson how well and how frequently we quarrel.'

'I didn't ask you to bring me here,' I tell her, stiffly climbing out.

Rain flecks the windscreen of the car: it falls on my grey and grizzled head: my arm in hers, the car door locked, we proceed up a flight of worn stone steps to a glass-panelled porch.

Lunatics are visible inside: a mosaic floor inset with a design which appears to incorporate, to my discerning eye, a flower. 'Didn't Van Gogh shoot his brains out,' I ask her, 'after visiting a place like this?'

She appears to know her way, gripping my arm beneath hers then, having negotiated a flight of stairs, we turn along a corridor which echoes (more mosaics) to a woman's high-pitched voice calling, 'I shan't! I shan't!' and then, as if re-programmed by someone as positive in their thinking as Etty, 'I shall!'

We enter a room: we have, a nurse informs us, been expected. We sit, with several others, on wooden benches: figures pass to and fro obfuscated by a layer of liquid which hangs, in permanent suspension, in front of my eyes.

I see a facsimile of a figure I knew before, erect, slim, balding: the epitome, I reflect, of a self-made man, except, I recall, so much more has gone into his creation: a suit as dark and as elegantly striped as Maidstone's, and singularly less creased.

'Forty-three years,' I tell him, 'is a very long time,' to which, unsmiling, he remarks, 'I make it nearer forty-five,' grasping, however, my outstretched hand – smiling at Etty (shaking hers), I convinced he has met her already.

'So much,' I tell him, 'is still the same. As if,' I add, 'we were back at King Edward's,' the smoothness of his chin (so many lunatics have passed his way before), the coolness of expression (eyes, light blue, cast, distractedly, to a far horizon). 'You announcing your intention of thrashing me in the mile.'

'I don't think I ran the mile,' he says. 'Cross-country,' he adds, 'I did for a while,' continuing, 'I've had a long talk with Doctor Raynor, and a longer one still with your daughter,' smiling at Etty again, and when I enquire, 'Did you come

309

to any conclusions?' he replies, 'We're not here to come to conclusions. We're only here to help.'

Put him in perspective.

'On the other hand . . .'

He indicates the way to a door marked 'Annexe': we pass along a corridor with a wooden floor: a line of elderly figures, holding hands backwards and forwards, approaches us from a lighted space: a key is taken from Robeson's pocket and a door inscribed with his name is opened.

He indicates, with an outstretched hand, a chair that Etty might sit in, directly to one side of a wooden desk – indicating a second as Etty signals I sit in the first. He takes his place not behind but, not unlike Maidstone, beside the desk so that, confronting Etty, he is diagonally across the desk from me.

'How are you?' he enquires, glancing from me to Etty, and when she replies, 'Not well,' he adds, 'Doctor Raynor, in his letter, sounded intimidated by your father.'

'He's more at home,' I say, 'with miners, at least, with those that used to be miners. Particularly,' I go on, 'their wives and children.'

Robeson's legs are crossed: long and lean, with prominent, sharply-pointed knees and one bared ankle above a sock which reminds me of the short-trousered, red-haired, lanky youth squeezing spots in a glass-fronted cupboard. Now consultant at Eastley Hall, re-named, he must, on not a few occasions, encounter not a few of his former chums (rivals, fellow entrants for the Horsfall fellowship to St Edmund's).

'Good old Edward's!'

'I beg your pardon?'

'One Old Edwardian to another,' (creatures from a bygone age). 'The parameters are perimeters only,' I tell him. 'Beyond them,' I continue, 'everything is allowed.'

'Let me,' he tells me, 'make a note.'

A pad, taken from the desk, replaces the file on his knee. A pen, taken from an inside pocket, is – Old Robeson! – carefully unscrewed: nothing changed in three thousand years. 'Perhaps you remember Beatrice?' I enquire. 'A putative beauty with magenta hair likened by some to a ptolemaic cat. A leading light,' I go on, 'at the High School.'

Previous medical history, he enquires, glancing at Etty, to which I reply, 'I was consulted by the infamous existentialist Robert (known as "Bobby") Mackendrick whose father was a Ukrainian cobbler who plied his trade in places as far apart as East Ham and Clapham, in years as divergent as 1906 and 1937, he killed by a bomb at the grand old age of seventy-two in an air-raid shelter with a suspect roof which received a direct hit in 1941. "Bobby" asked me if I would listen to his tapes, a preamble to his writing his celebrated *The Phenomenology of Experience*, an amalgam, not entirely inaccurate, of much of what I told him. It is, in short, a study of me, unannounced and something of a parody of my less successful but more influential *A New Theory of the Mind* and my equally influential *The Logic of Grief*, without a doubt,' I wait for acknowledgement, 'you must have read them all.'

'We read nothing, I'm afraid,' he says, 'up here.' He glances not at me, but Etty.

'In which case,' I tell him, 'let's stick to the facts,' giving him my date of birth and marital status, number of children and financial position. 'The future has been mortgaged to the past by mortgagees who made commitments which had nothing to do with me,' I tell him. 'Insanity is a motor impairment which, like everything else, has a spiritual dimension, one, however, which conditions, rather than is conditioned by.'

'What feelings, for instance,' he asks me, 'are you having now?'

'I might as well confess it, dissimulation is my ruling passion. I am that not uncommon phenomenon, a vocational liar. All my life,' I add, 'is a fiction. Not a day has gone by in which I have not added another word, another deed, another event, another action.'

'Is he,' he enquires of Etty, 'as defensive with you?' and when she answers in the affirmative, I add, 'Opposition, in the past, has been all I've had. (Me against the school, remember?) Not invited back in my final year at the Drayburgh, for – I was told,

311

by Sir Felix Pemberton, the Principal at the time – you've seen, I take it, his pictures at the Tate? – failing to attend statutory classes in Perspective, Anatomy and the History of Art and, a peculiarly venturesome subject for that time, the Moral, or was it the Immoral Principles of Design. I was, in reality, writing novels, not painting the pictures and drawing the drawings I should have done. Furthermore, for the next few years, I taught in schools in the East End of London which were – at least three of them – counted amongst the worst in Great Britain, the venomous Tudor Street School between the Whitechapel Road and Cable Street in Stepney, and the odious Windsor School in Hackney, to name but two, after which I applied for jobs as diverse as a refuse superintendent (the only white man in the queue of West Indians and Asians, losing out to one of the latter) at a departmental store in Oxford Street, as a stock-clerk in a steam-casings manufacturer's office in Clerkenwell, an exhibition-stand erector for a firm in Southwark, at the southern end of Blackfriars Bridge, as a copy-writer at the corner of Wardour Street and Shaftesbury Avenue, as a journalist on the in-house magazine of a well-known manufacturer of household soap: a cleaner, a bouncer, a washer-up. I ended up starving in a room above a sweet-shop in a street not far from where I am living at present, collecting discarded vegetables and half-rotten fruit from the gutters as the day-long street markets closed. Meanwhile of course,' I glance at Etty, 'our first two children were born and I was writing and painting every minute of every hour when exhaustion didn't engulf me.'

I laid it on the line:
I gave it to him proper:
no good not lying when you're down:
o give the sod a copper.

'And all the while,' I add, 'you were studying at the Radcliffe.'
He is writing with a thick-nibbed pen – a present from Mrs, or perhaps Ms Robeson at Christmas, or bought at the Swan

Press, the only bookshop in Linfield: no books by the author whose tortured revelations are a postscript to his life in Linfield.

'Then, of course, with *A Hero of Our Time*, I became,' I add, 'a household word.'

And so forth, as Isabella, in her retirement at Torquay would say ('nothing like the Riviera') when the delirium of recollection got beyond her: 'Those picnics that we had (when Bea was a child) in Ardsley Woods, *and so forth*,' waving her delicately wrinkled hand.

'How I loved her. Above all else,' I am about to add, but remark, 'And never looked back until, approaching my fiftieth year, but, more closely, my fifty-fifth, I was overwhelmed by forces which youth, energy, certainly passion had, until that moment, kept at bay, a species of terror, the intensity and extensiveness of which, even now, after all these years, I hesitate, indeed, am unable to describe.'

'Experiences,' Robeson says, referring to Raynor's letter, 'you've had since childhood.'

'I believe you were in Junior King Edward's?' I enquire.

'King Edward's Juniors,' he replies.

'Fee-paying at the time.'

'I was a fee-payer all the way through school,' he says, and adds, 'At least, my parents were.'

'I was at Onasett Juniors.'

'A good school, too, I hear,' he says.

'Only a few passed to the Grammar.'

'That's right.'

'Equality restored by administering to the sick in your home town,' I tell him.

'It wasn't my home town,' he says. 'My parents lived abroad and, when not, in a variety of places. However,' he pauses, 'I have made it my home town,' and adds, 'Would you say you were feeling depressed?'

'Dispiritation,' I tell him, 'has been my way of life. I wake each morning as do the bereaved. *Someone has gone.* In my case, my mother's eldest son who died six months before I was born.'

'Your mind harks back to it continually,' he suggests.

313

'Not,' I tell him, 'any longer.' (I have, I might have told him, outgrown it.)

'We all have our portion of bad luck,' he says. 'Some infinitely more than others. The question we have to ask isn't,' he continues, 'why or how, or even when and who, but what are we going to do about it?'

The words taken, or might have been, out of Maidstone's mouth (a pragmatist!).

'A life,' he continues, 'of initial hardship, followed by one of considerable success.'

'A classic pattern,' I tell him, 'of decline.'

Etty is subdued. 'Perhaps you'd feel easier,' I suggest, 'if my daughter wasn't here.'

'On the contrary,' he says, 'I'm interested in what she has to say.'

'Over the last few days,' she says, 'he has rambled in his speech, has been unable to focus his thoughts, is totally self-absorbed, and appears oblivious of any help anyone may give him.'

God help Cotman! is what I am about to say, but, if shocked, swiftly reply, 'That's not entirely true. I am more aware than ever of my faults and do my best, despite dispiritation and attacks of terror, to set them right.'

Robeson writes – left-handed, I note, recalling this mannerism in the Sixth Form Library, his pen held in such a way that, as he wrote, the nib was pointing at his chest: something narcissistic, careerist, even, in this gesture – less so, I reflect now, as if, self-possessed, he is privately lost.

'In addition to which there are,' I tell him, 'moments of self-preoccupation that induce a feeling of my being lifted from the ground. I float. A curious sensation I can't,' I conclude, 'otherwise describe.'

'Would you describe it as ecstatic?'

'On the contrary,' I tell him, 'I invariably feel reflective, as if this form of elevation is, or should be, my normal state of mind.'

A sense of normality, he might have written, he ascribes to an abnormal state of mind.

'Who, in this situation, is to define normality?' I enquire. 'Or do we take a hippocratic view that that which is not experienced by the observing mind is not to be considered normal – is, if not corroborated, to be considered pathogenic, etymologically deriving from, in short, a grief-stricken source?'

Such abstruseness (a view of Linfield's inner suburb – rows of semi-detached houses – visible through the window and, closer to the building, a mildewed, stone-flagged yard) is not to Robeson's liking: his pen, its cap towards me, is arrested in its track: the self-directed scribbler, the other-directed scribe, the silver clip enquires, have you come here to decide?

'Were you,' I enquire, 'at the Allgrave party that summer when "the best generation KEGS has ever had", as the Head described it, met for, as it turned out, the very last time?'

'I was one of the few,' Robeson said, 'who didn't go.'

'Why not?'

'Because,' he says, 'I wasn't invited.'

'I wonder why that was?' I ask.

'Because,' he says, 'I was in the bug-house,' smiling at Etty to add, 'The boarding-house where us poor boarders slept, socially unacceptable,' he goes on, 'to the town boys,' and, still smiling, 'You're the third person from that party I've seen in the past few months,' continuing, 'not socially,' the pen still in his hand, 'but in this room.'

'Depression of the kind I have described is the equivalent,' I tell him, 'of having your skin peeled back, or your skull removed. All those things that normally protect you have been displaced. The whole metabolism quivers and shakes, is ceaselessly tormented.'

I tell him this to have the satisfaction, the cap of the pen once more towards me, of watching him make a note on his pad.

'You're the seventh psychiatrist I've spoken to, at length, over the past ten years – one, roughly, every eighteen months – and though our encounters have never led to much – as

315

much a fulfilment of their expectations, I might add, as mine – it has nourished in me a scepticism of my own reactions. Am I, for instance, I ask myself each morning when I wake – gripped by alarm, anxiety, dread – *as mad as I make out*? Is this a reasonable expectation? i.e., a sensitive and intelligent man, imbued with understanding, sensibility, taste, even with the gift of self-expression. Will it, unless I am brutalised like everyone else, ever be any different? Am I condemned to be an aberration, a sensitised monstrosity, thrown up by nature which only evolutionary indiscretion will bring to an end? It's not, for instance, by chance, that when I look up the antecedents of a case like mine – unique, I would have thought, in many respects – I am not directed to psychology, or even analysis, let alone philosophy or God, but to teratology, the science of vegetable and animal monstrosities, and the famous Harrison and Schaadt experiments, at Berkeley, on pregnant mice.'

I am scarcely, at this stage, in a state to go on (his pen feverishly active on the paper before him – how like those lectures in Natural Science, he, as always, sitting at the front).

'I haven't heard of teratology,' he says, smiling at Etty, 'applied to this particular subject. Nor,' he goes on, 'of Harrison's – and did you say Shat's experiments on pregnant mice?'

'I want! I want!' comes a voice outside the door, followed by a banging at the one adjacent.

Robeson's pen is still. The adjoining door is opened: 'What is it, Hilary?' a male voice enquires.

'*Can* I smoke?' a woman's voice replies.

'Only if you have to.'

'You said only one a day.'

'Only one.'

'I've had one, Doctor Freeman, already.'

The door of the room is closed.

'What relevance,' Robeson says, 'do these experiments have for you?'

'My mother suffered,' I tell him, 'in a similar way when,' I add, 'she was pregnant with me.'

316

'You're not equating yourself,' he smiles once more at Etty, 'with a mouse?'

'With several.'

'Or even,' a further smile at Etty, 'with several.' Leaning to the file, he adds, 'Your psychiatrist at the North London Royal was inclined,' he consults an appropriate sheet of paper, 'in fact, was anxious to discount it.'

'We are talking about a physiological entity,' I tell him. 'Like having, for instance, red hair, or being born with only one foot.'

'At least, not three,' Old Robey laughs.

I laugh as well: so does Etty, who, until now, has watched Robeson's expression with a frown.

'If,' he goes on, 'it happens to be – shall we say, not "true", but relevant – it doesn't change in any way what you intend to do about it now. A mouse, I suspect, has no powers of reflection. Consciousness it might have, in a passive but not an active sense, of things mulled over and acted on. And we,' he smiles again at Etty, 'are mullers, and you, if I'm not mistaken – according to the *The Edwardian*, which I still receive, at the end of every term,' he gestures in the direction (I take it) of the school, 'are a muller-in-extremis, your books, whereas unread by me, have been commented upon almost, it seems, on an annual basis – until, that is, the last few years. I take that to be congruent with your illness.'

'It was more my illness was congruent with something else,' I tell him. 'My wife leaving me, for instance, first for the sake of science, then for the sake of the parliamentary private secretary to the Minister of Health and subsequently, in a reshuffle, to a junior minister in the same department.'

'Your wife's departure was congruent with your illness?' he enquires.

'Coincidental,' the patient declares. 'I was already in extremis,' (the foetal prodigy of those early months, locked in with its placenta, had, after sixty-odd years, finally shown its hand).

'What brought you to me?' he suddenly enquires and, as I

turn my head from the window, perceive that this enquiry is directed not at me but to the, until now, relatively silent figure beside me who, pre-empting my desire to say, 'Brought is the operative word: I didn't choose to come,' says, 'He appears, despite you being with him, to be speaking to someone else. That, and his irresponsible and at times nonsensical actions, his inclination to sit, his arms folded across his stomach, and rock himself in a chair, his tendency – which, at this stage, I wouldn't wish to put any higher than that – to weep, involuntarily, without provocation, sometimes, with only one or two intermissions, for several hours on end.'

'What do you weep about?' he asks, and adds, 'It's unusual for a man to weep so long,' as if, in reporting this behaviour, Etty is being, if not deceptive, misleading.

'I don't know why I weep,' I tell him. 'It happens, as it were, without my knowing. First of all,' I go on, 'there's fear, a feeling of desolation, of loss, so complete that, even after all these years, I couldn't begin to describe it.'

'Why not,' he tells me, 'make a start?'

'First of all,' I tell him, 'there's the fear that is on me the moment I wake. There is no morning, for instance, when it isn't there, and no day when it doesn't persist until the evening. At times it is so intense, so comprehensive, so all-embracing that, involuntarily, I weep.'

'What sort of fear?' the pen pointing once more towards his chest.

'A passive fear, synonymous with waking to the realisation that during the night a death sentence has been passed, and an active fear synonymous with the realisation I will never see another dawn, another night, my children, my wife, or anyone I love, again. Underlying this sensation is a feeling of guilt which not merely absorbs but consumes the mind entirely, so monstrous and complete, so all-pervading and all-enclosing, that there is no hope – no conception, even – of forgiveness or atonement: gripped by this dementia, the mind can think of nothing else. Yesterday, for instance, I persuaded myself I was on the threshold of going mad. This was prompted by the severity of a bolt depression which struck me, unaccountably, when I glimpsed my daughter's doctor, Raynor, in the village, doing nothing more significant than carrying a bag of shopping to his car. Immediately I thought, "My last hope has gone!" though what that hope was, and why it should be abandoned at such an irrelevant moment, I have no idea. This attack, appeared to be related to the shallowness of everything around me: the people in the street, the face of Raynor with his bag of shopping – the fact that he had something meaningful to do in life and I, transparently, had not – and with the face of Etty and the cleaning-woman as I came back inside the house. I immediately thought of Bea and the shallowness of our marriage, of a relationship diverted from its course by something as inconsequential as a laboratory experiment and a relationship with a one-armed opportunist whose name at school, I understand, was "Bandit". The fatuity, as I say, not only of all these people but of such reflections reducing me to a state not indistinguishable from that of a condemned man who steps out to the yard and, after one or two faltering steps, onto the scaffold. A certain complicity in what is about to take place absorbs him, alongside the feelings of terror and despair, a dispiritation so profound he can't even speak, as if, in desperation, he is about to slip the noose from around his neck. Yet the noose, in this allegory, is reality itself, and the irreality he would have to endure in taking it off is worse than the reality he faces at present, a realisation which pitches him into a despair greater than anything he has previously imagined.'

The room is quiet: a door opens in the corridor outside. 'One more,' says a woman's voice, followed, from inside the adjacent room, by, 'Perhaps you'll miss one tomorrow.'

A door is closed: feet fade towards the sound of distant voices.

All this, I reflect, is induced by what? Not hunger, not electric shock, not a lack of shelter, nor a lack of love but, despite the absence of such things, an organic, physiological condition endemic to my system.

'I think,' Robeson says, writing again, 'you give me a very clear picture.'

When I enquire, 'Of what?' he replies, 'A tired mind.'

'My God!' I cry. 'I only need a rest!'

'A rest,' he says, 'wouldn't do any harm.'

'What do you think, Etty?' I ask. 'Does that complete the clinical picture?'

'I think it's gone further,' she says, 'than that. We need,' she continues, 'a practical solution.'

Robeson raises his head: he is not sure what a remark like that is intending to suggest.

'You think your father,' he pauses, 'ought to come in.'

'I'm not sure I can handle him,' she says, 'in the mood he's in at present. He can't, quite clearly, be left in London or up here to live alone.'

'Do you want to come in?' Robeson says, addressing me.

'I'm quite all right on my own,' I tell him.

'You're currently living with your daughter,' he says as if, having identified a coffin, he is tapping in a nail.

'It was her, and her mother's suggestion I should come up here,' I tell him. 'My wife, as you know, has now re-married. "A run-away romance", it was described in the papers. Though where they ran to I've no idea. They were both back at work inside two weeks.'

'That is an indication of the difficulties my husband and I are under,' Etty says, obscurely, interrupting this remark.

'The only point,' I tell Robeson, 'I wish to make is that I was living contentedly in London, and though one or two neighbours had made complaints, they were nothing that, on reflection, I couldn't contend with.'

'What complaints?' Robeson says, closing the file on the desk and re-adjusting the pad on his knee.

'I solicited, in a wholly innocuous way, the wife of my next-door-neighbour and the wives of two other neighbours across the street. With women particularly I have difficulty in distinguishing between what I wish them to be – loving, warm, all-embracing, providing the affection I never had – and what they

320

are: attached to, and strongly imbued with the values of their husbands. Now I've recognised this as a characteristic of my illness – which, like most disabilities, requires a little while to get used to – I can and, indeed, shall refrain from doing the same again.'

'What would be the same?' he says, this a turn-up, his look suggests, for a former hero of King Edward's whose name, for several decades, has figured prominently in the termly published *Edwardian*.

'I commented on their make-up as well as their appearance, in terms which were approving but which were regarded by them as, if true, intrusive. Yet how can truth be intrusive? I'd enquire, their husbands, of course, taking a more forceful line, disinclined to have their wives approved of in any way at all.'

'How approve?' He re-crosses his legs, preventing the pad, as he does so, from falling on the floor.

'I embraced each one of them and, in one specific instance – that of my immediate neighbour – solicited a kiss.'

'Were you aware of this?' He directs his enquiry to Etty.

'It was my mother who visited him,' she says, 'and found him unable to work or even properly feed himself. Both his general practitioner and the psychiatrist, Maidstone, suggested it would be a good idea to bring him away, as an alternative,' she adds, 'to returning either to the North London Royal or Boady Hall.'

'I went prepared,' I tell him, 'to a group therapy session, with an account of my past history at my fingertips, to find only four other people there, in addition to the psychotherapist, as a consequence of which, on the therapist's instructions, we spent the entire hour playing Twenty Questions. How, with an intellect like mine, with a wealth of social, cultural, moral and spiritual, not to mention domestic experience behind it, am I supposed to recover? I'm afraid confinement, apart from keeping me off the streets, never did me the slightest good.'

'I had no alternative,' Etty says, 'but to bring him home. But I'm not sure his eccentricities fit into a home with two young children, and I'm loath to have him returned – since he so dislikes it – to Boady Hall.'

'Eastley Hall,' I enquire, 'is a suitable alternative?'

'Doctor Raynor,' she goes on, 'suggested we got in touch with you, not merely,' she adds to me, 'as a matter of form but because he believes we need advice.'

'There are halfway houses,' Robeson says – with, I notice, a return of his smile. 'But none that I know of would be suitable for a man of Richard's background.'

'Why not call me Fenny?' I ask.

'Fenny?'

'The name I had at school.'

'I don't remember that,' he says (his own, too, I presume, forgotten).

'I don't see why my wife should interfere,' I tell him. 'It's only guilt. She came, I might add, without any warning. Two days, as it happened, after she'd got back – though I wasn't to know it at the time – from an overseas trip with Albert. Tanned. I hadn't, she discovered, read about her in the paper – the sensational run-away bride and groom, and the difficulties both the Ministry of Health and the Medical Research Council might be in having the soliciting of funds, by the latter of the former, compromised by what was described as "practically an inter-departmental marriage". Politics,' I add in parenthesis, 'is a tricky business. As it is,' I continue, 'she caught me by surprise, opening the door, as I did so, to find her on the step, no food in the kitchen, a pile of unwashed pots, unshaven – "unapproachable," she announced, "merely the shadow of my former self, the man she had married some thirty-odd years before." Albert, I scarcely need to add, I never brought up. Sexual jealousy is the most painful of all the emotions, outside of anxiety and terror, and their cohort, despair, I being a specialist in all three. Nevertheless, if I had had the opportunity, I wouldn't have had the slightest compunction – would, indeed, have derived a great deal of pleasure from it – in killing Albert, and a great deal more, not from killing – I wouldn't like to do her down (after all, I love her) – but from conveying to my former wife the scale and intensity of what I felt at being abandoned in favour of a one-armed mandarin whose own species of suffering is infinitesimal beside my own.'

'I believe you were deeply affected,' Robeson says, 'by the death of Vivienne Wylder.'

'I was,' I say, 'and am,' and then enquire, 'Who is Vivienne Wylder?'

'Vivienne,' Etty says.

'I know no one of that name,' I tell her.

'You lived with her,' Etty says, 'for over five years.'

'It couldn't have been over,' I tell her, 'I would have noticed.'

'Under five years,' she says. 'The dates aren't that important.'

'She had a great deal of money of her own,' I tell her, 'but never any cash. The greatest disturbances to our relationship were less to do with drink and drugs and professional failure – the latter, otherwise, apart from Melvyn, her constant pre-occupation, but money. I'd given all I had to Bea who, unlike Etty, took it without the slightest hesitation. I've earned – or, perhaps, I deserve, she might have said, every single penny. For putting up with me,' I add to Robeson.

'She enjoyed being a mother,' Etty says.

'She enjoyed,' I tell her, 'being my wife, until she was per-suaded not to.'

'Who by?' Etty asks.

'I never found out,' I tell her. 'The place, the times. All the women at that time were giving up on marriage, only – within days, in some instances – weeks, months – taking up with someone else, invariably,' I go on, 'a facsimile of the one they'd left behind.'

'Like you, in Mum's case,' Etty says.

'I doubt it,' I tell her, and add, 'I wonder.'

'It had, nevertheless,' Robeson says, 'a profound effect.'

'My assets,' I enquire, 'or my wife's re-marriage?'

'The death of Vivienne Wylder.'

'That was several years ago,' I tell him, and add, 'Two and a half, to be precise,' or was it eighteen months (two weeks, three days, and thirty-seven minutes? according to the coroner's report). 'She'd been lying there for nearly two days, or was it

323

four, her suitcases packed and hidden in the garden shed, I assuming she was visiting friends, the few she had left, in L.A., one in particular, a diabolic presence, addicted to a diet which when she was over there, reduced Vi to little more than a match-stick, something she redressed with booze the moment she got back. Initially,' I go on, 'she came whenever she'd started drinking, having been turned out or down by most if not all of her other friends. In her final years she'd turn up directly from the airport, having flown in from L.A. or New York, or even Chicago where she used to go and dry out. A taxi-load of cases, like moving half a house, none of which she opened. Sometimes she'd stay a month, sometimes a day, sometimes – on two or three occasions – for only three or four hours. Sometimes six months. Sometimes a year. "Partners in distress," she'd say, and bed down, or otherwise, without another word. She'd been threatening to kill herself for seventeen years, and had even tried it two or three times, on one occasion driving a car into a motorway bridge, having previously, however, fastened her seat-belt. She came out with a dislocated shoulder and a broken wrist which, for two or three days, sobered her up. As for psychoanalysts: she joined me at the North London Royal. Maidstone, the Sub-Dean of the Medical School and the Longcroft Professor of Psychiatry, fell on his knees before her. "The most remarkable woman," he told me, "I have ever met," taken in by her assertions she intended to reclaim herself. "My Academy performance," she described it. He let her out after seven weeks on that occasion and two weeks later she was dead.'

I weep. 'In,' I tell Robeson, 'a disenchanted way (no notice to be taken of it: in another man such an affectation might just as casually be conveyed by the scratching of his head: an itch occurs which induces tears, a melancholia so profound it can neither be described nor analysed).'

The writer takes a rest, absorbing himself in thoughts of the countryside, or the wife of his next-door neighbour, the impracticalities of a relationship with whom must be as clear to her as they are to him: thoughts of immortality cross his mind, together with intimations of senility (currently undiagnosed).

'My principal concern,' I add, 'is to find a companion of the opposite sex with whom I can have a relationship at least as rewarding as that which, for the better part of thirty-odd years, I had with my wife. A woman, in short, who is companionable and strong, intellectually assertive, physically engaging, and who has lived a life, ideally, as unpredictable and as charged with adversity as my own.'

Robeson is writing once more on his pad.

'Do you require,' he suddenly enquires, 'a sedative?'

'I've dispensed with drugs,' I tell him, 'some time ago.'

'I'd recommend you re-start your course,' he says, 'of anti-depressants. We might,' he goes on, 'try a different kind. Once this phase is over I'd recommend a return to lithium. It doesn't necessarily require,' he adds, 'a lifetime commitment.'

'I'm afraid,' I tell him, 'I've been this way before,' glancing at Etty and adding, 'Have you brought me here to be sectioned? Is that what Raynor's up to?'

'No,' she says, and shakes her head.

'As a child,' I tell Robeson, 'she loved me very much. So did all the children. When I was a husband and a father, for days, quite often, at a time, I felt, in light of my temperament, unreasonably happy.'

'It's your welfare,' Robeson says, 'we're concerned about. But that doesn't preclude,' he goes on, 'the effect that that welfare, and the provisions we may make for it, may have on others.'

Maidstone said, 'I have never been depressed myself, as opposed to being dispirited, nor have I ever been anxious to a degree which makes it impossible to function, as a consequence of which I can only imagine what it's like, in your analogy the equivalent of endeavouring to imagine a new colour or the limits of a limitless universe. I have only your symptoms to go on, indications which, as you can see, distress me as much as anyone. If I respect your suffering there is an obligation on you, not to defer to, but to recognise mine. The

325

treatment I am recommending I am obliged, in all cases but your own, to prescribe with the knowledge that if I failed to do so I would be open to accusations of professional neglect. I have no alternative therefore but to insist you take the medication and, failing that, to make it mandatory that it is administered to you, if not by me, then someone else.'

Robeson says, 'If you don't take the prescription, in the doses I recommend, to the satisfaction of your daughter and/or Doctor Raynor, I shall have no alternative but to have you brought inside.'

I weep.

'The dispensary,' he adds to Etty, 'you'll find downstairs. If any further difficulties arise you will, of course, let me or Doctor Raynor know.'

On a separate sheet of paper he writes a number.

'Telephone that number at any time and bring your father in directly if you're in any doubt at all.'

To me, he continues, 'I'm giving you the benefit of the doubt. Freedom outside as opposed to confinement here.' He raises his arm, as he might on winning the mile that he says he never ran. 'The choice,' he concludes, 'is yours.'

'Not that it's any concern of mine,' I tell him, 'but at the time of the events I have previously described I was plagued by reporters, as indeed were my neighbours, who wished to take photographs of the shed in question. Though failure is a cloak that few people can afford and none, as far as I am aware, wholeheartedly welcome, despite its being so freely dispensed, it is not one which even now obscures me entirely. I am still susceptible to being recognised and responded to in a wholly unacceptable way.'

'I am sure your name,' Robeson says (his smile returning), 'will be of no interest, if it's known at all outside the pages of *The Edwardian*, to anyone at Eastley Hall.'

Eastley was a man of action and lived in a house the foundations of which are still, allegedly, in place beneath the present building: he built a five-arched bridge across the River Lin ('one for each of the senses'), hunted in South America, was famous for riding a crocodile with a bridle and bit, and built the first hospital in the district, in the grounds of his house, for the treatment of the mentally ill: a taxidermist, naturalist, water-colourist, philanthropist, engineer (his son assisted George Stephenson in the construction of the station in Linfield) he bequeathed his house and grounds to the hospital which bears his name.

'I gave,' I tell Robeson (Eastley, too, of course, was considered mad), 'all my money away, although a sum has been retained by my former wife, and is administrated by her and my children in conjunction with the bank and the Board of Inland Revenue. I have a residual income which would inconvenience the proverbial mouse, though not at all one of Harrison's and Schaadt's notorious menagerie who subsequently lived, despite their hereditary problems, in, I understand, luxurious retirement, in the form of royalties on plays and novels and from the sale of occasional paintings and drawings, most, too, of which, I gave away. I don't belong to the government scheme for paying authors on the basis of copies borrowed from public libraries, on account of the principle, adhered to, as much as possible, throughout my life, that an artist should be independent of statutory procedures, such independence being the only valuable thing he or she may have. I'd rather starve to death, and, on occasion, have almost done so, rather than accede to state support, not least – the most invidious of all motives – because it's well intentioned.'

I am about to continue but observe that Robeson has already risen (the slurring of his chair). 'The pills are to be taken initially,' he says, 'in very small doses. There'll be no effect for five or six weeks, during which time,' he confides to Etty, 'I want you to call me should you ever feel the need. I'll see your father this time next week. Will you be free,' he enquires, 'to bring him?'

'I,' she says, 'or someone else.'

'The other point I wish to make,' I tell him, unable to recall precisely what it is, 'is that there are certain qualities common to us all, the "all" I refer to,' I continue, remaining in my chair, 'being those afflicted by an unreasonable dependency on others.'

'I'll see you and your father out,' Robeson says (after all, at one point, he was courting Etty's mother and, should Albert fall at the final jump – a one-handed leap at the prime-ministership – might still see himself in there with a chance: from provincial anonymity to metropolitan (Kellsian) notoriety: fame, for fuck's sake! I can see it in his glance).

'This, in turn, is occasioned by what I would describe as an absence of self, a phenomenon I can only describe as being akin to a fall from grace, an absence of, or a removal from God. No language adequately describes it, and though it may have prompted Major Eastley to donate his home, in the late eighteenth century in an unprecedented fit of generosity, to the community in which he lived, for the healing, by seclusion, of those who were mentally ill, the only comment it would draw from me is that it is indistinguishable from a feeling of perdition, the absence of something within one's body without which communication with anything outside, temporal or divine, is not only indescribably painful but impossible. In short, I am not the person you thought I thought you thought I thought you thought I was.'

We are sitting in the dispensary amidst a multitude of over-coated figures who are waiting, via an illuminated sign, for their number to come up: Etty has gone off to get a coffee, returning with a plastic cup which, despite being encased in another, is still too hot to hold.

'Am I to be like this for ever?' I ask her. 'For ever like this to the end of my life?'

'You're lucky he didn't take you in,' she says.

'It's at moments such as this that reality becomes a mockery of my strongest feelings,' I tell her. 'A further reality takes over, comprised of violence, malevolence and destruction, the whole of it suffused by a feeling that life is comprised of nothing else – love, friendship, goodwill – not to mention hope – species of appearance, until appearance becomes our springboard for living and, the ultimate deception – the final irony, Etty – the core of life itself.'

She isn't listening (sipping her coffee) crossing her legs within the confines of the chair and glancing up at the illuminated sign above the dispensary porthole. We have, evidently (glancing at the ticket in her hand) several numbers to go.

'All this,' I tell her, 'is a waste of time. When you were young and happy, and we were living in Belsize Park, one big, happy family, or, if not happy, boisterous, things like this would have seemed unreal. Untenable. Inconceivable. Out of this world. As if I have been cast into inner darkness. Where,' I enquire again, 'did it go wrong?'

'I shall arrange for Charlie to come with you when you next see Robeson,' she says. 'He may be more constructive than I appear to have been.'

'You've been,' I tell her, 'constructive enough. What more could anyone want? My principal impulse,' I go on, 'is to protect you. You have done more than enough,' I add, 'already. No man, considering his history, could have been more sympathetically looked after than I have been. Manipulative, self-centred, cantankerous, uncaring – cowardly, to boot – what more could I have asked for?'

We are being observed by several attentive faces. ('Take no notice of these,' I tell her. 'Most of them are mad.')

'This is a general dispensary. Eastley Hall is part of a general complex,' she says.

'As for being sectioned, I don't believe my behaviour warrants it,' I tell her. 'As for these pills. I wondered if Bea and Albert wouldn't have me. Being a junior minister in the Ministry of Health, having a madman in his home might do him, professionally, a great deal of good. While life might seem to be vicious and bad he would have the invaluable satisfaction of proving it is not so.'

'I don't think, Father,' she says, formally and calmly, 'you have anywhere left to run.'

This phrase I not infrequently used with Bea: having written myself, as it were, to notoriety, and complemented this achievement by painting pictures – several of which, though rarely hung, were purchased by the Tate – and discovering that my propensity to subside at intervals into the profoundest gloom was, despite all my efforts to resist it, unassuaged, I frequently remarked, 'I have nowhere left to run,' to which Bea would respond, with her unfathomable stare, 'Except here.'

'The other thing I wanted to tell him,' I tell her, 'was that long into my adult life I was firmly convinced that everyone endured the things that I did. Everyone, I foolishly assumed, woke each morning to a feeling of terror and, throughout the day, their principal energies were engaged in attempting to overcome not only that but its indefatigable ally, dispiritation. Fear, combined with despair, produced an awesome dread, the most fearful of all the human emotions. Everyone, I was convinced, experienced the same. I took it for granted – in the same way I could assume that, despite wearing shoes, everyone had five toes on each foot. I even assumed Bea, even you, suffered in a not dissimilar way, that all the principal questions of human existence came terrifyingly to the surface at the moment of waking, but that she, and you, and everyone else, had not only a greater degree of resourcefulness in combating the condition but, the most debilitating emotion of all, infinitely more courage in covering it up. Only in the last few years have I come to recognise that the degree of fear and dispiritation that has greeted me each morning on waking, and which, in struggling not to show, I merely showed to everyone, is the prerogative, if not of me alone, of a small percentage of the human race who suffer in a not dissimilar fashion. Imagine my surprise when I discovered that what came to my mind as effortlessly as the joy of living was confined, in my personal experience, to me alone. Surprise, that is, and dispiritation, a fear and a despair at my isolation greater, terrifyingly, than the original symptoms. I was, as the saying goes, engulfed.'

'That's our number.'

My daughter stands: I repair to the porthole and, through the sliding panel, take the pills myself. When the pharmacist –

a girl, in appearance at least, of seven – enquires, 'Mr Fen-church?' I am more than convinced that in her unseemly made-up face there is a flicker of recognition.

'It was merely,' Etty says, when I point this out, 'the loudness of your voice. In respect of remaining anonymous, you having only yourself to blame.'

'As always,' I rejoin as we descend the steps to the car. 'Guilt at feeling guilt,' I add, 'and so on.'

Peas, broccoli, baked potato and ham are, peculiarly, all we have that day for lunch.

We eat in silence (a brief call from Etty to Charlie to tell him the outcome).

'I don't think,' I tell her when she returns from the phone, 'I'm ill. Some experts call it "a problem with living", varying degrees of experience of which are common to most if not all people's lives.'

To which, with typical Kellsian asperity, she replies, 'If you're not ill then I am.'

'Perhaps you are,' I tell her, to which, with not unKellsian vigour, she responds, 'That's how you used to undermine Mother. You won't do the same with me.'

'I was most gentle with your mother,' I tell her. ('There was no one I loved more,' etc. 'She couldn't have had a finer husband.') 'She was much envied by the women in the street (whichever street that was). There was no woman in the neigh-bourhood more idolised by her husband.'

'Why not make it London?' she says.

'Why aren't the children home to lunch?' I ask.

'I made arrangements,' she says, 'for them to have their lunch elsewhere. I didn't know,' she adds, 'how long we'd be.'

'Good job you did,' I tell her, yet wonder at the emptiness of the house. It was never, I reflect, as empty as this: there was always someone or something in it.

'We'll be leaving, in any case,' she says. 'There's a partner of Charlie's who's willing to buy it.'

'I never knew that,' I tell her, looking out, for the first time,

331

at the garden and trying to imagine, after all these years, those flowerbeds – and those trees, the beech hedge – in the hands of someone else. The last vestige of Isabella, with that garden, I reflect, will be gone, but say aloud, 'It sounds to me a good idea.'

'We've found a pleasanter house,' she says, 'closer to Linfield.'

'Not London?' I enquire.

'I've had enough of London,' she says. 'It's paradise on earth up here,' (a recent, and derisory conclusion, I reflect).

'You're beginning to talk like me,' I tell her, to which, without interest, she replies, 'I am.'

Nevertheless, consulting Robeson (not least, a figure of authority) has given her some relief: I hear her singing in the kitchen, later in the day, and moments later, humming on the stairs: shortly after that comes the sound of recorded music from her room (as she works, no doubt, on 'Greta Bridge' – all those tones and planes and textures, the miraculous abstraction and miracle invention). Mrs Otterman, who normally leaves each day after preparing lunch, returning later, if requested, to prepare dinner or supervise the children, comes in, around tea-time, and calls – from the back door of the house, 'I've brought you up some flowers, Mrs Stott,' naming the gardener as her source and, in response to a call from Etty, adding, 'I thought the house needed cheering up.'

'Oh, we're cheerful enough already,' Etty calls – on with 'Ships off Gravesend' now, no doubt. 'Which isn't to say they won't be welcome.'

I have, at her suggestion, remained throughout the afternoon in bed and when I go down to the kitchen, Mrs Otterman, who has evidently come in to prepare the dinner (several guests are due at seven), the miner's wife, daughter, grand-daughter and great-grandchild remarks, 'You're looking well. How did the hospital go this morning?'

'You'd better ask Mrs Stott,' I tell her. 'She did all the talking.'

'That's unlike Mrs Stott,' she says, and adds, 'Nevertheless, I

332

can see it's done some good. You're far less dark beneath the eyes.'

'That,' I say, 'is because I've washed. You should know, being the daughter of a miner.'

Her sharp-featured, dark-eyed face lightens with a smile.

'You're pulling my leg, Mr Fenchurch!' turning to the sink.

'I'm too old to pull anybody's leg,' I tell her, at which, turning once more, she cries, 'I'm sure you're much younger than I am!'

'I'm sixty-five,' I tell her, 'or nearly, and look half as much again.'

'I'm not quite as o'd as that,' she says. 'But feel it, at times, I can tell you.'

'I hope this house,' I tell her, 'will never change. That you, or I, or someone known to me, will forever be at work in the kitchen, in one or other of the rooms upstairs, in the garden or the yard outside. That the trees will bud, the flowers bloom, the fruit ripen, with a Kells or a Corcoran or a Fenchurch somewhere about, painting or writing or hammering or drawing, the window open, on a sunny day, to the sound of Celtic or Saxon voices. Too much has happened here, too much has been felt, endured, survived. Our blood is in these stones.'

'I thought you were from Onasett,' she says.

'What have you been saying to Mrs Otterman?' Etty says when, later, she comes up to my room. 'She was ever so bright when she first came in.'

'I won't, if you don't mind, come down to dinner,' I tell her, for the children, already, are playing in their room (the sound of Mrs Otterman's voice as, earlier, she bathed them) and Charlie has returned and is already dressed, his voice coming from the hall and then the sitting-room as he first greets then solicits with drink the first of his evening's guests.

'Everyone will expect you,' she says, (the occasion, she is about to tell me, will do me good).

'Tell them,' I tell her, 'I'm unwell. It's happened often

333

before,' and when she says, 'They won't believe it. You're supposed to be up here and getting better,' I respond, 'I am much better,' (in my shirt-sleeves, she in a gown that scarcely covers her shoulders). 'I intend in the morning,' I continue, 'to go back to London. There's nothing left for me up here.'

A look of extraordinary gravity lightens the skin around her eyes.

'When did you decide that?' coming one step further into the room.

I am sitting at the table, beside the window, where, from my youth onwards, I have sat many times before.

'I am writing up,' I tell her, 'my memoirs. The embryo, as it were, of *The Private Papers of Richard Fenchurch*, revealed to the world by his second eldest daughter or, failing that, the author himself, the ultimate, if unreliable, authority on the subject. Previous studies have merely moved my work on the one step from penultimate neglect to conclusive obscurity.'

'It's not a good time to discuss it,' she says, a flush rising from her throat, more nakedly exposed than ever. 'Which,' she adds, 'is probably why you chose it.'

'It's too late to ring up Robeson. He'll be out at dinner, or, if I'm any judge of character, in front of the television,' and when she turns to the door, I add, 'I welcomed seeing him this morning. I welcomed you taking me as well. Don't you see I've come full circle? Robeson and Linfield is where it began: the old school tie, the élitist education, that ardour that goes with the provincial grammar-school boy: that plum-cheeked look, like the crest of the school, which accompanies him throughout the rest of his life. There's one such youth, with that same parochial, charming, bright-eyed look, who presents a television programme on the arts in an identical manner, adenoidal, sincere, that earnest, community-serving expression (the persona of the actor not far behind). It's a world I eschew. I loathed it then. I loathe it now, buried, as it was, in the London mists, the London fog, the effete artistic drizzle that, throughout these years, has numbed me to the bone. I've buried my pills, by the way, in the garden, a foot apart. The worms, I can assure you, over the next few years, will turn into happy toads.'

And when, moments later, Charlie comes up, dressed for the evening, after Etty's gone down, I say something of the same again: 'Robeson has done me the world of good!'

'I hear,' he says, 'you're leaving, Father.'

'I feel much better,' I tell him, 'for seeing Robeson. It's brought my old motivation back, contempt for parochialism and an avid desire – which has nothing to do with you – to escape.'

'Where would you escape to, supposing we were inclined to let you?' Charlie says, sitting on the bed (very much, I reflect, in a pre-match fashion: elbows on thighs, a thick-necked stoop, leaning forward as he gathers his strength: an Old Edwardian, of course, himself, as was his distinguished father).

'Taravara Road,' I tell him. 'Apart from one or two tourists, curious to see where Vivienne swallowed her bleach, I should settle in quite quickly. I even thought,' I go on, 'I could rent or buy a miner's cottage – there are a lot standing empty in the back-way villages where the pits have gone – and paint and write to my heart's content. I've been admiring the sunsets since I came up here, specifically the one,' I continue, 'we had last night, with a lurid band of green above a screen of red, a crimson orifice darkening to blue, an orange sheen around the sun, a turquoise and magenta cloud one side, and fangs of vapour, like wings, gold and silver along each edge.'

He fists one hand in the palm of the other.

'The fields and hedgerows,' I conclude, 'where my youth and dreams began.'

He fists his hand once more (before he runs out with the First XV: 'Play up, KEGS! Play up, play up, for fuck's sake, play the game!').

'And you've buried all your pills.'

'I'm grateful to Raynor,' I tell him. 'And more grateful still to Robeson. And most grateful of all to you and Etty. Without the former, of course, and the latter, the second wouldn't be there. I've come full circle. I feel a new man. I can't tell you,

Charlie, how glad I am that you and Etty had the idea of bringing me here. It's done me, I assure you, the world of good. On top of which, the news of you selling up the house – too big, too impractical, too vulnerable – it scarcely needs explaining – has clearly done the trick. I gave away, over the past fifteen years, something in excess of half a million pounds, none of it recoverable. I have a house, of modest proportions, and a residual income which will enable me not to have to scour the gutters after the local street market has been cleared up. As I say, when I've settled in, with a little subsidy, perhaps, from you, or Bea, or both – or, even, the sale of a picture, an unexpected run on a book, a revival of a play – I can come up here, rent or purchase a cottage – one up, one down – and paint and write, and think. Respice finem, Charlie.'

'Are you coming down?' he says.

'I'm staying up here,' I tell him, 'to write.'

'We'll discuss it in the morning,' he says. 'I'll delay going in to Linfield. These phases,' he goes on, 'require that someone should be with you all the time.'

All is not well in the Land of Uz, said Hiro of the Chaldeans.

Cannibalism in Ardsley as the miners eat their wives.

'You can't be left alone,' says Charlie.

(I've been there all my life).

I remember very well how, in her last days, Vivienne was convinced she was being followed in the street – 'by an actress' who, 'portraying' Vi, was being filmed in a film commissioned by her former husband, 'in order,' she complained, 'to justify his life.' On occasion, out together, we would come across this woman disguised, variously, as a bus conductress, a police officer, and an usherette in a cinema – and once as a stranger who approached us in the foyer of a theatre and asked Vivienne the way to the ladies' toilet. 'That's *her*!' she said as the woman walked away. Much subsequent fleeing from scenes (she said were) being filmed while all I saw was a passing car, a woman glancing in her handbag, a tourist with a camera. 'They're everywhere,' she said, running videos of her films twice hourly

336

through the night, 'looking,' as she said, 'for clues. I'm convinced they hired her to watch me as I failed.'

Poor Vi.

Poor Hiro.

Poor wives.

Our telephone was tapped: a 'detective' followed her from bar to bar (from car to car, shop to shop): everywhere was somewhere.

'Why should they make a film?' I asked. 'They haven't got the rights.'

'Rights?'

'The rights,' I tell her, 'to your life.' (The rights to the story which, she says, time alone can tell.)

Her midnight calls to Hollywood: to a director she had worked with, to a dietician, to a Scotsman she had met on a studio lot who professed to have known her father: 'A saint! A saint!' The writing on large (discarded) sheets of paper, in coloured crayon, 'the story of how,' she'd cry, 'I was crucified by men!' ('That's why,' she'd say, 'I live with you: look at the way you treated your wife.').

'Look at the way,' I'd tell her, 'she's treated me.'

'With contempt! (Don't you think you didn't deserve it!),' lying on the couch in the tiny Taravara Road back kitchen. 'My admiration for your wife goes up in leaps and bounds. It wasn't large-heartedness that prompted you to give away your money.'

'I haven't gone back on anything,' I tell Etty when, her guests departed, she knocks on the door, seeing the light beneath. 'I promised nothing at Eastley Hall, nothing to Raynor, nothing to Robeson, nothing to you and Charlie, nothing even to Maidstone, who was far more pressing than all of you. I intend,' I go on, 'to make a new start.'

'I'm not sure Robeson, or Raynor, would agree to your going, nor your doctor in London,' she says, implying it only takes two of them to put me away for good.

'I'm so much better,' I tell her. 'I was telling Charlie, that meeting with Robeson has done the trick. I can't tell you how

337

grateful I am to you and Raynor. Without you bringing me up here nothing like this would ever have worked out.'

'It's too late to discuss it,' she says, and when I enquire, 'Too late in the day, or too late in the cycle of events?' she merely shakes her head. 'We'll discuss it in the morning.'

'In the morning,' I tell her, 'I'll be gone. My whole life has been based on spontaneous reaction. In such a way I got all my jobs, got to the Drayburgh, wrote my books, painted my pictures, became, in short, what I am today,' and when she replies, 'A fool,' I laugh. 'To be insane, with me, is to be dead with any other person.'

'That's not much of an endorsement of Charlie,' she says. 'And even less of me,' to which I respond, 'Charlie is as mad as I am. At least I represent a range of disaffection which would put me on a level with those iconoclastic heroes he and his chums affect to admire. How, for instance, would you have spoken to Van Gogh? Aren't I a Gogh of the northern counties, a parochial buccaneer?' she waiting in the door, arm raised towards the lintel (a childhood gesture) as if searching for support. 'I'll pack my bags,' I add, 'tonight. Without your help, as I told Charlie, I couldn't have achieved this peace of mind.'

'Is it peace of mind?' she says.

'I feel a new man,' I tell her, 'already.'

'This morning,' she says, 'you didn't feel well.' ('Creased over in that chair when I came in,' she adds, indicating the one in which I'm sitting – terrified (let's face it) of what might happen at Eastley Hall.)

'I shall miss this place,' I tell her, 'and yet it's necessary,' I add, 'to let it go,' while, from behind her back, across the landing, Charlie enquires, 'Why don't you leave it, Etty, tonight? There'll be plenty of time in the morning,' his voice no different from when, earlier, I had heard him calling, in the yard behind the house, 'Goodnight! Goodnight!' to his cheerily departing guests. ('He'll not do a midnight scarper.')

20

IN THE MORNING I am ill: 'A rheumatoid condition,' Raynor says when, alarmed, Etty calls him in. 'His blood-pressure,' he tells her, 'is far too high and there's congestion in his lungs. His glands, too,' he adds, 'are up. In other circumstances,' he addresses me directly, 'I'd have you taken in.'

I dream: there is an argument (in an ancient building, not unlike a temple, across a landing) about the medication I might be given. 'He planted the pills,' I hear, 'in the garden, and all sorts of peculiar things came up,' (flowers bloomed, plants burgeoned, the house, after a while, began to fall down).

'It's been coming on,' she says, 'for days. (Ever since I brought him up.) His feet were steaming in the car.'

'It's a wonder,' I tell her, 'I didn't die (He takes no regard of other people.) In sleep, the mind is disassembled, like petals close at sun-set, opening (I go on) at sun-rise. Figments,' I add, 'are the fruit of the tree that you have at the back of the house, adjacent to the Dell, into whose pool it drops its leaves (in autumn when they die).'

When she says, 'You needn't act, you *are* delirious,' I reply, 'Put me on the train to Taravara Road (or the bus to Camden Town),' the place, had I known it, I set out for sixty-five years ago (pushed beneath the bridge of Linfield Station while over-head a single drop of water falls, darkening the fabric of my mother's coat).

'I dreamt last night,' I tell Etty when she next comes in, 'that I fell ill,' and when she says, 'Like the time I called on you in London and found Vivienne, drunk, beneath the sink,' I

339

respond, 'She was. She was mending the plumbing,' recalling the incident far too well. 'She hit her head on a pipe.'

'What was all the vomit?' she says.

'Vomit?'

'She was,' she tells me, 'very sick.'

'Dizziness from the blow,' I tell her, perceiving the room through a veil of tears.

I make my way up the slope then across the fields and down the, at one time, winding lane (that led, by a circuitous route, to Ardsley Wood) – now a broadened, straightened highway – to the station.

'Where's the station?' I enquire of a man in a passing car and when the car has stopped and the man got out, enquiring, 'Are you all right?' I remark, 'It used to be here, by this bridge,' lines running off in both directions.

'The station hasn't been here for years,' he says – a youngish fellow, a woman still in the car, its engine running.

'I spent hours,' I tell him, 'by the siding. It was my principal occupation when I'd nothing to do. I drew the buildings, and an ancient metalwork bridge that crossed the lines and through the planks of which you could see directly down the engines' funnels (the demise of the steam engine the end of the world of course, for me).'

'The nearest station,' he says, 'is Linfield.'

'Isn't there one,' I enquire, 'much further away?'

'Further?' He glances towards the car. 'There's Darton,' he says, mentioning a village in the opposite direction.

'I might try that,' I tell him, looking along the road (any moment Etty and Charlie setting out to search).

'I can drop you there, if you like,' he says.

A sporty model, the car, like the man himself. 'I'd be much obliged,' I tell him.

The boot is opened, my suitcase placed in.

'We're giving this gentleman a lift,' the man remarks to the figure inside and, with signs of displeasure, the woman gets out: sliding the front seat forward, she indicates I get in behind.

340

'You get in, Shirl,' the man suggests, but churlish Shirl remains by the door and, hearing a car engine approaching from the village, I swiftly squeeze in.

A car – neither Etty's nor Charlie's – passes, throwing up a cloud of spray.

'We're going to Darton,' the man informs the woman and she – no comment – gets in in front. 'We almost knocked you down,' he adds to me, over his shoulder, as he closes his door.

The car moves off: the road, unfamiliar in its straightness, is neatly attenuated between their heads. They are young: a disembodied gesture of goodwill. 'It must be some time,' he goes on, 'since you came down here,' the last houses of the village, set amongst fields and against the profile – still there, thank God – of Ardsley Wood, passing by on either side.

'I was only,' I tell him, 'passing through,' noticing, for instance, the neatness of his hair (how ill-judged, I reflect, of Etty to suggest my interest in people has been impaired), the neatness, too, of hers, and the fragrance that comes through to the back of the car. 'Though I knew it well when I was younger. So much of my life,' I go on, 'was spent amongst these fields and woods, by Ardsley Dam, in Ardsley Wood,' gesturing as the trees of that – I now observe denuded – plantation disappear: a large, prefabricated structure – not unlike an aircraft hangar, and presumably a warehouse – has been set incongruously in the long-loved fields the other side.

Beginning his last adventure at the age of sixty-five.

'I'll be forty-six next birthday.' An incongruous message which has little effect on the heads in front.

I resist observing the landscape on either side or directly ahead and merely concentrate on the surface of the road itself: the alternate flicking of a broken line and the variegated texture of the tarmac.

'Nothing is what it seems,' I am about to add, but say instead, 'I hope it doesn't take you out of your way.'

'Hardly,' the youthful, clean-shaven, fair-hair-styled man declares. 'A couple of miles at most.'

341

He has, possibly speeding, almost knocked me down and is anxious, I reflect, to make amends.

'I thought I might make for Glasgow,' I tell him, reflecting ('Lunatic Picked Up by Disingenuous Couple'), should he be questioned, this should be enough to put pursuers off. Such a primitive device, however, depresses my spirits and, recalling there is no chemical agent in my digestive system that can arrest or subdue my current excesses, I add, 'Or Sheffield. Being,' I go on, 'of independent means, the world, as, indeed, it always was, is still my oyster,' on the absurdity of this confession wondering if I haven't gone too far. 'Or Blackpool,' I suggest.

All is not well in the Land of Ur.

'The advantages of the independent life – the independent mind apart – is that freedom and liberty are often confused, the one not being a concomitant of the other, defined, as they are, by separate rules which, on the surface, appear to confound the element they're defining. The man, for instance, in the middle of the desert might assume he is free, but, on further reflection, conclude he is not. At liberty would be a better description, for he is not free from hunger or thirst, or, let's face it, the longing for someone to love. Freedom, in short, has to be defined, and mine is defined by its limitations. I am free, for instance, from the burden of earning a living, for it's difficult to starve in a country with such a profusion of goods and so richly endowed with charities. Is one's freedom defined solely by the limitations one places on oneself, inculcated, the majority at least, in childhood, which in turn is the period when the adult mind brings to bear upon it the discipline required of the adult mind in order to function in an environment governed exclusively by technological prescription which is itself the product of an adult mind? Indeed,' I add as a car sweeps past to the young man's consternation, 'a vicious circle.'

Two vehicles are overtaken by the young man in turn: the car ahead – unfamiliar, not one I recognise – disappears over the brow of a wooded hill: we are moving through a landscape I recognise with a pang of pain: here I walked with Isabella, here I strolled, on summer afternoons, with Bea: here, on one occasion, I wheeled Etty in her pram, sitting down on a fallen tree and, admiring her sleeping head against the pillow, reflected, 'What on earth will become of her?'

'It's odd, Ardsley station being removed. It had such character,' I tell them. 'On the one hand, the expresses thundering through, approaching ninety miles an hour, on the other, the stopping trains, together with the long coal trains from Ardsley pit, and the long, returning trains of empty wagons,' while, further afield, at Onasett, as a child, I and my companions would follow a path across the fields, beside the golf-course, to the parapet of a bridge which allowed us access to a similar, cross-Pennine line where we laid coins on the rail to be flattened by engines.

'So you come from here?' the man enquires.

'A child of Ardsley, an old son of the village,' I tell him, 'who has seen,' I continue, 'better days. I came in by bus and couldn't believe my eyes, my favourite station, the one from which I left on many adventures, to school, to college, on holidays, on travel to foreign lands, had disappeared.'

'We haven't lived long in the village ourselves,' he says. 'Since the pit went we thought it looked quite pretty. We're in one of those new estates at the top of Ardsley hill, next to the old house and Rectory, close to the church.'

'A sort of mews,' the woman declares.

'The Hall,' I tell her.

'That's the one. Lived in by a solicitor,' she adds.

'A barrister,' the young man says.

'A lively place in the old days,' I tell her.

'You knew it, then?' She turns her head.

'I knew the family living there,' I suddenly explain.

'The ones there at present are relatives,' she says. 'A grandchild, or, at least, that's what they say.'

'You go to work in Darton?' I enquire.

'Near there,' the young man says, naming a town some miles away. 'We have a shop. We set up in business this time last year and so far,' he glances at the woman, 'so good.'

'Fashion and sportswear,' the woman says.

'It'll be quite late before you get back home,' I tell them. 'And hear the news in the village.'

'We don't hear much,' the woman says. 'Unlike the old days, I imagine.'

'The only village activity nowadays,' the young man says, 'is to do with the consumption and sale of drugs.'

'By which time I'll be in Glasgow,' I tell him.

'Or Blackpool,' the woman says.

'I think I'll press north,' I tell her. 'I've a particular reason for doing so,' I add.

'Relatives?' comes the man's enquiry.

'Someone, at one time,' I tell him, 'I thought I might marry.'

'Where do you live yourself?' the woman enquires.

'I'm on the move, at present,' I tell her and, the conversation having achieved a degree of tedium I can, in the comfort of the car, no longer sustain, the old rail junction of Dalton (lines from the east and west meeting those from the north and the south) comes into sight, its colliery, I notice, too, having disappeared.

Rows of terraced houses enclose the road: shops (the majority of them, eerily, boarded up) and, some distance through the village, beyond where the colliery at one time stood, the station is visible above an embankment of slag.

'It was very kind of you,' I tell the couple as I disembark and my suitcase is set down in the station yard.

'Any time,' the man says as he gets back in, waving, moments later, as the car drives off.

'They nearly knocked me down,' I inform the man I assume to be the station official but he merely remarks, 'Cold day for sandals. Off on your holidays?' indicating the overcast sky – resonant, still, of course, with winter, even though the flowers of spring, in one or two places (plastic tubs, for instance, on either side of the tarmacked entrance) are pushing through.

I plan a route that will take me not to King's Cross but Euston and, using the money I have taken from Etty's purse, a little more from a drawer in her desk, the children's piggy-bank

344

and the pockets of Charlie's overcoat (and Mrs Otterman's in the kitchen), I purchase the relevant ticket.

Trains of a local nature pass in and out, none, however, on the route I want: a phalanx of passengers finally alights. The name of my first destination is called.

My suitcase, I observe as the train pulls out, I leave behind, glimpsing it as I might a child deserted on a railway platform. It is midday by the time I arrive at Euston.

I catch a bus in Drummond Street: familiar shops and offices pass: the dull façades of Victorian houses, the Georgian lineaments of Mornington Crescent obscured beyond adjoining roofs, the detritus of Camden High Street and, after a change of bus, the oppressive, winding route, along a narrowing road, between decaying offices, shops, yards and blocks of flats: the darkening, suddenly, beneath a bridge, the emergence into the fracas of traffic and people the other side: within minutes of getting off the bus I am in Taravara Road, an interstice between the diminutive, butterfly-roofed houses with their ochre brick façades and white and cream-painted fascias.

I unlock the front door: an aroma of cold air, a hint of gas, perhaps of vegetation (the drains nothing to write home about), stale food: the welcoming hall (illuminated from the fanlight above the door): the room, to the left, knocked through from back to front and cluttered with canvases and sheets of paper – hardboard, easel, paints – the light suffused through dusty glass. Immediately ahead, beside the stairs, the passage leading, down two steps, to the room at the back: I open a door and reveal an interior divided between a sitting-room and kitchen: a gas-mantled fire (the cooking range the opposite end), a door and two windows looking out to the yard (a vista of encroaching houses).

I sit in a chair and allow the house to re-absorb me.

The telephone rings. Not many hours after that there's a knock at the door. 'What is madness?' Maidstone enquired. 'I'm not even here,' he went on, 'to discuss it.'

Food. Am I capable of living on my own? The cuckolded

husband, the writer and artist (incompetent father, improvident son). Where do I go, I reflected, from here?

I went out shopping; returning, I sat for hours: noises from the house next door: the clatter of pots in the adjoining kitchen. Voices.

All is not well in the Land of Ur.

From a curtained window I glimpse my eldest daughter Matt first getting out of then into her car parked down the street: the intervening ringing of the bell, the rush of blood to the heart: paroxysmal tachycardia (that rushes round the head): a tall, lean girl with her mother's freckled skin: long-skirted, booted, with a tight-waisted, round-cut jacket (secured by a single button): visible, behind the windscreen, Dan, her Scandinavian husband, taller, slimmer: blond: they gaze up at the house for several seconds: they must be discussing the possibility of summoning the police.

Christ crucified ('I know what I am doing'): he had it all worked out.

Looking for a cottage – vandalised, of course, while he was out: out-of-work miners trample on his goods, write 'Here we go' across his pictures: "the miracles of art outweigh," he wrote to Bea, "the miracles of science". "How are you?" she enquires in a letter I pick up, amongst circulars and bills behind the front door (recognise the writing). "I've suggested to Etty she takes you north," ("home" crossed out: 'at least,' he thought, 'we have that in common, our children and our past'), "there's plenty of room at Ardsley," enough, I reflect, to do her research, me in one wing, she in another, divorced from Albert, staining cells: all my pictures, from now on, will be in yellow.

The bell rings at the door: it's followed by a knock ('I know you're in there, Father!').

'Perhaps the door is jammed,' (Dan's voice the other side: the Scandinavian reporter).

'It's bolted,' (as the door is tried again).

Rain fell, the day we married, but the sun came out in the afternoon: Isabella's friend (from the WI) had a cinematic camera and took pictures of us walking, through the grounds and past the Rectory, to Church and – a single cut (no cameras allowed in the church itself) – walking back again.

Bea's daughter beats on the door the other side and, after a pause, calls, 'Dad?' and then, more formally, 'Father!'

Etty must have called her.

And pictures, too, of the reception on the lawn, the looming presence of the Hall, Fenchurch in his morning-suit (despite it being the afternoon), with his grey top hat, Bea in her tight-waisted, flare-skirted wedding dress (which lay like a lost cause for years in a cupboard above the sweet-shop in Camden Town), the relatives and friends – and Isabella, radiant, incandescent, like a bride herself – all fifty-seven years of her, Fenchurch subdued (fired from the Drayburgh the previous summer, his art in tatters, Bea still one year to do at college) the final shot on the station platform, the train to London drawing in: Bea, Isabella, Corcoran . . .

'Dad?'

Tenacity a Kellsian trait.

'I've gone to Scotland,' I tell her through the door.

'Open up,' she says. 'We want to come in.'

'Don't ring me,' I tell her, 'I'll call you:' cheeks suffused by the exertion of pushing, knocking, stooping, pressing – calling out to a recalcitrant father as I open up the door.

Who breathes, perspires, creates, aspires: 'You've got here, then,' she says.

'I'm just about to leave,' I tell her while Dan, smiling, brushes back his fringe of hair. 'Where are you going, Richard?' he says, as if other plans in mind.

'I thought I'd try the north,' I tell him. 'Or, then again, the south.'

'You're in the south,' he says, 'already.'

'Further south,' I tell him. 'Where the bluebird flies and the sea is green and people can lie all day in the sun,' only Mathilda says, 'You've done enough lying already. How much money did you pinch?' as if this invoking of the preceptorial self will bring the composite back in line.

'The awful irrelevance,' I tell her, 'of all we do – in art, that

347

is, as well as silence,' and when she says, 'Do you mean "science"?' her pale green eyes – almost grey in colour – looking into my darker ones, I add, 'Names of painters, poets and whores – dramatists, Mattie, and musicians – people whose work is of no consequence at all, while mine goes unattended. There was not one letter here when I arrived that has anything to do with me, Bea writing to a man at this address whom she assumes to be her former husband,' turning down the passage while the tall, slim figure of Bea's child casts a tall, slim shadow before me.

'My mind is in pieces,' I remind her. 'I have no intention it should be other than it is,' drugs which I took under Bea's influence, 'which wasn't true,' I add, 'at all,' uncertain which words of these I've spoken. 'Only the other day, for instance, I stood on the hill at Onasett golf-course and did a drawing of Onasett against its headland, Harlstone pit no longer there. It has a pre-industrial freshness, like an athlete in peak condition arriving at a race already run.'

Leather boots, creased horizontally around her instep: a full-length, full-skirted dress, the upper half of which, with its high-necked collar (secured by a glittering brooch), is concealed beneath her round-cut jacket (no corner on it anywhere): 'the turbulence of genius,' I might have said (the buzzing of a fly in a long-still room where, once, Vivienne, with the incongruity of the Hollywood whore she was, stretched out on a couch – where Danny sits, his wife still standing by the door).

Contemplates her father: all my previous triumphs – posters, of his plays – stored with the miscellaneous bric-à-brac of Vivienne's upstairs.

'I had her for weeks,' I tell her, 'on the mantelpiece in a plastic jar provided by the Golders Green crematorium, several of her drinking pals imbibing from the bottle while the priest intoned the non-sectarian rites and we chanted, absurdly, in the local church (no organist provided) the fifteenth psalm which identifies those who, in the last analysis, will not be allowed into the kingdom of heaven – excluding not only Vivienne herself, and all her pals, but yours truly, Richard

348

'Fenchurch,' my long-loved daughter at the peak of her career, her bronze hair, plaited, coiled in a crown at the top of her head, her pale, hollow-cheeked face turned not in my but her husband's direction ('Say something, Dan,' her look suggests).

'We've come,' Dan says, 'to take you back.'

'How can you spare,' I enquire, 'the time from work?'

'This doctor, Robeson, Etty has found, is prepared,' Matt says, 'to sign you into Eastley Hall.'

'It's all a question of rhythm,' I tell her, 'how and where you put the words, less the ones you've chosen,' and add, 'I shall be happy living here, much as I was before Etty fetched me.'

The telephone rings: Matt, half-startled, glances round.

'You're looking very well,' I tell her.

'That'll be Etty,' she says and when Danny picks it up, his tall figure uncoiling from the couch, stooping, dark-suited, to where the instrument lies by his feet, he listens for a while then says, 'Matt is here, if you'd like to speak to her,' and adds to her, 'It's your mother.'

'Immensely well. I've never seen you looking better. Your work, I conclude, is going well.'

She takes the phone and bows her head, raising a strand of hair from her brow and securing it behind her ear.

'No,' she says, and after a murmured enquiry from the other end glances up and answers, 'Do you want to talk to him?'

When I take the phone the receiver has been replaced the other end.

'I am,' I tell her, 'interned by love. I don't wish to go,' I add, 'to Eastley Hall, nor to the North London Royal. I am quite prepared,' I go on, 'to live on my own. A visit each day, or alternate days, or even alternate weekends, should be enough to reassure you. I intend, for instance, to go out shopping,' and when she says, 'It appears you've been already,' I conclude, 'That's what I mean: I'm perfectly capable of looking after myself.'

She sits, bemused, across the tiny room: a couch and two chairs confronting each other, the latter at right angles to the gas-mantled fire. Bea at one time accused me of loving Matt and Etty and Beckie too much: 'You are too fond of your daughters: your sons could do with care as well,' but when I pointed out I spent more time with Kenneth and Benjie, she blithely announced, 'Time alone will tell.'

'Aren't they daughters a father could be proud of?' I'd tell her. 'Aren't they daughters who, despite an inner-city education, have done immensely well, one a financial adviser and management consultant, another a scholar – and who knows what Beckie will become?' (she about to start at college). All, in any case, I concluded, gifts inherited from her.

Now when I declare, 'Your mother accused me of caring about our children far too much, supervising your education in those crummy schools without, so she said, a care in the world. Private education – which, she said, would have suited you better – was, I told her, an abuse, not least of a democracy's primary tenet that education was a right, not a privilege to be purchased by the few.'

'Isn't guilt part of your illness?' Matt enquires – or is it merely, I conjecture, her observation?

'I've forgotten all the parts,' I tell her. 'And all the questions and answers, too. Why don't you pop in in two or three days' time? Apart from the odd people who want to see where Vivienne died, and come, invariably at weekends, to take pictures, no one calls. I'll have no one to relate to and if you wish, on the front door, I can hang a notice which says, "Before you go out adjust your dress," and look in one of the drawings to see if I'm properly attired. No one, otherwise,' I conclude, 'would know I was here.'

When she continues sitting there, one booted foot swaying above the other, and Danny, close-cropped, continues sitting on the couch, I reclining in the other chair, I announce, 'To behave, in the past, in the way I've done, isn't a critique of anyone. Material possessions, to me, have always obscured what it was I wished to do. I've never felt so well, for instance, since the day I gave to Bea, and you, everything I had. My only qualm was the damage it might do. But Bea is used to wealth, or was, until her father died.'

I gave away everything I had in the hope that by getting rid of it I would re-vivify my talent: such a simple precept. Initially, of course, I was thought quite mad: I didn't realise what I was up to: the absurdity of giving up a house worth half a million pounds. 'You don't seem happy,' someone said. 'The world is bedevilled by material things,' I told them. 'I am better off without,' scrawled, or so she said, in a casual letter to Bea.

"Dear Bella, if only you could see me now."

How might the fallen rise, etc.

The airship drifted overhead while to the south (seventy-two miles, to be precise) her mother lay in the arm of her lover.

'Bea and I are now divorced. She has no rights of any sort. My sectioning,' I add, 'has been rescinded. I don't wish Etty to apply for it again, even though she has this psychiatrist and her own G.P., a man called Raynor, at her beck and call. Both are bedazzled by her books, though she only has one to her credit.'

I met a woman novelist once.

'Each day,' she said, 'I write a little.' 'Why, in that case,' I asked, 'don't you write a lot?' 'A lot would be a little too much,' she said. I asked her for a date. 'The plums,' she said, 'are not in season,' (the sea at the seaside, the cork in the bottle).

Jocular: the hieroglyphics.

'You want to be left alone?' Matt says.

'I do.'

'I'm not qualified to decide,' she says.

'Ring up Maidstone.'

'I already have.'

'Don't try Mackendrick,' I go on. 'He'd put me inside to prevent me writing the sequel to *A New Theory of the Mind*, the epilogue of which he wishes to write himself, having pinched, on his own admission, most of it already. "I am an anthologist," he said when, putting my mental life in his hands, I went to the trouble of pointing it out. What did Maidstone say?' I ask.

351

'He said he was retired and we should consult with his successor, which, as yet,' she says, 'we haven't done.'

'What have you decided?' I hastily enquire (like asking Joan of Arc to set herself on fire). 'Etty,' I tell her, 'even as a child, was always an alarmist.'

'You'll be all right on your own?' she asks.

'My sentiments exactly,' as I slowly rise. 'We had an argument before I left. Charlie, Etty and I. Etty was haughty, I was naughty and Charlie was very sad. I'd lost interest, he said, in the things that count. I had no interest, *she* said, in people. "I've got past what you mean by people," I said. (I am deep inside their minds.)'

After my daughter and my son-in-law depart (offering, the former, to go out shopping 'to buy anything you want') I walk, for a while (amounting, I suspect, to several hours), around the house. Danny is saying to Matt as they walk to their car, 'He has to make his own decision,' while Matt, waiting for him to release the door, says, 'What about the doctors?' ('Robeson' and 'Raynor' framed on her lips through the reflected light of the windscreen) while, with a cheerful wave, I watch them depart, their vehicle turning from our narrow street, enclosed by irregularly terraced houses, into the broader one beyond.

All is not lost in the Land of Ur, wrote Hiro (people's motives for doing what they do are never what they seem).

In the back-street kitchen, with its back-street yard and its back-street windows overlooking

a man as cantankerous as I.

'The peculiar thing is,' he told Etty when she rang, 'I left my suitcase on Darton station. My sketchbook and a life of della Francesca, Botticelli and Mantegna are also inside. (What have these three,' I ask her, 'in common?)'

The night, alone, with Sebastopol and Corunna Streets adjoining: the sound of music from The Spion Kop thundering through the weekend air: flats on one side, a house on the other.

"He was starting," Fenchurch wrote, "where he left off (to have no idea where he was going)," lying in bed, the glow from his neighbours' windows shining in his own. He had done too much: 'If I love you will you love me?'

'If you love me will I love you?'

"Such thoughts are reassuring."

His sleep: on a log, in Ardsley Wood, 'Would you give up writing and painting if it threatened to come between us (would you give up everything)?'

His heart, for instance, wasn't strong: the pills he took for tachycardia he had long ago dispensed with, along with those for (non-specific) anxiety and depression.

"I take nothing now but cups of tea (and have done away with alcohol and women)."

The house was falling into ruin: twice the size of Fenchurch's, it was nevertheless tall and narrow: the ceilings had broken away from the rafters, the stairs come away from the walls; rain, when it fell, poured through the roof: pots and pans, aimed at collecting it, were scattered across the upper floor. It was like, he often reflected, boarding a sinking ship, the swaying of the stairs (the creaking of the timbers), the tarpaulin sheets suspended like sails directing the rain ineffectually to the appropriate containers (the odour of decay and, unless he was mistaken, rats).

Yet Siobhan, alias Mrs O'Farrell ('Vaughan' to him and his fellow students at the Drayburgh forty years before) appeared to be above all this: ebullient – a Scottish mother, and Irish father – broad-bosomed, with a lyrical inclination to transmogrify in paint her domestic life, she had remained throughout three marriages, four children and as many live-in lovers ('my body is worn out, where not with love, of course, with kids'). Blonde, stout, the rotundity of her figure enhanced by shawls and gowns: 'Where have you been the last few weeks?' she enquiring, the door having fallen open at his knock.

'Ardsley,' Fenchurch said. 'They've been trying,' he told her 'to lock me away.'

He went inside to look at her pictures: scenes from her childhood, portraits of her children, one of a husband, two of a lover. 'My capacity for love is limitless,' she had often said, 'yet I never took money from any man.'

A turbulent, troublesome woman, her hair tumbling to her shoulders: pale eyes gazed out from a broadly-featured face, with a full-lipped mouth and red-flushed cheeks which, in the summer, shone like the sides of an apple. Furrows lined her brow over which a fringe fell in a frieze of curls: broad-beamed, broad-hipped, 'as long going across as coming up,' she had told him, taking him through to the kitchen: cats sprang off a chair (cat-food – brown and blood-coloured rusks – scattered across the floor). From the cluttered sink she removed a pot (pans and bowls from a week of cooking, more than the whole he had in his house). 'Coffee?' her fingers vivid with colour. 'So they want you back inside?'

'I intend,' I tell her, 'to put up a struggle.'

'You can come and stay here, if you like,' (the smell from the sink, the decaying food, the fissures in the walls, and holes directly through the ceiling, exposing the beams of the floor above).

'I'm all right where I am,' he told her.

'Nevertheless,' she said, 'it's always here if you want.'

Was this the 'success' (of failure) he had, in the past, gone on about: was this the antithesis to Vi, the bleach and mogadon-soaked killer? Was this what life was all about: the where not grease- graffiti-streaked walls, the (startling) pictures, pinned carelessly above the stove along with telephone messages yellow with age – a life he could not in any way encompass, or become a part of? This is Vaughan, he reflected, and I really have no place with her: out of chaos, order (her colours, shapes, her belligerent, sketched-in pictures: 'tactile', 'plastic', 'relevant', fine.)

The sister, he had told her, he had never had, not someone he could turn to (her method of support as helpful as a hammer to the head): someone with whom he could celebrate success, the opening out of his life at the publication of a novel, the production of a play, the completion of a picture,

354

events which, with a peculiar wryness, she never, as far as he could ascertain, very much enjoyed.

The greatest moment of his life: when Isabella acceded to those intimacies which, in their final stages, involved the removal of her clothes (and which she, with an intoxicating delicacy, effortlessly assisted). She wasn't vulgar, by any means, he reflected, 'her sensitivity and openness of an order I have never encountered in anyone before.'

'I've missed you, the past few days,' she said. 'I miss our talks about art. No one talks to me about painting, it's all about men or this bloody house,' a dribble of dust from the laths overhead.

The vomit from a cat lay in a pool on the table before him.

Having put on the kettle, and set down his pot, she wiped it away with a sheet of newsprint on which she'd idly drawn a head.

'Do they intend,' she says, 'to take you back?'

'I've been put,' he says, 'on my best behaviour. No more late-night phone calls to Bea, no more protests in the street, no more soliciting of neighbours' wives, nor, indeed, of anyone,' he adds. 'Or lapses of taste when talking to women. A by-product of my current disability, which might be likened to despair, is,' he goes on, 'I can't get women, either individually or corporately, into focus. I am, when addressing or merely observing them, whether old or young, thin or fat, degenerate or angelic, driven by a desire to be embraced,' whereupon, stooping, she places – as he has hoped – her arms around him, a difficult manoeuvre which he only finally eases by standing and allowing her to draw him to her.

His hands encompass her solid hips: his fingers delve at the flesh of her back.

'This is more like it,' he sighs as, behind him, the kettle gives out the shrillest shriek.

'I'd better get the coffee,' she says and he, releasing her, goes over to the kettle, turning it off and announcing, 'I've changed my mind to tea.'

Picking up his pot, he looks round for another (they are all

355

in the sink) and when she says, 'I've had one, thanks,' he puts in a tea-bag and pours in the water.

Steam rises in the chilly air: the house, other than by an electric fire, is unheated.

'Let's go to the studio,' she says, he reflecting with any other man she would have said the bedroom.

As he follows her up the swaying stairs – fresh areas of brickwork revealed behind the disintegrating plaster, fresh laths exposed by descending plaster, fresh areas of wall and ceiling stained by damp – these thoughts preoccupy Fenchurch unduly: 'Isn't Vaughan, in a unique way, an amalgam of all the women I have known as well as of certain aspects of myself I have protected or concealed in a way which she, within herself, has never felt obliged to? Isn't she the woman I thought I was working from but, in reality, towards, over all these years?' recalling the fresh face of the twenty-one-year-old he had glimpsed standing at her easel in the mixed life-room at the Drayburgh forty-five years before: the sturdiness of her figure, the candour of her look (which, despite her three husbands and four children, had never left her): the blueness of her eye, the curve of her smiling, if not laughing mouth, the cascade of curls from her tossed-back head (the fullness of her throat, the amplitude of her breast), the characteristic sway outwards and downwards as she walked or stood, legs parted, at her easel (no decorous jabs or titillations but broad, expansive sweeps of the brush: never anything less than primary colours).

'What do you think of this?' as they come into the principal first-floor room which, through a tall, uncurtained window, looks onto the car-parked street below (several streets' walk away from his own).

The scroll of colour, the streak of paint, the fractured, jagged, vibrant line.

'Based,' she adds, 'on my notion of a woman. One not altogether unlike,' (she gives a laugh, throat bared, curls cascading to her shoulders), 'myself.'

'One of your best,' he says, his mind not on the picture but Vaughan herself, the angle of her body, the way it superimposes

356

itself against the discarded drawings that litter the floor, a table, two chairs, the paint and crayon-scoured walls themselves, embodiments of plants and figures on the plaster. She was, he reflected, not merely a handsome but a beautiful woman – in a way that all women were to him now, but more so: she exuded grace, she exuded strength, she exuded beauty – to a degree he had, except in Isabella, never experienced in another woman. 'And this is someone,' he further reflected, 'who is perceptibly stiff-limbed, marked – vividly – by her experience as a wife and mother – as three wives, and four mothers: how could I have not noticed her over all these years?'

'Or this one?' turning to a section of the wall to which numerous sheets had been attached, aimlessly, or so it seemed, one on top of the other.

'Like all your pictures,' he said, realising, for the first time, she dyed her hair and that, unusual for her, she was wearing make-up. 'When I was first successful,' he added, 'I thought I would be besieged by women. When I wasn't, I felt let down – unaccountably so, in many respects – and, as a consequence, redoubled my efforts. When, with my second success, I met with the same result, I can't describe the degree – and intensity – of my frustration. Yet, once on with a fresh piece of work, it was quickly forgotten. Now,' he went on, 'the work has gone, and my reputation with it. Perhaps the work, which absorbed me so completely, was merely a distraction. I've certainly, in the past, made mistakes which can only be described as cataclysmic, and, to that extent, we have a great deal in common,' and when she said, 'I don't see my life in terms of mistakes, nor,' she continued, 'failure, either,' he responded, 'It's one of the things I have to give up, or, if not give up, at least control, a disinclination not to talk when neither thought nor feeling warrant it. You see why I frighten people off, not least of all my family.'

When, for a while, she gazed past him to the picture, he suddenly added, 'It's what has led to accusations that I have no interest in people: everything is reduced to verbiage. Nothing,' he concluded, 'matters any more.'

'I wouldn't say that,' she says. 'It matters to me,' continuing, 'You don't seem interested, at the moment, in pictures. I can't blame you,' and with an aimlessness he had always associated with her, 'Let's go back down and get more tea.'

So this is what it's like, he thought. All these years I never knew: all these years and I forgot. I don't wish to be shackled to anyone – not wives, not children – not art: the first time in my life I'm free, not merely, he reflected, at liberty.

Vaughan, he suspected, was relieved that he should leave (perhaps had been, in any case, expecting someone else). 'All is not lost,' was his immediate response (walking back through the streets). 'Going to Ardsley and coming away from it,' he further reflected, 'was the best thing I ever did. And although this feeling won't be with me all the time, on those occasions that it is I can recoup sufficient of its strength to carry me through the intervals between. I shall outlive the pain that engulfed me, outlive my art, outlive the means by which I put it into practice. Reality, after all, goes on for ever and, to the degree that I am part of it, so will I.' In the decadence of Vaughan's existence he had found a source of strength: in the arbitrary way she supervised – or refused to supervise – her life (disinclined to arbitrate in the existences of others) he had found an antidote to the way he had lived himself (the prescription he had written from an early age and which – in fulfilment through women, an unrepayable obligation – had driven him mad). He had – he had not been aware of the process, merely of the pain – been re-united, in a tangible way, with that source of reality which was within him, not outside. 'Such a casual visit,' he thought, 'and yet, as if, in a curious way, I've been planning it all my life: right up to that moment when (her bell not working) I knocked on her door, found her doodling on the newsprint in the kitchen, made the tea, went up to her room, looked at her pictures then, with a peculiar contentment, came away,' (she undismayed at his leaving): all those forces that had, waveringly, characterised his existence in the past had been brought into focus. 'Of course, at the instant she showed me the painting – the woman rising, as if

358

from a bed – I took it as an invocation, the one thought came to me, through the mists and clouds, of Isabella,' as if, with dread as well as understanding, with a sense of enchantment as well as fear, in fear and trembling, he were moving closer to the one he loved.